Inept: Impaired: Overwhelmed

Inept: Impaired: Overwhelmed
Tall Tales from West Virginia and Beyond

BIL LEPP

Quarrier Press
Charleston, WV

Quarrier Press
Charleston, WV

Copyright 2002 by Bil Lepp

Front Cover by Erin McKinnon
Book Design by Mark S. Phillips,
Marketing+Design Group

10 9 8 7 6 5 4 3 2 1

Printed in the United States of America.

Library of Congress Control Number: 2001119147
ISBN 1-891852-17-5

Distributed by:
Pictorial Histories Distribution
1416 Quarrier Street
Charleston, WV 25301

Table of Contents

Creation Mother Nature

Dedication:

First and foremost for Paula and Noah
because I love them so.

And then, because I treat them
so poorly throughout the book:
Buck-dog, Frank, and Scott. In that order.

And lastly, but by no means leastly:
Adele L. S. because I finished this today
and she was born today.

Mayhem Dressed Like an Eight Point Buck

At some point in my life I will learn not to go along with Skeeter Barth's ideas. Ever since his family moved down from Pennsylvania, the year we both turned four, Skeeter and I have been next-door neighbors. Since that fateful day there has not been a moment when either of our mothers rested easy. And it was all because of Skeeter's cockamamie ideas. Take deer season our senior year for example.

Skeeter showed up at my house at 3:30 in the morning wearing a grin so diabolical that I should have pled illness and stayed in bed, but instead I gave him a cup of coffee and listened to his plan. To skip ahead, our day ended early, about 7:00 that morning, with the two of us parked on the shoulder of Main Street receiving citations from an important public official for the heroic deeds we had accomplished. All the while a pack of astonished on-lookers shouted accolades.

The only problem was that the heroic deeds were only heroic in our eyes, the important public official was Sheriff Hasbro, the citations were tickets, and the accolades were all being shouted on behalf of the good Sheriff.

Sheriff Hasbro had had to radio into the courthouse

and disturb the judge's breakfast, but he proudly announced to the crowd that "Mayhem" was a crime and that it looked like he could charge me and Skeeter with it. A roar of approval burst forth from the crowd.

"Now," Sheriff Hasbro had said to us, "get out of those costumes, get that dummy off the hood of your truck, and follow me in."

The costumes to which the Sheriff referred had been handmade by Skeeter and were almost perfect replicas of eight-point buck deer heads. The only reason I even consented to putting the mask on was because it was the day before deer season, not actually deer season, and Skeeter had promised that we would not go anywhere near the woods, nor would we, under any circumstances, get out of the truck.

And then there was the dummy. Skeeter had filled an old pair of coveralls with hay, fastened on a pair of boots, gloves, and a hat, and then tied the whole thing to the front of his Ford. "It's simple," he said. "We put on the masks and drive around town with the dummy on the hood. Get it? Like we are deer and it's people season. And we bagged one! And then we pull up to Sullivan's store and say 'Can we check this here?'" I had to admit that it sounded funny. But funny in the sort of way that you hope your dad never finds out that it was you.

To keep our fathers from finding out, we left the house before dawn. I don't like to worry my mother, or lie to her, so I left her a note explaining my whereabouts. It said, "Out with the deer and the dummy." That way she would know I was doing something pertaining to deer season and that I was with Skeeter.

We had to wait until first light if we wanted anyone to see us so we hid in the state park, put the masks at our feet, and slept for a few hours. Usually the park is a safe place to hide. It is true that the park did not open until sunrise, but generally speaking the police did not bother you if you looked innocent, or if you were parked way up the service road where the patrol cars seldom ventured, as were Skeeter and I. The pre-dawn air was bitter cold. As usual, Skeeter's truck was low on gas; so we couldn't run the heater because we were, as usual, short on cash. And the wind was blowing, which normally wouldn't have mattered except that the passenger side window was frozen in the down position. Before long there was frost on the windshield, frost on the dummy tied to the hood, and frost in our veins. The only way to stay warm was to put on the deer masks.

We woke up to the sound of a car horn. Someone was sitting in their car facing us, their bright lights on. In the early morning gray I could just barely make out the silhouette of a police car. Of all the days in the year, this would be the day the cops decided to check out the service road. The driver's side door opened slowly and Sheriff Hasbro cautiously advanced toward us, his flashlight drawn. He had as bewildered a look on his face as I have ever seen. In retrospect, I guess he had good cause to look so confused. It is not every day that you come across a pick-up truck stopped in the woods with a man tied to the hood and two figures staring out from the cab; two figures who look remarkably like a couple of deer caught in your headlights. I stuck my head out of the window and grunted like a full-fledged buck. Sheriff Hasbro jumped sky high.

Skeeter started the truck and we pulled quickly around the police car and down the service road. Sheriff Hasbro had not asked us a single question nor suggested, in any manner that Skeeter and I could understand, that we were in trouble. Thus, we did not feel like we were "fleeing arrest." But, as we found out later that morning, Sheriff Hasbro saw things in a different light.

I turned the CB to the police channel. Sheriff Hasbro was saying, "Well, Tom, I don't care if ya do think I'm crazy! There was two deer driving Skeeter Barth's pick-up truck down the service road and, by God, I believe they had Skeeter tied to the hood!"

"We can only hope so," was the reply. The comment was not lost on us.

"Well," continued the Sheriff, "whoever it is, they're headed straight for Main Street. They won't get away."

The smartest thing to do when you are obviously caught is to give up, count your losses, and head home. Unfortunately, doing the smartest thing was not our strong suit. And as long as we were driving down Main Street in deer costumes with a man tied to the hood, it was a pretty safe bet that this was not going to be the day we turned over new leaves.

Small towns have many quaint traits that make them special and endearing, little traditions which you can count on to make you feel at home. One thing you could count on in Halfdollar, West Virginia, was that folks would be up and listening to their police scanners while drinking their morning coffee. As we came into town you would have thought Orson Wells was landing a space ship at City Hall. Throngs of people, most still in their robes and slippers, lined the street. Having heard the Sheriff's conversation about the two deer driving the stolen pick-up, they had come out in droves to see the show.

Sheriff Hasbro was still on the radio trying to figure out the best way to stop us. He was none too eager to pull over two heavily armed and obviously dangerous deer. Opting for the better part of valor, Sheriff Hasbro was not following us with lights a' flashin' and siren a' blarin', but was rather discreetly developing a plan. In fact, if we hadn't picked up his transmissions on the radio, we wouldn't have known that he cared about us at all. Unprovoked and un-impeded, Skeeter and I drove through town at a safe speed with no thought of surrender.

And then over the CB we heard, "...better call Skeeter's dad, Animal Control, and the FBI..." The words sent a shudder through our bones. It could only mean one of two things. Either Skeeter's dog, Axel, was an international terrorist and the Sheriff was calling Mr. Barth to let him know that Animal Control had been authorized by the Feds to have Axel "taken out," or Skeet and I were in a lot of trouble and they were about to call his dad. Our dads scared us a lot more than the FBI. We decided that it would be best to pull over and wait for the Sheriff. The rest, well, I've already told you about the citations and the accolades.

They say that true forgiveness only comes after absolute repentance, and that you must forever af-ter remain both contrite and sincere, struggling ev-eryday not to repeat your actions, nor ever take any glory from the original deed. I believe I speak for both Skeeter and myself when I say, from the bottom of my heart, that we might never be forgiven for our actions that day.

Woodpeckers Just Don't Make the Best Pets

When you are young, and desperate to become a lion tamer, or a big game outfitter, you are apt to run into trouble. Living in the heart of West Virginia, I found very little big game to hunt, and far fewer lions to tame. Especially when I was eleven. So, I did the next best thing. Every Saturday morning I would rise while the dew was still wet on the ground, wolf down a bowl of cereal, pull on my long johns, and watch cartoons. Cartoons can be just as dangerous as a charging rhino when you are pumped-up on choco-nuggets and at an impressionable age.

Though I never hurt myself dropping anvils off cliffs, or by strapping rocket-powered ice-skates to my feet, or even by accidentally swallowing a whole cake that had a stick of dynamite for a candle, I was still endangered. It was that woodpecker with the crazy laugh that finally got me into a jam. From the very first time I saw him I wanted a woodpecker for a pet. As a child I had not noticed that you hardly ever see anyone who has a woodpecker for a pet and so I didn't think twice about the fact that it might just be a bad idea.

We lived out in the country. In my backyard there was a rotten tree that was almost five feet tall, and hollow most of the way down. I was watching that tree one afternoon when a huge pileated woodpecker landed on it and started pecking away. As I watched, a hole grew in the tree beneath the reciprocating beak of that big bird. Bigger and bigger the hole grew until it was big enough for him to slip through. He looked to his left, looked to his right, and then slid into the hollow tree. In a few seconds he reappeared, only to launch himself into the air. For the next hour, I watched as he returned time and again with a beak full of twigs, or straw, or yarn. It dawned on me that he must have been building a nest. And then it dawned on me that this woodpecker might just make the perfect pet.

I knew that to have a pet bird, a person must also have a birdcage. My family was poor and earthy, that is to say, not the sort of family that had an antique, exotic birdcage in the attic. In fact, we did not even have an attic. I also knew that if I had asked my parents for a birdcage I would have gotten the same response I had gotten when I had asked for the anvil, the rocket- skates, and the dynamite. So, if I wanted a birdcage, I was going to have to build it myself.

I searched the woods high and low for the best assortment of sticks that I could find. I cut them to size and bound them together with binder's twine and wood glue. Like most things built by an eleven-year-old craftsman, the artistry of my cage was only surpassed by its pristine engineering. I put the finished cage on the dresser in my bedroom and then set out to capture my bird.

I had a plan to catch the woodpecker, but I was going to need an accomplice if the plan was going to be successful. My neighbor, Skeeter Barth, was always up to bagging wild game, so I shared my dream with him. I had to consent to his demands of half ownership and visitation rights, but that seemed like a really good idea. By claiming half ownership in the bird, Skeeter automatically became half-liable for any foul-ups or mishaps that might arise due to the ensuing woodpecker hunt. Though I strongly doubted that anything would go wrong, it was comforting to know that in the event of complete disaster or bodily injury, Skeeter would be in as much trouble as I would.

Really, our plan was ingenious, which leaves me wondering how Skeeter and I came up with it. All we needed was a burlap bag, a stepladder, and a bucket of water. Not since before we had been introduced to Tom and Huck had a plan of ours not required, at the barest minimum, a kerosene torch, or at least a dead cat. All we had to do was wait until the woodpecker came home for the night.

And when he did, we simply snuck up to the tree. Skeeter held the burlap sack over the hole the woodpecker had made and I climbed the ladder and poured the bucket of water down the hollow tree.

A terrible squalling burst forth from within the trunk. Old fungus covered bits of bark shook loose from the tree as the deluged woodpecker spun circles inside the stump trying to discover the source of the flood. Becoming more and more upset, the woodpecker sprang from his nest. Unfortunately for the bird, Skeeter had maintained his position and when the woodpecker flew out of the tree, he went right into the burlap sack. Just like that, Skeeter and I had caught ourselves one fine woodpecker. And this time, we hadn't even set the woods on fire. Congratulating ourselves on a job well done, we tied the bag shut and headed toward the house.

If I knew my mother, she would be by the back door wringing her hands and contemplating what

Skeeter and I were up to, so we went in the front door. It is not that I wanted to cause my mother worry, but she had an almost pathological need to know what I was bringing into the house. Rarely could I pass through the kitchen with a twitching, wiggling, yelping burlap bag that she didn't demand to know what I was bringing into her home. It was silly really, and I had learned to avoid the encounter. However, if she suspected that an unknown creature had made it into my room, she was much less likely to barge in. The time she found my pet skunk while vacuuming under the bed taught her, so far as I was concerned, a valuable if unpleasant lesson.

Skeeter and I slipped through the front door and up the stairs to my bedroom. Needless to say, Skeeter was visibly impressed with the cage I had built. When he said, "What a piece of junk! Did you find it at the dump, or down by the river? That'll never hold a woodpecker, it's made of dead wood!" I could hear the jealousy and wonder in his voice. I cast him an understanding glance, took the burlap bag from his hand, opened the door of my cage, and let the woodpecker hop into its new home. By that time, most of the glue had dried and the door only fell apart twice before I got it shut. We quickly discovered that woodpeckers make odd pets.

Even though they eat bugs and such, you can't really call woodpeckers "carnivorous" in the same sense that you would a man-eating lion or a Great White Shark. And yet we were soon to learn that woodpeckers can put on a ferocious front. The big bird sat on its perch, regaining its composure. It glanced at the cage, and then studied the room. The window was shut, as was the door. Satisfied with the room, the woodpecker leaned forward and tapped the cage with his beak, lightly, almost playfully. And then, he reared back and attacked the bars of his cage like a rabid jackhammer on a balsa wood sidewalk. Skeeter and I went from proud, calm, bird owners sitting on the edge of my bed, to screaming, horror driven eleven-year-olds in less than a second.

The woodpecker, now loose, swooped around the room and dove at us. We were jumping up and down, clutching each other for safety, yelling at the top of our lungs. The devil bird strafed our heads with its razor-like talons and then landed on the doorknob. Splinters flew as he cut into the door. With a blur of his yellow beak and his red head he bore through the wood like a carbide-tipped drill bit. As we watched the woodpecker's tail disappear through the hole he had cut in the door, Skeeter and I sighed and then fell back onto the bed, exhausted.

In our relief to be alive, it had not occurred to us that the woodpecker was not gone, but rather presently at-large in the house proper with my nervous mother. Already my mind was looking for a way to deny that I had had anything to do with the woodpecker, but the cage, the assorted feathers on the floor, and the perfect woodpecker sized hole in the door were pretty damning evidence. As my mind raced for an excuse, I hit on the idea of claiming that I was participating in a "catch and release" study being conducted by the Federal Game Commission. It was thin, but better than 'fessing up. I waited for my mother's screams.

When Mother failed to be alarmed by the hell-bird cruising the house on a search and destroy mission, I began to fear the worst. She had either seen the bird and just plain died, or the woodpecker had crept up on her, captured her, gagged her, and was now holding her hostage. Mustering our courage, we decided to investigate.

Before leaving the room we put our ears to the door. Hearing nothing, I looked out the woodpecker hole. Seeing nothing, I began to slowly open the door. I nearly fainted when the door was jerked from my hands, conjuring up images of the woodpecker landing on my face and going for the kill. And then I heard my mother's voice saying, "Well, what in the world are you two up to? All that screaming?" And then, her ire growing, "And what is that pile of rotten sticks on your dresser? And, my lands! How did you get this hole in your door!"

I looked up at my mother, tried to remember my lie, but all I could say was, "It was the woodpecker! That awful woodpecker!" Skeeter and I began sobbing.

"Don't you lie to me young man! You're grounded! A woodpecker putting a hole in your door, I've never heard such a thing. Forever more!"

To this day I do not know what became of that woodpecker. For the longest time I was sure it was in the house, lurking in some dark corner, waiting to strike. Mother thought I was crazy for wearing an army helmet and a neck brace around the house for the rest of the summer, but I wasn't taking any chances.

As I grew older, I began to assume that the woodpecker had just flown out the front door. If there was one thing Skeeter and I never did, it was close the door we came in through. Or, the woodpecker might have gone out one of the many windows in the house. Regardless of its route of escape, I was never so glad to have had a pet run away.

Yes, a boy has got to be cautious and has got to choose his pets carefully. Always remember that cartoons are fiction, and that woodpeckers, panthers, coyotes, roadrunners and skunks, no matter how loveable and ingenious they may be on TV, do not always make the best pets.

Please, Don't Print Any of This

I stood in the wet sand between the three-foot catfish and the waterline. My knees were bent and my feet were spread shoulder width apart. I was prancing to the left and right, trying to keep the catfish from getting back into the water. His eyes were on mine, his gills opening and closing with malice, and his jaw working in time with the lunges he made toward my feet and shins. It was an ugly scene.

My fishing pole was splintered, my net was bent, and my boat was a tangled wreck of twisted metal. To top it all off, my right arm was numb from the elbow down and my left arm was numb from my neck down. So, my arms hanging useless by my sides, I scampered back and forth between the fish and the water. There was no way I was going to let the fish that broke my pole, wrecked my boat, and paralyzed my arms get away.

I had been paying attention. He'd been playing with my bait, eight feet below the still surface of Skitter Creek. I had one hand on the grip and one hand on the reel. I was ready. He tugged, nudged, bumped, and dribbled my bait. My rod tip bounced, jiggled and twitched, ever so slightly. I held fast, my eyes fixed on the rod, my tongue in the corner of my mouth. Suddenly, the tip of my pole hit the water and the line started stripping out. I set the hook and began to finesse the fish into the boat. I could tell from the swift jabs, followed by moments of weightlessness, that this fish had been hooked before and knew how to defend himself. He was doing all he could to trick me, but I kept the pressure on and before long he was beside the boat. I'd never seen a prettier fish on the end of my line. He was half as long as the boat. I picked up my net and worked it under his thrashing body.

I have never been a great fisherman. I've landed a few big ones in the past, but more by luck than skill. Part of my problem, I suspect, is that I buy most of my gear in discount shops and at garage sales. It is, therefore, not the highest quality gear and carries no guarantees. Well, that's not completely true. It is usually guaranteed to malfunction at the most crucial time possible. Thus, I was not overly surprised when, just as I started to lift the netted fish out of the water, two things happened. First, the long, thin, worn, aluminum handle of the net began to crease, buckle, and then bend back towards the river, under the weight of the great green catfish. Second, the fiberglass at the apex of my bent rod began to splinter in long, sharp shards. I was about to be doubly foiled by my gear and I wasn't eager to tell folks that the fish got away because my net broke AND my rod busted.

Holding both the rod and the net in my hands, I threw myself backward in the boat. This motion provided sufficient force not only to drag the huge catfish over the gunwale and into the boat, but also afforded me enough kinetic energy to continue my backward progress until I somersaulted over the opposite side of the tiny craft and into the water.

I quickly surfaced and began pulling myself back into the boat. The catfish was jammed in the rim of the net like a walrus in a kayak, and crammed between the first two seats of the boat like an elephant in a Yugo. His whole body was flexed like Popeye's forearm and he had all the madness of John Brown in his eyes. As I pulled myself back into the boat, I managed to submerge the port corner of the stern for a few seconds. Water rushed onto the floor of the boat, flowed under the seats and, incidentally, lent enough buoyancy to the stuck catfish that he managed to wiggle free of the net and the seats. He lay in the bow glaring at me.

I turned and started the motor. I kept one eye on the fish as I fiddled with the switches and got us pointed toward shore. He had his head on the center seat and his tail coiled under him. That made me nervous. As I faced completely forward, that catfish sprang at me, mouth open, fins out, and tail thrashing. I let go of the rudder and, choosing to meet force with force, I threw myself at the fish, arms spread wide.

There are many reasons why you should never wrap your arms around a catfish, but I was caught up in the moment. Right away my right elbow was pumped full of pain from the barbed fin on the left side of that fish, and his dorsal fin scraped across my right collarbone. My arms went limp. That fish bounced off my chest and fell back to the floor of the boat.

Because the motor was running full-bore, the boat was headed straight for shore at a good clip and there was nothing I could do about it. My arms were useless and I was too emotionally spent to try and steer with my feet. Besides, the shore was flat, sandy and soft. I figured we would slide up it a few yards and then coast to a stop, at which point I would stand around until feeling returned to my arms. I was surprised at how far up the shore a johnboat can skid. Actually, the boat never did come to a natural stop. About three yards up the beach there were two young oak trees, maybe three feet apart. The johnboat headed straight toward those trees, and would have made it through without incident, except that that boat was about three and half feet wide. First, there was a tremendous thud as the boat impacted, then the starboard side peeled back like the lid on a SPAM can, then the port side of the boat tried to climb the other tree. The motor dug into the sand, the boat listed, and, unable to balance ourselves, the fish and I slid out.

The catfish lay on the ground, unable to get up due to biological and evolutionary reasons. I lay on the ground, unable to get up because I had been stupid enough to try and hug an airborne catfish. When my cell phone tumbled out of my knapsack we both just stared at it, disgusted. I couldn't call anybody because I was too ashamed, and it wouldn't have done him any good to call anybody because none of his friends could walk on land.

He started to thrash and leap toward the water. I rolled over onto my belly, got on my knees and, leaning against one of the trees that had stopped my boat, managed to stand up. I stumbled toward the waterline and headed him off. He was surprisingly agile and before long he had backed me up until my feet were in the water. I had just about given up hope when I saw someone coming down the path from the parking area.

"Thank heavens," I said, "can you give me a hand?"

To my great annoyance, the guy started taking pictures. While he was getting a light reading for a shot of the boat, the fish finally out-maneuvered me and got away. As it turns out, the guy was a reporter for the *Halfdollar Two Bits*, the local paper. Now, Halfdollar is not a big town so it doesn't take much to make the front page of the paper and thus I was not surprised when I saw my image under the headline the next morning. There I was, unable to lift my arms, courageously keeping that fish from getting back into the water. What did surprise me was the headline and caption under the photo: LOCAL CAT-FISH STRIKES BACK: Hometown man nearly nabbed by record size fish. While the catfish was unavailable for comment, Bil Lepp (pictured) had this to say of the events that wrecked his boat, broke his pole, bent his net, and temporarily paralyzed his arms: "Please, don't print any of this."

Fump. Tink. Whizzzz.

Angus Fester was a dairy farmer who was obsessed by a desire to have cows around him, so much so that his children all bore the names of bovine species. There were the boys: Angus Jr., Malvi, Guernsey, Jersey, Beefalo and Hereford. And then there was his daughter Charolais. Fortunately, Charolais' mother had intervened on her behalf and demanded that if the poor girl was going to be named after a cow, at least the name should sound feminine. It was a small victory.

Angus, Angus, Jr., Malvi, Guernsey, Jersey, Beefalo and Hereford were all brutes whose physical unattractiveness was only matched by their complete lack of personality. Charolais, on the other hand, was undoubtedly the prettiest girl in all of Halfdollar, West Virginia, if not throughout the greater tri-county area. And Skeeter had long been in love with her. The only problem was that Angus Sr. hated Skeeter, as did Angus' boys. Not to leave me out, they hated me too. Where all the hatred stemmed from is hard to say, but it was not helped by the fact that Skeet got a BB gun for his thirteenth birthday. Well, I guess that was innocent enough; it was the application of the BB gun that really got us into trouble.

You see, Skitter Creek was the best catfishing creek within walking distance of our houses, which meant it was the best creek around. To get to Skitter Creek, Skeeter and I had to cross Angus' cow pasture, which meant we had to deliberately ignore the "No Trespassing, This Means Skeeter and Bil" signs which Angus had nailed to every post along his fence. Many were the times when the whole male side of the Fester clan, followed by the bovine side, chased us through the fields.

Angus Sr. loved his beer, and always bought it at the little market, Shaffer's, across from Skeeter's house. As luck would have it, the window in Skeeter's attic opened onto a perfect, unobstructed view of the market's front door. Even without a scope, Skeeter and I could hit a soup can from 100 yards away with his new BB gun, and a soup can is just about the same size as a beer can. And the parking lot of the store where Angus bought his beer was only thirty yards away.

We watched, staked out really, Shaffer's convenience store for days. About 7:30 every evening Angus Sr. drove up in his beat up pick-up, parked, went in, and bought a six-pack. Then he carried it outside, laid it on the hood of his truck, and walked over to the bench on the far side of the lot where the old men sat and smoked. He'd put in a chew, fold his arms, and chat a bit.

So there we were. Skeeter drew a bead on the six-pack sitting on Angus' hood. There was the fump of the air gun going off, and then the tink of a brass BB impacting a full aluminum can. Then a beautiful stream of pure white foam arced out from the can and splashed onto the sidewalk with a distinct whizzing sound.

He handed me the gun. Fump. Tink. Whizzzzzz.
I handed the gun back to Skeeter. Angus Sr. had placed his six-pack, almost surely unintentionally, so that we had a clear line of sight to three of the cans and then a side view of a forth. Skeet tried the skill shot. "Fourth can, side shot." He announced. He drew a deep breath and let out half of it. Fump. Tink. No whiz. We waited a moment. "Well," he said, "I must have just winged it."

"Yep. I heard it hit. Hand me the gun."

Just then, Angus Sr. started saying his good-byes to the old fellas at the bench and walking toward his truck. He walked around the front of his pick-up and paused to look at the beer on the sidewalk and on the hood. He picked up the six-pack and could obviously feel that it was about 24 ounces light. He jiggled the six-pack, a perplexed look on his face. He pursed his lips, scowled, and then lifted the cans to his ear. He shook them. Even from across the street we could hear the BBs rattling around like the balls in spray paint cans. Angus Sr. scowled again. He was holding the defective six-pack right beside his ear. He gave the cans a mighty shake, listening closely.

Sometimes the world is a perfect place—and this was one of those times. Angus Sr. had no love for the law and Sheriff Hasbro had no love for Angus Sr. Angus had spent more than a few belligerent nights in the county jail for various offenses involving beer. As Angus was shaking the six-pack next to his ear, Skeeter and I saw Sheriff Hasbro come around the corner of Main Street in his cruiser and pull into the parking lot of Shaffer's store.

Suddenly, the can Skeeter had winged burst open. Apparently the BB had jammed into the side of can. Angus' vigorous shaking had caused the pressure in the can to build and the BB was the weak spot. A stream of foam shot straight out of the can and into Angus' ear. The beer quickly soaked his overalls and shirt. He spat out a few quick obscenities (Angus' ability to swear was about his only redeeming quality) and then deftly aimed the stream of beer away from his ear and into his mouth. Just then, he saw Sheriff Hasbro.

Cops are keen about picking up on sudden movements. They are used to people frantically trying to hide themselves and/or their actions at the very sight of a police cruiser. Sheriff Hasbro saw Angus lower his arm and spin around. He wasn't sure if Angus had had something in his hand, but he figured he ought to investigate.

Angus looked over his shoulder, a panicked expression creasing his face. Sheriff Hasbro noticed that Angus had both hands down around his mid-section. Later, Sheriff Hasbro would tell folks he thought to himself, "No. Couldn't be. I mean the guy has no class at all, but in the parking lot, at 7:30, taking a p...". There was an audible whizzing sound emanating from Angus, the strong smell of cheap beer, and a growing puddle of fizzy, yellowish liquid on the pavement.

The sun was setting at an angle that suited Skeeter and me fine. It lit the front window of Shaffer's store so that a perfect reflection of Angus' front side was visible to us. He was looking over his shoulder at Sheriff Hasbro, almost crying. All the while, we saw in the window, he was unzipping his fly and trying to shove the six-pack under his coveralls.

"Angus," Sheriff Hasbro said slowly, "what the Sam Hill are you doing?"

"Nothing officer, honest."

"You haven't been drinking beer?"

"No sir, honest."

"You smell like beer. You realize that public urination is a crime, right?"

"Sir?" Angus sounded utterly shocked at that accusation.

"Angus, turn around."

The stream of beer ceased to splash onto the sidewalk. Angus fiddled with his zipper. He lifted his left foot and jiggled his leg. He turned around, slowly. From his belt line, and growing steadily down both thighs, there was a dark, wet stain. Angus smiled awkwardly. "Is there a problem officer?"

A crowd had gathered and Angus was doing his best to act like there wasn't a six-pack in his pants, and his best to pretend that he didn't know it looked like he had wet himself. The crowd was snickering and Angus was turning bright red.

"OK, look," he said, as he undid his fly. There was a gasp from the crowd as Angus started to pull out the six-pack.

"Now, just take it easy there..." Sheriff Hasbro yelled.

Angus made it clear that he was pulling out the six-pack, and nothing else. He redid his fly. He held up the six-pack above his head as an explanation. He shook it gently so that everyone could hear the rattling sound. He pointed out the holes in the cans to the Sheriff. The Sheriff looked at the holes and rubbed his chin thoughtfully. Angus put the cans back on the hood of his truck just as they had been when he found them. Skeeter and I heard the words "BB" and "trajectory" as we ducked beneath the windowsill. We lay perfectly still. The temperature in the attic doubled, and then started to triple. Everyone knew where Skeeter lived, especially the Sheriff and Angus.

Skeet's folks weren't home at the time. So we let the Sheriff knock and knock. We could hear Angus yelling. They never proved a thing, but then, we knew Angus didn't care much about proof, and the Sheriff, well, he knew we'd do something else sooner or later and he could make us pay then. But for that one moment...

Luckless and Buckless

Dear Personal Ad Editor,
Please include the following ad in your upcoming publication:

Relatively new hunter, who has yet to bag his first buck, is seeking lasting, long-term relationship with trophy buck, preferably eight points or more (eastern or western eight points considered.) Am willing to travel to meet you. I will spend long hours in the snow sitting in front of brush, or in a tree, or in a field, or in a dell, or in a glade, or on a mountaintop, or in a ravine bottom to bag you.

I am six feet tall, handsome, woodsy, a cunning hunter, and given to wearing orange hats, wool pants and leather boots. I own a number of high-powered, high-priced hunting rifles, the cost of which you can help me justify. You should be mature, in your prime, wise and wary, as well as tall, well-built, with short brown hair and dark eyes.

I feel compelled to tell you that while I fully intend for this to be a long-term relationship, your services will be needed only for a relatively short period. After I track you in the deep woods, overcoming myriad hardships and perilous encounters with grizzlies and mountain lions, I will get you in my sights. Chances are, I will be off balance, standing on one foot (the other having been mauled by a griz), weak from hunger (since a mountain lion will have made off with my pack), and down to my last bullet (the rest will have been used up blasting myself out of the avalanche). You will be running away from me, full out, in a heavy thicket, behind a fallen log, and beneath a canopy of vines. You will then hear a loud BANG! Following the bang, I am in a position to offer you immortality.

Your features and noble qualities will be remembered by me for the rest of my days and many are the times I will tell people about you over a beer, by a campfire, or along the trail. You will be regaled as "My First Buck" and be the first in a long line of prestigious deer to fall at the hands of this up-and-coming, mighty hunter. No exaggerations will be too great to describe you as I grow older. In the days to come, you will stand ten feet tall and have a rack that would do an elk proud. You will, in short, become an everlasting icon in the front porch folklore of hunting camps. What more could you ask for?

Please send personal information, approximate location, and photo (if you have one) to "Up-and-Coming," Box 864.

Wildlife Management in a 100,000 sq. ft. Hardware Store

When I was in college, I spent at least half my time outdoors, devoting only cursory attention to the menial task of being formally educated. Instead, I learned how to ride trains and I mastered my fishing skills. A man can live longer than you'd expect on brim; and laundry gets just as clean if you wear it in the river as it does if you put it in a machine, more or less. Oddly, I had very few girlfriends in college.

After college I serioused up and developed strict criteria that any future employer would have to live up to before I would accept a job from them. Number one, they had to offer a job. Number two, well, I guess there was just the one. After turning a few organizations down because they could not live up to my standard, I got a job working at a camp for troubled youth in North Carolina. I did not have to buy a suit, I got to live in a tent year round, and I got to take twenty-day canoe trips whenever I wanted. Granted, I had to take ten irreverent youth with me when I went, but I was used to college life. After a couple years in North Carolina, I got married and had to move back to the real world, but not before I got accepted into another college.

Having a wife, tuition, a car, a house... I couldn't really afford to just go to school and then go adventuring. I had to get a job to go along with everything else. So, I decided to get a job that emulated the out-of-doors and yet paid well. I got hired at one of those super hardware stores that sell everything under one huge roof. The building was 100,000 square-feet huge with twenty-four foot ceilings and a greenhouse. Sometimes a low pressure zone would build in the greenhouse, get sucked through the air conditioning system, mix with the hot air blowing in from the loading dock, and we'd have scattered showers in the tool department. We sold a lot of umbrellas when that happened, but as time went on it got harder and harder to find guys to give power tool demonstrations.

My manager was a guy named Tupid Noraymus, and he wasn't all that bright. Tupid would sometimes jump on a forklift to show us how he was "just a regular guy." He'd drive out to the receiving area, pick up a pallet of birdseed and then drive through the store to the garden center. The problem was, Tupid was a poor forklift driver and would consistently put the tines of the forklift right into the bags of seed, three or four times, before he actually got them under the pallet. As a result, there would be gaping holes in the bags out of which birdseed would pour, creating a trail of birdseed a yard wide and a quarter mile long which attracted every kind of rodent and winged creature in a four county area.

Now, having a store full of squirrels, opossums, raccoons and sparrows might seem distasteful to the general public, but to someone who longed for the great outdoors, it was just the ticket. For the little old ladies that opened the dishwasher displays only to find a litter of chipmunks, the idea was revolting, but for me, coming to work was like clocking into an eight-hour mini-safari.

The birds and bats would nest way up in the rafters and the raccoons and such would crawl in any hole they could find. A lot of days I'd get a guy to lift me up on the forklift and drop me off on the top shelf, just below the ceiling. I usually tried to get a fellow employee to lift me up, but in a fix I'd get anyone who knew the difference between a factory outlet and an electrical outlet to drop me off.

Once, a guy asked me for a 4x4 and when I told him we had eight, ten, twelve and sixteen foot 4x4's, he said, "No. I need a bigger 4x4."

"Well, I can order a longer one if you need." I said.

He replied, holding his hands about half a foot apart, "No, I need a bigger 4x4."

I finally figured out what he needed and said, "Well, we have some 4x4's that are 6x6's."

"Yeah, that's what I need!" he said with a smile.

Needless to say, I didn't let him drive the forklift, much less lift me up.

Anyway, I'd go up to the top shelf, twenty-some feet off the ground, with my field guide, a set of binoculars and some jerky, then I'd build a blind among the boxes and see what flew by. My blinds were normally pretty sparse, but I did have one with a mattress and a comforter where a less ethical employee might have napped. I, however, kept those things solely as a reserve should my buddies forget to get me down before closing time.

We actually gathered a wide variety of birds in our rafters, including one small owl that fed on the mice and smaller critters. I counted, fed, and even tagged these creatures. Eventually I came to realize that I was not just an employee, but an unexpendable member of the staff. Though I was seldom seen actually working, I cultivated and preserved the habitat for the store's wildlife. I'm not positive Tupid knew what I was doing, but I feel sure he would have appreciated it.

Often I would select top grade lumber from the racks, borrow a hammer and some nails from the tool department, have a gallon of good paint mixed, and then retire to the saws where I would cut and shape bird houses. I put in a whole row of bat houses just inside the greenhouse door. With the sprinklers constantly watering the plants, a lot of puddles pooled up and never went away in the greenhouse. Dangerous flocks of mosquitoes would use these pools as resorts and maternity wards. Those bat houses I built kept the mosquito population down and stifled possible outbreaks of disease among staff and patrons. I am proud to say that in all the time I worked at that store, not one person died of malaria.

One day, while I was watching over my preserve high atop the lumber racks, I noticed the nose of a large, furry beast cautiously sniffing the air from beneath the treated decking boards, twenty-some feet below. I watched for what seemed like hours. So dedicated was I, that I even forced myself to endure over-time hours, at a meager time-and- a-half rate, in order to discover the nature of said beast. It was one of those hot, hot days the South is so famous for and thus the air conditioners in the store were operating at full power. Those conditioners, mind you, resembled the engines on a 747 and put out cold air at gale force. My blind, as coincidence would have it, was located directly under one of those vents. I was dealing with a deadly wind chill factor and had to be careful of frostbite and hypothermia, even if the temperature outside was nearing 110. But the hunter in me forced me to overcome such hardships and I continued my vigil, looking for the nose below. It was, however, all for naught. Sixteen hours into my hunt I was forced to climb down from my shelf and clock out.

That night, as I lay in bed, I hit upon an idea. The next day at work I climbed back up and watched faithfully until just before closing. When the beast failed to show itself, I was left with no choice but to set my plan in action.

I went over to the craft department and got a twenty-pound bag of plaster, then I went to the snack room and bought a handful of candy bars. I got the best electric screwdriver we sold and I built a wooden frame with some top grade 2x4's. I built the frame right in front of the spot where I'd seen the nose poking out. I mixed up the plaster, always keeping an eye on the beast's lair lest he should spring on me. I then poured the plaster into the frame in such a way that if the beast came out he would have no choice but to leave his prints. Then, just to be sure, I got more plaster and spread it halfway down the aisle in both directions. I had no idea what sort of beast I was dealing with and I wanted to make sure it could not jump clear of the plaster and thus elude detection. I then opened the candy bars and tossed them carefully in front of the den's entrance as bait. After all that, I clocked out and went home.

I could hardly sleep that night, dreaming of bears, or bobcats, or maybe even a wild boar hiding out in the store, preying on the lesser creatures Tupid had unwittingly invited to take up residence. I skipped breakfast the next morning and went into work early. I came around the corner of my project area and stopped cold. I had captured the prints of a beast all right. I recognized Tupid's boot print from the number of occasions it had been thrust toward my hind end. I could see that he had walked a few steps into the aisle before realizing he was walking in wet plaster. I could also see where he had picked up one foot to examine the bottom of it. He must have been looking down at his shoe when he started yelling because I could see the clear impression of some very harsh words frozen in the now dry plaster.

I decided not to look for other tracks just then. In fact, I decided it was time to resign from my position and look elsewhere for employment. Great outdoorsmen, like great artists, are seldom truly appreciated, or wholly understood.

Deer Hunting, Detroit Style

Deer hunters are always looking for ways to improve their edge over our antlered quarry and I believe I have come up with the best solution yet. It is a simple idea that will put an end to dousings in deer scents, the deer stand, and camouflage. In fact, the deer hunter will no longer need to hide at all, but rather make himself as loud as possible.

Now, I have a nice rifle and boxes of shells with various loads, but I believe that if I could shoot a car out of my gun, I'd have a much better chance of bagging a deer. Not because cars are larger than bullets, but rather because deer seem more inclined to be killed by cars. The next time you drive to your favorite shooting range, conduct a small scientific test. Count the number of dead deer along the shoulder of the roadway. Next, count the number of dead deer lying on the shoulder of the shooting range. I'll wager a fair amount that there are more dead deer on the road. Clearly, deer walk into the path of oncoming cars with much greater frequency than they do into the path of oncoming bullets. So, a car shaped projectile would certainly be more effective than a bullet shaped projectile.

Auto manufacturers make no secret of the fact that

they design cars to resemble bullets for all of the obvious aerodynamic benefits. So why should munitions companies be shy about making car shaped bullets? Experience testifies to the fact that any self-respecting deer would gladly step in front of your newest car. Your chances of killing a deer with your car multiply exponentially based on the car's make and model, how much you paid, and how much you love the car. If you buy a 1974 Honda Civic you will never, ever, hit a deer. If you buy a brand new Corvette with the Indy 500 package, you will hit a deer before you get off the lot. If Winchester or Remington would just make a Corvette shaped bullet you could step onto the porch of your hunting lodge, fire, and deer would line up to collide with your bullet.

Unfortunately, the car shaped projectile is just a dream. But fear not, brother hunter, for I have come up with an idea that you can apply the next time you head out into the woods. Instead of stopping at the sporting goods store on your way out of town, stop at your local hardware store. Buy about six hundred yards of roll roofing, a can of yellow spray paint, and a pair of roller skates.

Find a clearing in the woods and stretch out the roll roofing. Next, take the can of yellow paint and spray two parallel lines down the center of the roll roofing. When you are done, what you should have is a decoy roadway. You might want to add potholes or a construction site, just for authenticity. That done, put on the roller skates and speed back and forth yelling "VROOOOOOOOOOM!" at the top of your lungs. That should bring the deer right to you. They will think that a new road has been built and they will rush to the area to destroy your car. Much like trout fishermen who "watch the hatch" to determine the best fly to use, you might want to spend some time at an actual, nearby road to get a feel for what kind of cars are most prevalent in the region. Try and sound like the local cars.

In all my Boy Scout and ROTC classes on gun safety, I never once had an instructor mention gun safety while on roller skates. There are only two possible reasons for this. Either everyone who has ever tried it is dead, their wives having secretly buried the bodies before the information became public knowledge, or the idea has never been tried. I suspect the former is closer to the truth. Men will try anything, and the stupider the better. That means that somewhere out there a woman has forfeited her husband's life insurance policy, claiming he ran off, rather than living with the embarrassment of telling the truth.

The stickiest issue in this whole scheme is stopping before you broadside the deer. You want to shoot him, not ram him. While automobiles often win battles against deer, humans on roller skates generally fair worse. You have a number of options here. You can practice leaping the deer, like an ice skater leaping oil barrels, but that solution poses a myriad of difficulties. Unless you were captain of your 1974 high-school disco-skating team, you might want to steer clear of leaping the deer.

The next option is what I like to call Deliberate Use of Recoil. Use the biggest load you can find. Load your own shell if you can. Pack in enough powder so that as soon as you fire, your forward momentum is checked, knocking you in the opposite direction. You will want to practice skating backwards through the woods at high speed. Try and have a good idea where low hanging branches are.

The last option is still in the experimental stages. I

call it the Reentry Solution and use space shuttle technology here. Refit the butt of your rifle so that it sticks up and over your shoulder a good six inches. Install in this modified butt a parachute. Rig a small charge to the parachute so that when you pull the trigger, the bullet fires normally and the secondary blast discharges the parachute behind you. The parachute, if properly deployed, should slow you down dramatically, just as it does when the Endeavor lands.

So, there you have it. Good luck, good skating, and good hunting.

The Monster Stick's Last Ride

You know you are a real West Virginian when you consider a fishing pole a family heirloom. As some of you know, my brother Paul passed away in January of '98, but many were the times Paul stood on the stage of the Liar's Contest and bedazzled us all with stories of the Monster Stick. Now the Monster Stick was Paul's nine-foot surf casting rod complete with six miles of brand new fifty-pound test Stren carp cord. It was the castingest outfit he ever owned and he always talked about how dangerous the Monster Stick was in the hands of an amateur.

The reason the Monster Stick was such a hazard to the untrained was mainly because it was such a bear to cast. Casting the Monster Stick entailed a two-handed, full body twist that was a cross between an Olympic hammer throw and a ballet pirouette. Casting from shore presented a myriad of problems and casting from any vessel smaller than an aircraft carrier almost always resulted in the boat being capsized.

The Monster Stick was the Pandora's box of fishing equipment. Strange things happened again and again whenever the Monster Stick reared its head. Take the time my grandfather was bringing the Monster Stick to this country. He cast off the deck of a huge cruise liner and snagged what he thought was a whale. He only realized he was mistaken when he brought the thing along side the ship and the guy in the crows-nest hollered "ICEBERG!" To my grandfather's great embarrassment, that ship sank in something over two hours.

Needless to say, I was scared stiff of the Monster Stick. I never went near the thing. But this last April I was out in my garden tilling when I heard a voice say, "If you bait it, catfish will come." I looked around but didn't see anybody. And then I heard it again, "If you bait it, catfish will come." Even though I couldn't see anyone talking to me, I could tell from the slow West Virginia drawl that the voice could only belong to one of two people—it was either God, or my brother Paul. Either way, the revelation was clear: The Monster Stick needed one last fling and I was going to have to be the man to do it.

I snuck into my sister-in-law's house and stole the Monster Stick from its resting-place above the mantle. I bought a five-gallon bucket of raw beef livers and a bass boat, and then I set sail on the waters of the mighty Buckhannon River. Standing in that boat, with that rod in my hand, I felt as confident and as volatile as a Third World dictator with nuclear capabilities. I was heavily armed, crazy with power, and right likely to do something stupid enough to put all of humanity in jeopardy.

To be honest with you, I think the day would have come out just fine if I hadn't made one particular mistake. You see, I decided that I ought to bring my dog, Buck, out in that boat with me. For those of you who don't know, Buck is my super-dog whose mother was a German shepherd and whose father was a prolific and extremely determined basset hound. Like most of the men in my family, Buck is funny looking and none too bright. As a matter of fact, when God was passing out brains, Buck thought he said "drains" and so he asked for one that emptied quickly. On the other hand, when God was passing out noses, Buck thought he said "roses" and so he asked for one that smelled real good. Buck's nose is one of the best in the world. Just to give you an example of his nasal prowess, remember that fairy tale about the Princess who sleeps on the twenty-three mattresses and then finds the one with the pea on it? Well, that's nothing. I guarantee you that even if you had 23,000 mattresses it would take Buck less than a minute to find the one with the Princess's pea on it.

Anyway, I tossed Buck one whole beef liver to keep him quiet while I was fishing, then I put another whole liver on the hook at the end of my line. I stood up, closed my eyes, grasped the Monster Stick in both hands, and went into my cast. As I spun around I put all my weight on my right foot. That caused the boat to list in that direction and subsequently pushed all the water on the right side of the river against the right bank. Then I put all my weight on my left foot. That pushed the boat in that direction and so all the water on the left side of the river was pushed against that shore. With nothing to hold it up any longer, that bass boat plopped down onto the muddy bottom of the Buckhannon River. When I opened my eyes and saw those two walls of water on either side of me, and felt the power of that rod in my hand, I knew just what Moses must have felt like at the Red Sea. When I looked again, and saw those two walls of water collapsing on me, well then I knew just what Pharaoh's army must have felt like.

Just before those two walls of water crashed down I

noticed a few things. First, I noticed that the line of the Monster Stick was still feeding out nicely and that the bait was rocketing down the river. Then, I noticed that there was a strange looking blob on the end of my hook. The last thing I saw was that Buck-dog was no longer in the boat. As near as I can figure, Buck was jealous that I was going to give a whole liver to the catfish and so when I cast, he had sprung for the bait and in the process had caught his collar on the hook. I had just cast my dog away worse than the Swiss Family Robinson. Then the water crashed down.

The force of that water drove my tiny bass boat three feet into the mud and left me mired up to my hips in pure muck. But the line was still spinning out and I knew I was in trouble. Either Buck was going to drown when he hit the water, or he was going to be swallowed up by a huge catfish. And I didn't want to have to explain all that to my wife. If I was going to save my dog I was going to have to work fast.

I reached in my pocket and pulled out my trusty, seventy-four-function Swiss Army type knife. I quickly opened up the scuba gear and the flippers. I have the Jacques Cousteau special—I had to pay ten extra dollars for all that. I suited up, pulled myself out of the mud and headed to shore towing the Monster Stick and that five-gallon bucket of livers. I made it to shore just as Buck started his downward arch. I saw the railroad tracks and heard the whistle blow just as Buck was hitting the water. Now those weren't just any railroad tracks mind you, but Wierton's world-famous steel fashioned into CS&X railroad tracks stretching clear from Cowen to Grafton via Burnsville, Buckhannon, Carrolton and Philippi. And, as luck would have it, just then a six engine, 168 car CS&X monster train was rolling by.

I made it to the train just as Buck sank beneath the surface of the water. I jammed the Monster Stick into the rungs of the ladder of the last car on that train and jumped on. Monster Stick, meet monster train. For various physical and scientific reasons that I just don't have time to go into here, the momentum of that train going in the opposite direction of that cast was sufficient to pull Buck out of the water and drag him along. Buck got his feet under him and was cruising along like a water skier. He lifted his front paws, did a few rooster tails, and even flipped over a fallen log. All the while I was reeling away.

I got Buck about ten feet away from the train, just off the edge of the bank, and then I flipped my wrists and the Monster Stick popped Buck out of the water. I think everything would have been fine from that point on if a catfish the size of a Buick hadn't chosen that exact moment to strike for the bait. That catfish came out of the water faster than a White House intern from the Oval Office. The fish swallowed up Buck's hind end. I flipped the bait, Buck and the catfish out of the water and behind the train where they all plopped down on the tracks. That catfish was so big that he straddled the tracks and was coming along behind the train like a flatboat on the Erie Canal.

I had to get Buck out of that fish's mouth, so I took one of those whole beef livers and threw it at the fish. I figured that as soon as it got within range the fish would open his mouth and try to catch it. When the catfish opened his mouth for the liver, I would just reel Buck in. The only thing was, Buck smelled that liver coming and when it got within range he leapt up and swallowed it whole. I said, "Bad Dog! Bad Dog!" and tossed another liver. Buck swallowed that one too, and the next, and the next, until my five-gallon bucket was empty and my five-gallon Buck-dog was full. I was at my wit's end; I didn't know what to do.

Fortunately, Buck is not totally without means of his own. You see, all that fear and liver started to react with the natural juices inside of Buck, and, to put it politely, Buck's own personal gastrointestinal El Niño went into hyper-drive. He released enough methane into that catfish to put both Mountaineer and Columbia Gas out of business. That catfish swelled up like the Hindenberg and rose up off the tracks. As the fish and Buck shot skyward, I had to play out the line to keep it from breaking. Before long I had all six miles of line reeled out and Buck and that catfish were trailing behind the train like a kite.

Every time we went around a curve it would fling them way out around the train and it was everything I could do to hold on. We rounded a particularly sharp curve and it whipped those two way out to the side. The force was so great, and they were going so fast, that when the fifty-pound carp cord hit a mountain about twenty feet from the top, the line just cut right through it like a hot knife through butter. The top of the mountain lifted up and then crashed back down. Well, I smiled then. I mean, if nothing else had gone right that day, at least I had just completed the first, and only, totally successful mountain-top removal and reclamation operation.

I looked over my shoulder and saw that the train was going into a tunnel. I started reeling as fast as I could and had Buck and that giant fish right behind the train again when we hit the tunnel. The bloated catfish slammed into the tunnel entrance and his front lips filled the opening, but no more would fit in.

The line on the Monster Stick started to sing under the pressure, caught, as it was, between the immovable force of the catfish and the unstoppable force of the monster train. At the critical moment, when it seemed sure I would lose Buck forever, the catfish gave up. He parted his lips and Buck shot out like the cork from a bottle of champagne. The catfish flew backward out of the tunnel and danced around the sky like a deflating balloon until he finally dove back into the river.

I grabbed Buck, the Monster Stick, and the empty liver bucket and jumped from the train. I went straight to my sister-in-law's and hung the Monster Stick back in its place of honor over the mantle. It had had its last fling, and now, may Paul and the Monster Stick rest in peace.

How We Got Out in the Cold in the First Place

If you ask me, Global Warming was Mother Nature's plan all along and it would have come off without a hitch had hunters done what they were supposed to do. Think about bitter, wind howling, icicles-in-your-mustache, cold weather for a moment. What good does it do us? I think that it is overrated and outdated. Cold weather was probably just a tool designed to help humankind along, but, as usual, we failed to heed the lesson.

Imagine our original forefathers and foremothers existing in the mild to hot temperatures of Mesopotamia. There they were, living in caves, wearing fig leaves and eating raw meat: an undeniably sorry sight. When Mother Nature looked in on them from time to time she must have shook her head and said, "They just aren't progressing like I'd hoped. I see by the fig leaves that they've invented camouflage, but I really expected them to invent the 2x4, fiberglass insulation, and double paned, low E windows by now. If nothing else, I thought sure they'd have come up with the idea of cooking meat on their own." And then the idea struck her, "If it got cold, really cold, these boneheads might get to work, take that first step and invent fire. When they've invented everything they need, I'll just warm Earth back up again."

Suddenly, snow began to fall. The wind picked up, ice bit into the people's skin, meat froze, and there was no way to get warm. Caveman said, "Sheesh, it's right chilly. I wish we had invented and installed an insulated sliding glass door at the mouth of that cave."

It was too nasty to go outside, and there was no Sports Center, so Caveman just picked up two sticks and started rubbing. The sticks burst into flame and all of a sudden the cave was full of noxious black smoke. Right away Cavewoman came up with the idea of a chimney, so just as quickly, Caveman had to leave the warmth of the freshly invented fire and go outside to invent brick, mortar, a plumb line level and, at last, the chimney.

When he was finished with the chimney it looked wonderful. The chimney stood straight and proud in a field of tall grass and deepening snow. It was a beaut. This, however, was where Mother Nature's plan began to fail. Cavewoman took one look at that chimney and said, "Well, isn't that just darling. Wouldn't a nice Cape Cod, two story, multi-bathroom, picket fenced, cottage with a wraparound, screened-in porch look so nice beside that chimney?" Caveman had no choice but to get to work.

There were a few very brave cavemen, men brave enough that after having invented the chimney, and after then hearing about the house, just plain walked away. Every now and then you'll see a memorial to these souls: just a lonesome chimney in the middle of a field, or in a glade, the men who built them having long since suffered mysterious, violent deaths. Most of the cavemen just got to work.

Having built the houses to go with the chimneys,

Caveman was suddenly confronted with the fact that he had created a lawn. Left on his own, Caveman would not have seen anything but field. Cavewoman, however, was kind enough to point out that what was so recently nothing but tundra was now the front, back and side yards, respectively.

Pleased with her little experiment, Mother Nature let the earth begin to get warm again. Warmth brought on new growth, especially in this thing Cavewoman called yard. This, of course, meant mowing. When the mowing was done, Cavewoman pointed out that the house could use a fresh coat of paint. Then the windows needed cleaning...

Even though Caveman was tired from all the work he was doing, he still found time to invent the basement and the concept of tinkering. Soon, the high-powered rifle, the scope, the fly rod and the reel materialized.

Caveman began to grumble. Other cavemen heard him and they all concluded that they needed a week off. It was decided that they would tell their wives that they were out of meat and needed to go hunting. Reluctantly, Cavewoman agreed.

Mother Nature saw no harm in the men going off this one time to scout out some game, but it soon became apparent that hunting was not their only motive. And then they were going year after year. Lots of things weren't getting invented on time, if at all. Mother Nature realized that the only thing that could possibly keep the men from going hunting was the re-institution of cold weather. It was a devious plan.

Men would wake up on the first day of what was becoming known as "Deer Season" and the weather would be fine and warm. They'd pack their gear, head out into the woods, and by the time they were in their tree stands it would be thirty-below with forty-five mile an hour winds. Mother Nature, year after year, would create meaner and meaner weather, but the men stayed out. When that failed, she drove the deer into the thickest parts of the forest, painted them brown and made them swift and quiet. Still the men came, undaunted. And soon they weren't just hunting deer, but turkey, duck, antelope, squirrel, rabbit, and anything else that wasn't man, woman or dog. Caveman was even so bold as to cut a hole in the ice and go fishing!

So, as you can clearly see, Mother Nature intended all along for the world to be a mild, decent, game populated place. But once she got the cold started, she had to keep going, had to keep trying to keep the hunters at home. But it was no use; soon even the women started venturing out into the cold to get away from the Cape Cod with the lawn and the chimney. Mother Nature, I believe, has just thrown in the towel.

Stereotypical Clergy

As a pastor, I am often forced to attend various and sundry meetings— Sunday meetings, too. And thus, when I lived in Meadow Bridge, West Virginia, and was asked to attend a pastors' meeting in Halfdollar, I was not only willing to go, but I offered to drive the car in which we carpooled. "We" being the Baptist pastor, the Catholic priest, and me.

While we were at the meeting, I won a door prize. It was an offering plate, about as big around as a trash can lid and lined with plush velvet. A lovely thing. On the way home I put that offering plate in the front seat. Buck-dog, who had ridden along, found the offering plate to be a wonderful place to catch a nap. The Baptist pastor and the priest rode in the back. Being three members of the Cloth, and a dog, it was only natural that we had stopped on the way home and picked up a bucket of fried chicken. The chicken was sitting nicely between the front seats.

Well, this was January. And there was no way to get between Meadow Bridge and Halfdollar by car except to go up and over Sandstone Mountain, a 3,200 foot monster that is incline enough going up, but almost straight down on the way home. At the bottom is the New River. We were coming down that mountain and it was snowing so hard that I was eventually forced to pull over onto the shoulder. No sooner had I pulled over than I noticed a semi truck coming at us full steam ahead down that hill, and there was no chance he was going to stop. .

That ol' truck got bigger and bigger in my rearview mirror. The priest was Hail Marying so fast it sounded like he was speaking in tongues. The Baptist pastor was trying to get into his Big-Gulp, hoping to immerse himself one last time before doom struck, and I was, well I'm a Methodist, so I was just sitting there. Buck-dog, on the other hand, is a dog and thus was interested mainly in preserving himself.

Buck saw the truck, grabbed the bucket of fried chicken, pulled it into the offering plate, and hunkered down. When that truck hit, the impact shot Buck through the windshield, still in that offering plate with the fried chicken, like a Frisbee. The priest, the Baptist and I were next through the windshield. There we were, a Methodist preacher, a Baptist pastor, and a Catholic priest flying through the evening sky, and not a punch line in sight.

That ol' truck burst in two. It was carrying shoes and suddenly there were 100,000 pair of tennis shoes flying through the sky.

Buck-dog, in that offering plate, flew all the way down to the New River, which was frozen over solid. He hit the ice in that offering plate so hard that it knocked his hind legs out of the plate. But that fried chicken was still in there, so with his front half, Buck hung on tight. He slid out across the ice.

Me, the Baptist pastor and the Catholic Priest hit next. We slid across the ice in a somewhat tangled ecumenical movement, following Buck's path. The 100,000 pair of shoes dropped into the woods behind us. That's when I said to those other fellas, "Boys, I sure hope no one can see us. Here we are living up to all the stereotypes people have about clergy. I mean, look at us. Three pastors chasing a bowl full of fried chicken and half a Buck in the offering plate out onto thin ice while 200,000 soles are lost in the wilderness behind us."

A Picture of the Moose that Killed Us

Eventually Skeeter and I grew up and, surprisingly, our fathers still liked us despite all the wrecked cars, mayhem, debacles, lost power tools, et al. In fact, Skeet's dad, Frank, even liked us enough to ask us to go black bear hunting in Montana. Frank offered to drive, pay for the gas, do all the planning and see to it that we were fed. No one could pass up a deal like that. So, we packed everything we owned—and some stuff we bought extra just to ensure we had too much—into the minivan and headed west.

The thing about Frank and Skeeter is that God gave their family the optical genes of cave dwelling crickets. Frank got sent to the principle's office once in elementary school because when the nurse asked him to read the top line of the eye chart he said, "All I see is a blur." She thought he was being a smart aleck, but the fact is the poor guy couldn't see the "E" that we all take for granted. Frank and Skeeter are just this side of legally blind, sort of a work release probationary blindness. That's not to say that they are illegally blind, though I've seen that once or twice when we've spent too much time at Androczi's Vineyard. None-the-less, we made it across the country with little or no trouble due to visionary problems—

we are very rarely accused of anything visionary. The locals were glad to have us, and our money, for the first two weeks of May, but everyone in Swan Lake agreed that we were two weeks too early for bear hunting. "The last two weeks of May are the best for bear hunting," they told us. But that didn't stop Frank, Skeeter and me from scouring the woods looking for black bears. Of course, our greatest fear was that we would stumble onto the path of a grizzly, so I kept my eyes wide open and Frank and Skeeter looked as best they could. And that is how we almost got killed by a moose.

When you are looking for black bears and expecting to be eaten by grizzly bears, moose are often the last thing on your mind, especially if you are from West Virginia where the only moose are large, often over-stuffed, Lodge members. The moose, in my mind, is not a beast to be wary of, but rather a sort of large-horned wild bovine with all the malice of tofu. Especially compared to a griz.

It had been a long day. The three of us had hiked up a peak to Scott's Point, hoping to catch a view of Scott's Lake, but staying well away from the notorious grizzly area. We had, at times, been waist deep in snow and it was late afternoon when we finally got back to the minivan and started our long drive out. "Well boys, what now?" Frank asked as we hit the hard top. It was still light and I was hoping to catch a glimpse of the Swan River as the sun went down, so I suggested we take a drive down a short road that ended at the river. Frank obliged me and we made the turn. Frank pulled the van to a stop at the edge of the waterway.

It is Frank's nature to be a cautious man, always anticipating the danger we might encounter. You have to remember that he had known Skeeter and I for thirty years and was used to disasters befalling him while in our presence. As a result of his close association with the two of us, Frank always made it a point to turn the van around facing our escape route, before we went into the wilderness. That way all we would need to do to flee was pile in and hit the gas. But it was late, and our normally dull senses were even more depleted than usual, so Frank just pulled up to the river's edge.

I was in the backseat of the van looking through binoculars at the opposite side of the river. Everything was golden in the sunshine and I was impressed by the huge, honey brown stump of what must have been a massive tree. Frank and Skeeter were in the front of the van trying to figure out who could see least well. "See that picnic table over there?" Skeeter asked Frank. "Nope," Frank answered emphatically. "Me either," Skeeter replied smugly. They switched glasses and went through the same line of questions about the outhouse four feet from the van. Neither could see it. Nor could they see the trees across the river, the river itself, the hood ornament, the dashboard, or each other. I was putting considerable thought toward offering to drive for the rest of the trip, when the stump that I had been admiring moved.

"Boys," I said quietly, "did either of you see that stump move?"

"Shut-up" Skeeter answered, "we're having a serious, scientific discussion up here."

"No, really, across the river at two o'clock, that huge honey-colored stump just stood up."

Both of them lunged for their binoculars. "Two o'clock Eastern or Mountain time?" Frank asked. Then they saw it. We froze in position, staring through the lenses waiting for whatever it was to move again. All of us had grizzly on the brain, and huge honey-colored moving stumps in Montana, we knew, must certainly be grizzlies. The stump raised its head and the setting sun shone full on the huge, onyx eyes of the biggest moose I'd ever seen (granted, it was the only one I'd ever seen). "That's a freakin' moose!" I shouted, jumping straight up in the van and smashing my head into the ceiling.

"I think you might be right." Frank whispered, and then added, "Now let's not get excited. These things can be dangerous but I want to get out and take a picture. Everyone got their sidearm?" We checked and shook our heads. "Good. Now, very quietly get out of the van, but don't latch your doors, we might need to jump back in."

We slid out of the van, each of us again checking our pistols as though we might be about to duel with the moose rather than observe it. And though the .22 Magnum I was wearing might not be more than a cosmetic accessory, like a strand of pearls, Skeeter was wearing a .44 and Frank a .38. I figured any attacking grizzly would laugh at me as it charged, taking all six shots in stride, flinch as Frank unloaded, and stagger just enough after taking Skeet's load that one of us might have time to finish praying before being devoured. But we were ready for action, come Hell or hungry wildlife.

Each of us took a step from the van and snapped a photo. Then we advanced a few steps, snapped another photo, and moved up again. Our reasoning was that we were bound to spook the moose sooner or later so we would get the best picture we could by getting closer and closer until it bolted. The moose looked up from the tall grass on the other side of the

Swan River, munched a clump of straw between its jaws, turned its head toward us, and then bent for more grass. When you have been awakened the last six nights in a row dreaming of grizzlies pulling apart deer, elk and hunters, gnashing flesh and crushing bone—well the sight of an herbivore chewing cud just doesn't instill instant fear in your heart.

Wearing our blaze orange vests, and snapping pictures at a feverish pace, we moved from tree to tree, inching ever nearer the moose. Once a minute or so the huge moose would look up at us, shake its head lazily, and go back to chewing. Before long, we were directly across the river from the moose, not a hundred yards of shallow river separating us. The moose was so big that I had to switch to my wide-angle lens just to fit him in the frame. Skeeter, who seldom carried a camera, had borrowed his wife's twelve-dollar "Snap-o-Matic" and was forced to take a picture first of the moose's rear end, and then his front end, in order to get the whole thing. It should have registered with us that any beast big enough to require a panoramic shot was no beast to be trifled with. The moose looked up, and pounded his front paw into the dirt. He took a step forward.

"Time to go boys," Frank whispered while snapping one last picture. "For all we know he has a calf in the woods he's protecting."

"Frank," I said, "I think that it's the female of the species that care for the young in the moose world. Not the male."

"No reason to take any chances boys. For all we know, this is a very liberated moose that has sole custody of his kids. It is the new millennium after all, and this is obviously a very progressive moose."

"Dad," Skeet said in a hushed tone, "I'd like to try

and ride that thing. Do you think it would come over here if I offered it an apple?"

I don't know if Skeeter was joking, I pray he was, but as if in response to the question the moose leapt forward into the river and stood knee deep in the water, glowering at us. It quickly became obvious to us that this was no docile, flat horned bovine, but rather a couple of tons of very angry "prey" used to defending itself against large packs of hungry wolves. Frank jumped up, startled, and in the process, mashed the button down on his camera, simultaneously taking the last picture, cursing, and starting the loud, mechanical whirl of the automatic film rewind. Apparently moose do not like that sound.

The beast reared up, turned downriver toward our van, and started charging. It stayed across the river but was seemingly intent on finding a place to cross. Frank took to his feet like a sinner running for the Church during the Rapture. Skeeter grabbed my collar and jerked me to my feet and we both headed for the shelter of the van. I thought about drawing my .22, but only with the thought of tossing it away like unwanted ballast. In order to free his right hand for drawing his .44, Skeet was attempting to shove his wife's $12 camera into the cargo pocket of his pants. The moose was lopping just across the river, his eyes on us. The van was still a good twenty-five yards away. The moose was, I'm positive, calculating how to best cut across the angle.

Skeet's attention was focused on shoving the cheap camera into his pocket and so he didn't see the picnic table until he was, literally, on top of it. His feet flew up, his arms and legs went spread eagle, and he slid across the wet redwood on his belly. His wife's cheap camera spun into the air. Both Skeeter and I had recently married and we still had a lot to learn, but one rule that was branded in both our brains was, "Don't drop, break, lose or otherwise deface property belonging to your wife." We watched the camera spin through the air with that thought in mind. Skeet somersaulted off the table into the dirt. I stopped in my tracks and then dove for the camera. The moose found his ford and turned in the river. Frank made it to the van and cranked the engine to life. He was yelling, "Come on boys! This is no time for skullduggery!" The camera plopped down on the moist leaves covering the forest floor.

Skeet managed to gain his feet again and we both raced for the camera, oblivious to the moose now three quarters of the way across the river and making a beeline for my backside. Even though it wasn't my wife's camera, and even though both Skeet and I are married to two of the nicest, most understanding women you'd ever meet, it still seemed prudent to retrieve the camera. The moose landed on our shore like the Allies at Normandy and then, inexplicably, stopped in his tracks. Skeet grabbed the camera and, as if suddenly awakened from a deep sleep, both he and I were struck with the gravity of the situation. The moose was fifteen yards away, the van was ten, we were inadequately armed, and had just stopped our desperate flight to save a $12 camera. Frank was going to be red-hot, especially if the moose decided to ram the van.

"Crap," Skeet said softly, "do we let the moose kill us, or Frank?"

"Frank." I said. "He can't see worth a darn. He doesn't know you dropped the camera; tell him you dropped the .44. It will seem like a more reasonable thing to have stopped to pick-up."

"OK, that's good. But what now?"

The forest was silent except for the sound of the moose taking controlled, very deep breaths, and the engine of the minivan purring softly. Something, a pinecone maybe, fell in the distance and landed with a muffled thud. A squirrel was chattering above us on a branch. The moose lowered his head. Skeeter raised the camera to his eye and snapped a quick shot. The moose charged and Skeeter and I ran with everything we had. Frank started backing the van down the road with the side door wide open. We raced toward the dark, gaping hole that was salvation. Skeeter jumped in first with me right behind. I slammed the door shut as Frank threw gravel twenty yards in every direction executing a perfect 180, then flooring it down the quiet road. We watched the moose lope behind us, with a sort of satisfied look on his face. He followed us for a quarter mile or so, more for show than as a threat, and then he ducked into the woods.

Frank was pouring sweat, more from anger than fear, as he said, "Why on God's green earth did you two stop?"

"I dropped the .44," Skeet said sheepishly.

"Then why, for the love of God, did you snap a picture?"

"Well Dad, it's like this, I figured we were goners. I figured we were spending our last few moments on earth and I started to think about Grandma and how nice it was going to be to see her in Heaven. And I thought, wouldn't it be nice to have a really great picture of that moose so I could show her and say, 'Grams, this is my pal Bil. And this is a picture of the moose that killed us.'"

And the Winner Is?

There are two things in life you should never do if you are going to be in a car driven by my father for any length of time. The first is: Don't eat. The second is: Don't drink any liquid. You see, my father gets behind the wheel of a car, shuts the door, straps on his seatbelt, points the car in the direction he will be heading, embarks, and that's it. He will never, ever stop. If dad were driving to the moon he wouldn't stop, not even for gas. He would figure out a way to be refueled en route. Don't eat; don't drink, ever, if you plan to be in a car with my dad. I mean, a week ahead of time start your starvation diet. You want every last ounce of matter that can be purged from your body long gone before ever strapping into Dad's car. Hearse drivers are more concerned for the physical needs of their passengers than my father is.

"Have you emptied out?" Dad would ask as the family headed out the door for a trip. If you hadn't, it was your own fault. You were warned. You might be holding in the last glass of milk you drank clear to Bangor if you didn't empty out before getting in the car.

I knew all of this. I was aware of the situation. I tried to make all my friends aware of the situation as well, especially the rest of the guys in my Scout troop.

Dad was our Scout leader and thus he drove us to and from camp. That was all well and good because Dad is a good guy and he let us have our fun in the van, but God bless the poor boy that didn't heed my warnings. It wasn't so bad on the way to camp. All of us were at least eleven. So we were practiced in the art of holding it in, what with years of experience sitting through school, church and long car rides. It was easy to program our minds to exert control. You simply had to rely on timing and stamina. But coming home from camp, well that was a different matter all together.

It was August. We had been at Dilly's Mill for summer camp an entire week. It was our last day. Everyone was worn out, sunburned, and itching from bugs and poison ivy. We had shot rifles, blasted clay pigeons, sailed, canoed, fished, built fires, burned our fingers, cut ourselves with sharp pocketknives, and generally had a high time. Spirits were soaring. The thought of going home only added to the general merriment of the day.

At lunch that day we had been served tacos. Like all camp tacos, they were too salty and we had added way too much hot sauce. We were thirsty. It was hot in the lunchroom. There were sweating aluminum pitchers of water and fruit drinks making rings on the tables. I considered my options. We would leave in an hour. I was dying of thirst. It was a four-hour ride home, and Dad was driving. I reached for the pitcher and poured one more glass of water. I reckoned I could process that before it was time to roll on home. I sipped at the cool water.

Jimmy Sampson, a portly, sweaty kid who had less self-control than your average twelve-year old, filled his glass as well. He knocked it back and went for another. "Jimmy," I warned, "take it easy, we're leaving soon."

"I can handle it," he said. He downed another one.

"Jimmy," Pete Vichoff asked, "do you think you could drink that whole pitcher of water?"

"Sure I could," Jimmy said.

I looked at Pete. "Pete," I said, "don't do it."

Pete paid me no mind. "Jimmy, if you drink that whole pitcher of water in five minutes, I'll give you my new canteen."

It was a nice canteen. Pete had won it in an archery contest. It was a military canteen with a cooking pot/drinking cup that fit over the outside. They were twelve dollars in the Trading Post. Only the high-rolling Scouts could afford them that summer. Pete unhooked the canteen and laid it on the table for everyone to see. It was sharp, no doubt about that. Jimmy eyed it.

"All I gotta do is drink this pitcher of water in five minutes or less and I get that canteen?" He asked.

"Yep."

"Do I get to throw up part way through?" Jimmy queried.

"NO!" Everybody shouted. It was a standard rule of eating and drinking contests that you could not throw up halfway through, but you had to ask.

Jimmy looked at the canteen. He looked at the pitcher of water. He gripped his glass. He looked at the clock. Fifty-five minutes before we had to leave.

"Who has a stop watch?" Jimmy asked. Three guys volunteered to keep time.

Pete said: "You ready?"

Jimmy nodded.

"Set." Pete said.

Jimmy opened his mouth, put the glass in position, and lifted the pitcher to pour.

"Go!" Pete yelled.

Jimmy poured a glass and downed it in two gulps. He had half the pitcher gone in under a minute. Someday, he would make his frat brothers very proud. After the first minute he slowed considerably, pacing himself, resting here and there for twenty or thirty seconds. It now took him four or five swallows to down each glass. His breaths came in short, shallow gasps, but he kept drinking. Nine glasses in and he was moving like a drunken frog. "I gotta pee," he said. "I gotta pee bad!"

"Keep drinking," somebody called. "There's still about three glasses of water in the pitcher."

Jimmy poured another.

"Forty seconds!"

He drank the glass in one huge gulp and poured another. Barely a glass full was still sloshing around in the pitcher.

"Thirty seconds!"

Jimmy drank rapidly, not gulping, just steadily pouring the water down his throat, his head tilting further and further back. He slammed the glass down on the table. He looked like a bloated hippo sitting across the table from me. He poured the last half glass of water out of the pitcher.

"Twenty seconds."

Jimmy took six or seven deep breaths. As deep as he could anyway, all that water in his gut was pushing up into his chest cavity and compressing his lungs. At this point in the contest, his lungs were likely no larger than lima beans. He shut his eyes and pursed his lips. He lifted the glass.

"Ten. Nine. Eight . . ."

Jimmy started to turn the glass up to drink. The glass touched his lips and then his eyes bugged out. He choked once, turned toward Pete, and threw up water all over Pete's chest and into his lap. Pete jumped up from the table, grabbed his canteen and ran out of the room screaming. All of us were laughing—all of us except Jimmy. Jimmy had glassy eyes and his head was on the table. He stood up on wobbly legs, turned toward the door, and staggered outside. We watched him go into the woods about ten feet. He stopped. And then we heard the sigh of relief as he emptied the rest of the way out.

Jimmy made two more trips to the woods before it was time get in the van. All of us did. We had four hours of non-stop driving ahead. The thing about being at camp for a week was that it threw you out of practice. All your training and stamina went out the window because a boy in the woods doesn't need to be selective about where or when he goes. When you gotta go, you go. It was hard to get back into the mind-set of waiting and holding.

Dad pulled up in the van. "Everybody emptied out?" he asked. We all ran to the woods one more time. Jimmy and I sat in the first row of seats in the van. Pete and two other guys were behind us, the rest of the troop crowding in behind them. Most everybody fell right to sleep. Jimmy and I chatted it up a little. He was disappointed about not winning the canteen. "But," he said, "at least I threw up on him. That's something." I had to agree.

Pete leaned toward us. "Jimmy," he said, "I knew you couldn't do it. I knew you were just a loser. I would have bet a million dollars because I knew there was no way you were going to win. My new canteen was safe and sound the whole time." Pete showed us the canteen again.

Jimmy shrugged it off and then went to sleep. I fell asleep soon afterward.

I was having a dream. I was in a tunnel, a coal mine maybe, battling trolls. It was hot, very hot. I was trying to crawl through a hole in the roof of the tunnel, but a troll had grabbed my thigh at the last second, and he had it in a death grip. The troll was wailing. It was saying, "Mr. Lepp! Mr. Lepp! I gotta whiz!" The troll sounded like Jimmy. I woke to find Jimmy clutching my leg and pleading with my dad. "I gotta whiz Mr. Lepp. I gotta whiz bad! Please, please, please."

Dad turned his head and said, "Jimmy, you should have emptied out before we left."

"I did Mr. Lepp, Scout's Honor I did."

"Well Jimmy, we'll be home in an hour. You're a big boy, you can hold it."

Jimmy looked desperate. He swallowed hard, relaxed his grip on my leg, and sat back, cautiously. I went back to sleep.

"But Mr. Lepp," I heard him saying later, "I gotta whiz bad."

"Jimmy," my dad said, "we'll be home in half an hour. Just sit tight."

Jimmy was rocking back and forth in his seat. He had his elbows locked and his hands on his knees. He was taking deep breaths and staring straight ahead. Every so often I could hear him swallow. There was no way I was going back to sleep now. We were sitting on vinyl seats. I wanted to know if the flood was coming my way, and if it did I wanted to get out of the way.

I started thinking about how Jimmy had vomited all that water on Pete. He had just turned toward him and let it rip. I started to worry about Dad. Would Jimmy pee on my dad? "Dad," I said, "this is one time you might want to make an exception."

Jimmy joined me. "I gotta go bad Mr. Lepp. BAD! If you ain't gonna stop, at least roll down the windows, otherwise I'll flood the van and we'll all drown!"

"Twenty minutes now," Dad said. "If you really have to go Jimmy, use your canteen." Dad chuckled at his little joke. I looked at Jimmy. Jimmy smiled. We both looked over the back of our seat. Pete was asleep. His canteen was on the seat next to him.

Grabbled

Skeeter Barth and I watched the fishing shows on television together every Saturday morning. We were young and eager to grow up well versed in catfish fishing. Always ready to try new techniques, we were amazed to watch two guys in Mississippi swimming along the banks of the Sunflower River fishing for catfish using only their bare hands. The narrator called it "Grabbling," and was describing how these two guys felt along the bank under the waterline looking for catfish dens. When they found a hole, they would stick their arms into the dens and pull out huge catfish clamped on their forearms. It was one of the most fascinating things we had ever seen.

When the show was over we headed down to Skitter Creek, the best catfish stream within walking distance of our houses. We hiked up the bank until we found a place where there were a number of trees with root systems half submerged. The guys in Mississippi took nothing with them into the water but fearlessness and brawn, figuring any fish they reached into was no match for their prowess. Skeeter and I, on the other hand, scouted out a large stick in case we had to fight our way out of a catfish.

We jumped into the stream and I started feeling

along the bank just under the waterline. I found a large hole and stuck my hand into the opening. The inside of the hole was slick and cold—just as I had imagined the inside of a catfish might feel. When nothing happened, I stuck my arm in up to my elbow, then up to my shoulder. I was feeling around, hoping to discover a giant catfish uvula hanging down on which I could clasp my fingers for some sort of purchase. Skeeter was standing behind me, the big stick raised above his head. "I guess there's nothing in this hole," I said, turning toward Skeeter. Just then I felt something twitch inside the burrow.

"Wait a sec, something moved."

"Was it a catfish?" he asked.

"I don't know, I've never felt the inside of a catfish move before."

Skeeter made his way over toward me. "Let me see." He reached out and shoved his hand into the hole. "Feels like mud."

I felt something twitch again. Skeet's eyes widened. "Did you feel that?" he asked.

"Feel what?"

"That twitching."

"Yeah, but I thought it was you."

We looked at each other; there was surprise and wonder in his eyes. We were about to land our first monster catfish by hand. We were grabblers!

"What do we do now?" I asked.

"I guess we just wait for it to strike. Pull your arm out," he said.

"No, I found it first, you pull your arm out."

"You pull yours out!"

While we arguing, we were splashing water at each other and thrashing our hands about inside the hole, each trying to push the others' arm out. Suddenly, our arms were sucked deep into the hole, until our shoulders were underwater and our cheeks were pressed against the cold mud of the bank. A clamp closed around our arms like a steel trap slamming shut. Try as we might, we could not get free. I started to wonder if the catfish in the hole had been watching the very same TV show, and had spent the day waiting for an arm to reach into it's den. Horror driven and panic-stricken, Skeeter and I pulled with all our might. The catfish didn't budge. We put our feet as high up on the bank as we could and pushed, but our toes just sank into the slimy muck.

Skeeter had turned as white as a styrofoam bait cup and I was sweating despite the cool water washing by me. It dawned on me that those two guys from down south were better prepared than us for hand-to-gill catfish fighting. The arms on those guys were as stout and hard as chestnut limbs, compared to the lily stems that dangled from my shoulders. Furthermore, a ten-pound catfish was nothing to a 250-pound man, whereas the same fish was ten percent of me. It was going to be hard to go through the rest of our lives known as "Those two kids who lost their arms catfishing."

I noticed that Skeeter still had the stick we'd found in case of an emergency. I reckoned this was as good a time as any to deploy it. I took the stick from Skeeter's hand and wedged it into the hole. I forced it as deep as I could into the lips of the catfish. With our free hands we grabbed the top of the stick and pulled down. The lever action forced the fish's mouth open enough that Skeeter was able to wrench his arm free. He sprang from the water and rushed off into the woods, screaming at the top of his lungs. I hadn't remembered that as being one of the techniques used by the guys from Mississippi.

Now I was alone in the water, shoulder deep in a catfish that had no intention of letting go. I willed myself into believing that it was a catfish, and not some diabolical creature left over from a prehistoric age. I considered reaching in with my other hand and punching the catfish square in the nose, but I was loath to lose another arm. It was a great blow to my ego that I, a Second-Class Boy Scout who could start a fire with less than twelve matches, could not negotiate myself out of a catfish with a brain the size of a pea.

As I started to pray I got the funny feeling that God had run out of good ideas and was now testing a Daniel In The Lion's Den/Jonah In The Great Fish-hybrid on me. As the last flicker of hope was fading from my eyes, I heard a rustling and looked up to see Skeeter, holding about thirty feet of thick rope.

He tossed one end to me and told me to hold on. He put the other end of the rope in his teeth and started shimmying up the big oak tree towering over me. When he had climbed to the lowest limb, he made his way out over the water.

"You holding on?" he yelled down.

"Yeah, what are you going to...." Just then he leapt from the tree. The rope was lying across the limb, with me in the water on one side, and Skeeter heading toward the water on the other. When he was about halfway down he caught up with the slack in the rope. There was a split second when he hung, suspended in the air. I could hear the rope whining under the strain, and feel the force of Skeeter's weight pulling me up. I made a fist with my hand inside the catfish's mouth. I felt him slip toward the front of the hole, and then I was jerked out of the water. The catfish was holding on tight to my fist. We burst skyward like a waterspout. The great fish was big, green, ugly and mad. Mud dripped off his slick skin, his tail and fins thrashed wildly. I could almost hear him thinking, "And this is why you shouldn't bite the arm of every stupid kid that reaches into your hole."

We came to a stop just below the tree limb. Skeeter's feet were in the water. I looked down at him and smiled. "Good thinking, what now?" I asked.

"Now," he said, "I start pulling the rocks out of my pockets. As I get lighter you will start to pull me up. When I get to the top, you'll be in the water again. I'll tie you to the limb and you can hold onto the fish while I run home and get a net."

It was brilliant, the best plan Skeeter had had in weeks. One by one he pulled rocks from his pockets and slowly he started to ascend toward the limb. We smiled at each other as we passed halfway through the exchange. He was almost at the limb when suddenly, the massive catfish gulped in a breath of air. He opened his mouth completely and I found myself staring straight down into the endless pink vastness of his insides. His breath was as foul as the winds of Hell and his extended jaws were wide enough to swallow me whole. He glared at me, a menacing hiss escaped his gills, and then he turned his lithe body and dove back into the water with a great splash. And then he was gone. I let go of the rope and followed him in. Skeeter crashed into the river behind me.

"Well," I said, "at least no one will believe him either when he tells his pals about 'The one that got away'."

Das Buck

O n the one hand you have West Virginia, 24,181 square miles of beauty, 265 miles wide, 237 miles tall, located between 37th and 40th north latitude, the 77th and 82nd west longitude, and nestled quietly between Ohio, Pennsylvania, Maryland, Virginia, and Kentucky. On the other hand you have Buck-dog, my super hound whose mother was a German shepherd and whose father was a prolific and extremely determined basset hound. He looks like a German shepherd that swallowed a canoe. He's about three feet long from stern to bow and about a foot wide at his widest.

You wouldn't think one small dog, less than three square feet in area and surrounded by a cloud of flies and fleas, could pose much of a threat to West Virginia. But when you combine Buck-dog's low center of gravity with his high center of buoyancy, you are faced with a dog that has little tendency to roll, flip, pitch, yaw or in any other way go catiwampus. Add to this equation his long, cylindrical shape, and you have, in short, the perfect living submarine-cum-hound dog. Well, I guess since he's part German shepherd it wouldn't be appropriate to call him a submarine, but rather an unterwasserzoig, a U-boat, Das

Buck if you will. Now, you're saying to yourself, "But West Virginia is completely landlocked. We only have 111 square miles of water area (that's a pre-valley fill figure by the way). What possible harm can Das Buck present?"

Well, I asked myself that same question. You see, I had been reading a lot of Jack London recently and I was becoming more and more enamored by the idea of dog sledding. The idea of mushing a team of dogs across the frozen tundra in pursuit of fortune and glory has its appeal. The only problem is that we have very little frozen tundra in our state, and I only have one dog, and no dog sled. But, living in Fayette County has its advantages for those seeking Londonesque adventures. The way I figured it, frozen tundra is nothing more than land defined by its extreme natural conditions and covered in snow. And snow, we all agree, is just frozen water. Thus, I logically deduced that the New River is basically nothing more than unfrozen tundra. I mean, it is just a strip of land defined by its extreme natural conditions and covered in unfrozen snow. Am I right or am I right?

So, I had my tundra, and now all I needed was a dog sled and a team of dogs capable of taming this newfound unfrozen tundra. That was the easy part: I simply substituted Das Buck for the dog team and my wife's kayak for the sled. I harnessed Buck to the kayak and we headed toward the river.

Now, I figured anybody could dog-kayak the New River downstream. The trick would be to go upstream. We threw in at Charlton Heights and mushed around in circles for a few minutes until Buck got his sea legs and I got a feel for the craft, and then we headed upstream. Das Buck made short work of the Kanawha Falls, dodging and weaving his way through the current as easily as the People's Republic of China got through America's Department of Defense computer system. We cruised through Hawks Nest, under the New River Gorge Bridge, up the Rattle Snake Rapids, past Prince and then under the Mary Ingles Draper Bridge. After all that, the Sandstone Falls was like a mush in the park for Das Buck and me in my dog kayak. We were taking it easy as we passed Hinton, figuring to pull out at the base of the Bluestone Dam, when suddenly a flock of ducks flying north for the summer landed en masse all around us. In Jack London's stories it was always a pack of wolves that threatened the survival of the dog team and crew. You wouldn't right away perceive a flock of ducks as a danger, unless, of course, you knew Buck-dog.

Buck is strong, friendly, and makes for good company, but he is none too bright and scared to death of all other living creatures. This is a dog that was once backed into a corner by a rabbit; a squirrel once treed him; and the first time he saw a cow he flat out fainted. So when the ducks landed, Buck panicked. Now your average duck, all alone in a pond, is a fairly harmless creature, but you get a bunch of ducks together and they can sense fear. They felt Buck begin to panic and they turned toward us like they were the International Olympic Committee and we were a rich city in Utah. I had to work quickly if I was going to save Das Buck and my dog kayak.

I reached into the front of the kayak and pulled out one of the styrofoam blocks that helps keep it afloat. I then pulled out my stainless steel, seventy-four function Swiss Army type knife and quickly opened up the duck shaped cookie cutter and the hot glue gun. I cut out a perfect duck shaped figure from that styrofoam and then coated it in high strength, waterproof glue. Because I was trying to emulate Jack London exactly on my little trip, I was wearing a huge, down-filled, hooded parka. I ripped it open and grabbed a handful of feathers. I stuck the feathers to the glue on my styrofoam duck and then glued the duck to Buck's head. I quickly made two more ducks and stuck one to Buck's back and the other to his tail. Now he was completely camouflaged, utterly hidden. If he were a crime, Congress couldn't have covered him up better. He was the perfect Buck duck decoy ploy.

To the ducks, it must have appeared that Buck just disappeared, but they still had me in their sights. I was a sitting duck in the midst of a duck stampede and I can tell you that adrenaline was pumping out of my adrenal ducts faster than water off a duck's back. In his panicked state, Buck started barking. The barking startled the ducks and as quickly as they had come they lifted off the water and flew toward Canada. Buck-dog, seeing the ducks fly away, recovered himself and started to look around. He turned to look at me and suddenly saw the fake ducks I had glued to his back and tail. He then caught a reflection in the water of the mallard stuck to his head. He froze, realizing that he was surrounded. In Buck's mind the alarms were going off. He must have figured that if all the ducks had flown away, all but these three ducks, and they had chosen instead to pounce on his tail, back and head, then these must be the three baddest ducks in all the world. This is where the Buck duck decoy ploy suddenly backfired. Buck-dog dove!

He dove beneath the New River's surface and drug me in my dog kayak right behind him. He was back in his Das Buck mind set and he was cruising upstream, right toward the dam. Every time he glanced over his shoulder, those ducks were right there, never gaining on him, never losing ground. Buck shot up the spillway and to my surprise went straight into the center most drainage hole of that dam. Well that's when we got jammed up. The kayak turned sideways and filled the passage, blocking the flow of water out of Bluestone Lake. The force of the water all around us was so great that it washed the duck off Buck's head, then the one on his back pulled free. The way we were stuck, both Buck's heads and mine were in a tiny air pocket, so for the moment we could breathe.

My more immediate concern was that the entire state of West Virginia was in grave trouble—as well as parts of Virginia and North Carolina. Having completely blocked the flow of water out of the Bluestone Dam, the waters in the lake were rising at an unprecedented rate. Bluestone Lake was quickly going from the second largest body of the water in the state to the first. Water was backing up in the Greenbrier River and the Bluestone River. The southern half of the New was flooding all the way back to Blowing Rock, North Carolina. Bluestone State Park, Pipestem, White Sulphur Springs, Marlinton, Droop Mountain, Cass, Greenbank, Bluefield and Concord College were all being threatened by the impending floodwaters.

On the other side of the dam, the New River was drying up. The entire tourist based economy of Southern West Virginia was disappearing as rapidly as the tops on our mountains. If the New River dried up there'd be no more white water rafting, no more scenic fishing trips, and the New River Gorge Bridge would be forever more known as the Old River Dried Up Ditch Bridge.

That's when Buck noticed the duck still glued to his tail. Buck deftly spun around in his harness and grabbed that styrofoam bird by the head. He gave a vicious jerk and the duck tore off his tail. Buck spat the duck out and the headless decoy washed against the front of my pinned kayak. In an act of sheer bravery Buck lunged at the duck, hitting the nose of my kayak so hard that the vessel was knocked free of the drainage portal and was suddenly caught up in the wall of water pouring forth from the dam.

We rode the wave all the way down to Lick Creek where we managed to hang a right and get out of the flow. In the turmoil I had lost my paddle and I realized we were going to have to walk home. In retrospect, after being jammed in a dam in the unfrozen tundra with Das Buck, three styrofoam ducks, and the economic future of West Virginia hanging over my head, well, I figured there were worse ways the day could of ended than just being up Lick Creek without a paddle.

De-Livered from Stolen Gear

My oldest brother, Paul, was as avid a fisherman as had ever been created. He knew where to find catfish better than most of us know where to go on the first Tuesday in November (the only real difference being that Paul was interested in hooking the biggest slime sucking, mud eating, sewer dweller that he could bribe onto his line). But being ten years my senior, Paul was always reluctant to have his little brother tag along on fishing trips. As a result, I was left to learn the intricate details of catfish fishing on my own. Now when I say "on my own" of course I mean with the help of my neighbor and co-conspirator, Skeeter Barth.

By the time we were twelve, Skeeter and I had discovered that Paul had an abundance of fishing gear, more than any one man should have all to himself. Especially considering that that man was my brother and I had next to no fishing gear, save a rod with two eyes missing, a reel that had about eight feet of line, a handful of hooks, and a bobber made out of a milk jug lid.

Entering junior high, as Skeeter and I had the previous fall, had been a shock to our systems. Almost immediately teachers had begun assigning us two, three, even six page reports, which we had to complete using primary and secondary sources. As a result of such ridiculous assignments, Skeeter and I discovered the library for the first time. The concept of checking out books, on as many sorted and sundry subjects as the junior high librarian would allow, using them for whatever purpose might arise, and then returning them, all in the guise of scholarship, was just too close to criminal behavior for Skeet and I to pass up. The concepts of "checking out" and "borrowing" other people's property were all too lucrative to ignore, or restrict solely to the library. And so we began to borrow Paul's gear. It wasn't long until Skeeter and I had enough lures, flies, sinkers, hooks and beer bottle openers to be proper fishermen. It was, however, about that same time that Paul started to notice his tackle box was growing lighter and lighter.

As Paul's fishing gear dwindled he started to suspect foul play. Every fisherperson expects some gear attrition due to snags, hang-ups, strong fish and tackle box spills, but when suddenly half or more of your stock disappears, and from your bedroom at that, suspicion grows. I'm not sure Paul was onto us specifically, but he did start asking me a lot of pointed questions like, "Hey, did you and Skeeter steal all my gear?" and "Boy, that looks like my new lure. Where'd you get it?" These questions are hard enough to answer, but when he found Skeeter and me with a flashlight in his bedroom closet, hovered over his tackle box with said new lure in hand, and pockets bulging, well, that can be a tight spot to get out of. I looked him straight in the eyes and said, "Um, yes well, is uh.... YIKES! A spider!" At that moment I tossed a tangled mass of line at his head.

Paul had a pathological fear of spiders. Even the

smallest arachnid crawling across the floor on the other side of the room would send him into fits of panic. When the tangle hit him square in the face, he blanched, ran out of the closet and fell across his bed, arms flailing and tears streaming. It was a dirty trick, but necessary if Skeeter and I were to escape with our lives. We made a beeline for the door and didn't stop running until we got to Skeeter's house and had safely locked ourselves in Skeeter's bedroom. But we were had. Paul knew what we were up to and we knew that he would certainly exact some measure of revenge. As Skeeter and I saw it, we only had two chances.

Our first chance was a long shot and took a little work. Having written a report on voodoo for our World History class, Skeeter professed himself well versed in the art of black magic. We quickly built a voodoo doll of Paul, laid it on the bed, covered it in hand drawn spiders, and chanted all the magic words and spells we could devise. Our goal was to mystically knock Paul into a catatonic state. After all, if he were catatonic he couldn't hurt us (and the remainder of his fishing gear would be useless to him and so we could help ourselves). Being relative novices in the realm of voodoo we cast a back-up spell for amnesia, just in case.

Our second chance for survival, and the one I lay the most stock in, was to barricade ourselves in Skeeter's room for the rest of our lives. We slid the dead bolt home and pushed the dresser in front of the door. We crept to the window and watched my back porch to see if Paul was up and looking for us. He came out of the kitchen door with his fishing vest on and a pole in his hand. Our voodoo obviously needed work. He walked across the yard and stopped right under Skeeter's window. We both gulped audibly.

"Oh fellas? Skeeter, Bil, are y'all up there?" Paul called out in the most friendly of tones. It was nerve racking. "Listen, I was going fishing. I wondered if you two would like to go along?"

Now we were in a jam. Paul was asking us to go fishing with him. This was something for which we had begged and pleaded. I had pestered my mother to no end to make Paul take me fishing with him. Everybody knew that Skeeter and I dreamed of the day when Paul would willingly invite us to go fishing with him. I could see my mother in her flowerbed, smiling her approval at Paul for asking us. I could see Mrs. Barth by the clothesline, giving my mother a knowing wink. "Isn't that nice," she was saying.

If they only knew. It was obvious that this was Paul's plan to get us back for stealing his gear. He'd picked the perfect moment to ask us. Our mothers were present, it was a perfect day, the sun was up, and the fish were very likely biting. Many times he had recounted to us stories of days just like this one, complete with bright sunshine and cans full of fat worms. Days when fishermen simply had to drop a line near a river and the fish would leap ashore to strike. "And yet, despite all that," he would add, softly, "ordinarily good, decent fishermen forced by their mothers to drag their little brothers along with them sometimes just go mad. Completely out of their heads. I read in the paper just yesterday where a fisherman in California used his little brother, and his little neighbor, to lure sharks in close to his boat. The fisherman figured he'd have plenty of time to net the shark and save the lads at the decisive moment, but alas, he went stone cold crazy and let the shark swallow his little brother and neighbor. Then he netted the shark and had it mounted. Tragic."

It was clear to Skeeter and me that if we accepted Paul's invitation he would certainly chop us up and use us for bait. In short, if we accepted we were dead. On the other hand, we could not decline the invitation. Both our mothers were watching. If we said "No" they would probably call a psychiatrist right then and there. We would be committed for the rest of our lives. Short of that, we would never be able to convince my mom again to ask Paul to invite us along. Paul stood one story beneath us, smiling like a carp in a septic tank. He had us; we were dead men. Skeeter frantically shook the voodoo doll, thumping its head and hoping for amnesia.

I swallowed hard. "Yeah," I managed, "that would be great. We'll be right down."

"Great." Paul said. "Oh, and don't forget to bring all your new gear."

Hearing that, Skeeter put the voodoo doll on the floor and dropped a dictionary and three encyclopedias (volumes A, M and S) on its head. We were both pale and sweating bullets. But, there was nothing to do except face the music. We shook hands, grabbed our stuff, and headed out.

I walked straight to my mother, pale and wobbly from the weight of my impending doom. I hugged her long and hard. "I love you," I managed to whisper. She almost had to pull me from her, "Are you all right?" she asked. My mouth was dry, my voice horse, but I managed to say, "Yes, just excited." Skeeter was going through the same motions with his mother. Paul just smiled a devilish grin. If my mother suspected any wrongdoing in the works, she gave no hint of it. She just waved as Skeeter and I dragged our limp bodies into Paul's car, the Great Golden Carp Cruiser, or GC for short.

On the way to the river we stopped and picked up Paul's pal Charley. Charley, Paul had often told us, had been raised in the rivers of Africa by a school of piranha. According to Paul, Charley could single-handedly eat a cow to the bone in less than ten seconds. Charley was fond of telling us that he only left the river because he was bitten by a rabid polar bear while migrating to his traditional spawning waters in the Yukon. The bear bite turned him into a werebear and he was wanted in three states and two Canadian provinces for devouring his friends' little brothers and their neighbors.

When Charley got in the car he glanced at us in the backseat. Skeeter and I stifled screams and huddled together. Paul pulled off the main road onto a dirt track. We were headed for his secret fishing hole, a place so shrouded in mystery that Skeeter and I knew our bodies would never be found. Paul stopped the car and we got out.

"Skeeter," Paul said cheerily, "you come with me. Bil, you go with Charley." It was cold comfort to know that Paul was too emotionally attached to me to kill me himself. He would leave that to Charley.

Paul and Charley got their poles, tackle boxes and coolers from the trunk. Paul led Skeeter upstream; Charley and I went down stream. He made me walk in front of him.

"Charley," I said, mustering my courage, "you don't have to do it."

"Do what?" he asked.

"You know. Kill me." I stopped on the trail and looked back at him. He had a puzzled look on his face.

"Kill you? Why would I do that?"

"Well, aside from the fact that you were raised by piranhas, that you're a werebear, and that you are wanted for eating little brothers and neighbors, Paul caught me and Skeeter stealing his fishing gear this afternoon and he brought us out here to kill us. Didn't he?" "Not that I know of. Besides, I stole all my gear from my older brother, and Paul stole most of his from me, so he can't be too upset about that. That's just fishin'. In fact, he called me yesterday to ask if I wanted to take you and Skeeter fishin'."

I was visibly relieved. A giant weight had been lifted from my heart and soul. Paul was just taking us out for a good time! It was a miracle—or voodoo.

Charley sat down by the river and, seeing my battered rod, handed me one of the poles he had with him. He opened his cooler and pulled out a lidded plastic container. "I thought we'd fish for catfish today. Is that all right?" I nodded. He opened the container and I almost fainted. It was full of putrid liver floating in blood and water going green. "Rotten liver," he said, smiling, "drives them catfish crazy." He drew his filet knife from its sheath on his belt and reached into the bowl. He picked up the liver and started to cut a chunk off. I was suddenly overcome with nausea. Charley extended the piece he had removed to me. I took one look at the blob in his hand and screamed at the top of my lungs. I pushed his hand away with all my might. When I did, I upset the container and splashed blood all over Charley's shirt and pants. I sprang to my feet and dashed off into the woods like a startled fawn.

Hearing my scream, Skeeter jumped up from beside Paul. "So, that's your plan?" he yelled. "Separate us, get us to drop our guard and then use us up for bait!" He dashed down the river toward my scream. Skeeter burst through the underbrush and stopped dead in his tracks. In the distance he saw bloodstained Charley standing on the bank. Paul had followed right behind Skeeter and was coming out of the woods just as Skeeter fainted. Paul managed to catch him before he hit the ground. Utterly baffled, Paul and Charley laid Skeeter down and made him comfortable until he came to.

I had regained my composure by then and was threading my way back to the river when I began to hear laughter. I could just make out Skeet's voice. "So you see," he was saying, "when I heard Bil scream, I thought you were finishing him off. And then I came through the bushes and saw you standing there covered with blood, and holding that dripping knife in one hand and the bleeding liver in the other. I guess I figured you'd killed Bil and were cutting him up for bait. It must have knocked me out." Paul and Charley roared with laughter. Skeeter smiled too.

I walked up to the three of them and Skeeter and I waited for Charley and Paul to stop laughing. Then they cut up the liver, showed us how to bait our hooks, where to cast, how to prop up our poles, and, after awhile, how to get a catfish off the hook without getting stung.

Lessons Learned Bear Hunting

I don't know much about Flathead County, Montana, but I do know this, and the locals will back me up. The first two weeks in May are not the best time to go there if you want to hunt black bear. They will all be happy to tell you, after you have arrived, that the bears are much more likely to be awake and awandering during the latter two weeks in May. But nobody told us that ahead of time and so there we were, guns at the ready and nothing to shoot.

I will also readily admit that before that trip, the sum of my bear hunting knowledge was what I had learned from Liver Eating Jeremiah Johnson: When a grizzly attacks, ram your knife deep into his chest and then break off the blade. It was not a tactic I was eager to employ. I was, in fact, planning on steering clear of grizzlies all together. But I was an apt pupil and was with two experienced hunters, albeit West Virginia raccoon hunters by the names of Frank and Skeeter. Nevertheless, they had boned up on bear hunting, had each been bear hunting once, and were reasonably decent folks, even if they did make fun of me for wearing a .22 and an Arkansas Toothpick as my last ditch grizzly repelling gear.

The next important lesson I learned was that bear

expect their hunters to be macho, or at least manly. This means that even if you eat beans out of the can the whole trip, play stud poker at night, cut your chaw from a plug with a well-honed knife and carry a powerful, well-oiled firearm, the bear will still not let you kill him if you arrive on the scene in a Ford Aerostar. No self-respecting black bear wants his hide carried home in a minivan, even if it is all-time four-wheel drive. The bear, I believe, prefer pick-up trucks or a suitable derivative there of.

The first thing I learned in the wilderness was that not every large, black object dotting a clear-cut hillside is a bear. Most of those objects are in fact stumps. Then I learned that no matter how long you stare at a bear shaped, fire blackened stump through binoculars, it will never, ever become a black bear. Not even if you try and catch the stump off guard by turning away, feigning disinterest, and then snapping your focus back onto the stump. Stumps remain stumps; it is the Law of the Jungle. I further came to understand that honey colored boulders, dark shadows, derelict cabins, elk, deer, Canadian Geese and slumped-over pine trees are also not black bears, though one slumped over tree gave us a hell of a start.

We were walking up a snow-covered road. Snow had fallen steadily all night but the sun now shone full. Snow had collected on the windward side of the pine trees and the smaller trees bent under the weight until they eventually leaned over all the way to the ground. It was beautiful, yet unnerving. As the snow melted off the trees, they would spring up out of the snow like released snares. Our first experience of this phenomenon was in the curve of a narrow road just after noon on that sunny day.

We had actually found a set of black bear tracks and a fresh pile of scat. The prints traced an uphill route in the snow, following the road. As we came around a bend we froze dead in our tracks. There, not twenty yards ahead of us, was a huge bear lying in the snow. We could see the curve of his back and the ends of his fur swaying in the breeze. We each gazed at the marvelous creature through our binoculars. It was a giant, at least eight feet long, but the snow and landscape obscured its full form. Because the figure was obscured we could not make out for certain what type of bear it was. We could not determine if it had the characteristic humped shoulders and dish-shaped faced of a grizzly. The prints we were following had obviously been made by black bear, but the bear ahead of us was not necessarily the owner of the tracks. The only other physical way we knew to determine the difference between black bear and grizzly was that a black bear's claws are shorter and darker than those of a griz, but none of us was willing to get close enough to play manicurist.

A grizzly starting from a prone position can cover twenty yards in less time than it takes a grown man to whimper, "Mommy." We decided it would be prudent to back down the road a ways and find a suitable spot from which to watch our quarry. The road was slippery and the footing unsure, but we thought it prudent not to turn our backs on the beast in front of us.

As we were edging up the road bank to position ourselves behind a boulder, Frank, the eldest of our party, slipped. His son Skeeter reached out to steady him and succeeded only in grabbing the strap on Frank's binoculars. The effort caused Skeeter to lose his footing and he too began to fall. I instinctively lunged for the pair, while at the same time stepping backwards to find a better purchase. I managed to grab Skeeter's hunting vest and jerk him backwards. Just then, our bear reared up, throwing snow in every direction. Terror stricken at the sight of a ten-foot grizzly standing on his hind legs, I fell rump first into the snow, still holding Skeet's collar, and Skeet still holding Frank's binocular strap.

My posterior landed on a snow covered pine tree. Breaking through the ice I freed the tree from the snow and it immediately sprang upright, two or three branches catching under my fanny pack. I was swept off my feet and duly flipped upside down like a Christmas tree angel fallen, but still suspended, from Grace. Since I was holding his vest in a death grip, Skeeter was subsequently jerked up into the branches of the tree, followed by Frank, thanks to Skeet's lock on his binocular strap. I was thankful for the extra ballast the two hunters provided lest I be catapulted a good distance up the road, into the path of the charging grizzly.

The three of us being heavier, and a good bit denser than the snow, caused the tree to bow gracefully to the ground yet again. Skeeter and Frank were beneath the tree and I was caught on top. I let go of Skeet's collar and managed to free myself from the branches, rolling off before the tree could spring its deadly trap again.

I was sure our charging grizzly would be on us any second so I lay perfectly still. Nothing. I waited. Still nothing. Skeet got up cautiously. I rose to my knees. Frank had passed out and was pale. We roused him by stuffing snow down his collar. After we found out he was OK, we laughed at him for fainting. He casually explained that he passed out on purpose. "I knew," he said, "that the best defense against a bear is to play dead. I reckoned that if I passed out it could only help my ability to play dead. And, I figured that if I turned pale it would help camouflage me."

I peeked up the road. The bear was still standing where we had left him, only now he was a dark green pine tree recently freed from the snow, much like the one we had just battled. Even though I knew that no amount of staring would turn the tree into a bear, still I looked away quickly, hoping to squelch any sympathetic magic and mollify any bad mojo.

The last—and possibly most important—lessons I learned bear hunting in Flathead County, were, first, fear the trees. Second, if you have to hike out of the woods on a cold spring day in bear country while wearing wool long johns and wool trousers, don't pee your pants out of fear. It can be rather uncomfortable. And finally, if you do pee your pants out of fear think of a good cover story before you walk into the Swan Lake Tavern because the locals laugh at hunters who are that scared of trees.

"The trees around here," the bar keep explained with a wink, "are coniferous, not carnivorous!"

Hot Dog and Flies

Summer for you and me can be hot, so hot that we are reduced to sitting under the air conditioner in our boxer shorts sipping on a sweating glass of anything legal, and often something illegal. The sort of sipping drink that your great-grandpap invented with the sole intent of doing serious damage to the central nervous system, so that even if you were to burst into flame, you would feel as cool as the bottom of a well.

Summer for Buck-dog is not nearly so easy. He would much rather be shaved naked and stuck into a potter's kiln than endure July underneath his insulating coat of jet-black fur. Just as faith in God protected Shadrach, Meshach and Abednego as they sauntered through Nebuchadnezzar's furnace, so Buck's faith that winter will come keeps him from bursting into flame. In the interim he just perseveres, finding ways to stay cool.

It was mid-July last year and the thermometer had been soaring. The grass had all gone brown and the wells were drying up. Buck-dog spent the cool hours of the morning digging deep holes in the yard, way down into the cool earth where he could take shelter from the coming heat. He would lie in his hole perfectly still; with just his eyes peering over the edge, watching the day go by and the weeds along the fence line wilt.

Buck was laying in just such a hole while I was packing up the Jeep to go fishing. He was staring at me and I knew he wanted to go so that he could frolic and then lounge in the cool waters of the New River. I opened the back door of the Jeep and he jumped out of his hole and into the backseat. As soon as we got to the river he sprang into the water and swam around a good bit while I was setting up my gear. When he tired of swimming he drew up close to the shore and proceeded to dig one of his trademark holes in the mud. He let it fill with water and then plopped down into his homemade spa. It made me think of how Reverend Francis Asbury, passing through the spa rich areas of the Eastern Panhandle on his first visit to West Virginia, had remarked that the place was "Good for the body, but intolerably hard on the soul," or some such theological rhetoric. Buck rested his head on the lip of the hole so that just his nose and eyes were above the water. I couldn't help but note that he looked like an alligator in the Mississippi Delta swamps.

The sun was climbing high and by this time I had my rod resting on a forked stick while I sat in a lawn chair sipping Grandpap's cooling tonic and considering what my bait must look like on the bottom of the river. Just a blob of rotten chicken liver emitting its putrid essence, but turning the catfish on like a good perfume on a pretty woman turns on a man. The liver smell luring the fish in, enticing him with all the splendor of nature, only to deliver a hook in the cheek and life on a string. "It is a hard world for men and catfish alike," I thought out loud. I sat for another half hour with not so much as a tug on my line. My attention drifted to the bucket of chicken livers cooking in the sun next to me. Flies were buzzing around the lidded container. I reeled in my line and was getting ready to put more liver on my hook when I got an idea.

My thought process was simple (it always is). Catfish like to eat things that have been dead for a long time, things that smell terrible, and things that are otherwise gross. Flies spend their days going from pile to pile of foul smelling garbage and long dead animals. Flies, I concluded, ought to be covered in every sort of thing that a catfish covets. Therefore flies must be the perfect catfish bait!

I quickly caught a handful of flies and baited up my hook. My line hit the water, there was a pause, and then my pole bent over and the line started to spin out. I grabbed my rod and the fight was on. I could tell that it was a relatively small catfish as it wasn't all that hard to crank in, but he was smart. He kept trying to hang me up on various items under the surface. When I had him within twenty feet of the shore he shot out of the water and hung in midair for a few seconds, turning his body in all directions as though looking for something. Then his eyes spotted a fallen tree with a mass of tangled branches lying in the water ten feet downstream. He dove back underwater and sped toward the tree. I tried to reel in enough line to cut off the angle, but he was too quick for me.

But he was not too quick for Buck-dog, who is a heck of a good fishing dog. Buck saw the fish leap from the water and must have guessed his intentions. The route the fish had chosen to the tree cut just in front of Buck's hole. The catfish, unaccustomed to having dogs lying in wait for him, obviously had not spotted Buck's nose and eyes peering above the water's surface. As the fish cruised by his hole, Buck sprung for him, nearly catching the fish's tail. Alarmed, the fish redoubled its efforts to get into the branches of the tree. I felt the fish pulling harder and harder on the line. Buck, undaunted by his initial failure to snag the fish, swam in pursuit. I hauled back on the pole as hard as I could to slow the fish down.

The rocks along the shore were searing my bare feet. The sun was directly above the river and the water was evaporating so quickly that the haze made it impossible to see the far bank. I could just make out the fallen tree through the glare of a heat induced mirage. I could see the lithe figure of Buck cutting through the river like a snake and the slight roiling of the water just beneath the point where my line submerged. The fish was headed for the nearest branch with determined malice, intending to wrap my line in the tangle. Buck, reading the fish's mind, sped around the catfish and turned him like a collie herding sheep. The fish managed to slip by Buck and again headed into a tangle. Buck deftly turned the fish. Now Buck was solidly positioned between the tree and the fish. In a last ditch effort the fish dove. Buck followed him down.

I saw the tree trunk bob up and down and shake a bit as the fish and Buck bumped it underwater. Buck was swimming back and forth along the edge of the trunk protecting it like a hockey goalie protects the net. Suddenly, and counter to all predictable forces in nature, the fish bolted straight toward me, faster than I could reel in the slack. I was dumbstruck as the small fish swam right up to where I was standing and flopped up on the shore. And then I saw why.

Buck was swimming back upstream making frequent turns and backtracking now and then in small semi-circles. In front of him, dodging and weaving to no avail, were the dorsal fins of three huge catfish. Buck was herding them straight toward me. I grabbed my net and one by one scooped them up. Thirty-one pounds of prime catfish cut right out of the herd. All I could figure was that they had been nesting in the cool waters under the fallen tree and the action of the little fish had attracted their attention. When they came out of their holes to see what was up, Buck simply drove them my way. I was so pleased that I let the little fish go.

Buck-dog walked back to his hole and plopped down, hot and exhausted. I put some more flies on my hook, took a sip of Grandpap's coolant, cast, and sat down. "Yes sir," I said to myself, "nothing better when you're fishing on a summer day than a hot dog and flies."

Dad's Never Lost

Generally speaking, it is hard to get perilously lost on a pond, complicated to get lost on a lake (the Great Lakes and the Salt being obvious exceptions), and difficult to become wholly disoriented on your average river, considering you have only upstream or downstream to choose from. However, there is no real trick to getting lost in the woods, but even a marginally experienced woodsman ought to be able to get himself un-lost if he uses his head. Still and all, it is only a bonafide, ultra-frontiersman himself who can be led blindfolded through the thicket, over hill and dale, and left dizzy beneath an overcast sky, who, upon opening his eyes, can say with confidence, "We're not lost. I know exactly where we are. I've been lost here before."

Such a man is my father. Dad has a natural born knack for never getting lost. As a child, I was amazed at his ability to set off from the well-traveled path, guide us deep into the forest, and yet, within mere hours of our projected E.T.A., deliver us from the woods to the exact spot where we had been headed. As I reflect on those days, hoping to glean a bit of that ability for myself, I have noticed a few key traits that enable the ultra-frontiersman to never be lost.

First of all, Dad spent hours in the woods. He would say to us kids, "Well, I'm going to take a little hike. I'll be back in an hour or so, if I don't get distracted." Then he would saunter off into the dawn lit forest. Later, much later, he would come home covered in mud, scratched, shivering and favoring one tender ankle or the other. "Boy, did I see some things today!" He would announce. "I'm starved. The Ranger who gave me a ride home was cranky and wouldn't let me stop to get a burger." Having spent so much time in the woods, and having the good fortune to have gotten so many private tours by forest rangers, Dad almost always knew where he was in the forest surrounding our house.

Another technique Dad employed, especially if we were away from home, was to limit the area in which he could get lost. For example, when we vacationed, we almost always went to an ocean. Dad liked the ocean because it gave him one solid, guaranteed border. "You see son," he would explain, "with the Atlantic to the East, your chances of getting lost in that direction are greatly reduced." His favorite place to vacation was, by far, Islesboro Island, Maine. The nice thing about Islesboro is that it is an island. Dad would proudly announce: "Australia is an island, afloat in the greatest ocean on this earth. Australian adventurers take what they call walkabouts. A walkabout is where you simply head off into the outback and take what comes your way; it's real Man against Nature kind of stuff. That's why I like Islesboro Island. It's just like the Australian outback." And the island was just like the Australia outback in every way, except, that Islesboro is only about eight miles long, a mile wide, positioned in the North Atlantic rather than the South Pacific, and more closely resembles a rainforest than a desert. Our cottage sat right on the water, so all you had to do to not get lost on your walkabout was find the shore, choose a direction, and keep walking. Eventually, barring heavy fog or nightfall, you would see the cottage as you came by.

A third important factor in not getting lost that I learned from Dad is that you should never commit to, or state, a definite destination. Instead of saying, "Let's take a hike to Seneca Rocks," Dad would say, "Let's take a hike and see what we see," or, "Let's take a hike, I've got something I want to show you." I can't count how many hikes I took with Dad that ended with him declaring something to the effect of: "Well, there it is. Ain't she a beaut? Mile marker five-thirteen."

And last, but certainly not least, Dad had patience. If you have patience, you can never be truly lost. Sooner or later one of two things was bound to happen to us. Dad would either say, "Son, we're not really lost. We know the ocean is to the East, the Mississippi to the West, the Great Lakes to the North and The Gulf of Mexico to the South. Eventually we'll come to one of those things and know exactly where we are." Or, and this was more often the case, Dad would stop dead in his tracks, study a boulder, a huge tree, an outcropping, a waterfall, or whatever, and then say with a twinkle in his eye, "Wait a minute. I know where we are. I've been lost here before."

Code 70

When the bear came out of the woods I almost missed it. Its fur was the same golden brown color as the pine needles and fallen leaves carpeting the forest floor. It was standing in the tall grass at the edge of the field looking around. I put down my pen and picked up the binoculars that were lying on the table. When I focused in on the bear, he looked right at me and then turned back into the woods. I had just enough time to notice that he had a yellow tag in his ear and a radio collar around his neck.

I was working at Pueblano in the backcountry of Philmont Scout Ranch. Pueblano was a late 19th century logging camp and we taught troops passing through about wood lore. We were also supposed to keep a sharp eye out for bears.

When we spotted a bear, we had to get on the CB radio and call down to base camp. A bear sighting was called a "Code 70" on the radio. We had to let base camp know about the bears because Philmont does everything that it can to protect the animals within the ranch's borders. Bears that are not afraid to be around humans are dangerous and often have to be trapped or killed because they will rummage through garbage, backpacks, or even houses looking for something to eat. Because of that, it was important to try and keep the bears away from the campsites.

Most bears at Philmont have been seen before and the bear experts try to put a numbered tag in each bear's ear. Every bear has a different number so that it is easy to identify which bear is which. Sometimes the experts even put radio collars on the bears so that scientists can study their habits in the wild. If a bear without a collar or tag is seen lurking in the woods, an expert is sent out right away to check on it.

I got up from my chair and went into the cabin. Each backcountry camp had a small, solar powered CB so that we could call in daily reports to base camp about troops passing through, report bear sightings, or keep in touch during emergencies. I picked up the microphone, pressed the button that allowed me to talk, and said, "Pueblano to Base Camp, come in Base Camp." We never used our own names on the radio, just the campsite name.

A voice came back saying, "This is Base Camp, go ahead Pueblano."

When you called in a Code 70, Base Camp asked a few questions about the bear like, "Does it have a tag in its ear?" "Is the bear wearing a collar?" "How much do you think it weighs?" and "Where is the bear now?"

I told them that the bear I had just seen had a tag and a collar, but that it went back into the woods before I could see the number on the tag or get a good estimate of the bear's size. The man at Base Camp took all the information and thanked me.

The evening was cool and the sun was setting. Adam, my camp mate, was calling in the daily report and I was on the porch sipping coffee and talking to some scouts who had gathered to hear stories about the old days. That's when Adam said, "Bil, you'd better come listen to this." I got up and walked to the door of our cabin. It was a heavy wooden door and, like all the doors in the backcountry, it opened in. I pushed it open just in time to hear someone on the CB say, "Miranda to Base Camp. Come in Base Camp." I recognized the voice automatically. My cousin Andy worked at Miranda and he was on the radio.

"This is Base Camp, go ahead Miranda," came the reply.

"Yeah, uh Base Camp, I got a Code 70 up here." Andy's voice was calm but he sounded like he was far away from the microphone.

"Roger that Miranda. Does the bear have a tag in its ear?"

"Yes," came Andy's answer.

"Can you still see the bear?" asked the guy from Base Camp.

"Yes," said Andy, "I can see him well."

"Good. Can you read the number on the tag?" The guy from Base Camp sounded bored. He probably answered as many as ten Code 70s a day.

"Yes," said Andy, "56."

"What color is the bear?"

Andy sounded sort of out of breath. "The bear is black with cinnamon tints."

"How much would you say the bear weighs?"

"I'd say he weighs enough to push over a wood stove and crush a metal cot. Probably about two hundred, two hundred and fifty pounds." There was an impatient tone in Andy's voice now.

"Where is the bear now and where is it heading?" The guy from base camp suddenly sounded a little more interested.

Andy was laughing sardonically when he said, "The bear is in my cabin. He pushed open the door; got the sandwich I had left on the counter, knocked the wood stove over and crushed my bed. I think he's asleep now. Don't reckon he's headed anywhere for awhile."

"Where are you?" the guy from Base Camp asked, with wonder in his voice.

"I'm in the rafters of my cabin."

"How are you using the CB?"

"I grabbed a broom the second the bear pushed the door open. I took a swat at him, and then jumped up here. I'm using the handle of the broom to cue the radio."

The guy from base camp started to say something else, but Andy cut him off.

"Look, I've really enjoyed this conversation, but I was actually calling to find out if you could send me some help. I don't want to spend the night up here with that bear lying on my bed."

Adam and I didn't wait for Base Camp's answer to that question. We grabbed a couple of flashlights and headed down the trail. It took over an hour to get to Miranda and when we got to Andy's cabin he was on the front porch with a screwdriver. "Oh," he said, "the bear left about twenty minutes ago. I was just fixing the hinges on this door so that it opens out, instead of in. The next bear that tries to steal my sandwich is going to have knock this dab-blame door down!"

Bathing Buck

Buck-dog is a thirty-seven inch irony. Despite being half German Shepherd, Buck is somewhat less than brave, and though he is half basset hound, he couldn't track a bunny rabbit in a shoebox. As a matter of fact, Buck is useless in the woods and is basically the equivalent of five Second Class Boy Scouts, in combat boots, trying to sneak up on Chief Cornstalk in autumn.

When I found out that dogs are descendants of bears, right away I set out to trace Buck's genealogical background in hopes of finding some noble bear in his past. I wanted to counter his inabilities with, if nothing else, distinguished ancestors. I was expecting to find in Buck's line perhaps the bear from Grizzly Adams, or Kipling's Baloo. Heck, I would have settled for Winnie-the-Pooh. What I found instead were strong family ties linking Buck-dog with Fozzy, Yogi, Booboo, and about half the bears that showed up in The Far Side cartoons.

Another thing I discovered was that bears like to roll around in the worst smelling stuff they can find in the forest in order to camouflage their scent. This trait Buck has not only inherited, but also mastered, even revolutionized. At least once a week he finds someone's left over catfish bait, a cow patty, a diaper, or a dead gopher to roll around in. He's even pointed out a skunk that lives along the route of our nightly walk. Each night Buck tries to get loose and chase the thing. I honestly believe he wants to get sprayed.

Here's the thing though, Buck's mighty abilities to disguise his scent aside, he ain't worth wet socks in a blizzard when it comes to getting game. There is not a bird, mammal or snake in the five state radius that fears Buck. I mean, let's face it, as much as I love Buck, he was born in the city. Durham ain't New York, but a city is a city and Buck spent his formative year on the mean streets and tobacco roads. He might be street smart, but he is yet to catch up with his country cousins. Truth be told, when we moved back to West Virginia I went so far as to borrow a neighbor's coon-dog to sort of tutor Buck in the finer points of country living. That's where his primal urge to roll in s it was re-ignited. And thus, Buck is essentially a four-legged compost pile headed your way.

I've taken the liberty of listening in on a few conversations the local wildlife have had recently, and it isn't pretty. I overheard this conversation four squirrels were having at the base of an old oak tree as Buck approached, up wind.

"Hey, do you hear something coming?"

"Yeah, but from the racket it's making I bet it's that dog, Buck. He's harmless, let's just sit tight."

"Geez-o-wheeeeezel! Whatever it is, it smells like a swine barn."

"That's Buck all right. You can bet your bottom acorn that anything still alive that smells like that has got be Buck."

It isn't easy for me, Buck's faithful owner, to hear things like that. The other day, bless his heart, Buck got loose and rolled in the carcass of what must have been a very dead, very rotten scavenger who must have died long ago of a serious lower bowel blockage. A whole day passed before I could even get close to Buck, and then I had to wait for the company to leave and my wife to go shopping before I could do anything about the stench. Once everyone was gone though, I dragged Buck into the guest bathroom and locked the door. I ran into the good bathroom and raided it for supplies.

I grabbed my wife's wildflower shampoo, daisy soap, lilac aromatherapy crystals, and apricot bubble bath. Then I gathered up the luffa, the back scratcher, the Ajax and a pair of latex gloves—I meant business. When I opened the door of the guest bathroom, Buck backed into a corner and started baying a mournful dirge. I turned the water on in the tub and dumped in a liberal dose of lilac crystals, bubble bath and detergent. I put on an old terrycloth bathrobe over my good jeans and t-shirt, pulled the latex gloves on my hands, and tied my handkerchief over my mouth and nose.

I turned to look at Buck. Buck hates to take a bath and I am used to him being despondent about the prospect, but now the baying had been replaced by a quiet cry, saturated with misery and fear. When I caught my own reflection in the mirror I understood why. I made for quite a picture. There I was, wearing a long white coat, rubber gloves and a bandana, that looked like a surgical mask, tied around my face. The water in the tub was steaming and the bubbles were oozing over the sides. I looked just like a mad scientist standing before a boiling cauldron, in desperate need of basset-mix gizzard. And Buck was plumb scared out of his head.

On a good day there is no chance of coaxing Buck into the tub, and this was not a good day. His hair bristled and he almost growled. I chuckled at him, and then lunged. I grabbed him just before he could slip behind the toilet, and wrestled him into the tub. The fight was on. I had one hand on his collar and with the other I was scrubbing, lathering, rinsing and repeating as fast as I could. Buck was bucking, diving, squirming, thrashing and turning with all the agility of an alligator. Giving Buck that bath was like trying to circumcise a Brahma bull during a rodeo.

When I was finally done, the water had gone from warm and soapy to something that resembled tepid borscht. I was half drowned; Buck was thoroughly upset and mostly washed. The Ajax was gone and the bathroom was flooded. As soon as I let go of his collar, Buck sprang from the tub.

Buck, starting from the very tip of his tail, started to shake, slowly at first, but before long he was as consumed as a Holy Roller in the presence of the Spirit. Tiny droplets of water flew in every direction, coating the walls, the mirror, the doors and the ceiling. When he was utterly shook, he looked up at me. And then he stuck his nose as far back along his spine as he could. He slowly brought his nose forward, leaving not one hair unsmelled. And when he was done, he looked up at me and smiled. A peace filled the room, and for a moment all I could smell was bleach, wildflowers and water. It was as though I was standing in a spring field after a light rain. And then something crawled into the field and died. I figured out why Buck was smiling. He smelled worse now than he ever had before. He smelled like a bouquet of flowers to be sure, but a bouquet growing out of a cow patty atop a landfill.

There was nothing to be done. I waited until dark and took Buck on his nightly walk. When we got to the yard with the skunk, I just plain dropped the leash.

Mississippi's Big Sunflower River Blues

I grew up in what some people consider to be the North, what some people consider to be the South, and what I have always considered to be West Virginia. But, as quickly as I could, I married a girl from the Mississippi Delta. Some people marry for money, some people marry for fame, but I married for love. Well, love and desire. You see, for as long as I can remember I have heard tales about the mighty blue catfish which swim the waters of Mississippi's rivers and canals, and I greatly desired to fish for them.

As luck would have it, my in-laws live right on the Big Sunflower River. Sometimes, when the rains come, they live in the Big Sunflower River. Having been told this information by my wife, I made sure to pack a fishing pole the first time we visited her parents. We also brought my dog, Buck. Buck is an extraordinary dog whose mother was a German shepherd and whose father was a prolific and extremely determined basset hound. Like most of the men in my family, he's funny looking, he's not all that bright and, odd as it may sound, he loves to eat insects. So when he looked in the back of the Jeep and saw the cricket sitting quietly on my fishing pole, he sprang for it.

Now, if you've never driven down the highway with

your new wife, in your new Jeep, with your dog howling like mad because there is a crappie lure stuck in his upper lip, then you really haven't lived. I pulled to the shoulder as quickly as I could and opened the back door of the Jeep. Buck flew out of the truck and into the woods dragging my brand new catfish rod behind him. The reel busted when it slammed into the guardrail, and the rod snapped when Buck bit it in two. We were late getting to my in-laws because we had to find a veterinarian in Cleveland, Mississippi, in the middle of the night, and I was ten feet from a river with 300 yards of tangled line and nothing to tie it to! But I still had my dream and my resolve.

Early the next morning I found a cane-pole in my father-in-law's shed. I untangled about twenty feet of line, and recycled the hook from the lure Buck had bitten (I'd asked the vet to save it for me). I got some cheese from the 'fridge and found a place to sit along the muddy bank. To my great surprise, I only had to wait six hours before I landed my first Mississippi catfish. And it was a dandy! Three pounds, at least. My head danced with visions as I dreamed of all the fish I would catch on future trips, when I had a new pole, a reel, and a bucket of rotten liver.

It was not to be so.

I feel certain that if you read through enough Top Secret documents published by the Third Reich you would discover that after laying hundreds of miles of barbed wire and anti-personnel obstacles along the beaches of Normandy, the Germans figured they had better lay a supply in along the bed of the Big Sunflower River, too—just to make sure. If you've ever fished the stretch of water just behind my in-laws' house then you know exactly what I mean. You could get a dry fly snagged on the bottom of that river before it ever left your boat. In the decades since the Second World War, and mind you this is pure speculation, I believe that the Forest Service discovered the tangle of barbed wire and immediately decided that it provided the perfect testing area for an experimental underwater bramble-brush. To cover their experiment, they made the water so muddy that a cubic foot of it weighs more than a cubic foot of granite.

Alligators, dragging prey to the bottom of that river, have been known to become lost in the tangle and are never heard from again. Trees are embarrassed to fall into the river because the possible tangles they can offer are no worse than a stick in your bathtub compared to what is already on the bottom of the Big Sunflower. So, why fish there at all? Well, the Big Sunflower River flows right through some of the best cotton and soybean fields in the world. It is fed by the run-off of these fields and the waters are rich with dead bugs and fertilizer. Moreover, squirrels, mice and light raccoons are often swept into the current after mistaking the muddy waters for very wet ground. All of these nutrient rich tidbits cannot help but get washed down into all of that tangle at the bottom of the river, and there, lying patiently and content, are thousands of catfish just getting bigger and bigger.

Knowing full well that those fish are there, I cannot, in good conscience, not fish for them. I have been making the trip to my in-laws' for five years and I am proud to say that I have fished every time I have visited. I have lost enough weights to ballast a submarine, enough hooks to build the bridge over the river Kwai, and approximately twelve miles of line. And I have thoroughly exhausted four reels trying to bring up Third Reich surplus. But all three of the fish that I have caught have been magnificent, proud bearers of the Mississippi catfish tradition.

People say that the best time to fish the Big Sunflower is when the water is either going up, or going down. They also say that a hungry catfish will bite on anything. If that is the case, then it is my solemn belief that that river has gone neither up nor down in five years, and, furthermore, that those catfish are the best fed gilled creatures in the world. I've tried worms, beef-liver, rotten cheese, chicken liver so spoiled it was green and I had to wear a mask until it was below the surface, road kill, and most of the left-overs in my in-laws' freezer (sorry Crazy Mama).

I have developed some theories as to why I've caught only three measly fish in a river where others frequently bring forth six-foot cats. For starters, I drop the theory that I am a poor fisherman before seriously considering it; my ideas are much more complex than that. Take "The Theory of Holiday Fishing" for example. Most of the time when I am at my in-laws' it is either Thanksgiving or Christmas. I believe that it is shortsighted of us humans to assume that our aquatic brothers and sisters don't celebrate these holidays as well. Surely catfish gather their families around them during these festive holidays and celebrate much the same way we do. Certainly they pull out the card table and the fine china and cook up a meal so replete with yummies that everyone gets stuffed to the gills on turkey and sweet potato pie. Now, I ask you, what catfish who has a 'fridge full of cold turkey and mayonnaise at home is going to stop long enough to snack on a wet piece of cheese defying all the laws of nature by maintaining a solitary position in the midst of the current? I have yet to find one who will.

Then there is "The Theory of My Patience Relative to Inclement Weather." I will sit in a johnboat on the river for hours on a warm, sunny day, just waiting to catch a fish of any size or shape. Why, if it's nice, I might even be inclined to take a nap. Snags hardly bother me in nice weather. I can put new line on my reel ten times on a July day, provided I have a nice breeze and a cool drink. But let the temperature drop below forty with a stout cross wind and, mysterious as it may sound, I suddenly loose all desire to re-line my reel or take a nap. And if a cold rain starts, well, my patience plummets faster than a blind mule off a cliff.

Generally, in such conditions, the only thing that keeps me on the river at all is the "they" who are so fond of saying, "Fish won't bite in this kind of weather." I'll prove them wrong, someday. Out there somewhere is a fish just as dumb as I am.

Five years and three fish later, I still sit by the Big Sunflower whenever I can. The fact of the matter is that even without the thrill of catching the fish, it's a nice place to be. I love the in-laws, I love the Delta, I love the Big Sunflower, and I love to fish. So, if you need me, I'll be the one in the lawn chair, covered with mud, smelling like rotten liver, fighting a snag just behind the in-laws' place down in Holly... wait a second! Just because my fishing hole has yet to yield hundreds of huge fish, and you think it's a rotten place where seldom a gill or fin appears, that doesn't change the fact that it's my secret fishin' hole, so, HANDS OFF!!

Buck and the Contemplative Life

B uck has never been a dog that minded chewing something up. For that matter, Buck has never been a dog that minded at all. But back to chewing, Buck values things more in terms of their tenacity than anything else. He operates on the Rawhide Standard, judging all things according to their rawhideness (he made that word up). He would thus much rather chew up a combat boot than a slipper, or a hard bound copy of Tom Sawyer than any "1,000,000 copies sold!" Grisham novel. Lately, I've been tossing him spent shell casings and used circular saw blades to gnaw on. No matter what I give that dog, he chews it to pieces, swallows it, and then passes it on, if you catch my drift.

Recently, Buck was diagnosed with heartworms, *Dirofilaria immitis* for my vet readers. This, of course, came as a great shock to us. We had had no idea that he was sick. The treatment is not too complicated, but it came as a shock to Buck, me, and the heartworms alike. Essentially, straight poison is injected directly into the dog's blood stream. The dog suffers little ill from the procedure and it is relatively safe. Unless you are a heartworm.

I was a little worried when I dropped Buck off at

the veterinarian's office that the local chapter of Parasites' Rights might stage a demonstration, but evidently they were needed elsewhere that day. The doctor took Buck into the exam room, pulled out a syringe, and shot Buck full of poison. That was it. Well, except not quite.

The worst part of the whole ordeal was that Buck was ordered to stay calm and confined for the next thirty days. As the poison worked, the doctor explained, it would kill the worms. The heartworms, which had attached themselves to the veins inside Buck's heart, would slowly dissolve into Buck's body and be purged. If he were to get too excited, or run too much, or otherwise get his system in a tizzy, there was a danger that whole worms would detach into Buck's system and get jammed up in his heart and lungs. That, naturally, would kill Buck, and none of us wanted that. So, it was bed rest for Buck-dog.

I shortened Buck's run to about six feet, quit letting him run loose, canceled his nightly walk, and made him a bed inside the house. The bed in the house was the only part of the recovery that he enjoyed. Since he was going to be laid up for a bit, and because Buck always enjoys a good book, I provided him with a selection of library books. I piled up the classics. London, Abbey, Faulkner, Dante, Aristotle, Plato, Luther, Wesley, Barth, Lao Tzu, the whole bit. As is Buck's nature, he quickly consumed and digested quite a bit of information. Like any literary critic, after Buck was done there wasn't much left of the books except chunks of the covers and an unrecognizable pile in the backyard. I can't decide if I should shovel what's left of the books into the library drop box, or just come up with the fines.

Having absorbed all of that literature, wisdom and

religion, Buck became as lethargic and sophomoric as a freshman philosophy major. But, if all the thinking and confinement did anything for Buck, it had surely helped him become a much more contemplative—even introspective—dog. Whereas in the beginning of his confinement he would go to the end of his six-foot run and bark viciously at the rabbits eating my wife's garden, by the end he would just lie in his doghouse and cogitate on the notion of rabbithood.

It was difficult in the beginning to get Buck to understand why he needed to be fettered. He never once felt ill and never showed the first sign of being infected. We only discovered the malady via the course of a normal check-up. It was tough to get the message across. Actually, I suppose I am partly to blame for Buck's misunderstanding. I kept referring to his illness as "Heartworms," even after he had read all those books. It wasn't until I spelled out *dirofilaria immitis* during a Scrabble game (this was after he'd been through the books, or, well, I guess it would be better to say, after the books had been through Buck) that he understood his condition completely. After that, he was even more resigned to the contemplative life.

Buck really took to the notion that the unexamined life is not worth living, or however that saying goes. I often caught Buck deep in thought, carrying himself with the aloof air of an academician. Once I even found him burying a pair of horn-rimmed glasses and a pocket protector in the back yard.

Out in the yard, on his shortened tether, Buck adjusted to the quieter life. I think the basset hound genes in his system began to exert themselves, though "exert" and "basset hound" are probably oxymoronic. It might be better to say that the basset genes slowly began to wax toward dominance, much the same way the New Orleans Saints are waxing toward dominance. But, whatever was going on, it was wearing Buck out and he was forced to sleep more and more. At times he rolled over on his back and stuck his legs straight toward the heavens before falling asleep. But when he was awake, his eyes were on the rabbits.

I honestly believe that Buck went from dreaming about eating rabbits to actively supporting the idea of the rabbits' place in the cosmos as sentient beings whose lives have meaning and purpose beyond dinner. I believe that Buck strongly hopes to foster a dialogue between rabbits and dogs wherein they can establish a harmonious relationship, sharing the land and the resources while respecting the differences in culture and species. To such an end, Buck continually invites his new friends closer and closer to his house through his peaceful demeanor. The rabbits remain weary of his motives. Perhaps it is the prejudices of a zillion years of animosity between the dog and the rabbit, or perhaps it is the way that Buck so recently treated rabbits, but they refuse his invitations.

Of course, it might also be the fact that no matter how calmly, how serenely, Buck looks at the rabbits, no matter how peacefully he lies in his house, no matter how much Buck believes that he has achieved a higher plain of a contemplative dog, still, when he stares at the rabbits, his tongue laps across his canines and the drool drops onto the ground.

Impaired: Inept: Overwhelmed

Rock climbing is a sport involving much skill and technique. Therefore it is clearly not a sport Skeeter and I were in any way prepared to undertake. It also involves a lot of gear, like rope, harnesses, carabineers, D-rings, and special shoes. And thus it involves a lot of money. Skeeter and I, being sophomores in high school, had little money. With no skill and no money, we were utterly unqualified to be rock climbers. All we had were our amazing powers of reason and our motto, which we had borrowed from the Marine Corps: "Improvise; Adapt; Overcome." (My father, always willing to encourage our endeavors, suggested the motto might better define Skeeter and me if it was: "Impaired: Inept: Overwhelmed.") But we wanted to be rock climbers and so we put our amazing powers of reason to work.

First of all, we reasoned, everyone has rope. Why buy expensive climbing rope when there were miles of rope in dad's shed just waiting to be used? We figured we could make a harness out of just about anything. As far as special shoes, we reckoned that if the 82nd Airborne could win World War II in parachute boots then we could rock climb in parachute boots. As for carabineers and D-rings, well, we had enough money to buy a few of those, provided they were absolutely necessary.

So there we were, standing under the New River Gorge Bridge, its massive primer red arch spanning the canyon above our heads, the pounding flow of the rapids in our ears and the dry rock of a cliff beckoning us. We had looked at a map of the canyon's best climbs and had chosen an area called "Where Real Men Dare," for obvious macho reasons. This was a climb that was supposedly for beginners. In retrospect, I think the idea was that it was a climb for beginners who were properly versed and outfitted in rock climbing. No one bothered to tell Skeeter and I that bit of information—not that it would have made any impression.

Furthermore, we'd decided on "Where Real Men Dare" because our other choices had included climbs called "Beginners Only," and "Monkey See-Monkey Do." We were too proud to do "Beginners Only" and "Monkey See-Monkey Do" hit a little too close to home. We had also avoided the more advanced climbs, including "Leave It to Jesus." We skipped that one because as sophomores in high school we were certain that Jesus was sufficiently unimpressed with our behavior and would likely not come to our aid.

The main reason we decided to start on a beginners level climb wasn't because we couldn't handle a more advanced climb, but because we were testing experimental equipment and thought it might be better to start slow.

"Skeet," I said, staring up the rock face, "if the rope is supposed to keep us from falling off the cliff, shouldn't it be tied to something above our heads?"

He pondered that and said, "Well, that does seem prudent. But how do we get it up there?"

"I've told you a thousand times," I said accusingly, "that you should have bought that grappling hook at Sullivan's Flea Market."

"And I've told you a thousand times that it's not a grappling hook. It's an anchor."

Just then someone above us yelled, "ROPE!" A coil of brightly colored climbing rope arced above our heads and the loose end fell to the ground nearby.

"I bet," I said, "that they tied the other end of that rope to a tree or something up there and that now they are going to rappel down and then climb back up."

"You," Skeeter mocked, "are a genius."

A silhouetted figure appeared on the cliff above our heads. She was clad in a helmet, a T-shirt and stretchy pants. She looked down and said "Hi." We waved. She was fastening a rope to a ring tied to her harness. She stepped to the very edge of the cliff and pulled the rope taut.

She said, to someone we couldn't see, "Rappelling."

"Rappel on," a voice replied.

As if she were sitting down in space, she leaned out over the edge of the cliff until her legs were perpendicular to the face of the rock and only the rope supported her weight. She bent her knees and then pushed herself off the cliff. Her body arced out from the rock and she zipped down the rope. As she swung back toward the cliff she bent her knees, hit the rock gracefully, bounced, and landed softly beside us. She set about unfastening the rope. She was about twenty years old and fantastically beautiful.

"Wow. You're pretty good at that." I said. "So now that person up there is going to come down?"

She nodded.

"And then you'll climb back up?" Skeet asked.

She nodded. She tilted her head and examined our

gear, and us. Her eyes narrowed in wonder, or maybe awe. Or maybe plain old confusion. She looked at us the same way my mother had looked at us just before querying, "Now, tell me again why you put the cat in the dishwasher?" And then our newly descended acquaintance asked, "Have you guys ever climbed before?"

We nodded our heads, emphatically, "Oh yes, sure, lots of times, all over this canyon, up and down."

She raised her eyebrows. "You've climbed down?"

I looked at Skeet; he shrugged. I said, as confidently as I could, trying to sound aloof, "How else do you get down?"

"Usually," she said, "you rappel."

"Sure," Skeet rejoined, "I mean that's the easy way."

"Tell me," she asked, "why do the two of you have knapsacks on your rear ends?"

Skeeter and I both glanced self-consciously at our posteriors. In our efforts to improvise and adapt we had invented our own harnesses. All the harnesses we had seen in the climbing store were made of heavy webbing. The harnesses wrapped around the waist and inner-thighs, much like a diaper. They were also expensive. The knapsacks that we had carried our lunches in, however, were not expensive and the shoulder straps were made of the same heavy webbing as the harnesses. Both packs had waist straps as well. I pointed out to Skeeter that we could simply step through the shoulder straps, pull them up like pants, cinch them tight, put the waist straps through our belt loops, and viola, a harness. As an added benefit, the pouches of the packs were just at our hind-ends. So we stuck pillows in them to act as seats, or serve as cushions should we fall.

Whoever she was, our new friend was doubled over,

pointing and laughing. She finally managed to cough out, "Karen, come down quick. You gotta see this." Karen, who was still at the top of the cliff, finished rigging the rope, leaned over the cliff, gave the commands, and slid gently down to us. Karen took one look at our harnesses and started laughing with her friend. Even the cleverest ideas of a sophomore boy seem stupid and awkward when said boy is suddenly being laughed at by beautiful young women.

Skeeter and I stood stock-still. With luck, I was thinking, we could come up with a good story to cover our appearances and still get a date with these girls.

"We're testing this equipment for the Army. We're Special Forces," Skeeter said. I grimaced, so much for a date. While Skeeter was busy letting the women in on our top-secret mission for the Pentagon, I was doing what I could to nonchalantly cover our coil of rope before it too was spied. Having seen the compact, brightly colored, sleek climbing rope the women had used, I had come to the conclusion that our rope was not, in any way, proper climbing gear. It was, instead, eighty feet, and about 200 pounds, of the three-inch diameter brown rope used for mooring naval cruisers to giant cleats in deep sea ports. It was identical to the rope we had to climb in gym class, and since our teacher always referred to that rope as the "climbing rope" we naturally assumed that three-inch naval line was what we needed in the New River Gorge. It had taken both of us to lug the rope to the base of the cliff, and now I was trying to push it behind a rock without being noticed.

"Is that your climbing rope?" Karen asked.

"This? No..." I stammered. I was loath to follow Skeeter's Special Forces lie, but I couldn't come up with anything else. "This is the rope the helicopter

used to lower our Jeep into the canyon. We were prac-
ticing early afternoon heli-drops into hostile landing
zones. Part of our training involved getting out of the
gorge by climbing."

"So where's the Jeep?" Karen's friend asked.

"It fell in the river. Inexperienced pilot." Skeet said.

"So," Karen asked, obviously humoring us, "then
where's your climbing rope?"

"In the Jeep." I said.

"So your orders," Karen's friend asked, "were to be lowered into the gorge, with a Jeep, and then climb out?"

"Yes."

"So how were you going to get the Jeep out?"

"I shouldn't be sharing this information with you,"
Skeet said, lowering his voice and looking around.
He paused, beckoned the women closer, and whispered, "The Jeep was just a decoy. I'm afraid that's
all I can say on the matter." He grabbed the shoulder
straps of the knapsack he was wearing upside down
around his legs and hiked it up, as though it were a
gun belt with a six-shooter slung low.

They smiled kindly. "Look," Karen said, "it's obvious that you guys are experienced climbers, trained
the Army way." We nodded. "But," she continued,
"well, my friend and I are instructors here at the New
River Gorge. We were just about to start a class. We
are meeting right here, in about twenty-minutes. I
bet you two could make it back up to town, sign up
for the class, and still be back here in time to sit in.
The proper gear, including helmets and harnesses,
are provided. That is, if you would like to learn the
civilian method of climbing and if it wouldn't interfere with your mission." We smiled, slipped out of
our knapsacks, and jogged to the car.

For once in our lives, we sat still in class and actually excelled.

The Great Narwhal and Naugahyde Habitat

In our county there were two branches of law enforcement. There was Sheriff Hasbro, who served and protected the general population, and Warden Rake Sogbottom, who almost served and protected the wildlife and natural resources in our region. Well, Hasbro and Sogbottom represented the two branches of law enforcement recognized by the state constitution, but there were always Acts of God and some girl's daddy with a shotgun.

Skeeter and I were familiar with Sheriff Hasbro, thanks to the special interest he had taken in our lives ever since we lit Mrs. Crankberry's lawn on fire. We sort of had an internship going on with the Sheriff's office, in the sense that he was nearly always threatening us with internment. But Sheriff Hasbro was good people. My father used to say, "Hasbro might be a cranky, narrow-minded sod, but he is the kind of guy that won't get mad if your dog pees on his tomato plants."

Skeet and I were also familiar with Acts of God. We practically precipitated a few events that might have been mistaken for Old Testament like-catastrophes, had we not gotten the holes patched and the flood gates shut, so to speak. We had managed to steer clear of fathers with shotguns, excepting Angus Fester, but that had nothing to do with his daughter, Charolais.

As for Warden Rake Sogbottom, well, suffice it to say that he had an uncle who was a state senator and a mother who worked on the Governor's staff. Warden Sogbottom had started his career in public service as the Vice-Deputy Commissioner for the Department of Natural Resources. He had slowly and steadily worked his way down the ladder until he was the most reprimanded, and lowest paid, warden in any of the fifty states. But, he wasn't a proud man, so he seldom gloated. He just showed up for work two or three times a month and spent the rest of his time looking for poachers at Billy the Kid's Tombstone, the local tavern. Every now and then he would wander through the woods and write a ticket, or check a fishing license. He would clamber up behind you (he thought he was sneaking) and say, "Freeze, now jus hold ih righ hair well wha do we have hair reach for ah sky bussed I gaw you boy boy hu boys aah ah sa-asion aren goona believe hiss one son yer going up ha river yes sir wha in ha Sam Hill do you hink you are up ooh?" Only, he said it all as one word. It took many hunters many years to finally decipher and deduce that Sogbottom was actually saying: "Freeze. Now just hold it right there. Well, what do we have here? Reach for the sky. Busted. I got you boy. Boy, the boys at the station aren't gonna believe this one. Son yer going up the river. Yes sir! What in the Sam Hill do you think you are up to?" Only without the benefit of the letter "T," or punctuation. Sogbottom talked fine in normal conversations, when he had them, which wasn't often, but his string of cop clichés just ran together in one fast, dry, T-less, multi-syllabic command.

Warden Sogbottom gave the otherwise respectable West Virginia Department of Natural Resources a bad name, and he was the nemesis of all decent, law-abiding outdoorspeople. For that matter, most of the crooks disliked him as well. That was unfortunate for everyone except Skeeter and me. You see, Skeet and I rarely set out to break the law, but then we rarely set out to make fools of ourselves either, and yet both happened more often than one might imagine. We weren't murderers or poachers, but before we were old enough to carry guns we sometimes trespassed, just for purposes of exploring, or, like any boy will, we set up snares and rodent traps with a box balanced on a stick. We had no idea such things were against the law, but every so often Sogbottom would nab us, and haul us into town wearing handcuffs. The up side of this was that we got to ride in Sogbottom's Jeep with the sirens blaring, and Sheriff Hasbro was always able to talk Sogbottom into letting us off with a warning, instead of the twenty years of hard labor that Sogbottom demanded. The down side was that Sogbottom was a big, heavy guy and there were few saplings strong enough to suspend him, and few boxes big enough to hold him, so he almost always escaped from the snares and box traps we set. Contrary to popular belief, Sogbottom could indeed find his way out of a cardboard box.

Once, when were about eighteen, Sogbottom took me and Skeeter down to the Sheriff's office and said, "Hasbro, lock these two up for me while I call the FBI."

"What?" Sheriff Hasbro asked.

"The FBI. Lock these two up."

Sheriff Hasbro smiled at us, and shrugged. "I reckon they've done something to warrant me locking them up for a minute. Come on boys." As we were following the Sheriff to the cell he said to us, "I just want to hear what he says to the FBI. I'll put him on the speaker phone so you two can hear, too." He shut the door to the cell, but didn't lock it.

"Warden Sogbottom?" Hasbro asked, "Would like to use the phone in my office?"

"Yeah, sure. That'd be great. Give me a little privacy." He stepped into the office and shut the door. Sheriff Hasbro waited a few seconds, and then flipped on the speaker phone.

The phone rang twice and then a woman's voice came over the line saying, "Hello. Federal Bureau of Investigation. How may I direct your call?"

"I need to talk to somebody in the Deranged Species department."

"Sir, it is a federal offense to make prank calls to the FBI."

"This ain't no prank call! This is Warden Rake Sogbottom of the West Virginia Department of Natural Recourses and I need to talk to someone about deranged species!"

"Did you say the 'Department of Natural Recourses?'"

"Yes, Natural Recourses."

"Are you some sort of revenge-oriented group?"

"Do what? No! Natural Recourses! Like wildlife and forests and streams and rivers."

"OHH! Natural Resources," she said, chuckling.

Sheriff Hasbro muted the speaker phone so that Rake wouldn't be able to hear our laughter.

"Yes, yes, Resources. Now, let me talk to someone about deranged species."

"Sir," came the voice from the FBI, obviously around a laugh, "do you mean endangered species?"

"That's what I said!" Warden Sogbottom shouted.

"No sir, you said . . . well, never mind. I'll connect you."

There was a brief silence, a ring, and then a man's voice said, "Department of Endangered Species and Large Animal Theft, Agent Rustler speaking."

"Agent Rustler? This is Warden Rake Sogbottom of the West Virginia Department of Natural Rec . . . from the WVDNR calling."

"How may I help you, Warden?"

"I got two boys locked up here who openly admitted that they were hunting narwhal and naugahyde. And they don't have a license for either. I checked."

"Warden Sogbottom? Do you know that it is federal offense to make prank calls to the FBI?"

"This ain't no prank call! I heard one of them boys say 'I'm gonna hunt the narwhal. I'll try and flush one your way.' Then the other said, 'No. I'll hunt naugahyde.'"

There was a silence on the other end of the phone. It persisted. Then the silence lasted a little longer. Finally, Agent Rustler said, "And after you heard the accused say that, what did you say?"

I said what I always say when I catch folks up to no good: "Freezenowjusholdihrighhairwellwhadowe havehairreachforahskybussedIgawyouboyboyhu boyysaahahsaasionarengoonabelievehissonesonyer goinguphariveryessirwhainhaSamHilldoyouthink youareupooh?"

"You said what?" the agent asked, perplexed.

Sogbottom repeated it.

We heard the agent say, to someone else at the FBI, "Ed, get Behavioral Science on the phone. We got a live one here." And then Agent Rustler asked, "Warden, is there someone else I could talk to, just to, ah, verify your position. We get all kinds of pranksters calling here."

"Well," Sogbottom said, a little put-off, "the Sheriff is here. And the two boys I caught."

"I'm listening on the speaker phone, and so are the boys," Sheriff Hasbro said. "Agent Rustler, let me just say that I believe there might be some mistake here. Warden Sogbottom sometimes misunderstands things. May I ask him a few questions, maybe clear this up?" Sheriff Hasbro asked.

"Shoot," the agent replied.

Sheriff Hasbro looked through the window of his office at Warden Sogbottom, who was still on the phone. The Sheriff said, "Sogbottom, do you know what a 'narwhal' is?"

"Sheriff, I am a game warden. 'Course I know what narwhal is. It's a deranged species. I read about it in a fishin' magazine."

"Boys," the Sheriff turned to us, "do you know what a 'narwhal' is?"

Skeeter said, "Um, I think it is an arctic whale."

"With a big, long, spear-like nose," I added.

"Warden," the Sheriff began, "do you know where the Arctic is?"

"Mason County?" he replied, lamely.

"Warden," the voice of Agent Rustler came over the phone, "do you know how to hunt whales?"

"Well, with a harpoon gun, I reckon."

"Were the boys carrying a harpoon gun?" the agent probed.

"Well," Sogbottom puzzled, "I must say I didn't check their pockets yet."

"So," the agent continued, "you think they might have harpoon guns in their pockets?"

"They're crafty boys. Crafty."

"And," the Sheriff probed, "when is the last time you saw a naugahyde in the area, Warden?"

"Well, like I said," he said, "they're deranged animals. You hardly ever see them. That's why almost

nobody sells anything covered in naugahyde any-
more. It's against the law. Which, I might add, is why
I arrested these two no-goods." Warden Sogbottom
smiled triumphantly at his logic.

"Skeeter," the Sheriff turned toward us, "were you
hunting narwhal?"

"No, Sir."

"Bil," he asked me, "do you have a harpoon gun?"

"No, Sir. We were hunting deer, with regular guns."

"Warden," the Sheriff was in his Perry Mason mode,
"where were the boys hunting?"

"Up by Conrad's Ruins."

"The ruins with the two walls? The walls everybody
and their mother call the Far Wall and the Near Wall?"

"Yep, that's exactly where they were."

The FBI agent cleared his throat and said, "Sheriff,
I think you have this under control, if you need me
later, just give us a ring." He hung up without another word.

Sogbottom stepped out of the Sheriff's office and
into the main room. He was a little pale.

"Sogbottom," the Sheriff was on a roll now, "Did
the boys maybe say, 'I'll go hunt by the Near Wall,'
instead of 'narwhal'?"

"Maybe." Sogbottom was turning a bit pink.

"And, considering 'naugahyde' does not actually
come from an animal, and further considering that
you are the only 'deranged species' in the county,
could the boys have said, 'No. I'll hunt. NOW GO
HIDE'?" The Sheriff rarely let himself lose his tem-
per, but when he did, Sogbottom was almost always
the cause.

Sogbottom faltered, his whole body moved as
though a mild bolt of lightening had passed through
him. He gulped. He opened his mouth to talk,

squeaked once, smiled, and said meekly, "Gosh y'all, I was only kidding around." He laughed a sickly little laugh, turned, and ran.

The Sheriff faced us and said, "Come on boys, I'll drive you back up to the famed West Virginia narwhal and naugahyde habitat. You be careful though, them narwhal can run a man through."

Scars and Calamities

There are only a finite number of awards the average dog can expect to win in his lifetime, especially when that dog is a mutt like Buck. There are no American Kennel Association awards for dogs of less than full breed, and the only papers Buck has ever had are the ones we spread on the kitchen floor when he was a pup. So, as far as national awards and recognition go, Buck is pretty much out of the loop.

Furthermore, Buck is not what you would call a "cultured dog." He cares about as much for arts and culture as he does for warts and torture. The closest Buck-dog has ever been to actually engaging in art was when he peed on a museum. It was a sad day in Buck's life when he found out that NEA stood for the National Endowment for the Arts and not, as he had supposed, Nice Eats for Animals.

Therefore, it came as quite a surprise when I found out that Buck was a finalist for an animal award. It seems that each and every year the animal community celebrates those members of the various species who really did right by their fellow creatures. And Buck-dog was getting the award. Just as we in West Virginia gather each year to celebrate the Governor Awards for Arts and Humanities, so the animal world gathers for their own Governor's Awards; that would be the Animal Governor Weasel H. Overgood Awards for Scars and Calamities. The awards are given to those creatures who did the most over the past year to disrupt normal, peaceful life for humankind as a whole.

You see, it was just this past fall and Buck-dog was sleeping in the front yard. It was getting dark and I had just hooked him to his lead. His lead, by the way, consists of a fifty-foot, plastic-coated, quarter inch, steel cable bolted to an eighteen inch yard anchor secured in one cubic yard of concrete. Buck is a strong dog and your average yard screw just won't hold him.

So there he was, sound asleep, not even considering disrupting the normal ebb and flow of humanity. But, he was dreaming. He was dreaming that a skunk was walking through the yard. Now I am sure you are familiar with the term "attributes." Attributes are those qualities of a creature that are good, or outstanding. Buck-dog is woefully lacking in the attribute column, but he does have an abundance of what I like to call "Ain'tributes." For example, he ain't too smart, he ain't too good looking, and most importantly, he ain't about to let a skunk wander through our yard unmolested.

As coincidence would have it, while Buck was dreaming that a skunk was walking through the yard, a real skunk actually wandered in. Well the skunk saw Buck, and froze. And Buck, dreaming like a good dog will, was chasing the skunk in his dream. He was laying on his back and had all four feet moving at full RPM's. Quite suddenly, Buck awoke. He saw the real skunk and without even pausing, he rolled over. His feet hit the ground going full speed. The skunk took off running and Buck shot out after him.

Buck was going so fast and so strong that when he got to the end of his run, he just plain pulled that yard anchor, and cubic yard of concrete, right out of the ground.

We were living in Fayette County at the time, and for reasons unbeknownst to me, that skunk ran straight to Route 60 and headed north toward Charleston. Buck-dog followed him and the chase was on, with Buck pulling that fifty-foot cable with the cubic yard of concrete behind him.

The eighteen inch anchor stuck out of both ends of that cubic yard of concrete, so as Buck ran down the road the concrete pushed that steel anchor against the pavement. Buck was moving so fast that that steel spike was shooting an arch of sparks twenty-five feet behind him. This was in the middle of that drought we had last year and so as each spark hit the ground, a fire flared. Buck, ashamed as I am to admit it, started a line of forest fires from Hawks Nest to Marmet while chasing that skunk. And you might think that that alone would win him the Animal's Award for Scars and Calamities, but that ain't a fourth of it.

You see, that skunk blasted through East Bank, just dodging the high school, but Buck-dog managed to grab the skunk's tail just on the edge of town. Buck grabbed that skunk's tail and started shaking him from side to side while continuing to run full-out. Well, that skunk skunked. Suddenly Buck-dog found his mouth full of skunk stink and he spit that skunk out just as hard as he could. About the same time, that cubic yard of concrete hung up on the corner of East Bank High School. Buck was in such a fury that he just leaned into his tether and literally dragged that high school off its foundations and north toward Charleston. Meanwhile, that skunk flew clear up to Dupont and landed right in the middle of the Dupont High School lunchroom. The students at Dupont grabbed their noses and started running south, all the while Buck was running north, dragging East Bank High School behind him. And then— BAM! Those students from Dupont ran smack into East Bank High School just outside of Quincey. The Panthers met the Pioneers and a huge high school Reese Cup was formed.

You might think that the forest fires and the forced school merger alone might have won Buck-dog that Scars and Calamities Award—but that ain't the half of it.

You see, that skunk kept right on moving. He cruised up Route 60, merged onto I-64/77 and then cut across the 35th Street Bridge into Kanawha City. He took a right on Route 61 and headed toward South Charleston. Here's the thing though, that skunk was getting winded and so he tried to outsmart Buck. He ran under the South Side Bridge on-ramp. Buck was hot on his trail though, and as he gave chase, Buck managed to get that 50-foot, plastic-coated, steel cable wrapped around all the pillars holding the on-ramp up. With one mighty surge Buck pulled those pillars clean loose of their moorings and the Department of Transportation had to close the South Side Bridge on-ramp for repairs until just recently.

"Now," you're saying to yourself, "surely forest fires, mergers, and bridge demolition are good enough qualifications for the Scars and Calamities Award," but the best—or the worst—was yet to come.

The skunk climbed up onto the I-64/77 bridge and started heading north toward Morgantown, and then hung a quick left onto I-77 toward Parkersburg. Buck, too, made that sharp left turn, but that fifty-foot steel cable didn't. The cable swung out across the Elk River and that cubic yard of concrete smashed into those big Pennzoil tanks, ricocheted off them and bounced into a tanker sitting by the shore, punching holes in the tanks and the tanker. That dumped somewhere in the neighborhood of 137,000 gallons of diesel onto the ground and into the Elk River. That spill, in turn, caused the demand for petroleum products in West Virginia to skyrocket, increasing the demand for oil in the United States, and thus the World. That put a bind on crude oil production in the Middle East and so, thanks to Buck (and a healthy .23 cent a gallon state tax) you are now paying a $1.57 a gallon at the gas pumps. And that, my friends, is how you win the Governor Weasel H. Overgood Award for Scars and Calamities.

The moral of this story, by-the-by, should be quite clear. Like Buck, you can set the world on fire chasing your dreams, but if you mess up the schools and tear down all the bridges, well, then all you're doing is passing a lot of expensive gas.

burning all the bridges behind you

Cost of Living

My father was in the passenger seat of my Uncle Gerhard's Land Rover saying, with pink coins of mirth on his cheeks, "Sheriff Hasbro, bless his heart, is a good man, a charitable man, and even, keeping charity in mind, a smart man. Nevertheless, he is of the flesh, especially around the belly, and thus Fallen and subject to the human condition, just like the rest of us; even if he is an elected public servant. While he should, by all rights, know better than to let the prejudices and stereotypes of society at large dictate his thoughts and habits, he still falls prey to the pressures of circumstance, nature, nurture, and just plain bad sense. Therefore, Gerhard, seeing as how you were driving a brand new Land Rover, with Ohio plates, through the economically depressed town of Halfdollar, West Virginia, with a bumper sticker that says 'Vegetarians do it with Relish,' he had to pull you over."

"The bumper sticker is a joke," Uncle Gerhard said, with an angry color still visible on his face and beneath his stubble. "He ought to know it is a joke since there are three dead deer tied to the hood and cargo rack."

"You're not listening," Dad chuckled while running a hand over the dashboard. "I was just saying he has succumbed to the influences of what sociologists and anthropologists probably call a rural xenophobic mind set. As such, and as the rightfully elected Law in this county, he really had no choice but to pull you over. You are an outsider, in a great car, breaking the speed limit, and to top it all off, you have come to West Virginia and taken three fine deer which you will export to the Buckeye State, where, everybody knows, they got their own damn deer."

"I didn't even kill those deer. None of them! You, Skeeter, and Edison got them. All I got was a head cold, and now a ticket for going twenty-eight miles an hour in a twenty-five zone!"

"Calm down. What you got was your 'come-upins' for being a Yankee."

"I was born in this state!"

"Well, you got Ohio tags now. And everybody knows that if you ain't from here, it's your fault."

"What's my fault?"

"It is your fault that this land has been raped and pillaged. Obviously, if you are not from here, you are guilty. You become a vicarious member of the carpetbaggers that took all the profits from the mines and the timber, screwed the workers, and moved all the money to New York."

"That's ridiculous, and you know it. Dad was a coal miner not fifty miles from here. I've never been to New York, and I have Ohio tags, not New York tags. And that Sheriff gave me a ticket! That's just wrong."

We were nearing the turn off to the house.

Dad pointed at our mail box and said, "I know it, and you know it, and the boys in the backseat know it. Even Sheriff Hasbro knows it, but he has, as I've tried so hard to point out, succumbed. He has a civic duty to his voters to pull you over, whether he wants to or not. What if someone saw him see you drive down Main Street with this nice car and the deer and the Buckeye tags, and him not even pull you over? It would be an affront to the sensibilities of all the decent, and indecent for that matter, folks who voted for him. Pulling you over, more importantly, having people see him having pulled you over, right there on Main Street, will win him both votes and moral support."

"And," Uncle Gerhard said, "the eighty dollars for the ticket."

"No," Dad said, "we'll go down to the station on Monday and he'll fix the ticket for you. He doesn't want the money. The wrong that needed righted was sanctified by the act of pulling you over. Taking the money would be immoral, like an indulgence. Obviously you cannot actually be held accountable for the sins of the coal barons, made to suffer for them, as it were. You are more along the lines of a sacrificial pigeon, not a lamb."

"Pigeon? Thanks." He turned down our road.

"Would you prefer martyr? Look at it this way, he pulls you over and all the folks here are happy. On Monday we go get the ticket fixed, it won't even show up on your insurance or driving record. You will go back to Ohio and tell all the folks at work, and all your friends, and anyone else who will listen, that you got a ticket from some backwoods cop in Halfdollar, West Virginia, for going twenty-eight in a twenty-five zone. Everyone will immediately understand that you actually got the ticket for having Ohio tags. You will neglect to tell anyone that the ticket was removed from the books, and no one will ask about that because people like to know that someone else got screwed by the injustices of the system.

And if anyone does ask 'How much was the ticket?' You will say, 'Eighty dollars,' again, failing to mention that the ticket was written off the books. And the next time those freaks from Ohio drive through here, they will be going twenty-four miles an hour. Everyone wins."

"So what was that crack about high priced scotch and caviar?" Uncle Gerhard asked.

Dad stared out the side window, tilted his head, and said, "Now that I think about it, maybe that's what got you the ticket."

"How's that?" Uncle Gerhard asked, confused.

"Sheriff Hasbro is not a friend of the rich and well-to-do, unless they are campaign contributors. And even then, he keeps his distance. Like many of us, he would naturally assume that if you had a cooler full of high-priced scotch and caviar in a Land Rover, you were well-to-do. And uppity for not offering him some."

"But I don't have scotch, and certainly not caviar, in the cooler."

"But the Sheriff did ask you what you had in there, right?" Dad queried.

"Yes, so?"

"And you said?"

"Beer and fish bait."

"No, think about it. What did you say, exactly?"

Uncle Gerhard creased his brow, smiled, and said, "I said, 'Black Label and fish eggs.'"

"Sheriff Hasbro," Dad deduced out loud, "is a beer drinker to be sure. But they don't sell Black Label around here, so he probably wasn't thinking beer. I do, however, remember him telling me, just the other day, that at a sheriffs' conference on the Jersey shore he had had Johnny Walker Scotch, Black Label. He told me it was a rich man's drink. So he must have figured that you had high priced liquor, not very cheap beer, in the cooler. And if you had high priced liquor, obviously you must have meant 'caviar' when you said 'fish eggs.'"

"And," Uncle Gerhard added while pulling into the drive, "He probably thought to himself, 'That pompous, Buckeye son-of-a-bitch thought I was too dumb to know that caviar was fish eggs, so he dumbed it down for me. I'll show his ass with a ticket!'" He smiled, shook his head, and got out of the car. "Oh well," Uncle Gerhard continued, "at least I know you won't be voting for him next election, after the way he treated your little brother and all."

Dad smiled. "Don't be crazy. My tax dollars pay his salary, and he just did exactly what I pay him for."

Primeval drawls - ~ sex
~ scrounged
~ Food
Its' Fishing - Which makes all
those other things possible

Homer's Stinky Cheese

I have heard it said that Time exists so that everything does not happen at once, and Space so that
it doesn't all happen to you. Because God is gracious,
there are only a finite number of things that can go
wrong in one person's life during any given day. But
there are certain combinations of individuals whom
God never intended to get together. Sometimes these
individuals perform certain tasks, which God did not
create them to perform, and thus chaos sometimes
ensues.

Time
&
Space

It was January and the New Year had dawned crisp
and cold. It was so cold that the power lines had been
ripped down by frozen, falling limbs, thereby shutting
off all electricity to Halfdollar, West Virginia. Before long,
the propane and heating-oil tanks ran dry and the water lines froze. We were living off the heat of fireplaces
and cook stoves, fueled by coal and fallen limbs. We
had two choices if we wanted water. We could melt snow,
or fetch water from the creek. Melting snow was all
right if you only needed a little water, but it took a long
time to melt gallons of it, which also burned up a lot
fuel. So, if you wanted more than a glass of water at a
time, you had to hike to Skitter Creek. That winter,
Skitter Creek was a sheet of ice nearly a foot thick and

the only way to get water was to bust through the ice and lower in a bucket. It was almost, Skeeter and I agreed, too cold to go fishing.

But, the thing was, as the youngest children in our families, we were the ones who had to trek through the snow to Skitter Creek with a big auger, an axe, and a bucket to get the water. And if we were going to Skitter Creek anyway, well, we might as well fish. A boy is only a boy for so long. At fifteen years old, people were already expecting Skeet and me to do less fishing and more non-fishing related activities. So, we grabbed a pole, the auger, axe, and a bucket, and headed off to the creek where the catfish were buried warm and snug, deep beneath the mud.

Skeet said, "I have on my new battery-powered socks. They keep my feet toasty. I can set the temperature as high as eighty degrees."

"Lord," I said, "your feet smell bad enough when you wear flip-flops. I can't imagine what it must be like inside that rubber boot with the temperature cranked too high."

"Well," he replied, "to tell you the truth, after a few minutes it gets kind of squishy."

"Yuck."

"But, it's warm. Like walking barefoot in a swamp on a summer day."

"Yuck."

We walked on quietly for a few minutes, the crunching of the snow the only sound we could hear. Well, the crunching snow and the squishing noises from inside Skeet's boots.

I broke the silence. "Think we'll catch anything?"

"Dunno," he said, shrugging beneath his layers and layers of wool clothes. "Let's go by Homer's house. If anyone knows, he will."

Homer Goldenseal was a tall, lanky, philosopher who lived on the outskirts of town and ran a small cheese processing plant, as a hobby. He had been a professor and an editor, but had retired with his dreams of opening a wine and cheese inn in Halfdollar. We liked Homer, and, more importantly, he liked us. Homer was also a class "A" catfish fisherman. If anyone knew how to ice-fish for catfish, it would be Homer. We knocked on his front door. Homer invited us in, telling us to take off our coats and sit down.

"Boys," he said, looking at us over his reading glasses and sniffing the air, "you stink!"

"Well Homer," I replied proudly, "we're doing our part to conserve water by not bathing."

The city had asked that citizens conserve water in any way possible. Skeeter and I, though young, were contentious members of our community and thus determined to do our part to save water. We decided not to bathe until the weather lifted and the pipes thawed. It wasn't long until we were so immersed in our efforts to save water that we were unwelcome in most establishments. We could freely walk around the stockyard, the chicken houses, and the sewer plant, but no one else would have us.

"Hum, well, we all have to do our part." Homer said, crinkling his nose. "I imagine that with the two of you not bathing all winter, the city may conserve two, possibly three gallons of water."

"At least that much." Skeet said, smiling.

Homer looked at the bucket we were carrying, the auger, and the axe, and said, "I assume you intend to go down to Skitter Creek to do a little catfish fishing and you want some cheese? Well, I have been saving a particularly effective morsel for you. Hold on one moment." He left the room and we heard him going down the creaky stairs into his basement. A few minutes later he emerged with an old coffee can with a duct-taped lid. The lid was swollen convex and pulling on the tape until you thought it would burst right off. I could see the tiny white threads straining underneath the gray adhesive of the duct-tape. Homer said, "I surmised the two of you would be by eventually, wanting to go winter fishing. So, when I found this bit of cheese in a dark corner, where it had been sitting for Lord knows how long, I set it under the heat lamp for a few days, so it could swelter and ripen. That lid popped off three times due to the gases that built up. It sounded like a shotgun."

Homer looked at us with his best professorial demeanor, "Catfish, by nature, are reclusive creatures, lying on the floors of our waterways, presumably pondering the mysteries of the deep, or at least waiting for a tasty morsel to wash their way. To a catfish, tasty morsel is a relative term defined by two things. First, scent, or odor, and second, texture. Catfish expect their meals to be rank and soft. And in winter, especially in weather such as this, they hibernate, digging deep into the mud to stay warm. They will only come out to eat if they are absolutely famished, or overwhelmed by the scent of something irreverently odoriferous." Homer held up the can of cheese and smiled at us. "You boys be careful with this stuff. Don't shake the can and for Pete's sake don't drop it! Oh, and don't open it in your house and don't tell your mothers where you obtained it!" With that he shoved us out the door.

"Must be good stuff," I was saying to Skeet, when we heard Homer behind us.

Homer caught up to us and said, "One more thing."

He pulled a pair of nylon pantyhose out of his left pocket and held them up. Skeeter and I looked at each other askance. "You boys know what these are?" We smirked. "Oh, no, not that," Homer said with a blush, "these here are for fishing."

"Well, thanks all the same Homer," I said, looking at the ground and wondering about the sanity of our benevolent friend, "but I think we'll do without."

"Yeah," Skeeter added, "I ain't puttin' those on, no matter what kind of fish I might catch."

"Ah jeez Louise boys, just shut up and listen! These are not for wearing. If you take out your pocket knives and cut you a little strip off of these hose, then you can put your bait right in that little piece of cloth. After that, you wrap the cloth around the cheese, tie it off, and then put the whole thing on your hook. That way, the scent of the bait still leaks out, and when the fish comes to investigate, and feels the bait, it'll feel soft. When he bites, the hook will still go through, but you won't lose your bait because the pantyhose will stay snagged on the hook. You can just pull the little baggy out of his mouth and cast again! That way you don't have to freeze your hands off trying to re-bait, or touch that cheese too often."

We thanked him and headed out.

Even though it was nigh on twenty-three below zero, it was still hard, hot work busting through a foot of ice. We knew our families needed the water and that our triumphing over the elements could mean the difference between life and death, but in the end, it was the urge to fish that drove Skeet and me on.

While I attacked the ice with the auger and axe, Skeet braved the cold air, barehanded, to rig the pole, tie on a hook, pinch on some sinkers, and fasten on the bait.

"You got the hook ready?" I asked Skeet as I finished busting out the hole.

"Yeah. But boy, this cheese stinks! It's like glue, sticky, stinky, glue. I can't get it off my hand and I don't want to put my glove back on over it, but my hand is freezing." Skeet was shaking his hand in the air. It was orange from the cheese and purple from the cold. I was embarrassed for him. Even as a teenage boy, raised in Halfdollar, West Virginia, I was well aware that purple and orange are not colors that ought to be worn together.

"Skeet," I said, "reach in the hole and wash your hand off."

"No way, nope," he said emphatically. "Not with this stuff on my hand. I remember all too well the last time a fish latched onto my hand, and that was in the summer. If that happened today, I'd die before you could help me!"

"Well, you gotta do something, or you'll get frostbite. Take off one of your electric socks and stick your hand in it."

"Then my foot will freeze. Crap!" He was starting to look worried. He thought for a second, and then said, "I know, I'll take these panty hose Homer gave us and wrap my hand in it. It'll be like a big warm mitten. I read somewhere that hose have the same insulating value as long-johns." He pulled the hose from his pocket and did as he had said.

"OK. Is the line ready?" I asked.

"I already told you it was."

"OK, don't get testy. I'll just make the hole a little bigger. We don't want to catch a huge fish and only have a small hole. You get ready to drop in the line. Wait. Do you think we should fill the bucket first, or fish first?"

"Let's fill now, so we don't forget."

"OK. Watch out." I took a half dozen more swings with the axe. I grabbed the bucket, stuck it under water, and pulled it out full. As soon as the bucket was clear of the hole, Skeet dropped the baited hook into the stream. I laid the bucket behind me and we stood stock still, watching the water flow past the hole. Nothing happened. A half hour passed, then forty-five minutes.

"Maybe it's just too cold." Skeet said.

"Maybe." I said. I had been looking down the hole, watching the flowing water, waiting for the slightest indication of a fish. Homer's super-bait just wasn't working. When I looked up for the first time I was startled to see that Skeet was at least six inches shorter than he had been three quarters of an hour ago. "Skeet!" I yelled, "You're shrinking!"

He looked up at me, surprise in his eyes. "Oh my goodness!" He bellowed. "You're right! I used to be as tall as you. Now I'm looking up at your chin!"

We both looked down, I at the top of his head, he at the ice. "Maybe," I said, grasping for an explanation, "it's the cold. Maybe your body is contracting to save heat. Or maybe, my gosh, maybe it's Homer's cheese! Maybe when you got it on your hand it caused some biochemical reaction that caused your cells to shrink."

"Maybe," Skeet said with a gulp, "or maybe it is my electric socks." His voice was plaintive. "Maybe the bottom of my boots got so hot they melted the ice and I slowly sank in. And then maybe the batteries died and now my feet are stuck in the ice."

I looked at his feet, well, where his feet should have been. Instead of feet, there were just two shins sticking out of the ice like tree trunks. "Goodness." I said. I took a step backwards to better examine the situation, and in so doing managed to step right into the bucket of water we had filled. The water was more than half solidified and as my foot sank into the bucket I could feel the icy slush begin to seep over the top of my boot. My foot came to a stop very deep down in the bucket. My boot was wedged. Try as I might, I could not free my foot. "Crap," I said.

Panicked, I tried to step out of the bucket. I kicked my foot in the air and thrashed about. It is harder than you might think to walk on ice with a bucket on your foot, and so it came as no surprise to me when I quite naturally lost my balance and stepped through the hole we had bored in the ice.

"Well," Skeeter said, "that was clearly the smartest way to handle the situation."

I was sitting on the ice, my leg completely submerged, the three-gallon bucket on my foot full of icy water and caught in the current below. I felt as though my leg was slowly being torn off.

And then something struck on the bait. But not a fish, and not the bait on the hook wrapped in the pantyhose, and not somewhere beneath my bucketed leg in the water. No, no, nothing as simple as all that.

"Uh-oh," I heard Skeet whisper. "It looks as though Homer's stinky cheese won't wake sleeping fish, but apparently hibernating bears are not immune to the fetid bait."

I looked toward the woods, and sure enough, a sleepy looking black bear was standing on his hind legs sniffing the air. He saw us. I looked at the can of cheese.

"We have to get rid of that cheese," Skeet said. "I bet that's what he wants. Throw it to him, or throw it into the woods, just get rid of it."

"You get rid of it!" I whispered harshly.

"In case you haven't noticed," he countered, "I'm stuck in the ice."

"Well, so am I! Do something. Grab the can with the fishing pole, drag it over to you."

Skeet started to reel in the line so he could use the pole to reach the can. He looked at me quizzically as I started to shriek at the top of my lungs, "QUIT REELING! QUIT REELING! CUT THE LINE! CUT THE LINE!"

"Shhhhhhhhhhh," he hissed, "you'll upset the bear!"

"The hook," I said as calmly as I could, "is in my tush! Please stop reeling and cut the line!"

He giggled. "The hook is where? Did you say it was in your 'tush'?" He leaned this way and that on his frozen legs, laughing hysterically. Every time he laughed, the hook jiggled and stung like the dickens.

"Yes! It is in my TUSH!" I hollered.

The bear was approaching, leading with his nose.

"Skeeter," I said sternly, "the bear is coming this way. You had better toss him the can of cheese. Remember, he wants the cheese and you are frozen in the ice. And you have cheese all over your hand, under the pantyhose mitten you are wearing."

That brought him up short. To both my relief and consternation he dropped the fishing pole. He started to furiously unwrap the pantyhose from around his hand. He had the hose about halfway unwound when he looked at me on the ice and started laughing again.

"What?" I said, a bit angry.

"You have the cheese on your tush! And here comes a bear. And I have this cursed cheese-glue on my hand and it has rendered the removal of these pantyhose impossible. And here comes the bear." He stood there above me with the hose hanging from his hand like the skin molting off of a snake.

"Skeet," I asked, looking up at him, "why is it that every time we are about to die it is in situations where our main motive for living is not the preservation of our lives, but rather to escape the embarrassment our deaths would cause."

"What do you mean?"

"You just said it pal, you have pantyhose glued to your hand and I have cheese stuck in my tush. And here comes a bear. We have to get out of this right now or else people will know how stupid we are! There will be questions, lots of questions, concerning pantyhose and cheese!"

"I see what you mean," he agreed. "It would be a lot more glorious to be killed by a hungry bear while fetching water for our families during a blizzard, then to die wearing pantyhose."

I reached around and grabbed the line that was tied to the hook that was stuck in my tush, which was connected, on the other end, to the fishing pole. I pulled the pole toward me. I got my pocketknife out of my pocket, cut the line, and used the pole to snag the can. I slid it toward me. The bear was growing less cautious, approaching with much greater speed. In fact, he was almost running. "Here Skeet," I said, "hold the can."

"Don't be crazy, just throw it!"

"Hold the can!" I reached up and shoved it into his hands. I made my way around the perimeter of the hole my leg was in until I was beside Skeet. With a mighty effort I lifted my bucketed leg partially out of the flow and grabbed the back of Skeet's jacket. Holding fast, I then let the weight of my bucketed leg drag me back down. With his feet bound six inches in the ice, Skeet bent backward like a catapult arm. When the back of his head touched the ice, I let go. He sprang forward just as I had hoped he would, letting go of the cheese can as he crossed through the apex of his movement. The can rocketed downstream four feet above the ice, traveling just under mach speed. It hit the bear right between the eyes. He went down for the count.

I was feeling pretty impressed with myself until I realized that the can was coming back. The sticky cheese on Skeet's hand had saturated the pantyhose and when I shoved the cheese can into Skeeter's hand, the pantyhose had fastened on tight. Now they were acting like a giant, powerful, rubber band. The can sailed just over my head and passed Skeeter just off his left shoulder. It was moving so fast that it nearly pulled his arm out of its socket as it cruised behind him. There was a sharp CRACK! For a brief moment I thought Skeet's arm had come off. When I looked up, he was gone.

The force had been so great that it had pulled Skeet free of the ice and he was now sliding on his rump across the surface of the river. When his feet were ripped free of the ice, the hole we had dug was enlarged and I was thus able to pull my leg out of the river, bucket and all. The bear was still out cold.

Skeet and I assembled on the shore and managed to start a fire. We thawed out, collected our gear, and headed for home.

"Know what?" Skeet asked.

"What?"

"I think from now on, when we go to fetch the water, I should leave my electric socks at home."

"Yeah," I said, "that seems like the solution to all of our problems."

A Kind of Charitable Man

Where we hunt in eastern West Virginia the deer are seldom huge or notable, but they are the deer we have, and so we are satisfied. The deer Frank shot, however, was especially not huge or notable, but Frank was trying his level best to work up a hint of satisfaction. He was trying to trick his psyche into believing that the deer would yield more than three steaks and a burger by calling in for help.

"This is Hangnail," Frank said over the radio, "I just got a nice one in the ravine and I need some help dragging him out."

I volunteered to give him a hand and started walking his way. As I started into the ravine I could see Frank at the bottom standing over what I thought might be a dead cat, or possibly a groundhog.

"What's that?" I asked as I got to him, pointing to the tuft of fur between his feet. "Har, har," he said, "that's my buck.""Looks more like two-bits to me," I said."No, no, he just looks small from the angle you're seeing him. When I get him all dressed out and butchered he'll fill the freezer." "When you get him all skinned," I said, "he might fill a hot-dog bun, if you don't cook him too long."

The deer, in all honesty, was bigger than any I had

shot in recent history, but then I was entering into my fourth season of a deerless drought. It was a six point, but the rack sat on the deer's head like a ten-gallon cowboy hat on an infant. It just wasn't right. And though the shot Frank had delivered was clean, it was high, almost too high.

"Why," I asked, "did you shoot him so high?"

Frank blushed a little. "I thought," he began, "I thought he was further away. It was a perspective thing."

"Where was he when you shot him?" I asked.

"Right here, he dropped straight down."

"Where were you?"

Frank pointed vaguely across the ravine, "Over there."

I looked far down the creek bed but saw no sign of Frank's position. As my eyes drifted back I noticed a tree stand about fifteen yards up the hill on the other side of the creek.

"That your stand?" I asked.

"Yes," Frank seemed a bit angry about the question.

I pressed him, "That's your stand, fifteen yards away, and you thought the deer was further away?"

"Just drop it," he said.

"No, wait a second. You hit that deer high. Way high. It looks like you thought he was maybe 150 yards away."

"I told you," he said with finality, "it was a perspective thing."

And then I understood. The deer had that nice rack, so Frank had assumed that he must have been big, bigger than he was anyway. Therefore, Frank figured that the deer had to be far away to look so small, and so he aimed high.

Frank said, "Who are you anyway? Columbo? Quincey? Just help me drag this beast up to the road."

I looked at the deer again and scratched my head. "Are your pockets full?" I asked.

"Why?" he asked.

"Well," I said, "I thought if you had an empty pocket you could just drop that beast in it and hike out."

Frank didn't find that nearly as funny as I did. He did, however, produce from his pockets an array of tow lines and, working deftly, tied the deer's front feet over the rack. He handed me one line and then picked up another for himself. We positioned ourselves on the uphill side of Frank's monster and leaned into the harnesses. The terrain was rough, since we were at the bottom of a deep ravine, but the going was not all that tough. Dragging that deer out of the ravine was just slightly more physically taxing than riding an elevator with a small bag of potatoes on your shoulder. Frank huffed and puffed to make a show of it, but I knew he was faking.

At the top of the hill we managed to pull the deer through the woods and onto the shoulder of the dirt road. Frank, pretending to be out of breath, said, "We'd better walk back to camp and get the truck, rather than drag this giant all the way back."

I nodded in agreement and we started the long, arduous, quarter-mile hike back to the truck. Just as we got back into our campsite another bunch of hunters in a pick-up were pulling out, headed in the direction we had just come.

"We better hurry," I said, "those guys are likely to see that deer of yours and steal it."

Frank considered that and then said, "Well, if they steal it, they probably need it more than I do."

"Yes," I added, "many a starving family man would be willing to risk the loss of his hunting privileges just to steal that deer. Why, with that deer and a package of bologna a man could feed his family for a meal, provided the package of bologna was full. A fella might even be able to make a nice buckskin glove out of the hide. Yes sir, any man who needed a sandwich and one glove would readily steal that deer."

I could see that Frank was enjoying my commentary immensely, even if he was pretending to turn red in the face and growl. We got in his truck and headed back down the road. When we had covered the quarter-mile back to where we had left the deer, it was gone. Frank's mood sank. He backed the truck down the road to see if we had passed the deer.

Nothing. We drove well passed the spot we had left the deer, but it was gone.

"Maybe," I ventured cautiously, "when those guys drove by, the wind from their truck blew the deer off the road?"

"I will be go to Hell," Frank muttered. Frank had a way of swearing without regard to coherency or style. "They stole my deer." Frank suddenly shoved the truck into gear and headed full-bore down the little, rutted, dirt road. I struggled to put my seat belt on as the truck bounced and bucked, narrowly avoiding disaster at every turn. I wasn't sure what Frank was up to, and I wasn't sure I wanted to find out, but I was sure that I didn't want to die in a fiery car crash.

"Frank," I said cautiously, "maybe we should slow down."

"They stole my deer!" He shouted. "They stole my deer!"

"Frank," I reasoned, "did you see those guys? There were four of them in that truck, and they were big, nasty looking guys. Are you sure you want to catch them?"

He drove on.

"Frank? Remember how you said that if they stole it, they probably needed it more than you?"

He drove on.

"Frank! For the love of God! I don't want to die." I pretended to scream like a sissy and cry like a baby until I was consumed in a theatrical sob that would have done Oscar proud.

He drove on.

Within minutes we were pulling onto the hardtop road and burning rubber. Frank flew down the mountain to the little store that served as a checking station in the little town below.

The thieves' truck was not to be seen. Frank jumped out of the cab and ran up to the shopkeeper who was sitting on the front porch. "Did anyone in a pickup truck check a huge deer in here today?"

The old shopkeeper said, "Son, they was all in pickup trucks, they been comin' in all day, and they all thought their deer was huge."

Frank glanced over his shoulder at me, looked to be making up his mind, and then said to the shopkeeper in a hushed town, "Did four guys just come by with a little deer, looked like a small, brown sheep with a six-point rack?"

The shopkeeper busted out laughing. "Yes sir, those boys came by, they live down the road a piece. Why? You want a photo for Ripley's or somethin'?"

Frank swallowed hard, climbed back in the truck, and we headed down the road a piece.

I was just signing my last will and testament, which I had scratched out on a napkin, as we rounded a bend. Frank stood on the brakes. Below us, just off the road, was a house. In the driveway was the pickup truck that had driven by with the four big guys in it. In the bed of the truck, just barely visible from twenty-five yards away, was Frank's deer. Surrounding the truck bed, and staring up at us with a hint of malice, were the four tough guys. They all stood erect and started walking toward our truck. As they drew near Frank grabbed the inside door handle, undid his seat belt, and started to open the door. Then he looked over at me. I was acting like all the blood had rushed out my head and I was deathly pale. The four guys were flexing their fingers, wrists, arms, chests and necks as they drew closer. Suddenly, Frank stepped on the accelerator and we shot down the road. He was silent for a moment and then he commented, "I don't think that was my deer. And besides, whoever stole it, they probably need it worse than I do."

About the Stories

Mayhem Dressed as an Eight Point Buck: When I went to graduate school I was under the impression that I was the only West Virginian in the crowd. I was, therefore, surprised one day to see a battered pick-up truck in the parking lot with West Virginia tags. On the rear window of the truck there were two stickers. On the left side there was a Duke Divinity School sticker, on the right there was an NRA sticker. Right away I knew I had found a pal. I hung out in the parking lot until the guy showed up. After I explained to him that I was not a stalker, we hit it off. Our only regret is that we did not have the opportunity to grow up together and so I set out to invent our memories through the Skeeter Tales. *Mayhem* is the first story in the Skeeter series.

Woodpeckers Just Don't Make the Best Pets: Woodpeckers is the second Skeeter tale I wrote. The sequence of events described in this story actually transpired, more or less, it's just that Skeet and I were not actually involved. The outline of this story was related to me at a picnic in Meadow Bridge, WV. A fellow was telling me that as a child he had caught a woodpecker using the bucket of water method, and that he had built a cage out of wood. In real life, he left his bird in the garage. In the lives of me and Skeet, well, it is only natural that we would take the bird in the house.

Please, Don't Print Any of This: It has long been my goal to publish a story in *Field & Stream.* They reject my tales, as my brother would say, with all the regularity of a bran muffin with a prune juice chaser. The editors suggest that a person submitting stories should read a few issues of *F&S,* to familiarize themselves with the publication, before submitting stories. I didn't. I just kept writing and submitting and getting rejected and writing and submitting and getting rejected.... Finally, I broke down and read all the humorous stories *F&S* published going about three years back. Following that, and duly familiarized with the sort of thing they publish, I sat down and wrote this tale. I sent it off with all the confidence of a bear in a fish hatchery. It was rejected faster than any other story I had ever submitted to them.

Fump. Tink. Whizzz: Don't try this at home. This story is fiction, pure fiction. I don't know how or why it came to me, it just did. When I write stories like this I understand why Skeeter and I did not get to grow up together. God had a plan, and that plan was to keep us apart. We would, I'm sure, have come up with this, or similarly ridiculous schemes.

Luckless and Buckless: You never know what a deer might read. This offer remains good. Feel free to contact me.

Wildlife Management in a 100,000 sq. ft. Hardware Store: I worked at two different giant home improvement stores while I was in grad school. Well, "worked" might not be the best word. Let's say I was employed by them. Generally speaking the stores were well run and management really did good by me. But there is always, in every work place, that one screwball who has risen to the top by voodoo and/or witchcraft. Tupid didn't actually exist, but you know the guy.

Deer Hunting, Detroit Style: I saw these ideas in a vision just before I went hunting one year. This is just good sense. I mean, somebody should run with this idea. I wrote this piece for my column "Time Well Wasted" which ran for a while in the *Fayette Tribune*.

The Monster Stick's Last Ride: My first book, *The Monster Stick*, was put together just after my brother Paul died. I collected a bunch of his tales and a bunch of mine, and sent them to August House. Paul had been dealing with August House off and on but had never finished a whole book's worth of tales. The good folks at August House were very receptive to the collection I sent in and it became the book, but I had a nagging feeling in my gut. Paul's saga of the Monster Stick itself was cut short. The collection of tales needed an end. The 1998 Liars Contest was coming up and I figured I'd do a tribute to Paul and finish the Monster Stick thread in one fell-swoop. The end result is this tale, my last Biggest Liar winner. And now, may Paul and the Monster Stick rest in peace.

How We Got Out in the Cold in the First Place: This is another tale that showed up first in my column in the *Fayette Tribune*. Once again, it is just pure logic. Sometimes I wonder how a deductive, anthropological, evolutionary, archaeological genius like myself never got discovered.

Stereotypical Clergy: Each year on the Prairie Home Companion they run a contest called something like "Talented People From Towns Under 2000." It is a neat idea as it gives folks from small towns a chance to show off their talents on a national level. I figured I had as a good a shot as anybody to get on the show, so I wrote this tale. Your act had to be no more than three minutes long. I crafted this tale to fit the specifications nicely but, alas, I think it was too good. I suspect that Mr. Keillor took one listen and decided he ought not have me on the show lest I displace him.

A Picture of the Moose that Killed Us: This story is mostly true. We really were chased by a moose in the wilds of Montana, and Skeet really did stop to get that one last photo.

And the Winner Is?: Again, true but conflated. My dad really did tell a guy to pee in his canteen, but I'm pretty sure he was joking. And the kid really did, though I think he was quite serious. I, however, was not present. The rest of the tale is constructed from bits of my past.

Grabbled: People really do this. Who knows why, when God gave us perfectly good fishing poles to use for just this purpose. Skeet and I did not do it. I should point out that the reason why we did not do it is because we did not actually grow up together. Given the opportunity, I believe I can say that we probably would have given grabbling a shot. I wrote this in hopes of getting published in *In-Fisherman* magazine. This tale did not get published in that journal but it did help foster a relationship with the editor, Doug Stange. Mr. Stange is a stand-up guy as far as I can tell.

Das Buck: This was my last lie in the West Virginia Liars Contest. After the 1999 contest, I was hired by the West Virginia Department of Culture and History, the governmental agency that runs the show. This story, thankfully, won first place, bringing my total Biggest Liar titles to five and my winning streak to four in a row. As I said, following that contest I was hired by the government, which just goes to show that if you lie good enough and long enough, eventually the government will hire you.

De-Livered from Stolen Gear: Were do any stories come from? This just ended up on the computer one day. It's like that theory that if you had enough monkeys, eventually one would type out a Shakespeare sonnet. I ain't saying this is Shakespeare, I'm just saying that there are enough monkeys in my office on a day to day basis. . . .

Lessons Learned Bear Hunting: When Skeet, his father, and I went to Montana we had a lot to learn. West Virginia is plenty wild and wonderful, but anytime you add grizzly bears (and moose) to the equation, well, things get more complicated. I wrote this piece, actually, for a lecture I was asked to give on crafting tales. What I did was first write out as true an account as I could recall about our trip, and then I went back and rewrote it as a tall-tale.

Hot Dogs and Flies: I believe I might have been sipping Granddad's tonic when I put this together.

Dad's Never Lost: All true. This was another shot at *Field & Stream.* I was going for their back page, where they publish the true but often humorous bits about hunting and fishing. Once again I studied up on the style they seem to like and, once again, they sent me a very pleasant form letter letting me know how sorry they were that they could not respond in person.

Code 70: There is a legend at Philmont that this really happened, but there are lots of legends at Philmont. This did not actually involve my cousin, or me and we have pretty solid alibis for the rest of the things that happened the summer we were out there together.

Bathing Buck: I think this was in my column in the *Fayette Tribune* as well. If you have a dog, especially a big, outside dog, you have likely experienced much the same thing while attempting to bathe him or her. I guess if God had intended dogs to be clean, God would have made them cats.

Mississippi's Big Sunflower River Blues: This story first appeared in *Mississippi Game & Fish.* The editor said that it had enough fishing substance and technique in it that he wasn't even going to bill it as a humorous story. Whatever. He was going to print it and if he wanted to market it as a how-to article I wasn't going to argue. This was the first tale I had in a magazine that was published outside of my region. I was pleased to get it in.

Buck and the Contemplative Life: There's just nothing like having a dog, is there?

Scars and Calamities: For the past three or four years the West Virginia Division of Culture and History and the Governor's Office have joined together to award those artists and folks involved in the arts who made a significant contribution to the humanities in the state. The award ceremony is a black tie affair and offers West Virginia performers as entertainment between the awards. I was asked, after much begging, to be one of these performers. Our Governor at the time was Cecil Underwood, thus my animal governor, Weasel Overgood. The real Gov was sitting in the front row of the theater when I delivered my tale. I think I heard him laughing, and I still have my job, so I guess it went OK.

Cost of Living: Sometimes I try and write serious stories. The result is usually something like this story, except I generally don't like them, except as fire starters. I like this tale though. I hope that it deals with some real issues in a fun but serious way.

Homer's Stinky Cheese: I get these ideas lodged in my head. Ideas like being frozen in the ice while ice fishing, ideas like really smelly cheese that a guy concocts in a basement laboratory as if it were an illegal drug, just ideas that need a home someplace in a story. Eventually, those ideas meld into a tale.

Impaired: Inept: Overwhelmed: I write fairly regularly for a magazine called *Wild Wonderful West Virginia.* It is published by the WV Division of Natural Resources and generally promotes the State and its wonders. The editor asked me if I would do a piece on rock climbing. Because I have a pathological need to please editors, especially those editors who pay me, I agreed. The problem was that I know nothing about rock climbing, except that it involves rocks and climbing. I've been once or twice, but most of the information didn't sink in. So, I figured the best way to approach the tale was to appear dumb about the whole procedure. This was not a stretch. As long as I was going to come off looking dumb I figured I'd better drag Skeeter down, too. I think it worked out well.

The Great Narwhal and Naugahyde Habitat: This story started as a typo. I inadvertently typed Department of Natural Recources, instead of Resources one time, and the idea was born. I knew I had to use it, I just didn't know how. At long last I conjured up Warden Rake Sogbottom. The thing is, Skeeter and I need a nemesis and Sheriff Hasbro has begun to turn into a pretty decent guy. I can't have Hasbro be our bad guy if he is a good guy, so I was in a fix. Sogbottom is, however, not modeled after any game warden I have ever met. I think the WV DNR does a great job. But, I have worked in state government long enough to have run into a few characters who got their jobs through connections and who have subsequently lived down to everyone's expectations.

A Kind of Charitable Man: Frank is a mild mannered man not given to getting excited. He is, however, serious about deer hunting and has hunted deer every conceivable way short of parachuting into a herd of deer armed only with a glue-gun and a staple remover. This story is pretty much true. A lot of people say to me, "I'll have to be careful around you, or I'll end up in a story." More often than not they are wrong—not everything that happens is story worthy. Frank, on the other hand, does little that is not worth a tale. I would also like to note that, knowing full well there might be trouble, Frank took his brother's truck to run down the thieves, not his own.

About the Author

Bil Lepp has been writing and telling original tall tales for over a decade. He has performed throughout the country and written for several national magazines. A graduate of Duke Divinity School, Bil is a United Methodist pastor, though he is not presently serving a church. He works full-time for the West Virginia Dept. of Culture and History, but also presents concerts, workshops and seminars on storytelling at schools, festivals, banquets and other events. *Inept: Impaired: Overwhelmed* is his second book, following *The Monster Stick* (August House Publishers). He also has one audio recording entitled *Buck Meets The Monster Stick* (August House). Bil lives in Charleston, West Virginia, with his wife Paula, their son Noah, and, of course, Buck-Dog. Yes, he is a real dog. You can visit and contact the Lepps at www.buck-dog.com.

UNGUIDED MISSILES

Also by Fen Osler Hampson

Securing Europe's Future (co-author)
Forming Economic Policy
Hawks, Doves, and Owls (a contributor)

UNGUIDED MISSILES

HOW AMERICA BUYS
ITS WEAPONS

□

Fen Osler Hampson

W. W. NORTON & COMPANY

NEW YORK · LONDON

Published simultaneously in Canada by Penguin Books Canada Ltd., 2801 John Street, Markham, Ontario L3R 1B4.

Printed in the United States of America.

First published as a Norton paperback 1990

The text of this book is composed in 11/13 ITC Garamond Book, with display type set in ITC Garamond Book Condensed. Composition and manufacturing by the Maple-Vail Book Manufacturing Group.
Book design by Suzanne Bennett & Associates.

Library of Congress Cataloging-in-Publication Data

Hampson, Fen Osler.
    Unguided missiles: how America buys its weapons / Fen Osler
Hampson.
        p.   cm.
    Includes index.
    1. United States—Armed Forces—Weapons systems.   2. United
States—Armed Forces—Appropriations and expenditures.   I. Title.
UF503.H36   1989
355.8′2′0973—dc19   88–15356

ISBN 0-393-30641-0

W. W. Norton & Company, Inc., 500 Fifth Avenue, New York, N.Y. 10110

W. W. Norton & Company Ltd., 37 Great Russell Street, London WC1B 3NU

2 3 4 5 6 7 8 9 0

CONTENTS ·

FOREWORD

In the early 1980s, America's defense budget rose a dramatic 50 percent as a willing electorate heeded Ronald Reagan's warning that our nation stood in danger of falling well behind the Russians on a variety of military fronts, but especially in the twin areas of technology and weapons systems. Expenditures in all areas shot up, and stayed up, for about five years until the pendulum of public and congressional opinion swung back toward a reordering of priorities. Driving this momentum away from more defense spending were widespread concern about waste and fraud in the weapons-procurement world and sky-high budget deficits that powered the national debt to new heights.

Many of those who seek to explain how weapons procurement and defense budgeting and planning processes work assume much familiarity on the part of the reader with the intricacies of Washington life. Fen Hampson does not make this mistake; rather, he explains for a general audience how the procurement system works, why it is so relevant to weapons development, and what the key problems are. There is an irony here—it has taken a dispassionate Canadian to place the American defense reform debate into a wider perspective. Not that Hampson is unfamiliar with things American. He began this work over four years ago as part of the Avoiding Nuclear War Project at the Center for Science and International Affairs at Harvard's John F. Kennedy School of Government. Hampson's resulting cases are a treasure of research and interviews.

Unguided Missiles also avoids a mistake common to many books about defense spending—an overconcentration on corruption and waste. To be sure, there are corruption and waste in all areas of

public life, but that is not the heart of the matter. It is the politics and decision-making devices of defense that we should concentrate on. And Hampson does. Before focusing on any particular weapon, one must first understand the life cycle of modern weapons systems through the steps of the acquisition system. These are, of course, intimately entwined with the mechanics of the defense budget and programming systems in the Pentagon and in Congress. Both are fully and cogently described in *Unguided Missiles*. Only after absorbing these all-important introductory chapters is one ready and able to fathom the stories of those names so familiar, yet so mysterious, to most Americans: the Trident submarine and missile, the MX and the Midgetman, the B-1 bomber, the air-launched cruise missile, the M-1 tank, and last, but certainly uppermost in the public mind today, Reagan's Strategic Defense Initiative.

Hampson has a convincing argument to put forward here—that America's defense is driven by the dictates of political compromise and the "politics of consensus" more than by compelling strategic military doctrine or logic. In the stories he tells, the march of new technology, the "arms race," and the hostility between the superpowers are less important in weapons development than is commonly thought. To the extent that these strategic factors hold center stage, they do so only after making their way through Byzantine domestic debate about weapons development.

The difficulty of modern weapons development does indeed lie in an "iron consensus" between various areas of government and business, between the White House, the armed services, the intelligence agencies, and the defense industries. Many see reason to start up weapons systems and few see reason, or have the will, to stop them. The resulting incrementalism and confusion are systemic problems. How to reform the system and to restore political control to weapons acquisition and the budget process? Intelligent and well-informed answers are here.

Unguided Missiles is anchored in a model of the budgetary process drawn from economics and game theory. Some of Hampson's conclusions, taking these theories into account, may seem counterintuitive: less coordination and cooperation, rather than more, among different government agencies and interests to sharpen defense planning and budgeting priorities; less scrutiny of the details of the budget if Congress means truly to oversee and control

weapons development; simplification and synchronization of the budget cycle if political accountability is to be strengthened. In short, *Unguided Missiles* is a book that uses stories—long and interesting stories of national importance—in the interest of much-needed reform. Fen Hampson's message is a message well worth listening to and this book well worth reading.

—Joseph S. Nye, Jr.

ACKNOWLEDGMENTS

The idea for this book germinated while I was a fellow at the Center for Science and International Affairs at Harvard's John F. Kennedy School of Government. I would like to thank the co-directors of the School's Avoiding Nuclear War Project, Graham Allison, Albert Carnesale, and Joseph Nye, for their encouragement and support. I also thank Brian Tomlin, director of the Norman Paterson School of International Affairs, Carleton University, and Geoffrey Pearson, executive director of the Canadian Institute for International Peace and Security, for creating a supportive research environment at their respective institutions. The following individuals provided constructive criticism and advice on various drafts of this book: Robert Art, Jane Boulden, Michael Bryans, Philip Hampson, Brian Mandell, Jim Moore, Steven Miller, Michael Nacht, Joseph Nye, Ron Purver, Harald von Riekhoff, Jane Sharp, and Lynn Page Whittaker. I thank them for their efforts although I alone remain responsible for any errors of fact or interpretation. Nicholas Swales was a dogged research assistant and I am very pleased to include his own study of the M-1 Abrams tank in this book. Sue Connell and Lynne Cardinal provided resource and library assistance above and beyond the call of duty. Doina Cioiu kindly typed part of the manuscript. I am particularly grateful to Ruth Gordon and George Hampson, who carefully proofed the manuscript. Finally, a special word of thanks goes to Ed Barber and the editorial staff at Norton for their work on this book.

Unguided Missiles

1

□

INTRODUCTION

Dead reckoning is a term sailors use to describe navigation by the wind and ocean currents when clouds cover the stars. It is navigation by improvisation. And it requires more luck than skill. Dead reckoning also describes the way the United States buys its weapons. It is a process dominated by improvisation and "ad hocery" in response to shifting political and bureaucratic winds, where politics too often substitutes for careful planning and well-designed policies.

Ask any American, "Who built the MX missile, the Trident submarine, or the B-1 bomber?" and he or she might well answer "The air force," "The navy," "Rockwell, Boeing, General Dynamics," or "The Pentagon." The answers would be only half right. Imagine that person's surprise if you told him or her that Congress and the President were just as important, if not more so, in designing and building those weapons.

In recent years it has become fashionable to lambaste the Pentagon and the armed services for "gold-plating" weapons, cozying up to defense contractors, and allowing them to overcharge the American taxpayer for $200 nails, $400 hammers, $600 toilet seats, and $8,000 coffee pots. Such complaints are justified, but some of the biggest cost increases, inefficiencies, and reasons for bad weapons decisions lie in the political arena and the "process" of deciding what weapons to buy, how, and when.

Buying major weapons is a supremely political and controversial process. That it is so is no accident. The founding fathers intended it to be that way. By placing the authority to raise armies and buy weapons in the hands of the federal government, they

sought to provide for a strong common defense. Alexander Hamilton trumpeted the reasons in *Federalist 23.*

> Whether there ought to be a federal government intrusted with the care of the common defense is a question in the first instance open to question; but the moment it is decided in the affirmative, it will follow that that government ought to be clothed with all the powers requisite to complete execution of its trust. And unless it can be shown that the circumstances which may affect the public safety are reducible within certain determinate limits . . . it must be admitted as a necessary consequence that there can be no limitation of that authority which is to provide for the defense and protection of the community in any matter essential to its efficacy—that is, in any matter essential to the *formation, direction, or support* of the National Forces.[1]

Checks and balances were built into this central authority. Although the President is the designated Commander-in-Chief of the armed forces, he cannot buy arms and raise armies without first obtaining approval from Congress. Article 1, Section 8 of the Constitution gives Congress the power "to lay and collect taxes, duties, imposts and excises, to pay debts and provide for the common defense and general welfare of the United States. . . ."

Has the system worked the way America's founding fathers intended? Yes and no. On the one hand, congressional control over defense spending ensures that most major weapons programs come under scrutiny. On the other hand, a combination of long lead times from the inception of a weapons program to its eventual development and the incremental nature of the budgetary process itself exacerbates program delays, raises costs for major weapons systems, and, most important, erodes political accountability. The four-year term of presidential appointments contributes to program instability because weapons usually take longer to build than the time their presidential sponsors hold office. A new incumbent with a new set of defense priorities often puts his predecessor's pet projects on the back burner while moving others to the fore. This also contributes to delays, inefficiencies, and bad management in the process of buying weapons.

Efficiency is not one of democracy's virtues. Modern technology and long lead times for modern weapons system development,

however, make the democratic process even more inefficient and cumbersome. This would be a small price to pay were it not that political accountability is also weakened because major weapons programs outlive their political sponsors (and critics) and assume uncontrollable lives of their own. This book is, in essence, a biography of those lives, the lives of weapons.

2

□

THE WEAPONS ACQUISITION CYCLE

How are new weapons chosen? Who are the relevant actors and institutional interests? What are their roles in planning and design? There are no simple answers to these questions. In theory, weapons should be chosen to perform new or ongoing missions in response to new or existing military threats. The requirements for new weapons should therefore be determined by the armed services, after which a manufacturer is chosen to produce them. In practice, however, "conception, development, and production of defense systems are supported by a broad spectrum of government and private organizations,"[1] including organizational units of the government, "in-house" laboratories, and private industry. All have a close working relationship in the development of new weapons. The continuous involvement of these interests in planning and development makes it difficult, if not impossible, to pinpoint exactly the genesis point of new weapons.

The presence of these interests also creates problems of control both in the early stages of weapons design and later when a program has entered full-scale development and production. Successive reforms have failed to improve planning, enhance oversight, and rationalize procurement practices. As a consequence, special interests continue to undermine policy by advancing their own preferences on weapons design and development.

This chapter describes the formal stages of the weapons acquisition cycle and the relationship among the key actors and interests involved.

PROGRAM GENESIS

Much of the initial research and program development for new weapons proceeds in great secrecy. Provenance is murky. As Gordon Adams points out,

> Secrecy permits the contractors and the [Defense] Department to decide the nation's military future without having to deal with dissident or alternative views. In theory, at least, the Department decides what it needs and then shops around for a contractor who can fill those needs. In practice, however, needs, fulfillment, missions, and weapons systems are so intertwined that it is almost impossible to tell where one stops and the other starts. Generally, the Department defines a "mission"; it then doles out R&D money to the companies who refine a weapons system over a series of stages and in consultation with the Defense Department. On the other hand, the companies themselves often take the initiative. Once a major weapons system exists, momentum is created within the company, the DoD and Congress to buy it, particularly since the Government has already heavily invested in the company R&D.[2]

The defense contractors maintain large R&D (research and development) operations. Paul Cherrington and Ralph Gillen argue that for "companies primarily in the defense business, the share of time and effort devoted to R&D marketing is very high, since many of the production contracts have their genesis in R&D contracts."[3] Industry plays an important role in defining and providing input into the Mission Element Need Statement, which provides the basic justification for a new weapons system. Defense contractors will anticipate the needs and deficiencies of their Pentagon clients. As a former officer of the Raytheon Corporation states, "The day is past when the military requirement for a major weapons system is set up by the military and passed on to industry to build the hardware. Today it is more likely that the military requirement is the result of joint participation of military and industrial personnel, and it is not unusual for industry's contribution to be a key factor. Indeed, there are highly placed military men who sincerely feel that industry currently is setting the pace in the research and development of new weapons systems."[4]

Eight major companies dominate defense contracting: Boeing, General Dynamics, Grumman, Lockheed, McDonnell Douglas,

Northrop, Rockwell, and United Technologies. In the 1970s, for example, 37 percent of all new DoD R&D contracts fell to these companies, not to mention funds for major ongoing weapons procurement programs such as the B-1 bomber, the MX missile, cruise missiles, laser weaponry, space satellites, etc.[5] These eight companies also pulled another $11 billion in contracts from the National Aeronautics and Space Administration (NASA) in this same period.

These prime contractors are highly visible, but attached to the defense business are literally thousands of subcontractors who manufacture many of the parts for systems assembled by the majors. For instance, "[p]arts for Northrop's F-5 fighter are made by York Industries of Emigsville, Pennsylvania; Superior Manufacturing of Long Island City, New York; the CECO Corporation of Portland, Oregon; Breeze-Illinois of Wyoming, Illinois; and many other firms."[6]

The top firms maintain offices in Washington, and employ former employees of the Pentagon. Knowing the corridors of the Pentagon helps business. Something of a revolving door exists between the Pentagon and industry, which gives special meaning to the "iron triangle" of the defense industry, the Pentagon, and government interests. According to the Council on Economic Priorities, in an eight-year period almost 1,500 officers above the rank of colonel went to work for defense contractors, and slightly over 200 went the other way from industry to the Pentagon.[7] As J. Ronald Fox, a former Assistant Secretary of Defense, states, "The availability of jobs in industry can have a subtle, but debilitating effect on an officer's performance during his tour of duty in a procurement management assignment. If he takes too strong a hand in controlling contractor activity, he might be damaging his opportunity for a second career following retirement. Positions are offered to officers who have demonstrated their appreciation for industry's particular problems and commitments."[8]

The companies also maintain PACs (political action committees) through which individuals and corporations can make campaign contributions to elected officials. This is particularly important when it comes to lobbying Congress, as we will see in Chapter 4.

The Pentagon's in-house labs also play a crucial role in weapons systems development, particularly in helping to define the solution to operational needs. The navy has the largest institutional structure because of the specialized nature of naval warfare. By

contrast, the air force has little in the way of indigenous R&D centers. The country's major universities also do R&D for their government, a relationship that goes back to World War II. For example, the Johns Hopkins University Applied Physics Laboratory and M.I.T.'s Lincoln Laboratories were established in the 1940s under government sponsorship and, though independent, continue to rely on government contracts.

A variety of independent nonprofit corporations are also linked to defense R&D. These include the RAND Corporation, the Aerospace Corporation, and the MITRE Corporation. These R&D centers bridge the military and industry. They help "integrate the diverse ingredients necessary to formulate solutions to the appropriate need" and "bring to this central function special qualifications stemming from their firsthand experience in the test, evaluation, and support of operational systems, and in their orientation to problem solving rather than to a product line."[9]

The weapons labs—Lawrence Livermore near Berkeley, California; Los Alamos in New Mexico; the Jet Propulsion Laboratories (JPL) in Pasadena, California; and the Oak Ridge Labs in Oak Ridge, Tennessee—also play a key role in basic research. Some of these labs were also set up during World War II and played an important role in the Manhattan Project, which built the atomic bomb. The Oak Ridge lab, for instance, separated U-235 from U-238. Los Alamos took on much of the bomb's basic research and engineering. Lawrence Livermore, established after the war, was likewise active in the basic research for the hydrogen bomb. These labs continue in these research and development roles even today, as witness their involvement in the Strategic Defense Initiative, or "Star Wars," program.

FORMAL STAGES IN WEAPONS ACQUISITION (FIGURE 2–1)

Milestone 0. Weapons begin at the mission need determination and concept formulation stage.[10] At this stage the military service will explore a particular problem and seek a remedy. It will look to ways to upgrade a current system or develop an entirely new one. Comparative cost calculations are important here because the cost of upgrading or modernizing an old weapon is usually considerably less than the cost of developing a new one. On the other

Figure 2-1. The Cycle for Major Weapons Acquisition

Source: Adapted from Alexander Kossiakoff, "Conception of New Defense Systems and the Role of Government R&D Centers," in Franklin A. Long and Judith Reppy, eds., *The Genesis of New Weapons: Decision Making for Military R&D* (New York: Pergamon Press, 1980), p. 73.

hand, development costs for a new weapon may be offset by the shorter lifetime, higher maintenance, and lower performance of an old weapon. The particular present and future needs and missions of the service are assessed during this exercise.

Its mission properly defined, the project moves to the "requirements-validation" phase, still a part of the initial assessment. The services play an especially important role here by defining the technical and operational requirements of systems that might perform the mission and assessing alternative approaches and designs. The government's own R&D centers are also on this scene, often working closely with private industry by conducting feasibility studies and exploring the engineering and technical requirements of alternative ways of addressing the threat.

The military service–contractor interface has been criticized on several grounds. One of them is that the services' intimate technical involvement in the development of a system inhibits contrac-

tor creativity. According to former Secretary of Defense Harold Brown, one measure "that would improve the application of technology and the effectiveness of modernized weapons systems would be to give the systems contractors performance specifications rather than technical specifications." Argues Brown, "The prime contractors need to have some leeway for trade-offs among the various performance specifications, giving substantial weight to maintainability and reliability."[11] The F-16, discussed below, was built under this approach. But it is also true that contractors are in the enviable position of being able to shape service preferences and to press the services to buy the latest technology and hardware. It is the old problem of whether the tail wags the dog.

Although, theoretically speaking, specific weapons are not considered during this initial stage, the close involvement of industry in concept definition inevitably means that alternative weapons designs are discussed and evaluated. Alexander Kossiakoff points out, "The ... process develops the concept to the place where approval can be sought to proceed to validation and demonstration of selected options, that is, alternative weapons designs. If the requirements-validation process has been carried out properly, a solid basis for competition should have been developed."[12]

Milestone I. At the end of this initial exercise, a Decision Coordinating Paper (DCP) is drafted. The DCP has two purposes: it assesses the costs, operational advantages, and technical risks associated with the development of a new weapons system and it makes a recommendation for the Milestone I review, which is undertaken by a top-level committee responsible for supervising the entire acquisition process. This committee, called the Defense Systems Acquisition Review Council (DSARC) and renamed the Defense Acquisition Board (DAB) in 1987, comprises the Under Secretary of Defense for Acquisition; the Vice Chairman, Joint Chiefs of Staff; the Service Acquisition Executives of the Army, Navy, and Air Force; the Assistant Secretaries of Defense for Production and Logistics, and Program Operations; the Comptroller of the Department of Defense; the Director of Defense Research and Engineering; the Director of Program Analysis and Evaluation; and the chairs of Acquisition Committees, as appropriate.[13]

The DSARC system, born in 1969, was the initiative of then Deputy Secretary of Defense David Packard. Packard aimed to

introduce a "sequential structure" into the procurement process whereby weapons programs would be formally reviewed at key points in their life cycle. Dissatisfaction had lingered over Secretary of Defense Robert McNamara's personal acquisition style in the 1960s. Major cost increases, schedule slippages, and performance shortfalls in a number of key projects including the F-111 fighter-bomber and the C-5A jumbo transport aircraft had been much publicized. Shortly after entering office, President Richard Nixon set up a blue-ribbon panel, chaired by Gilbert Fitzhugh of the Metropolitan Life Assurance Company, to study ways to improve the system. The panel's principal recommendation was that major weapons systems should not be bought as a "total package." Development should be slow enough so there would be sufficient opportunity to test and review systems and their subcomponents before the actual production. As Tom McNaugher explains: "At each point, testing, hopefully of real hardware prototypes, was to be used to generate information on which proper decisions could be based. As it was characterized at the time, Packard was seeking a 'fly before you buy' policy, with OSD [Office of the Secretary of Defense] and the services meeting at appropriate DSARCs to review the information so generated. With their emphasis on prototypes and testing, and with the promise of a more regulated and less disruptive OSD role in weapons acquisition, the Packard initiatives seemed like a thoroughly sensible approach to squaring the need for management oversight with the need for managerial flexibility in handling fast-moving technologies."[14]

DSARC/DAB therefore is continuously involved in the research, development, testing, production, and procurement phases of all major weapons systems. Once DSARC/DAB initially approves a new weapon, the project moves to the second stage—"demonstration and validation." At this stage, the objective is to narrow the range of alternatives and develop a clear idea about what the weapon should do. Any deficiencies in the requirements of the system or technical approach are supposed to be found at this stage. The sponsoring service(s) and the potential contractors for the system work closely together in deciding the practical and feasible. Although one aim of the Packard reforms was to encourage a genuine search among alternative technologies and a full airing of the options, in practice the system has not worked this way. The services usually have a fairly fixed idea about the kind of system they

would like to build and they "thus work to exclude genuine alternatives from the very start; for them the development of competing models after DSARC I has at best been a way of holding contractors' feet to the fire. In fact, RFPs [requests for proposal] have grown neither shorter nor less technically detailed in the years since Packard introduced his initiatives, suggesting that competing 'alternatives' differ only modestly in technical detail."[15]

Milestone II. At the end of the demonstration and validation stage, the project undergoes a second full and complete review known as Milestone II, which includes limited production for operational testing and evaluation.[16] At this point a decision is made whether or not to build the prototype. For major systems, the decision will involve millions of dollars. Approval to proceed with full-scale development usually means the Secretary of Defense intends to deploy the system. During Milestone II the system and the principal items necessary for its support are designed and here interservice rivalry may intensify because of the level of resources involved. Once made, a commitment becomes difficult to reverse. "Because of this, few large weapons systems will be canceled after this stage is reached."[17]

The early stages of R&D for a new weapons system cost little compared to subsequent expenses in developing, producing, and operating the weapon. However, for the millions spent on R&D millions more will go toward system development. One study has calculated the following distribution of costs during the life cycle of a typical weapons system: 3 percent for early R&D; 12 percent for full-scale development; 35 percent for production; and 50 percent for operation and support of the system (see Figure 2-2). Thus, one problem with weapons development is that "attractive concepts, even rough designs, are cheap to produce, but they provide temptations to high budgets and new risks years later."[18]

Once a system has moved to full-scale engineering and development, changes become extremely costly and difficult. In theory, the system's design is frozen; in practice, it is not. Often, despite the expense, at the initiative of the sponsoring service(s), new performance characteristics are specified that must be built into the system by the contractor. Inevitably, this impedes progress, disrupts development schedules, and inflates costs.

The problem of "gold plating" is vividly depicted by James Fal-

Figure 2-2. **Phases in the Life of a Major Defense System**

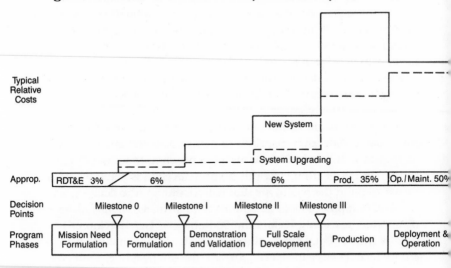

Source: Adapted from Alexander Kossiakoff, "Conception of New Defense Systems and the Role of Government R&D Centers," in Franklin A. Long and Judith Reppy, eds., *The Genesis of New Weapons: Decision Making for Military R&D* (New York: Pergamon Press, 1980), p. 72.

lows in the story of the F-16, which was originally designed as a lightweight combat fighter plane. It was not loaded with fancy hardware or aviation electronics so that it would be both small and versatile and work well in dogfights. The prototype YF-16 "was so small and so hard to see, either by eye or by radar, it maximized the advantage of surprise. Its projected cost was about half that of the F-15." James Schlesinger, then Secretary of Defense, authorized production of the fighter because he was impressed with its performance and its low cost and was able to persuade the air force and Congress to go along with the project.

However, production had to be supervised by the air force and as soon as it went into engineering development the blueprints were changed. According to Fallows, "technical specifications that had been so deliberately avoided up to this point" were added to the plane along with "roughly two tons of new electronic equipment and other modifications. ... This stage represented nothing less than the rejection of the entire philosophy under which the plane had been designed."[19] In the end, the air force got a plane

almost twice as expensive as the original prototype, considerably heavier and therefore less agile in the air, and harder to maintain because of all of its equipment. Although considered a superb aircraft and a "success" compared to its predecessors, the F-16 was not nearly as good as it might have been.

"Gold plating" is not the only problem, however. The decision-making process eventually consumes more resources and must satisfy an increasingly larger constituency well beyond the initial sponsoring service or agency. "[T]his consensus-building process tends to drive the requirements for a new system to higher levels of technical risk. ... Indeed, consensus-building [continues] ... over the course of the development project. Successive DSARCs open the ongoing project to reexamination, during which the consensus-building process that generated the initial requirement may be reenacted. ... Meanwhile, new technologies may have arisen since the previous DSARC, each proferred with great optimism about cost and performance, and some no doubt will find their way into the 'new' requirement."[20]

Another problem is program concurrency. Systems are often rushed into production before the individual components and subcomponents of the system have been adequately tested so as to make sure that they work together as a complete system. Although the DSARC review system is intended to prevent this, in practice these controls are not exercised. Parallel as opposed to sequential development can lead to major problems and performance short-falls. In the case of the B-1B bomber, for example, the subject of Chapter 7, the plane entered service without all of its working parts in order because of program concurrency. The plane's radar-jamming equipment, terrain-following radars, and controls all had serious problems because they had not been tested together as a complete system before the aircraft entered production. Some of these problems could have been averted had there been less haste in design and development.

Milestone III. The final procurement stage is production and deployment. It begins with the Milestone III decision which starts production approval and it goes forward until the last system is delivered, accepted, and provided to the active forces. This stage may be marked by conflict among the services and often between the services and OSD, especially if several major programs are competing for funds at the same time.

Thus, the total weapons cycle is often quite lengthy, involving years rather than months. And it may be ten or fifteen years after the project was initially conceived that the actual weapons system enters service. Throughout this process, from beginning to end, industry and the Pentagon work closely together. Stages I through III are funded through the Department of Defense's Research, Development, Test, and Evaluation (RDT&E) budget accounts. When the system enters full-scale production, it is funded out of the Department's Procurement account. Additional funds are also provided through the Military Construction and Operation and Maintenance accounts. Funds to continue testing the system and exploring ways of improving and upgrading are provided through the RDT&E budget. At this stage two further milestone reviews may be conducted. *Milestone IV* encompasses a review one to two years after initial deployment to assure operational readiness and support objectives are being achieved and maintained during the first several years of the operations support phase. *Milestone V* encompasses a review five to ten years after initial deployment of a system to determine if major upgrades are necessary, or if the system should be replaced.

SYSTEMS ACQUISITION WITHIN THE SERVICES

To this point, I have discussed only the general characteristics of weapons acquisition. Important differences mark the way this process works for each branch of the armed services. I will describe each service's procedures briefly, in turn recognizing that it is virtually impossible to show all the interrelationships between individuals and groups during systems acquisition.[21]

Army. The army process begins when an operational need is identified by the combat developer, normally the Training and Doctrine Command (TRADOC), in coordination with the matériel developer, normally the Matériel Development and Readiness Command (DARCOM). The need is documented in either a Justification for Major System New Start (JMSNS), for major programs requiring the approval of the Secretary of Defense, or a TRADOC and DARCOM jointly prepared and signed letter of agreement (LOA). LOAs are approved by the matériel and combat developers

unless the advanced development costs are expected to exceed $25 million, in which case approval must be sought from head-quarters. A favorable decision on the Mission Need Determination Statement may signal the formation of a special task force or special study group to develop the concept. For the Milestone I decision review, the army requires the preparation of a System Concept Paper (SCP) for all programs. For Milestones II and III a Decision Coordinating Paper (DCP) must be drafted. For major programs requiring the approval of the Secretary of Defense and for Designated Acquisition Programs (DAPs) requiring Secretary of the Army approval, the Army Systems Acquisition Review Council (ASARC) will review the DCP/DAP before it is submitted to the Secretary of Defense and/or the Secretary of the Army. All other programs are reviewed in-house. The ASARC membership list consists of top managers in the army including the Vice Chief of Staff, who serves as Chairman of the Board; the Assistant Secretaries; and the various Deputy Chiefs of Staff for Research, Development, and Acquisition, Operations and Plans, Personnel, and Logistics. In addition, the army's top intelligence officers will sit on the board.

Navy. Generally speaking, the navy begins buying when the Chief of Naval Operations (CNO) approves an Operational Requirement (OR) or the Commandant of the Marine Corps (CMC) approves a Required Operational Capability (ROC) report. If the program involved is considered to be a major one ($200 million or more for research, development, testing, and engineering, or $1 billion or more for procurement), the navy prepares a Justification for Major System New Start, or JMSNS. After the OR, ROC, or JMSNS has been internally approved, the document is incorporated into the Department's next Program Objectives Memorandum (POM)—these are discussed in the next chapter. If the POM is approved, the program may enter the concept exploration phase. Milestone reports for smaller programs are reviewed internally by the navy's own Defense Naval Systems Acquisition Review Council (DNSARC) or Office of the Chief of Naval Operations before being presented to the Secretary of the Navy, the Chief of Naval Operations, or the Commandant of the Marine Corps for approval. The DNSARC comprises the Assistant Secretaries, the Deputy Under Secretary, the CNO, the CMC, the Chief of Naval Matériel, and other senior officials. Milestone reviews of all major programs are reviewed by the

DNSARC and the Secretary of the Navy, before being submitted to DSARC and the Secretary of Defense for approval.

Air Force. Systems acquisition begins in the Air Force when an operating command submits a Statement of Operational Need (SON) with a Mission Element Need Analysis (MENA). If a determination is made by air force headquarters that the SON represents a major program, a JMSNS is prepared and then submitted to the Secretary of the Air Force. This might be approved by the Secretary himself if it falls within an already designated acquisitions program, or, if it represents a major new program, it may be submitted as part of the air force's new Program Objectives Memorandum for approval by the Secretary of Defense. Once the JMSNS is approved and the necessary Planning, Programming, and Budgeting System (PPBS) action has been taken, the concept exploration phase begins. A System Concept Paper is eventually prepared, which will be reviewed by the Requirement Assessments Group (RAG) and then the air force's own Systems Acquisition Review Council (AF-SARC). The council's membership includes the Assistant Secretaries of the Air Force, the various Deputy Chiefs of Staff, and the senior advisers. Minor programs can be authorized by the Secretary of the Air Force. Major programs must be forwarded to the DSARC to make its own recommendation to the Secretary of Defense. Subsequent milestones are handled in a similar manner.

INTELLIGENCE

Throughout each procurement stage intelligence estimates about hostile nations' programs play a key role in bureaucratic and political decisions about weapons development. These estimates feed into programming, planning, and budgetary decisions about ongoing and future weapons programs. Estimates about an adversary's military capabilities are just that: estimates. It is not easy to answer key questions: How much are they spending? How much will they spend five or ten years from now? What weapons will they deploy in the future and in what numbers? In particular, enormous uncertainty exists about Soviet military programs and intentions because the Soviets are secretive about their forces. In arms control negotiations, for example, Western diplomats have had to rely on their own independent assessments of Soviet forces and capabili-

ties. And sometimes even Soviet negotiators and diplomats have had to turn to Western sources because their own military will not give them the necessary information.[22]

The problem, however, is not simply that Communist societies are closed and their military secrets tightly kept—though perhaps less so under Gorbachev. Strategic forecasting is a difficult exercise even in open societies. Obvious difficulties are involved in projecting Soviet military capabilities, but similar difficulties would be encountered if one were asked to describe U.S. weapons programs and force requirements five, ten, and fifteen years ahead. Too many imponderables cloud projections of the future. We don't know how governments will respond to future threats (or perceive them); nor do we know what resources will be available to them to meet future challenges to national security.

Intelligence estimates try to predict the future and specify what and how many forces will be deployed by hostile nations. The judgments that inform these estimates play a major role in subsequent resource allocation and in decisions about the number of weapons to build once a system has proved itself on the testing ground and is waiting to be developed. This process is, of course, highly political. In the competition among different interests in the Pentagon and the rest of the bureaucracy, intelligence forecasts are used to advance key interests. Not every kind of weapon the military wants can be deployed in the numbers it wants. A great deal of lobbying ensues. Intelligence assessments that support the special interests of a particular service are eagerly seized upon to justify the weapons programs and interests of that service.

The government and the armed services often differ in their view of various external threats. The Pentagon and the armed services have traditionally stressed the severity of the Communist threat, more so than, for example, the CIA (Central Intelligence Agency), which is staffed almost entirely by civilians. This difference is undoubtedly rooted in the organizational imperative of the armed services to build and acquire weapons. The "missile gap" with the Soviets in the late 1950s and early 1960s was largely created by the air force.[23] When the gap proved mythical and the air force's intelligence estimates were temporarily discredited, the CIA assumed a greater role in intelligence gathering and assessment. However, the CIA was to some extent eclipsed in the late 1970s and early 1980s by the Pentagon, which used its own Soviet

assessments to justify its new defense programs. Intelligence estimates have oscillated between excessive pessimism and excessive optimism. The "bomber gap" and "missile gap" represent cases when Soviet capabilities were overestimated. But Soviet ability to acquire new technologies and to develop new weapons systems has also occasionally been underestimated. This is particularly true of intelligence estimates that underestimated how quickly the Soviets would develop the atomic bomb in the 1940s and the H-bomb later on in the 1950s. When the Soviets shot down Gary Powers' U-2 in May 1960 this came as a surprise—nobody thought Soviet air defenses could reach that high. Soviet air defense capabilities during the B-1 bomber debate in the 1970s were also underestimated, especially the Soviet capability to locate, track, and shoot down low-flying bombers.

Although technology and intelligence gathering have improved dramatically over the years with the development of satellites and other sophisticated reconnaissance capabilities, this has not eliminated uncertainty in intelligence forecasting.[24] Even today, intelligence assessments are extremely contentious and politically sensitive. This will not change because intelligence is not only a matter of "facts" but also of judgment, of intention.

One striking fact about the U.S. intelligence network is just how many agencies exist to gather and collect data about foreign governments, the Soviets in particular (see Figures 2-3 and 2-4). The CIA has traditionally been responsible for developing the National Intelligence Estimates (NIEs) about Soviet forces. However, the DIA (Defense Intelligence Agency), which is part of the Pentagon's own independent intelligence network, also works with the CIA in formulating the NIEs. Other participating agencies include the National Reconnaissance Office (NRO), the State Department's Bureau of Intelligence and Research (INR), and the National Security Agency (NSA).[25] The major military services also have their own intelligence divisions, which report to an Assistant Chief of Staff for Intelligence.

The Pentagon's intelligence estimates are included in the mission element need and authorization reports and in the other reports that must be prepared for the milestone reviews. They are also incorporated into the Joint Strategic Planning Document prepared by the Joint Chiefs of Staff in response to the Secretary of Defense's Defense Guidance Statement (described in the next chapter). The

Figure 2-3. The Intelligence Community

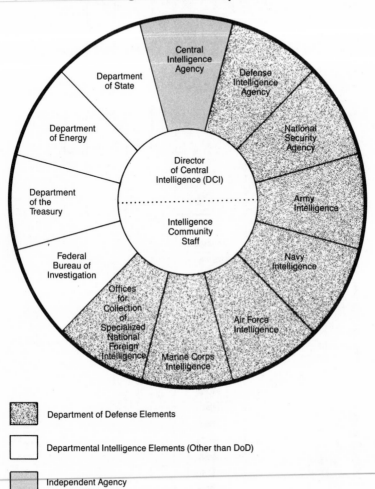

Source: Scott Breckinridge, *The CIA and the U.S. Intelligence System* (Boulder, Colo.: Westview, 1986), p. 48.

two key intelligence documents are the Joint Intelligence Estimate for Planning (JIEP) and the Intelligence Priorities for Strategic Planning (IPSP), both of which are prepared annually by the Office of the Joint Chiefs of Staff (OJCS). The JIEP contains short- and mid-term intelligence estimates on situations and developments

Figure 2-4. **Intelligence-Related Functions of the Department of Defense**

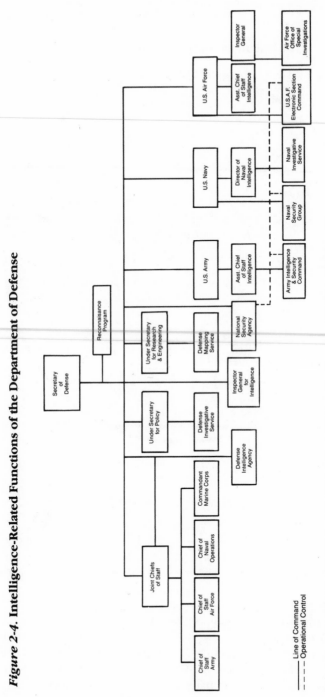

Source: Scott Breckinridge, *The CIA and the U.S. Intelligence System* (Boulder, Colo.: Westview, 1986), p. 52.

around the globe that could affect U.S. security interests, as well as a global appraisal and estimates of the nature of military threat including those posed by Warsaw Pact and Asian Communist forces. The IPSP provides guidance for DoD intelligence production, collection, and support activities.[26]

RECENT REFORMS

On February 28, 1986, David Packard, Chairman of the President's Blue Ribbon Commission on Defense Management, submitted an interim report to President Ronald Reagan. The Report's indictment was blunt: "Today, there is no rational system whereby the Executive Branch and Congress reach coherent and enduring strategy, the forces to carry it out and the funding that should be provided—in light of the overall economy and competing claims on natural resources. The absence of such a system contributes substantially to the instability and uncertainty that plague our defense program. These cause imbalances in our military forces and capabilities, and increase the costs of procuring military equipment."[27] The Report recommended some thirty changes affecting the management structure of the Pentagon and the upper echelons of the military services so as to clarify lines of authority, require more accountability, and improve communication across the defense establishment. The recommendations included giving more authority to the Chairman of the Joint Chiefs of Staff, who would still report to the Secretary of Defense and advise the President, but who would have his own staff and the responsibility of forcing the services to produce a coherent five-year military program under spending guidelines set by the President; lengthening the budget cycle and reducing the amount of "micromanagement" by Congress by having it approve a five-year budget plan for defense and vote on defense appropriations every two years instead of every year; creating a new Under Secretary of Defense specifically responsible for weapons acquisition; and expanding the authority of the U.S. regional military commanders-in-chief (the CINCs) by having subordinate commanders report directly to them and expanding their spending authority.

Some of these recommendations have been adopted by Congress in the Military Retirement Reform Act of 1986, chief among them creation of a new position—Under Secretary of Defense,

Acquisition.[28] Responsibilities also were defined in the Defense Acquisition Improvement Act of 1986 and approved in the 1987 Defense Authorization Bill. Military department and service headquarters reorganizations were directed in the Department of Defense Reorganization Act of 1986.

The legislation defines the scope of the acquisition function as including "procurement, research and development, logistics, development, testing, and contract administration," and defines acquisition specialties as "including contracting, logistics, quality, program management, systems engineering, production, and manufacturing."

The Under Secretary heads the major engineering organizations (Research and Engineering; Command, Control, Communications, and Intelligence; Atomic Energy) and logistics organizations (Acquisition and Logistics; Small and Disadvantaged Business Utilization). He is the senior procurement executive for the Department of Defense and has the authority to direct the Secretaries of the military departments and all other elements of the Department of Defense on procurement matters. He is assisted by an Under Secretary of Defense for Acquisition or procurement "czar."

The procurement "czar's" authority was the subject of an intense battle between the House and the Senate. The House wanted the official to "supervise" the weapons procurement process, which is in the hands of the separate services, whereas the Senate preferred a stronger version by which the Under Secretary would "direct" the services' purchases. The House prevailed on this count and also in keeping the Director of Operational Testing, a job created by Congress in 1983 to ensure that the services subject new weapons to realistic tests under battlefield conditions, independent from the Under Secretary.[29]

The Defense Acquisition Improvement Act also requires the Secretaries of the individual services to establish a "baseline description" for a major defense acquisition program before the program enters full-scale engineering development—and before it enters full-scale production. In the full-scale development stage, the description must include the performance goals for the weapons system to be acquired under the program, the technical characteristics and configuration of the system, total development costs, and a schedule of development milestones. The same items, along with testing, initial training, initial provisioning, and total procurement costs, must be provided for the production stage.

The Act also enables the Secretary of Defense to streamline the management and funding of some major weapons programs by establishing designated "defense enterprise programs." These programs have their own special executive program officers. Program officers can report directly, without intervening review or approval, to the senior procurement executive of the military department concerned, thereby removing several layers of bureaucracy and procedural regulations, except basic federal purchasing rules. However, programs must go through regular procedures for milestone review and authorization, although the Secretary of Defense can request congressional authorization of funds for a program to cover periods of up to five years for either full-scale prototype development and testing or full-scale production. He would agree, however, to a so-called "baseline"—a cost limit, performance specifications, and timetable for the program. Once granted a multiyear authorization, a program would not be dealt with in the annual Defense Authorization Bill unless it fell short of the stipulated cost, performance, or schedule limits. In that case, Congress would have to reauthorize the program after the Defense Secretary informed Congress of the revised baseline. However, all enterprise programs continue to require annual appropriations from Congress. The Pentagon must also have at least two competing contractors build prototypes of any major proposed weapon and must require realistic testing of that weapon. But these requirements can be waived by the Secretary of Defense if they are deemed impractical and the decision is explained to Congress.

The Under Secretary for Acquisitions is supported by two major boards, the Defense Science Board and the Defense Acquisition Board.[30] The latter replaces the Defense Systems Acquisition Review Council. DAB assumes responsibility for the DSARC milestone reviews, for defining and validating new system requirements, for assessing cost/performance trade-offs, for reviewing alternatives to new R&D starts, and for issuing full-scale development and high-rate production recommendations in joint and major programs. The Board is intended to provide a forum for addressing the broader defense acquisition improvement concerns, early commitment to programs, and increased program stability.

The Defense Science Board, established in 1956, remains unchanged. The Board consists of 150 members appointed from the civilian sector by the Secretary of Defense on recommenda-

tion by the Under Secretary for Acquisition and the chairs of the army, navy, and air force respective scientific advisory panels or boards. It is there to advise the Secretary of Defense and the Under Secretary for Acquisition on overall scientific and technical research and engineering.

The acquisition reforms are intended to create "a single uniform system whereby all equipment, facilities, and services are acquired, maintained, and disposed of within DoD. The system entails establishing policies and practices which govern acquisitions, determining and prioritizing resource requirements, directing the process, internal management control, and reporting to Congress."[31] However, as one senior DoD official explained to me, the reforms have involved more of a "reorganization and relabeling" of existing departments rather than a fundamental overhaul of the system. This is certainly true in the case of the procurement "czar" who simply replaces the Under Secretary of Defense for Development, Research, and Engineering (DDR&E) in the organizational chart. Moreover, responsibility for weapons acquisition still rests in the hands of the independent services, and their relationship with OSD remains essentially unchanged. (It is interesting to note that the first Under Secretary for Acquisitions, Richard Godwin, quit in frustration after being in office only a few months because he felt his authority was too limited to do his job properly.) Although the new system of "defense enterprise programs" removes several layers of bureaucracy, thereby making the decision-making process somewhat more efficient, programs must still go through the "milestone" review process. However, the system does give those programs that qualify for this special status some immunity from the process of congressional authorization, which will be discussed further in Chapter 4.

CONCLUSION

This chapter has reviewed the formal stages of the weapons acquisition cycle and some of its major problems. Recent reforms, like the establishment of a special Under Secretary of Defense for Acquisitions, may bring about greater order and efficiency, but as long as the armed services bear primary responsibility for weapons acquisition, system performance requirements and specifica-

tions will continue to respond to service and contractor needs and priorities. Other problems, such as the dangers of consensus building in milestone reviews (which can increase program risk) and of program "concurrency" (whereby systems are rushed into production before their subcomponents are adequately tested), are only partly addressed by the reforms. Moreover, these reforms have focused primarily on DoD and less so on the relationship between DoD and Congress in programming and budgeting. In weapons acquisition nothing can be done without money, and the defense budget plays a critical role in weapons acquisition and procurement. The next two chapters examine the politics and structure of the budgetary process in the Pentagon and Congress, respectively.

3

□

THE PENTAGON AND THE DEFENSE BUDGET

During the Grenada invasion of 1983 a group of soldiers lost touch with the main U.S. force. Pinned down by heavy fire from the Cubans their situation grew critical. In a desperate bid for help, the group's commander tried to call in air support from the navy's carriers on his radio. No reply. His radio operated on a different frequency from the navy's, making communication impossible. Suddenly, one of the soldiers saw a telephone. To his surprise, it was in working order. Using his AT&T calling card, he placed a long-distance telephone call to Fort Bragg, North Carolina, where an incredulous but helpful operator was able to relay his SOS to the invading U.S. force. Within a matter of minutes, air support arrived.

Such a story illustrates the perverse effects interservice rivalry can have on military operations. In this case, the services owned radios that operated on different frequencies.

Students of the weapons acquisition and defense budget process have eagerly seized upon the interservice rivalry model to explain how the process works in the Pentagon.[1] But conflict is only half the story. A lot of cooperation—some would say collusion—defines the "essence" of the bureaucratic relationship not only among the services but also among the other players in the Defense Department and the government. An understudied aspect of government behavior, the effects of cooperation are often just as pernicious and pose their own special problem for public policy, as we see in the case of the defense budget.

Although the armed services and different bureaucratic and organizational interests in the federal government are in a fundamen-

tally competitive relationship with one another, the defense budgetary process encourages a cooperative approach to decision making and the fashioning of political compromises which, once forged, are hard to break. What this usually means is that even competing programs in the budget will be funded at sufficient levels to remain viable. When resources are scarce, funds will be cut but rarely will major programs be canceled outright. Faced with the trade-off between efficiency and bureaucratic harmony, efficiency will get the short end of the stick in programming and budgeting choices. Over the long run, funding shortfalls and budgetary instability take their toll in higher program costs, schedule slippages, and poor performance in weapons development. The problems posed for weapons development by cooperative bureaucratic strategies in assembling the defense budget are the subject of this chapter.

INCENTIVES FOR COOPERATION

Game theorists note that cooperation among potential adversaries is enhanced by games with frequent and regular interactions among players and incremental decision-making processes such that present actions and cost-benefit calculations are undertaken with an eye to the future (see Appendix A). Conversely, competitive or conflictive strategies are more likely when costs and benefits are experienced immediately and players have little chance of encountering each other again; that is, when the game has a definite beginning and end and is not likely to be repeated by the same contestants.

Cooperation is also enhanced under conditions of what economists call "oligopoly." In an oligopolistic setting, where there is a limited number of producers of any given good or commodity, cooperative, price-fixing strategies will prevail as producers seek to divide up markets among themselves and to limit the number of competitors. Unlike pure monopoly, with only one producer, there is some competition. But the degree of competition is restrained and producers will not actively try to erode one another's market share by competitive pricing strategies as they would in a free market. This "competitive-cooperative" relationship is usually managed through a process of tacit bargaining or informal "signal-

ing" because of anti-trust prohibitions against price fixing and direct collusion among firms.

In the bureaucratic setting, bargaining strategies are similarly "competitive-cooperative" when it comes to deciding the defense budget for many of the same reasons game theorists and economists note. Cooperation is facilitated by incremental budgeting processes, frequent contact among the bureaucratic players, and definable limits to the number of institutional interests involved. Moreover, unlike the economic marketplace, there are no prohibitions to prevent direct communication among the parties. Bureaucratic preferences are therefore signaled directly through formal bargaining and negotiation.

Changing Stakes. In the initial stages of development, the sums of money involved in relation to a weapon's total procurement costs and the defense budget as a whole are usually quite small. Funds are never committed to a program as a lump sum. Individual budgetary decisions rarely commit the sponsoring service or the government as a whole, particularly in the early stages, to actual deployment of the system. Thus a program will rarely be challenged in its early stages of development. But the cumulative effect of these decisions builds momentum into a program and by the time it reaches the prototype development stage it will have already consumed significant resources.

A decision on production and deployment, however, raises the bureaucratic stakes because of the level of resources involved. At this point, interservice rivalry intensifies, especially if a number of different programs are competing for scarce funds. The services will not hesitate to look for allies in the Pentagon, in other branches of the bureaucracy, or even in Congress to ensure that their projects get top priority. If a program does come under serious challenge from its opponents in the Pentagon, the bureaucracy, or Congress, a service or OSD may try to reduce the visibility of the program in the budget or reach a political compromise by deferring major costs until later and by "stretching out" procurement and deployment of the system.

Frequent and Regular Interaction among Players. Government is not entirely unlike business and an important part of doing business is getting along with your business partners. Officials in

the Pentagon and other branches of government continually meet with their counterparts in the bureaucracy. This is especially true of the budget process. The defense budget is not drafted in isolation by some lone official in the Department of Defense or the Office of Management and Budget in the White House. It has architects in different branches of the bureaucracy who are constantly consulting with one another, deciding and re-deciding what to do, when, and how. It is a team effort and, like any team effort, there are rewards for being a team player and penalties for trying to go off on one's own or playing by a different set of rules. This is not to say that conflicts do not occur. But when they do, strong incentives remain to strike a compromise by trading off competing interests so that the process does not become bogged down.

A service will be extremely reluctant to challenge directly the programs and interests of another service unless, of course, a major commitment of resources is involved, because it may find its own programs under challenge at some later point, and it will have to pay a price for its earlier "defection." Furthermore, on a purely personal level, strong incentives force individuals facing one another across the same table on a weekly or monthly basis to cooperate because they know they will be seeing one another again.

Time and Organizational Constraints. Because of the sheer number of budget decisions, the tendency is to split the difference so that decision-making procedures do not break down or get held up. Key deadlines constrain the time available to assemble the budget. Too many challenges and too much confrontation can lead to a breakdown of organization and decision making.

These three factors help to explain why a major weapons program, once it gets started and develops an organizational constituency within the Pentagon, is hard to kill after it has entered production and why it will continue to receive some level of funding. When there is conflict, and difficult choices and trade-offs must be confronted, the players will try to "split the difference" and reach a consensus satisfactory to all interested parties in some measure. This often explains why weapons programs are "stretched out," why unit costs (and ultimately total program costs) are driven up, and why deployment levels are not what the original sponsors intended. In the process, key programming priorities may be undermined. In these budgetary games, no clear "winners" or "los-

ers" emerge. Nobody gets everything he or she wants. By the same token, nobody is left empty-handed.[2] Once they have acquired sufficient momentum and the backing of major organizational interests, systems rarely die.

THE BUDGETARY SYSTEM

The structure of the budgetary process has, of course, changed substantially over the years. Under President Eisenhower's administration, the Secretary of Defense did not issue program guidelines to the services and there was no formal effort to integrate military policy with fiscal policy. Instead, the Secretary would issue fiscal guidelines in the form of budgetary ceilings the services could not exceed. This left the services to buy what they wanted without any sort of policy directive from the Secretary of Defense. Defense planning was therefore under the proprietary control of the military.

The architect of the current defense budgetary system was Secretary of Defense Robert S. McNamara, who served in the Kennedy and Johnson administrations. McNamara was a former professor of management at Harvard who had helped pull the Ford Motor Company out of virtual bankruptcy in the 1950s. A strong believer in the virtues of cost-benefit analysis, he initiated reforms that led to the introduction of PPBS (Planning, Programming, and Budgeting System) in the Department.

These reforms tied together military defense and financial planning in order to strengthen the role of the Secretary of Defense in military planning. As Alain Enthoven and K. Wayne Smith, two former members of McNamara's staff, explain,

> The main job of the Secretary of Defense, we believe (and McNamara believed), is to lead the Department in the pursuit of the national interest. He cannot do this job by passively administering a predetermined budget ceiling, rubber-stamping his approval on agreed JCS recommendations, and adjudicating Service disagreements. He has to take the initiative, raise the issues, provoke debate, demand studies, stimulate the development of alternatives, and then decide on the basis of fact and merit. PPBS has proved to be a valuable instrument for helping the Secretary of Defense be an effective

participant in the strategy, force, and financial planning process in DoD.[3]

The purpose of PPBS was to introduce explicit criteria for measuring the adequacy of defense programs and for judging trade-offs among the alternatives. One of the key measures was cost, but as McNamara himself explained: "I do not mean to suggest that we can measure national security in terms of dollars—you cannot price what is inherently priceless. But if we are to avoid talking in generalities, we must talk about dollars: for policy decisions must sooner or later be expressed in the form of budget decisions on where to spend and how much."[4]

The key elements of PPBS were the Five-Year Defense Plan (FYDP), the Draft Presidential Memorandum (DPM), the creation of the Systems Analysis Office in OSD (Office of the Secretary of Defense), and the Development Concept Paper (DCP).[5]

The FYDP was developed not only to provide a record of current costs and manpower but also to project this information far enough ahead to estimate future costs in the defense budget. The FYDP produced a series of tables giving an eight-year projection of forces and a five-year projection of costs and manpower covering ten major military programs: strategic forces, general-purpose forces, intelligence and communications, airlift and sealift, guard and reserve forces, research and development, central supply and maintenance, training and medical services, administration, and support of other nations. The FYDP in an important way tied force and financial planning considerations together into one package, providing a basis for planning throughout DoD.

The Draft Presidential Memorandum originated in 1961 with the preparation of President Kennedy's "white paper" on U.S. nuclear strategy. By 1965 the DPMs had become the chief program decision-making document and had expanded to cover the whole defense program (not just strategic forces). They were actually drafted by the Office of Systems Analysis and provided the basis for subsequent discussions in the services and by the Joint Chiefs of Staff on strategy, force requirements, and financial considerations. (The DPM is the forerunner of the modern-day Defense Guidance Statement of the Secretary of Defense.)

McNamara's innovative DCP represented a further attempt to

examine performance, cost, and schedule estimates, as well as technical risks, with the specific purpose being to overcome the tendency of the services to overstate the performance of a new weapons system while underestimating its development costs and risks. (It is similar to the JMSNS statement, discussed below, which is used today.)

These basic management tools are still used in the preparation of the defense budget. According to Larry Lynn and Richard Smith, however, McNamara's hope that PPBS would stimulate interservice rivalry and lead to more design options by forcing information and options to the Secretary of Defense was not realized. Each service's " 'essence,' or self-defined primary mission . . . limit[s] the options it is organizationally capable of producing. . . . Even when competing programs [exist], the service and congressional support that each [develops] severely [restricts] the ability of civilian managers to exploit the overlap." Thus, "if an idea [gathers] momentum, even if only in the development stage, it [is] hard to kill or deflect."[6]

McNamara's objective to make the budgetary process more "rational" by making it conform to planning and programming guidelines set by the President and his Secretary of Defense was also not

Figure 3-1. **The Defense Budget Process** (Steps 5, 6, and 7 are discussed in detail in Chapter 4)

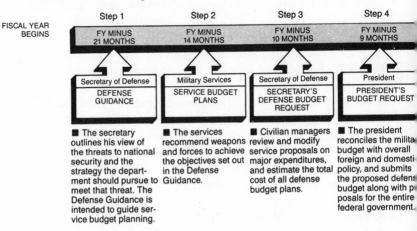

	Step 1	Step 2	Step 3	Step 4
FISCAL YEAR BEGINS	FY MINUS 21 MONTHS	FY MINUS 14 MONTHS	FY MINUS 10 MONTHS	FY MINUS 9 MONTHS
	Secretary of Defense	Military Services	Secretary of Defense	President
	DEFENSE GUIDANCE	SERVICE BUDGET PLANS	SECRETARY'S DEFENSE BUDGET REQUEST	PRESIDENT'S BUDGET REQUEST
	■ The secretary outlines his view of the threats to national security and the strategy the department should pursue to meet that threat. The Defense Guidance is intended to guide service budget planning.	■ The services recommend weapons and forces to achieve the objectives set out in the Defense Guidance.	■ Civilian managers review and modify service proposals on major expenditures, and estimate the total cost of all defense budget plans.	■ The president reconciles the militar budget with overall foreign and domesti policy, and submits the proposed defens budget along with pi posals for the entire federal government.

Source: Mark Rovner, *Defense Dollars and Sense: A Common Cause Guide to the Defense Budget Process* (Washington, D.C.: Common Cause, 1983), pp. 18–19.

realized. As we see below, continued involvement not only in establishing programming priorities but also in shaping the budget enables the services to undermine or circumvent the goals and priorities of their political masters.

BUDGET STAGES (FIGURE 3-1)

The defense budget must pass through four basic phases before it is submitted by the President to Congress.[7] This process is characterized by regular interactions between OSD and the armed services from the initial formulation of the budget to the end. Frequent opportunities exist for the services to present their demands and shape the process as it moves along. OSD, which is responsible for planning and for ensuring that service interests fit into the President's and the Secretary of Defense's objectives, is in a potentially competitive relationship with the services. Occasionally, conflict will erupt over resource allocation decisions for different programs. But close institutional linkages between OSD and the services in budgetary programming moderate the degree of bureaucratic rivalry and struggle.

Step 5	Step 6	Step 7
FY MINUS 4½ MONTHS	**FY MINUS 4 MONTHS**	**FY MINUS 1 MONTH**
Congress	Congress	Congress
CONGRESSIONAL DEFENSE BUDGET CEILING	DEFENSE AUTHORIZATION	DEFENSE APPROPRIATION
■ Congress establishes spending ceilings for various categories of federal spending, including defense.	■ House and Senate Armed Services Committees draft a law setting out the Pentagon's approved shopping list in detail.	■ House and Senate Appropriations Defense Subcommittees draft a law essentially similar to the defense authorization, but covering more of the defense budget.

Step 1. The budgetary process begins with the Secretary of Defense's Defense Guidance Statement (DG). In this classified paper, the Secretary of Defense sets down what he sees as the key threats to vital U.S. national security interests and how they should be met. The paper, delivered each January, represents an attempt to translate broad strategies and plans into specific military terms; it tells the military not only what its goals are but also how much money it will have to spend over the next five years to meet them. However, what is crucial to the military is the budget for the first year of the planning period.

The DG in a real sense initiates a dialogue with the armed services about the contents of the defense budget. Although it is intended to be a directive to and a guide for the military services in drawing up their own budgets, the services' own priorities and plans often conflict with those of the Secretary of Defense and can only be resolved through the elaborate system of bargaining encouraged by the way the defense budget is prepared.

Preparation of the DG begins with the Joint Strategic Planning Document (JSPD) submitted to the Secretary of Defense by the Joint Chiefs of Staff. The JSPD presents the Joint Chiefs' view of the threat and contains a projection of U.S. force requirements over the next seven years to deal with it. It is a "wish list" because the projections are not based on any kind of appraisal as to what financial resources will be available to the military. However, it is intended to serve as a "baseline" against which affordable programs can be measured and risk assessments undertaken.

The JSPD is studied carefully by the Defense Resources Board (DRB) in OSD.[8] It is intended to provide guidance in the drafting of the DG, although whether it achieves this purpose is doubtful. As Richard Stubbing, a former official in the Office of Management and Budget, writes, "Over the years, the members of the JCS, recognizing their mutual need to promote individual service goals, have tacitly agreed not to criticize the programs of the other services. Thus, the advice which comes out of the JCS—in documents like the JSPD—is likely to be uncritical of existing programs and dedicated to increasing each service's forces and budget."[9]

This reflects a more general tendency in the JCS toward consensus. In a major study of the official record of JCS recommendations in the 1950s and 1960s political scientist Arnold Kanter found that the proportion of "split" decisions only occasionally exceeded 1

percent annually, the rest being unanimous.[10] Kanter attributes the paucity of split recommendations to several factors. First, only about 25 percent of JCS recommendations in the period he studied were actually decided by the Chiefs themselves, and this figure dropped to 5 percent in the 1960s.

Second, explains Kanter, "the growing volume of JCS decisions increases the danger that the staffing machinery simply will break down under the load. Unanimous recommendations also create an atmosphere more conducive to coping with the workload by reducing conflict among the Chiefs and within the staff." This is particularly important because the JCS must make literally thousands of decisions during the course of any given year. As former JCS chief General Maxwell Taylor observed many years ago, since "one dissenting Chief can prevent action on an issue for long periods, it is difficult to force consideration of matters unpalatable to one or more of the services."[11]

Third, according to Kanter, "the services' bargaining advantages vis-à-vis the Administration are enhanced to the extent that they are able to cooperate with one another and adopt unanimous positions." Thus, it is exceedingly rare of the JCS actually to challenge a weapons program that is strongly supported by a service.

As various sections of the DG are drafted, they are circulated to different branches and sections of the armed services for comment and revision. The JCS present their own risk assessment (JSPD) and by early January the final version of the DG is ready, which essentially completes the first step in the preparation of the defense budget.

Step 2. The second step involves the preparation of the military service budgetary requests. During the spring, the army, navy, air force, and marines respond to the DG and put forward their own proposals as to how the goals in the DG are to be achieved. The individual program requests, known as Program Objectives Memoranda (POMs), contain a five-year blueprint for each service's needs and are the key building blocks in the defense budget.

The POMs address such key questions as "How many personnel? How many weapons? What kind? How much support? How will forces be deployed?"[12] However, the answers are supposed to conform to the Secretary of Defense's budget and program guidelines. The POMs also include budgetary requests for the develop-

ment of new weapons systems, which is how new weapons find their way into the budget. Before these requests can be made, though, the services must prepare a Justification for Major System New Start (JMSNS) statement and have it approved by the Secretary of Defense.

The POMs go on to detail service plans for systems already under development. Occasionally systems may be canceled to permit funding for a new system, or requests for funding may be increased to accelerate programs already under development.

The services usually begin working on their POMs well before (usually the year before) they get the DG from the Secretary of Defense. As one senior DoD official explained, their usual tactic is simply to "rewrite" the POMs "so that they conform with the Secretary of Defense's DG statement [interview, 1987]."

The relationship between the services and OSD is also close. There is little one can do without the approval of the other, which encourages cooperative bargaining strategies when interests and priorities conflict. The army's Director of Program Analysis and Evaluation, Major General Patrick M. Roddy, explained it this way.

> Here I am right here, that is, Director of Program Analysis and Evaluation. I have a counterpart in OSD. He is called Program Analysis and Evaluation also. Here are the budget folks, the OSD Comptroller, the Army Comptroller and Director of the Army Budget, because everything he does ultimately has an impact on me and vice versa. So we in essence get handcuffed to one another early on in the process and we chair something called a Program and Budget Committee.
>
> Every dollar that gets moved around in the Army budget must be approved by this committee. The same thing is true in programming. So there is no element of the Army program or the Army budget that gets moved around without it coming through this committee. I sit there. He sits there. And we co-chair the committee. I can't have a meeting without him there and he can't have one without me. . . .
>
> From there it goes through the Secretary of the Army, to the Deputy Secretary of Defense, or SECDEF, who chairs the Defense Resources Board. . . . The Secretary of the Army sits on DRB. All of the other service secretaries sit on the DRB as do all the principal assistant secretaries of Defense and the Chairman of the Joint Chiefs of Staff.

All decisions relating to the program approval or disapproval process as it relates to the services are done by the DRB.[13]

In early summer, the POMs are reviewed by the Secretary of Defense and the Joint Chiefs of Staff in a process managed by the DRB, which will carefully screen major projects involving requests over $25 million (smaller projects are only reviewed by the sponsoring service). The JCS will submit their own evaluation in a report known as Joint Assessment Planning Memorandum (JPAM) which ascertains whether the POMs fulfill the objectives of the DG of the Secretary of Defense.

The Secretary of Defense will then review any appeals of DRB decisions and adjust the POMs.[14] Once approved, the POMs become Program Decision Memoranda (PDMs), and they contain the rough outlines of the final budget. At this point, in theory at least, the planning and programming parts of the PPBS cycle and the work of the DRB are complete, although in practice DoD continues to tinker with planning and programming priorities.

Step 3. The third step in the budgetary cycle is to take the PDMs and translate them into specific budgetary accounts such as procurement, operations and maintenance, etc. This task is performed by OSD's Comptroller and OMB, and the competition among the services to protect their "wish lists" from OSD's and OMB's pruning shears is often intense.[15] The Secretary of Defense will then make any final changes before the budget request is submitted for approval by the President.

The Secretary of Defense has the opportunity to change the PDMs and veto any new weapons procurement initiatives. He occasionally will exercise this power although instances are rare. "Within the budget cycle ... the Defense Secretary's options are usually limited to either approving or not approving new service weapons, and then setting the timing and rate of production once a program is approved. What's more, the issues normally raised in the summer program review generally focus on in-depth technical assessments of a weapon's cost, its performance characteristics, and its mission effectiveness. Seldom is a new program challenged for a perceived failure to meet the broad defense strategy."[16] Furthermore, a Defense Secretary's options are limited by the role of the Under Secretary for Defense Research and Engineering (now

Under Secretary for Defense, Acquisitions), who is the third-highest official in DoD and is responsible for weapons development. "Over the years the USR&E bureaucracy has assumed the role of technology advocate, working with the services to design ever more technologically advanced weaponry. The Under Secretary—usually a career defense-industry executive—generally supports the weapons projects suggested by a military service, making it difficult for the Defense Secretary to direct that weapons programs be cancelled or drastically altered."[17]

Because the Secretary of Defense is an advocate for the Pentagon and is only making a budgetary recommendation to the President that he knows will probably be pruned, there is a strong institutional and bargaining imperative for him not to chop service requests too drastically.

Instances where a Secretary of Defense has tried to overrule service interests by mandating a new weapons program are rare. But when he has, the outcome has usually been unsuccessful or disastrous. The most celebrated case was the TFX decision by former Secretary of Defense Robert McNamara. McNamara tried to get the navy and the air force to build a common tactical fighter. McNamara supposedly got the idea after accompanying President Kennedy on a tour of a carrier where he was overwhelmed by the diversity of aircraft. Both he and Kennedy wondered why there were so many different planes and when he was presented shortly afterward with proposals from the navy and the air force to begin development of two separate planes, he arranged a shotgun marriage of the two designs.

McNamara refused to accept the judgment of the services that a biservice program was not feasible.[18] The navy wanted a plane that could operate at high altitudes, from aircraft carriers, and could carry air-to-air missiles. The air force, on the other hand, wanted a plane that could fly close to the ground using terrain contour matching radar and that would have the capability to destroy ground targets with either conventional or nuclear bombs. In the resulting design competition, the military favored a design by the Boeing Aircraft Company. However, the Secretary of Defense liked the design of the General Dynamics Corporation because it was cheaper. The contract for the TFX was awarded to General Dynamics, but McNamara won only a Pyrrhic victory over the services.

Although the plane was built, it conformed only to the air force's

specifications and was too heavy for the navy's aircraft carriers. The navy ended up buying the F-14, and the TFX, renamed the F-111, became an air force plane.[19] After McNamara left his job, the air force got the plane it really wanted, the F-15.[20]

Step 4. From August to January, the defense budget is scrutinized by the President and his staff in the Office of Management and Budget.[21] Other agencies, such as the State Department, the CIA, and the Arms Control and Disarmament Agency, may also express views on the defense budget informally through the National Security Council.

During this fourth and final step of the budgetary process within the executive branch of government, the defense budget competes with other budgetary requirements and fiscal objectives. This is when the classic "guns versus butter" issues are resolved and the President decides how much to spend on defense versus other national social, economic, and political priorities, although rarely will the trade-off be posed so starkly. OMB plays a crucial role and will trim, cut, or (rarely) add items to the budgetary requests of the individual agencies.

If an agency doesn't like OMB's decision it can appeal to OMB or directly to the President himself. However,

> None of that applies to the Defense Department. Because of the length and complexity of Pentagon budget making, OMB has long held that its early involvement in the PPBS process was essential. Acknowledging that abandonment of their customary detachment might cost them some objectivity, OMB examiners reasoned that having a better idea of what was going on would compensate. Thus, OMB participates in the entire budget process within DoD. OMB defense budget examiners spend much of their time at the Pentagon, rather than at the Executive Office Building with the rest of their colleagues. Moreover, OMB's Associate Director for National Security Affairs is a voting member of the Pentagon's Defense Resources Board, thus ensuring some Presidential involvement in every step of DoD's budget process.[22]

Former OMB director David Stockman vividly depicts how the defense budget and growth levels were settled in the early days of the Reagan administration.

The next problem was settling on what the "real growth" should be, since Reagan had been all over the lot on that one. . . .

In a parting "up yours" gesture at the new administration, the Carter lame-duck budget had already provided 5 percent real growth through 1986. But Frank Carlucci now maintained that the Carter lame-duck budget would not provide for the kind of weapons modernization, force structure expansion, and readiness and sustainability funding that was needed. We had to think in terms of the 8 or 9 percent growth range, he said. . . .

But I knew Marty Anderson, back at the Office of Policy Department, was a flinty anti-spender on everything. If I came back to the White House with the higher figure, he'd go off the deep end. The last thing I wanted was a time-consuming punchout at the White House. So I suggested we split the difference down the middle and go with an interim 7 percent real growth increase. . . . Weinberger thought about it a moment. "In light of the disgraceful mess we're inheriting," he said, "seven percent will be a pretty lean ration." But he agreed to go along.[23]

But this did not end the negotiation. As Stockman soon discovered the 7 percent real growth calculation was based on constant 1982 dollars after the "get-well" package had been added to the defense budget. When the constant-dollar figures were translated into current-dollar values, as Stockman exclaims, "I nearly had a heart attack. We'd laid out a plan for a five-year defense budget of *1.46 trillion dollars!*" Stockman had to wrestle with Secretary of Defense Caspar Weinberger to get the figure down. OMB's Slower Growth Alternative (SGA) provided a budget of $1.33 trillion. But as Stockman observes:

> You practically had to look at the difference closely in order to avoid a rounding error. Weinberger could keep 92 percent of his budget. . . .
>
> We had taken the utmost care to ensure that SGA conformed to the Administration's highest defense priorities. . . . No cut was proposed at all, for example, in any of the basic strategic modernization programs.
>
> The Pentagon's proposed funding levels for the B-1 bomber, the MX-missile, the Trident submarine, the new sea-based strategic missile, and the cruise missile program would all remain unscathed. These programs would receive more than $150 billion over five years.

Likewise, SGA accepted most of the Pentagon's plans for modernizing key conventional weapons systems. . . . With ships, it was much the same. . . . The bottom line was that you could do a *lot* to strengthen the military with $1.33 trillion.[24]

Important differences mark the way different Secretaries of Defense have approached their jobs and budgetary planning. According to former Under Secretary for Defense Robert Komer, McNamara's successor, Melvin Laird, did not rely as heavily as did McNamara on OSD and gave the services much greater authority in defense planning. His directives were largely in the form of fiscal guidance to which the services were expected to adhere in their POMs. Secretary of Defense Harold Brown reinvigorated systems analysis and instituted an annual consolidated guidance (CG), "which combined all the policy, fiscal, and programming guidance for preparation of the next budget and the FYDP." The first chapter of the CG, which provided general strategic guidelines, was drafted by the Under Secretary for Defense Policy, a new post created by Brown. Brown also formed the DRB to review the POMs and resolve programming and budgeting disputes before they reached the Secretary of Defense.

Defense Secretary Weinberger and his successor, Frank Carlucci, relied heavily on the DRB, which was the principal vehicle for planning and programming. "No consolidated guidance for service POMs is issued, only a defense guidance which is now prepared by the USDP [Undersecretary of Defense, Policy]. . . . Thus, the DRB has become a more powerful instrument for defense planning and programming. . . . With the service secretaries (and, informally, the service chiefs) in attendance, the DRB is a much more collegial forum in which the services not only submit the programs, but sit in judgment on them." According to Komer, "[t]his procedure, in effect, puts the service secretaries back into the policy-strategy business, from which they had been debarred at least since McNamara. Moreover, by its very nature, it focuses primarily on programs, rather than strategic issues, thus making programs drive strategy even more."[25]

BUDGETARY IMPACT ON WEAPONS ACQUISITION

A major problem with the budgetary process has to do with its impact on the weapons acquisition cycle. Although a major weap-

ons system program that has moved to the production stage rarely gets cut from the budget, the program may get stretched out to reduce immediate costs, particularly—though not exclusively—during periods of increasing fiscal austerity and budgetary belt-tightening. This has the long-term effect of driving up the unit costs of the system because the system cannot be produced efficiently by the contractor.[26]

Upon assuming office in 1981, Secretary of Defense Weinberger initiated a thirty-two-point program to improve the way DoD buys weapons. Several of the initiatives were designed to discourage stretching out a weapon's production schedule so as to avoid un-economically low production rates, including efforts to maintain programs at planned schedules, quantities, and funding; contracting for more than one year's deliveries at a time for certain programs; budgeting to "most likely cost"; and buying weapons systems at economic production rates. Although the Defense Acquisition Improvement Plan (DAIP) did improve the acquisition process, it nevertheless fell well short of its goals. According to the General Accounting Office (GAO), implementation of twenty-three of the thirty-two initiatives was less than complete and program managers surveyed by GAO characterized their programs as unstable more often in 1985 than at the beginning of fiscal year 1983.[27]

An earlier review of forty-one acquisition programs by the GAO found that all experienced some change in total program costs ranging from a decrease of more than 50 percent to an increase of more than 37 percent in the course of one year, but none was completely eliminated from the budget. During the same period fourteen program schedules changed, ranging from an acceleration of one month to a slippage of fifteen months.[28]

In its A³ (Affordable Acquisition Approach) study, the air force looked at 109 programs and found real growth of about 5 percent per year traceable primarily to program instability which in turn was derived from large unplanned changes in program funding. This caused, for example, 729 F-16s to cost $2 billion more than originally planned as the production schedule was stretched out three years. Lieutenant General James W. Stansberry (USAF), a former administrator in the Office of Federal Procurement, explained the program planner's dilemma this way: "Defense systems take several years to bring into being, and we cannot afford to change our plans every year along with budget changes. Inevitably in the

annual competition for scarce Federal dollars, we change, defer, delay, stretch out and almost guarantee cost growth. As Commander of a major acquisition division, I was faced with the same problem every year. My input to Air Force Systems Command for our portion of the Federal budget dollar was terribly constrained (obviously) and I had too many programs to fund. There was a terrible temptation to 'nickle and dime' all of the programs and hope that next year there'd be more money."[29]

Poor linkage between planning and programming in the budgetary process contributes to the problem. According to the GAO, "[t]he program and budgeting phases' predominant focus on the first year of the 5-year defense program obscures future costs and affordability of today's program and budget decisions." Moreover, "[f]unds are budgeted (as well as executed) in terms quite different from those in which they are programmed, and no clear link between the two exists."[30] This is because programming emphasizes missions, or outputs, whereas budgets are formulated in terms of inputs, namely, personnel, procurement, and operating expenses. Program budgets are prepared and submitted long before they are actually approved, so adjustments are often required because pricing and other key assumptions have changed. Reluctance to undo existing bureaucratic compromises, however, makes it difficult to effect these changes.

Poor oversight of budget execution, which is not defined as a formal part of the PPBS, creates another set of problems. Execution is the primary responsibility of field personnel in DoD and the services. Those in headquarters spend the bulk of their time formulating and justifying the plans, eventual programs, and the final budget. There is insufficient attention paid to the execution and monitoring of programs and the way funds are spent.

Underfunding, inefficiency, and lack of effective monitoring create delays and cost overruns in the acquisition process. As Jacques Gansler explains: "Even after development is complete, the high costs of each weapon mean that only a few can be purchased per year, so that the deployment of any significant number is delayed still further. An added effect of lengthened acquisition cycles is reduced efficiency in the acquisition process and, therefore, still greater unit costs and still lower quantities. Thus, the lengthening acquisition cycle has a compound military effect. First, it results in a decline in America's technological advantage over the Soviets,

since most of the systems deployed in the field are older designs; and, second, the longer cycle itself causes higher costs and, therefore, reduced quantities."[31] But the problem is not simply the Pentagon. In some ways, it is far more serious in Congress, as we will see in the next chapter.

CONCLUSION

This chapter has argued that the budgetary process plays a key role in shaping the behavior of organizational and bureaucratic actors in the Pentagon and in the rest of the government on weapons procurement matters. Although the armed services, the Department of Defense, and the Office of Management and Budget have conflicting interests and budgetary goals, the way the budgetary process is structured encourages horse trading and compromise. But once commitments are made and a program that has acquired support in the Pentagon bureaucracy and in the contracting community moves to the prototype testing and production stage, interservice competition and rivalry usually intensify, especially if a number of major programs cannot all be funded at once. Major programs, though rarely canceled, will invariably be cut to accommodate competing demands and interests in a finite pie.

Procurement budgetary decisions are, for the most part, incremental. Funds are rarely committed in a lump sum to cover the entire lifetime development costs of a major weapons system. They are usually secured on a piecemeal basis. In the early stages of basic R&D and prototype development, the level of resources committed to a new weapons program is relatively small in relation to the system's total development costs, and it is relatively easy to get support for a new R&D program in the budget. Key actors and institutions in the Pentagon and in the rest of the government that formulate programming and planning priorities consult regularly with one another in such a way that encourages a cooperative approach to decision making. The Secretary of Defense's Defense Guidance Statement, which initiates the planning process, is not so much a directive as a means for initiating a dialogue with the Joint Chiefs and the services so that their own interests and programming priorities can be taken into account. The POMs, which contain a five-year blueprint of service needs, are the basis for fiscal planning in DoD and the key building blocks in what eventu-

ally becomes the budget proposal to the President. The budgetary process is supervised by the Defense Resources Board, which has representatives from the services, OSD, and the Office of Management and Budget. The Board meets frequently and plays an integral role in shepherding the budget through its various stages.

Time and organizational pressures also play their role. The budgetary cycle is repeated each year and preparation must adhere to a tight schedule. Faced with impending deadlines and a multitude of programming and budgeting decisions, overt conflict and deadlock resulting from "all-or-nothing" bargaining strategies are simply not viable. Thus, compromise is one of the key rules of the game. And although the services will rarely get all that they want in the way of new weapons, they are rarely left empty-handed.

While this decision rule may be optimal for reconciling competing institutional demands and making difficult trade-offs, it results in program "stretch-outs" and higher unit costs for individual weapons systems. This creates enormous difficulty for the defense industry, frustrating competition and breeding inefficiency, as Jacques Gansler and others have noted.

When the President delivers his budget to Congress in January, the focus of the debate and decision-making process shifts to the Congress. As we will see in the next chapter, however, the same decision rules seem to apply to congressional behavior. To a significant extent, the budgetary process, in combination with other factors, has a similar effect on Congress's approach to difficult weapons procurement choices.

4

□

Congress and the Defense Budget

In the spring and summer of 1983 Congress made a number of crucial decisions by which it approved flight testing and basing of the MX missile. Looking back on those decisions, *New Yorker* correspondent Elizabeth Drew observed:

> [G]iven the MX's bizarre history, the convoluted reasoning that went into its most recent justification, the serious misgivings of those who were most responsible for helping the weapon win congressional approval, and the potential consequences of their actions, the story is an unusual one. It is a story of well-intentioned people acting out of a combination of their own sense of what it means to be "responsible"; their own sense of what they needed to do to "position" themselves politically or lay the groundwork for political advancement; and political fear. Almost none of those who made the President's victory possible thought that the missile was, in itself, a good idea. . . . It was the politicians searching for some middle ground—painstakingly trying to pick their way through nuclear politics—who gave the President his victory on the MX.[1]

Congress is a strange institution even to a veteran Washington correspondent like Elizabeth Drew. That the MX was able to secure congressional approval despite widespread opposition is puzzling.

Many believe that political self-interest and opportunism motivate Congress.[2] If congressmen were motivated solely by self-interest, however, the machinery of government would quickly grind to a halt when those interests clashed. As Elizabeth Drew and others note, the situation is more complex and political self-interest is only part of the story.[3]

Pluralist or interest-based models overlook the important ways that issues and interests are redefined by Congress in the legislative process and through discussion.[4] The *process* of arriving at decisions and the *norms* or *rules* of decision making together shape and define policy choices in a way that is not adequately explained by reductionist theories of decision making. When it comes to the defense budget, cooperation and consensus are prized almost as highly as the desire for political advancement. The prevalence of these norms helps to explain why Congress will rarely kill a major weapons system program, even one that is unpopular with many congressmen. However, these norms are reinforced by the structure of the budgetary process and the incremental manner whereby Congress authorizes and appropriates funds for defense. What are these norms? How do they define policy choices? How does Congress deal with the defense budget? These questions form the subject of this chapter.

THE ROOTS OF CONSENSUS

Consensus. What does consensus mean? As Congressman Les Aspin (D.-Wis.), Chairman of the House Armed Services Committee, explains, "Consensus, of course, does not mean unanimity. What it means is at least a majority. Consensus does not mean taking the middle ground on every issue. It means a package that makes sense to the common-sense middle."[5] Finding the right formula is not easy. As Aspin suggests, the consensus must be created and the process is anything but tidy.

Frequent and Regular Interaction among Members. Institutional processes encourage cooperative behavior on the part of Congress's members. Game theorist Robert Axelrod notes that one of the principal requirements for a cooperative strategy is the strong chance of interacting with other players. "[I]f there is a large enough chance that a member of the legislature will interact *again* with another member, there is no one best strategy to use independently of the strategy being used by the other person. It would be best to cooperate with someone who will reciprocate that cooperation in the future, but not with someone whose future behavior will not be affected by this interaction." And he goes on to observe that in the case of the U.S. Congress, "the chance of two members

having a continuing interaction has increased dramatically as biennial turnover rates have fallen from about 40 percent in the first forty years of the republic to about 20 percent or less in recent years."[6]

On defense budgetary matters, as we will see below, interaction is regular and frequent among members of the congressional budgetary authorization and appropriation committees and subcommittees. Contacts between members of the two houses are also extensive. The high level of communication encourages a cooperative approach to budgetary issues in the legislature for the reasons Axelrod notes.

Reciprocity. The importance a congressman will attach to any given vote on the defense budget is also quite small compared to the value or sum of all of the votes he may be asked to cast in any given year. Another way of saying this is that future votes matter and congressmen will approach budgetary issues as non–zero sum. They will be more willing to make concessions and to cooperate with rival interests in order to ensure that their own interests are not sacrificed in future votes. Reciprocity means "Don't vote against programs in my district and I won't vote against programs in your district."[7]

Incrementalism. Incremental decision-making processes encourage reciprocity by casting a long "shadow of the future" over present decisions. There is never a single, decisive vote on the defense budget. Many votes will be taken in any given year on a wide range of budgetary items having to do with authorization and appropriations. Congressmen never need feel they are committing themselves to anything. Decisions can be reversed later on by adding or deleting funds from the budget. Programs cut from the Defense Appropriations Bill can be resurrected in the form of "supplemental appropriations" the following year. The low discount rate attached to future votes or "payoffs" helps secure the consensus that Congressman Aspin and others value so highly.

Although incrementalism facilitates consensus, it also helps erode it as priorities change and political coalitions shift. In a series of successive votes on the budget, new pressures may emerge as special interests mobilize and lobby Congress. A weapons program may find itself under attack as groups try to cut its level of funding

or have it canceled. Although major programs rarely die as a result, political uncertainty breeds program instability, raising costs for major weapons systems.

Congress rarely funds programs on a multiyear basis. When Congress looks at the cost of a weapons system or a major R&D program, it generally wants to know how much must be paid this year rather than the program's complete cycle costs. Procurement and R&D represent a relatively small portion of total current expenditures or "outlays" in the defense budget, as we will see below. The incentive to cut procurement items from the current budget for fiscal reasons is therefore reduced because the immediate benefits are generally quite small.

THE BUDGETARY PROCESS

Debates about defense in the budgetary authorization and appropriations process have to do with the marginal allocation of resources. Congress almost never addresses the fundamental question "Should we fund this program?" Rather, the question is *"How much?"* Once we understand the logic of this process, it becomes easier to see why major weapons programs rarely die at the hands of Congress.

In contrast to the budgetary process within the executive branch, congressional review of the defense budget is relatively open to public scrutiny. It is not so difficult to understand who the players are and where they stand on particular issues. The debates in committee hearings and on the floor of the Congress are open and often carried directly to the public by the media.

A trend has emerged, what Gregg Easterbrook has called "government in the sunshine." But every vine grows in the sun and Congress quite literally has become a jungle of confusion.[8] The breakdown of the seniority system, the proliferation of subcommittees, recent changes in the budgetary system, and the growth of congressional staff all contribute to the chaos. Most important are the changes that came in 1974 when Congress passed a "subcommittee bill of rights," giving subcommittees the right to hold hearings any time they want and creating a system of "multiple referral" so that several subcommittees can review the same bill or topic at the same time. These reforms, says Easterbrook, have transformed Congress "from an institution in which power was

closely held by a few to an institution in which almost everyone had just enough strength to toss a monkey wrench." But, "[m]ore than any other factor, the deregulation of subcommittees has increased Congress's workload and decreased its cohesion." John Tower (R.-Tex.), former chairman of the Senate Armed Services Committee, echoes these concerns. He observes that his own committee spent a good deal of its time "trying to fend off competition from other committees and monitoring what the other committees are doing," thus wasting precious time and energy.[9]

The year 1974 was also a turning point for the way Congress spends money. The reforms undertaken in the Congressional Budget and Impoundment Act increased Congress's involvement in the details of the budget and its influence over spending decisions. Prior to 1974, Congress had no formal mechanisms for reconciling revenues with expenditures in the budgetary process. The committees that actually spent the money, the authorizing and appropriations committees, were not responsible for raising the money they spent. Instead, taxation was the responsibility of the Senate Finance Committee and the House Ways and Means Committee. This division of responsibility had its own special problems because the authorization and appropriations committees did not have to worry about the fiscal consequences of their spending decisions or whether there was enough money in the federal treasury to cover the programs they approved. As one former congressman remarked, "No one, including myself, in Congress in the 1960s ever asked what anything would cost. All we thought about was, Does this sound like a good program? Can we get it through?"[10]

The Act of 1974 created new budget committees in the House and the Senate. The purpose of these committees was to integrate spending with revenues in the legislative process. The membership of the House Budget Committee is drawn from the membership of the Ways and Means Committee, the Appropriations Committee, and from other standing committees. The Senate Budget Committee has no fixed representation from other committees, but its membership includes senators from the finance and appropriations committees.

The budget committees are assisted by the staff of the Congressional Budget Office, also established in 1974. The CBO has a large staff and prepares reports and other key materials for the committees on a wide range of budgetary issues, including defense. The

budget committees are involved continually in turf battles with the authorization and appropriations committees. "Wedged in between powerful taxation and spending committees, the new panels have contended with suspicion, mistrust, and outright hostility from their older counterparts."[11]

More recently, budget committee practices have angered authorizing panels such as the armed services committees. The budget panels have avoided serious confrontation largely by focusing on broad revenue questions and appropriation totals. By staking out the " 'How much?' questions, the panels have left to the appropriating and authorizing committees the traditional questions of how totals should be allocated."[12]

PREAPPROPRIATION*

Step 5 (Figure 4-1). Congressional involvement in the federal budget formally begins when the President submits his annual Budget Message to Congress, usually in late January or early February. The House and Senate Budget Committees hold hearings, consider reports from the CBO and other congressional committees (such as the House Ways and Means Committee and the Senate Finance Committee), and "mark up" different versions of the budget. The full House and Senate then vote on their alternative resolutions and send them to a Joint Conference Committee on the Budget which hammers out a compromise. The House and Senate then vote on the Conference Committee proposal leading to a congressional budget resolution that theoretically must be adopted by May 15, although this deadline is almost never met in practice.

The First Budget Resolution sets spending targets for each category in the federal budget, of which national defense is one. All in all, federal spending is divided into some twenty categories known as "functions." Although the spending ceilings are not binding, subsequent action on authorization and appropriation bills usually falls below the ceiling. In addition to providing targets for the next fiscal year, the resolutions also stipulate spending targets for the next two years. But these are not binding and will be changed in subsequent annual budget resolutions.

*Figures 4-1, 4-2, and 4-3 explain in detail Steps 5, 6, and 7 of the defense budget process shown in Figure 3-1.

Figure 4-1. The First Budget Resolution

• The First Budget Resolution sets target spending levels for each category of federal spending, including national defense. Although the spending ceilings are not binding, subsequent action on Authorization and Appropriations bills generally does stay below the ceiling.

• The law requires that congressional action on the First Budget Resolution take place within a strict timetable, but in practice it often slips badly. What follows is the officially mandated schedule:

Late January — Early February
The president sends his annual Budget Message to Congress.

Mid-February — April 15
House and Senate Budget Committees hold hearings, consider reports from other committees, and "mark up" different versions of the budget.

April 15 — May 15
The full House and Senate then vote on their alternative resolutions and send them to a joint Conference Committee on the Budget which reconciles the differences in a compromise budget.

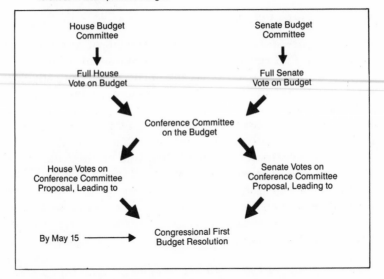

Source: Coalition for a New Foreign and Military Policy, *How Congress Acts on the Military Budget and Arms Control* (Washington, D.C., December 12, 1984).

The Budget Act also calls for a Second Concurrent Resolution in September, the purpose of which is to take the "targets" and make them into binding "ceilings." Originally intended as an instrument that would enforce budgetary procedures and spending guidelines, it has been circumvented in practice. Congress has simply used the Second Resolution to rubber-stamp or approve spending decisions subsequent to the First Resolution. Thus, the targets in

Figure 4-2. **The Defense Authorization Act**

• The annual Defense Authorization Act, taken up once the First Budget Resolution is completed, allocates funding to various military programs and sets conditions under which money can be spent.
• Major congressional battles over weapons programs, like the MX or the B-1 bomber, are first raised during work on the Defense Authorization Bill.

Mid-February — Early May
House and Senate Armed Services Committees hold hearings and "mark up" different versions of the Defense Authorization Bill.

Anytime from May through June or July
House and Senate floor votes on the Defense Authorization Bill.

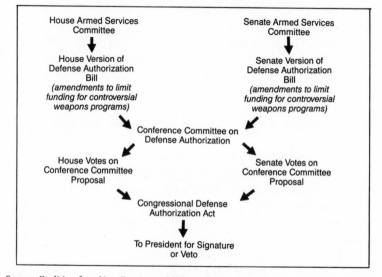

Source: Coalition for a New Foreign and Military Policy, *How Congress Acts on the Military Budget and Arms Control* (Washington, D.C., December 12, 1984).

the First Resolution have in fact become the key benchmarks for federal spending.

Step 6 (Figure 4-2). The Department of Defense cannot spend a single cent of taxpayers' money until it gets detailed approval from Congress telling it how much it can spend, for what, and when. The first stage in getting such approval is defense authorization. The annual Defense Authorization Act is taken up once the First Budget Resolution is completed. The Act allocates funding for various military programs and stipulates the conditions under which the money can be spent. Major congressional battles over key

weapons systems, such as the MX missile, the B-1 bomber, and the Trident submarine, have begun during the deliberations on the Defense Authorization Bill.

From mid-February until early May, the House and Senate Armed Services Committees will hold hearings and "mark up" different versions of the Defense Authorization Act. In doing so, they will hear from literally hundreds of witnesses from DoD, the Congressional Budget Office, the General Accounting Office, and occasionally from industry and other private organizations. Once the House and Senate versions of the Defense Authorization Bill are completed, often including amendments to limit funding for more controversial weapons programs, they are sent to a Joint Conference Committee on Defense Authorization. The House and Senate will then vote on the Conference Committee Proposal. Once passage of the Congressional Defense Authorization Act has been secured by vote in the House and Senate, it will be sent to the President for his signature or veto. This can happen any time from May to July.

The Defense Authorization does not cover the entire defense budget—in fact, only about three-quarters. However, key items subject to the bill include DoD's budgets for Procurement; Research, Development, Test, and Evaluation; Operation and Maintenance; and Civil Defense. The bill does not authorize sums for personnel, but it does set limits on the number of people DoD may employ, and it sets other personnel policies.

This system did not always exist, but in 1961 Congress mandated annual authorization for procurement of weapons systems including missiles, aircraft, and ships. Arthur Maas explains:

> Previously the military departments had had permanent, open-ended authorizations to purchase any weapons they needed, and congressional control over this important activity had, therefore, been limited to annual appropriation procedures. Soon after the Armed Services Committees had begun to consider annual authorization for weapons systems, they realized that they had not achieved effective control by attending to procurement alone; that the vast expenditures for research, development, tests, and evaluation of weapons systems, which preceded procurement, pretty well determined which weapons would be bought. They therefore extended the annual authorization requirement to these antecedent activities as well. Thereafter Congress progressively broadened annual au-

thorizations to cover all research, development, test, and evaluation carried on by the Department of Defense (to commence in 1964); procurement of tanks and other tracked combat vehicles (1966); personnel strengths in each of the reserve branches (1967); procurement of other weapons (1969); personnel strengths of the regular forces (1970); operation and maintenance expenses (1982); ammunition and communications and supply equipment (1983).[13]

The expanded roles and scrutiny of the armed services committees in the preparation of the budget increase the potential for conflict with the appropriations committees, and the number of jurisdictional battles has risen. The service committees, who are strong congressional allies of the military, tend to support the Pentagon's requests for funding increases. This is also the case with the House Appropriations Committee where, since 1976, members voted to a committee can pick their own subcommittee assignment. "It is common for 'hawks' and congressmen who represent large defense interests to become members of the defense subcommittees of Appropriations and vote to express their policy preferences or to benefit their constituents rather than to consider the balance of public spending."[14] During much of the Reagan defense buildup in the 1980s, the House and Senate Armed Services Committees largely ignored demands from other quarters to cut military spending to reduce the growing federal budget deficit.

Senator Sam Nunn (D.-Ga.) reorganized the Senate Armed Services Committee, which he chairs, to strengthen what he calls a "mission approach" to defense spending and policy issues. He has created four subcommittees which are responsible for specific DoD missions. Two subcommittees—Readiness, Sustainability, and Support; Manpower and Personnel—have a functional orientation. A Conventional Forces and Alliance Defense Subcommittee deals with NATO and East Asia, while a Projection Forces and Regional Defense Subcommittee oversees military missions in the defense of Southeast Asia. The Strategic Forces and Nuclear Deterrence Subcommittee reviews U.S. deterrence policies and oversees the Strategic Air Command, the U.S. Space Command, and the North American Aerospace Defense Command. Nunn also formed a special Defense Industry and Technology Subcommittee "to marshall defense resources and policies in such a way to ensure U.S. technological superiority."[15]

CONGRESSIONAL INTERVENTION

The "explosion" of congressional involvement in defense policy is illustrated by the following figures. The annual average number of pages in the reports of the House and Senate Armed Services Committees and the Defense Appropriations Subcommittees was 231 pages in the period 1961–1969, rising to 829 pages in the 1970s and to 1,186 pages in 1980–1985. The number of floor debates and amendments to the House and Senate Defense Authorization Bills has also risen over the years. As James Lindsay observes, "In 1969 Congress made 180 changes to the defense authorization bill and 650 to the appropriations bill. In 1975 these figures were 222 and 1,032, respectively. In 1985, however, Congress made 1,145 adjustments in the authorization bill and 2,156 in the appropriations bill (representing more than a sixfold and threefold increase, respectively, in changes to the defense authorization and appropriations bills) [see Table 4-1]."[16]

According to Robert Art, several factors explain the rising importance of the armed services committees in the defense budgetary process. Among them was the House Armed Services Committee's increasing concern in the early 1980s that military readiness was getting short shrift in the defense budget and that the Operations and Maintenance (O&M) accounts were being cut disproportionately by an increasingly fiscally minded Congress.[17] More than any other account O&M involves the biggest annual outlays. The committee extended its mandate to cover O&M by setting up a Readiness Subcommittee and also by authorizing annually items in the account for "Other Procurement" that affect readiness, such as procurement of non-combat items like trucks and electronic equipment.

In addition, Art suggests that "both disillusionment with the 'imperial presidency' and the antidefense mood of the country after Vietnam pushed Congress into ever more detailed scrutiny [of the budget]." Possibly "the single most important factor in enabling Congress to engage in more detailed action on the defense budget was the expansion in the staff capability of the two defense committees."[18] The staff of the House and Senate Armed Services Committees is approximately forty staff members each—a threefold increase from the early 1950s.

Table 4-1. Characteristics of House and Senate Debate on the Annual Defense Authorization Bill, 1961–1985

Calendar Year	House		Senate	
	Days of Debate	Amendments	Days of Debate	Amendments
1961	1	2	1	0
1962	1	7	1	0
1963	2	2	1	2
1964	1	10	1	1
1965	1	0	1	0
1966	1	1	1	0
1967	1	5	1	0
1968	1	7	3	8
1969	3	21	37	34
1970	3	23	28	31
1971	3	21	13	30
1972	2	14	8	15
1973	2	14	9	50
1974	2	11	8	35
1975	3	15	6	28
1976	2	12	4	18
1977	3	16	2	6
1978	2	19	2	18
1979	3	33	3	11
1980	4	26	3	24
1981	7	49	3	17
1982	7	78	7	58
1983	8	64	13	68
1984	6	52	10	108
1985	9	140	9	108
1986	10	116	7	83
Average:				
1961–69	1	6	5 (1)*	5 (1)*
1970–79	3	20	8	24
1980–86	7	75	7	67

* These numbers reflect the Senate averages for the 1960s if the 1969 ABM debate is excluded.

Source: James M. Lindsay, "Congress and Defense Policy: 1961 to 1986," *Armed Forces and Society,* Vol. 13, No. 3 (Spring 1987), p. 374.

Congressional staffers enjoy considerable power because of the tight demands on the time of elected officials. They often have a greater substantive understanding of the issues than the elected representatives for whom they work. A staffer, like Anthony Battista of the House Armed Services Committee, may, in fact, be a more important player on certain arms control and defense policy issues than the congressmen who serve on the committee for which he works. Complains Senator Warren Rudman (R.-N.H.), "Unfortunately, because of the system of hearings and other duties, you become heavily reliant on committee staff and your staffs. As a result, I think staffs, particularly committee staffs, play far too important a role in the running of the Senate."[19] Congressional staffs set the defense agenda in Congress not only by planning the timetable of hearings, but also by deciding who will testify and what questions will be asked. They have enormous control over the political agenda and getting hold of a key staffer may be more important than seeing his boss. Congressional staffs are the not-so-invisible hand which shapes, guides, and manipulates the political agenda in Congress. This has prompted one observer to express concerns about the future of representative government given the power nonelected officials exercise over the political process.[20]

The impact is also felt on management and oversight. As a report of the Washington-based Center for Strategic and International Studies explains, "Each staffer and each new piece of legislation ultimately adds an incremental burden to the management of acquisition resources. Given the intense political atmosphere and the huge increase in attention to oversight issues, one unhappy tendency has been to view each anomaly in the acquisition business as an indication of malfeasance (demonstrating the need for government regulation)."[21]

The growth of congressional involvement in the details and management of the defense budget contrasts directly with the decline of congressional power over the federal budget as a whole. This is because the "uncontrollable" entitlement and other statutory programs portion of the budget has grown to over three-quarters of the total budget, "while that portion of the budget Congress desires to 'control' has been squeezed from 41 percent in fiscal year 1967 to 23 percent in fiscal year 1982." Defense accounts for almost 75 percent of the controllable federal budget.[22] As we will see below, however, even this figure is misleading because Congress's control over the defense budget is limited by other factors.

Figure 4-3. The Defense Appropriations Act

- Appropriations bills formally allocate funds to programs which have been authorized.
- In recent years, Appropriations bills have become important in battles over major weapons programs. Often the Appropriations Subcommittees can be expected to shave funding for particular minor programs.

Mid-February to June
Defense Subcommittees of House and Senate Appropriations Committees hold hearings and ''mark up'' the Defense Appropriations Bill. Full Appropriations Committees then revise and approve the bills.

Anytime from late June to September or later
Full House and Senate vote on Defense Appropriations Bills.

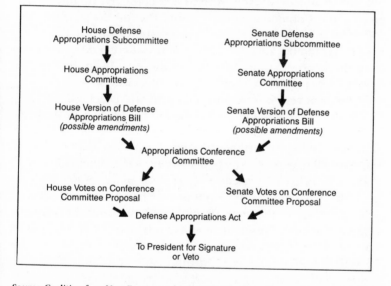

Source: Coalition for a New Foreign and Military Policy, *How Congress Acts on the Military Budget and Arms Control* (Washington, D.C., December 12, 1984).

APPROPRIATIONS

Step 7 (Figure 4-3). Once the defense budget has been approved, it moves to the appropriations committees for review and action. The House and Senate Appropriations Committees are two of the most prestigious and important committees in Congress. They are divided into subcommittees including one for defense. The annual Defense Appropriations Bill *is* the defense budget and it is usually tailored closely to the Defense Authorization Bill. It gives an item-by-item breakdown of DoD expenditures and regulates the Department's spending and accounting practices.

Unlike authorizations, appropriations cover virtually every aspect of DoD expenditures except military construction, nuclear warhead programs, civil defense, and other non-DoD defense activities (for which separate appropriations accounts exist).

Like the armed services committees, the Defense subcommittees of the House and Senate Appropriations Committees hold lengthy hearings before which numerous witnesses (many of whom have also testified before the armed services committees) appear. The subcommittees then "mark up" the Defense Appropriations Bill, which is subsequently revised and approved by the full Appropriations Committee of each house. The full House and Senate will then vote on the Defense Appropriations Bill any time from June to September or even later. Often Congress does not complete the appropriations bills before the new fiscal year, which starts October 1. Theoretically, DoD must close shop if this happens, but it never does because Congress will enact a Continuing Resolution to provide funds until the Bill has made it through the appropriations process. Once this is done, the Defense Appropriations Bill is submitted to the President for his signature (or veto). This formally completes the budgetary cycle for the fiscal year.

Agencies often go back to Congress for more money for programs that have run short of funds or have failed to obtain congressional approval in the appropriations bill, however. This usually happens when the President submits his budget for the new fiscal year, which includes a request for supplemental appropriations for the year already under way. In the case of the MX missile, for example, President Reagan was able to secure continued funding of the system in his fiscal year (FY) 1984 budget—funds which Congress had stricken from the FY 1983 budget. Not only may programs be revived through the supplemental appropriations process, but budgetary ceilings that Congress fought hard over before may also be exceeded.

Although budgetary authorization is supposed to precede appropriations so that the appropriations committees know what figures they are working with, delays and the resulting slippages in the authorization and appropriations schedules ensure that in practice this never happens. "Appropriating and authorizing committees work concurrently and nearly year-round; the appropriating committees choose dollar amounts before, from the standpoint of policy, they know how the money will be used. ... Thus the

process leads to a continuous frenzy of activity but few decisions that count."[23] In the end nobody knows exactly what's in the defense budget. As one exasperated House Appropriations Committee staffer exclaimed: "The defense bill, defense as an entity, is one of the most confusing damn things in this town to follow. The number of defense figures you can hear for 'the defense budget' in the course of the year—and at any time they are right, depending on what you are counting—is about 365."[24] Complains Congressman Les Aspin, "We're humming a merry tune while jogging into quicksand. The silly season lasts too long when we end up with a defense budget that has mismatched budget authority and outlay numbers, purchasing and maintenance figures that are out of line, and gimmicks to tie all the disparate pieces together. The process demands repair."[25]

Turf battles between the defense authorization and appropriations subcommittees often occur. However, disputes are usually over marginal resource allocation questions (how much to fund a program) as opposed to fundamental policy (should it be funded at all). Some argue this is because the defense committees and appropriations subcommittees are generally sympathetic to the Pentagon's interests.[26] Others point out that the appropriations committees and subcommittees have to struggle with two sets of conflicting requirements—a desire to fund programs that have been authorized by Congress and the need for economy—so the picture is not quite so simple. The House Appropriations Committee has "adapted to these expectations by concentrating its budget-cutting efforts within a 'safe' zone, defined at the upper level by the President's budget and, at the lower, by last year's expenditures."[27]

The Senate Appropriations Committee does not conduct the same detailed review of the budget as the House, but sits rather as an appeals board "to which departments and interests that are dissatisfied with what the House has done make a case for increases above those amounts."[28] However, its willingness to restore service requests has diminished over the years. A study that compared the fiscal years 1947–1969 to the period 1970–1979 found that the Senate had become more hostile to service requests than the House in this latter period. Although the House and the Senate usually end up splitting the difference in the Joint Conference Committee, the Senate has been the conservative spender.[29]

In the appropriations process, cooperation prevails. Disagree-

ments are ironed out in the particular subcommittees and issues are generally treated in a nonpartisan manner. The recommendations of the particular subcommittees are rarely overturned or changed by the full committee or the House as a whole. To quote Arthur Maas once again:

> Reciprocity prevails among the subcommittees, since this is a way of making unity effective. Members of the subcommittee on appropriations for agriculture will vote for the markup and report of the subcommittee on appropriations for defense in the expectation that the latter will in turn support them. As a result the full committee makes few changes in the subcommittees' recommendations. Also due to the norm of unity, it is infrequent that a committee is challenged and overruled on the floor. When it is, it usually requires a combination of several factors: an issue of significant policy importance that is easily understandable to the ordinary member; a split in the ranks of the Appropriations Committee; and participation, cooperation and direction by the House leadership in the effort to overrule the committee.[30]

Similarly, cooperation defines the rules of engagement between Congress and the executive branch on budgetary matters. It is what Richard Stubbing calls the "cut insurance" game. Although Congress has consistently maintained a budget-cutting approach to the defense budget in fifteen out of the past sixteen years (usually cutting the President's budget anywhere from 2 to 7 percent), "the executive branch anticipates the congressional need to lower defense spending and therefore includes in its requests extra funds for the removal by Congress." Although the Secretary of Defense and other Pentagon officials will justify their programs in open hearings before Congress, "in the back rooms DoD and congressional staff are working out mutually acceptable lists of reductions which will cause little or no damage to the program DoD really wants to pursue. These 'cut insurance' funds can then be slashed from the defense-budget request by Congress, permitting members to demonstrate their fiscal toughness to their constituents without harming the defense program."[31] The process is akin to Carl Friederich's "rule of anticipated reactions" whereby the President's policies are altered in anticipation of the way Congress is likely to respond.[32]

For highly controversial weapons programs, the politicking between the executive branch and Congress is intense and a consensus may be difficult to reach when priorities conflict. This may well be the key arena where a program's fate is decided and where policy outcomes are best explained by Robert Pastor's "interbranch politics" model of government. According to Pastor, in some policy arenas, policy is best explained "by the interaction between the two branches" of government as opposed to what goes on within each branch.[33] Because Congress has the power of the purse, its influence over weapons procurement is substantial. It can block a program by denying funds if it disagrees with the President's priorities. A strong incentive for the President to cooperate and accommodate congressional preferences and priorities on defense therefore exists, although the question "Who has co-opted whom?" may be difficult to answer when all is said and done.

BUDGET AUTHORITY AND OUTLAYS

How do authorization and appropriations committees deal with defense budgetary requests? Are some programs more immune to cuts than others? As noted above, service committees in recent years have tried to protect O&M accounts from cuts by deficit-conscious colleagues. But does this mean that these accounts are more prone to cuts than other key accounts such as Personnel, Procurement, Research, Development, Testing, and Evaluation? The evidence suggests they are.

Although one study found that in the period 1960–1970 Congress focused its attention almost exclusively on Procurement and RDT&E and basically ignored other budget titles,[34] more recent data suggest greater congressional involvement in all budget categories with the greatest growth of interest, measured by changes in budgetary outcomes, in the Personnel category.[35]

Several factors explain why Congress is reluctant to attack the Procurement and RDT&E accounts except at the margin. The first has to do with the relationship between budgetary authority and outlays. When Congress gives the Pentagon budgetary authority, it is in fact giving the Pentagon the authority to write checks for contracts and spending obligations it has entered into.[36] However, in many instances, the Pentagon will not actually spend all of the money it has earned in one year. What it doesn't spend will be

carried over as credit into subsequent years.

What the Pentagon spends in any given year is called an *outlay,* and outlays are usually less than what has actually been appropriated. Thus, for example, in the case of the Procurement account for FY 1988, only about 15 percent of the funds appropriated will be spent in the first year, 30 percent in the second, 27 percent in the third, and smaller amounts in the fourth, fifth, and sixth years (see Tables 4-2 and 4-3). By contrast, 94 percent of the funds allocated to Personnel will be spent in the first year. (The figure is also high for the first year in the Operations and Maintenance account.)

For a fiscally minded Congress interested in attacking the budget deficit, what matters are outlays not appropriations—that is, the money that is actually spent by the Treasury Department in any given year. As Brookings Institution defense analyst Joshua Epstein explains:

Deficits, of course, are a function of outlays, not budget authority. Congress, however, appropriates the latter not the former . . . [and] it is easy to see why fast-money accounts (associated most closely with the readiness of forces) should be most vulnerable when deficit reduction becomes a congressional imperative. A dollar cut from procurement budget authority reduces outlays (and the deficit, other things being equal) a mere 15 cents in the first fiscal year, while a dollar cut in operation-and-maintenance budget authority saves fully 73 cents in outlays.[37]

This explains why Congress is usually anxious to shear the Personnel and O&M accounts instead of Procurement when it attacks the defense budget. But even if the defense budget was reduced to zero tomorrow, the Pentagon would still be spending money from previous appropriations. "This built-in spending explains why *outlays will grow even if budget authority does not.*"[38]

The problem is vividly illustrated by the Reagan administration's military buildup. The administration asked for $312 billion for its defense programs in FY 1988 and another $332.4 billion in FY 1989 for a total of $644.4 billion in the two years. Defending the planned increases, former Secretary of Defense Caspar Weinberger complained that defense spending had suffered what he termed a "real" decline over the past several years. He was right

Table 4-2. Defense Outlay Rates by Appropriation Title, Fiscal Year 1988
(percentage of first-year budget authority spent)

Appropriation Title	First	Second	Third	Fourth	Fifth	Sixth
"Slow-money" investment accounts						
Procurement	15.00	30.17	26.69	13.59	6.30	1.24
Research, development, test, and evaluation	50.20	38.20	7.57	1.40	—	—
Military construction	12.36	39.05	22.99	12.86	5.57	3.52
Aggregate for investment group	26.33	33.22	20.28	9.59	4.21	0.95
"Fast-money" operation and support accounts						
Military personnel	94.09	5.30	0.03	—	—	—
Operation and maintenance	74.28	19.85	2.65	—	—	—
Family housing	49.44	27.13	12.13	4.64	2.24	1.00
Aggregate for operation and support group	82.87	13.31	1.64	0.10	0.05	0.02

Source: Joshua M. Epstein, *The 1988 Defense Budget* (Washington, D.C.: The Brookings Institution, 1988), p. 10.

Table 4-3. Defense Outlays If Budget Authority Were Zero for Fiscal Years 1988–1992
(millions of dollars unless otherwise specified)

Appropriation Title	1988	1989	1990	1991	1992	Five-Year Total
Investment						
Procurement	70,175	42,654	18,695	6,555	1,065	139,144
Research, development, test, and evaluation	17,011	3,251	514	0	0	20,776
Military construction	4,435	2,383	1,180	486	189	8,673
Operation and support						
Military personnel	3,953	22	0	0	0	3,975
Operation and maintenance	17,800	2,111	0	0	0	19,911
Family housing	1,408	600	237	98	31	2,374
Other	415	96	25	0	0	536
Energy	3,511	668	105	0	0	4,284
Total	118,708	51,785	20,756	7,139	1,285	199,673
Investment as percentage of total	77.2	93.2	98.2	98.6	97.6	84.4

Source: Joshua M. Epstein, *The 1988 Defense Budget* (Washington, D.C.: The Brookings Institution, 1988), p. 10.

Figure 4-4. **Real Growth in Defense Budget Authority**

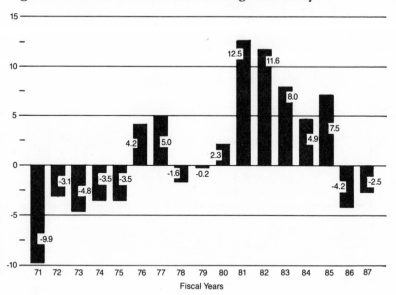

Fiscal Years

Source: Hon. Caspar W. Weinberger, Secretary, Department of Defense, *Fiscal Year 1988 Defense Posture,* in Subcommittee on the Department of Defense, Committee on Appropriations, House of Representatives, *Hearings on Department of Defense Appropriations for 1988, Part 1,* 100th Congress, 1st Session, 71-858-0 (Washington, D.C.: U.S. Government Printing Office, 1987), p. 13.

insofar as defense budget authority (see Figures 4-4 and 4-5) was indeed cut by Congress by 4.2 percent below a zero real growth level in FY 1986 and by 2.5 percent in FY 1987. However, defense outlays, or what the Pentagon actually writes in the form of checks to pay its bills, rose steadily from the time Reagan came to office (see Figure 4-6). In FY 1981, for example, defense outlays totaled $157.5 billion in *current* dollars; in FY 1986, annual defense outlays had risen to $272.2 billion, according to the Office of Management and Budget. In all, from FY 1981 to FY 1986, defense outlays totaled $1.3 trillion. National defense outlays as a percentage of the gross national product amounted to 4.7 percent of GNP in 1979. They rose steadily to 6.4 percent of GNP (about $280 billion) in 1987. Complaints about congressional reductions in budgetary authority are also somewhat misleading and must be viewed

Figure 4-5. **Department of Defense Budget Authority** (FY 1988 dollars in billions)

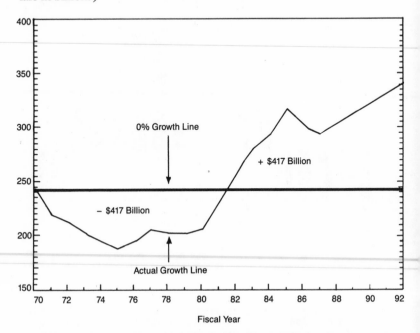

Source: Hon. Caspar W. Weinberger, Secretary, Department of Defense, *Fiscal Year 1988 Defense Posture,* in Subcommittee on the Department of Defense, Committee on Appropriations, House of Representatives, *Hearings on Department of Defense Appropriations for 1988, Part 1,* 100th Congress, 1st Session, 71-858-0 (Washington, D.C.: U.S. Government Printing Office, 1987), p. 12.

in a broader context. CBO calculates that defense budgetary authority rose from $117 billion in 1978 to $290 billion in 1987, representing an increase, after adjusting for inflation, of nearly 48 percent.[39]

Even if defense spending were to hold to zero real growth in coming years, with only enough increase to deal with inflation, CBO projects that defense outlays will total $1.8 trillion from FY 1987 to FY 1992 (as compared with the $1.3 trillion spent from FY 1981 to FY 1986).

The amount of unspent funds has risen steadily. In 1975, unobligated balances for the Pentagon totaled $62 billion; by FY 1981 unobligated balances had risen to $112.8 billion, by FY 1982 to

Figure 4-6. **Defense Budget Authority and Outlays, Fiscal Years 1950–1992** (billions of 1988 dollars)

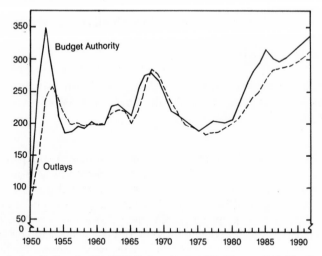

Source: Joshua M. Epstein, *The 1988 Defense Budget* (Washington, D.C.: The Brookings Institution, 1988), p. 2.

$142.2 billion, by FY 1983 to $172.1 billion, by FY 1985 to $205.1 billion, by FY 1986 to $262.2 billion, and by the end of FY 1987 to $299.7 billion. The mismatch between defense budgetary authority and outlays is what some call the "bow wave effect." As more and more authority gets carried over from year to year, funds unspent from previous years' appropriations become a progressively larger amount of new defense outlays, edging up from 30.2 percent in FY 1982 to 40.8 percent in FY 1987. For FY 1988, DoD estimates put the figure at 40.6 percent of outlays for which the government is already contractually bound and therefore is not controllable by Congress. As one individual observes, "These amounts are virtually entitlements."[40]

Purchases of new weapons and equipment also do not make up the lion's share of the defense budget. In FY 1984, for example, 42 percent of the defense budget went for manpower-related costs (pay allowances for active duty personnel, reserve and retired personnel, family housing, personnel, etc.), whereas procurement of all kinds came to 33 percent of the budget.[41] In FY 1987, 29 percent went to procurement, 27 percent to operations and maintenance, 25 percent to military personnel, and 14.2 percent into

research and development and military construction. Thus cuts in the procurement category tend to have less impact on the overall budget than those in other categories. With "bow wave" amounts and pay and allowances in the defense budget almost fixed, Congress is more or less forced to hit DoD O&M and investment accounts to make a dent in outlays.

Another reason Congress is usually reluctant to attack procurement in the defense budget is politics. Les Aspin explains why a congressman is selective about the kinds of defense cuts he will favor.

> A Congressman who wants to ... cut military spending but protect jobs ... is likely to focus, for example, on such defense issues as manpower questions, cutting troop strength in Europe, and disbanding divisions; these would reduce the defense budget but would not directly affect employment at home. (The demilitarized troops, of course, will add to unemployment, but not significantly for any one Congressional district.) An amendment to slow down the production of a given weapons system will gain more votes than an amendment to eliminate it entirely. Finally, when it comes down to cutting a weapons system, one whose economic benefits are localized in a single state, or in one or two Congressional districts, is more likely to be cut than one that, through contracting and subcontracting, has managed to spread its economic largess throughout the country.[42]

The B-1 bomber is a classic case. Although the principal contractor for the bomber is Rockwell International, the program has over 5,000 subcontractors, suppliers, and vendors in forty-eight states and the District of Columbia, including important geographic areas like California, Washington, New York, and Massachusetts. "Rockwell has made use of this subcontractor network to encourage support for the B-1 in Congress. Representatives Les Aspin and John Seiberling (D.-Ohio) have both reported Rockwell initiatives encouraging their support for the B-1 and informing them of the value of subcontracts in their districts. Friendly members of Congress are usually allowed to announce the award of subcontracts for their districts."[43] It is interesting to note that even Senator Alan Cranston (D.-Cal.), one of the most vociferous critics of the Pentagon who has voted to cancel almost every new strategic

weapon, voted for the B-1 because it would be built in his home state.

Les Aspin argues that another important factor affecting defense votes on the floor of the House is constituent pressure. The two main lobbies are the arms control and peace groups and the defense community. Neither group can mount a campaign for every issue and so it usually comes down to a question of "countervailing pressure, i.e., whether or not the services want a budget item more than the arms-control community and peace groups." Aspin also believes that the services have greater resources at their disposal so they usually prevail. "For the arms-control community and the peace groups to have an impact on a Congressman's vote, they not only have to find an issue on which they can agree, they must also be extraordinarily committed. Half-hearted efforts will not produce sufficient votes."[44]

It is also true that Congress will be reluctant to turn down a request for funding, even in the very early stages of research and development, for a weapons system that is fundamental to a military service's "essence" or mission. "There are ... some weapons systems that are so fundamental ... that cutting a program even at this early state is difficult ... [for example] the Air Force's drive to keep manned strategic bombers and the concomitant Navy commitment to aircraft carriers." If cuts are made, they will be marginal. This is also true for major procurement decisions involving deployment of a system. "To turn down an important weapon system becomes a major confrontation with often heavy political costs. ... Rather than engage in such behavior, a compromise is often struck to procure fewer than originally planned ... [but] even this limited purchase approach does not necessarily save money, primarily because of cost overruns and the loss of economies of scale."[45]

EFFECTS ON INDUSTRY

Many would agree that the turbulence and unpredictability of the congressional appropriations process make life difficult for industry. Complains Thomas G. Pownall, Chairman and Chief Executive Officer of the Martin Marietta Corporation:

> The most destabilizing effect on procurement of major weapons systems is the annual budget process. Congressional committees,

the military departments, and industry firms are constantly caught up in this process. There is great uncertainty in many cases regarding program authorizations and funding levels.

This affects capital investment, planning and efficiencies in production, and it encourages stretchout of programs at inefficient production rates. This is almost entirely a responsibility of the Congress and should receive priority attention in any effort that Congress makes to improve the Defense Procurement System.[46]

Cost changes to programs dictated by Congress or even by the Department of Defense itself have a disturbing ripple effect and will increase the costs of a program by a minimum of anywhere from 3 to 5 percent. A study that calculated the cost-driver effects between a change in total defense procurement spending and its subsequent impact on program stability found that even a modest 2 percent reduction in the defense budget would shrink acquisitions by 6 percent and drive up the unit costs of any given stretched-out program by 5 percent (see Table 4-4).[47]

Congress's proclivity for micromanaging various details of the budget, while ignoring others, also comes in for heavy criticism. Jacques Gansler points out that in 1983 alone Defense Department witnesses testified on the 1984 budget before 96 committees and subcommittees and that all in all some 1,306 witnesses provided 2,160 hours of testimony. (In 1986, for example, the printed record for authorization hearings before the Senate Armed Services Committee alone amounted to 4,759 pages, of which 2,100 pages (44 percent) were prepared statements for the Committee.)[48] Gansler argues that "[t]hese redundant hearings are time-consuming (for both Defense management and the Congress) and focus all of the attention on the infinite detail of the budget, rather than on the policy and oversight required."[49] A survey of ten companies found that visiting days of government and corporation personnel cost industry almost $2 billion a year.[50]

Sensitive to these criticisms, the House and Senate Armed Services Committees have tried to put increased attention on "the formulation and articulation of U.S. strategy" as opposed to micromanagement. In 1987 the Senate Armed Services Committee changed fewer than 200 of the line items in the President's defense budget request. However, when the Bill finally came to the Senate floor in September, lawmakers tried to attach 117 amend-

Table 4-4. **Changes to Total Defense Procurement Spending and the Impact of Program Stability**

Start of Fiscal Austerity

Unplanned Budget Change	Effect on Acquisition Budget	Effect on Non-Major Weapons System Portion	Quantity Change	Unit Cost Change
+12%	+22%	+22%	+24%	+ 3%
+ 8	+14	+14	+14	0
+ 4	+ 6	+ 5	+ 4	+ 4
+ 2	+ 2	+ 1	− 1	+ 5
0	− 2	− 3	− 6	+ 8
− 2	− 6	− 8	−11	+ 9
− 4	−10	−12	−16	−12
− 6	−14	−17	−20	+14
− 8	−18	−21	−25	+16
−10	−22	−25	−30	+19
−12	−26	−29	−34	+22
−14	−30	−33	−39	+25

During Period of Fiscal Activity

Unplanned Budget Change	Effect on Acquisition Budget	Effect on Non-Major Weapons System Portion	Quantity Change	Unit Cost Change
+12%	+22%	+22%	+26%	− 2%
+ 8	+14	+14	+14	0
+ 4	+ 6	+ 6	+ 4	+ 2
+ 2	+ 2	+ 2	− 1	+ 3
0	− 2	− 2	− 6	+ 4
− 2	− 6	− 6	−10	+ 5
− 4	−10	−10	−15	+ 6
− 6	−14	−14	−19	+ 7
− 8	−18	−18	−24	+ 8
−10	−22	−22	−28	+ 9
−12	−26	−26	−32	+10
−14	−30	−30	−35	+11

Source: The CSIS Defense Acquisition Study, *U.S. Defense Acquisition: A Process in Trouble* (Washington, D.C.: Center for Strategic and International Studies, Georgetown University, March 1987), p. 56.

ments, most of them so-called policy amendments. There was similar dissatisfaction in the House where representatives tried to attach 124 amendments. The House's total was short of the record 140 floor amendments in 1985. The amount of floor time spent on

debate has also increased from an average of three days of floor time from 1975 to 1979 to an average of seven days from 1980 to 1984.[51]

Jacques Gansler believes that savings of some 20 percent in weapons programs could be achieved by stabilizing the Department of Defense budget in Congress and suggests that this should be done by adopting multiyear defense budgeting:

> Two- or three-year budget cycles would introduce the stability necessary for contractors to plan more efficient production runs and lower unit costs of procured systems. Furthermore, multiyear budgets would encourage DoD and the Congress to consider the long-term, strategic implications of budget and procurement decisions.[52]

As Robert Art cautions, however, "it is not self-evident [multiyear budgets] . . . would enhance the quality of policy oversight . . . as long as the armed services committees adhere to their budgeting approach. . . . By giving Congress more time to budget, moreover, Congress may take more time to budget. Budgeting could expand to fill the time available, and the Congress could become more, not less, preoccupied with it."[53]

Nor is multiyear procurement a panacea from the point of view of the Pentagon's program managers, although important savings have been realized in programs funded under multiyear procurement. The navy, for example, reported savings "in excess of $500 million" for fifty-one multiyear contracts authorized since FY 1982. The air force reported savings of $3 billion for six major programs funded under multiyear procurement. However, the effect of multiyear funding is to lock funds into programs, making it difficult to adjust and reallocate budgetary resources later on if required. General Lawrence A. Skantze, Commander of the Air Force Systems Command, explains: "When we sign a multiyear procurement contract, it helps program stability and reduces costs. But at the same time it limits our programming flexibility. With a large percentage of our resources tied up in MYP [multiyear procurement] contracts, it can be very difficult to solve funding problems that arise when we put the annual Air Force budget together. Ad-

ditionally, many in DoD and Congress perceive a loss of Federal budget flexibility when we sign a multiyear contract."[54]

No shortage of proposals for reform exists including suggestions for greater policy oversight, "milestone" authorizations, multiyear fundings for specific account items like R&D and Procurement, advance authorizations for appropriations, and so on.[55] At the time of this writing, the congressional committees that oversee the military are struggling with legislation to finance the Pentagon's operations for two years instead of annually.[56] The Pentagon was required to submit a two-year budget, covering its requests for FY 1988 and FY 1989, for the first time in 1987 under an amendment offered by Senator Sam Nunn and attached to the FY 1986 DoD Authorization Bill. However, it was impossible for the House and Senate Armed Services Committees to vote a complete Authorization Bill for the second year (FY 1989) because the administration's overall budget for FY 1989 did not meet the reduction targets set by Gramm-Rudman-Hollings, legislation mandating automatic, across-the-board spending cuts if specific targets for reducing the size of the federal deficit are not reached. It is unlikely that Congress will be able to work out a true two-year budget. Explains Les Aspin, "We will never authorize everything for two years," because of disputed programs like the Strategic Defense Initiative. Additional problems exist on the appropriations side. From the time the Pentagon submits its budget in January until Congress considers DoD appropriations in the fall, many of the Pentagon's original calculations for program costs are lowered or raised because of changes in inflation, fuel costs, and other variables. Under two-year appropriation the quality of estimates would be a lot worse and many appropriations committee members are skeptical that much can be gained from two-year appropriations.[57] As Robert Art explains, "The dysfunctions in defense budgeting stem from powerful political forces built into the very structure of the defense policy process. ... Even with significant structural change ... the habits of nearly a quarter century will not easily wither."[58]

Table 4-5. **Congressional Reductions to the President's DoD Budget Requests** (current $ billions)

	1984	1985	1986	1987
President's request	273.4	305.0	313.7	311.6
Congressional reductions	−14.7	−19.5	−35.3*	−29.9
	(5.4%)	(6.4%)	(11.3%)	(9.6%)
Enacted†	258.7	285.5	278.4	281.7

*Includes $11.0 billion sequestered under Gramm-Rudman-Hollings.
†Excludes Contract Authority.

Source: Hon. Caspar W. Weinberger, Secretary, Department of Defense, *Fiscal Year 1988 Defense Posture,* in Subcommittee on the Department of Defense, Committee on Appropriations, House of Representatives, *Hearings on Department of Defense Appropriations for 1988, Part 1,* 100th Congress, 1st Session, 71-858-0 (Washington, D.C.: U.S. Government Printing Office, 1987), p. 10.

CONGRESSIONAL ACTION ON THE FY 87 AND FY 88 BUDGETS

For the first five years of the Reagan presidency, the Pentagon had enjoyed almost 8.9 percent average annual growth rates in its budget. Real growth in budgetary authority declined by 4.2 percent and 2.5 percent in FY 1986 and FY 1987, respectively, but these declines were offset by a Supplemental Budget Request of $2.8 billion in the FY 1988 budget. However, actual spending through FY 1992 would continue to grow at a rate of 21 percent because of funds appropriated but not spent from previous years.[59]

Massive federal deficits in the mid-1980s were a growing worry to Congress. After dragging its feet Congress finally decided to attack the defense budget with its pruning shears. In 1984 Congress trimmed the President's request by 5.4 percent, in 1985 by 6.4 percent, in 1986 by 11.3 percent, and in 1987 by 9.6 percent (see Table 4-5). Where were the "cuts" made?

In FY 1987 the Defense Authorization Bill had a number of arms control compromises that continued a congressional ban on tests of anti-satellite missiles, barred production of certain chemical weapons, and cut 34 percent from the President's $5.3 billion request for the Strategic Defense Initiative by leaving it at $3.5 billion. The readiness of Operations and Maintenance accounts was cut from the President's request from $87 billion to $79.5 billion (9 percent). (It is interesting to note that both the House and

Senate Appropriations Committees approved O&M funding levels that were less than either the House or Senate Armed Services Committee had authorized in their separate Defense Authorization Bills.) In an unusual departure from previous practice, Procurement and Research and Development accounts were also cut by fairly substantial amounts. The army suffered the biggest cuts: 13.8 percent from its procurement request and 15 percent from R&D. The air force had its procurement and R&D requests clipped by 13 percent. The navy fared slightly better: 9 percent for procurement, 12 percent for R&D.

However, if one looks at the FY 1987 DoD Authorization Bill for major procurement and R&D programs, the picture was really not that bad from the Pentagon's standpoint. None of the twenty-five programs listed in Table 4-6 was actually eliminated. Some were clipped more than others. But in the case of major weapons programs, the Pentagon got almost everything it wanted. For example, in the case of the Trident II missile, although funding was cut, authorization was still given for the twenty-one missiles requested by the navy. The navy also got approval for four new attack SSN-688 submarines and one new Trident submarine, which were in the initial request. It also got its 324 Tomahawk cruise missiles. The air force did not get all of the twenty-one MX missiles it wanted—the number was cut to twelve—but the program was not eliminated. And the Midgetman missile R&D program got almost as much as DoD had requested in its initial budgetary submission.

For the FY 1988 DoD Authorization Bill, deficit pressures were even greater and the specter of automatic cuts from Gramm-Rudman-Hollings led to a "deficit summit" between Congress and the White House in November 1987. President Reagan's defense request to Congress stood at $312 billion, which would have meant a 3 percent net growth in the defense budget after inflation. The final omnibus Continuing Resolution signed into law on December 22, 1987, by President Reagan contained $291.5 billion in defense budget authority, $20.5 billion less than the President's original request. The reductions amounted to a 3.5 percent loss relative to the previous year's budget of $291 billion, taking into account a 4 percent rate of inflation. The Continuing Resolution, which would fund federal spending for the rest of FY 1988, was a makeshift budget adopted by Congress nearly three months after the new

Table 4-6. FY 1987 and FY 1988 DoD Authorization Bill Conference Agreement for Major Procurement and Research, Development, Testing, and Engineering Programs (current $ millions)

		DoD's Request			House Authorization			Senate Authorization			Conference Agreement		
		RDT&E	Number	Proc.	RDT&E	Number	Proc.	RDT&E	Number	Proc.	RDT&E	Number	Proc.
SDI	FY87	5,347.0	—	—	3,125.0	—	—	3,953.0	—	—	3,530.0	—	—
	FY88*	5,198.7	—	—	2,546.0	—	—	4,120.0	—	—	3,604.0	—	—
F-16	FY87	81.3	216	2,881.9	0	150	1,926.3	81.3	192	2,646.9	65.4	180	2,353.0
	FY88	36.5	180	2,223.7	0	180	2,123.7	36.5	180	2,173.7	33.5	180	2,173.7
F/A-18	FY87	59.1	120	2,896.3	35.0	84	2,140.6	59.1	96	2,466.4	59.1	84	2,250.0
	FY88	17.3	84	2,316.6	10.0	84	2,316.6	17.3	84	2,316.6	12.0	84	2,316.6
Trident II	FY87	1,632.9	21	1,124.4	1,500.0	21	1,124.4	1,632.9	21	1,124.4	1,595.0	21	1,124.4
	FY88	1,098.5	66	1,931.3	1,000.0	72	1,931.3	1,098.5	66	1,931.3	1,073.5	72	1,931.3
DDG-51	FY87	0	3	2,448.0	0	1	871.7	0	3	2,466.0	0	3	2,390.3
	FY88	—	3	2,122.3	—	0	0	—	0	0	—	0	0
SSN-688	FY87	18.3	4	2,047.8	18.3	4	2,047.8	18.3	4	2,047.8	18.3	4	1,966.0
	FY88	21.4	3	1,519.4	15.0	3	1,519.4	21.4	3	1,519.4	21.4	3	1,459.4
F-15	FY87	209.0	48	1,675.4	0	24	975.0	209.0	48	2,047.8	179.0	42	1,543.0
	FY88	118.6	42	1,384.2	0	42	1,334.2	118.6	42	1,334.2	115.6	42	1,334.2
M-1	FY87	3.8	840	1,643.6	3.8	840	1,578.6	3.8	840	1,643.6	3.8	840	1,578.6
	FY88	—	600	1,354.7	—	720	1,533.2	—	720	1,626.7	—	720	1,607.6
CG-47 Aegis	FY87	38.4	2	1,913.8	28.5	3	2,715.1	38.4	2	1,913.8	38.4	3	2,715.1
	FY88	—	2	1,926.5	—	4	3,328.9	—	5	4,127.0	—	5	3,328.9

C-5B	FY87	—	21	1,937.4	—	21	1,908.4	—	21	1,937.4	—	21	1,919.3
	FY88	—	—	—	—	—	—	—	—	—	—	—	—
MX	FY87	352.3	12	1,418.1	200	12	1,114.7	322.3	21	1,418.1	290.0	12	1,114.7
	FY88	642.6	21	1,260.0	281.2	12	864.0	451.2	21	1,160.0	351.2	12	864.0
Trident submarine	FY87	51.8	1	1,362.7	41.0	0	0	51.8	1	1,362.7	41.0	1	1,300.0
	FY88	31.6	1	1,193.7	31.6	1	1,193.7	31.6	1	1,153.7	26.6	1	1,153.7
Midgetman	FY87	1,375.5		—	1,375.0		—	675.5			1,200.0		—
	FY88	2,233.2		—	2,063.2		—	700.0			1,500.0		—
AH-64	FY87	12.9	144	1,189.3	12.9	120	1,050.2	12.9	120	1,064.3	12.9	120	1,032.8
	FY88	0	67	654.6	0	77	752.8	50.0	90	880.2	23.8	80	836.1
Bradley IFV	FY87	20.0	870	1,121.8	10.0	593	830.0	20.0	720	926.8	15.0	720	895.8
	FY88	—	616	699.4	—	616	684.4	—	616	699.4	—	616	699.4
Patriot	FY87	40.2	700	951.5	0.0	585	921.5	40.2	700	920.0	40.2	700	920.0
	FY88	—	715	851.4	—	715	836.4	—	715	851.4	—	715	836.4
F-14 A/D	FY87	268.4	15	541.1	240.0	10	360.6	268.4	15	541.1	260.0	15	520.4
	FY88	—	12	676.8	—	12	676.8	—	12	676.8	—	12	676.8
Tomahawk SLCM	FY87	68.4	324	721.7	68.4	324	643.5	68.4	324	666.7	68.4	324	666.7
	FY88	47.4	475	915.9	20.0	475	787.2	47.4	475	835.9	17.6	475	787.2
ALCM	FY87	10.9	—	12.4	4.1	—	12.4	6.1	—	12.4	4.1	—	12.4
	FY88	3.6	—	2.3	3.6	—	2.3	3.6	—	2.3	3.6	—	2.3
KC-135 re-engine	FY87	—	50	865.8	—	50	836.6	—	50	997.4	—	50	997.4
	FY88	—	—	—	—	—	—	—	—	—	—	—	—
C-17	FY87	612.3	—	182.3	587.3	—	145.3	547.3	—	182.3	547.3	—	145.3
	FY88	1,219.9	2	617.9	979.9	2	600.0	1,195.5	2	617.9	1,170.0	2	617.9

(Cont.)

Table 4-6. (Continued)

		DoD's Request			House Authorization			Senate Authorization			Conference Agreement		
		RDT&E	Number	Proc.	RDT&E	Number	Proc.	RDT&E	Number	Proc.	RDT&E	Number	Proc.
M1-A	FY87	12.8	840	1,643.6	3.8	840	1,578.6	3.8	840	1,643.6	3.8	840	1,578.6
	FY88	—	720	1,533.2	—	720	1,533.2	—	720	1,626.7	—	720	1,607.6
AV-8B	FY87	48.6	42	623.3	65.0	42	623.0	48.6	42	623.3	56.6	42	623.3
	FY88	13.1	32	564.2	13.1	0	0	13.1	32	591.7	13.1	24	427.8
AMRAAM	FY87	19.0	260	656.6	0	135	387.6	19.0	260	656.6	19.0	180	587.3
	FY88	—	630	832.9	—	500	680.8	—	630	832.9	—	500	743.1
AGM-88A	FY87	3.9	2,130	493.4	0	1,450	362.5	3.9	2,130	493.4	3.9	1,655	374.4
	FY88	—	1,748	423.0	—	1,748	402.7	—	1,748	402.8	—	1,748	402.7

*Excludes Department of Energy authorization figures.

Source: U.S. House of Representatives, *National Defense Authorization Act for Fiscal Year 1987: Conference Report to Accompany S-2638*, 99th Congress, 2d Session, Report 99-1001 (Washington, D.C.: U.S. Government Printing Office, October 1986), pp. 281–456; and U.S. House of Representatives, *National Defense Authorization Act for Fiscal Years 1988 and 1989, Conference Report to Accompany H.R. 1748*, 100th Congress, 1st Session, Report 100-446 (Washington, D.C.: U.S. Government Printing Office, November 17, 1987), pp. 251–601.

fiscal year began substituting for nearly thirteen appropriations bills including defense.

Despite the cuts, the net decline involved no major weapons cancellations. In fact, the legislation reprieved a number of programs including the navy's A-6F attack aircraft and the air force's Midgetman small ICBM, while also providing $6.3 billion for two aircraft carriers and $3.6 billion for the Strategic Defense Initiative, plus $300 million in SDI funds in the Energy Department budget. The $700 million in research and development for Midgetman overruled the Senate Appropriations Committee recommendation to terminate Midgetman, and included $350 million for the rail garrison MX basing system and $36 million for the MX program itself. In addition, the budget summit pact set a figure of $285.4 billion for outlays, a mandatory ceiling that derived from Congressional Budget Office calculations and the Gramm-Rudman-Hollings baseline via the budget resolution. According to some, however, the budget package figures setting budget authority at $292 billion and outlays at $285.4 billion were mismatched because the $292 billion figure had been picked quite literally "out of the air" as a midpoint between the high- and low-tier levels of the budget resolution and the $285.4 billion in outlays did not translate into $292 billion of budget authority but rather a figure closer to $290 billion.[60]

CONCLUSION

Congress's obvious difficulties in achieving reductions and deciding among competing programs in the defense budget at a time of mounting fiscal austerity are all too apparent.

This chapter has argued that "process" matters when it comes to the way Congress deals with the defense budget. Congressional approval of the defense budget is a multilayered process marked by piecemeal decision making and incrementalism. Congress does not sit down with the defense budget as a whole and then make one set of final decisions about funding. Rather, its deliberations involve "budget resolutions," "budget authorizations," and "appropriations."

What bearing do these different legislative actions have on each other? The answer seems to be a qualified "not much," because

they are carried out simultaneously rather than in the sequence in which they are intended. The process seems chaotic—which it is, even to those who are responsible for "managing" it.

Key norms inform congressional decision making: those of co-operation and consensus. When interests conflict, strong institutional incentives exist to strike a bargain to accommodate competing demands halfway. Half a loaf is generally recognized as better than none.

Regular interactions among congressional players in the "formulation" of the defense budget, the incremental nature of decision making, and the recognized importance of reciprocity encourage cooperation and facilitate "consensus." Thus, the key focus of much of the debate about the defense budget in general, and weapons programs in particular, involves marginal resource allocation questions like "How much do we give this program?" rather than questions on fundamental choices like "Do we need this system?" The consensus is messy and may mean different things to different people depending on where they stand on the issues. Incremental approaches to budgeting and shifting political coalitions also cause the "consensus" to shift over time.

Congress's failure to address fundamental trade-offs by funding high-priority programs while eliminating others is further encouraged by the annual nature of defense appropriations. Although Congress has moved to multiyear authorization for some non-controversial programs, it avoids examining the total costs of most programs through their life cycles. For this reason, weapons programs have tended to fare somewhat better at the hands of a deficit-minded Congress than other expenditures, like Personnel and Operations and Maintenance, because procurement outlays are lower in the current year compared to other programs.

What this all means is that a major weapons system or program, even an unpopular one like the MX, will rarely die at the hands of Congress although its future may, at times, seem uncertain. A program will generally get enough money from Congress to keep itself going—though not as much as its supporters or as little as its opponents seek. The chapters that follow will explore the origins and development of controversial weapons programs including the Trident, MX and Midgetman, B-1 bomber, cruise missile, M-1 Abrams

tank, and Ronald Reagan's Strategic Defense Initiative. These programs survived the onslaught from those who wanted to see them canceled, but they failed to secure the levels of funding and degree of budgetary stability their sponsors had sought.

5

□

THE TRIDENT SUBMARINE AND MISSILE

On April 7, 1979, the nuclear-powered submarine *Ohio,* officially described as the most formidable strategic weapons system ever devised, was launched after being christened by the wife of U.S. Senator John Glenn of Ohio, in a ceremony marked by controversy. Senator Glenn used the occasion to warn the Carter administration that the chances of Congress approving the SALT II agreements, then under negotiation, were slim unless the United States could verify Soviet compliance. This statement prompted the President's wife, also visiting the Electric Boat Yard at Groton, Connecticut, to lay the keel for another ship, the *Georgia,* to chide the Senator for "premature debate on these issues."

It was another two years before the first Trident, the *Ohio*, was to set sail in Long Island Sound for sea trials. Again controversy, but of a different kind, marred the ceremony. Demonstrators ringed the facility at Electric Boat protesting the deployment of the submarine. Admiral Hyman Rickover, the father of the atomic reactor that powered the submarine, had to sneak into the shipyard and hide from reporters behind a mattress when he boarded the ship. No sooner had the *Ohio* made its way into the Sound than it stopped dead in the water—a mechanic had forgotten to install a crucial component for its engine. As a Soviet patrol vessel hovered suspiciously close by, protest boats continued to harass the submarine as it lay still. It took several hours for the missing part to be taken by launch to the ship and installed for the trials to resume.

Why was the Trident built? Why did it take so long to deploy? What problems did the system encounter in its various stages of development? Trident was built because the navy wanted it. But it

might not have been built had not certain events, particularly in arms control, worked in its favor. As it was, the submarine had a troubled voyage. Although Congress never took the initiative to kill the program, funding cuts and changing strategic and fiscal priorities under different administrations contributed to program delays and cost overruns experienced by Electric Boat, the submarine's builder.

Unlike the submarine, the Trident II missile was not the subject of intense congressional scrutiny or criticism. It had a smoother ride and enjoyed the strong support of the Reagan administration for early deployment. Why?

Should these systems have been built? Compelling arguments can be made on both sides. But one thing is certain—the Trident program somehow survived in the face of formidable opposition in the Pentagon and Congress.

PROGRAM INITIATION AND DEVELOPMENT

Threat assessments about Soviet strategic programs played a key role in the early formulation and development of what eventually came to be the Trident submarine and missile program, as did concerns about the aging Polaris/Poseidon submarine force. By the mid-1960s, the key elements of the current U.S. strategic force posture were in place. Secretary of Defense Robert McNamara had approved procurement and deployment of 41 Polaris submarines for the navy, 1,000 Minuteman ICBMs (intercontinental ballistic missiles) for the air force, and the development of a new missile for the Polaris submarine, the Poseidon. His plan was to rearm Polaris with the Poseidon missiles by the 1970s. Each sub would carry 16 Poseidons with up to 14 warheads apiece.[1]

Indications surfaced from U.S. intelligence services that the Soviets were initiating a major buildup of their own forces, including a large ICBM and submarine force and an ABM (antiballistic missile) defense against ballistic missiles. In 1966 McNamara ordered the STRAT-X study to assess U.S. strategic requirements in the next decade in the face of the mounting Soviet threat. This was a follow-up to the PEN-X (penetration of enemy missiles, experimental) study, which had speculated that the Soviets would achieve greater accuracy in their ICBMs as well as antiballistic missile systems, thereby putting the new U.S. Minuteman force at risk. The STRAT-X

study, headed by General Maxwell Taylor, argued for counter-measures to this problem. The navy was also represented in the study,[2] with senior naval officers Rear Admirals George H. Miller and Levering Smith. Miller was a leading naval strategist and would become head of the Navy Office of Strategic Offensive and Defensive Systems.[3]

STRAT-X reviewed 125 new proposals for missile basing systems. The air force lobbied for a replacement for the Minuteman ICBM. The navy proposed a new submarine concept called ULMS (underwater long-range missile system). Other proposals included missile-firing submersibles, ICBMs carried on trucks, surface ships, or barges, new bombers, seabed platforms, submarines in the Great Lakes, etc.

The STRAT-X panel concluded that the navy's ULMS represented the least costly and most survivable alternative. The panel envisioned development of a slow submarine with a small nuclear power plant. The panel also urged development of a new, long-range, 6,000-mile missile.

> From its inception, ULMS was envisioned as the eventual successor to Polaris and Poseidon. The principal difference between ULMS and the older Polaris-Poseidon missiles was that from the outset ULMS was to incorporate very-long-range missiles into submarines of a rather conservative design, based largely on existing submarine technology, but with more quieting of machinery.[4]

One idea called for missiles to be carried horizontally outside of the submarine so it could carry different missiles of different sizes without modifying the hull, thereby permitting greater flexibility in firing. However, the idea was eventually killed because of fear of collisions which would damage the missiles.

Vice-Admiral Hyman Rickover, head of the Naval Reactors Branch, Assistant Chief of Nuclear Propulsion, and also a member of the Atomic Energy Commission, insisted in the early stages of design that the submarine have an S8G reactor capable of generating 60,000 horsepower. If Levering Smith was the founder of the nuclear submarine and the Polaris program, Rickover was second only in technical reputation. Rickover had helped to develop the technology of nuclear propulsion and had successfully developed the natural circulation reactor, which could operate without the use of noisy

pumps at low speeds, thereby providing greater quietness. Rickover had even deployed such a reactor in an experimental attack submarine, the *Narwhal.* He was something of a national hero, particularly in Congress.

Combative and fractious by nature, Rickover ridiculed Smith's idea of a smaller submarine in the Joint Committee on Atomic Energy: "The origin [of the Trident] was that we have a large submarine that could only make four knots and would most of the time rest on the Continental Shelf of the United States."[5] His insistence on a bigger reactor for greater speed was challenged by systems analysts in the Pentagon. But there was little doubt that if the bigger reactor was used, it would give Rickover substantial control over the new submarine program.

Admiral Elmo Zumwalt, who became Chief of Naval Operations in July 1970, did not like the idea of a larger power plant, but he felt it important to get Rickover's support for ULMS "because you couldn't get Congressional support without it."[6] Zumwalt realized it was important for the navy to speak with one voice to the Congress.[7]

However, resolution of the Smith-Rickover confrontation presented a serious problem to Zumwalt and other top navy officials. "Even informal discussion of the behemoth design was sufficient to inspire outrage in Deputy Secretary of Defense David Packard in late 1970. Perceiving such signals of trouble, then Under-Secretary of the Navy John Warner and Chief of Naval Operations Admiral Elmo Zumwalt knew that they would have to force a redesign, and they began to probe for options." The result was a classic compromise rather than an exploration of options.

Some navy analysts recognized that, given the absence of a known threat to Poseidon survivability, the construction of a new submarine could wait and that procurement of a longer-range missile for Poseidon boats would provide an ample margin of safety. This option (labeled EXPO option, for "expanded Poseidon") would have restored sole control to Smith. ... When the top admirals held a critical meeting in January 1971, the unacceptability of EXPO was the only point of major agreement. Needing some constructive solution, Admiral Zumwalt settled on a fallback position which Rickover's office had prepared, a submarine design of 14,000-ton displacement with a single 30,000-shp [standard horsepower] reactor. The missiles associated with this design were smaller but,

through the use of technical advances, still would have extended range. . . . Zumwalt named Rear Admiral H.E. Lyon as Project Manager 2 of the Trident program and gave him overall responsibility, i.e., he was to mediate between Smith and Rickover.[8]

But Trident supporters in the Pentagon actively worked to exploit the compromise to their own ends. "Both the submarine and the missile grew incrementally in size to their current dimensions—the missile by six inches in diameter and four to five feet in length; and the submarine by 5,000 shp in reactor output and 4,700 tons in displacement . . . without any change in the perceived threat of the goals of the system."[9] The reactor and vertical, inner-tube missile arrangement drove up the size of the sub to a length of 560 feet and a displacement of 18,700 tons (versus the original plan of 443 feet and 8,240 tons).

The ULMS schedule was accelerated, as was the date for initial deployment (to 1979), and funding for the first reactor was included in the 1973 budget (one to two years in advance of actual need) to defend the design against its detractors.

Funding for ULMS during this early period came from the navy's general R&D appropriations. The figures came to $21.1 million in FY 1968 and $24 million in FY 1969, of which $600,000 went to ULMS in 1968 and $5.9 million in 1969. Another $110 million went to ULMS research in the budget of the Atomic Energy Commission.

On February 1, 1968, Admiral Thomas Moorer, Chief of Naval Operations, issued an Advance Development Objective Memorandum, and in May 1968 DoD formally recommended a program to develop a replacement for Polaris and got $5 million to initiate study for general system requirements.

On October 4, 1969, the Chief of Naval Operations established the ULMS to centralize the project. The project was placed under the control of the Special Projects Office, created in 1955, which had pushed through the development of Polaris. This gave the Office a modicum of independence over the system's design and construction. But by early 1970, ULMS had begun to attract attention from lobbyists who saw support for the program as a way to force abandonment of the B-1 bomber and ABM programs. A report by the Members of Congress for Peace through Law (MCPL) recommended continued work on ULMS calling it "the epitome of the

blue-water option at a time when the probable obsolescence of fixed-base [silos] has become clear." The National Urban Coalition in its 1970 *Counterbudget* called for a reduction in defense spending but expanded funding for ULMS.[10] Many legislators supporting the program who had otherwise had a consistent record of opposing defense expenditures "looked at it as an alternative to the proposed antiballistic missile system, which the defense community hotly debated during the Trident's early funding controversy. One of the major purposes of the ABM was to protect a set of ICBM silos, another was to defend other soft targets such as Washington, D.C. But if the Trident could offer a safer 'version' of the ICBM and ABM, then it presented an opportunity to slash the military budget by opting for the strategically 'cleaner' Trident program instead of the more complicated ABM/advanced ICBM concept."[11]

RESEARCH AND DEVELOPMENT

From 1969 to 1972 Congress appropriated $165 million for ULMS research. But this did not include separate funding for sonar and torpedo improvements and the Atomic Energy Commission absorbed the costs associated with development of the submarine's reactor.

In January 1970, President Richard Nixon's Secretary of Defense, Melvin Laird, asserted that if the Soviet Union continued with its strategic weapons buildup it would be in a position to destroy most of U.S. Minuteman missiles by 1974 (a date he forecast to Congress in the spring of 1969). And he went on to declare that if the buildup could not be curbed, either through arms control or Soviet self-restraint, the United States would seriously consider the construction of a successor to the Polaris submarine and a new strategic bomber.[12] The administration's enthusiasm for ULMS was rising. But Congress's apparently was not.

The ULMS office had been working on a Development Concept Paper to present to the House and Senate Armed Services Committees, but the report fell flat and ULMS funding for a new hull design and missile studies was cut by both armed services committees from $20 million to $10 million. The opposition came principally from members of Congress and the air force; the latter saw the advanced submarine competing for resources for new land-based missiles. It was clear that the atmosphere in Congress had

changed from the days of its unequivocal support for Polaris.[13] Nevertheless, ULMS was still able to garner enough bipartisan support. Senator Richard Schweiker (R.-Penn.) chided the House Armed Services Committee for lacking a "sense of priority."[14] ULMS subsequently received $43.7 million in FY 1971 for R&D. The following year (FY 1972), JCS Chief Admiral Moorer requested $111.3 million for the program and got $104.8 million.

In 1971, the Pentagon decided on a missile and a contractor for the ULMS program. The STRAT-X study had recommended a missile with a range of 6,000+ miles. Defense Secretary Melvin Laird and Deputy Defense Secretary David Packard realized that they needed a transitional missile capable of fitting into the existing Polaris/Poseidon submarine. Although retrofitting might delay ULMS deployment, they ordered the development of the C-4 (Trident I) missile.

The contract was awarded to the Lockheed Missile and Space Company (which had built other missiles for the navy). The bidding was not opened to other companies because Lockheed was encountering financial difficulties at the time and desperately needed the business. At the same time, the Development Concept Paper for ULMS was presented to the Secretary of Defense, who ordered practical development of the project in the summer of 1971. An additional $20 million was given to the program to keep it going.[15]

The Development Concept Paper outlined four options for ULMS: (1) do nothing and cancel the program (this option reflected some sensitivity to the views of congressional critics); (2) build a new Poseidon missile with greater range and continue with the ULMS research program; (3) build the ULMS submarine only; and (4) build ULMS and an extended-range Poseidon, and deploy both in the future.

DoD leaned toward Option 3 but there was little chance that a submarine could be built in time to replace the Polaris, which would finish production at the end of the decade.

PROCUREMENT

Deputy Defense Secretary David Packard, however, did not want to go ahead with the new submarine. Cost conscious and ever skeptical of the services' apparently insatiable demand for new weapons, he had deep-seated reservations about whether the United

States needed a new submarine just then. In September 1971, he issued an official Development Concept Paper on the Trident program (Defense Concept Paper 3b 10c). The paper substituted for the EXPO option (which had been proposed earlier) and suggested that the navy could modify the missile tubes in the Poseidon submarine to carry the new, extended-range missile intended for the ULMS. This would extend the operational life of the Poseidon submarine force and defer any new submarine construction until the early 1980s. "The finesse looked brilliant. It forced out the option which the Navy had labored to suppress, and Packard could expect an increasingly skeptical, economy-minded Congress to find that option attractive. Congressmen would be loath to resist a program involving the primary component of the strategic arsenal, but they would presumably welcome a version of that program that was cheaper and at least as effective."[16]

The navy option survived with the intervention of the White House, however. In October 1971, President Nixon ordered Secretary of Defense Melvin Laird to increase defense spending substantially during the next fiscal year (FY 1973), especially in strategic forces modernization. The Moscow Summit had just been announced and the President intended to sign the new SALT agreements. Nixon felt that sizable and visible increases in defense spending were necessary to appease congressional hardliners, like Senator Henry "Scoop" Jackson (D.-Wash.) and his assistant, Richard Perle (who later went on to become Assistant Secretary of Defense in the Reagan administration), who worried that an arms control agreement with the Soviets would weaken U.S. defense.

In addition, the President was also concerned about the status of the negotiations on offensive weapons.

It was already certain that the offensive agreement would allow the Soviets 400 to 500 more ICBMs than the United States, but it was most uncertain whether the Soviets would agree to limits on missile submarines, which they were building at the rapid rate of seven or eight per year and which we were not building at all. Threatening to accelerate the U.S. submarine missile program might encourage the Soviets to agree to limits on future construction. If the threat failed, the accelerated program would help mollify the allies and the conservatives. . . . Hence, given the President's commitment to "bargaining chips," he wanted a construction program under way to help the subsequent negotiations.[17]

The President's initiative effectively scuttled the Packard plan to defer deployment of ULMS. In October $81.3 million was released out of the FY 1972 budget for ULMS, with a request to accelerate the program by two years.

In November 1971, the ULMS group in the Department of the Navy completed its own study for the Secretary of Defense. None too surprisingly, it concluded that ULMS was the only option for the navy. But it did not formally recommend acceleration because of fears about the political risks of appearing too enthusiastic. A special funding order was issued on December 23, 1971, by Defense Secretary Laird (Progress Budget Decision 317) which opened up $104.8 million for ULMS construction to be available in FY 1972.

Laird not only approved the program, he also urged the navy to complete the system for deployment in 1978. For this purpose, he requested $942 million from Congress for ULMS and another $445 million for engineering of the B-1 bomber.[18] He gave four reasons for the request: (1) since ULMS was already under way as a high-priority program it would not disrupt other programs such as Poseidon modernization and construction of nuclear attack submarines; (2) ULMS was the best technical option for modernization: the submarine would be very quiet and could carry a wide variety of missiles of different payloads; (3) ULMS could carry a large number of missiles and would therefore need fewer boats and crews; (4) ULMS missile development would enable the navy to continue the life of the Poseidon submarine force.[19]

In subsequent congressional hearings, Admirals Rickover, Smith, and Lyon argued that the decision to accelerate was not based on "any single additional or recent threat but on an assessment ... [and] analysis" of Soviet strategic improvements overall.[20]

This view was backed up by the Joint Chiefs and other administration officials. Admiral Thomas H. Moorer, Chairman of JCS, told the Senate Armed Services Committee that "the Soviets are believed to be working on a number of new antisubmarine warfare developments which could significantly improve their antisubmarine warfare capability in those waters in which our submarines are now required to operate." Dr. John S. Foster, Jr., Director of Defense Research and Engineering, told the same committee, "We know that the Soviets devote a significant amount of their resources to antisubmarine warfare development and exercise." But

in a rather telling statement, surprising for its frankness and honesty, he explained, "Unfortunately, we are not able to adequately assess the effectiveness of such a capability."[21]

Advocates of the accelerated program gave two reasons for ULMS. Polaris/Poseidon would reach obsolescence by their twentieth year (between 1979 and 1987 depending on when they entered service) and they were becoming increasingly unreliable because of Soviet improvements in antisubmarine warfare. However, this assessment did not go unchallenged. One government report argued:

> The Polaris boats were originally designed with great and expensive emphasis on reliability. They have been operating at low speeds; they have been carefully maintained; and they have compiled an outstanding record of operational reliability to date. Indeed the Defense Department itself has proposed that a new cruise missile be developed for deployment on the older Polaris submarines, thereby admitting that they still have years of useful life. Second, sudden and unpredictable improvements in Soviet antisubmarine warfare capabilities could render the current force vulnerable. Again, the argument does not withstand scrutiny. The large size of the planned boat has *at best* no effect on vulnerability, and some have argued that the larger size may increase vulnerability. As for extra speed, even at twenty-five knots the boat would be outrun by attack submarines which travel at thirty knots or better. Moreover, no submarine seeking to avoid or escape detection would ever run at twenty-five knots since at such speeds it can be detected at very long range. The natural circulation reactor can operate without inherently noisy pumps only up to a power output corresponding to approximately ten knots of speed. Current submarines routinely operate below this speed. The increases in missile range do provide a significant hedge against vulnerability by forcing the Soviets to search for them in a vastly greater ocean area. But since current ASW [antisubmarine warfare] technology cannot detect submarines in the area from which they now operate, the first increment in range offered by the Trident I missile appears sufficient.[22]

The same report stated that the "Trident program was not the most logical choice from the available options. A more sensible approach would have been to continue R&D for another five years and then to have reassessed the technical situation. If an actual

deployed hedge against ASW improvements were irresistible, however, the Navy could have procured the Trident I missile for a number of existing Poseidon boats, gaining a major decrease in vulnerability without engaging in an expensive submarine construction program."[23]

But this was to suggest closing the door after the horse had fled the stable. "No one in the STRAT-X group had been instructed to analyze all of the eventualities involved in mating a new missile to a new submarine (as demanded by the study's guidelines), nor had anyone been ordered to consider the advantages presented by increasing the size of the sub."[24] Thus, the navy had seized the initiative in transforming a platform concept into an actual weapons system, while ignoring intermediate and less costly alternatives.

As ULMS finally moved toward actual production it gathered more opposition. Just after the January 4, 1972, announcement of Progress of Budget Decision 324, which allocated an additional $35 million from FY 1972 to ULMS, Senator William Proxmire (D.-Wis.) challenged the rate of development. In a letter to Hyman Rickover, Proxmire asked, "Why are we rushing into ULMS at such a fast pace[?]" Referring to the navy's policy of testing a weapon, or at least a prototype before purchase, Proxmire wondered "where is 'fly before you buy'?" He predicted ULMS ultimately would cost $30 billion and warned that the navy and Congress were "moving toward another procurement disaster."[25]

Defense critic Morton Halperin charged that "[t]here is at present no sign of any Soviet technological breakthrough in the direction of being able to find and destroy the Polaris/Poseidon [fleet]. . . . A new fleet designed to be immune to an unknown threat would probably be wrong for its purpose." He called the project "politically motivated, strategically unnecessary and wasteful"[26] and suggested that some of the Poseidon missile's warheads could be offloaded to lengthen the range of the missile to forestall the Soviet ASW threat.

Herbert Scoville, Jr., President of the American Federation of Scientists, had a similar reaction:

So far, no convincing case has been made for the need to proceed with a replacement for the Polaris-Poseidon system and for making a commitment to a new large, high-speed submarine. Russian construction of SLBMs is no justification for ULMS; the Russian missile

submarines do not in any way threaten the Polaris deterrent ... all authorities agree that the U.S. is far ahead qualitatively and can deliver from submarines about 5,000 warheads to fewer than 700 for the U.S.S.R. Even if we foolishly choose to race the Russians in the number of SLBMs, ULMS is certainly not the way to do it; each ULMS system will probably cost five or more times per missile launched than the Russian Y-class system ... no evidence has yet been presented that the Russian ASW program could present a threat to the Polaris deterrent in the next decade.[27]

Senator Thomas McIntyre (D.-N.H.), Chairman of the Senate Armed Services Subcommittee on Research and Development, opined that the ULMS "promises to be one of the major and most controversial issues to be considered by the Congress because of the size of the fiscal commitments involved."[28] He was not far off the mark although the degree of controversy turned out to be less than he expected. The Senate Armed Services Committee on February 25 rejected the administration's request for an immediate appropriation of $35 million in supplemental or emergency funds to accelerate the development of ULMS. And in the initial Senate vote on the program in April 1972, $942 million was rejected when Congress learned the navy had not completed design studies.

The vote occurred at the same time the United States and Soviet Union were completing the SALT I negotiations. The Treaty was signed by President Nixon in May 1972 with much fanfare. As anticipated, the United States accepted unfavorable numerical limits in strategic submarines and missiles. To get the JCS to support the Treaty, the administration and Congress struck a deal with Admiral Thomas H. Moorer, JCS head, that the strategic modernization package, which included Trident, would obtain the necessary funding for acceleration. Moorer and the JCS publicly had expressed their misgivings about numerical superiority in land-based missiles granted to the Soviet Union under the SALT agreement. Secretary of Defense Melvin Laird also said that he would not support the Treaty if Congress refused to proceed with the modernization plan of the administration, including provision of funds for the Trident and B-1 bomber if it is to maintain "a realistic deterrent" during the freeze on offensive weapons.[29]

Most of the funding went toward adapting the Poseidon/Polaris fleet to carry new Trident I or C-4 missiles. Only $110 million

went to new submarine development and construction and another $30 million to the development of a new, longer range missile, the D-5, that would be the follow-up to the C-4. This new missile would have a range of 6,000 nautical miles and would be larger in diameter and length than the C-4.

The new missile meant that the hull for the submarine would have to be considerably longer than the Poseidon/Polaris. The navy favored a hull that would displace 18,000 tons, one capable of carrying a full load of twenty-four missiles (versus sixteen for Poseidon/Polaris). However, congressional critics were quick to accuse the navy of being arbitrary in its design for a new boat. Vice-Admiral Rickover was also blamed for choosing an oversized reactor to power the boat which also increased the hull size.[30]

Laird requested $977 million for the program, of which more than half was for accelerated funds for the program ($508.4 million).[31] The Senate Armed Services Committee approved Laird's acceleration of the Trident program even though some of its members believed that despite its major costs Trident did not add much to national defense. The Senate Foreign Relations Committee was even less enthusiastic about the *quid pro quo* and criticized the administration for trying to couple approval of the agreements with increased spending on strategic arms. Senator J. William Fulbright (D.-Ill.), the committee Chairman, blasted the package on the grounds that "more force, greater spending and additional weapons will not make either side more secure. . . . More can only lead to a deepening of the balance of terror which has enslaved this world for more than a decade."[32] He also challenged the administration's assertion that the Soviets were beginning contruction of a new Y-class submarine like the Trident. Fulbright scolded Laird: "I am hopeful Senators will be able to vote on the weapons without being scared to death by your misinformation."[33]

However, congressional action did not go much beyond rhetoric. Congress voted for the program and much of the subsequent debate in both houses focused on the marginal issue of program acceleration rather than the fundamental merits of the program itself. For two years running, 1972 and 1973 amendments cutting the ULMS program back to the more leisurely schedule envisioned by David Packard were defeated by very close votes both in the Armed Services Committee and on the Senate floor.[34] In the FY 1973 vote taken in 1972, the navy's request for a $508.4 million

package in accelerated funds for ULMS was dropped by the Senate Armed Services Ad Hoc Research and Development Subcommittee, in effect putting the program back on its old schedule. The full committee found itself tied on the vote, which was broken by its chairman, Senator John Stennis, (D.-Miss.), who cast his vote in favor of accelerated development. However, Senator Lloyd Bentsen (D.-Tex.), who was worried about the cost of the program and was a member of the R&D subcommittee, carried the fight to cut funds to the floor of the Senate in which he was only narrowly defeated in a 47–39 vote.[35]

The *New York Times* supported the Bentsen amendment which would have delayed production but continued development work on ULMS: "To replace the Polaris-Poseidon fleet a decade or two before its normal retirement—to seek to counter an anti-submarine threat that does not exist and may never materialize or may take an unpredicted form—is the height of folly." [36] However, only $852.9 million was actually appropriated in FY 1973, representing a cut of $124 million from Laird's original request of $977.1 million. (This represented a cut of $127.2 million from the navy's original request.)

Senator William B. Saxbe (R.-Ohio) argued that "accelerating the [ULMS] submarine could prove a negative factor in the development of our new-found relations with Russia." Senator Edward Kennedy (D.-Mass.) expressed his belief "that going forward with an advanced weapons system at a stepped-up pace clearly flouts the spirit of the SALT accord and threatens the ... success of the subsequent SALT discussions." Stuart Symington (D.-Mo.) attacked the program's costs and argued that the navy should follow the "fly before buy" concept.[37]

These arguments were addressed by Vice-Admiral Philip Beshamy in hearings before Congress. He argued that refitting older vessels had its limits and that Poseidon could not accommodate new sonars or power plants. American subs were getting noisier as engines wore out and maintenance and operational costs were rapidly rising with aging systems. He pointed out that the industrial base was also eroding and the navy wanted to avoid having to make "block" replacements because shipbuilders would not be able to handle a massive surge in demand for replacements. He also argued that the system was a stabilizing deterrent because of its reduced vulnerability.[38]

In May 1972, the ULMS program was renamed Trident. The first submarine did not get its name until 1976, however—the *Ohio,* which broke the tradition of naming submarines after famous Americans or personalities.

PROCUREMENT AND DEPLOYMENT

In spite of political opposition in Congress (which was dying after the crucial votes in 1972–1973), Trident began to move to the contractors and subcontractors. For the missile, "Motorola, RCA, and T.I. worked on microelectronics devices, Rocketdyne prepared the small motors, Union Carbide made the nose caps, and Ensign-Bickford together with Exploration Technologies supplied pyrotechnics materials. For the submarine itself, all of the early subcontractors (as well as some new ones) commenced production. For example, National Forge began producing the main propulsion shafts, HYBO hull machinery . . . Uncle Sam provided many large items under SARs (Selected Acquisition Requests)," which are classified requests that do not appear in specific budgetary outlays.[39] In the FY 1974 budget request, the Department of Defense asked for $1.5 billion for Trident, of which $285 million was to go to General Dynamic's Electric Boat Yard for the initial contract for the submarine, $302 million for materials procurement, $685 million for R&D, and $182 million for Trident refit complex and support facilities. On August 1, 1973, the Senate Armed Services Committee trimmed the Trident program by $885 million.[40]

In a crucial vote Senator Barry Goldwater (R.-Ariz.), who was absent when the vote was taken, announced that Senator Strom Thurmond (D.-S.C.) had miscast his proxy vote. Goldwater had voted for two consecutive years against Trident acceleration. But Admiral Rickover personally lobbied the Senator to change his mind, and change it he did.[41] On August 3, the Senate restored the $885 million to the program by a hair's 49–47 margin. The House had earlier approved the full $1.5 billion package so Trident did not go back into joint Conference. Senators Thomas McIntyre and Pete U. Domenici (R.-N.M.), two of the major opponents to Trident, decided to carry the fight to the floor and offered an amendment to cut funds from the program. The administration sent a formidable team of Admiral Zumwalt, Admiral Rickover, and Secretary of the Navy Warner to the Hill to give a closed-door, classified

briefing detailing Soviet advances in ASW, which led to the amendment's defeat—but not until after a knock-down, punch-out floor fight in the Senate directed at the votes of eighteen "undecided" senators in which the administration was criticized for resorting to scare tactics. The House Appropriations Committee, however, decided to cut $253.9 million from the House bill of $1.5 billion. The Senate agreed even though the cuts would affect the long-range procurement for Trident subs 5-7. The Senate Appropriations Committee, worried about further program delays, agreed to seek supplemental funding of $240 million for the program, if deemed necessary.[42]

Congressional action on the FY 1974 budget for Trident was as follows:

> Navy requested $1.5 billion.
> House approved $1.5 billion, July 31, 1973.
> Senate Armed Services Committee removes $885 million, September 1, 1973.
> Senate Armed Services Committee restores $885 million, September 3, 1973.
> Conferees approve $1.5 billion, October 20, 1973.
> House Appropriations Committee removes $240 million, December 1, 1973.
> Senate Appropriations Committee agrees with House to remove $240 million, December 13, 1973.
> Final Navy appropriation $1.26 billion.[43]

The first Trident was ordered from Electric Boat Yard on July 25, 1974, with a delivery date specified for April 30, 1979. But the contract also contained a clause stipulating, "In recognition of the high national priority assigned to the Trident program the contractor has promised to use his best efforts to support a December 1977 delivery date for the lead ship."[44]

The key elements of the Trident program—the submarine, missile, and base—had begun to take shape by 1974. However, some still wanted development of a smaller submarine, while others wanted to know why the program was not moving faster. The administration, in its efforts to tackle inflation, was also trimming budgets. Even Trident did not remain unscathed in the ensuing cuts, which caused further program delays.

In FY 1974 the contract price of the submarine was set at $780 million (excluding reactor components and fuel core). Gordon Rule, head of the procurement and clearance division of Naval Material Command, blew the whistle and publicly rejected the contract figure as being "imprudent."[45] But he was reprimanded and overruled by his navy and Defense Department superiors.[46] Representative Les Aspin (D.-Wis.) of the House Armed Services Committee asked for a House investigation into Rule's charges, but the navy successfully defended its contract with Electric Boat.

The FY 1975 request for Trident was for a total of $2.04 billion, of which $107 million was to go to continued component development of the submarine, $927 million to complete funding for second and third Trident submarines, $240 million for advanced procurement for two Trident submarines in FY 1976 and FY 1977, $662 million for the Trident I missile, and $107 million for Trident base construction. In FY 1976 the navy also requested $16 million for a conceptual and feasibility study for an SSBN-X, intended to serve as an alternative to the Trident design by having a cheaper hull design and a smaller reactor, but the request was subsequently dropped, largely in response to critics who continued to oppose Trident's size and cost.[47]

Congressional critics pointed out that Trident's budget was already $3 billion higher than originally predicted. Representative Les Aspin accused the navy of "hiding at least $2.8 billion" and related missile development of at least $15.2 billion in increased costs.[48] The navy, however, defended the program on the grounds that changes in development, scheduling, and inflation were contributing to overcosts—$922 million, for example, was due to two scheduling stretch-outs from an annual building rate of 1-2-2-2-2-1 submarines to 1-2-1-2-1-2-1; and from 1-2-1-2-1-2-1 to 1-2-1-1-2-1-2.[49] Admiral Albert L. Kelln also cited "fiscal constraint reasons" because the "navy was trying to do all the things that had to be done within allowed funds." But Electric Boat had its problems, too. As Admiral Rickover's biographers point out:

> With the Trident and the SSN-688 class being built side by side at Electric Boat, it becomes difficult to distinguish their separate problems. There were design changes—thousands of them—to both classes. The Navy claimed there were not an inordinate amount. EB claimed there were. Rickover put the blame squarely on EB's work-

ers. "For many years," he said, "there has been a large amount of loafing at Electric Boat. I have personally observed this problem in both shops and ships during my inspections, and recently I have received reports that loafing is so bad that some workers do not even make an effort to appear busy."

Many old-timers at the yard agreed with Rickover, but others suggested that management should share the blame. During the turmoil over Trident and the SSN-688s, EB had three general managers in three years. In a single year, one hundred and eighty of the top three hundred management positions changed hands.[50]

And they go on to state that "[i]nadequate budgets and efforts to continue a balance—or compromise mix of strategic-bomber aircraft (the B-1) and land-based missiles (the MX), as well as Trident—caused a loss of support for the submarine program. Soon the first ten boats were stretched out—in paper plans—to six years and then to seven. Even that schedule was not to be. And the lead submarine, named *Ohio,* was far behind schedule."[51]

However, the design of the Trident, according to L. Emmett Holt of Electric Boat, was only 10 percent complete when the contract for eight Tridents was signed in 1974. The company contended that cost overruns of about 50 percent would be only 3 percent if the expense of design changes and the effect of seven years of inflation were taken into account.[52]

On November 29, 1977, the navy's Trident program managers, Rear Admirals Albert L. Kelln and Donald Hall, both nuclear submariners, announced that the lead submarine had increased in cost from $780 million to almost $1.2 *billion*—a 50 percent increase. They said that the lead submarine was still three years from completion. "Asked why the program was delayed, Admiral Hall could state only that Electric Boat has 'not stated a reason, they have indicated that they would not make the contract delivery date.' Asked about higher costs, the answer was also vague: 'It's primarily associated with the longer construction period, the stretch-out of the program.'"[53] The blame was being put on Electric Boat, but it was obvious it also lay in the political arena and the delays, uncertainties, and vagaries of the budget process.

On December 6, 1974, Secretary of Defense James Schlesinger stated that the proposed new arms agreement with the Soviets (the Vladivostok agreement) would have little impact on the defense budget. Depending on what the Soviets did he saw a "prob-

able need" to build two Trident missile submarines beyond the ten already planned and to keep ten Poseidon submarines in operation longer than planned, plus a new strategic bomber and a larger intercontinental missile force.[54] However, the Vladivostok agreement was never signed.

On February 6, 1975, the Pentagon, in secret portions of the R&D budget presented to the Senate and House Armed Services Committees, requested funds to develop a "good, hard, target capability" for the Trident II missile. Senator Thomas McIntyre, Chairman of the Senate Armed Services Subcommittee on Research and Development, sent a letter to Schlesinger asking, "If we develop an effective hard-target capability [that is, an ability to destroy enemy missile silos] in our Trident missile, won't this radically change the character of our sea-based missile force, the inherently limited accuracy of which has given us the sure capability of destroying soft targets, such as cities, while avoiding a destabilizing threat to the Soviet's own deterrent of land-based missiles?"[55]

By 1976, the Trident program was far enough along that many of its critics had given up or were focusing on other programs up for consideration, such as the B-1. Some still continued the fight, however. In hearings on the FY 1976 budget, IBM Defense Analyst Richard Garwin called the Trident program "entirely premature" and argued that it "ought to be terminated with either the second or third ship." Stanford physicist Sidney Drell called Trident "an elegant 'Cadillac of the sea.' " Others, including Representative Joseph Addabbo (D.-N.Y.), opposed much of Trident's subsystem development.[56] However, Congress went on to appropriate $1.3 billion for the Trident in FY 1976. "The FY 1976 funds matched the Administration's request: one Trident at $791.5 million plus eighty missiles at $349.8 million, totaling $1,141.3 million. Originally the House had passed funds for two Tridents (a $1,520.3 million total), but the Senate reduced the number back to one, reasoning that Electric Boat's personnel hardly could work any faster."[57]

In the House Armed Services Committee, the chief critics of the program were Les Aspin and Patricia Schroeder (D.-Colo.). The Committee was unhappy about the navy's cost estimates. In its FY 1976 recommendation, the Committee recommended $1.75 billion for Trident, although it cut other defense programs. One member, Robert Legget (D.-Cal.), tried to delete $559.9 million

from Trident construction funds, but was opposed by other members of the Committee. Representative Morris Udall (D.-Ariz.), a presidential hopeful, also indicated his opposition to the Trident program on the grounds that there were "deadly risks" in letting the arms race escalate.[58]

Opponents of the Trident slowly began to shift their attention from the submarine to the Trident I missile and the development of the Trident II missile. Senator Hubert Humphrey (D.-Minn.) led the opposition to the testing of a MaRV (maneuverable reentry vehicle) warhead for Trident in the Senate and achieved a 43–41 victory. But the ban was later dropped in Joint Conference. "On August 2, 1975, the conferees provided $602.6 million for fiscal year for the fourth Trident. This figure represented a cut of $10 million from the Administration's own request but retained the bulk of the actual construction funds. The House committee deleted $48.6 million in Trident II missile funds in October, but a month later the entire House restored $38.6 million."[59]

The keel for the first Trident, the *Ohio* (Figure 5-1), was laid on April 11, 1976. Katherine Whittaker Taft, wife of Republican Senator Robert Taft, Jr., welded her initials onto the hull of the ship. The navy had accepted the first submarine, the *Holland,* from Electric Boat seventy-six years ago to the day.[60]

With the election of Jimmy Carter in 1976 the size of the defense budget became a contentious political issue. Carter considered cuts to the defense budget because of the upcoming SALT II talks. But strong opposition to defense cuts in Congress encouraged Carter to abandon plans for cutting this budget in 1977. "Ultimately a compromise weapons bill with funds for a nuclear-powered carrier, which Carter opposed, emerged and was passed, but the B-1 bomber was canceled, leaving just four prototypes." Trident absorbed $671.1 million of the Pentagon's $19 billion in new weapons estimates. In July Carter ordered Minuteman II production to be shut down.[61]

In his last budget message to Congress in 1976, President Ford had proposed eight Tridents over the next five years. But Carter and Defense Secretary Harold Brown cut back the number to six and then to five Tridents.[62]

In FY 1978 defense budget appropriations, the Trident program got funds for Poseidon refitting with Trident I missiles, Trident submarine construction, and base construction. But one Trident-

Figure 5-1. U.S.S. *Ohio* (SSBN-726), the Navy's First Trident Submarine, on Sea Trials

Source: Natural Resources Defense Council, Washington, D.C.

related program was already the subject of a tough legislative battle: Seafarer, a proposal to build a massive underground radio antenna for ELF (extremely low frequency) communication with deep-diving subs. The House tried to cut funds for this project, along with funds for NAVSTAR (an intelligence satellite communication system), both of which were restored by the Senate. As Douglas Dalgleish and Larry Schweikart observe, "The fact that the SEA-FARER, TACAMO, NAVSTAR and other projects complementary to the Trident vessel now in the R&D stage commanded the center of attention in 1977 underscored the almost routine nature of Trident funding bills among the vast majority of legislators. Congressional approval with little quibbling of all funds requested for the eighth Trident in the series further emphasized this standing."[63]

Electric Boat, the contractor, was still having severe difficulty meeting contract schedules and prices for the Los Angeles class attack submarines. "Partially because of the fear that shipbuilding

problems might spill over to the Trident as well as because the Tridents already were behind the original 1974 accelerated 'best honest effort' schedule, legislators renewed their infatuation with an adumbrated version of the Trident. On August 5, 1978, a House committee added $3 million for continued research on a less-expensive sub to follow Trident and, on January 27, 1979, the Senate Armed Services Committee increased to $10 million the original request for this purpose."[64] On June 14, 1978, Senator Thomas McIntyre, Chairman of Senate Armed Services Subcommittee on Research and Development, urged that the figure be increased to $16 million to start "concept and design" studies for a submarine that would "complement" the Trident program.[65]

In the FY 1979 budget request for another Trident submarine, the request for $40.6 million for the Trident II missile was deleted by the Senate Armed Services Committee because it felt the missile was not needed, especially in view of the development of the MX missile by the air force. Opponents also worried about the much-touted hard-target kill capabilities of the Trident II missile. The arguments were summarized by the Congressional Research Service's *Trident Issue Brief* of 1981. "To acquire a hard target capability . . . might cause the Soviets . . . to launch their ICBMs on warning of attack, in which case computer malfunction or human error could lead to nuclear war. . . . [The] Soviets would [also] have less warning than they would for an attack by ICBMs."[66] The Trident II missile has great accuracy at a range of 4,000 nautical miles, almost double the range of the Poseidon missile, which can drop 10 warheads within 1,800 feet of their targets. These advances, made possible by marked improvement in the submarine's navigational system, included the submarine's inertial navigation system; navigational aids, or signals from shore-based radio transmitters and satellites circling the earth; improvements in the submarine's firing control system, which recomputes the path to the target every few minutes; and in missile guidance and stability.[67]

Budgetary constraints encouraged DoD to make Trident II and MX more alike in order to save costs. The "dual-use" concept that had White House support was reportedly developed by Under Secretary of Defense William Perry. Perry suggested two options: the navy could be assigned the task of designing both land- and sea-based versions of the missile, or the air force could be allowed to develop its own system but would have to use some navy com-

ponents. However, remembering the problems when McNamara tried to force the two services to collaborate on the TFX fighter, some air force officials expressed skepticism about the idea, while others felt this was the only way it would get a new missile.[68] Eventually the idea was dropped.

Trident I funding dropped in FY 1979 relative to the previous year because Defense Secretary Harold Brown wanted to redirect funds to the development of an intermediate-range nuclear force in Europe.[69] There had also been continuing problems with the missile system, which was not living up to the revolutionary advances its advocates had originally promised.[70] With congressional approval, the navy also lost one Trident in the defense budget.

> Trident was in trouble, and everyone knew it. There had been one Trident authorized in fiscal 1974, two in 1975, one in 1976, one in 1977, two in 1978, and then none in 1979, a total of seven submarines in six years. The plan had been ten Trident submarines authorized in four years. (In the Polaris era, forty-one submarines had been authorized in a similar period.) Congress resumed funding Trident submarines in fiscal 1980—at a rate of one per year.[71]

In 1979 public and congressional concern about the Soviet threat rose, reinforced by the Secretary of Defense's 1979 annual report, which declared that "a Soviet surprise attack in which our forces 'ride out' the attack poses a severe test" to U.S. strategic capabilities. This led to funding requests for one new Trident in the 1980 budget, as well as funding for the Trident I and II missiles.[72]

The FY 1979 defense budget request made no mention of the SSBN-X option, but the FY 1980 report indicated that an alternative submarine design to follow Trident was under consideration.

In 1979, in testimony before Congress, Dr. David Mann, Assistant Secretary of the Navy for Research, said that he believed a new Trident submarine, capable of carrying 24 missiles, with a displacement of 15,000 tons, could be built for 30 percent less than the cost of an *Ohio*-class submarine. He also proposed to refit the Los Angeles class of attack submarines with a center section that could carry 16 missiles. The SSBN and SSN forces would therefore have the same power plant as other systems, which would greatly simplify logistics and operations.[73]

Despite cuts to the B-1 bomber program in the Carter defense

budget, Trident remained unscathed. The FY 1980 defense budget secured congressional approval without too many cuts because of mounting concern over the Soviet invasion of Afghanistan and the "discovery" of a secret Soviet brigade in Cuba. Secretary Brown was personally opposed to Trident II missile funding, but "[e]ventually ... Congress directed the Pentagon to transfer $33 million from other projects to the Trident II missile development."[74]

On April 7, 1979, the *Ohio* was launched, but it would be another two years (June 18, 1981) before the ship could go on its first sea trials with Admiral Rickover aboard. The *Ohio* had been under construction for more than six and a half years, and the remaining subs were delayed by more than two years each.

Part of the delay of the *Ohio* had been caused by metal worker strikes at Electric Boat,[75] and much of the initial work on the submarine had to be redone. One Defense Department official complained that "thousands of welds have been done improperly and have to be redone, hundreds of pipes and valves are in the wrong place ... the boat's a mess."[76] As a result, both armed services committees apparently favored delaying the tenth Trident for a year. "Both committees followed through by delaying exercise of the option for the tenth contract on May 9, 1981, although they later added $110 million for parts procurement for the following two Tridents."[77]

THE REAGAN ADMINISTRATION

President Reagan was elected to office in 1980 with a commitment to increase the defense budget. In his 1981 defense budget, Reagan announced an ambitious new strategic modernization program for 100 MX missiles (to be deployed in Minuteman silos) and 100 B-1B bombers, as well as development of the Trident II (D-5) missile for deployment by 1989, plus a major buildup of the navy and other goodies.[78] However, the House Armed Services Committee deleted funds for the eleventh Trident, citing problems at Electric Boat, although it did leave $330.7 million for funding in the future.

Trident had found a protector in the Reagan administration. In the FY 1983 budget, Reagan requested two additional Trident submarines and funds for the Trident I and II missile programs for a

total of $4,355.8 million. In spite of an attack by House liberals and fiscal conservatives on the defense budget, the White House and the Senate secured appropriations for these programs.[79]

The administration's plans called for building a total of twenty Trident submarines over a ten-year period. Reagan's Trident program escaped much of the controversy surrounding the MX land-based missile, largely because submarines are considered more secure from Soviet attack than MX basing schemes. Some of the opponents of the MX, like Senator Ernest F. Hollings (D.-S.C.), recommended increasing the Trident force instead of the MX force.[80]

In June 1982, Secretary of Defense Caspar Weinberger announced that he was restructuring the Trident II (D-5) program to avoid procurement of Trident I (C-5) missiles for fiscal years 1981–1984 and that he planned to introduce the D-5 system into the fleet in slightly greater quantities over the current schedule. This would extend some submarine construction time frames, primarily as a result of Trident II government-furnished equipment not being available to support the construction of these submarines.[81]

Not everyone was happy about the Trident II missile program. Congressman Thomas J. Downey (D.-N.Y.) chastised fellow liberals, who supported Trident while criticizing MX, on the grounds that "it will be the most destabilizing first-strike weapon ever built, far more than MX ... [because] it could be fired from submarines near the Soviet Union thus allowing no more than 10 minutes warning."[82] These concerns were echoed by Herbert Scoville, Jr., President of the Arms Control Association, who said, "Trident II is a serious arms control problem—I think it's basically a mistake" because it would give Soviet leaders a strong incentive to put their missiles on hair-trigger alert, thereby increasing the possibility of accidental war. Defense analysts Michael Altfeld and Stephen Cimbala stated the case against Trident II as follows:

> The implications of Trident II for crisis stability are uncertain, but potentially quite negative. The combined accuracy and yield of Trident II will put most Soviet hard targets at prompt risk. Moreover, the possible employment of SLBM in depressed trajectories could reduce Soviet warning time following Trident II launch to 15 minutes or less. Finally, the improved range of Trident II will allow U.S.

forces to launch an attack from many different azimuths simultaneously, thus further stressing Soviet warning, control and defense systems.

In a coordinated attack, a fleet of 15 Trident submarines would be sufficient to place two warheads on each of the Soviet Union's 1400 silos. . . . this would mean an American ability to destroy 87 percent of the Soviet Union's land-based missile force. . . .

As a result of all this, the pressure on Soviet leaders, in the midst of a major crisis, to preempt rather than lose a counterforce war would probably be immense, especially if Trident II constituted the U.S.'s only significant counterforce system. Additionally, the pressure on U.S. leaders to preempt rather than have the "plug" pulled on their only major counterforce option would also be immense. Under such circumstances it is hard to see how a major crisis could be kept from escalating to war.[83]

This view is not shared by all in the defense and arms control community. Joel S. Wit, a Washington arms control and defense consultant, called Trident "an attractive option" and certainly more attractive than MX or Pershing II because of its invulnerability to a Soviet first strike and long-term survivability in the absence of significant developments in antisubmarine warfare.[84]

In November 1984, the navy stopped buying Trident I as production of the Trident II system began (Figure 5-2). The missile would have an initial operational capability by 1989. Although the program enjoyed widespread support on Capitol Hill as a relatively safe and stable way to buy nuclear weapons, it still had some critics. Representative Les AuCoin (D.-Ore.), a member of the House Defense Appropriations Subcommittee, said, "I'm looking forward with considerable apprehension to the day when both sides have large numbers of heavy accurate SLBMs positioned near the other's borders." Representative Norman Dicks (D.-Wash.) shared this concern: "There are a number of us who are concerned when you look at the mix of Trident IIs and MX's that we will go beyond a theoretical point and possess a first-strike capability against the Soviet systems."[85]

A Congressional Budget Office study said that the administration's goal to have Trident II missiles deployed on all 20 Trident submarines by the year 2000 would result in a force of approximately 4,800 nuclear warheads "with a significant capability to destroy a hardened target." This increase "would represent a fun-

Figure 5-2. Open Hatches on a Trident Submarine Showing Tubes for Trident Missiles

Source: Natural Resources Defense Council, Washington, D.C.

damental shift in U.S. capability, enabling the United States to conduct large-scale attacks on hardened targets in the Soviet Union."[86] And it would raise the cost of the Trident submarine force from $69.8 billion to $85 billion, making it the most expensive program in U.S. defense history.[87] Congress approved the plan anyway by approving funds for acceleration of Trident II deployment.

CONCLUSION

The story of Trident was marked by political controversy from the program's origins to subsequent decisions about procurement, deployment, and modernization. Different institutional and political influences also affected the program in its long gestation and development cycle. The difficulty of identifying a single factor (or set of factors) to "explain" why the system was deployed is readily apparent. An action-reaction model of arms races, though, helps to explain the early origins of Trident. Fears about the Soviet stra-

tegic buildup in the mid-1960s resulted in the STRAT-X study which made the initial case for a follow-up system to the Polaris/Poseidon submarine. Concerns about the eventual aging and obsolescence of the Poseidon/Polaris fleet also played an important role in the search for a successor. However, these assessments did not go unchallenged, and many felt that a new submarine was premature.

However, the ULMS/Trident program had strong advocates in the navy and the Pentagon. Once the bureaucratic machinery to guide the program was set up, the program developed a political momentum of its own, over and above the objections of rival services like the air force.

Leading personalities also played a very important role in the program's design and eventual implementation; it was not simply a case of bureaucratic politics. Vice-Admiral Rickover, in particular, was crucial in deciding the power plant for the submarine, which helped to determine the ship's size and ultimate performance characteristics. Had a less powerful and commanding personality been in charge of the reactor and propulsion branches of the navy, the submarine might have been sized differently and the option of building a smaller sub pursued more vigorously.

Throughout the system's development, from program initiation to deployment, Congress's presence was felt, but perhaps most acutely on key questions of procurement and deployment. The Trident program had its detractors not only in the bureaucracy, but also on Capitol Hill. Congressional enthusiasm for the program prior to 1972 was lukewarm, even in pro-defense constituencies like the Senate Armed Services Committee. Why did Congress eventually vote for procurement and deployment of the system?

The answer lies in a remarkable set of political bargains that were struck within the executive branch and among the President, Congress, and the Pentagon, with the signing of the SALT I arms control agreements. Just prior to the signing of SALT I, President Richard Nixon ordered his Secretary of Defense, Melvin Laird, to accelerate a number of strategic programs, including Trident, and to increase defense spending. Nixon anticipated a tough fight to secure congressional approval of the SALT I treaties and did not want to appear "soft" on defense. He therefore overruled a plan put forward by the Deputy Secretary of Defense which would have effectively put Trident on hold. When the SALT I agreements were submitted to Congress, the Secretary of Defense and the Joint Chiefs

of Staff made their approval conditional on congressional approval of this strategic modernization package, including Trident acceleration. To congressional hardliners, these conditions were not only acceptable, but desirable and necessary. For congressional "doves," it was bitter but necessary medicine which had to be swallowed in order to get a major new arms control agreement. Arms control and the nature of the political bargain struck by Nixon to get the Pentagon and congressional hardliners "on board" in SALT I played a major role in explaining ultimately why Trident was bought.

Had there not been a new arms control treaty in 1972, it is quite likely that Trident procurement would have been delayed or deferred, perhaps indefinitely, and that some other system would have been built as a follow-up to Poseidon/Polaris.

As it was, however, there was no shortage of delays in Trident construction and deployment. Some were the result of contractor difficulties at Electric Boat. Some were the result of improper planning and design, and a set of military requirements that were far from complete when the first contract for the first Trident submarine was signed. Some were also the result of fiscal pressures, particularly during the Carter administration. But Congress's cuts played a role, too.

Under Reagan, the Trident program found a more secure home. Reagan expanded the program and embarked on a costly decision not only to build more ships, but to accelerate production and deployment of the Trident II missile. However, by the time Reagan entered the White House, Trident had gained political acceptance. The decision to proceed with Trident had long since been made by a previous Republican president, and the issue was not what to buy, but how much.

6

□

MX and Midgetman

In December 1986, thirteen years after its inception and with its future still in doubt, the MX missile became operational. Ten new missiles installed in refurbished Minuteman silos went to full alert beneath the plains of Wyoming near Francis E. Warren Air Base.[1] The MX had survived four presidential administrations, thirty different basing modes, legal threats, popular demonstrations, legislative obstacles, and multiple lobbying pressures.[2]

But the program bore little resemblance to an original vision. At one point, MX had been intended to address the increasing vulnerability of the U.S. Minuteman ICBM force. The problem was to develop a basing mode that would render the land-based leg of the U.S. strategic triad less vulnerable to a Soviet preemptive strike. But no solution, particularly one politically acceptable to Congress, could be found. In the end, MX went into Minuteman silos. The vulnerability problem was not solved but the missile was deployed anyway. Why did the system survive? Why was it deployed? Why was "Midgetman," a single-warhead missile, designated MX's successor? These are the questions to be examined in this chapter.

PROGRAM INITIATION AND DEVELOPMENT

The United States Air Force began exploring the concept of an advanced ICBM to replace Minuteman in the late 1960s. Interest was strongest in the Strategic Air Command (SAC), but the Department of Defense saw little need for a new missile since Minuteman had only just been deployed. But the impetus from technological innovation was strong and designers in the weapons

laboratories saw a need to improve and surpass old designs.[3] They began work on a new ICBM that would be more accurate and more powerful than the Minuteman, could carry a larger number of nuclear warheads, and would harness new technologies in guidance and rocket propulsion.[4]

The weapons designers found an enthusiastic customer for their ideas in SAC, which was constantly trying to perfect its mission to destroy Soviet nuclear weapons and missiles in their silos. Work started in the late 1960s on a larger warhead (larger than the Mark 12 carried on Minuteman III) to be carried by a bigger missile. The program was named WS 120.

Secretary of Defense Robert McNamara, however, was not very keen about the program. Ever skeptical of the military's unquenchable thirst for new weapons, he argued that a larger warhead would not be big enough or accurate enough to destroy Soviet ICBMs in hardened silos. He persuaded the air force to adopt MIRV Minuteman (that is, placing several warheads on one Multiple Independently Targetable Reentry Vehicle missile) rather than going for a bigger warhead on a new missile, on the grounds that this would be more cost effective.[5]

Many, including members of Congress, were not pleased about the counterforce, hard-target kill capability implications of the new warhead system. They supported the decision of the Office of the Secretary of Defense (OSD) to stop funding for the WS 120 program.

The air force circumvented this barrier simply by renaming the program WS 120A and research continued on the development of an even larger MIRV warhead system. In 1971, the air force submitted a Required Operational Capability (ROC) request to begin study of a larger, MIRVed missile as an eventual replacement of Minuteman, with 1977 as the anticipated date for deployment. It also sought funding for a land-based deployment mode that would be invulnerable to a Soviet strike.[6] It succeeded in getting funding and approval for both programs.

MX had its official beginnings with the establishment of the U.S. Air Force MX Office at Norton Air Force Base in San Bernadino, California, in June 1973. By late 1973, the air force had already begun to define the specifications for the Missile X.[7]

With the formalization of the MX program in 1973, the air force began to look at different ways of deploying the missile. Of these,

the air-mobile and covered-trench basing modes seemed most promising. Under the air-mobile basing scheme, the missile would be carried by and launched from an aircraft. The covered-trench mode would see the missile placed on a rail car which would move around on a set of tracks in a dug-out trench.[8]

In 1974, the air force successfully launched a Minuteman missile from a C-5A transport plane flying over the Pacific and found that four ICBMs even larger than a Minuteman could be carried in a C-5A jet or jumbo airliner.[9]

Less than a year later, however, the air force rejected the air-launched system as a mid-1980s replacement for Minuteman. The reasons were outlined in the Secretary of Defense's statement to Congress in support of the FY 1976 defense budget request. Schlesinger indicated that the air-mobile version was unacceptable because of cost and accuracy constraints and that DoD was planning an advanced deployment of MX in existing Minuteman silos. "By far the most difficult problem which must be resolved . . . is the selection of the basing mode. Fixed silos may become vulnerable to a Soviet counterforce attack, but they have some very important advantages, namely, accuracy, good two-way communications . . . general responsiveness to control by the National Command Authorities and low operating costs."[10] By 1976, the air force had pretty much decided on the interim solution of basing MX in existing Minuteman silos until a survivable basing mode could be found.

Soviet development in the mid-1970s of a whole generation of new missiles (the SS-16, SS-17, SS-18, and SS-19) prompted the air force to lobby the Office of the Secretary of Defense (OSD), the President, the National Security Council (NSC), and Congress for accelerated development of a follow-up missile to the Minuteman. SAC was not interested in taking the Minuteman missile and making it mobile. Minuteman lacked both the accuracy and explosive power to knock out Soviet missiles.[11] Instead, SAC wanted a new missile that could carry ten warheads or more (compared to Minuteman's three) and would also be more accurate. Defense analysts Holland and Hoover argue:

> The movement of support for MX was stimulated by two developments in the modernization of Soviet strategic forces that significantly bothered many U.S. strategic analysts. U.S. intelligence

concluded in 1974 that the Soviets had made critical strides in reducing the vulnerability of missile targets. This had been achieved by the intensive hardening of potential Soviet target sites such as ICBM silos. A successful destruction of those Soviet targets by U.S. ICBMs necessitated increased hard-target capability. Moreover, Soviet modernization of their strategic forces threatened survivability of U.S. ICBMs.[12]

These developments led in 1973 to a thorough reexamination of U.S. strategic policy—a reexamination that was to have important implications for MX.

The reassessment of U.S. strategic policy was undertaken by direct missive from President Nixon, who indicated that he wanted a broader array of strategic options than suicide or capitulation in the event of nuclear war with the Soviet Union. A reappraisal had actually already begun in the Office of Systems Analysis in DoD in 1971. That project was headed by Dr. John Foster, Director of DDR&E (Directorate of Defense Research and Engineering), who had been appointed chairman of a special committee to evaluate targeting doctrine in the SIOP (single integrated operational plan, the Pentagon's master plan for conducting nuclear war with the Soviet Union) in July 1972. Foster's committee recommended greater "flexibility" in the SIOP, an implicit requirement for more accurate and deadly weapons.[13]

This and other studies eventually culminated in National Security Decision Memorandum 242, issued by President Nixon and then publicly declared by Secretary of Defense James Schlesinger.

NSDM 242 expressed the Nixon administration's formal commitment to develop a more flexible targeting capability. The key elements of the new doctrine were escalation control, war termination, and the maintenance of a secure strategic reserve force. If deterrence failed and led to nuclear conflict, the United States would try to use its nuclear weapons in a way that would limit damage and casualties and hopefully terminate the conflict on terms favorable to the United States.

NSDM 242 also sought to expand the number and scope of options available to the President in a nuclear conflict, including limited nuclear options involving the employment of hundreds of weapons, so that the President could deal with Soviet aggression in a proportional way, rather than being forced into a large-scale

nuclear response. As James Schlesinger explained in his FY 1975 Report to Congress:

> It quickly becomes evident that there are many ways other than a massive surprise attack in which an enemy might be tempted to use, or threaten to use, his strategic forces to gain a major advantage or concession. It follows that our strategic forces and doctrine must take a wide range of possibilities into account if they are to successfully perform their deterrence functions.[14]

The doctrine also included the concept of a *secure reserve force.* "With a reserve capability for threatening urban-industrial targets . . . we could implement response options that cause far less civilian damage than would now be the case."[15] And, if escalation could not be controlled, the United States would target remaining Soviet forces to impede recovery.

Schlesinger, a strong supporter of the MX research and development program, was instrumental in overcoming resistance in OSD to the development of performance criteria for the new ICBM—which OSD had rejected in previous years.[16]

For the FY 1975 defense budget Schlesinger requested $37 million to explore a basing system for the MX. His FY 1976 budget request, by contrast, deemphasized MX development because of President Ford's concerns about a breakthrough in arms control at the Vladivostok talks. But by the summer, there was growing support for MX in the air force and among conservatives in the Senate, reflected in a direct appeal by a number of senators to the administration to deploy MX on an interim basis in Minuteman silos. President Ford asked Congress for $294 million for FY 1977 to support continued engineering for MX and further research on development of mobile-deceptive basing modes. Outgoing Secretary of Defense Donald Rumsfeld (who had recently replaced Schlesinger) subsequently proposed $1.5 billion in authorization for MX in the FY 1978 budget.

Rumsfeld's decision to accelerate the program was the outcome of a number of critical decisions that had been taken within DoD. In March 1976, the air force presented a series of alternative proposals for a new ICBM to the Defense Systems Acquisition Review Council (DSARC) designed to address growing concern about Soviet strategic capabilities and ICBM vulnerability. "The options

ranged from the Pave Pepper Program (increasing the warheads on Minuteman II from three to seven) and the MX missile in one of two sizes, either an eighty-three-inch [diameter] or a ninety-two-inch ICBM, to basing mode alternatives of superhardening Minuteman silos and various mobile-deceptive basing schemes. The DSARC recommended to the DDR&E that the larger MX design be readied for final engineering, construction, and deployment and that three basing alternatives for MX be further explored with the possibility of interim deployment of MX in Minuteman silos." [17] The recommendations were accepted by the new DDR&E head Malcolm Currie, who forwarded them to Rumsfeld for approval.

The air force's interest in the mobile basing scheme, however, clashed with U.S. arms control policies during the ongoing SALT negotiations following the Vladivostok talks. U.S. arms control negotiators were opposed to any sort of mobile basing schemes because mobile missiles would be difficult to find and count, even with advanced satellites and reconnaissance techniques, which would make it difficult to verify an arms control agreement.

Although the United States was unable to get the Soviets to agree to a ban on mobile basing schemes in SALT I, the United States issued a unilateral declaration of opposition to mobile basing in the SALT I Interim Agreement on Offensive Weapons. In the SALT II negotiations, the United States continued with its opposition to mobile basing, even though the Pentagon continued to explore actively trench and air-mobile basing systems for MX.

Both Schlesinger and Rumsfeld lobbied President Ford to reverse the United States' opposition to mobile basing, over the objections of Secretary of State Henry Kissinger, on the grounds that MX was a useful bargaining chip and a hedge against the impending vulnerability of the U.S. ICBM force to Soviet missiles. [18]

Congress exercised an important influence over the early development of MX. It forced the air force to abandon its immediate plans to retrofit Minuteman silos with MX missiles by vetoing authorization funds for research and development on silo basing in 1976. The move was spearheaded by Senator Thomas McIntyre (D.-N.H.), Chairman of the Research Subcommittee of the Senate Armed Services Committee, over the vigorous objections of his more hawkish colleagues like Senators Henry Jackson (D.-Wash.) and John Tower (R.-Tex.). McIntyre believed that MX should not be deployed unless a survivable basing mode could be found. His

views prevailed and the air force was sent back to the drawing board. "This action, in combination with the need for a MX basing mode compatible with the verification stricture of the SALT regime, led the Department of Defense on a path that eventually produced the MX in a multiple protective shelter mode (MX MPS)."[19]

CARTER AND THE MX BASING PROBLEM

Jimmy Carter was elected to the presidency in 1976. He was not a great fan of MX and saw it as little more than a bargaining chip in arms control with the Soviets. Vice-President Walter Mondale and Deputy National Security Assistant David Aaron were also skeptical of MX. Secretary of Defense Harold Brown and the new head of DDR&E, William Perry, were likewise suspicious of the need for MX. The Carter team's reservations about the new missile went right to the core of its strategic rationale, namely, the missile's hard-target, silo-busting capabilities. If MX could attack and destroy Soviet missiles in their silos, the Soviets might be tempted to launch their own missiles first in a crisis because of fears of losing them.

These concerns prompted Carter to postpone previous Secretary of Defense Donald Rumsfeld's request to put $294 million in the FY 1978 military budget to move MX into full-scale development, including testing. Carter also decided to cut the missile's budget by more than half for FY 1978.[20]

Carter then ordered a full-scale reevaluation of MX and a review of all of the studies conducted by the Ford administration on the missile. Presidential Science Adviser Frank Press directed the review, which was spearheaded by the Office of Science and Technology. Secretary Brown also assigned his own Defense Science Board to study the problem. In anticipation of a potential challenge to the program, the Air Force Systems Command undertook its own evaluation of the MX program.

In a news conference on April 1, 1977, after the Soviets rebuffed initial U.S. arms proposals, President Carter threatened to accelerate the development and production of the MX missile.[21] But it was more of a bluff than a serious threat because the administration had still not made up its mind about the missile.

On October 3, 1977, there were press leaks that Brown had

tentatively requested $245 million to put MX into full-scale development. It seemed that Brown had changed his mind. News of Brown's "decision" sent shock waves through Capitol Hill and a sharp rebuff from Senator Thomas McIntyre, who complained bitterly that DoD had not even completed the study of the weapon that Congress had ordered the previous year. Brown decided to go public by defending the program to reporters accompanying him on a trip on the U.S.S. *Saratoga*, seventy miles off the coast of Naples.[22] He was reprimanded for his indiscretion by the White House. Carter decided to turn down the Pentagon's request for full-scale funding, much to the embarrassment of his Secretary of Defense. The National Security Council advised the President against full-scale development on grounds that doing so could have an adverse affect on the SALT II negotiations. The Office of Management and Budget also favored delaying the missile until research on a basing mode was further along and proposed cutting the FY 1980 air force request of $580 million for MX in half. The General Accounting Office urged delay for similar reasons.[23]

In November 1977 the air force and DoD officially abandoned the trench concept as a basing option.[24] In closed-session testimony before the Senate Armed Services Committee, William Perry said the scheme is "no longer viable." Lieutenant General Alton D. Slay, Commander of the Air Force Systems Command, expressed similar reservations: "I think that since we are talking of a program that could exceed $25 billion, including operational and support costs for 10 years, we ought to make very, very sure we know what we are doing on the basing mode."[25] The Senate Armed Services Committee unanimously recommended $158.2 million for ongoing program development, but not for production.

The idea that gained the most interest was a vertical-silo Multiple Aim Point (MAP) proposal of the Defense Science Board panel, calling for the construction of some 4,000 empty concrete launching silos, between which 200 MXs would be moved in a random fashion by truck. In Pentagon jargon this was known as the "shell game." It was an idea that was to acquire growing appeal, particularly in the face of new fears about the Soviet missile threat.

In October 1977 the Soviets conducted a successful test of their giant SS-19 intercontinental ballistic missile with MIRVed warheads from the Turatam rocket base in the southwestern Soviet Union. Over the next several weeks, the Central Intelligence Agency

(CIA) and the Defense Intelligence Agency (DIA) poured over their monitored data of the test results. In December, the results were delivered in a secret memo to CIA Director Admiral Stansfield Turner and Secretary Brown. The memo informed them that the Soviet Strategic Rocket Corps had made a dramatic breakthrough in upgrading the accuracy of its missiles and now had the capability to bring warheads within a few hundred yards of their targets, including the 1,054 U.S. Minutemen in their silos.[26] As *New York Times* correspondent Richard Burt reported:

> This finding abruptly ended a drawn-out and divisive debate in intelligence circles over when, if ever, Moscow would have the capacity to launch a "first-strike" attack against the American land-based nuclear deterrent ... Mr. Carter's national-security aides acknowledge that this could happen as early as 1981, when the Soviet Union should have completed deploying some 500 SS-19 missiles and about 300 SS-18s (an even bigger ICBM that is equipped with 10 warheads).[27]

Proponents of MX in the administration "argued persuasively that the improved Soviet accuracy accelerated the ICBM vulnerability problem for the United States. Even for skeptics like William Perry, Under Secretary for DDR&E, the evidence suggested that the vulnerability problem was very real and did not lie the decade away that some had thought. "MX provided the potential means to cope with growing Soviet strategic capabilities and the menacing war-fighting doctrine ascribed to the Soviets by many U.S. analysts."[28]

The vertical-shelter MAP mode was reviewed at Norton Air Force Base and then presented to a DSARC meeting in April 1978, but it had some problems: it would take almost twenty-four hours to move a missile into another silo if the position in one silo was in any way compromised, and silos were categorized as launchers under SALT regardless of whether there was a missile in one or not. The 4,500 silos required for the basing system would also violate SALT counting rules for missiles.

MAP was heavily criticized by an independent group of scientists working under the auspices of the Program in Science and Technology at the Massachusetts Institute for Technology. These scientists (M. Callaham, B. T. Feld, E. Hadjimichael, and K. M Tsi-

pis) argued that, in any such system, because "the aim points are far apart, an opponent would be able to attack them simultaneously with relatively inaccurate warheads, without the impediment of fratricide [in which the detonation of one incoming missile would destroy another]." They also cited the obvious security problems of trucks roaming around the American countryside.[29]

In August 1978 there was a critical meeting between President Carter and his advisers at Camp David, the presidential retreat in Maryland, concerning MX. Secretary Brown wanted the meeting because of fears about growing Soviet missile accuracies. Other officials believed that the missile was necessary to get Congress to support the new SALT II Treaty. Brown indicated his support for the vertical-silo MAP alternative, but others expressed concern about potential verification problems with MAP and the dangers of keeping the location of the missiles a secret. The MAP scheme was rejected as being unacceptable.[30]

The State Department and officials in the United States Arms Control and Disarmament Agency (ACDA) favored development of a smaller, eighty-two-inch-diameter missile which would work on a fast-track racetrack. National Security Adviser Zbigniew Brzezinski and top SAC officials, however, favored a heavier missile (ninety-three inches in diameter), particularly if the United States was unsuccessful in negotiating MIRV limits with Soviets in SALT. The heavier missile would be able to carry more than ten warheads.[31]

In December 1978 the air force submitted a second evaluation to a new DSARC meeting. Once again, it indicated its preference for a ninety-two-inch missile in a vertical-silo MAP system. The proposal was accompanied by a five-volume Environmental Impact Statement for MX, Milestone II. The administration approved engineering development, construction, and deployment of MX in response to the positive recommendation of DSARC, but deferred the question of missile size and deployment mode.

MAP, however, quickly proved itself to be a public relations disaster. The designation of "multiple aim points" was dropped when Congress recognized that the scheme was intended to provide thousands of different targets or "aim points" for Soviet bombs. People were scared out of their wits by air force officer briefings that the system was intended to serve as a "sponge" for "soaking up" enemy warheads.[32]

The air force was subsequently directed to consider the possibility of an air-mobile basing system—an idea previously rejected. A supplemental Milestone II on air-mobile basing was completed in March 1979. The administration requested supplemental authorization for full-scale engineering of MX following the December DSARC meeting.

In May 1979 a Presidential Review Committee (intra-governmental committee to review national security policy) submitted five options for dealing with the ICBM vulnerability problem. "The options were: (1) to go to sea with a new, more accurate SLBM known as Trident II, or the D-5 SLBM program (which was to be supplemented by deployment of a large number of cruise missiles on B-52s); (2) the MX MPS missile option; (3) the MX land-mobile system of truck launchers on the nation's interstate highway system; (4) an air-mobile system; and (5) an option that accepted the present strategic situation."[33]

At a June 1979 NSC meeting, the administration decided to deploy the system in a mobile basing scheme to begin in 1983, with specifics of the system to be worked out in the fall of 1979. "This decision was linked both in time and in concept to the Administration's initialing of the SALT II Treaty later in that month. Although the decision was opposed by [CIA Director Admiral Stansfield] Turner, former opponents such as Vice President Mondale and Secretary of State Vance were apparently supportive given the linkage of MX to SALT II. At this time Carter apparently accepted Brzezinski's argument for a ninety-three-inch missile. This decision to engineer and to deploy MX was linked to the need to build the support of the JCS, the air force, and later members of the Senate for the SALT II Treaty."[34]

The SALT II Treaty also addressed the numbers problem of silos and shelters. It specified limits on MIRVed ICBM warheads and restrictions on launcher ceilings and RV warheads, thereby dealing with the problem of saturation attack on a MAP or MPS system of 4,600 shelters or silos. This would freeze the strategic situation to the satisfaction of some congressional critics.

CONGRESS

In the Senate Armed Services Committee, Senators Jackson (D.-Wash.), Tower (R.-Tex.), Jake Garn (R.-Utah), and Barry Goldwa-

ter (R.-Ariz.) were the champions of the new ninety-three-inch MX missile. They urged rapid deployment of the missile in Minuteman silos as an interim solution until a long-term basing solution was worked out. Garn thought the vertical-silo MAP was the best solution for the long term, that it would offer a better opportunity for hardening than horizontal shelters. Senator McIntyre of the R&D subcommittee favored a smaller missile in a mobile basing scheme. Senator John Culver (D.-Iowa), who replaced McIntyre in 1978 as head of the subcommittee after McIntyre's electoral defeat, shared McIntyre's views. Senator John Stennis (D.-Miss.), Chairman of the Armed Services Committee, also supported MX but did not want to tie the administration's hands to any particular basing scheme.

Congressional interest in the MX in the 1977–1979 period was largely confined to the armed services committees. There was little support for or opposition to MX on the floor of either House.

On May 3, 1979, the Senate approved 79–12 a Defense Supplemental Authorization Bill for MX, with some senators expressing their support for multiple protective shelter basing. The Senate also recommended $75 million to study the air-mobile basing mode to mollify arms control advocates.

> A pro-MX coalition in the House, with important prodding and information from members in the Pentagon, gave Carter a more direct message and erased any doubts about that chamber's position on MX deployment. ... First, the House defeated (100 to 291) an amendment attempt by Berkeley Bedell to reverse the legislative bias toward MPS basing. ... Then members deleted the funds for the air-mobile version. As passed out of conference ... the final bill contained several fairly explicit directives to the Carter Administration. All of these elements were the result of compromises forged *in advance* by the air force and a few critical members of Congress ... and mandated that the air force proceed "immediately" with "full-scale engineering development" of MX in the MPS mode unless the Secretary of Defense himself certified that another system was superior.[35]

Supporting the coalition for modernization were National Security Adviser Brzezinski, Majority Leader Robert Byrd (D.-W.Va.), Minority Leader Howard Baker (R.-Tenn.), and key members of the Senate Armed Services Committee, including Sam Nunn. Op-

posing it were Secretary of State Cyrus Vance, the State Department, and ACDA, who urged a more cautious approach toward the Soviets.[36]

In the middle of this brewing storm over MX stood the President. Jimmy Carter had never liked the missile but he found himself under strong attack on defense because of his handling of the B-1 bomber (which he had canceled) and the neutron bomb (where he reversed himself on an earlier decision to cancel the program). He was under mounting pressure from Congress to increase defense spending and to continue with ICBM modernization. This pressure became particularly acute after the Soviet invasion of Afghanistan and the Iranian hostage crisis.

Carter felt it necessary to give his firm support to MX after signing the SALT II Treaty with the Soviets in Vienna in July 1979 and hoped that this would strengthen the support for SALT among congressional hardliners and symbolize his commitment to stand tall to the Soviets.[37] The MPS basing was essentially proposed to bring the services and hawks on board. JCS Chairman David C. Jones announced that he would have "deep reservations" about supporting SALT without mobile MX MPS.[38]

Executive branch representatives in congressional hearings on the SALT II Treaty pointed out that without limits on Soviet warheads, MX MPS would enter service in 1986 already behind the Soviets in the race between shelters and warheads, which was the system's rationale.[39] But there was some concern whether the Treaty itself might impose a ban on deliberate concealment measures and construction of new ICBM launchers which would allow the United States to construct the multiple launch point "shell game." The Foreign Relations Committee was not satisfied with the administration's assurances that MX MPS could be deployed under SALT II and added an understanding to the ratification document that declared U.S. intent to deploy a verifiable MX system.[40]

Many liberals were opposed to MX MPS because of its first-strike capability and its potentially destabilizing effects on deterrence. They also expressed their displeasure with the Carter administration's commitment to increased defense spending.[41] "But Carter reasoned that the aversion of liberals to MX and MPS basing would not cause them to imperil the success of an agreement whose consequences for arms control were significant. SALT was used to jus-

tify MPS basing to anti-MX groups; MX MPS was used to woo conservatives, moderates, and anti-SALT individuals to support the arms control treaty."[42]

On Friday, September 7, 1979, Carter announced that the $33 billion racetrack was the preferred basing system. A supplemental $2.2 billion request budget in November included $200 million in funding for full-scale development of MX. (The submission was made necessary by Carter's decision in August to veto the Defense Authorization Bill for FY 1979 because it included unwanted money for a new nuclear aircraft carrier.[43])

The basic plan called for building 200 road loops, each 15 to 20 miles long, in the deserts of Nevada and Utah. In each loop there would be one missile aboard a mobile launching vehicle (called a transporter-erector-launcher, or TEL). A motorized shed on wheels would surround the TEL and accompany it whenever it moved along the loop. The shed would be used to hide the missile's true location from the Soviets. Around each loop, at 7,000-foot intervals, would be 23 underground garages made of thick concrete to resist the blast of incoming missiles. The TEL would hide the missile in any one of the garages and periodically move it to a new site unbeknownst to the Soviets. Once every six months or so, slats in the roofs of the shed would be opened to reveal that there was, in fact, only one missile in each shed, in order to comply with arms control agreements with the Soviets (see Figure 6-1).

The scheme encountered heavy opposition almost as soon as it was announced. Defense scientists Sidney Drell, Director of the Stanford Linear Accelerator, and Richard Garwin of IBM argued that the racetrack would be just as vulnerable as Minuteman during the early part of its construction, because the Soviets would have enough warheads to aim two at each missile garage. Only when construction was complete would the Soviets be presented with targeting problems, but by then the SALT II Treaty (due to expire in 1985) would no longer be in effect and the Soviets would be free to place more warheads on their missiles and/or build more missiles to target the whole system.[44]

A study by the Congressional Budget Office (CBO) for the Senate Committee on the Budget arrived at similar conclusions. It pointed out that the costs of an MPS basing system would be sensitive to the number of Soviet warheads available to attack it, and that "[o]ne Soviet response would be to increase the number of

nuclear warheads available to attack an MPS basing complex." The study concluded that "[t]he survivability and costs of an MPS basing system would be substantially more certain if there were permanent, verifiable limits on ICBM forces."[45]

Paul Nitze, then head of the Committee on Present Danger and a former member of the SALT I negotiating team, said the dragstrip system would be clumsy and conceptually inelegant. He recommended instead that the United States build hundreds of new silos in the far West and then move the missiles secretly from one silo to another in a different kind of "shell game." Others said that the best solution was to put the MX missiles into existing Minuteman silos and then build an antiballistic missile system, contrary to the provisions in the SALT I Treaty, to defend the missile fields.[46]

The key blow to MX MPS, however, was Carter's withdrawal of the SALT II Treaty from Senate consideration in January 1980 following the Soviet invasion of Afghanistan. Without SALT, the strategic viability of MX MPS was uncertain because there was no theoretical constraint on land-based missiles and warheads deployed on them. The Soviets might therefore be able to overwhelm the MX MPS system by deploying more missiles and/or warheads.

The unease of liberals, who were not happy about the missile from the start, grew after the withdrawal of the SALT agreement for Senate approval.

The MX MPS coalition also began to erode as congressional delegates from states where MX would be deployed began to feel heat from their constituents. These congressmen were worried because Michigan and Wisconsin residents had blocked construction of the Trident ELF (extra-low-frequency) communications system in their states some years earlier.

The Governor of Kansas wrote to the President expressing his concerns:

> [T]he U.S. Air Force is proposing that potentially 8 percent of the entire state of Kansas be removed from civilisation ... I find this proposal unbelievable and inconceivable. I urge you and the Air Force to immediately suspend any further consideration of sites in the State of Kansas for the mobile missile program.[47]

Representatives from Nebraska and other midwestern plains states were also upset that Milestone II identified the South Platte plains

Figure 6-1. MX MPS Basing

Launcher

Missile Launch Sequence

AFT Equipment Module

Cannister

Forward Equipment Module

Launcher Characteristics

Length	155 Feet
Diameter	110 Inches
Weight	500,000 Pounds

Closure opened.

Launcher emerged and erected to launch position.

Source: Office of Technology Assessment, *MX Missile Basing* (Washington, D.C.: U.S. Government Printing Office, September 1981), pp. 46–47.

as geotechnically suitable for MX deployment. In response to pressures from their constituents, they drafted an amendment to the FY 1979 DoD Supplemental Authorization Bill that effectively eliminated the region from consideration. "The sense of the Congress is that the basing mode for the MX missile should be restricted to location on the least productive land that is available for such purpose."[48] This increased the likelihood that Nevada and Utah would be chosen for the site.

The governors of Utah and Nevada at first expressed their unequivocal support for MX with an obvious eye to the economic growth that would come with the program. Defense contractors from their states also lobbied hard for the system. "The MX system promised to give a boost to the marginal economies in the Great

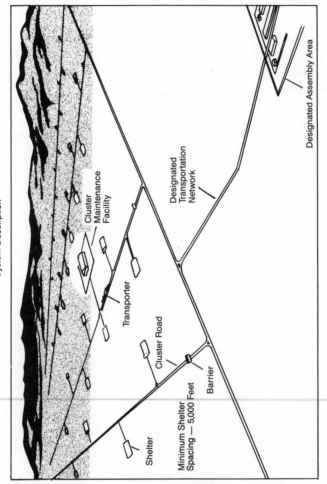

Cluster
Maintenance
Facility

Transporter

Cluster Road

Shelter

Minimum Shelter
Spacing — 5,000 Feet

Barrier

Designated
Transportation
Network

Designated Assembly Area

Basin area, and residents in both Nevada and Utah have a long tradition of support for the Pentagon. In this respect, Senators Orrin Hatch (R.-Utah), Jake Garn (R.-Utah), Howard Cannon (D.-Nev.), and Paul Laxalt (R.-Nev.), and Representatives Dan Marriott (R.-Utah) and Gunn McKay (D.-Utah), had served their constituents well. They were strategically placed on committees that allowed them to exercise considerable influence on the MX debate. Garn and Cannon were members of the Senate Armed Services Committee, and Laxalt and McKay were ranking members of the military construction subcommittee, Appropriations Committee of the Senate and House respectively." [49]

The only opponent was Representative James Santini (D.-Nev.), who was uneasy about the environmental, socioeconomic, and cultural implications of MPS. The air force's environmental impact statement had showed that natural resources would be depleted, wildlife harmed, and people displaced by the system.

He attached an amendment to the 1980 Defense Fiscal Authorization Bill that would prevent more than 25 percent of shelters for MPS being placed in any one state. (Santini could not attack MX itself because he was pro-defense and from a pro-defense state, but had to do something to mitigate its impact on Nevada). The amendment was defeated 84 to 289. The liberals wanted to attack the system itself; some conservatives favored the system, but many just did not care. However, Santini did get the House Interior and Insular Affairs Committee to authorize the Office of Technological Assessment (OTA) and the Congressional Research Service to assess the adequacy of the environmental impact studies conducted by the air force on the program. His action effectively prevented approval of fast-track legislation for MX introduced by the air force in 1979.

In the 1980 election year, opposition to MX began to mount, especially with the demise of SALT II. The House Budget Committee in its report on the Defense Budget Resolution for 1981 expressed reservations about MX. The Pentagon responded by announcing modifications to the racetrack scheme that would reduce costs and environmental impacts.

The air force's environmental meetings with local residents in January 1980 in Nevada and Utah met with critical public reaction. There were also signs of growing apprehension over the racetrack system among state and local politicians. [50]

In April, appearing before the House Appropriations Subcommittee on Military Construction, Utah's Democratic Governor Scott Matheson and Nevada's Republican Governor Robert List reversed themselves and attacked the MPS plan on the grounds that it would do irreparable harm to their states and damage the fragile ecosystem of the area. According to Matheson, the invasion of construction crews would also change forever "the chosen way of life" of the people in the region's rural communities.[51]

In March, the air force indicated that it had reversed its support for the vertical basing mode and endorsed the horizontal mode as having greater mobility and verifiability. Air Force Chief of Staff General Lew Allen, Jr., informed Congress that "the additional confidence offered by the horizontal version of MPS approved by the President is well worth the additional cost."[52]

The Committee on the Present Danger, in its 1980 report, emphasized the need to "proceed urgently with the MX and Trident programs. To cover the period of danger before MX is available in useful numbers in 1989, Minuteman III should be redeployed in the most effective and timely way; that is, in the multiple vertical protective shelter system."[53]

MX was also the heated subject of debate in the 1980 presidential campaign. At the Democratic convention one delegate tried to delete language supporting the missile from the Democratic platform. This was followed by a bitter fight in which Secretary Brown lobbied delegates on the floor and President Carter sent them handwritten notes. Ronald Reagan in a September television debate with candidate John Anderson stated, "I am not in favor of the plan that is so costly . . . and will take thousands of square miles out of the West." He had earlier said that the plan "should be scrapped because it is unworkable."[54]

MX MPS also began to take the heat from some of its former supporters, such as John Stennis, Orrin Hatch, Jake Garn, Howard Cannon, and Paul Laxalt. They told Carter that the racetrack would not work without arms control and good cooperation with the Soviets. They emphasized the need for a quicker and cheaper basing mode than racetrack. Cannon introduced an amendment to limit the initial phase of construction of MX MPS in Utah and Nevada to 50 percent until a feasibility study was conducted on how to house the remaining 50 percent of the system.

The 1981 Weapons Authorization Bill was $5.9 billion fatter

than Carter had requested, but the bill for MX research was $1.4 billion, or $60 million less than what Carter wanted. The Military Construction Bill of 1981 would not allow appropriations "until terms, conditions, and requirements of the National Environmental Policy Act (42 U.S.C. 4332) are met, which will include a complete analysis of a split-basing alternative."[55]

What role did changes in strategic doctrine play in the Carter administration's policies on MX? In 1980 Carter signed Presidential Directive 59. PD-59 had begun with PD-18 in which Carter essentially endorsed retention of NSDM 242 and directed that three further major studies be undertaken: a Nuclear Targeting Policy Review (NTPR), a modernization of the ICBM force, and a strategic reserve force study. NTPR was headed by Leon Sloss in the Pentagon. There were numerous supporting studies including an extensive survey of Soviet doctrine and plans. Policymakers shared the conclusion that Soviets sought to win in a nuclear war. They believed that the Soviets expected a nuclear war to be short and decisive, although Soviet writings did not deny the possibility that the conflict might be prolonged.

NTPR concluded that the U.S. command, control, and communications system needed improvement and that U.S. strategic forces should be more robust than they were. The report also suggested that more options be added to the SIOP to give U.S. strategic forces more flexibility and "that relatively less emphasis be accorded to the destruction of the Soviet economic and industrial base and that greater attention 'be directed toward improving the effectiveness of our attacks against military targets.' "[56] NPTR served as the basis for PD-59, drafted in early 1979 and formally signed by the President on July 25, 1980. PD-59 focused greater attention on destroying Soviet general-purpose forces and Soviet command structure and authorized Secretary Brown to issue a New Weapons Employment Policy (NUWEP 2), which gave priority to targeting Soviet military capabilities, including nuclear and conventional forces. MX was clearly necessary to support the new, refined strategic orientation.

Defense Secretary Brown stressed that the new "countervailing strategy" was intended to deny to the Soviets their principal strategic objectives. He nevertheless emphasized that PD-59 was "not a new strategic doctrine ... [but] a refinement, a codification of previous statements of our strategic policy."[57] It did not require

superiority in nuclear forces but "essential equivalence." If MX was central to this policy, then the administration had come up short by failing to win congressional approval for deployment of MX in the multiple protective shelter basing mode.

REAGAN AND MX

Reagan was elected to office having discredited the MX MPS plan in the election campaign, but committed to developing an extended war-fighting strategic capability.

On March 16, 1981, Secretary of Defense Caspar Weinberger announced the formation of a committee of leading defense scientists and senior retired military officers to be headed by California physicist and Nobel Laureate Charles Townes. The Townes group was asked to solve the basing problem by reviewing all data assembled by the Pentagon over the previous eleven years.

The mountain states were now pretty much opposed to MX MPS. Senator Laxalt, Reagan's campaign chairman, was now opposed to MX MPS. In May 1981, the Mormon Church came out against MX MPS. Other hawks had come out against the system. Arms controllers did not like MX much anyway, and there was growing suspicion generally about its military and economic implications.

Ralph Regula (D.-Ohio) and Bo Ginn (D.-Ga.) on the House Appropriations Committee were annoyed that the air force was still spending money on MX, despite a 1981 mandate in the Defense Appropriations Bill barring design funds from being spent until a basing mode decision was made. The House Appropriations Committee passed an amendment by Regula and Ginn ordering the Pentagon to stop work on MX until such a decision was made.

The Senate Appropriations Committee retained provision of the House bill and voted to delete an additional $4 million from MX planning funds and to approve $36.2 million for development of an ABM LoAD (Low-Altitude Defense) for MX.

The 1982 Defense Fiscal Authorization Bill, however, contained the first major financial commitment to construction of the MPS basing mode. If approved, the program would move out of R&D and construction would begin by 1984, with the aim of completing the system by 1989.

Defense critic Ron Dellums (D.-Cal.) tried to get the House to

kill the program outright, but his amendment was defeated 96 to 316.[58] In the Senate, Harrison "Jack" Schmitt (R.-N.M.) and William Roth (R.-Del.) tried to get the President to deploy the system on an interim basis in fixed silos and to defend it with an ABM system. Garn and Laxalt felt the move was premature. Senator Carl Levin (D.-Mich.) and Representative Paul Simon (D.-Ill.) tried to get amendments that would require congressional approval of an MX basing mode in advance of any appropriations for the system. Levin's bill passed 59 to 39, but Simon's lost by 201 to 205.[59]

On June 4, 1981, the House passed a bill introduced by Representative Dan Marriott to withhold funding for MX until the Defense Secretary submitted to Congress a plan to minimize the economic, social, and cultural impact of the weapons system on the states and communities affected by its deployment.[60] This reflected Congress's changing attitude toward MX, but it is important to note that the amendment was not an attack on the fundamental merits of the system itself.

In July 1981 the Townes commission delivered its report to the President. Although its contents were never made public, on October 2, 1981, President Reagan proposed to deploy temporarily 100 MX missiles in heavily armored underground silos until a decision for a permanent basing mode could be made. He suggested three alternatives for the long term: (1) put the missiles on planes; (2) place them in deep underground launchers; or (3) rebuild an antiballistic missile defense system to protect the missiles in ordinary silos.[61]

The interim arrangement would have a minimal impact on Utah and Nevada and was applauded by governors and senators from the two states.[62] Of the long-term solutions, Secretary Weinberger apparently favored the idea of an air-launched MX. On October 2 he told reporters, "I'm very hopeful that the continuous airborne patrol research will show that it is feasible."[63] This reportedly had been one of the preferred options in the Townes report. The idea called for the missile to be put in randomly flying aircraft constructed largely of plastic reinforced with carbon fibers to make the plane extra light. The plane would stay aloft for several days while carrying one or two missiles with up to ten warheads apiece.[64]

Reagan's interim solution and airborne plan for the missile were opposed by John Tower, other conservative senators, and the air force, which favored MPS.[65] "The proposal for the MX missiles

won't be rubberstamped," predicted Henry Jackson, second-ranking member of the Senate Armed Services Committee. Senator Goldwater told Caspar Weinberger, "Forget the air-launched missile, please. It is dead." The military had only learned of the plan just before the President's speech. The Joint Conference on the Defense Authorization Bill in November directed that some $25 million be used to study a smaller version of the MPS shuttle system, and eliminated research funds for the airborne scheme.

In September 1981, Congress's Office of Technology Assessment (OTA) issued its own report on MX basing. The report examined five possibilities: (1) MPS basing in several variants; (2) antiballistic missile defense of MPS basing; (3) launch under attack; (4) basing on small submarines; and (5) basing on large aircraft. It concluded that "no basing mode is likely to provide a substantial number of survivable MX missiles before the end of this decade." MPS survivability would depend on "preservation of locational uncertainty," that is, "preventing the Soviets from determining which shelters hold the actual missiles." A system of 200 MX missiles and 4,600 shelters "would not be large enough if the Soviets chose to continue to increase their inventory of warheads." MPS "would severely impact the socioeconomic and physical characteristics of the deployment region" because of very rapid population growth in rural communities associated with project construction and the large area covered by the system.[66]

During the October–November 1981 hearings before Senator John Warner's (R.-Va.) subcommittee on strategic warfare, JCS Chairman General David Jones said that he personally preferred President Carter's "shell-game" plan to deploying MX in super-hardened silos, but also said he would support the President's decision not to adopt the plan.[67] The Pentagon was not prepared to defend the interim silo basing plan.

On October 28, 1981, the Defense Appropriations Subcommittee gave a flat thumbs down to further funding for MX.[68] But in the FY 1982 Defense Appropriations Bill, Congress did not kill the system. Instead it approved the Nunn-Cohen amendment prohibiting the use of more than 5 percent of MX R&D funds for development of super-hardening silos and mandating that the administration adopt a permanent basing mode by July 1, 1983, rather than 1984 as planned.[69]

On November 6, 1981, the Senate in a voice vote on the De-

fense Authorization Bill voted to delay appropriations of $300 million for basing the MX.[70] Secretary Weinberger and other senior OMB officials indicated that they would not be upset if Congress voted down the plan to base MX in hardened silos.[71] It seemed a forgone conclusion when, in May 1982, the Senate voted to cancel MX R&D funds for interim silo basing. On July 19, two days before the House was to vote on the same issue, Reagan abandoned the interim silo basing plan and announced he would adopt a permanent mode by December 1, 1982. The House then narrowly approved production of the first nine MX missiles 212 to 209, but fenced in the funds.

The Defense Fiscal Authorization Bill was approved on September 8, 1982, with 90 percent of MX basing procurement funds sequestered until thirty days after Congress was informed of the President's decision and a permanent basing mode was accepted.

During the summer, Weinberger and the Pentagon had searched for new basing ideas. They came up with close-spaced basing, or "dense pack." The idea, originally proposed in the 1970s by a young air force officer, worked on the so-called fratricide concept. The missiles would be arrayed in a small area so that radiation, blast waves, and debris generated by initial detonations overhead would destroy or deflect other incoming warheads, unless the explosions were timed with nearly impossible precision. The ability of MX to withstand the attack would be enhanced by the construction of super-hardened concrete silos. Surviving MX missiles would be launched through the debris in a retaliatory attack. The technical case was hampered by provisions in the 1963 Partial Test Ban Treaty prohibiting atmospheric tests. Without conclusive evidence, it was difficult to prove the system would work and skeptics argued that warheads with earth penetrators would minimize the effect of fratricide and that they could be timed to detonate on cue.

On November 22, 1982, Reagan recommended deployment of MX in a dense-pack scheme in southeastern Wyoming. Anticipating the announcement, Senator Ernest Hollings (D.-S.C.) said he would lead opposition to the plan in the Senate while Congressman Joseph Addabbo (D.-N.Y.) said he would do the same in the House. Senator Gary Hart (D.-Colo.) and thirty-seven other members of the Senate signed a statement in October opposing closely spaced basing.[72]

But "Reagan tied MX to arms control, a tactic intentionally gauged to defuse the growing sentiment for a nuclear freeze ... [and] during the 97th Congress, U.S. arms control policy and the nuclear freeze were two of the most important issues on the legislative agenda.... The fear of nuclear war and the belief that such a war was becoming more likely fueled the dramatic growth of grassroots movements."[73]

Senators Edward Kennedy (D.-Mass.), Mark Hatfield (R.-Ore.), and Alan Cranston (D.-Cal.) denounced the President's speech and the need for "Peacekeeper"—Reagan's new name for MX. On March 10, 1982, Kennedy and Hatfield had introduced a Joint Resolution on Nuclear Weapons Freeze and Reductions (Senate Joint Resolution 163) urging that "as an immediate arms control objective, the United States and the Soviet Union should: pursue a complete halt to the nuclear arms race; decide when and how to achieve a mutual and verifiable freeze on the testing, production, and further deployment of nuclear warheads, missiles, and delivery systems; and give special attention to destabilizing weapons whose deployment would make such a freeze more difficult to achieve." It was followed by the Jackson/Warner Resolution (Senate Joint Resolution 177) of March 30, 1982, proposing a "long-term, mutual and verifiable nuclear forces freeze at equal and sharply reduced levels of forces." The first Freeze Resolution in the House of Representatives (House Joint Resolution 521) was defeated 204–202 on August 5, 1982, but a Joint Resolution for a Mutual and Verifiable Freeze on and Reductions in Nuclear Weapons (House Joint Resolution 13) passed on May 4, 1983.

The House voted to tie up MX funds pending approval of the dense-pack scheme by Congress. It quickly became apparent that nobody liked the idea. It was theoretically troublesome and the problem was compounded by the lame-duck atmosphere in Congress owing to the 1982 congressional elections. Representative Jack Edwards (R.-Ala.) told Under Secretary for Research and Engineering Richard DeLauer: "I am supposed to be one of the hawks on the [Appropriations] Committee, I guess, but I swear the more I sit up here and listen to this, the more I wonder what in the world we are up to.... This whole world has got to be foolish.... This sounds like Dense Pacman."[74]

The JCS split on support of dense pack. The army worried about the theory behind the fratricide concept, and the navy worried

about the theory of hardened silos. However, Congress did not kill the system outright. "On December 7 the House voted to accept an amendment by Addabbo . . . to deny procurement funds for the MX missile while retaining R&D monies. . . . However, to gain even that legislative concession the White House had engaged in a vigorous lobbying campaign that included intercontinental telephone calls to Congress from the President and Secretary of State Schultz in Brazil, and Weinberger in Belgium."[75] And the House also decided to fence the funds allocated for basing until April 30, 1983.

On December 14, 1982, Reagan and senior senators from both parties met to work out a proposal under which Congress would fund MX procurement but bar expenditures pending selection of a basing mode. Cranston tried to introduce an amendment to delete all funds for MX procurement, but the motion was tabled 70 to 28.

In the final bill, Congress agreed to eliminate all funds for MX procurement, prohibit flight testing of MX, and fence R&D funds for the basing mode until congressional acceptance, through concurrent resolution. The President was also required to submit a technical assessment report of dense pack and alternative basing modes as well as an evaluation of an alternative ICBM to MX. The bill contained enough loopholes so that the air force could still build as many as twelve missiles, making the MX operational at the same time as a basing decision was made, "thus allowing the Air Force to actually circumvent the proposed delay of full implementation of the weapon system."[76]

On January 3, 1983, on the advice of Robert McFarland, Deputy NSC Adviser, the President appointed a bipartisan commission headed by Brent Scowcroft, former NSC adviser in the Ford administration, to study the MX problem. The Scowcroft Commission was told to coordinate and consult with Congress and to reach a consensus before it released its report, due to the President by February 18, although the final report was not issued until April 6, 1983.

The Commission consulted closely with Representative Les Aspin (D.-Wis.) and Senator Sam Nunn (D.-Ga.), and split into two groups: technical and information. The technical committee dealt with strategic problems and how to choose a politically acceptable option; the information committee kept the President and

Congress informed and sought advisers from outside of government.

On April 6, 1983, the Commission recommended deployment of 100 MX missiles in Minuteman silos with continued exploration of a more permanent home; called for development of a new, smaller, single-warhead missile, known as Midgetman, to shift forces away from MIRVed ICBMs; and urged the United States to negotiate a new strategic arms limitation agreement with the Soviets to reduce the number of warheads on both sides.[77]

The air force wanted MX more than it wanted a single-warhead missile. Weinberger was also not keen about going ahead with Midgetman. Senator Jackson wanted MX, as did the President. However, many Democrats in the House were not keen on MX but, so it was thought, might accept MX if the package included a commitment to Midgetman and arms control. In the words of Elizabeth Drew:

> And so the Scowcroft Commission produced a report that was designed to be acceptable to various constituencies: Democrats on Capitol Hill, the White House, and the Pentagon. This is why the report had such an odd shape.... To justify placing the MX in fixed silos, the commission dismissed the hypothetical "window of vulnerability"—the possibility that the Soviet Union could destroy all our land-based missiles in a single strike ... [it] described the MX as a transitional weapon, and recommended the deployment of Midgetman single-warhead missiles, and it stressed the importance of arms control.... In addition to recommending the deployment of the MX, the commission threw a sop to the Pentagon by giving Weinberger the leeway he had sought over whether the Midgetman would be proceeded with. The commission also couched its recommendation on arms control in terms that Pentagon officials would find useful.... It said that the deployment of MX, since it would give the United States a hard-target kill capability, might induce the Soviet Union to negotiate and also to shift its land-based force to a force of single-warhead missiles.[78]

Explained commission member James Woolsey, "The report seeks to compromise a bunch of views and accepts partially a number of arguments, so I'm not surprised that [it] appears [self-contradictory].... It's an effort to put together several pieces of the puzzle, and an attempt to say that people who have talked about strategic

weapons in different ways each in part have some legitimacy in what they're saying."[79]

The President accepted the report on April 19, 1983.

TESTING AND PROCUREMENT

The Scowcroft Report effectively closed the "window of vulnerability" and presented MX as a bargaining chip for arms control. Liberals and moderates were not happy about the Scowcroft recommendations. But Representatives Les Aspin and Albert Gore (D.-Tenn.) got them to accept the package because of its arms control "build-down" provisions, and also got the President to issue a letter reaffirming his commitment to arms control.

The opponents in the House were led by Addabbo, Les AuCoin (D.-Ore.), and Thomas J. Downey (D.-N.Y.). Said AuCoin: "There has been no strategic weapon that has passed this stage of funding that has ever been permanently cancelled."[80] He was right, but in the minority.

On May 2, 1983, Gore wrote to the President asking for assurances that proceeding with MX would also result in "a major effort ... to bring sharper focus to the proposed single-warhead ICBM, and to allay concerns that it cannot be realized in a reasonable period of time." (Many on Capitol Hill were concerned that the air force would delay Midgetman to deploy MX.) The President wrote back with a pledge: "We will promptly undertake a major effort to bring the proposal of a small, single-warhead ICBM to fruition on a high priority basis."[81] On May 25, 1983, the House voted affirmatively on flight testing and development of silo basing.[82]

But there was little progress on START (Strategic Arms Reduction Talks) and the pro-MX coalition began to come apart preceding legislative consideration of the 1984 Defense Authorization Bill.

On May 4, the House approved the Freeze Resolution. Nevertheless, on July 20, 1983, the House narrowly agreed (220 to 207) to authorize funding for procurement of the first twenty-seven MX missiles. It adopted two amendments on "voice votes"—one by Armed Services Chairman Melvin Price to prohibit procurement and deployment of Peacekeeper from outrunning the development of Midgetman; the other by Gore and Representative Nor-

man Dicks (D.-Wash.) to cut the number of MXs authorized from twenty-seven to eleven.

How could members vote for the freeze and then MX? Said one House Democrat: "These are people who had doubts about the freeze. They aren't doves who became hawks; they went with the freeze and then wanted to get back to the center."[83] Or in the words of Congressman Dicks, a member of the House Defense Appropriations Subcommittee who had actively backed the Freeze Resolution: "I'm getting identified as a freezie and I've got to get back."[84]

Senators Sam Nunn, William Cohen (R.-Maine), and Charles Percy (R.-Ill.) wrested more concessions from the administration. The President incorporated their build-down concept (which would commit the United States and Soviet Union to retire two existing warheads for each new one deployed) in a new set of instructions to the START delegation; appointed James Woolsey, a former Pentagon official, to the START delegation; and prescribed limits in Midgetman weight and total warheads.[85]

On May 25, 1983, the Senate voted funds for MX flight testing and silo basing. "Following the vote nineteen Republicans, whose support for MX was contingent upon the administration's commitment to START, informed Reagan that their support would be reversed unless real arms control progress was forthcoming."[86] But on July 26, the Senate defeated the Hart/Hatfield amendment to delete MX procurement funds from the Defense Authorization Bill.

On October 4, 1983, the President announced a new START position and two days later the START talks resumed with James Woolsey joining the team. On November 1 and 7, respectively, the House and Senate approved $2.1 billion for the purchase of eleven MX missiles and R&D for Midgetman, defeating attempts by opponents to delete funds for production of the MX missile.[87]

The decision to push ahead with MX deployment was consistent with the spirit of changes that were taking place in U.S. strategic doctrine under the Reagan administration (Figure 6-2). A new review of targeting policy was conducted by Fred Ikle, Under Secretary for Defense, Planning. In October 1981 National Security Decision Directive 13 was prepared to succeed PD-59, and in July 1982 Secretary Weinberger issued NUWEP 2, which served as a basis for a new SIOP "in which increased attention was ac-

Figure 6-2. Vehicle Launch Validation Test of an MX Prototype, Mercury, Nevada, November 1982

Source: Natural Resources Defense Council, Washington, D.C.

corded the requirements of nuclear weapons employment in a situation of prolonged or protracted nuclear conflict."[88] The new SIOP, formally designated SIOP-6, took effect on October 1, 1983.

The national security objectives of the Reagan administration

were officially described in the Secretary of Defense's FY 1984 report:

> To deter military attack by the USSR and its allies against the United States, its allies, and other friendly countries and to deter, or to counter, the use of Soviet military power to coerce or intimidate our friends and allies ... [and] in the event of an atttack, to deny the enemy his objectives to bring a rapid end to the conflict on terms favorable to our interests, and to maintain the political territorial integrity of the United States and its allies.[89]

THE MOVE TO DEPLOYMENT

In 1984 the administration requested $3.172 billion for FY 1985 for MX procurement, including forty missiles. Congress ultimately approved $1 billion for MX procurement other than the FY 1985 missiles and sequestered another $1.5 billion for the procurement of twenty-one missiles. The "fenced" money was released by a House vote on March 28, 1985, which completed release procedures spelled out in the FY 1985 Defense Department Authorization Act. Under a compromise reached the previous year, each chamber had to vote twice to release the $1.5 billion. There was a strong lobbying effort by House Democratic leaders to get supporters of the missile to switch their vote, but the effort narrowly failed (217 to 210). Many on both sides of the House said that MX would not have won approval without the onset of the arms control talks in Geneva and the desire to express solidarity with the President and his negotiating team. In addition, some contended that the forty missiles would be far less dangerous than the hundred missiles because the smaller number could never be construed by the Soviet Union as intended for a surprise attack.[90]

In action on the FY 1986 defense authorizations, Congress limited to fifty the number of MXs that could be deployed in non-superhardened Minuteman silos, and reduced the number of MXs to be procured with FY 1986 funds from the forty-eight requested to twelve.[91] In response to the rising chorus of complaints about MX in Congress from opponents on both the left and the right who were worried that the fixed missile would be vulnerable to attack, the President agreed to limit deployment of MX until a suitable basing for the rest of the missiles could be found.[92] Crucial to the majority was a swing group of Democrats, including Sam Nunn,

member of the Senate Armed Services Committee, and Les Aspin, Chairman of the House Armed Services Committee, who believed that MX placed in old Minuteman silos would be too vulnerable to attack. They believed that the missile was useful primarily as a bargaining chip for arms control.[93]

Under the agreement, Congress permitted more than fifty missiles to be procured only for testing, and noted that twelve to twenty-one missiles "should" be procured for testing in FY 1987. These restrictions on procurement and deployment would not apply if "a basing mode other than existing Minuteman silos was specifically authorized by legislation."[94] The year 1986 was quiet because the FY 1987 request contained funds for only twenty-one missiles, within the bounds of the legislation. R&D was even less controversial than deployment because the FY 1987 MX R&D request was $360 million (plus another $390 million for basing R&D).

Midgetman caused increasing controversy because it was scheduled for full-scale development, the last stage of R&D before procurement. A decision to proceed was crucial because it would lock in many aspects of the system, including missile characteristics and basing mode; would imply a deployment decision eventually; and would require substantially higher appropriations.

By 1986 there were signs that enthusiasm for Midgetman was cooling in the Defense Department, particularly as budgetary pressures forced the system to compete for funds with President Reagan's Strategic Defense Initiative.[95] Under Secretary of Defense Donald A. Hicks stated that "Midgetman is not the most efficient way to do the job . . . [and] I don't personally believe that the small ICBM is the proper solution for the American people in terms of the amount of money you'd have to spend." Secretary of Defense Caspar Weinberger and Assistant Secretary of Defense Richard Perle were openly critical of the costs of the system.[96] But a special Pentagon advisory panel headed by John Deutsch, professor at the Massachusetts Institute of Technology, concluded in a report delivered in February that Midgetman would make U.S. nuclear forces more capable of surviving a Soviet attack, whether or not the United States and the Soviet Union agreed on arms control.[97] The report was careful to point out, however, that "[a]t current Soviet accuracies and current U.S. cost estimates," MX is less expensive than Midgetman, but that "as Soviet accuracies approach 300 ft. Circu-

lar Error Probable (CEP)," the cost advantage switches to Midg-etman.[98]

Reports began to surface that the Pentagon was thinking about putting three MIRVs on Midgetman, which would mean buying fewer missiles and saving money over the life of the program. However, this would mean a larger missile to be carried on a big-ger launcher and would almost certainly exceed the 30,000-pound weight limit imposed earlier by Congress to prevent the air force from loading additional warheads on the missile.[99]

In April, President Reagan ordered DoD to launch a new study to investigate whether the United States should deploy a new mo-bile MIRVed warhead missile about the size of Minuteman. This was in anticipation of the upcoming decision on whether or not to proceed with Midgetman development, to be made at the De-cember meeting of the Defense Systems Acquisition Review Coun-cil.[100]

Word leaked out that a compromise was being forged on Midg-etman between Representative Les Aspin and Defense Under Sec-retary Donald Hicks. Hicks favored two warheads for the missile; Aspin, one warhead for one missile. The compromise would in-volve a further change to the missile once it entered production. Under the concept, the Midgetman would be produced initially as a single-warhead missile until 250 were built. At that point, a de-cision would be made whether to continue producing the missile to the full complement of 500 or retrofitting the 250 already built with an additional warhead. The decision would be made in 1995.[101]

On June 24, the House Armed Services Committee voted to sharply limit the deployment of MX missiles until major develop-ment began on Midgetman. Under the measure, no more than ten MX missiles could be deployed until the major components of the Midgetman missile were tested, contracts were awarded for full-scale development of the missile, and the Secretary of Defense affirmed that the Midgetman missile would be deployed by 1992. Said one congressional staff member, "We sent a signal that we are going to play hardball with their weapon system, if they are going to play hardball with our weapon system."[102]

With its hands tied by Congress, the Reagan administration ap-proved full-scale development of a 37,000-pound small intercon-tinental ballistic missile with a single warhead. But top administration

officials publicly continued to express skepticism about the plan.[103]

The administration also requested funds to proceed with a rail garrison basing mode for fifty MX missiles in addition to the fifty planned for stationary deployment. Under the rail garrison basing plan, MX missiles would be placed on railroad cars that would be housed at military installations around the country. In a national emergency, the cars would be dispersed at classified sites along the more than 200,000 miles of track in the nation's rail system.[104] The idea received full support from SAC Commander General John T. Chain, who said the missiles were needed to buttress the U.S. deterrent. The dispersal "would help stabilize" the world crisis "because a train could not be attacked if the adversary can't locate it ... [and if] the day should ever come that we would have to move these trains out onto the tracks, the American people would be standing by railroad crossings waving American flags because these trains would very well be the last action this country could take to keep from being attacked."[105]

The House of Representatives cut in half the money requested by the President to study the proposal in its vote on the Defense Authorization Bill in April. Some argued it would take too long (three hours) to get the missiles dispersed on the rail lines, which would still leave the MX vulnerable to a "bolt-out-of-the-blue" attack, and that the plan would be costly. Some favored a fifty-missile cap on MX. In the words of Representative Robert Badham (R.-Cal.), a member of the House Armed Services Committee, "none of the alternatives to the rail-garrison basing is palatable." Continued funding for the rail-garrison scheme up to and including the FY 1988 budget seemed to confirm that.

The controversy did not end there. In June 1987, a special panel of the Committee on Armed Services composed of the Subcommittee on Research and Development and the Subcommittee on Procurement and Military Systems conducted a review of the program for a key component of the MX missile and guidance control system: the Inertial Measurement Unit (IMU). The review was prompted by reports of repeated IMU delivery problems and the air force's suspension of payments to the prime contractor, Northrop Electronics Division.

The IMU determines the missiles position in flight and compares it with the programmed course. Errors are then corrected by the flight control system. The House Armed Services Commit-

tee's report asserted that there were "serious questions of confidence" in operational MX missiles because of problems with this device. When the missile was tested it fell "outside the current accuracy requirements" for the system. The report condemned Northrop's management practices which included, among other activities, "false certification of test results . . . acceptance of faulty parts from subcontractors and charging the government for rework costs, improper time card billings, and use of dummy corporations that resulted in the procurement and use of parts that were not inspected and certified."[106] But the report also recognized that political uncertainties about MX's future and pressures from the air force lay at the root of the problem and contributed to Northrop's difficulties.

> Notwithstanding the uphill struggle of the MX, evidenced by repeated amendments to kill the program during consideration of the annual defense bill. . . . Despite the uncertainty and confusion over the pace and ultimate size of the program, the Air Force continued to press for rapid production of the MX.
>
> Consequently, a mixed message was being delivered to the defense industry. On the one hand, questions of program stability were raised. On the other hand, a premium was placed on pushing components and missiles out the door as quickly as possible and on minimizing any program difficulties. Thus, at the same time that an acquisition strategy was forcing NED to transition rapidly and an R&D facility of 500 employees to a full-rate production facility of 5,000 employees, the future of MX was in doubt. Simply stated, Northrop management was neither equipped nor prepared to cope with this environment nor to meet the established production schedule.[107]

Conclusion

Like Trident, the story of MX is one of controversy from almost beginning to end. And like Trident, different technological, political, and institutional influences affected the development, procurement, and deployment of the system. No single factor or set of pressures explains how and why the system was deployed.

In the beginning, the single most important factor was technological momentum and the desire of the air force, and Strategic Air Command in particular, to perfect its hard-target kill capability

and ability to destroy Soviet missiles in their silos. But there was resistance to the program, most notably from then Secretary of Defense Robert McNamara and other senior officials in DoD who doubted whether and if such a capability could or should be developed. Nevertheless, the air force eventually got its way, eased by McNamara's departure, and MX became an established research program in the early 1970s.

It was not a smooth ride for the program and its Pentagon proponents. There was opposition from the Congress and also from senior administration officials in the White House. Soviet advances in MIRV technology and the deployment of a whole new category of missiles by the Soviets in the early 1970s helped to build bureaucratic and political support for MX. New thoughts about the value of counterforce and limited war-fighting capabilities, which officially became enshrined in NSDM 242 (and later PD-59), also provided a strategic rationale for MX, although it is difficult to tell whether this was a case of the doctrinal dog wagging the strategic tail, or vice versa (or perhaps a bit of both). One thing is certain, though—the architect of the Nixon administration's (and then Ford's) new strategic doctrine was Secretary of Defense James Schlesinger, who was a key supporter of the MX program and intervened at a critical point in the program's development over the objections of arms controllers to ensure its continuation and secure funding.

President Carter came to office no fan of MX. His first and foremost priority was arms control and MX seemed to be more of an obstacle than a hindrance. But as the SALT II talks stalled in the sands of Soviet intransigence and dramatic new evidence of Soviet missile capabilities was unearthed by U.S. intelligence, MX seemed both a useful bargaining chip and a useful insurance policy if the talks failed. The talks did not fail, but so lukewarm was domestic political support for the SALT II agreement that Carter needed MX to appease congressional hardliners who worried that arms control would lull the United States into a false sense of security. Much of the administration's political capital and effort went into devising a basing mode that would address growing fears about ICBM vulnerability. But the "solution," MX MPS, was no panacea. And it became increasingly obvious that the President and his advisers had not worked out a careful political strategy for selling the idea to Congress. When Carter was forced to withdraw SALT II from

Congress for ratification, the entire package he had so carefully put together unraveled. Those who had doubts about MX MPS expressed them, and MX MPS found itself the target of a growing environmental movement in the states where it was to be deployed.

In spite of his enormous political popularity and the initial public support for his military buildup, Reagan fared little better with MX. Although MX fitted in nicely with his administration's commitment to the development of a limited war-fighting capability, Reagan had difficulty getting congressional approval for a suitable basing mode for MX. Reagan himself did not like racetrack. But dense pack, and various schemes for putting MX into the air on giant airplanes which would stay aloft for several days, got the proverbial congressional "thumbs down." Eventually, Reagan hit upon the right political formula. And again, our story is one of compromise in which everybody got a little bit of what they wanted, but not everything. The Scowcroft Commission's proposal to temporarily deploy MX in Minuteman silos until a more suitable, long-term basing solution could be found, in exchange for arms control reductions in nuclear warheads and the development of a new, single-warhead ICBM, won congressional approval. Congress voted to deploy MX, although in far fewer numbers than the administration wanted. The bargain was tenuous and was renegotiated each time additional funds were requested from Congress to continue procurement and deployment of MX, but in its essentials it remained intact.

The first fleet of MX missiles was finally deployed in December 1986. Research and development on Midgetman was also under way and Midgetman passed a crucial hurdle in the procurement cycle at the same year's end, in spite of lukewarm support from the air force and the objections of the Secretary of Defense and some of his key deputies. Midgetman deployment will depend on whether Congress can impose its strategic preferences on the air force and the Pentagon.

Like Trident, however, the fundamental story of MX is one of haggling, delays, and the search for a politically acceptable compromise to Congress and the President. Although the arms race, doctrinal and technological innovation, and even arms control played important roles in program development, the final shape of MX ultimately reflected a number of crucial bargains struck between the executive and legislative branches of government—the

key bargain being reflected in the report of the Scowcroft Commission. Worries about ICBM vulnerability were all but swept under the rug of political expediency. The "temporary" solution for MX deployment (to put MX into Minuteman silos) turned out to be just what the air force had proposed some ten years earlier—a solution that was anathema to widely expressed concerns about the vulnerability of fixed-silo basing modes. The strategic arguments and counterarguments had clearly gone full circle.

7

□

THE B-1 BOMBER

In May 1960, the Soviet Union shot down an American U-2 high-altitude reconnaissance plane, piloted by Gary Powers, with a sur-face-to-air missile (SAM). The United States had regularly con-ducted flights over the Soviet Union and always with impunity. Never before had the U-2 faced the threat of SAMs at such high altitudes. The Soviets had obviously perfected a new weapon. The airspace over the Soviet Union was no longer safe. Not only did the Soviet action scuttle hopes for a diplomatic summit between President Dwight Eisenhower and Soviet leader Nikita Khrush-chev, but it also sent jitters through the air force by dramatizing the new vulnerability of the U.S. strategic bomber force to Soviet air defenses.

The air force's response was surprising. Instead of abandoning the manned bomber in the face of this new and emerging threat, it defended it with renewed vigor, while pressing ahead for the development of a new strategic bomber to replace its aging fleet. Ultimately, it succeeded in getting the B-1, or B-1B as it came to be known, but not until a lengthy and prolonged battle with its critics in other branches of the armed services, the President, and Congress. The system's development was delayed and, when it was finally bought, the price was astronomical.

The story is not one of technological innovation, but rather of a service clinging tenaciously to an old technology and an old mis-sion. It is also a story of which a skeptical Congress nevertheless continued to go along with successive administrations' changing policies on the B-1: to develop, then cancel, then deploy.

By contrast, the story of the air-launched cruise missile, which

is discussed in Chapter 8, is one of a system being imposed on a reluctant service by an innovative and forward-thinking civilian leadership in the Pentagon. It is not so much a story of technological innovation as cost-conscious analysts in DoD who looked for new ways to refine existing technologies to curb the military's appetite for more expensive weapons. Again, it was a system years in the making because of bureaucratic squabbling and the difficulties encountered in forging the right political compromise to satisfy all interested parties.

ORIGINS

Throughout the 1940s and 1950s, the air force's long-range bomber was the centerpiece of U.S. strategic deterrent. The navy possessed only limited capability to attack targets in the Soviet Union with carrier-borne aircraft and, from 1955, with the submarine-launched Regulus I cruise missile. In 1960, virtually all of the United States' strategic eggs were in one basket. The Strategic Air Command had 2,000 bombers (the B-47 and B-58, which were medium range, and the B-52, which was long range). In 1958, the United States deployed Thor and Jupiter medium-range missiles in Western Europe, although the new force of ICBMs (intercontinental ballistic missiles) and SLBMs (submarine-launched ballistic missiles) was entering service.[1]

The U-2 incident stimulated a spate of studies by the air force on the problem of how to circumvent Soviet radar and air defenses by low-altitude penetration. If a high-flying plane was vulnerable, then maybe the answer was to go low, beneath the operational range of Soviet sensors. The idea seemed promising and the program was consolidated into a project called AMSA (Advanced Manned Strategic Aircraft) in April 1964.[2]

The idea of a low-altitude bomber was not new. During World War II, while conducting fire-bombing raids over Japanese cities, U.S. planes often flew low to avoid anti-enemy aircraft fire. This low-altitude capability was also mentioned in the requirements for the B-58 and B-70 supersonic bomber programs, although these aircraft were designed primarily for high-altitude missions.[3] Indeed, during the 1950s, air force intelligence projections pointed to the growing threat to the U.S. bomber force posed by advancing Soviet air defense capabilities. A December 1951 General Operational

Requirements report for the B-58 stated, "The potential enemy's defensive capability indicates that after 1957 the USAF strategic weapons systems must be able to perform at both low and high altitudes and at very high subsonic to supersonic speeds. This requires that these weapons systems become available to operational units in early 1957."[4] In March 1958, two years before the U-2 incident, an air force requirements statement argued that the B-70 "must provide flexibility in the selection of cruise penetration, and bombing altitudes from high to on-the-deck. The ability to perform a low altitude (approximately 500 feet or lower) mission is required." As Michael Brown indicates, "these intelligence projections and warnings were ignored [by the air force] once they were included in the formal requirements statements. They were ignored because they complicated the case for high-altitude programs and because the projections themselves were rather tentative. The future was of course uncertain and the distant future was especially uncertain."[5]

The air force remained an ardent supporter of bombers that could fly higher and faster, like the B-70, well into the 1960s. Air force officials affirmed that high-altitude missions could still be successfully conducted with advanced electronic countermeasures and corridor-clearing tactics.[6]

Opposition to the high-altitude mission grew outside the air force. The U-2 incident had impressed upon many the potential vulnerability of the manned strategic bomber. In March 1961, the Kennedy administration decided to cancel the B-70 program. Almost immediately the air force began its AMSA studies to initiate a replacement for the canceled bomber and a follow-up system to the B-52. As Brown explains, "The cancellation of the B-70 was a critical event for the air force because it meant that there was no ready successor to the B-52, which was about to complete its production run, or the B-58, which was something of a disappointment and only a medium bomber in any event. The cancellation of the B-70 meant that there might soon be a deterioration in the air force's (and the nation's) strategic capabilities and that the air force's core mission, strategic bombardment, was in the process of being phased out by the Kennedy Administration. It was widely known that Secretary of Defense McNamara, for one, felt that ballistic missiles were more survivable and more cost-effective than strategic bombers. The air force, in other words, faced a *political*

crisis of the most serious kind; it was a matter of political and bureaucratic survival."[7]

In January 1962, Secretary of Defense Robert McNamara informed Congress that his office had done studies demonstrating that the speed and altitude advantages that the B-70 had over the B-58 and B-52 were minimal and had no effect on its vulnerability to SAMs. Nor was B-70 performance appreciably better than these two other bombers at low altitudes. In testimony before the House Armed Services Committee, which was to decide whether to vote funds for the RS-70 (a reconnaissance-strike version of the B-70 designed to go after remaining targets in the Soviet Union after the United States launched its ICBMs and SLBMs in retaliation), McNamara stated, "We think that the B-52s and B-58s, arriving after our missiles have suppressed the enemy's air defense, could penetrate as well, or almost as well, as the RS-70 [and that the RS-70 would] require the development of new air-launched strike missiles [that] because of their limited size and warhead yield would have to be far more accurate than any strategic air-launched missile now in production or development."[8]

The air force clung tenaciously to the high-altitude mission, however. For many years, the AMSA and B-1 program featured dual mission capabilities—subsonic and supersonic.

Over the period 1961–1964, the studies continued. The option of designing B-52s and B-58s for low-altitude missions was rejected by the air force. It seemed that neither plane could be successfully redesigned. The B-52 and long wings, not the short, stubby kind necessary to handle the stresses and strains of greater air pressure and turbulence at lower altitudes; and the engines of both the B-52 and the B-58 did not perform efficiently at low altitudes. The B-52 was also based on the technology of the 1940s. The air force was keen to use the more advanced technologies that had been developed by aircraft designers in the intervening years. The Air Force Systems Command even suggested that the answer to the B-70's vulnerability problems was to go even higher and faster by developing a hydrogen-fueled craft capable of hypersonic flight that would skim the upper reaches of the earth's atmosphere.[9]

The rest of the air force had little enthusiasm for such a high-tech approach, after the painful experience of the B-70. Many realized that it was more important to develop a more modest and flexible system, and one that would appeal to the cost-conscious

systems analysts in the Office of the Secretary of Defense. It was also important to design a plane that would survive before it was used. The Soviets were also building ICBMs and SLBMs. The new bomber would have to be able to scramble off the ground out of harm's way if the Soviets ever decided to launch a preemptive attack against U.S. bomber bases.

One of the first reports was the Subsonic Low-Altitude Bomber (SLAB) Study, initiated in 1961 and completed in March 1962, and conducted by the Aeronautical Systems Division (ASD) of the Air Force Systems Command (AFSC). It focused on the subsonic, low-altitude system and strategic bombardment mission.

In September 1961, the RAND Corporation concluded its own study on "future low-altitude intercontinental bomber designs." The study examined three possible variants to the strategic bombardment mission: (1) a boost-glide hypersonic approach similar to the AFSC study; (2) a supersonic-cruise, high-altitude approach, like the B-70 and RS-70 programs; and (3) a low-altitude approach. The study concluded that the third option was the most promising and could be conducted at subsonic or supersonic speeds. The study also examined various propulsion systems for the aircraft, including chemically powered and nuclear-powered options. It concluded that the propulsion system would have to be chemical because a nuclear-powered engine would take far too long to develop. The report indicated that a supersonic system would have range problems (because of fuel consumption), although a limited supersonic dash capability might be desirable.

In May 1962, a follow-up RAND study examined the feasibility of a "parasite penetrating bomber," that is, a bomber carried near its target by another plane. The idea was not considered viable and the study concluded that "[o]f the designs considered herein, our judgement favors aircraft of 11,000 Nautical Miles or greater range at high subsonic speed for low altitude penetration in the post B-52 period."[10]

Both RAND studies concluded that supersonic capabilities would add little to the survivability of the bomber, and serve only to lengthen development times and increase costs. If the goal was to develop a system quickly, then the subsonic route was definitely the preferred way to go.

The air force was under heavy pressure to come up with something. McNamara had already canceled one strategic bomber pro-

gram (B-70) and it was known that he was not keen on the idea of a new bomber program in general, although he preferred a system that would be flexible and would have high pre-launch survivability. The problem was this: a strategic penetrating bomber with short wings would require long runways and a greater takeoff distance than the B-52, which would adversely affect the bomber's pre-launch survivability. The problem was eventually solved when the air force came up with the idea of the variable-sweep wing, which could be extended for landings and takeoffs but retracted for supersonic flight.

In 1963, the air force initiated a second round of studies: LAMP (Low-Altitude Manned Penetrator Study), AMP (Advanced Manned Penetrator Study), and AMPSS (Advanced Manned Penetrating Strategic System).

LAMP focused on a low-level system with a variable-sweep wing that would enable aircraft to take off in distances less than a mile. AMP examined the feasibility of four different requirements: all subsonic low- and high-altitude capabilities; subsonic at low altitude with medium supersonic at higher altitudes; subsonic at low altitude with high-altitude, high-supersonic capabilities; and vertical and short takeoff and landing capabilities. These studies were conducted by North American Rockwell (subsequently renamed Rockwell International), Boeing, and General Dynamics. AMPSS was originally oriented to all subsonic designs but then expanded to cover medium- and high-supersonic capabilities.

The air force also formed two high-level study groups to examine the future of the manned bomber: Project FORECAST and the Manned Aircraft Systems Steering Group. Both groups concluded that a supersonic Mach 2.2 (medium) high-altitude capability would be required of any new bomber that was built, along with low-altitude capability.

RESEARCH AND DEVELOPMENT

In March 1964, all of these programs and subgroups were consolidated into one coordinating group officially named the Advanced Strategic Manned Aircraft (ASMA) only to be renamed the Advanced Manned Strategic Aircraft (AMSA) a month later.

By year's end 1964, the basic configuration and system requirements of the advanced strategic manned bomber were set. They

were to change little between 1964 and 1977 when the B-1 program was canceled by President Jimmy Carter—if only to be resurrected four years later by President Ronald Reagan.[11]

In August 1965, the Office of Operational Requirements and Development Plans in the air force issued a statement on the "Characteristics, Cost, and Effectiveness of the AMSA." It noted that $2.3 million had been spent on contracted studies alone and that the air force itself had examined over 5,000 point designs before setting the final program requirements, which were: (1) to fly an unrefueled mission for 5,000 nautical miles; (2) to take off in a distance of less than 6,000 feet; (3) to sustain a top speed of Mach 2.2 at 50,000 feet; (4) to sustain a speed of Mach 0.90 at low altitude over rolling terrain; and (5) to dash supersonically at an altitude of 200 feet over flat terrain.[12]

But the major story of the AMSA during this period was one of conflict between Secretary McNamara and the air force. McNamara insisted that "manned bombers of the future are simply going to be launching platforms for missiles," and was firmly convinced that the program had no real future.[13] In a secret briefing paper to President Lyndon B. Johnson, McNamara reportedly argued that AMSA would be rendered obsolete by the development of MIRV (Multiple Independently Targetable Reentry Vehicle) technology, which would be able to saturate the Soviet Union with nuclear warheads for half the cost of a new manned bomber.[14]

Early in December 1965, McNamara announced his decision to begin phasing out the B-58 bomber fleet, which was extremely costly to maintain, and the oldest B-52s and B-52C through F models. He proposed to replace these aircraft with the new FB-111, the bomber version of the F-111 (a medium-range fighter-bomber). McNamara also sought to cut costs by reducing the size of the air force from approximately 680 to 465 operational B-52s, keeping all 80 B-58s, and phasing in 210 FB-111s.

McNamara's plan was attacked by the air force and Congress. A Report of a Special Subcommittee of the U.S. House Armed Services of April 4, 1964, concluded that replacing B-52s and B-58s with the FB-111 was a mistake because the plane lacked the necessary range, payload, avionics, and flexibility to be a useful strategic system. The Report rejected the designated bomber role for the FB-111, arguing instead that AMSA should replace aging B-52s.

Wearied by the long round of studies and reports, the air force

was keen to move the AMSA program into the project definition phase. General Curtis LeMay (head of the Strategic Air Command, who had once said that SAC's main objective was to reduce the Soviet Union "to a smoking, radiated ruin") expressed his frustration: "I think we have reached a position where we ought to stop studying and go into the program definition phase."[15] But McNamara remained steadfast, permitting work to be done only on some elements of the propulsion and avionics systems. He also axed the budget for the AMSA program, forbidding the air force to spend the full amounts authorized by Congress. In 1965 Congress authorized $52 million for AMSA, of which McNamara spent $28 million. In 1966 he spent $46 million, more than double Congress's appropriated amount of $22 million, but most of that (as in previous and subsequent years) went into propulsion ($24 million) and avionics ($14.3 million) compared to a modest sum of $7.7 million in systems studies (where the air force wanted to devote the lion's share of its resources). McNamara believed that, whatever happened to the AMSA itself, these avionics and propulsion studies would be useful to other air force programs and for other systems. During the period 1965–1968, only 20 percent of the AMSA budget went into systems studies.[16] As Michael Brown notes, "it would have been politically difficult for . . . [McNamara] to kill the AMSA program outright, given the air force's and Congress's position on the subject, so he kept the program alive, but barely. And he spent as little as possible on the AMSA system itself. This helped McNamara control the program in two ways. First, it kept sunk costs in the program to a minimum, making AMSA relatively vulnerable to cancellation at any time; the work done on propulsion and avionics, moreover, was transferable to other aircraft programs. Second, it kept the program from building any momentum toward full-scale development."[17]

McNamara argued that the program was vaguely defined and that the system requirements were not properly specified. He refused numerous pleas from the air force, and even the Joint Chiefs of Staff, to move the program ahead on the grounds that the FB-111 was still the best alternative to AMSA.

For the firms angling to build the system, this was not good news. In 1967, Boeing dropped out of the systems effort study because it felt that the program was permanently stalled.

In the meantime, the vulnerability problems of the existing

B-52 fleet had to be addressed. The air force argued that the B-52 would be vulnerable to projected Soviet air defenses in the mid-1970s and that steps had to be taken to enhance its ability to penetrate Soviet airspace. Two important steps were taken to address this problem: first, a decision was made in the fall of 1968 to equip all late-model B-52s with SRAMs (Short-Range Attack Missiles); second, studies began on a new decoy missile to replace the existing Quail decoy missile. The need for a decoy had emerged from a series of bomber penetration studies undertaken by the air force in 1966–1967.[18]

In December 1965, McNamara had announced that SRAMs would be deployed on the controversial TFX (which later became the FB-111A). The SRAM development decision had been made in 1964, with development beginning in 1965.

In February 1968 McNamara resigned as Secretary of Defense, apparently frustrated by the Vietnam War and increasingly convinced it was a war the United States could not win. A new Secretary of Defense, Clark Clifford, took over. Clifford was much more enthusiastic about the manned bomber program (although later he was to condemn it) and on July 19, 1968, he authorized the Deputy Defense Secretary to order the Secretary of the Air Force and DDR&E (Directorate of Defense Research and Engineering) to explore ways of accelerating the AMSA program and shortening development times to move into production. This decision paved the way for the AMSA Development Concept Paper, a key hurdle on the path to deployment.

The air force wasted no time, and in November of that same year the AMSA DCP circulated its way through the offices of the Secretary of Defense, DDR&E, and the Office of the Secretary of the Air Force (OSAF). The DCP argued that the B-52 G/H models would be structurally sound until the early 1980s, and that it would take about eight years to develop and produce the AMSA. It also argued that the aircraft would require a low-altitude subsonic capability and a high-altitude supersonic capability, while calling for an "all-supersonic bomber."[19] It predicted that a supersonic capability would increase the aircraft's costs by some 24 percent and proposed four development options: (1) to have two contractors engage in a limited, three-year design competition that would not include competing prototype aircraft; (2) to move directly to the selection of a single contractor; (3) to continue with advanced

development for another year, postponing the move to engineering development; and (4) to have two contractors bid with completed design studies of an all-subsonic aircraft.

The first and fourth options preserved competition in the program, and also gave more time to study potential systems and assess the air force's future needs. But the disadvantages were the lack of full-scale prototype development and "paper" competitions that would only delay production. The second option was the fastest but it eliminated the possibility of competitive development and meant that the design would have to be frozen in its early stages to allow for full-scale, early production.

The authors of the DCP also worried about their inability to project the evolving nature of the Soviet threat over the eight-year period that would be required to bring this system to deployment. "We are unable to project our threat assessments eight years ahead with any degree of confidence. Nor are we able to forecast accurately the degree of technological improvement possible over such a span. Yet, to structure properly an incentive contract, we must be able to make such a projection."[20]

The third option would postpone development for another year while building on earlier studies, especially in avionics and propulsion. It represented a nod to McNamara's preference for keeping the program on the back burner.

The fourth option represented a departure from earlier thinking insofar as it proposed development of an altogether separate subsonic bomber. However, the DCP pointed out continuing uncertainties about the ability of such a system to contend with future Soviet air defenses without an additional supersonic capability.

John Foster, the director of DDR&E, indicated his preference for Option 1 because it gave greatest flexibility in program design (low and high speed). Alan Enthoven, Assistant Secretary of Defense for Systems Analysis, recommended Option 4 on the grounds that Option 1 would "not permit the timely evaluation of alternative aircraft designs that provide flexibility, through larger payload rather than higher speed." Harold Brown, Secretary of the Air Force (later to become Jimmy Carter's Secretary of Defense), joined in the DDR&E recommendation of Option 1 on the grounds that separate design of a subsonic AMSA would delay development unnecessarily and not provide sufficient flexibility for the system. Paul Nitze, writing for the Secretary of Defense, on November 20, 1968,

formally approved Option 1 with a supersonic capability "with the stipulation that continuing attention be given to trade-off studies of an equal cost subsonic system optimized for survivability and assured destruction."[21]

OSD requested $97 million for AMSA for FY 1970. The request was lowered by the administration to $85 million and then to $77.2 million. The AMSA budget had nevertheless tripled as the system moved into system development and source selection.

Under the new Nixon administration, Deputy Secretary of Defense David Packard initiated a thorough review of the AMSA program. On the basis of the review, he decided to accelerate and revise the development program. In 1969, the performance requirements for the system were modified, a new DCP was issued, and a new development program was put into place requesting full-scale development. Packard also pushed for source selection in FY 1970, almost two years earlier than recommended in the November 1968 DCP.

In order to issue the RFPs (requests for proposal) to industry Packard was forced to take a phased approach to avionics for the system that would allow for "growth." He also had to lower the low-altitude speed requirement for the system and eliminate its supersonic dash capability to keep costs and weight down. The air force was not happy about these changes in performance specifications but had no choice but to go along. Packard believed that cost reductions were more important than the performance and high-tech whims of the air force.

A new DCP was issued on October 1, 1969, with four options: (1) allow for a six-month proposal and source selection period which would result in a single system contractor and a single propulsion contractor for engineering and development; (2) allow for a three-month proposal and source selection period which would result in two contractors who would be given six months to design a system that would then be chosen on a competitive basis; (3) extend the competition in #2 to permit construction of test aircraft; and (4) postpone the initial competition phase and continue studying the program's requirements, costs, and risks.[22]

DDR&E, OSAF, and the Office of Systems Analysis were asked for their comments. DDR&E's John Foster opted for Option 2 on the grounds that it would have the shortest development lead time. Robert Seamons, Secretary of the Air Force, recommended Option 1 because he felt that there had already been enough analysis and

it was time to move the B-1 into full-scale development. The Acting Assistant Secretary of Defense recommended approval of Option 4 because the alternatives to the B-1 program had still not been properly addressed, including the use of standoff weapons and "less penetration" by bombers or more penetration aids and less speed. He felt that a proper risk analysis of costs and options to the program had not been done and did not want to narrow requirements of the program at this point. Packard, however, opted for Option 1 and the release of RFPs to the contractors. Issuing his directive, he also emphasized the need to assure the pre-launch survivability of the AMSA force.[23]

Surprisingly, Packard did not choose Option 3, which would have ensured a greater degree of sequential development and prototype competitions, and would have been consistent with his own procurement reforms. He wanted the program to enter full-scale development in FY 1970, and by November 1969 the RFPs had been released. North American Rockwell, Boeing (which had since reentered the competition), and General Dynamics were asked to submit their system proposals, and in June 1970 North American Rockwell was announced the winner.

Rockwell and General Electric (the contractor for engines) also received an incentive fee of $115.75 million if they met performance, cost, and time estimates in their engineering development contracts.[24] This was a new innovation intended to keep the program on schedule and within the stipulated contract costs.

Many changes were made in the initial design during the first few months of the development contract. In September 1970, Project Focus was initiated to refine the aircraft's basic design. The key changes were a reduction in the airframe's titanium content in order to reduce the cost of the materials going into the aircraft, and a lowering in the takeoff thrust of the engines which increased the aircraft's takeoff distance, thereby exceeding initial specifications.[25]

Now officially named the B-1, the plane was designed to have a shorter escape time and greater resistance to nuclear effects than the B-52. It would be able to respond more quickly than the B-52 to tactical warning of SLBM attack by Soviet submarines off the United States' coast. The B-1 was also expected to have a much smaller radar cross section than the B-52 and would therefore be more difficult to shoot down by Soviet interceptors or missiles.

The plane was also designed to carry twice the internal payload of the B-52; a total of 24 SRAMs, short-range ALCM (air-launched cruise missile)-As, and gravity bombs. The plane's range, however, was slightly less than the B-52H's range of 5,900 nautical miles.[26]

In January 1971 Project Focus was followed by Project Innovation, which was to look at ways to reduce the level of investment and the sunk costs in the program until after the production decision was made. Its report led to a decision to reduce the number of test aircraft to be developed from five to three. "To ensure that one full year of flight testing would precede the production decision, the date of the production decision was pushed back several months, from September 1974 to April 1975. The Packard philosophy, 'fly before buy,' was clearly at work here."[27]

During this period, the program moved back and forth between concurrent and sequential development. Grant Hansen, Assistant Secretary of the Air Force for Research and Development, testified before Congress that "a complete test and 'fly before buy' isn't really possible at all because if you built airplanes and then went away and tested them the people who built them would have gone away by the time you wanted to build some more."[28]

But as the B-1 moved further along the development track, it began to generate controversy. Senator George McGovern (D.-S.D.) and Representative John F. Seiberling (D.-Ohio) unsuccessfully sought termination of studies leading to the advanced manned-bomber program. Members of Congress for Peace through Law (MCPL) tried to slice $10 billion from the FY 1972 defense budget, recommended that the supersonic capability for the B-1 be dropped on the grounds that it was not cost effective, and asked that the aircraft be redesigned to carry long-range air-to-ground missiles.[29]

The B-1's political problems were not helped by growing technical difficulties in the program. In 1972 problems surfaced in the crew escape module, an alternative to ejection seats. Tests revealed that the ejection module did not work reliably and that the system would have to be redesigned at considerable expense.

In July 1973, Acting Secretary of the Air Force John McLucas announced that the B-1 program was being "rephased" (stretched out) because of cost and scheduling problems encountered by Rockwell, the prime contractor. The first test flight was pushed back to mid-1974 and the production decision was deferred from

1975 to 1976. However, "[t]he Air Force felt that Congress was at least partly responsible for this delay; according to the Air Force, the program was not receiving enough funding to adhere to the original schedule. While it was true that Congress, the Senate in particular, was beginning to become increasingly vocal in its criticism of the program and increasingly judicious in its support of the program, it was also true that Rockwell and the Air Force to a lesser extent were having some troubles in managing the program."[30]

The "stretch-outs" led to a gap between completion of the last development aircraft and the start of production. This created serious problems for the contractor, which would be forced to lay off its idle work force in the interim and would have difficulty attracting them back once production had to start. The eventual solution was to reinsert a fourth aircraft into the program in February 1974.[31]

With each delay and political compromise, the design of the plane changed. Under Secretary of Defense David Packard forced the air force to drop the plane's low-altitude supersonic capability in 1969 and its top speed capabilities were cut in 1973 and again in 1974 because of the pressure of rising costs. "The survival of the program was clearly at stake and, again, this political crisis forced the Air Force to do something that it preferred not to do."[32]

Program delays only exacerbated the political problem. Rising development costs and increased *estimated* production costs became the focus of intense congressional criticism. The annual reports of the General Accounting Office showed that unit costs for a fleet of 244 bombers were approaching the $100 million mark versus the original estimate of less than $50 million in 1970.[33]

Critics of the SALT I accords seized on the B-1 as confirmation of their concerns that the agreements had failed to restrict development, construction, or deployment of modern long-range bomber aircraft. The Center for Defense Information, an independent Washington defense lobby group, argued that modernization of the B-52 G/H bomber would make it just "as useful as the B-1 through the 1980s" and that the B-1 was therefore redundant and unnecessary.[34]

Secretary of Defense James Schlesinger publicly defended the B-1 program and system requirements in early 1974. He pointed out that the U.S. strategic bomber force needed general improve-

ments, including "(1) faster airfield escape and greater protection against the effects of nuclear detonations in order to avoid destruction by SLBMs which might be launched on depressed trajectories from Soviet SSBNs operating close to our shores, and (2) a capability to fly at very low altitude at high subsonic speed in order to penetrate Soviet air defenses."[35]

It seemed in private that Schlesinger was no great enthusiast of B-1. Confiding to Congressman Les Aspin (D.-Wis.), he reportedly described it as one of "the Cadillacs I inherited." He also quietly tried to promote a reassessment of the structure of U.S. strategic forces and made a significant if little-noted observation in his defense posture statement to Congress in 1975. "Each leg of the triad is not required to retain independently a capacity to inflict in a second [that is, retaliatory] strike unacceptable damage upon an attacker. Instead, the three legs of the triad are designed to be mutually supporting. . . . Missiles, for example, could help clear the way for bomber penetration, and bombers, in turn, could help to fill the gap of those important targets missed by missiles."[36]

The program was threatened by continuing attacks in the House and Senate as it neared a decision on production, including efforts in 1973 and 1974 to kill the program entirely. But they were rebuffed.[37]

In an attempt to address congressional concerns and head off the critics at this pass, the air force decided to review the entire program and address its cost problems. In the words of the air force's Vice-Chief of Staff, General R. H. Ellis, "Cost increases in the B-1 development program and projected cost estimates associated with the production phase, if allowed to continue, may diminish the likelihood of obtaining approval to proceed with acquisition of the system." The Corona Quest Review Board was established on September 23, 1974, to address these issues and its hearings lasted until December 1974.

The Board's recommendations were quite drastic: to simplify and redesign the movable engine inlets with fixed inlets, which would reduce the aircraft's top speed from Mach 2.1 to Mach 1.6. The crew escape module was also jettisoned because of rising costs and problems in the design.[38]

The B-1 took its first test flight in December 1974, the same year the ALCM program (discussed in Chapter 8) began.

THE DEBATE OVER PRODUCTION

Congressional concern over increases in projected costs continued to mount,[39] and interest in identifying and comparing the cost effectiveness of alternatives to the B-1, such as rigging the B-52 with ALCMs, grew. The Ford administration decided to preempt these initiatives by moving the program into production, but Congress was lukewarm and decided that the production decision should be deferred because it was a presidential election year. "The real question was whether it was sensible to purchase 244 of these planes at $80 million to $100 million apiece when equally effective alternatives might be available for substantially less money."[40]

The challenge to the B-1 on Capitol Hill was led by Senator John Culver (D.-Iowa), a member of the Senate Armed Services Committee, who at the Committee meeting on May 13, 1976, proposed to delay funding of the bomber until February 1977 so that the next President, whoever it might be, could make the production decision. Culver's amendment lost, but there was enough support to show that it might win on the Senate floor. It was evident that the vote would be close so opponents of the program decided to hold the vote on a day when some of the key senators favoring B-1 might be out of town, May 20.

In the meantime, the Federation of American Scientists organized a petition whose signatories included former Secretary of Defense Clark Clifford, McGeorge Bundy (Kennedy's and Johnson's National Security Adviser), and former CIA Science Director Herbert Scoville. A story of the mounting opposition to the B-1 was carried on "NBC Nightly News" on May 18, publicly indicating for the first time that the B-1 was in trouble.

On the day of the vote, opponents of the B-1 arranged for George McGovern to first offer an amendment deleting all funds for B-1 production. The amendment predictably lost, but the Culver amendment seemed a good compromise by comparison and was narrowly accepted (44 to 37).

Culver's amendment was attached to the FY 1977 Defense Authorization Bill. Wisconsin Democrat William Proxmire took up the amendment in the appropriations cycle, presenting it to the Senate Appropriations Committee. But the Committee split 14 to 14 on the amendment and the tie had to be broken by Senate Majority Leader Robert Byrd (D.-W.Va.), a defense conservative,

who nevertheless voted for it. House conferees also accepted the Proxmire amendment to delay full production and Congress directed that procurement funds for the first eight B-1s be allocated at the rate of only $87 million per month through January 31, 1977, effectively deferring the future of the program for decision by the next administration.[41]

In an effort to mute criticism of the B-1 in Congress and elsewhere, outgoing Secretary of the Air Force Thomas C. Reed assembled an outside committee headed by Courtland Perkins, President of the National Academy of Engineering, to determine any technical risks that might be encountered when the system entered production. He also formed a panel chaired by Edward E. David, Jr., Chairman of the National Security Council's ad hoc strategic panel, to review the alternatives to the B-1. The panel reported that the B-1 should be procured.

The air force and Rockwell also joined forces to deal with congressional fights over the program. They had shown considerable foresight by awarding subcontracts on the plane to firms in forty-eight states. Armed with lists of every B-1 subcontract cross-referenced by town, state, and congressional district, air force and Rockwell lobbyists descended on Capitol Hill. As Nick Kotz observes: "This information allowed the lobbyists to show members of Congress, down to the last dollar, how their constituents benefited from the B-1. The data became even more potent as subcontractors, mayors, and union leaders were enlisted to lobby their members of Congress."[42] Rockwell even mounted a secret "grassroots" campaign code-named Operation Common Sense headed by James Daniell, a marketing representative with the company, which included a special promotional film on the B-1 called *The Threat: What One Can Do.*[43]

However, a strong national campaign known as the National Campaign to Stop the B-1 Bomber, orchestrated by the American Friends Service Committee (a Quaker-founded pacifist group), had developed. The Committee comprised more than 1,000 local organizations and 50 campaign offices throughout the nation and during the 1976 presidential campaign it had successfully lobbied Carter to take a stand on the B-1 when he knew very little about it. In a statement to the Democratic Platform Committee on June 12, 1976, Carter stated, "The B-1 is an example of a proposed system which should not be funded and would be wasteful of tax-

payers' dollars." He later equivocated, saying that "at this point" he didn't favor construction of the B-1, although his decision wasn't included in his post-election promise book.[44]

A DECISION TO CANCEL

Upon entering the White House, Carter reduced the planned purchase of the B-1 from eight to five planes and ordered Harold Brown to reexamine the cost effectiveness of an alternative bomber force. The Assistant Secretary for Program, Analysis, and Evaluation chaired the study with the assistance of the air force, JCS, and DDR&E.[45] The air force was understandably nervous about the review, although it drew some comfort from the fact that Harold Brown, as Secretary of the Air Force, had been a supporter of the B-52 follow-up. The report to the Secretary of Defense was prepared in just three weeks, but its answer was equivocal: "cost-effectiveness does not provide a clear choice" among the alternatives.[46]

President Carter was presented with four choices: (1) build 244 B-1 bombers at a cost of $30 billion; (2) deploy long-term ALCMs on B-52s and cancel B-1; (3) do nothing and let the B-52s wear out and eventually move from a strategic triad to dyad; or (4) go slow with B-1 and scrutinize cost and capabilities closely as the system develops.

The President's National Security Adviser, Zbigniew Brzezinski, and Bert Lance, head of the Office of Management and Budget (OMB) and the President's close friend, urged him to choose the fourth option while the State Department and the Arms Control and Disarmament Agency (ACDA) favored the third. The President's group felt that the B-1 would help sell SALT II to Congress, keep up pressure on the Soviets, and reduce pressures to deploy MX. The State Department and OMB looked at the problem from the arms control standpoint.[47] However, Secretary of Defense Harold Brown apparently recommended that the bomber not be built, a recommendation Carter noted in his presidential diary as being "very courageous" because of the political interests that had developed for it.[48]

Carter reviewed the evidence and on June 3 decided to cancel production of the B-1 but to keep it in the development and testing stage (including avionics) and to monitor the program's progress. The Joint Chiefs were informed on the day of the decision.

Carter stressed that his decision was not directed against the B-1, but was rather a decision in favor of the cruise missile.

> My decision is that we should not continue with the deployment of the B-1, and I am directing that we discontinue plans for production of this weapon system. . . .
>
> The existing testing and development program now under way for the B-1 should continue to provide us with the needed technical base in the unlikely event that more cost-effective alternative systems should run into difficulty. Continuing efforts at the research and development stage will give us better answers about the cost and cost-effectiveness of the bomber and support systems, including electronic countermeasures techniques.
>
> During the coming months, we will also be able to reassess the progress toward agreements on strategic arms limitations, in order to determine the need for any additional investments in nuclear weapons delivery systems. In the meantime, we should begin deployment of cruise missiles using air-launch platforms such as our B-52s, modernized as necessary.[49]

The President's decision was based in part on a perceived change in the calculated capabilities of penetrating and standoff bombers to deliver weapons to targets and on a reassessment of the projected magnitude and sophistication of Soviet air defenses. The March 1977 tests of cruise missiles had also been most positive. The Secretary of Defense stated: "I have more confidence in our estimates of the effect that the low detectability of the cruise missile will have on Soviet radar than in the effect that the B-1's radar countermeasures would have had."[50] Although arms control considerations were a potential black mark against the cruise missile, in April 1977 the United States had proposed a maximum range limit of 2,500 kilometers on ALCMs in the SALT negotiations with the Soviets. Ultimately, the B-1's program costs were a key consideration, but as one observer correctly notes, "It needs to be emphasized that most of the controversy over the B-1's costs focused on the program's *estimated* production costs, rather than on *actual* cost overruns."[51]

Carter's cancellation decision was also based on support for the new Stealth bomber and the air-launched cruise missile development for the B-52. Stealth would depend on new technologies in aerodynamics, materials, and electronics to enable a bomber to

evade enemy radar. Although the program was still in the very early stages of research and design, these new technologies looked promising. But Carter was also worried about the impact of an affirmative production decision on the defense budget. In the congressional election campaign of 1978, Republicans accused Carter of violating the nation's security with the cancellation, but he refused to change his decision.

Although production was canceled, the B-1 did not die immediately. It still had life support in the form of continued funding for R&D. This support enabled the program to be resurrected quickly a few years later under Ronald Reagan. As Carter noted in his memoirs, "the enormous B-1 lobbying octopus was still alive and writhing. It would live to fight again after I left the White House."[52]

The House supported Carter's decision by the narrowest of votes (202 to 199), and the plane's supporters got a short-term boost when the House Appropriations Committee voted to have the Carter administration build six prototypes instead of the four he said were enough for continuing research. But this small victory was short-lived because the decision was subsequently overturned by the Senate.[53]

A coalition of forces in the Pentagon and Congress worked hard to keep the B-1 program in a holding pattern until the President could be persuaded to change his mind or a new President came along. Secretary of the Air Force Dr. Hans Mark and Deputy Under Secretary of Defense Dr. Seymour Zeiberg were unhappy about Carter's decision, and succeeded in channeling almost $450 million into Rockwell's B-1 program under the guise of funds designated for "penetration studies, advanced avionics, cruise-missile carrier studies, radar-absorbent-material studies, electronic-countermeasure studies, or strategic-bomber enhancement."[54] They got help from the B-1's supporters on the House Armed Services Committee, including Anthony Battista, the committee's staff director, Congressman Richard Ichord (R.-Mo.), and Congressman William Dickinson (R.-Ala). Taking Carter's directive to Congress to investigate the development of a new cruise missile carrier to replace the B-1, the two congressmen and Battista worked on the idea of turning the B-1 into an advanced cruise missile carrier (CMCA). The air force liked the idea and Hans Mark slipped CMCA into the 1980 defense budget. OMB, however, warned the President that

CMCA was simply a resurrected B-1 and Carter cut it from the budget he submitted to Congress. The second try was to give the program a new acronym—the long-range combat aircraft, or LRCA—while Battista and B-1 supporters in the House Armed Services Committee lobbied to have the B-1 included in the budget as the strategic weapons launcher, or SWL.[55]

Carter threatened to veto the entire defense bill if it included the B-1 appropriation. But Carter was in a difficult position. The Iranian crisis and Soviet invasion of Afghanistan had weakened his presidency, and attacks on his defense policy, including some by presidential candidate Ronald Reagan, were growing. The compromise that was eventually forged was to fund Stealth and to allow the administration to come up with a new plane instead of B-1. In September 1980, the House Appropriations Committee added $175 million to Carter's defense budget to study "new technology such as Stealth."[56] The FY 1981 Defense Authorization Bill passed by Congress in 1980 contained a directive that the "Secretary of Defense shall vigorously pursue full-scale engineering development of a strategic multi-role bomber," with an IOC "not later than 1987"—"which maximizes range, payload, and ability to perform on missions of conventional bomber, cruise missile launch platform, and nuclear weapons delivery system in both tactical and strategic role. Congress authorized and appropriated $350 million for this purpose."[57] It was a none-too-subtle attempt to revive the B-1 or some variant thereof.

THE B-1 GETS A NEW LEASE ON LIFE

Ronald Reagan came to the presidency with a new set of defense priorities. Committed to building up America's defenses, Reagan wasted no time implementing his plan as President. This was good news for supporters of the B-1. Early in 1981, the air force prepared a recommendation to Secretary of Defense Casper Weinberger calling for immediate production of a new version of the B-1 bomber while proceeding to develop a new, radar-evading Stealth aircraft.[58] Some senior officers in the Strategic Air Command, who had longer memories and were concerned that Congress would not fund the President's defense budget, argued that the FB-111 should be chosen as the interim bomber, because converting it would be cheaper and faster than building the B-1 variant. But

Figure 7-1. **B-1B Bomber on Test Flight**

Source: Natural Resources Defense Council, Washington, D.C.

they were a minority and the option was eventually dropped because the FB-111 could not carry cruise missiles and would become obsolete too soon.[59]

General Richard Ellis, Chief of the Strategic Air Command, preferred to go ahead with the advanced Stealth bomber and forgo
building B-1 or an interim alternative altogether. He was supported by critics like former CIA director Admiral Stansfield Turner,
who called the B-1 "obsolete" and compared it to the sailing ships
that nineteenth-century admirals preferred when they could have
had steam-driven warships. This group contended that Soviet radar
would be so advanced by the 1990s that the B-1 would be unable
to penetrate Soviet airspace.[60]

But Weinberger was not persuaded. In October 1981, the Reagan administration announced that it was reviving the B-1 bomber
program in the form of the B-1B, which would incorporate some
of the new Stealth technologies to help hide the system from Soviet defenses by reducing the plane's radar cross signature (Figure
7-1). The air force still saw the B-1B as a penetrating bomber,
although some defense analysts argued that it would have only a
standoff capability. One hundred B-1Bs were planned for production. At the same time, the administration requested $30 billion
for development of an advanced-technology bomber for introduc-

tion in the mid to late 1990s. The White House statement of the administration's proposal read:

> The Reagan Administration believes the B-1 is necessary to bolster our strategic forces during the critical 1980s, and the advanced technology bomber is needed to provide high confidence that our bombers will be able to penetrate Soviet air defenses into the next century.
>
> The U.S. must depend heavily on bombers (and sea-based forces) in the 1980s while we take steps to strengthen our land-based missiles. We can't afford to wait until the 1990s for a new bomber.
>
> ... There are currently technical and operational uncertainties about the advanced technology bomber. We believe these uncertainties will be resolved during development and that the advanced technology bomber will be a very effective aircraft when ultimately deployed.
>
> Without the B-1, however, there would be pressures to accelerate the advanced technology bomber, which would increase program risks and possibly result in less capable aircraft being deployed.
>
> ... The B-1 will be able to penetrate Soviet defenses initially and will make a good cruise missile carrier and conventional bomber after the advanced technology bomber is deployed and all B-52s are retired in the 1990s.[61]

The plan called for the first squadron of B-1Bs to be operational in 1986 and deployment of all 100 bombers by 1988.

Early in 1981 Rockwell International, the prime contractor, estimated total system costs at $11.9 billion. In May 1981, the air force issued a revised estimate somewhere between $15 billion and $18 billion. In July, it told Congress the plan would cost $19.7 billion. By October, some were even saying it would cost $27.9 billion.[62]

A GAO report in November 1981 put program costs at $39.8 billion and said that the Pentagon was artificially deflating costs by leaving out critical support features to the system. The unit cost of each plane had risen from $100 million under the Carter administration to anywhere from $200 to $250 million. Doubts were also growing about its penetration capabilities. A secret report of the Central Intelligence Agency (CIA) delivered to the House and Senate indicated that the penetration of Soviet defenses through 1990 would be no greater with the B-1B than with existing B-52s. Some in Congress expressed doubts about the need for and afford-

ability of two bombers.[63] However, the B-1B program did get multiyear procurement funding, despite efforts by Representative Joseph Addabbo (D.-N.Y.) to introduce an amendment that would have allowed the air force to buy ten B-1Bs in FY 1984 with elimination of the multiyear procurement aspects of the program.[64]

Congress committed the air force to a $20.5 billion (FY 1981 dollars) funding "cap." By 1984, however, many felt that the program had too much money because it seemed to be coming in under costs. Despite the air force's insistence that it needed these extra funds for unforseen contingencies, a little more than $1 billion was removed from the program, albeit with the promise that it would be restored if needed.

In its FY 1985 Defense Authorization Act, Congress imposed restrictions to prevent diversion of funds from the B-1B for the Stealth advanced-technology bomber because of its concerns that the air force might try to keep B-1B production lines open after its 100 aircraft were delivered. These fears were justified. Air force planners launched a campaign early in 1985 to keep Rockwell's production line "warm" and to build a B-1C follow-up that would be modified to meet some of the new Stealth requirements. But they encountered stiff resistance from Secretary Weinberger, who was strongly opposed to production beyond the approved 100 bombers, and from Air Force Secretary Verne Orr, who said there were "no internal plans whatsoever to buy the B-1."[65] The campaign nevertheless continued. Rockwell International proposed selling the air force forty-eight more B-1s at a "cut-rate" price of $195 million per plane compared to the $275 million per plane for the 100 B-1s already ordered.[66]

DEPLOYMENT PROBLEMS

By May 1986 reports surfaced that the primary contractor expected to exceed the $20.5 billion target, plus allowance for inflation since 1981, by $500 million.[67] This news came just before the first fleet of B-1Bs went on full-alert status at Dyess Air Force Base, Texas, in October 1986, marking the beginning of the first regular operations for the canceled plane since its resurrection five years earlier. The plane had barely gone into operation when air force officials announced that they were withholding more than $250 million in payments to companies that had produced it because it was found to have faulty electronic radar-jamming equipment (devices that

warn the plane's crew of radar signals emitted by missile sites on the ground and allow the bomber to jam the signals, confusing the defense) as well as defects in its flight-control and missile-firing systems. The plane had also developed small fuel leaks in its wings and fuselage.[68] Nevertheless, air force officials continued to defend it as "the most responsive bomber aircraft that any of us have ever flown. It is a superb flying airplane, and the crews all love the way it flies."[69]

The air force requested another $600 million for FY 1988 and FY 1989 to pay for the added costs faced by its contractors to fix the plane's electronic equipment. Total contract costs were now reported at $28 billion, with each plane running around $285 million.[70]

The House Armed Services Committee accused the air force of mismanaging the program in a report issued after a half year of investigation. The report charged that "[p]romises about aircraft performance and capabilities" were not met "and are not all expected to be met any earlier than 1991," and that "current limitations, particularly with regard to the electronic countermeasure/defensive avionics system, degrade the B-1B's effectiveness as a manned penetrating bomber." The reasons for these problems were found to lie in "[t]he extreme level of concurrency in the program [which] provided inadequate time for test and evaluation" (the last bomber would be delivered in 1989, six months before the flight test program is to be completed) and in insufficient "checks and balances" by the program's managers in the Department of Defense. But the report also found that the cost cap of $20.5 billion "failed to serve as a disciplinary measure"; instead "management initiative was diverted to find ways to escape the cap." The air force was accused of underestimating costs in order to bring the program under the $20.5 billion ceiling.[71]

Congress's multiyear funding of the program and its consistent support in return for a hands-off policy that avoided congressional micromanagement had also clearly not worked. Although officials within the B-1B program office were aware as early as October 1982 that major program modifications would be required, senior air force and Department of Defense officials were not made aware of these problems until the fall of 1985, and Congress was not officially informed of these changes until January 1987.[72]

A special report by the General Accounting Office of Congress also indicated that air force plans to correct deficiencies would

not be fulfilled until the 1990s.[73] Lawrence Skantze, Commander, Air Force Systems Command, responsible for air force research, development, and weapons acquisition, defended the program against these criticisms. He argued that electronic countermeasures in the B-1 were the biggest developmental challenge and the "largest ECM [electronic countermeasure] system ... ever attempted." Although "the black boxes checked out individually, they do not function as a system as well as we want," but the problem would be corrected "within two years." However, Congressman Les Aspin expressed the widely shared view that an extra $3 billion and four years' time would be needed to bring the bomber up to desired specifications, and launched a special House inquiry intended to apply the B-1B management lessons to other advanced weapons.[74] It had been a rocky road and the B-1B's technical and political problems had not ended with the system's deployment.

CONCLUSION

The B-52 bomber was designed in the 1940s and deployed in the mid-1950s, less than ten years from project conception to deployment. The basic design for the B-1 bomber began to take shape in the early 1960s, but it was almost twenty-five years before the bomber entered service. And it did so mired in political controversy and plagued with technical difficulties that probably will not be worked out before 1990.

Why was the B-1 built even though in the early 1960s the future of the manned bomber was in serious doubt? Why was it built even though no one outside of the air force, including successive Secretaries of Defense and at least one American President, Jimmy Carter, liked the B-1? The program did not die because no one wanted to kill it. Instead, the B-1 program was delayed, kept on hold, and simply stalled by civilians who held the purse strings to the defense budget. So central was the manned-bomber program to the air force's perception of its own mission and institutional survival, and so vigorously and ardently did the air force defend the program, that the political costs of outright cancellation and denial of all future funds for the program seemed prohibitively high, even to a strong Secretary of Defense like Robert McNamara. When Jimmy Carter decided to cancel production of the bomber, he felt compelled for political and strategic reasons to give just

enough money to the program to allow continued prototype research and development. The conflictual relationship about the bomber between the air force on the one hand and OSD and the White House on the other was also marked by cooperative behavior insofar as neither group was willing to jeopardize the fundamental interests and values of the other.

Programs have a way of outliving presidential incumbents, and the B-1 simply had to wait for a new President with a new set of defense priorities to give it a new lease on life. That President was Ronald Reagan.

Had the B-1 been built in 1977 it would have cost approximately $100 million a plane. Instead the "delay" resulting from Carter's cancellation of production led to a plane, albeit with some important modifications, costing almost $300 million. Whether the plane should have been built or not is a question on which reasonable men can differ. But there is little doubt that the system's growth in costs occurred because of the presidential cycle, changing presidential priorities, and Congress. If Congress had not deferred the production decision in 1976 to the next administration, Carter, upon entering office, would have been presented with a *fait accompli* that would have been difficult to reverse. But that is history.

Aside from this particular instance, however, Congress did not play a major role in the development of the B-1. It went along with Carter's decision to cancel the plane and then Reagan's subsequent decision to resurrect it. In an innovative measure, it agreed to multiyear funding for the program and took a "hands-off" approach to the system's development, until it became concerned about cost overruns and the technical difficulties the program was encountering. Even then, it was content to look for "lessons" for future programs, like Stealth, rather than becoming involved in reorganizing and micromanaging the details of the existing bomber program.

Those who see the arms race as the product of the ineluctable drive of technological innovation will find little evidence to support their claim in the B-1 or B-1B, or in the air-launched cruise missile, the subject of the next chapter. The technology and mission for the B-1 were for the most part old, notwithstanding its Stealth and advanced avionics features. Indeed, that was the basic charge of B-1's critics: the manned bomber was obsolete!

8

□

THE AIR-LAUNCHED CRUISE MISSILE

The B-1's development and early fate were intimately linked with the air-launched cruise missile, or ALCM (Figure 8-1). Unlike the B-1, a system that was highly desired by the air force and tied to that service's own image of its essential role and mission, the ALCM was not. The ALCM was foisted on the air force over its objections by civilian planners in the Pentagon and from outside. From its early beginnings, the ALCM was viewed as a threat to the future of the long-range manned bomber, and it was only accepted by the air force when it became apparent that its refusal to do so would jeopardize the bomber program. It was a system grudgingly accepted under political duress even though it has since come to be accepted as a potent and useful weapon in the American strategic arsenal.

ORIGINS

The origins of the cruise missile go back to World War II. The first cruise missile was the German "buzz" or "flying" bomb, the V-1. It was powered by a pulse-jet engine operated by a venetian blind device that opened to admit air and then closed to fire at 50 cycles per second. The Germans used the V-1 to attack British cities from launching platforms in France and Holland. They flew at a speed of 340–400 miles per hour, which allowed Allied fighters about six minutes to track and shoot them down. Because the missiles were small, however, they were difficult to detect. The British ended up using a variety of defensive measures against them including fighters, guns, and balloons. In all, the Germans fired over 10,000 V-1s against Britain. About 20 percent of them crashed before they

Figure 8-1. **Air-Launched Cruise Missile (AGM-86B)**

Source: Natural Resources Defense Council, Washington, D.C.

reached the English Channel. Out of the remaining 7,500 missiles that did reach the Channel, British defenses were successful in destroying just over 50 percent.[1]

The ALCM's more immediate predecessors were two air-breathing intercontinental missiles, the Snark and Navaho, which were developed for the U.S. Air Force in the early 1950s. Intended to precede the ballistic missile in the sequence of deployment, the Snark was a subsonic missile whereas the Navaho was supersonic. However, both systems were plagued by deficiencies in design and repeated test failures that delayed development. Eventually, the programs were overtaken by events with the imminent deployment of ballistic missiles in the late 1950s. Although cruise missiles were cheaper than bombers, these early systems did not perform as well as aircraft and did not have the same level of accuracy or targeting flexibility. Air force flyers were also not very keen on the system and service opposition to cruise in these early years also helped kill these programs. As one air force officer wrote in 1954:

Unfortunately, the actual reaction within the Air Force [to the guided missile] appears to be the exact opposite of that which might logically be expected. The attitude of Air Force personnel, individually throughout the Air Force and collectively in the major commands, seems to best be described as a combination of skepticism, indecision, and indifference. This is a sweeping statement, but it appears to be well supported by the facts.[2]

The other important forerunner of the modern-day cruise missile was the SCAD, or subsonic cruise armed decoy, developed in the 1950s and 1960s and carried by U.S. bombers to foil Soviet radars and draw enemy fire away from the bomber fleet itself. One of these was the "Quail," built by McDonnell Aircraft, which was designed to operate at high altitudes at subsonic speed at a range just under 500 nautical miles. It could be programmed to change its direction and air speed and it produced an image similar to a B-52 bomber on the radar screen. The system was operational in SAC for more than ten years.[3]

In the early 1960s, interest in the potential role for the cruise missile as a standoff system (a system that could be fired at some distance from its target while not placing its carrier, be it a plane or ship or submarine, in immediate danger) was rekindled. One of the early supporters was Secretary of Defense Robert McNamara who, along with civilian analysts in the OSD, sought to push the air force toward developing a long-range air-launched missile. But the air force, which did not like the cruise missile, resisted. As Robert Art and Stephen Ockenden explain: "Without exception, the military services did not want cruise missiles if they threatened their respective dominant missions or ate into their scarce funds, both of which in general were the case." This would be a continuing theme in the story of the cruise. "The cruise missile would not have proceeded as fast and as far, if indeed at all, had it not been for the intervention and support of high-level political figures in the Pentagon, the White House, and even the U.S. Department of State.... Technological innovation therefore did not create an irresistible force.... Technological innovation, however, only creates the necessary, not the sufficient, condition. At every crucial stage in the development of each type of cruise missile, high-level political intervention was necessary either to start it or to sustain it."[4]

In January 1968, SAC (Strategic Air Command) issued a Required Operational Capability Statement for a new decoy missile to replace the Quail decoy and the air-to-surface missile (Hound Dog) which were developed after the U-2 incident to prolong the life and mission of the B-52 (both had been initially designed in the 1950s). The Defense Science Board within OSD, however, took the position that the decoy should be armed.

The replacement for the Hound Dog was the SRAM (short-range attack missile). The missile had a supersonic capability, could be carried inside a bomber, and had a maximum range of 100 miles, compared to 600 for Hound Dog. Its mission was to suppress Soviet air defenses. According to Art and Ockenden, "The SRAM project team was careful to moderate any claims and to downplay any characteristics that might threaten existing air force doctrine. As one of the team noted: 'The trick in any innovation is to balance the demands of the innovators with political reality. We always took care to list modifications as refurbishments rather than as upgrades. We kept everything as incremental as possible. It's a lot less threatening that way.' "[5] SRAM quickly won air force acceptance and entered production in 1972.

Unlike Hound Dog, the Quail project was mired in controversy. The Quail missile was useful only at high altitudes and was not an especially good decoy for a low-level penetrating bomber. The air force, SAC, and respective agencies in DoD undertook a series of studies between 1967 and 1969 to establish criteria for a decoy that could be used against new Soviet air defenses. The major requirement was that the decoy had to fit inside the existing bomb bay of a B-52 and be used on the launching rack of the SRAM. This affected the size and range of the decoy. Even equipped with a small turbofan engine it would have a limited range of 500 miles.

In January 1969, the project was unveiled as a subsonic cruise armed decoy, but it was attacked by the air force because of its dual-mission capabilities. The air force distinguished clearly between the role of the SCAD and that of Hound Dog and the SRAM. Unlike the first systems designed to attack military targets like air fields and air defenses, SCAD "[was] designed," in the words of Secretary of the Air Force Robert Channing Seamans, Jr., "primarily as a decoy (armed or unarmed) to provide the capability to saturate enemy area defense radars and thus enhance the survivability of the bomber force. Even though the Soviets may be able to discrimi-

nate between a bomber and a SCAD, they would be forced to attack all radar objects if only a few SCAD were armed with a nuclear warhead."[6]

OSD pressured the air force to view the SCAD as a standoff weapons system. In the forefront of OSD opposition was John Foster, Director of DDR&E. Foster argued, "The SCAD carries a nuclear warhead and has adequate range to be used as a stand-off missile so that the bomber does not have to penetrate."[7] Foster supported McNamara's view that bombers could be used as platforms for missiles. The armed SCAD was also presented by critics in the Pentagon's Office of Planning, Analysis, and Evaluation (PA&E) as an alternative to the costly B-1.

OSD did not prevent AMSA from progressing to the B-1 but they did succeed in preventing the rapid development of the SCAD as a decoy. The air force's request for $30 million for SCAD in 1968 for FY 1970 was cut by OSD to $17.1 million and by Congress to $9.1 million. In the FY 1971 request, the air force and DoD agreed on a request for $33.6 million but Congress denied all. Foster helped scuttle the program in skeptical testimony before Congress.

The air force, in turn, "responded by monitoring and managing the program's development as closely as possible in order to ensure that the decoy did not become a full-fledged standoff weapon. The Air Force Systems Command took the unprecedented step of acting as subsystems integrator, a role normally reserved for the prime contractor.... Such close monitoring ensured that the decoy—now named the subsonic cruise armed decoy, or SCAD—would remain an augmentation of, rather than a replacement for, the penetrating bomber."[8] The air force revised the program to split SCAD into SCAD A, with a decoy and an "optional" warhead capability for the B-52, and a longer range SCAD B, with a warhead option for the B-1.

With budget cuts and mounting pressure against SCAD, the air force reviewed the entire program. It nevertheless decided the program was sufficiently urgent to request an additional $45 million for FY 1972, which OSD cut to $10 million.

DoD and the air force also began to take seriously the idea of a long-range stand-off missile. However, the air force took the position that cruise missiles and bombers would both be vulnerable to Soviet air defenses and argued rather disingenuously that the unit

cost of B-1 would be reduced if all the stand-off penetrating features were taken off it: "the stand-off cruise missile—since it must be subsonic to achieve the necessary range—becomes quite vulnerable to SAMs which have improved capabilities against targets at low altitude. Therefore to retain an effectiveness for the stand-off force ... the number of stand-off cruise missiles had to be increased—correspondingly increasing the necessary number of stand-off bombers to the extent that the stand-off force would cost more than the penetrating force even though each stand-off bomber was cheaper."[9] The air force also believed that against Soviet SA-3 SAM and follow-up missiles, cruise missiles were vulnerable.

The battle between OSD and the air force intensified as the former made it clear it wanted an armed decoy, while the latter preferred to keep it unarmed. The air force feared that an armed decoy could easily grow into a long-range stand-off weapon and, if it did, this would scuttle the case for the B-1.

SCAD's list of technical difficulties also grew. The problem with making the SCAD decoy was to make it look big so that it would look like a B-52 or B-1 bomber on a Soviet radar screen. But if it was to be used as a weapon, the problem was to make it as small as possible to hide from enemy radar and defenses. The $10 million requested for the SCAD program in FY 1972 was authorized by Congress, but the Senate Armed Services Committee made its support conditional on the air force making SCAD more accurate and dual capable. The full Senate also defeated amendments offered by Senator William Proxmire (D.-Wis.) to fund studies for a stand-off bomber like a B-52 equipped with SCAD and a wide-bodied cruise missile carrier.[10]

The bad news for SCAD program supporters was that, in the summer of 1971, an ad hoc panel of the President's Scientific Advisory Board concluded that long-range cruise missiles were feasible and effective in nuclear war.

Interest in SCAD diminished in almost inverse proportion to growing enthusiasm for the cruise missile. Senator Proxmire viewed the air-launched cruise missile as a good substitute for the B-1. He said, "It makes sense to develop a strategic cruise missile as a hedge against threats to our current strategic forces. But the Pentagon is developing the wrong missile at the wrong time. The Navy's SLCM program has little more merit than a nuclear warhead fired from a

crossbow, while an attack missile version of SCAD could provide us with an alternative option to the B-1 for preserving our strategic bomber force."[11]

Some congressmen were also suspicious that the air force was delaying development of the armed SCAD for the B-1 so that the system would not be ready by the time the production decision on B-1 had to be made. Nevertheless, the full $48.6 million for SCAD requested by the air force for FY 1973 was authorized and appropriated.

In February 1973, the GAO released a study that was highly critical of SCAD. It argued that the system would be vulnerable to the new and emerging threat of Soviet aircraft possessing a "look-down, shoot-down" capability. (The Soviets deployed the TU-126 MOSS in 1970, which already had a "look-down, shoot-down" capability over water.[12])

RESEARCH AND DEVELOPMENT

Later, in March–April 1973, the Defense Science Acquisition Review Council (DSARC) met to review the program and decide upon SCAD engineering and development. Three options were laid out: (1) to develop a decoy with an arming option but no actual development work on the armed version; (2) to develop a decoy followed by development later of an armed decoy; and (3) to develop a decoy and an armed version concurrently. Advocates of the stand-off replacement made it clear they saw it as an alternative to the B-1, but PA&E analysts said the system should be armed or canceled.

When it heard about this, the Senate Armed Services Committee expressed its anger that priority had not been given earlier to the development of an armed decoy. Worried about the rising costs of the B-1, the air force now argued, in a surprising turnabout, that the plane did not require SCAD capabilities after all, because this feature would add only modestly to its penetration capabilities. The air force also asserted that the B-52 "was not about to fall apart and that the United States could look forward to a mixed force of B-1s and B-52s for some time to come."[13] In words that later came back to haunt them, air force officials asserted, "The best available information at this time indicates the service life of the B-52 G/H aircraft to be early to mid-1990s."[14]

John Foster attacked the air force plan to proceed simultaneously with development of a decoy and an armed, extended-range version of SCAD at a DSARC meeting on April 13, 1973. He ordered the air force to return with a revised plan for simultaneous IOCs (Initial Operational Capabilities). The SCAD program was reconsidered by DSARC on June 28, 1973, but again failed to persuade OSD's top officials. They decided to cancel the program. Authorizing the decision, Deputy Defense Secretary William Perry Clements, Jr., said that $22 million of the $72.2 million for SCAD would be used to pursue cruise missile technology. OSD had decided to take the plunge.[15]

But Congress was not quite so enthusiastic as OSD about cruise missiles and halved the request for ALCM appropriations to $11 million, while insisting that money be used only to develop system components and subcomponents.

On December 19, 1973, Deputy Secretary of Defense Clements issued DSARC Directive 174 to the air force to begin development of a formal ALCM program using SCAD technologies for propulsion and the navy's TERCOM system then under development for guidance and navigation.

The TERCOM system was one of the most important technological advancements in cruise missile technology. One of the major problems with cruise missiles of the 1950s was how to get them to arrive on target after traveling thousands of miles. The development of microprocessor computer technology gave engineers the tool to do this. With this technology, a terrain map derived from a contour map or satellite reconnaissance could be stored in the missile's on-board flight computer. The missile would then use its radar to measure ground elevations and check them against the digital map stored in its computer memory. If the missile found itself off course, it could make the necessary adjustments to its flight controls to get back on course again.

Recognizing the inherent potential of this new technology, Clements considered it essential to incorporate it into any new air-launched cruise missile design. He also ordered the air force ALCM project to be phased back and coordinated with the navy project. The navy, however, actively resisted pressures from OSD to develop its cruise missile to be compatible with those launched from an aircraft. It argued that its own cruise missiles needed more range and greater weight. The air force was only too willing to

concur with the navy's assessment in order to maintain full control over its own program.

The ALCM program was further affected by the Joint Strategic Bomber Study prepared by the air force and DoD and delivered to Congress in December 1974. The JSBS was followed by an independent study on the future of the U.S. bomber fleet conducted by the Washington-based Brookings Institution a year later. The JSBS looked at various mixes of existing and potential aircraft and concluded that the B-1 was the most cost effective, whereas the Brookings study suggested that the B-1 was unnecessary and that the new bomber would not have to be as sophisticated. The JSBS came in for heavy criticism because of its assumptions and methodology, and various congressional critics took to calling it the "Joint Strategic B.S. Study."[16]

In hearings on the FY 1976 budget, the air force continued to argue that the B-1 was necessary and essential while the ALCM would help to prolong the life and mission of the B-52 in the interim. One senior air force official expressed the view that, while cruise missiles were not particularly effective against sites defended by SAMs, "[a]gainst undefended targets, cruise missiles are cost effective compared to B-1s and B-52s carrying SRAMs or gravity bombs."[17] As Charles Sorrels notes, "the Air Force . . . was skeptical about the ALCMs potential, expecially regarding its accuracy and adequacy of range," but the civilian director of research and engineering for the Department of Defense, Dr. Malcom R. Currie, was considerably more enthusiastic. He endorsed both the ALCM and SLCM "because they are designed for use on existing carrier vehicles and therefore have relatively low cost, and are potentially very high leverage systems. They stress the air defenses in a different way than our penetrating bomber forces (i.e., they are effective against advanced fighters and are countered by extensive advanced-capability SAMs)."[18]

OSD tried to accelerate ALCM funding in FY 1976 by doubling the funds requested by the air force, but in response to congressional concern over navy/air force duplication, it kept ALCM in an advanced development holding pattern in order for the navy's SLCM program to catch up. In fact, the ALCM was almost canceled in favor of an air-launched version of the SLCM, and the navy was asked to keep the B-52 in mind while it worked on SLCM.

Arms control also drove the pace of cruise missile development.

In the negotiations leading up to the SALT I agreements, cruise missiles did not figure prominently because of the program's infancy. Although the possibility of limiting the number of long-range ground- and sea-launched cruise missiles was raised during the course of the negotiations, it did not make its way into the final agreement. The cruise missile program, however, was a lucky beneficiary of SALT I. Secretary of State Henry Kissinger pushed acceleration of cruise missile development along with a number of other programs, including Trident, as a bargaining chip with the Joint Chiefs of Staff whose approval of the accords was necessary to secure the support of Congress. The State Department, through Kissinger, wrote the requirement for an air-to-surface strategic missile. In October 1973, Boeing was given a contract for full-scale engineering development for what was for the first time called an air-launched cruise missile. However, the missile still had the original specification laid on it, which was that it must be physically and functionally interchangeable with SRAM (short-range attack missile) weapons systems. This imposed severe performance limitations on the system, which was subsequently named ALCM-A.

At the Vladivostok meeting in November 1974 between Soviet leader Leonid Brezhnev and President Gerald Ford, the two sides agreed to limits on the number of strategic delivery vehicles (2,400) and the number of ICBMs and SLBMs equipped with MIRVs (1,320). In the published text of the tentative accords (which were never formally approved), the MIRV sublimit applied to ICBMs and SLBMs only. However, in subsequent negotiations two years later, cruise missiles were a contentious issue. The question arose whether bombers armed with ALCMs should be regarded as MIRVed systems, because the accords also covered "certain long-range air-to-surface missiles." The air force took the position that ALCMs were exempt from the restrictions. Secretary of the Air Force John L. McLucus firmly stated: "We are continuing development. Someone would have told us if there was an effect."[19] However, meeting with the Russians in January 1976 Henry Kissinger offered to include American bombers with cruise missiles in the 1,320 MIRV launcher ceiling permitted under the Vladivostok accords. It is not evident from the historical record whether he saw this as a bargaining "chip" or a bargaining "whip" to extract concessions from the Soviets. (The Soviets had made it clear they wanted to ban all cruise missiles with ranges over 600 kilometers.[20])

The year 1976 was important for the cruise missile program because of the impending decision on the B-1 bomber. In anticipation of the decision, DDR&E undertook a detailed examination of the viability of replacing the ALCM with an air-launched version of SLCM.

In March 1976, the air force conducted its first successful bomber-launch test of a cruise missile. Nevertheless, the air force continued to press the view that the air-launched cruise missile lacked the ability to reach all targets assigned to the bomber force under SIOP (Single Integrated Operational Plan) and had the additional problem of penetrating SAM-defended targets. The ALCM program was further constrained by the lack of variable terrain along the missile's flight path, which made it difficult for the TERCOM system to work efficiently. Thus, according to the air force, the B-1 was still necessary to reach heavily defended targets deep inside the Soviet Union. But the air force's apparent enthusiasm for the cruise missile was growing. Said Thomas Reed, Secretary of the Air Force, "The air-launched cruise missile . . . has a technology with tremendous growth potential."[21]

Continuing negotiations in SALT II raised the potential of further constraints. Air Chief of Staff General David C. Jones suggested that the MIRVed ICBM force might have to be cut if cruise missiles equipped with B-52 G/Hs were to be counted as MIRVed systems. But in its FY 1978 defense budget, the Ford administration tripled its request for cruise missiles to 2,328 (a figure which included the B-52 and proposed B-1 force; the decision to arm the B-1 with ALCMs had probably been made by OSD).

A second DSARC meeting in January 1977 led to a further restructuring of the ALCM program. Cooperation of the air force and navy was formalized through the creation of a joint project office. A decision was also made to accelerate the development of the extended-range ALCM-B so that it would be available in December 1980. The air force's preoccupation with the shorter range ALCM-A was seen as a way to protect the role of the penetrating bomber. DSARC II-A supported the view that the cruise missile could not be relied on to penetrate defended targets, but it also supported the idea of stretching ALCM-A to the ALCM-B rather than putting an extra fuel tank under the missile (the air force's preference). This had the effect of ruling out the B-1 as a long-range cruise missile platform because a longer missile would not

fit into its bomb bays. But DSARC II-A did take the position that a common missile for both navy and air force launch platforms might compromise the performance of both systems and therefore gave the go-ahead for full-scale engineering of each system independently.[22] The January 1977 DSARC II-A recommendation therefore stood as follows:

- Proceed with full-scale engineering development managed by the Joint Cruise Missile Program Office under navy direction
  - ALCM-B (long range); IOC by mid 1980, priority over ALCM-A; optimize B-52 for long-range ALCM carriage
  - Land-attack Tomahawk (long range) for sub and ship launch and ground launch
  - Anti-ship Tomahawk for sub and ship launch; demonstrate over the horizon target acquisition before DSARC III[23]

PRODUCTION

Jimmy Carter's negative decision on the B-1 bomber came as a shock to the air force, which thought it would at the very worst get approval to build at least ninety B-1s.[24] Carter's decision was followed by an amendment to the FY 1978 budget requesting an additional $325.4 million for cruise missiles. Fifty million dollars would go for ALCM-B development and the ALCM-A would be canceled because of its prohibitively short range. One hundred and six million dollars would go for an air-launched version of SLCM to compete with the ALCM-B, $60 million for preparation of cruise missile production, and $90 million to explore the concept of a wide-bodied cruise missile. The number of ALCMs to be procured also increased to 3,424 to arm 173 B-52G bombers.

Carter's decision forced the air force to take the cruise missile issue seriously and to consider whether it wanted to adopt a shared ALCM/SLCM system with the navy. The two programs were proceeding in tandem. General Dynamics was working on SLCM development while Boeing was working on ALCM. The General Dynamics model was longer and heavier than Boeing's, which meant that a B-52 rotary launcher could carry only six missiles instead of eight, but the two systems relied on the same technology and engine and guidance systems.[25] Because it was not a clear choice either way, on September 30, 1977, the new DDR&E chief, Wil-

liam Perry, ordered a direct competition between the two systems.

> It is a matter of the highest national priority, especially in light of the B-1 decision, to develop an air-launched cruise missile (ALCM) with optimum performance and minimum cost and schedule delays. I believe we can best accomplish those program objectives by conducting a competitive flyoff between Boeing and General Dynamics to determine which of their missiles will be the ALCM to be flown on the B-52 and, as appropriate, other cruise missile carriers.[26]

The competition would be conducted by the Joint Cruise Missile Program Office (JCMPO) while the selection itself would be recommended by a Source Selection Advisory Council composed of an equal number of representatives from the air force and navy. During full-scale development of the ALCM, decisions were made by a special Executive Committee chaired by DDR&E Chief William Perry. The air force also pursued the development of competitive opportunities in subsystem and component development to reduce redundancy and to promote efficiency. However, McDonnell Douglas was the designated supplier for guidance for competitors and all of the cruise missiles and they selected Litton and Honeywell to supply the basic hardware including the inertial navigation system and missile radar altimeter. Williams Research was the designated source for all of the small fan engines for the cruise missiles.

While the competition got under way, Carter's cruise missile decision came under close scrutiny from Congress. Some worried about the arms control implications of the decision, although Carter firmly stated that bombers armed with cruise missiles would not be considered MIRVed systems under SALT. The standoff range for the missiles would be 2,500 kilometers. Nevertheless, questions were raised about the ability of the Soviets to detect bombers at this range. The administration countered that bombers could fly below radars before they got within range of Soviet defenses.

In July 1977 radar towers were observed under construction along the Soviet borders in Romania and Poland, raising new fears in Congress about the penetrability of cruise missiles even though NATO officials were quick to dismiss these new Soviet countermeasures. But then some seized on rumors that the Soviets were

developing a new hypersonic SAM (the SA-10) to be used against cruise missiles. DoD officials quickly dismissed these rumors, saying that operational deployment of such a system was many years away.

In March 1977, the Carter administration's comprehensive arms control proposal to the Soviets included a proposal to limit cruise missiles to a maximum range of 2,500 kilometers. This was followed by an April 1977 proposal in which ALCMs were limited to 2,500 kilometers and SLCMs and GLCMs to 600 kilometers if deployed within a three-year period following the signing of SALT II (after which they would not be limited). The final Treaty restricted the number of ALCMs that could be deployed on a single aircraft and limited the total number of ALCMs that could be deployed by counting all aircraft fitted with ALCMs under 2,250 and 1,320 aggregate limits on strategic delivery vehicles and strategic delivery vehicles with multiple, force loadings. The protocol banned deployment of sea- and ground-launched cruise missiles with ranges greater than 600 kilometers, but not their development or flight testing.[27]

Tests of SLCMs launched against U.S. SAMs and simulated Soviet SAMs in January–October 1978 showed that Soviet air defenses would not be effective against cruise missiles. The FY 1980 defense budget requested $475.4 million for the ALCM-B cruise missile program, of which $90 million was for R&D and the rest for procurement of 225 missiles. The wide-bodied and advanced cruise missile program got an additional $65 million.

In late 1979, the fly-off competition for the contract took place between Boeing and General Dynamics. Two hundred navy and air force officers assisted the Source Selection Advisory Board in assessing the results of the competition. On March 25, 1980, Secretary of the Air Force Hans Mark declared Boeing's AGM-86B the winner. The decision was reinforced by a favorable DSARC III recommendation in April 1980 and a DoD review on May 1, 1980. The Boeing selection was attributed to the AGM-86B's superior guidance system, software, and aerodynamics. Boeing's missile could fly lower and over rougher terrain than General Dynamic's Tomahawk missile. The contract remained fixed at 3,418 missiles.[28]

Modifications were also made to incorporate the ALCM missile into the B-52 G/H payloads. These included development of a rotary-launch system to be incorporated in the bomb bay of the

B-52G to permit it to carry ALCMs.[29] In 1984 work also began on the development of a cruise missile launcher for the B-1 bomber, but there were no immediate plans to deploy cruise missiles on the B-1 before the 1990s.[30]

Although the air force and navy had gone their separate ways on cruise, the air force's AGM-86B and the navy's SLCM programs were structured to have maximum commonality in engine and navigation/guidance subsystems. The ALCM and SLCM also shared a common W-80 nuclear warhead, developed by the Department of Energy. The SLCM and GLCM engine, navigation/guidance, and mission planning projects were jointly managed through the JCMPO. However, after the April 1980 production decision, management of the ALCM was transferred to the air force's Strategic Systems Program Office (SSPO).

DEVELOPMENT PROBLEMS

Boeing's AGM-86B was plagued with development problems and continued bouts of testing failure. On its much-publicized first test flight on August 3, 1979, the missile crashed. Although it went on to six successful tests out of an initial round of ten, the image of failure stuck.

Subsequent tests of the system revealed more serious deficiencies, however. Out of fifteen tests conducted during the period 1980–1982, the AGM-68B suffered four failures and one crash. In 1980, the Air Force Testing and Evaluation Center (AFTEC) rated the system satisfactory in thirteen areas, deficient in three, and inconclusive in another eight. The reliability of the system's Offensive Avionics System (OAS) was singled out for special concern. In 1981, the AFTEC rated the operational effectiveness and suitability of the system "deficient." The second round of testing, begun in 1982, was marred by further crashes and serious software problems. Boeing was also forced to make significant changes to the design of the missile's nose and its housing and engine. The missile's guidance system continued to be plagued with problems. Many of these were still being worked out in 1988, long after December 1982 when the first "operational" ALCM squadron went into service at Griffiss Air Force Base in New York.[31]

The program also exceeded its development costs. In 1981 ALCM program manager Colonel Joseph G. Rutter reported that since the

initial development and procurement estimates had been made in early 1977, costs had grown about 35 percent in development and 10 percent in procurement in constant dollar terms. When the air force became aware in 1978 that development costs for work needed to be done would exceed available funding by well over $100 million, it had to decide whether to let the program schedule slip or to obtain funds from other sources to keep it on schedule. It opted for the latter and scooped an additional $66 million from the ALCM procurement line through reprogramming and an additional $33 million from the FY 1979 supplemental appropriation.[32]

Many of ALCM's difficulties can be traced to high levels of program concurrency, particularly in the ALCM and OAS development programs.[33] Concurrency was necessary to meet compressed time schedules mandated by the politicians. Colonel Rutter explains:

> The ALCM program, after the B-1 bomber decision was made, came under heavy emphasis to meet some very early initial operational capabilities. First of all we started the development program in February 1978, and we had to have hardware on the ramp at Griffiss Air Force Base by September of this year, a 3½-year cycle, which is relatively short in the development world.[34]

Time pressures also created problems at the organizational level because management responsibility was split between those in charge of the B-52 launch vehicle and those in charge of the ALCM program. Although the Joint Cruise Missile Program Office was formed in Washington, D.C., the responsibility for the B-52 remained at Wright Paterson Air Force Base. The two elements of this system had to meet common milestones but were under two different program managers.[35]

Cost overruns and program difficulties would not necessarily have been improved by multiyear procurement. It is interesting to note that the air force was asked in the DSARC III review to consider whether multiyear funding would lead to quantifiable potential savings, efficiency, and a steeper learning curve. According to J. R. Ray Utterstrom, when the air force put the question to Boeing,

> [o]ur position in a nutshell was that we favor multiyear procurement, but we did not think we had the experience to price [the program], certainly not price it firm, which was to be the rule.

Before we built missile 1, how could we sign up to build 2,200 missiles at a firm price? So we resisted. We said we would wait. We would like to do that in 1982. If you will buy the program out, we will give you these kinds of savings, something like 10 percent.[36]

Boeing eventually did submit its plans for multiyear procurement in FY 1983 based on the production experience of the first fifty units.

OTHER CRUISE MISSILE DEVELOPMENTS

Since 1980, the Defense Department's Advanced Research Projects Agency (DARPA) has been pushing ahead with "Teal Dawn," a program designed to integrate Stealth radar-evasion techniques into an advanced cruise missile (ACM) design. The system would be launched vertically from a Minuteman silo or equivalent and then fly on a horizontal path at supersonic speeds toward its target where, just before hitting the target, it would go into a ballistic trajectory.[37] The air force envisions acquiring about 1,500 advanced cruise missiles, although the final total would depend on whether the new missile would be available soon enough to interfere with the existing AGM-86B program. The ACM would have a range in excess of 6,000 miles, enabling it to be fired from U.S. airspace. The aim is also to develop a maneuverable system that would be able to evade Soviet air defenses. In early 1987, Secretary of Defense Caspar Weinberger announced that a site had been chosen for the Stealth missile and that the new missile would begin arriving at the base by 1989, although deployment would not begin until later in the 1990s.[38]

Another important cruise-related program is the MRASM (medium-range air-to-surface missile), a joint tactical missile of shorter range which uses a terminal guidance system to home in on its target and carries a variety of conventional munitions (versus a nuclear warhead). The program lingered near oblivion until Defense Under Secretary William Perry spurred it to life in 1980 on the grounds that it was a matter of "national importance" that MSRAM "be added to our strike warfare as soon as possible." The contract was awarded to General Dynamics, the loser in the ALCM competition. Under the development concept, MSRAM would be used to

attack runways and other targets inside enemy territory with cratering submunitions. But the air force would also like to use it for defense suppression, anti-armor, and electronic countermeasure and reconnaissance roles.[39]

CONCLUSION

The story of the ALCM, like the B-1, is interesting because it is marked by a mixture of conflict and cooperation among competing institutional interests. The air force was willing to humor its civilian leaders by supporting research on an armed decoy missile up to the point where the ALCM did not appear to pose a significant threat to the future of the B-1 manned program. As soon as the threat became apparent, however, it dug in its heels and did all it could to delay and arrest further work on cruise missiles. As the threat to the manned-bomber program intensified and it became evident to senior air force officials that if they did not compromise on cruise development the future of the B-1 would be jeopardized (or worse, they would lose control of the cruise missile program to the navy), they took a keener and more active interest in the program, and ingeniously searched for ways to ensure the compatibility of cruise missile development with the B-1. Congress played a passive role in the development of the air-launched cruise missile. It supported the proddings of successive administrations to get the air force to take the cruise missile more seriously, although it rarely gave any administration all of the funds requested to accelerate the program.

In the case of both the B-1 and the ALCM, cooperation and conflict were evident during different stages or phases of the weapons' procurement cycles. Like the B-1, the technology behind the cruise missile was not new—cruise missiles had been around since Hitler's "buzz" bombs of World War II. But a combination of new technologies for propulsion and guidance gave an old idea new appeal, apparent first to the civilian defense planners in the Pentagon.

9

□

THE M-1 ABRAMS TANK

BY NICHOLAS SWALES

On July 21, 1978, the XM-1 (experimental M-1) tank was unveiled to the press at the Aberdeen Proving Ground, Maryland. With finely calculated showmanship, the army put the XM-1 through its paces side by side with an M-60. "Either the M-60 wasn't trying its hardest, or the XM-1 has considerably better acceleration and speed and shoots more accurately," reported one observer.[1] The M-60's comparatively weak performance was not surprising since it was the product of 1940s technology. However, the M-1's performance was not up to scratch, either. The system still had major teething problems even though the U.S. Army had been working on building a new tank for over twenty years. The M-1 was finally delivered to operational units in 1981 (Figure 9-1), the same year the Soviet Union was deploying its fourth new tank since World War II.[2]

That the final-production M-1 and the improved M-1A1 turned out to be the world-beating tanks they are was due more to good luck and well-timed technological advance than to good planning and foresight. Although few denied outright that the United States needed new tanks of some sort by the early 1980s, advances in anti-tank weaponry in the 1970s raised disturbing questions about the future of the heavy tank, and the debate over standardization within NATO threatened to derail the program several times.

Congress, the Department of Defense, and the army all had different objectives and missions for the new tank. The army, as the user of tanks, sought the best equipment that money could buy. As the junior partner, however, its priorities suffered from the desire of Congress to control the price of the tanks. In addition, Con-

Figure 9-1. **M-1 Abrams Tank**

Source: United States Army.

gress used the program as something of a test case to affirm its control over the military on defense procurement. DoD, which took a longer view of the military threat, saw the tanks as a key issue in NATO alliance relations and was prepared to interfere with the tank's technical development for political purposes. As a result, the M-1 was the product of many compromises forged between Congress, the Defense Department, and the army, combining the latest innovations in United States, German, and British tank design. But this was only achieved at substantial political cost to each of the main political and bureaucratic actors, to NATO, and to the program itself.

While the M-1 was eventually produced in accordance with its original timetable, delays within the process caused rushed development of key components such as the engine. The resulting modifications, and the effects of inflation in particular, significantly raised the costs of the program by the time the system was deployed.

This chapter will explore the following questions. Why did the objectives of the main political actors conflict? How were these conflicts resolved? How did the resolution affect the final design and production of the M-1 tank?

PROGRAM INITIATION AND DEVELOPMENT

In December 1971 the XM-1 program was established to develop a Main Battle Tank (MBT) for the U.S. Army. But it was already the army's third attempt to develop a new MBT to replace the aging and increasingly obsolescent M-60 series. The first effort began in 1963 when the need for a new tank was not pressing (the M-60 only entered service in 1961).[3] Then Secretary of Defense Robert McNamara initiated a joint project with West Germany to develop the MBT-70 tank, a logical decision in view of the much longer tradition of tank design in Europe, as well as the prospective benefits from larger production runs and greater standardization within NATO.[4]

In 1969, Melvin Laird, the new Secretary of Defense, initiated an intensive review of major weapons system projects in the Pentagon. It was evident that the MBT-70 program was in serious trouble because of an escalating price tag and technical problems that were forcing the program seriously behind schedule, including several problems with the Shillelagh gun-missile system, particularly the reloading mechanism (for which the automatic loader did not work) and the barrel (which did not clean itself as intended). Also the suspension was weak, the power train did not deliver enough horsepower, and the turret-mounted driver became easily disoriented. In that year, Senator Thomas F. Eagleton (D.-Mo.), who was to prove a consistent opponent of heavy tank development, succeeded in halting funding for the MBT-70 program pending a GAO (General Accounting Office) cost study.[5] The outcome of that study was the cancellation of the MBT-70 program by Congress on January 20, 1970, because of its excessive cost (nearly $1 million per copy) and complexity. As one NATO observer put it, "It was an all singing, all dancing thing. Everybody thought it was absolutely marvelous, but far too expensive and far too complicated for any crew to handle."[6]

While Germany went on to develop the Leopard tank, the United States proceeded to develop an austere, "scrubbed-down" version of the MBT-70 designated the XM-803 which retained such features of the MBT-70 as the squatting suspension, the turret-mounted, counterrotating driver, and the Shillelagh gun-missile system but at a cost of only $600,000. Congress was not convinced by army assurances that this price tag was feasible, and first cut and then

restored $59.1 million in XM-803 production money from the FY 1972 Authorization Bill,[7] and then canceled the program altogether on December 18, 1971, once again citing technical difficulties and excessive cost.[8]

Concept Formulation. By the beginning of the 1970s, however, it was becoming evident that the army needed a new tank, so Congress included $40 million in the FY 1973 defense budget for contract termination costs of the XM-803 and for the initiation of a new program, the XM-1. In January 1972, the army set up a thirty-three-man task force at Fort Knox, Kentucky, with user, developer, and army staff participation, headed by Major-General William Desobry, an armor officer.[9]

The task force presented its report on August 1, 1972, in the form of a Mission Need Determination Statement containing "the performance, cost, technical and development schedules of various alternative configurations of a new tank. These alternatives ranged from modest product improvement programs for the current M60A1 tank to prototype development of a completely new main battle tank."[10] On the basis of this, the XM-1 Project Manager's Office was established in September, headed by Brigadier General Robert Baer, and a DSARC review was convened on November 14. At this review, DoD decided "to initiate a program to develop a new tank, which will be more capable than an improved M60 series tank, but simpler and less costly than the XM-803."[11]

The Material Need Document was then reviewed by the army to remove unnecessary features in order to keep costs down, and on January 18, 1973, the Development Concept Paper was approved by the army and DoD and was issued to potential contractors.[12] The DCP required the contractors, General Motors Corporation (GMC) and Chrysler Corporation (Ford was invited to submit a bid, but declined, commenting that the other two contractors had the tank business pretty well "locked in"[13]), "to achieve significant improvements over the baseline M-60 series in the areas of armor protection, mobility, firepower and RAM-D (Reliability, Availability, Maintainability, and Durability) at an average design-to-unit cost for a production run of 3,000 tanks of $507,790 per tank in FY 1972 dollars. Government furnished equipment would account for $55,790 of the cost per tank."[14] A degree of latitude was allowed

in the designs, and specifications could be traded off against each other within limits,[15] although it was later to emerge that these limits were in some cases fairly arbitrary.[16] The fundamental shape of the tank, though, was already decided by the choice of armor.

The design-to-unit cost limit, a design-to-production time limit of seven years, and an insistence on two prototype contractors to encourage competition were all imposed on the army by Congress which, starting in 1972, kept the XM-1 program under close scrutiny to try to avoid some of the problems encountered with the MBT-70 and XM-803. "The Congress ordered a low risk tank. We didn't want to get into any highfalutin' technology," commented Representative Samuel S. Stratton (D.-N.Y.), Chairman of the House Armed Services Committee Investigations Subcommittee,[17] who was to have a significant impact on the future direction of the program. In September 1973 Senator Eagleton failed in an attempt to give the cost ceiling the force of law in an amendment to the Defense Appropriations Bill.[18]

Chrysler and GMC submitted their initial proposals in May 1973. In June, the validation contracts were awarded: one worth $68.1 million to the Defense Division of the Chrysler Corporation, which planned to power its prototype with an Avco-Lycoming gas turbine engine, and one worth $87 million to the Detroit Diesel Allison Division of GMC which planned to power its prototype with Teledyne Continental's variable compression ratio diesel engine.[19] Each contractor was required to deliver to the army one prototype tank, one automotive test rig, and one hull and turret for ballistic tests.

DEMONSTRATION AND VALIDATION

Yom Kippur War. On October 6, 1973, the relative peace of the Jewish holy festival of Yom Kippur was shattered by a massive combined Egyptian-Syrian attack on Israeli defensive positions in the Sinai desert and along the Golan Heights. Israeli armored counterattacks encountered a new tactical situation. In the words of one Israeli tank commander:

> We were advancing, and in the distance I saw specks dotted on the sand dunes. I couldn't make out what they were. As we got closer, I thought they looked like tree stumps. They were motionless and

scattered across the terrain ahead of us. I got on the intercom and asked the tanks ahead what they made of it. One of my tank commanders radioed back: "My God, they're not tree stumps, they're men." For a moment, I couldn't understand. What were they doing out there—standing quite still—when we were advancing our tanks toward them? Suddenly, all hell broke loose. A barrage of missiles was being fired at us. Many of our tanks were hit. We had never come up against anything like this before.[20]

The Israelis had come up against new Soviet-supplied precision-guided anti-tank missiles (PGMs), and these took a substantial toll on Israeli tanks in the first few days of the war. The apparent ease with which relatively inexpensive PGMs were able to destroy relatively expensive U.S.-supplied tanks provided significant fuel to those in the United States who felt that tanks were becoming obsolete. Prominent in these arguments was Senator Eagleton, who had been saying, as early as November 1971, "The role of tanks is becoming more restricted and the tank itself is becoming more vulnerable."[21] Early in 1974 he visited Israel to get firsthand information on the Israelis' experience with tank vulnerability, and returned observing, "The advent of cheap anti-tank weapons has made it imperative that we build less costly, more agile tanks."[22] He requested a GAO inquiry into the tank program on the basis that they were becoming obsolete.

On June 29, 1976, the GAO report was made public by Eagleton and Representative Les Aspin (D.-Wis.). It argued that the Defense Department was rushing into developing a costly new MBT in the face of major uncertainties about the future of armored warfare. A similar report was also issued by the Senate Armed Services Committee based on a study by Senators John C. Culver (D.-Iowa) and Sam Nunn (D.-Ga.), noting that there was "a need to re-evaluate the role of the tank on the modern day battlefield" before committing any more money to development.[23]

The army response was to establish a Tank Special Study Group to review the XM-1 Material Need Document. Its recommendations, however, were relatively minor, suggesting increased engagement ranges and on-board ammunition storage, enhanced turret external stowage protection, and substituting a machine gun as coaxial weapon (light weapon mounted alongside the main tank gun) for the Bushmaster cannon, which was encountering techni-

cal difficulties anyway.[24] The army continued to believe in the effectiveness of tanks, frequently arguing that the tank remained the best anti-tank weapon.[25] Furthermore, army officials argued that the tank was not expected to operate alone on future battle-fields, and that most anti-tank missiles were even more vulnerable to countermeasures.[26]

The army's case was greatly helped by the development of new "special armor" by the British in the late 1960s, armor much more resistant than normal steel to hollow-charge rounds (such as those carried on most PGMs). The United States had been offered the armor technology in 1972 just as the XM-1 project got under way, and it was made a principal feature of the new tank design, its special nature accounting for the slablike shape of the XM-1.[27] According to Dr. Percy A. Pierre, Assistant Secretary of the Army for Research, Development, and Acquisitions in the early 1980s, the XM-1 was "impervious to any known Soviet anti-tank missile in service or development."[28]

Despite all this, the army was not able to silence completely the doubts about the obsolescence of the heavy tank, which were to surface periodically throughout the XM-1's development. There seems to be little doubt that the XM-1 will be the last of the heavy-weights. While the development of special armor has permitted the tank to survive the latest onslaught of anti-tank technology, the XM-1 is at the upper limit of tank size and weight, so future tank developments will have to incorporate some means other than making tanks bigger. Speed, concealment, and rapid reaction weaponry will increasingly become the important characteristics of tank design. The need to move tanks strategically also decreases the usefulness of large tanks because road and rail bridges and tunnels, as well as aircraft, can support only limited weights. Present United States Army future tank programs reflect these trends.[29]

Another event occurred during the prototype construction period that was to have far-reaching consequences in the development of the XM-1. In a throwback to the MBT-70 program, the Pentagon signed a Memorandum of Understanding with the Federal Republic of Germany on December 11, 1974, agreeing to test the German Leopard II against the winning U.S. prototype in the fall of 1976. The Memorandum was somewhat vague about what would then happen, but there developed a "popular belief, reinforced from time to time by official statements of both governments ...

that both the XM-1 and the Leopard were bidding to become the Army's next main battle tank."[30] This seems to have been a unilateral initiative on the part of Defense Secretary James R. Schlesinger, and it was not well received by the army. In conjunction with this, the Ford Motor Company, which had stayed out of the initial competition, began studies with Krauss-Maffei, the makers of the Leopard, to determine if it was feasible to produce the tank in the United States.[31]

TESTING AND DELAYS

Chrysler and General Motors handed over their prototype tanks to the army on schedule on February 3, 1976. The tanks were then subjected to the first phase of Developmental and Operational Testing (DT/OT 1), which continued to the end of April. The winning prototype was due to be decided by the army at the end of May, then endorsed by DoD, and the Full-Scale Engineering Development (FSED) contract awarded to the winning design by July 20.

While similar in appearance, the prototypes exhibited numerous differences, the most important being in the suspension and engines. Chrysler employed the Avco-Lycoming AGT-1500 engine, a revolutionary gas turbine, and the first-ever jet engine installed in a tank, with conventional torsion bar suspension. GM employed a more conventional diesel engine, the Teledyne Continental AVCR-1360, but with hydropneumatic suspension. During the two tests it was reported that there was only about a 2 percent difference in performance, with GM having the edge.[32]

While the decision process for the FSED contract award was under way, furious activity erupted in OSD and in West Germany concerning the planned testing of the Leopard II against U.S. tank requirements in September. It was obvious that the comparative testing was way out of phase with the United States' own schedule for tank development, and it was felt in both Bonn and the Pentagon that if the FSED contract was awarded on that schedule, then sunk costs of up to $106 million could be expected to work against any possibility of choosing the Leopard, even if it proved to be clearly the superior tank in the fall testing.[33] It was also becoming increasingly obvious that institutional pride and domestic political pressure in the United States were going to make the selection of

a foreign tank to equip the U.S. Army next to impossible. The GAO noted this in its July report: "The Leopard's chances for selection as the main battle tank are slim."[34] The Germans were not interested in buying the XM-1 in any case because they wanted their new tank by 1979 and the XM-1 could not be produced in Germany until 1981–1982.[35]

The outcome of meetings in June and July between Secretary of Defense Donald Rumsfeld, Under Secretary of the Army Norman Augustin, Deputy Director of Defense Research and Engineering Robert Parker, and their German counterparts was an Addendum to the 1974 Memorandum of Understanding. This was agreed to in early July, but could not be signed until August 4 because of U.S. Army contractual obligations to Chrysler and GM, which terminated August 1. The Addendum called on the two nations to use common tank components; in particular the United States agreed to redesign the turret of the XM-1 so that it could accept a 120-millimeter gun such as the one fitted into the Leopard, as well as the 105-millimeter gun already planned. The Germans in turn agreed to evaluate the XM-1's turbine engine for possible installation in the Leopard from July 1, 1977, on. Fuel, fire control, tracks, transmission, and common metric fasteners for both tanks were also to be standardized.[36]

On July 20, the date originally scheduled for the awarding of the FSED contract, Army Secretary Martin Hoffman delayed the announcement, and then on July 22 he announced that both contractors would be required to submit "alternate proposals. This additional step represents an extension of the validation phase of the XM-1 program and will call for the companies to submit revised proposals in which each will be asked to bid on the basis of both advanced engine technology and new key components selected as those which dominate field maintenance and logistics tank support in the field, and which will lead to a higher degree of standardization within NATO."[37] Requests for proposal were sent to the contractors on July 26, with an October 28 deadline.[38]

The reaction to the Defense Secretary's action was uniformly unfavorable from the army, the contractors, and Congress. Army objections were so strong that XM-1 Project Manager General Baer apparently threatened to resign in protest, and had to be convinced that this would do the program more harm than good. General Motors President E. M. Estes also sent a stinging letter to

Rumsfeld on August 2 calling the reopening of the competition "improper" and observing that, up to that point, the program had "been a model of constancy and good planning."[39]

Congress's reaction was even more severe. House Armed Services Committee Chairman Melvin R. Price (D.-Ill.) appointed Representatives Samuel Stratton and Elwood Hillis (R.-Ind.) to investigate the delay imposed by Hoffman on July 22. Stratton himself observed to Price that "by executive ukase, the Secretary of Defense has provided the German developers the additional time they want, in flagrant disregard of the will of Congress," and that the "eleventh hour change of plans is a shocking breach of sound competitive procurement practices."[40]

The army expressed its objections before Stratton's panel on essentially four grounds: (1) they were being asked to include in their new tank German components, which had not yet been tested and evaluated in the United States, since testing of the Leopard II was not due to be completed until December 20, 1976; (2) the need to submit new proposals imposed cost and time delays on the program of up to $943 million and two years; (3) the adoption of the 120-millimeter gun would represent a diminution of standardization in the U.S. tank fleet (which was armed with the 105-millimeter gun) and in NATO, where standardization on the 105-millimeter gun was almost complete at the time (Rumsfeld claimed that the 120-millimeter gun would represent an advance in standardization as it would be similar to the gun on the German tank); and (4) the 120-millimeter gun was possibly inferior to the new types of ammunition being developed for the 105-millimeter gun (the M735 and M774 rounds) and was, in any case, definitely unnecessary in the face of any forseeable threats in the future. Stratton's panel thus concluded that there was "no support for the smooth-bore 120-mm gun in the uniformed leadership of the U.S. Army."[41]

The House Armed Services Committee had objections of its own to the Secretary of Defense's actions, which were also contained in the panel's report:

The decision-making process in the case of XM-1 involved a revision of required procedures, a revision designed to avoid leaks of the source-selection information, which aborted the normal safeguards of the weapons-procurement process. These revised proce-

dures prevented the review by an Army Systems Acquisition Review Council (ASARC) and a Defense Systems Acquisition Review Council (DSARC). This prohibited the careful consideration of program alternatives with which the ASARC and DSARC are charged by regulations. The revision as implemented resulted in the uniformed leadership of the army being cut off from the decision-making process and the users of tanks did not have any input into the changes prescribed in the tank with which they may eventually have to fight.

The Secretary of Defense never approved an established DSARC position on the XM-1 program as required by Defense Department regulations. The Director of Defense Research and Engineering, if the testimony of his principal deputy is to be believed, took formal positions both for and against the XM-1 delay on the same day.

The change ... violates the terms of congressional approval and in the opinion of the panel is improper without congressional authorization of reprogramming of funds.[42]

Rumsfeld, either by accident or by design, avoided the panel, which further angered the congressional investigators.

As a result of the report, the House Armed Services Committee unanimously adopted a resolution attacking the agreement with the Germans and noted that the objective of fielding an effective tank as soon as possible "must take precedence over secondary objectives such as standardization or interoperability of components."[43] Nevertheless, the Committee's options beyond verbal censure were limited since funding for the program had already been approved through FY 1978, and the Senate took a much milder view of Rumsfeld's actions.

On October 28, Chrysler and GMC submitted revised bids. Chrysler simply fitted its turbine-powered prototype with a hybrid turret for 105- or 120-millimeter guns, but lowered its bid by 11 percent ($25 million), which brought it under GMC's revised bid. GMC submitted three further proposals: an upgraded version of its original diesel-powered design, the upgraded diesel-powered version with a hybrid turret, and a variant powered by the Avco-Lycoming turbine.[44] Their bid actually rose by 12 percent, prompting fears that Chrysler had "bought in" to the program—fears flatly denied by Army Secretary Hoffman.[45]

Following a DSARC Milestone II review, the Chrysler Corporation's prototype was selected for Full-Scale Engineering Development on November 12, 1976, even though the German Leopard II

was still undergoing testing when the announcement was made. The contract was worth $196.2 million, and was to produce eleven pilot tanks and associated hardware. Total army requirements at this stage were for 3,312 tanks.[46]

FULL-SCALE ENGINEERING DEVELOPMENT

DoD's decision to award the FSED contract to Chrysler, before the tests of the Leopard II AV (Austere or American Version—the Leopard II had been modified, including the addition of new armor, to compete with the XM-1) were completed on December 20, 1976, effectively put an end to any hopes of a competition between the two tanks. This was made explicit in an Addition to the August (1976) Addendum, which was signed on January 12, 1977. It stated formally that the competition between the XM-1 and Leopard had ended, and that the evaluation of the Leopard system would be limited to those subsystems designated as standardization candidates in the Addendum to the basic Memorandum of Understanding.[47]

In fact, the Leopard II failed to meet U.S. requirements for the new tank on four grounds deemed "essential" by the army: cost, weight, width, and schedule.[48] German observers at the tests were apparently happy with the results, noting they were the most extensive and severe tests the Leopard had ever been subjected to. Nevertheless, a nasty little diplomatic row took place in March when the United States announced that the Germans had short-weighted one of the test tanks to allow it to perform better. The row also concerned the choice of tank gun for the XM-1, a subject that was to dominate XM-1 development for the next several months.

THE TANK GUN DECISION

An important provision of the August Addendum was the U.S. agreement to test the German 120-millimeter smoothbore gun for possible use in the XM-1, and to decide this by January 15, 1977. In accordance with the agreement, the United States conducted its tests in December 1977. Also present at the tests was a British rifled 120-millimeter gun in accordance with a U.S. / U.K. Letter of Understanding signed on July 14, 1976, which agreed to the testing of 120-millimeter guns for possible future collaboration.

While the United States refused to make public any results of the gun trials, there were rumors that the British gun had placed first, the U.S. 105-millimeter with M774 ammunition second, the German gun third, and the U.S. 105-millimeter with M735 ammunition last. This time the Germans were apparently not pleased with the tests, citing unfair advantages given to the British, in particular as to the types of ammunition allowed.[49]

Partly as a result of the German complaints and partly as a result of U.S. Army objections to choosing the 120-millimeter gun until it proved unquestionably the better gun (objections backed up by the House Armed Services Committee), Army Secretary Hoffman went to Bonn in January to discuss a delay in the U.S. decision on tank guns beyond the original January 15 deadline. On January 11, it was announced from Bonn that the decision would be put off until December 30, 1977, before which time there would be another set of evaluations of the guns. Finally, at the end of January, the United States and Germany announced that they were going to begin producing separate tanks with different guns and engines according to their own schedules, while continuing to seek to standardize components in the future.

During March, the Germans began to turn up the heat on the Pentagon to choose the German gun by introducing an additional element into the discussion. The Pentagon had been trying to persuade European NATO allies to buy AWACS aircraft. The Germans were not enthusiastic, having made no provision in their defense budgets for the following few years for such equipment. Consequently they argued that if the United States was not prepared to buy their tank gun, then they would probably not be prepared to contribute toward the purchase of NATO AWACS aircraft.[50]

On October 20, 1976, shortly before the second round of gun trials was due to begin, Representative Stratton issued a report of his House Armed Services Committee Investigations Subcommittee that looked into the tank gun issue. It was particularly concerned with what it termed "a curious, but nonetheless pervasive interrelationship between the Leopard–XM-1 agreement and the purchase of AWACS."[51] It implied that the tank gun decision might involve political factors other than the pure military requirements, especially since the army appeared opposed to the larger gun. The report noted that the U.S. choice of the German gun had become a "symbol of U.S. commitment to the principal of standardization,

and as such has become the necessary candidate for Federal Republic of Germany's participation in the AWACS program."[52] It sent a pointed warning to the Pentagon to choose the tank gun on the basis of "military merit, not political considerations," or face the prospect of a confrontation between the administration and Congress in the spring.[53]

The second round of gun trials took place between November 7 and December 21. In this set of trials, the German smoothbore apparently placed first, an experimental British 120-millimeter rifled gun second, and the U.S. 105-millimeter third. Such was the importance of impartiality in this decision that a special independent "Red Team" of experts was added to the normal evaluative procedures to question weak points in the army's recommendations.[54]

On January 17, 1978, the army selected the smoothbore German 120-millimeter gun to install in later model XM-1s. This decision was transmitted to Congress on February 1 along with a reprogramming request for $10.9 million in FY 1978 to initiate an R&D program based around the gun to develop, among other things, an appropriate breech for the XM-1 and new types of ammunition.[55]

The army, however, still seemed divided on the issue of the gun. Army Vice-Chief of Staff General Walter T. Kerwin said that the uniformed army concurred with the decision, but reports indicated that this was not, in fact, the case. Secretary of the Army Clifford Alexander seemed to be hedging his bets at the press conference announcing the decision when he stated that actual use of the German gun was "dependent on successful completion of essential development and test efforts."[56]

The House Armed Services Committee Investigations Subcommittee released another report, which was unfavorable toward the decision. It noted:

There is no reliable intelligence to support a conclusion that the Soviets are likely to field a tank that can defeat the 105mm but not the 120mm. OSD and the Army Secretariat do not even agree about the nature of the potential threat, and therefore are unable to state a requirement for a tank gun that cannot be met or greatly exceeded by the 105mm gun with its improved ammunition. . . .

The Army's decision to adopt the German gun was based pri-

marily on the perceived desirability of demonstrating US commitment to the establishment of a two-way street in weapons procurement with the Federal Republic of Germany. There is no convincing evidence that the decision was based upon military requirement.[57]

Alexander flatly denied these charges and told the press the "driving force" for selecting the German gun was the size of the German tank fleet, and that the German gun had demonstrated a faster "first round kill probability," which was the essential criterion in the gun decision.

Apparently Congress as a whole agreed with Alexander because both the House and Senate Armed Services Committees appropriated (and in fact increased) funding requests for FY 1979 for development of the German gun, though they still avoided committing themselves outright to buying it. During this period, the proposed XM-1 purchase was increased from 3,312 to 7,058 tanks. The army was not prepared to detail how many of these tanks would be produced with the 105-millimeter gun before the 120-millimeter could be ready sometime in 1984.[58]

As discussions over the tank gun drew to a close, the eleven pilot-production XM-1s were delivered to the army on schedule between February and July 1978. The second phase of Developmental and Operational Testing (DT/OT II) began in March of that year but was suspended for three weeks in August following thirteen engine failures in June and July.[59] It was somewhat ironic that this should happen to the gas turbine engine, which had been chosen over the variable compression ratio diesel partly because it promised great gains in reliability and durability over diesels. Predictions made in 1977 suggested a time between engine overhauls of 12,000 to 18,000 miles, three to four times the durability expected for the diesel. The turbine also had 30 percent fewer parts than the diesel, and the majority of those parts could be replaced without removing the engine from the tank.[60]

The most serious problem was dust ingestion as a result of a defect in the air induction system that allowed dust to enter the engine and significantly erode it. Two other problems were caused by quality control and inadequate engineering design. Various modifications were made before testing resumed on September 5. However, there were six more failures between resumption of

testing and November, two being due to dust erosion. Of these two, one was the result of human error, and the other was because all damaged parts were not removed when the engines were modified to correct the dust ingestion problem. Of the nineteen engine failures in early DT/OT II, only four had not had their causes identified and adjustments made to account for them by December 1979.

Part of the problem was undoubtedly the sheer brutality of the testing, forced by the need to "cram 9,000 miles of testing into a very short period of time"[61] in order to stay on the seven-year developmental schedule laid down by Congress at the beginning of the program, which had already been thrown off by the delay in awarding the Full-Scale Engineering Development (FSED) contract.

Initially the army did not appear particularly concerned about the engine problems, noting, "This experience is typical of all engine development efforts," and "The XM-1 turbine program is paralleling industry programs by making a concerted effort to assimilate operating hours and miles, thereby expanding the identification of failure modes and corrective action before the system is fielded."[62] But concern was growing. Army Secretary Alexander acknowledged on March 3 that there were "serious problems in engine testing" but he did not think they were "program stoppers."[63] In spite of the difficulties and apparently unfavorable results from Developmental and Operational Testing II, an ASARC review nevertheless recommended the XM-1 for an initial low-rate production of 110 units funded in the FY 1979 budget.

Secretary of Defense Harold Brown appointed a "Blue Ribbon" panel of engine and tank experts from industry and the Pentagon "to assess the adequacy of the test program" and the status of the tank engine. The panel reported in April, shortly before the DSARC Milestone III meeting, that the engine problems could be expected to persist. By this time the engine had failed 37 times in 12,500 miles of testing, equating to a failure every 337.8 miles.[64] Nonetheless, the panel concluded that the turbine engine was the right choice. Program Manager Major-General Donald Babers, in testimony before the House Armed Services Committee in early April, acknowledged that the engine had not lived up to expectations and was in need of improvements, but noted that "100 percent of its problems are fixed, or there are fixes underway," and that no new problems had surfaced since November.[65]

Then, just before the DSARC was due to convene on April 17, the GAO weighed in with a report urging the Pentagon to delay the decision to go into Low-Rate Initial Production. "In our opinion," the report stated, "it would be preferable to defer the initial production decision until there has been a demonstration through further testing that design changes and modifications have indeed corrected the problems. . . . We recommend that, to avoid the possibility of producing a large quantity of unacceptable tanks, you defer or slow down the XM-1's production until acceptable reliability and durability levels are demonstrated."[66] The GAO observed that some 270 modifications had already been made to date, and that these could not be adequately tested before the start of production if the original schedule was adhered to.

In spite of all these warnings, on May 7, 1979, Secretary Brown gave his qualified approval for initial series production of 110 XM-1 tanks for FY 1979. Recognizing that "testing ha[d] not demonstrated the reliability we would have liked at this point,"[67] DoD reserved the right to decide in 1980 whether to hold FY 1980 production at the same level or increase it to the originally planned 352 for that year if further tests were still not encouraging. Observers noted, however, that such a delay could add significant costs to the program (perhaps as much as $200 million), which would create an impetus to authorize the 352 whatever the results of further testing.

The uncertainty surrounding the reliability of the XM-1 engine led the Senate, in the FY 1979 Defense Authorization debates, to seek to reserve $14.2 million to develop a backup diesel for the XM-1. The Pentagon had already awarded a $2.8 million contract to Teledyne Continental in March 1979 to continue development of its variable compression ratio AVCR-1360 diesel, which had lost out to the turbine in the original XM-1 competition, but it emphasized that this was not a backup. At the same time, Rolls-Royce lobbied the Pentagon to consider its new CV12 diesel engine as a backup power plant, a forlorn hope in view of the availability of a U.S. alternative.[68] The House accepted army arguments that a backup program would delay the XM-1 program and add significantly to costs. They did not wish to slow fielding of "this critically needed weapons system."[69] But the Senate ended up getting its way and an official backup program was initiated.

PRODUCTION AND DEPLOYMENT

Further Testing and Improvements. The Office of the Secretary of Defense ordered new tests of the XM-1 to commence in August 1979 to determine whether production should be stepped up in 1980 as planned or held at Low-Rate Initial Production. For these tests at Fort Knox, three-pilot vehicles were modified to eliminate earlier problems. Improvements included

> new steel sprocket hub with mud discharge ports, hull-mounted scraper to remove mud and sand as the track turns and inside steel blocks and an outside retaining ring to prevent inside and outside throwing of the track. To help align the track and prevent damage to the suspension in the case of an inside throw a new inside steel plate was mounted above the final drive. The suspension torsion bars were re-indexed at each road wheel and a more robust pressure valve applied to the track adjusting arm, which redistributed ground pressure and increased track tension and helped prevent the tendency toward thrown tracks. Turbine and blade failures due to the entry of dust and other matter through the seals in the engine air induction and filtration system were solved by fitting positive seals throughout the system.[70]

The XM-1 was put through some 12,000 miles of tests in an effort to achieve a Mean Miles Between Mission Failures (MMBF) of 272. Mean Miles Between Mission Failures is the United States Army's primary measure of vehicle reliability and durability (part of RAM-D). It measures the average distance traveled by a vehicle on a combat mission before something breaks so severely that the vehicle cannot finish its mission. The longer the distance, the more durable is the vehicle under combat conditions. A target of 320 MMBF was also assigned to the end of Developmental and Operational Testing III in February 1981. The M-60 had an MMBF of 423, but was a much more mature system.

The army was greatly encouraged by the results of the Fort Knox tests, claiming a 306 MMBF result. An army spokesman stated: "the test data ... indicate that the major problems encountered earlier have been solved.... It is evident that reliability of sub-systems affecting the mobility of the tank has been greatly improved. It now appears possible to meet the final stringent reliability and durability goals on the original schedule." Unfortunately, the fixes

themselves caused their own problems as the tank gained in weight until it surpassed the original fifty-eight-ton limit. This seems to have been generally accepted as unavoidable, especially with the prospective addition of the larger gun.[71]

In December, the Defense Secretary reconvened his "Blue Ribbon" panel of April to review the progress of the engine after the latest tests. The panel reported on February 5, 1980, that progress had been "outstanding" and concluded that "mission reliability of the XM-1 now exceeds both the OSD threshold and the requirement with a demonstration of 306 MMBF."[72]

Shortly before the end of January the GAO issued its own report acknowledging that the XM-1 was making "steady progress in overcoming many of its reliability problems,"[73] but it recommended that Congress limit further procurement of the tank to a low rate and that "the Department of Defense initiate a full-scale diesel engine development program for the XM-1 if the turbine problem persists."[74] The report further questioned the validity of the methods used to evaluate the Fort Knox test results and doubted the army's MMBF figures.

By this time, the Pentagon had already approved full-scale production of the XM-1 on January 20, permitting the army to order 352 tanks for 1980 at a cost of $711.3 million. Production was then scheduled to build up to 569 XM-1s in the FY 1981 budget, then to 720 in FY 1982, up to 1,080 tanks by FY 1985. Congress limited its actions to calling a number of senior army people involved in the program, including Project Manager General Babers and Army Vice-Chief of Staff General John W. Vessey, Jr., before the House Armed Services Committee Investigations Subcommittee chaired by Representative Stratton. The army's presentation appeared to sooth some of Congress's concerns, but not before Stratton strongly protested that the army was dragging its feet over the backup engine program and charged that "in the past, Congress has been bamboozled by Pentagon civilians and the army. You can't blame us for being skeptical."[75]

DEPLOYMENT OF THE M-1 ABRAMS

On February 28, 1980, the first-production M-1 was handed over to the army at a ceremony at Chrysler's tank plant in Lima, Ohio. The tank was christened by Julia Harvey Abrams, the widow of

General Creighton W. Abrams, a noted World War II tank commander under Patton and commander of U.S. forces in Vietnam for a time, after whom the army had decided to name the new tank. At the ceremony, Chief of Staff General Edward C. Meyer observed that the M-1 "will be better than anything the Russians have or anything we know they have on the drawing board."[76] He strongly disagreed with the GAO's January report and noted, "The soldiers who have to use it out there are satisfied and therefore I am satisfied."[77] Assistant Secretary of the Army for Research, Development, and Acquisition Dr. Percy Pierre noted the simultaneous arrival on the scene of the new Russian T-80 tank, but wouldn't speculate on the M-1's relative superiority over it.

FINAL TESTING

The third and final phase of Developmental and Operational Testing of the M-1 began in May 1980 and was to last until early 1982. The army maintained throughout that the tank was proving itself and that field testing "has demonstrated conclusively that it moves, shoots and survives better than any tank in the world."[78] However, the army did acknowledge that durability was not at its best. While evaluation reports from DT / OT III stated that the requirement of 320 MMBF was being met, independent analysis by the private Project on Military Procurement observed that the M-1 would travel only 43 miles before something broke. The army response was that this included the most minor of repair problems.[79]

Other significant problems brought out by the tests included dangerously flammable hydraulic fluid, and the tendency of the tank to consume fuel at too great a rate.[80] The addition of extra fuel tanks improved this situation to the extent that a comparative evaluation of a Leopard II and an M-1 in Switzerland in 1982–1983 saw the M-1 outrange the Leopard.[81] By the end of Developmental and Operational Testing (DT / OT) III the only RAM-D requirement not met or exceeded by the M-1 was for track life, though new tracks were under development.

While the M-1 was undergoing DT / OT III, all was not well with Chrysler and the M-1 subcontractors.[82] In spite of being assigned "highest national priority" in February 1980 (the "DX priority") by President Carter,[83] production of the M-1 was already two months behind schedule by December. The problem was apparently with

Avco-Lycoming, the engine subcontractor, which was not supplying enough engines. This problem was to persist through to 1983, but responsibility was equally shared between Avco-Lycoming and the army, with the latter diverting engines because of inadequate repair facilities.[84]

The cost of the tank was also becoming a matter of concern. With the original congressional price target of $500,000 a tank to purchase 3,000 tanks having receded over time, the tanks were costing up to $2.5 million each by mid-1981. "While the M1 tank is impressive in meeting its three other major combat requirements—firepower, mobility and armor protection—these advantages are offset to a considerable degree by shortcomings in reliability and maintenance, and its rising cost," observed Walter Shelley of the GAO.[85] Inflation was the chief cause but the decision to use German components also contributed to cost increases. This stimulated a debate in the press over the value of smaller numbers of expensive tanks versus larger numbers of cheaper ones.[86]

Finally, the Chrysler Corporation, experiencing a period of serious financial difficulties, decided to sell its Defense Division on February 19, 1982, to General Dynamics for $348.5 million in order to provide itself with a cash buffer in its efforts to recover profitability.

MODERNIZATION

The M-1A1. With the concluding of a U.S. / F.R.G. 120-millimeter gun license deal in 1979, the army and the Pentagon effectively committed themselves to upgunning later production models of the M-1 with the 120-millimeter gun.[87] Initially it had been hoped that M-1s with the larger guns could begin production in August 1984, but delays in negotiating the license pushed this back to August 1985.

Starting in FY 1978, funds were appropriated for R&D on the 120-millimeter gun and on its integration into the M-1 hybrid turret. The program originally designated the new tank the M-1E1, which was changed to M-1A1 when production began. The 120-millimeter gun was designated the M-256, and the first-production barrel was completed in early 1980. Trials of the gun began in 1981, and operational testing of the whole tank (DT / OT I)

took place in 1983. By mid-1984, DT/OT II had been completed with most RAM-D requirements met. DT/OT III began in 1986.[88]

The T-80 Debate. While the M-1A1 was going through its initial testing stages, a rather remarkable reversal of attitudes concerning the threat it was likely to face took place. In 1976 and 1977, the army had maintained that the 105-millimeter gun would be adequate for all foreseeable threats. The introduction of the T-80 into Soviet tank inventories in the early 1980s, an event easily foreseeable in 1977, saw the army reversing itself, with the support of the Pentagon.

The army argued that with the new Soviet tank and "in [the] face of the overlapping succession of new tank developments we are no longer on safe ground contending that our ... XM-1 will be vastly superior to Soviet models."[89] Taking their position further, they later stated before Congress that the 105-millimeter gun was unable to penetrate the frontal armor of this new tank.[90] Public concern was increased by a description in the 1981 edition of *Soviet Military Power* of the T-80 as "a new class of main battle tank," along with a highly misleading artist's impression of the tank.[91]

More sober assessments eventually prevailed, the British in particular viewing initial U.S. claims about the vehicle (which they believed was merely an improved version of the T-72) as "pure conjecture." By 1983, genuine photographs of the T-80 were appearing in *Soviet Military Power,* but the scare had undoubtedly contributed to the army securing the funds for an increase in M-1s from 7,058 to 7,467.[92]

Final Engine Problems. The final episode in the M-1's turbulent history has been called "The Great Tank Engine War of 1983." This was a rather curious battle between the army and Congress over whether or not the gas turbine engine for the M-1 should be "dual-sourced" (use of two engine producers, presumably in competition, instead of one). The army supported dual sourcing eventually for six different reasons: (1) to disperse production facilities to minimize labor strikes and sabotage; (2) to provide more total capacity in time of war; (3) to achieve greater monthly production; (4) to achieve better production quality; (5) to create competition to stimulate lower costs; and (6) because they did not like the present manufacturer.[93]

Congress argued that none of these arguments was valid, and that the army was really trying to punish Avco-Lycoming for initial difficulties in its production processes. The quality problems were addressed by a power train durability retest between July and December 1983 over 46,671 kilometers. Required specifications were passed satisfactorily. The army's request for second sourcing was also attacked as "a lousy analysis" by Under Secretary of Defense for Research and Engineering Dr. Richard DeLauer.[94] Senator Mark Andrews (R.-N.D.) suggested that Avco-Lycoming provide warranties for the engine and transmission.[95] And Congress prohibited second sourcing in the FY 1984 Defense Authorization Bill.

In 1982 production of the M-1 had risen to 60 units per month from 30 in 1981. This was maintained until January 1984, when it was increased to 70 per month despite an attempt by DoD to remain at the lower level. The original army FY 1984 request was for 840 tanks, but this was cut to 720 by DoD before submission to Congress. The Secretary of the Army stated:

> The reason for the stretch-out related to affordability. There had been previously, referring back a year ago and even later, some quality problems that related to the engine and those were addressed. . . . I feel rather confident that the engine quality problem has been resolved, and the stretch-out is one that related to affordability.[96]

Part of the reason for DoD's budget decision was undoubtedly that the army had a large number of new systems coming into production at the same time and it was proving difficult, even with the financial boosts provided by the Reagan Administration, to afford all of them.[97] The army appealed the DoD Program Budget Decision and, in a somewhat unusual move, succeeded in getting the 840 tanks approved by Congress. "The reduction of 120 tanks in FY 1984 is contrary to the clear intent of Congress to allow the Army to procure at least 840 tanks in FY 1984," commented an army spokesman.[98]

Production has been maintained at 840 tanks per year since then (see Table 9-1). By December 1985, 3,058 had been delivered, and production of the M-1 ended in May 1986, being replaced by the M-1A1 which began to come on stream in August 1985. The U.S. Marine Corps intends to reequip with the M-1A1 begin-

Table 9-1. Procurement of M-1

Year	Congressional Authorization ($ million)	Units
FY79	n/a	90
FY80	711.3	309
FY81	1,354.5	569
FY82	1,495.7	665
FY83	1,752.2	855
FY84	1,429.0	840
FY85	1,538.0	840
FY86	1,986.1	840
FY87	2,150.6	840
FY88*	1,537.5	600
FY89†	1,443.8	534

* Budget request.
† Anticipated budget request.

Sources: World Armored Vehicle Forecast 1987 (Greenwich, Conn.: Defense Marketing Services Inc., 1986), pp. 445–447, 1246; Richard Halloran, "Pentagon Approves Main Battle Tank," *New York Times,* January 21, 1980, p. A11 (the $711.3 million value); and *Jane's Armour and Artillery 1986–87* (London: Jane's Publishing Company, 1986), p. 118 (the $1,986.1 million and $2,150.6 million values).

ning in 1989, and Canada and Egypt have expressed an interest in buying that model.

CONCLUSION

The story of the M-1 is marked by controversy and sometimes bitter political battles between the various governmental organs charged with its development and deployment. The tank they ended up with was significantly different from that with which they began.

The initiation of the program was largely the result of systems obsolescence among the army's present fleet of tanks, but was helped by a carryover of impetus developed from the defunct MBT-70 and XM-803 programs. Indeed these two influences were so strong that few in a position to make the decisions seriously questioned the need for tanks. Almost nothing was heard against the tank from the other armed services, despite the presence of many arguments

about the increasing obsolescence of tanks and the program's considerable cost (it has been in the top ten of United States military R&D and Procurement outlays since at least 1984). The other services seem to have recognized that the army viewed the tank as central to its military role, in the same way the navy viewed the aircraft carrier and the air force the manned bomber. The dominance of an "Armor Mafia" in the tradition of World War II General George Patton ensured the prominence of this view.

The program was very strictly delineated from the start by Congress, which was imbued with a sense of urgency about the need for a new tank but also wanted to avoid the problems that had led to the cancelation of the previous tank programs. This led to sometimes intense micromanagement of the program under the scrutiny, in particular, of the House Armed Services Committee Investigations Subcommittee chaired by Samuel Stratton. Stratton himself seemed to consider the program something of a personal crusade. He wanted to get the best tank but within the program limits established by Congress at the outset.

Congress's desire to maintain its control over the program and its dominance of the procurement process was particularly noticeable during the validation extension and tank gun episodes. The Office of the Secretary of Defense, having to deal with a number of outside actors in the management of defense affairs, included the wider picture in its considerations of how to mold the XM-1 program. It saw no difficulty in including German input in the tank if it improved alliance relations and helped secure the AWACS contract.

Congress, however, was concerned with more parochial matters. Having laid down the timetable and cost limits for the program, it resisted interference, especially in the interests of denying America production of its own tanks. Nevertheless, congressional haste in getting the program into production subsequently tied Congress's own hands because additional monies had to continue being appropriated to keep the program moving. But each time Congress appropriated funds, it increased the sunk costs involved in the program, and thereby increased the impetus to continue even in the face of subsequent difficulties.

To permit the fastest possible introduction of the M-1 into the army, it was developed under a test, then fix, then test again program schedule devised by the army to speed the introduction of

new equipment into front-line use. Under this system, development programs were permitted to continue on schedule even when serious problems were encountered, which allowed the army to press on with procurement even though the tank's power train consistently failed to live up to durability expectations. The army fought to maintain its production schedule over the frequent objections of the General Accounting Office. In any event, it appears that much of the furor that arose over the M-1's engine problems was overstated. As one might expect, as the technology matured its reliability eventually improved.

The manipulation of threat assessments to suit the army's case at different stages of the program is another interesting feature of the story. The assessments seemed to flatly contradict each other at times, with the threat being minimized to reduce German involvement and then maximized to increase the number of tanks.

In the end, the M-1 was built because everyone wanted the army to have a new tank, but its development was also the subject of intense controversy because Congress, DoD, and the army each wanted to control it. In spite of this, the M-1 emerged as an effective fighting vehicle.

10

□

THE STRATEGIC DEFENSE INITIATIVE

On March 23, 1983, President Ronald Reagan went before the nation to declare his bold new vision of a nuclear-free world. Appearing on national television he said:

Let me share with you a vision of the future which offers hope. It is that we embark on a program to counter the awesome Soviet missile threat with measures that are defensive. Let us turn to the very strengths in technology that spawned our great industrial base and that have given us the quality of life we enjoy today.

What if a free people could live secure in the knowledge that their security did not rest upon the threat of instant U.S. retaliation to deter a Soviet attack, that we could intercept and destroy strategic ballistic missiles before they reached our own soil or that of our allies?

I know this is a formidable, technical task, one that may not be accomplished before the end of the century. Yet current technology has attained a level of sophistication where it's reasonable for us to begin this effort. . . .

I clearly recognize that defensive systems have limitations and raise certain problems and ambiguities. If paired with offensive systems, they can be viewed as fostering an aggressive policy, and no one wants that. But with these considerations firmly in mind, I call upon the scientific community in our country, those who gave us nuclear weapons, to turn their great talents now to the cause of mankind and world peace, to give us the means of rendering these nuclear weapons impotent and obsolete.

Tonight, consistent with our obligations of the ABM treaty and recognizing the need for closer consultation with our allies, I'm taking an important first step. I am directing a comprehensive and

intensive effort to define a long-term research and development program to begin to achieve our ultimate goal of eliminating the threat posed by strategic nuclear missiles. . . .

My fellow Americans, tonight we're launching an effort which holds the promise of changing the course of human history. There will be risks, and results take time. But I believe we can do it. As we cross this threshold, I ask for your prayers and your support.[1]

Thus was born the Strategic Defense Initiative, or SDI, which also came to be known as "Star Wars." This chapter examines the origins and development of SDI, focusing primarily on the domestic political debates and the role of Congress in SDI development. SDI is not a single weapons system but a research program involving a myriad of technologies and potential weapons systems. Unlike the other weapons programs discussed in this book, it is also a program still very much in the early stages of development. No weapons have been built yet and SDI's future is at best uncertain. However, it is a research program that has already cost billions of dollars and is now entering the testing stage for certain technologies. What is striking about the story that follows is that SDI has acquired considerable momentum as a research program despite formidable opposition and skepticism not only in Congress but also throughout the research and scientific community. This momentum will be hard to stop even by a new administration with a new set of defense priorities. If past history is any guide, SDI may be slowed but it is unlikely to die at the hands of a new administration or Congress. The story of SDI is one of budgetary compromises that have given the program just enough resources to sputter (some would say run) along.

ORIGINS

Although SDI was something of a Reagan invention, the idea of ballistic missile defense is certainly not new. U.S. defense efforts began in the 1950s with the development of the Nike Series surface-to-air missile to be used to attack Soviet bombers. With the development of the Soviet ICBM threat, against which there seemed to be no defense, the Eisenhower administration cut back on spending against the bomber threat and began to spend heavily on the development of anti-missile defenses. Nike evolved into the

Nike-Zeus system and "Project Defender"—a top-secret program to explore new and exotic technologies for ballistic missile defense—got under way. One project, code-named "Bambi," envisioned literally hundreds of space-based battle stations, which would use infrared sensors to track Soviet missiles and fire a huge sixty-foot rotating wire net into enemy rockets. By 1962, General Curtis E. LeMay, head of the Strategic Air Command, was predicting the development of lasers that would destroy enemy missiles "with the speed of light."

The Nike-Zeus program's days were numbered, however. Scientists in the Pentagon under the direction of Herbert York felt that the system had serious technical limitations. Robert McNamara, the new Secretary of Defense, also did not like the system. McNamara was persuaded by defense scientists in the Pentagon to turn the interceptor into one that would attack enemy missiles not in space but in the earth's atmosphere after any lightweight decoys had had a chance to burn up. Thus was born the Nike-X program, the predecessor to Sentinel.[2]

In September 1967, in response to anti-missile developments in the Soviet Union, the Johnson administration announced it would build the Sentinel ground-based ABM (antiballistic missile) system, which would carry nuclear warheads and be used to defend the United States from a Chinese missile attack or attack by some other party or accidental missile launch. The idea of using ABM as a bargaining chip for arms control also gained credence in the 1968 congressional debate on the Sentinel system. In 1969, the new Nixon administration scrapped the Sentinel program and with it the idea of defending cities. The army's Sentinel program was revamped into the new Safeguard program intended to defend missile silos. However, opposition to ABM had grown considerably in Congress as well as within the scientific and academic community. Safeguard also was not popular with people living near designated ABM sites, who believed that they would be more, not less, vulnerable to Soviet attack. Many feared that the technologies were inadequate and a race to deploy defenses would touch off a new race in offensive weapons to penetrate defenses. But the administration was able to persuade Congress it needed Safeguard as a bargaining chip for the upcoming SALT I (Strategic Arms Limitation Talks). The SALT I talks with the Soviets, which began in June 1969, were successfully concluded in 1972. The ABM Treaty

allowed each side a token force of two ABM missile sites with 100 missiles apiece. It prohibited testing and deployment of sea-based, air-based, space-based, or mobile-land-based ballistic missile defense systems or components. Two years later the number of ABM sites was reduced to one site with 100 missiles. The Soviets continued to maintain one site around Moscow. The United States had one site at Grand Forks, North Dakota, which went into operation in 1975 but was scrapped shortly afterward because it was considered too expensive and ineffective.[3]

SDI had its more immediate origins with President Reagan and Dr. Edward Teller, father of the hydrogen bomb. In January 1982, Teller met with Reagan to discuss new technologies for defense against ballistic missiles. There were four meetings with Reagan before the now-famous "Star Wars" speech of March 23. Other briefings took place with the President's science adviser, the Joint Chiefs of Staff, and the National Security Council. Reagan's interest in strategic defenses, however, pre-dated his election to the presidency. As Governor of California he paid a courtesy visit to Lawrence Livermore Laboratory in Livermore, California, one of the country's top weapons labs, founded by Edward Teller in the 1950s. Said Teller, "We showed him all the complex projects. . . . He listened carefully and interrupted maybe a dozen times. Every one of his questions was to the point. He clearly comprehended the technology. There was no skimping on time. He came in the morning and stayed over lunch." According to William Broad, author of *Star Warriors*, the picture of this third generation of nuclear devices made a lasting impression on Reagan and crystallized his vision of a future in which nuclear weapons would be rendered obsolete.[4]

Much of the scientific work for SDI was spawned at Lawrence Livermore under Teller's direction. In the early 1970s a special department known as the "O Group" was formed, comprised of young scientists who were sponsored by the Hertz Foundation, founded by John Hertz of the rental car company. The Hertz Foundation offered fellowships to students with outstanding potential in the applied physical sciences. This nucleus of Hertz Fellows helped to develop the concepts later sold to President Reagan as the basis for a multilayered space-based defense.[5]

During the 1980 Republican presidential primary campaign, candidate Reagan spoke about his visit to the North American Aerospace Defense Command headquarters inside Cheyenne

Mountain at Colorado Springs. "They are actually tracking several thousand objects in space, meaning satellites of ours and everyone else's, even down to the point that they are tracking a glove lost by an astronaut. I think the thing that struck me was the irony that here, with this great technology of ours, we can do all of this, yet we cannot stop any of the weapons that are coming at us. I don't think there's been a time in history when there wasn't a defense against some kind of thrust, even back in the old-fashioned days when we had coast artillery that would stop invading ships."[6]

The Republican Party's election platform presented on July 15, 1980, called for "vigorous research and development of an effective antiballistic-missile system, such as is already at hand in the Soviet Union, as well as more modern ABM technologies."

Upon being elected, Reagan pursued his idea with Senator Harrison F. Schmitt (R.-N.M.), former astronaut and Chairman of the Senate Subcommittee on Science, Technology, and Space. Recalls Schmitt, "We were talking about science and technology in general. Then, about halfway through the session, he [Reagan] made a statement that he was concerned that we could not just keep building nuclear missiles forever—that ultimately their proliferation would get us into serious trouble. He asked what I thought about the possibility of strategic defense, especially with lasers. We spent half the conversation talking about it."[7]

Teller wrote to the President a few months after the "Star Wars" speech to urge development of exotic, new technologies for defense. He argued that "converting hydrogen bombs into hitherto unprecedented forms and then directing these in highly effective fashions against enemy targets would end the MAD [Mutual Assured Destruction] era and commence a period of assured destruction on terms favorable to the Western alliance." This was the so-called nuclear X-ray laser. Along with Teller, the key scientist to lead the breakthroughs that laid the groundwork for the weapon, was Lowell Wood, a charismatic and gifted scientist who was recruited to Livermore by Teller and headed the O Group's laboratories there. A hydrogen bomb would explode, sending out a charge of X rays directed at enemy missiles or warheads to render them inoperable. The first test of the idea was conducted on November 14, 1980, beneath the Nevada desert. The test was code-named Dauphin.[8]

In 1981 the Heritage Foundation set up a working group on

strategic defenses whose members included Edward Teller, beer executive Joseph Coors, industrialist Jacquelin Hume, former Under Secretary of the Army Karl R. Bendetsen, and a former head of the Defense Intelligence Agency, Lieutenant General Daniel O. Graham. The group eventually split into two, those who favored development of exotic and advanced technologies for space-based defense and those who wanted to use "off-the-shelf" technologies for defense. The first group was headed by Teller and Bendetsen and enjoyed direct access to the President. The second was headed by Daniel Graham and did not enjoy the same access to the White House. Bendetsen and Teller successfully lobbied the President to go for the basic research option rather than the "off-the-shelf" technologies. Graham, in frustration, went public with his ideas, presenting them in a book called *The High Frontier,* published in February 1982, as well as directly to General John W. Vessey, Jr., who would soon be appointed Chairman of the Joint Chiefs of Staff.

In 1982 government analysts looked at the High Frontier idea, which called for a network of 432 space-based battle stations to fire kinetic-energy weapons at Soviet missiles as they rose over Asia. In a State Department Memorandum dated January 20, 1982, Richard Burt of the Bureau of Politico-Military Affairs said that "General Graham's High Frontier Approach has much more technical risk than he describes and is optimistic in the extreme on both cost and schedule." A joint study conducted by the air force and army concluded in a memorandum dated March 31, 1982, that "[t]he concept, as proposed, is not technically feasible for near term application using off-the-shelf or under-development hardware." On November 24, 1982, Secretary of Defense Weinberger wrote to Graham, stating, "We are unwilling to commit this nation to a course which calls for growing into a capability that currently does not exist. . . . With the substantial risks involved, we do not foresee 'cheap and quick' solutions to support the shift in policy you seek."[9] But all that was soon to change.

On January 14, 1983, Presidential Science Adviser George Keyworth visited Lawrence Livermore Laboratory and praised the "bomb-pumped X-ray laser program" in the first public announcement of the program, which had hitherto remained secret, reflecting the White House's growing interest in strategic defense. It was followed by meetings between Reagan and the Bendetsen-Teller

group. On February 11, the President met with the Joint Chiefs of Staff to discuss the future of the MX missile, although the meeting apparently drifted to include the subject of strategic defense. The President's March 23 speech was drafted by Robert C. McFarlane, Deputy National Security Adviser.

According to John Bardeen, a member of the White House Science Council at the time, there was "no prior consultation either with technical experts in the Pentagon concerned with research in the area or with his own Science Adviser George Keyworth" prior to the speech. "Although we met only a few days before the speech was given, and had a panel looking into some of the technology, we were not consulted. We met on Friday and left for home. Keyworth first heard about the planned speech late that afternoon and sent telegrams to some of the Council members involved to return to Washington on Saturday. With the speech scheduled for the following Wednesday, there was no time to make more than minor changes."[10]

Congressional reaction to Reagan's March 23 speech was mixed. Most were caught off guard. Congressman Les AuCoin (D.-Ore.) found "the President's views simplistic and dangerously out of step with the people of my district." And he stated, "I have regrettably come to the conclusion that this President is not content with deterrence. He wants instead military superiority." Representative Howard Wolpe (D.-Mich.) had this to say: "Last night the American people were treated to one of the most outrageous and misleading pieces of political propaganda that this Nation has seen in many years." Congressman Thomas J. Downey (D.-N.Y.) was just as scathing: "The only thing the President did not tell us last night was the Evil Empire was about to launch the Death Star against the United States." But the President had strong supporters, too. Congressman Ken Kramer (R.-Colo.) introduced House Resolution 3073 on May 19, 1983, the People Protection Act, endorsing a shift in U.S. policy to one that would "seek to save lives in time of war, rather than to avenge them." He called the President's program a "Manhattan Project for Peace." Kramer's bill was followed by hearings on November 10, 1983, at which the majority of witnesses, which included Edward Teller and Daniel Graham, expressed their overwhelming support for the program. But there were opponents in the scientific community, too. Nobel Laureate Hans Bethe, in a written statement to the House Armed Services Subcommittee on Research and Development, stated, "we must avoid a commitment

to global BMD [ballistic missile defense], for that will produce precisely the opposite result: a large expansion of nuclear forces aimed against us, combined with a vastly complex defensive system whose performance will remain a deep mystery until the tragic moment when it will be called into action."[11]

THE HOFFMANN AND FLETCHER REPORTS

To put meat on bare bones the administration commissioned a number of expert studies to further examine the problem of strategic defense. The first major study was prepared by Mr. Fred Hoffmann and a study team of outside experts for the Institute for Defense Analysis at the request of the Office of the Under Secretary of Defense for Policy. This panel's work complimented the efforts of the Defensive Technologies Study (DTS) and the Future Security Strategy Study (FSSS), interagency studies intended to assess the role of defensive systems in U.S. security strategy. The Hoffmann Report argued for a modest, intermediate defensive program. "The new technologies offer the possibility of a multilayered defensive system able to intercept offensive missiles in each phase of their trajectories. In the long term, such systems might provide a nearly leakproof defense against large ballistic missile attacks. However, their components vary substantially in technical risk, development lead time, and cost, and in the policy issues they raise. Consequently, partial systems, or systems with more modest technical goals, may be feasible earlier than the full system" (see Figure 10-1 and Table 10-1). Such intermediate systems, the panel argued, would "greatly complicate Soviet attack plans and reduce Soviet confidence in a successful outcome at various levels of conflict and attack sizes, both nuclear and nonnuclear. Even U.S. defenses of limited capability can deny Soviet planners confidence in their ability to destroy a sufficient set of military targets to satisfy enemy attack objectives, thereby strengthening deterrence. Intermediate defenses can also reduce damage if conflict occurs. The combined effect of these intermediate capabilities could help to reassure our allies about the credibility of our guarantees." The panel advocated development of a "flexible research and development (R&D) program designed to offer early options for the deployment of intermediate systems, while proceeding toward the President's ultimate goal . . . of the 'full system.' "[12]

Table 10-1. Hypothetical Multilayered BMD System

System Level	System Elements	Description	Comments
Level 1 **Terminal Defense** (defense of hardened sites using endoatmospheric rockets to intercept reentry vehicles (RVs) as they approach their targets)	Early warning satellites; ground-based radar; airborne optical sensors; ground-based battle management computers; fast endoatmospheric interceptors.	Warning of launch provided by high-orbit satellites; RVs detected and tracked in region of ground targets by ground radar and airborne sensors; ground computers assign interceptors to RVs; kill assessment* permits reassignment of defense interceptors; atmospheric interception used; air effects used to discriminate between RVs and decoys.	Homing either infrared (IR) or radar; interceptors should be relatively inexpensive, since many need not be nuclear or nonnuclear.
Level 2 **Light Midcourse and Terminal Defense** (additional layer added with some interception capability in midcourse and some ability to discriminate RVs from decoys in space to reduce burden on terminal layer; some area defense)	Level 1 plus: exoatmospheric homing interceptors, range hundreds of km; pop-up† IR sensors (possibly satellite-based instead); self-defense capability for space assets.	As in level 1 for terminal defenses; longer range interceptors added which can intercept some RVs above atmosphere, providing some area defense; this requires some discrimination capability, furnished by passive IR pop-up sensors, launched toward cloud of decoys and attacking RVs; the new layer reduces the burden on the terminal layer.	Passive IR sensors used for crude discrimination and possibly kill assessment; data base of Soviet RV and decoy signatures needed; sensors must be able to function in a hostile nuclear environment.
Level 3 **Heavier Midcourse Layer** (effective midcourse layer added, giving realistic two-layer system, with each layer highly effective)	Level 2 plus: ultraviolet laser radar (ladar) imaging on satellites; highly capable space-based battle management system;	Satellite-based ultraviolet laser radar (ladar) used to image objects; discrimination provided by comparing images with data base of Soviet RV and decoy characteristics; RVs attacked by in-orbit kinetic-energy weapons, which also defend all	Ladar imaging rapid with resolution good to 1 meter or less for adequate discrimination and birth-to-death tracking of RVs; kinetic weapon homing capability good to less than a meter.

	space-based kinetic energy weapons; effective self-defense in space; significant space-based power.		Extremely capable battle management system needed; kill assessment required for boost phase as well as midcourse.
Level 4 Boost-Phase Plus Previous Layers (boost-phase intercept added to kill boosters or post-boost vehicles before RVs and decoys dispersed)	Level 3 plus: ground-based high-intensity lasers (either excimer or free electron); space-based mirrors for relay and aim; high resolution tracking and imaging in boost phase; self-defense for all phases.	This level adds a boost- and post-boost-phase layer, consisting of very bright ground-based laser beams directed to their targets by orbiting mirrors; sensing by infrared sensors, imaging by ultra-violet ladar; battle management to handle all layers doing discrimination, kill assessment, and target assignments and reassignments. Boost- and post-boost-phase layers may be combined, since post-boost phase could be shortened to 10 seconds or so.	
Level 5 Extremely Effective Layer (Level 4 with better capability; meant to permit only minimal penetration to targets by enemy RVs)	Level 4 plus: more terminal and exoatmospheric interceptors; electromagnetic launchers for midcourse and boost-phase intercepts; large capacity space-based power; all systems extremely reliable.	More interceptors are added in terminal and mid-course layers; electromagnetic launchers used for boost, post-boost and midcourse intercepts; high capacity space power needed; all systems, including battle management must be extremely reliable.	Essentially same as Level 4, but more of it and higher reliability; newer technologies used as they become available.

* Kill assessment refers to the process of determining whether a struck target has been effectively disabled.

† Pop-up components are ground-based assets which are launched into space for action upon warning of an enemy attack.

Source: Office of Technology Assessment, *Strategic Defenses: Ballistic Missile Defense Technologies* (Princeton: Princeton University Press, 1986), p. 199.

Figure 10-1. Multilayered Space Defense

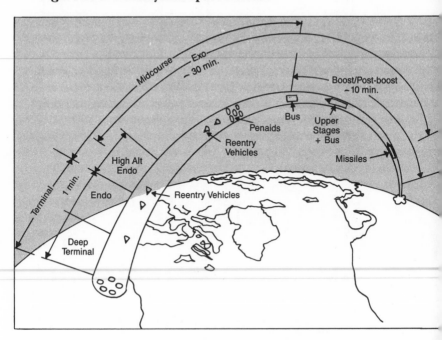

Source: Office of Technology Assessment, *Strategic Defenses: Ballistic Missile Defense Technologies* (Princeton: Princeton University Press, 1986), p. 142.

The Defensive Technologies Study was prepared by Dr. James C. Fletcher, on direct orders from the President after his March 23, 1983, speech to the nation. A classified and an unclassified version of DTS were presented. The goal of the Study "was to provide a basis for selecting the technology paths to follow when a specific defensive strategy is chosen." But it also tried to identify "near-term demonstrations of some system components ... that could provide for early deployment and meaningful levels of effectiveness against constrained threats."[13]

The Study reviewed "a set of strategic defense system concepts and supporting technologies in various states of development," including "concepts constrained by fiscal limitation," and argued that advances in defensive technologies justified a reevaluation of ballistic missile defense. New approaches to the problem of boost-phase intercept, such as particle beam and lasers and kinetic-energy

target destruction mechanisms, were now possible. Similarly, a variety of new sensing technologies showed promise for mid-course interception of nuclear warheads and for discriminating dummies and other debris from the warheads themselves. Likewise, technological advances since the 1960s in computer hardware and software and signal processing allowed new possibilities in command, control, and communications for battle management. DTS concluded: "powerful new technologies are becoming available that justify a major technology development effort offering future technical options to implement a defensive strategy; focused development of technologies for a comprehensive ballistic missile defense will require strong central management; the most effective systems will have multiple layers, or tiers; survivability of the system components is a critical issue whose resolution requires a combination of technologies and tactics that remain to be worked out; [and] significant demonstrations of developing technologies for critical ballistic missile defense function can be performed over the next ten years that will provide visible evidence of progress in developing technical capabilities required of an effective in-depth defense system."[14]

These assessments did not go unchallenged. The first salvo was fired by Dr. Ashton B. Carter in *Directed Energy Missile Defense in Space,* prepared for the Office of Technology Assessment in April 1984, which described and assessed current concepts of ballistic missile defense in space and "the prospects for fashioning from such weapons a robust and reliable wartime defense system resistant to Soviet countermeasures."[15]

The study's judgment on the President's Strategic Defense Initiative was harsh. "The prospect that emerging 'Star Wars' technologies, when further developed, will provide a perfect or near-perfect defense system, literally removing from the hands of the Soviet Union the ability to do socially mortal damage to the United States with nuclear weapons, is so remote that it should not serve as the basis of public expectation or national policy about ballistic missile defense." However, even "[l]ess-than-perfect defenses would still allow the Soviet Union to destroy U.S. society in a massive attack." It pointed out that some of the critical technologies for "Star Wars," such as directed-energy weapons and other devices needed for boost-phase intercept, "have not yet been built for the laboratory, much less in a form suitable for incorporation in a

complete defense system." Further, "[i]t is unknown whether or when devices with the required specification can be built." One of the report's key findings, however, was that the technological challenge was not to design devices to meet particular specifications for controlled situations but "to fashion from these devices a reliable defensive architecture, taking into account vulnerability of the defense components, susceptibility to future Soviet countermeasures, and cost relative to those countermeasures." Thus, "[f]or modest defensive goals requiring less-than-perfect performance, traditional reentry phase defenses and / or more advanced midcourse defenses might suffice. Such defenses present less technical risk than systems that incorporate a boost-phase layer, and they could probably be deployed more quickly."[16]

Carter's report was attacked by the Defense Department but its principal conclusions were not changed in a subsequent OTA expert review of the study. Undaunted, the administration continued to press ahead with its SDI program. On April 15, 1984, fifty-two-year-old Air Force Lieutenant General James Abrahamson was appointed to head SDIO (the newly formed Strategic Defense Initiative Office). SDIO was set up to streamline channels of communication and direction within services and agencies conducting work on the program and to maintain responsibility to the Secretary of Defense for SDI planning, programming, and budgeting. In consultation with service and agency staffs, its director would designate lead organizations responsible for execution of SDI projects and tasks. By the end of 1983, the Defense Department had swept some 150 ongoing military technology projects under the control of SDIO. Under Abrahamson and chief SDI scientist Gerold Yonas, eight program offices concerned with systems, sensors, survivability, lethality, key technologies (kinetic-energy weapons, directed-energy weapons), innovative science and technology, resource management, and external affairs were established. Meanwhile top aerospace companies, such as Lockheed Missiles and Space Company and RCA, formed special SDI divisions or named vice-presidents to preside over SDI work. The three national weapons laboratories—Los Alamos, Sandia, and Lawrence Livermore—also accelerated their research.[17]

On April 24, 1984, appearing before the Senate Subcommittee on Strategic and Theater Nuclear Forces, Lieutenant General James Abrahamson argued that "effective defensive systems could assist

[the United States] in achieving the arms control goals of reduced ballistic missile forces and enhanced stability." An arms control effort and strategy are "fundamental to everything." He also stated that he could see the need at some time in the future for modifications in the Antiballistic Missile Treaty but believed that Soviet concurrence in such modifications would be "the only way we could go forward" when that future point was reached.

> We are frequently asked whether the purpose of the Strategic Defense Initiative is to defend people or military forces. Accomplishment of both these missions is essential to the ultimate goal, which is to provide security for the people of the United States and our allies. The immediate objective is to conduct research on those technologies which might enable the development of defensive systems capable of intercepting ballistic missiles after they have been launched and preventing them from hitting their targets. Once proven, these technologies could be used for the design and development of an appropriate system of defenses. The highly effective defenses that we envision have three attributes which, we believe, would contribute to the ultimate objective. First and foremost, an effective defense against ballistic missiles would improve stability and reduce the likelihood of war by eliminating the military utility of a preemptive nuclear strike. Second, in the unlikely event—whether planned or accidental—that nuclear weapons be used in the face of effective ballistic missile and other defenses, such defenses would save lives and limit damage. Third, by reducing the value of offensive nuclear forces, both military and economic incentives would be created for negotiated offensive force reductions.[18]

Congress authorized and appropriated nearly $1 billion for FY 1984 for the development of technologies relevant to defense against ballistic missiles. The services and defense agencies had plans to increase spending for those relevant technologies to $1.7 billion in FY 1985.

SDIO moved quickly to streamline and accelerate management and procurement processes for ballistic missile defense technology programs. Emphasis was placed on speeding contract completion and contract performance. SDIO would use a "blanket determination and finding" to cover ballistic missile technology as opposed to contracts given out to specific projects. Another innovation was a "racehorse" request for proposals—a ten- to fif-

teen-page document laying out the program objective. The concept was to solicit industry's approaches to resolving technical issues as opposed to detailed specifications from the Defense Department. But Abrahamson had to work hard to stave off funding cuts in the $1.7 billion being sought for FY 1985. The House cut $407 million from the FY 1985 Strategic Defense Initiative program while the Senate sought $150 million in cuts.[19]

In testimony before the Senate Armed Services Committee in March 1984 Richard DeLauer, Under Secretary for Research and Engineering, said that the Pentagon's current goal was to be able to decide by the early 1990s "on whether and how to proceed with development of ballistic missile defenses." He said it was "impossible to estimate now, with any precision, the full cost of developing and deploying" a complete system. The task of combining these key technologies into a meaningful system would demand "breakthroughs in eight key technologies," each "equivalent to, or greater than, the Manhattan Project."[20]

Richard Cooper, Director of the Defense Advanced Research Projects Agency, told the same panel that "if we decided, say in 1995 or the year 2000, to do this [build a strategic defense system], it would take us 10–20 years to put it in place."

Richard Perle, Assistant Secretary of Defense for International Security Policy, said that the research program would lead later to decisions on development and even later to decisions on deployment. He rejected the criticisms of Ashton Carter's OTA report and asserted that there are "compelling reasons" to embark upon the SDI research program.[21]

THE PROGRAM EVOLVES

The idea of shooting down missiles with lasers or particle beams was certainly glamorous, but many years away. "Kinetic-energy weapons," the high-tech version of cannonballs, raised prospects of more immediate deployment. The first such weapon was successfully tested on June 10, 1984. A Minuteman I missile was launched at the Vandenberg Air Force Base in southern California toward the South Pacific in a homing overlay experiment. Twenty minutes later another Minuteman I was launched from the Kwajalein test site in the Marshall Islands carrying an interceptor vehicle—the kinetic-energy weapon—toward the warhead. The

interceptor tracked the warhead with an infrared (heat) sensor linked to an on-board computer and opened a fifteen-foot umbrella-like structure to improve the chances of a hit. The interceptor struck the warhead at 20,000 feet per second and destroyed it. Defense officials were quick to point out that while not capable of the protection provided by a layered system, the airborne sensors and kinetic-energy interceptors could provide the initial elements of a ballistic missile defense capability in the early 1990s.[22]

This and other tests whetted the appetite of some officials in the administration for a scaled-down version of strategic defense in the intermediate term before a full-scale version of SDI could be deployed. In secret testimony before the Senate Armed Services Committee, Under Secretary of Defense for Policy Fred Ikle said, "It stands to reason that as you move toward deployment of the full system there are some intermediate steps which have intermediate utility." In his prepared statement to the Committee he stated: "It seems plausible that components of a multi-tiered defense could become deployed earlier than the complete system. ... Such intermediate versions of a ballistic missile defense, while unable to provide the protection available from a completed multi-tiered system, may nevertheless offer useful capabilities."[23] This did not square with the President's own apparent vision of the future. Earlier, President Reagan promised that the system is "not going to protect missiles. It's going to destroy missiles."

The administration's increasing confusion about SDI was apparent to all. Wayne Biddle reported in the *New York Times:* "Taken together, these statements have helped make the issue of so-called interim deployment—specifically a defensive system for American ICBMs as a stepping stone to a full-fledged population shield—one of the most touchy in the current debate. A review of recent testimony by Administration officials shows far from perfect consistency on the matter. ... On any day of the week, it seems, Star Wars can mean just about anything."[24]

By 1985 year's end, scientists in charge of research for the administration's strategic defense proposal were saying that the plan had been substantially scaled down, from attempting to create an impenetrable shield to protecting the country's land-based force of intercontinental ballistic missiles. This change reflected the growing realization that the goal of an impenetrable defense was impossible, even though it remained the long-term aim. Dr. George

Keyworth explained: "Now what we're addressing more and more is what people call the transition, from the first deployment to the second and so on." Dr. Gerald Yonas, DoD defense scientist in charge of the research program on space defense, argued that some of the technology being developed for the full shield could be put to use as part of a scaled-down system which research continued toward the goal of total protection. "What was missing when we talked about very advanced technology in the next century was that it ignored all the evolutionary steps. . . . Now what we're saying is, hey, as we proceed down this evolutionary path there will be opportunities to apply these even more limited technologies if the country so desires."

As if to underscore the point, a study by the Union of Concerned Scientists concluded that "total Ballistic Missile Defense—the protection of American society against the full weight of a Soviet nuclear attack—is unattainable."[25] The report argued, "Even if individual technologies could be developed to the needed performance levels, fashioning them into a workable, deployable, and survivable system would pose insurmountable difficulties. The system would be immensely more complex than existing weapons and could never be tested under realistic conditions. In addition, it would have to be fully automated, responding instantly upon warning of attack without presidential involvement, given the very short reaction time available for boost-phase interception. Yet the defense would have to work with near 100 percent reliability. It would have almost no margin for error because even a minute 'leakage' rate would mean hundreds of nuclear explosions on U.S. territory—and millions of fatalities—in the event of a large Soviet attack."[26]

The limited-shield idea had its critics, too. Some argued that it would upset the ABM treaty—that limited defense of ICBMs might be perceived by the enemy as fundamentally offensive. Former Secretary of Defense James Schlesinger, now senior adviser at the Georgetown Center for Strategic and International Studies, observed: "One might be willing to upset the ABM Treaty to provide protection for every man, woman and child in North America. But to upset it for possible improvements in deterrence is a much more difficult decision . . . [and] there is no serious likelihood of removing the nuclear threat from our cities in our lifetime or in the lifetime of our children."[27]

A 147-page report by Stanford University's Center for International Security and Arms Control concluded that space-based defense was technologically unfeasible and strategically unsound. According to one of its authors, Dr. Sidney D. Drell, a Stanford University physicist and adviser to the Pentagon, "Technical people in the Defense Department realized the limits all along. I just don't know whether the others are just learning this or have known it and been sailing the treacherous waters between a declared Presidential goal and technical reality. I don't know. But it's created a fundamental confusion about a major part of our strategic posture. The President and the Secretary of Defense still talk about total defense."[28]

Still, some, like former Secretary of State Henry Kissinger, endorsed the idea of limited defense. Writing in the *Los Angeles Times* on September 23, Kissinger explained, "Even granting—as I do—that a perfect defense of the U.S. population is almost certainly unattainable, the existence of some defense means that the attacker must plan on saturating it. This massively complicates the attacker's calculations. Anything that magnifies doubt inspires hesitation and adds to deterrence. . . . The case grows stronger if one considers the defense of Intercontinental Ballistic Missile launchers. A defense of the civilian population would have to be nearly 100 percent effective, while a defense that protected even 50 percent of land-based missiles and air bases would add hugely to deterrence. The incentive for a first strike would be sharply, perhaps decisively, reduced if an aggressor knew that half of the opponent's ICBMs would survive any foreseeable attack."[29]

Soviet responses to SDI were also a growing source of debate and concern. Pentagon officials argued that the Soviets were on par with the United States in basic research on directed-energy weapons like lasers and subatomic particle beams that might be used for land- and space-based missile defense, but trailing in technologies needed to make energy beams into workable weapons. Top administration officials publicly expressed the belief that U.S. space-based defense would force the Soviets to give up reliance on offensive land-based intercontinental ballistic missiles and to build a similar defense system of their own. This view was challenged by experts on Soviet policy and weapons and by the Soviets themselves. Former Soviet party leader Yuri V. Andropov stated on March 27, 1983, "Should this conception be translated into

reality, it would in fact open the floodgates to a runaway race of all types, both offensive and defensive."[30] Sayre Stevens, former Deputy Director of the Central Intelligence Agency, said it would be enormously difficult to move from strategic deterrence to defense: "I don't quite see how you get from here to there." Stephen M. Meyer, a Soviet expert at the Massachusetts Institute of Technology, argued, "It's not going to be a race between our 'Star Wars' and their 'Star Wars,' but a race against our system and their efforts to overwhelm or neutralize it." Said Meyer, "one of the first things the Soviets could do is to drag out all of the 1,000 or more ICBM boosters they have lying around. They would not even need warheads or decoys." Launching such boosters along with armed missiles would automatically increase the number of targets, complicating the task of U.S. sensors and defensive weapons. According to Richard L. Garwin and Kurt Gottfried, members of the Union of Concerned Scientists, the Soviets might also try to develop "fast-burn boosters" that would finish burning before leaving the atmosphere, where they are immune to present-day laser technology. The Soviets could also spin their boosters, which would require major increases in the power of defensive lasers. In the longer run, the Soviet Union could increase its arsenal of ICBMs fitted with warheads and penetration aids such as "decoys and chaff" so that the United States might face 30,000 or more hostile warheads, three times the number in the current strategic arsenal. The Soviets could do this by fitting their heavy SS-18 ICBMs with thirty warheads instead of the ten allowed under the unratified SALT II Treaty.

Another Soviet countermeasure, according to these critics, would be to fire ballistic missiles from offshore submarines on "depressed" or low-angle trajectories so that they would spend much less time outside the atmosphere where they would be vulnerable to space-based defenses. This would further complicate the problems of defense. "Precursor attacks" would be another Soviet ploy. Such attacks would be timed to take place shortly before the salvos of missiles were launched. This would involve detonating nuclear weapons in space to blind or cripple or destroy space-based defenses or attacking ground stations in the United States that would relay the information to and from the space stations for battle management. Another possibility, raised by Richard DeLauer in congressional testimony in 1983, would be direct attack of the

defense by anti-satellite weapons. The Soviets could also resort to a variety of "passive measures" for defense including reinforcement or hardening of missile silos, dispersal of missiles and other crucial facilities, and civil defense.

Still others, like a special panel convened by the Office of Technology Assessment, expressed concern that the President's idea of a defensive shield could also be used for offensive purposes. Under one scenario, offensive missiles would be launched against enemy forces while the defense would be held in reserve to cope with any retaliatory strike. Defenses could also be used to attack enemy space satellites, easier targets than ballistic missiles. Defenses might even be used to conduct strikes against "soft" ground targets like airplanes, oil tankers, power plants, and grain fields, causing instantaneous fires and damage which, in the words of John D. G. Rather, a laser expert and supporter of SDI, could "take an industrialized country back to an 18th-century level in 30 minutes."[31]

Some challenged the idea that the United States would be safer even if it were protected by a highly effective defense against nuclear attack. According to Charles Glaser, a fellow at Harvard's Kennedy School of Government, "A situation in which both superpowers deployed nearly impenetrable defenses would be extremely sensitive to even small improvements in one country's ability to penetrate its adversary's defense. ... The country that first acquired even a small capability to penetrate the adversary's defense would have attained an important coercive advantage; it could threaten nuclear attack with impunity since effective retaliation would be impossible given the adversary's inability to penetrate its own defense."[32]

ARMS CONTROL

President Reagan increasingly viewed SDI as a useful bargaining chip in bringing about reductions in offensive weapons at Geneva talks in 1985. In a speech to the National Space Club he said, "The Strategic Defense Initiative has been labelled 'Star Wars,' but it isn't about war, it's about peace. It isn't about retaliation, it's about prevention. It isn't about fear, it's about hope, and in that struggle, if you want to pardon my stealing a film line, the force is with us. ... Our activities in space are already helping to keep the peace, providing us early warning and enabling us to verify arms agree-

ments. And far from being a violation of existing arms control agreements, once our adversaries fully understand the goal of our research program, it will add new incentives to both sides in Geneva to actually reduce the number of nuclear weapons threatening mankind. By making missiles less effective, we make these weapons more negotiable. If we are successful, the arms spiral will be a downward spiral, hopefully to the elimination of them."[33]

But U.S. arms control negotiator Ambassador Paul Nitze believed that the equation was not quite so simple. In a speech to the World Affairs Council of Philadelphia on February 20, he outlined a set of conditions to be met before strategic defense systems should be deployed. First, the technology "must produce defensive systems that are survivable" against preemptive attack. Otherwise, "the defenses would themselves be tempting targets for a first strike." Second, the systems would have to be "cost-effective at the margin, that is, they must be cheap enough so that the other side has no incentive to add additional offensive capability to overcome defense." If not, the system "would encourage a proliferation of countermeasures and additional offensive weapons to overcome deployed defenses, instead of a redirection of effort from offense to defense."[34]

If SDI was necessary for arms control, it was also necessary because the Soviets, according to the administration, were not living up to the spirit or letter of past arms control agreements. On April 11, 1985, in a speech to the American Society of Newspaper Editors, Secretary of Defense Caspar Weinberger charged that the Soviets "may be preparing" to violate existing treaties by deploying a nationwide defense against nuclear missiles. He argued that Soviet development of movable radar systems and high-speed missiles to intercept enemy missiles and their investment in laser research presented "the ominous possibility of a deliberate and rapid unilateral Soviet deployment of strategic defenses."[35]

The Reagan administration's key assessment of the Soviet threat was delivered in the Pentagon's annual publication *Soviet Military Power,* first issued in 1981. The DIA (Defense Intelligence Agency) had a major hand in drafting this annual review. The publication gained considerable public attention and was intended to provide information about Soviet military developments and programs. It consistently conveyed an image of the Soviets as engaged in the unrelenting pursuit of strategic and conventional military superi-

ority and was undoubtedly intended to buttress the administration's efforts to increase defense spending and promote the SDI program. The 1986 edition, for example, argued that "[p]aralleling the offensive strategic developments of 1985, the Soviet Union pressed forward with advanced new strategic defense systems. Construction continued on new over-the-horizon radars and large phased-array radars capable of tracking greater number of targets with increased accuracy. Two new classes of silo-based ABM interceptor missiles in the Moscow ABM system were in advanced stages of testing. More important, advanced research continued on the components that are necessary to achieve a rapidly deployable nationwide ABM system." It stated that the Soviet Union "also continued to work on advanced strategic defense technology programs focused on the development of high-energy lasers, kinetic energy weapons, radio frequency weapons, and particle beam weapons," so that "[b]y the late 1980s, the USSR may well advance to the testing of lasers for targeting ballistic missiles in flight."[36]

In its February 1985 *Report on Soviet Noncompliance with Arms Control Agreements,* the administration argued that "the USSR has violated the ABM Treaty."[37] One of the key issues had to do with the development of Krasnoyarsk radar in central Siberia in the Soviet Union. The administration argued that the radar was constructed for early warning with an ABM battle management capability and its location was in violation of ABM Treaty provisions regarding location and orientation of early-warning radars.The Soviets responded by arguing that the radar was set up to track satellites and to verify U.S. compliance with the Outer Space Treaty.

Similar concerns were expressed in the President's own December 1985 *Report on Soviet Noncompliance to Congress.* The Report stated: "The Krasnoyarsk radar appears even more menacing when considered in the context of other Soviet ABM-related activities. Together they cause concern that the Soviet Union may be preparing an ABM territorial defense ... [which] would have profound implications for Western security and the vital East-West strategic balance."[38]

These assessments did not go unchallenged. For example, the National Campaign to Save the ABM Treaty, headed by a group of prominent scientists, charged the administration with willful deception and argued that

the facts do not support the case that the Soviets are on the verge of a breakout of the ABM Treaty. While the Soviets have the potential for such a breakout, the Administration has failed to provide any convincing evidence that they are actually making such a move. ... There is little doubt that the new ... components could be deployed as part of a nationwide defense ... [yet] these activities—no more than similar American activities such as the Site Defense effort of the early 1970s—are not necessarily preparations for breaking out of the Treaty. In isolation, any ABM component could be regarded as preparations for a defense of national territory.[39]

A later study by the Center for International Security and Arms Control of Stanford University on *Compliance and the Future of Arms Control*—whose signatories included distinguished scientists and former officials like Sidney Drell, Deputy Director of the Stanford Linear Accelerator; former Presidential Science Adviser Dr. Wolfgang Panofsky; Raymond Garthoff, member of the SALT I delegation; William Perry, former Under Secretary of Defense for Research and Engineering; and Sidney Graybeal, U.S. Commissioner of the Joint U.S.-Soviet Standing Consultative Commission from 1973 to 1976—reached a similar conclusion. The report charged, "A perceived compliance crisis has been created, in part, by the Reagan Administration's exaggeration of the military significance of alleged Soviet 'violations.'" The report found "no evidence of a Soviet policy of violating arms control agreements, or of a consistent Soviet pattern of violations." Although it viewed the Soviet Union's large, phased-array, early-warning radar at Abalakova, Siberia, to be in violation of the ABM Treaty, it found "one area of questionable compliance" on the U.S. side: "the U.S. program to replace or construct new early warning radars at Thule, Greenland; Fylingdales Moor, U.K.; and through the PAVE PAWS programs in the U.S."[40]

M.I.T.'s Stephen Meyer argued, "It is true that the Soviets have the largest SDI program in the world, but that effort is overwhelmingly an air-defense effort." According to Meyer, the Soviet effort relies on radar systems, interceptor aircraft, surface-to-air missiles for anti-cruise missile defense, all designed to protect targets just before they are struck; even the largest radar being constructed at Krasnoyarsk is not particularly impressive. "The systems do not move ... and there is great uncertainty here about both the operational reliability of those systems and, more important, the

computer-processing capabilities."[41] Meyer argued that exotic weapons systems like lasers, particle beams, and orbiting accelerators are on Moscow's research agenda but are twenty to thirty years away and that research "is not linked to weapons programs at all." Moreover, the Soviets have "had serious difficulties making particle accelerators ... [and] no evidence suggests that they have successfully solved the problems besetting kinetic-energy weapons, which have rails that tend to warp after repeated firings, or gas-dynamic and electrical-discharge lasers."[42] According to Meyer, the Soviets are also very weak in the key areas of sensing, tracking control, and targeting—areas crucial to strategic defense.

There were skeptics in Congress too. Senator Albert Gore, Jr. (D.-Tenn.), rejected suggestions that the United States should "vigorously pursue research on strategic defenses" with the aim of developing a limited defense system for U.S. missile silos. "If Star Wars is a genie out of the bottle, then rather than discarding the President's concept of leakproof population defense, we should insist that the research program remain focused on that goal." He argued that the United States should continue to support the ABM Treaty and not test system components or subcomponents in space but confine testing to the laboratory because "[o]nce we or the Russians introduce such experiments in space, we shall have passed beyond research into a gray area at the threshold of weapons development."[43]

CONGRESSIONAL ACTION

President Reagan requested $3.7 billion for FY 1986, a substantial expansion from the $1.4 billion in FY 1985.[44] Senator John Warner (R.-Va.), Chairman of the Senate Armed Services Subcommittee on Strategic Theater and Nuclear Forces, said that he favored giving the President what he requested although he "would not commit ... to the entire request." Senator Ted Stevens (R.-Alaska), Chairman of the Senate Subcommittee on Defense Appropriations, called SDI "the highest priority I have." Representative Les Aspin (D.-Wis.) predicted that Congress would cut some money back, while Joseph Addabbo (D.-N.Y.), Chairman of the House Subcommittee on Defense Appropriations, said he hoped to keep the program at current levels of spending. Les Aspin summed up the legislative dilemma: "There is an important underlying debate there but it's

hard to see how the issue will get joined in a legislative context. As long as the program is only research, there is no legislative issue on which the opponents and proponents can line up on opposite sides. Even the most vociferous opponents say we ought to do research." The only issue, said Aspin, is how much to spend.[45]

Congressional interest in SDI grew during the Second Session of the 98th Congress. Hearings took place before Senate and House Armed Services Committees and the Appropriations Subcommittees on SDI funding and led to sharp debates on Defense Authorization Bills in both Houses. The House Committee on Foreign Affairs and the Senate Foreign Relations Committee also held hearings on outer space. Discussion of SDI on the floor of the House was limited. But in the Senate floor debate Charles Percy (R.-Ill.) introduced an amendment to cut $100 million from the SDI program in the Defense Authorization Act for FY 1985. He emphasized that his amendment was "a deficit-reduction amendment . . . a vote for fiscal responsibility. It is not a referendum on 'Star Wars.' " Senator William Proxmire (D.-Wis.) warned that SDI would "plunge this Nation ahead on a spending binge that will . . . cost our Federal Government a trillion dollars or more." He was rebutted by Senators John Tower (R.-Tex.) and Barry Goldwater (R.-Ariz.), who defended the research program. The amendment was narrowly defeated by a vote of 47 to 45. A final sum of $1.4 billion was authorized for SDI research in FY 1985 by Joint Conference Agreement adopted by House and Senate. The Senate had earlier given voice approval for DoD to provide to Congress annual reports clarifying SDI objectives. A concurrent Joint Resolution introduced in October 1984 by Senator John Chafee (R.-R.I.) encouraged the President to comply with the ABM Treaty, but the Committee on Foreign Relations took no action on the resolution.[46]

On April 4, 1985, the Senate Armed Services Committee reported to the full Senate for FY 1986 a Defense Authorization Bill providing $3.42 billion for SDI research. The Committee's recommendation was $300 million below the administration's budget request, but it gave its support for the SDI concept and for continued consultation with U.S. allies.

But the Senate had already cut FY 1986 budget authority for the Defense Department by $9.1 billion, which meant that SDI would have to take some share of the cuts. After several floor amendments the newly recommended amount was $2.97 billion, $750

million below the administration's request. Senator Larry Pressler (R.-S.D.) had this to say:

> When the Senate debated authorizations for ASAT and SDI research funding in May and June 1985, the mood in the Senate concerning space weaponry had been altered by a new development. Foremost was the return of the Soviets to the negotiating table in Geneva. It was widely believed that Soviet apprehension about the SDI had been a major factor in the renewed desire to negotiate. Many senators felt a responsibility not to undercut U.S. negotiators by voting to cut funding for programs that could be used as 'bargaining chips' in Geneva. It was in this general atmosphere that debate took place during consideration of the Department of Defense authorization bill for fiscal year 1986.[47]

An amendment on May 24, 1985, offered by Senator John Kerry (D.-Mass.) calling for a moratorium on ASAT (antisatellite weapons) testing was defeated by a vote of 35 to 51. On June 3, Senator Kerry introduced an amendment to freeze SDI funding at $1.4 billion. His amendment would have eliminated parts of the SDI program that might violate key provisions of the ABM Treaty. He made the familiar argument that the Soviet Union "would turn its resources into improving or replacing a portion of its weapons to sidestep the defense." He received strong support for the amendment from Senator William Proxmire and Senator Paul Simon (D.-Ill.), but the amendment was attacked by SDI supporters in the Senate. In a strange twist of logic Senator Barry Goldwater indicated that he did not "look upon the SDI exactly as my friend from Massachusetts looks at it. I look upon it as an antiweapon. . . . For every weapons system that has been developed, there has been an antiweapons system developed against it, and they are always successful." Kerry's amendment was defeated by a vote of 21 to 78. Senator Proxmire then offered an amendment to fund SDI research at $1.9 billion, inserting into the record three letters from Robert McNamara, Clark Clifford, and Elliot Richardson agreeing that that level would be sufficient. This amendment was also defeated, by a vote of 38 to 57. Senator Albert Gore then offered an amendment to fund SDI research at $2.5 billion but to impose restrictions on certain projects that might lead to ABM Treaty violations. It, too, was defeated, by a vote of 36 to 59. Senator John

Glenn (D.-Ohio) offered a final amendment to cut SDI funding to $2.8 billion. After brief debate it, too, failed, by 36 to 59. An amendment was introduced by Senator Malcolm Wallop (R.-Wyo.) to earmark $800 million for the development of ballistic missile defenses that could be deployed within five to seven years. Said Wallop in defense of his motion: "The strategic defense initiative as it is right now would not spend a single penny to build any device or any components of any device that would shoot down a missile.... And so this amendment goes against the grain of today's Pentagon, and so against the grain of what this body has done in the field of strategic weapons. This amendment proposes, strange to say, that we use a little of the money we spend to actually give something useful to ourselves." His amendment failed by a vote of 33 to 62, demonstrating, according to his colleague Larry Pressler, "that many senators who approve research may have second thoughts about actual deployment."[48]

The Senate left the FY 1986 budget for the SDI program intact at $2.97 billion. Senate Bill 1160 made deployment dependent on written certification from the President that such systems would survive a concerted attack sufficiently intact to meet their mission and would be economical enough to be maintained against the offense at costs lower than those for developing offensive counter-measures, including proliferation of the adversary's ballistic missiles. The debate reflected growing skepticism on Capitol Hill about the program. Supporters of the amendment argued that rapid development of the program would jeopardize arms control talks with the Soviets and set off a new weapons race. "We don't know what it will cost, we don't know what it will do," said Senator J. Bennett Johnston (D.-La.). "The only thing we're sure of is that the President is wrong. It won't make nuclear weapons obsolete." Senator Sam Nunn (D.-Ga.) said that the anti-missile project would not violate existing treaties because it was still at the research stage and not testing. He believed the amendment amounted to "micromanagement" of the Pentagon and added, "Congress is not in a position to do that."[49]

The House of Representatives approved only $2.5 billion for continuing research on SDI, a total well below President Reagan's request for $3.7 billion. There were five different attempts to raise or lower the total, all of which were defeated by sizable margins. The House position also reflected the ambivalence of lawmakers.

"What you're seeing is a number of members who are uncomfortable with the issue, and they're approaching it very cautiously," said Les Aspin, Chairman of the House Armed Services Committee. "It's a highly technical subject, and people are trying to find a middle position." Although some lawmakers supported the President's research program because it would bring pressure on the Soviets to bargain more seriously at the arms control talks in Geneva, many others opposed it, but feared that if they rejected it outright they would be labeled "soft on defense."[50]

The House also attached two amendments to the FY 1986 Defense Authorization Bill that would create a commission to monitor the Strategic Defense Initiative, and they were approved by voice vote. One amendment created an eight-member Congressional Commission on Strategic Defense to run through 1990, and the other established a five-member Strategic Defense Initiative Commission to run for six months after enactment of the Defense Authorization Bill. Barry Goldwater, Chairman of the Senate Armed Services Committee, admitted that "as one who has lived with SDI since its inception, there is an awful lot of it I do not know anything about. I think I am pretty safe in saying that about most members of the Senate." Representative James R. Olin (D.-Va.) commented, "I seriously doubt that normal committee oversight procedures will be sufficient for us to do the careful objective job we must do. Nor can we rely on the Pentagon program managers or other government agencies alone. . . . We have the responsibility to see that SDI does not acquire a life of its own before it has a clear plan, a realizable objective and is understood well enough so we can manage it."[51]

OPPOSITION MOUNTS

On June 21, 1985, a bright blue-green laser beam streaked up from the Hawaiian Islands, bounced off a mirror on the space shuttle *Discovery,* and zoomed back to the ground station at Maui, thereby completing the first successful experiment conducted by the Strategic Defense Initiative Research Team. Spokesman Lee DeLorme, press aide to General James Abrahamson, described the experiment as "a complete success." The experiment was designed to demonstrate that low-power laser beams can be fired with precision despite the distorting effects of the atmosphere. Scientists hoped

that experiments of this nature would verify whether more powerful lasers could be aimed accurately enough to knock down enemy missiles as they left the launching pad.[52]

President Reagan defended the anti-missile plan before entering Bethesda Naval Hospital for surgery on July 13, 1985. He tried to downplay the nuclear aspects of the program: "A nonnuclear strategic defense makes good sense. It is better to protect lives than to avenge them." He asserted that the Soviet Union had been working vigorously on its own anti-missile plan. "The Soviets have diverted huge sums of their military budget to a sophisticated strategic defense program which, in resources already allocated, far exceeds what the United States anticipates spending in the current decade."[53] Reagan reiterated this theme in an August 22 speech to the Republican Party of California.[54]

On September 23, 1985, the Department of Defense activated its first unified space command to oversee military programs in space consisting of systems devoted to intelligence gathering, watching for attack, and facilitating communications and navigation. But perhaps in the future it would also operate the SDI system. Leadership of the new command went to General Robert T. Herres, head of the North American Aerospace Defense Command and the United States Air Force Aerospace Command, which has its headquarters inside Cheyenne Mountain, also at Colorado Springs. General John W. Vessey, Chairman of the Joint Chiefs of Staff, said that the purpose of the new command was to extend the armed services' current strategy of deterrence. "There are several things the command will not become," he said. "It is not a force built to escalate the arms race. It is not a force built to achieve dominance for the United States. The command will make its contribution to that fundamental element of United States strategy, the prevention of war."[55]

Opposition to SDI among scientists and engineers across the nation's college and university campuses, however, began to mount. A campaign, spearheaded by scientists at Cornell, M.I.T., and the University of Illinois but with supporters on thirty-nine campuses, was formally announced in Cambridge, Massachusetts, on September 12, 1985. The movement began to get prominent scientists and engineers to sign a pledge to refuse to participate in research on strategic defenses, but not everybody was about to sign. Lieutenant Colonel Lee DeLorme said that the SDIO had considered

2,600 applications from individual researchers and universities to participate in the SDI program in 1985.[56] The scientific community was obviously divided.

Congress's Office of Technology Assessment released a 324-page report on September 24, 1985, commissioned by the House Armed Services Committee and the Senate Foreign Relations Committee to assess the opportunities and risks involved in an accelerated program of research on ballistic missile defense technologies. The report concluded that development of such defenses might make nuclear war between the United States and Soviet Union more likely unless the two countries could develop an "extremely capable" leakproof shield against nuclear weapons. But it expressed strong doubts that such a leakproof shield was technologically feasible and argued that a highly effective defense would require both sides to agree to significant reductions in their offensive nuclear forces. "If the Soviets chose to cooperate in a transition to mutual assured survival, it would probably be necessary to negotiate adequately verifiable arms control agreements on reducing present and restricting future offensive forces and on the manner, effectiveness, and timing of defensive deployments." But it went on: "There is great uncertainty about the strategic situation if BMD deployments took place without agreement between the United States and Soviet Union to reduce offensive forces as defenses grew. Until the actual offensive systems (including ICBMs, SLBMs, bombers, and cruise missiles) and defensive systems (including BMD and air defenses) were specified and well understood, no one could know with confidence whether a situation of acute crisis instability (i.e., striking first could appear to lead to 'victory') could be avoided." In such an environment, a "fear on either side that the other could obtain such a first strike capability could lead both sides to build up both their offenses and their defenses. Such build-ups would make it even more difficult to negotiate a cooperative transition from offense dominance to defense dominance."

The report also argued that the use of defenses in a more limited mode to reduce ICBM vulnerability would not necessarily "be the best way to provide missile survivability." It also said, "It is impossible to say at this time how effective an affordable BMD system could be." Although "SDI offers an *opportunity* to substantially increase our nation's safety *if* we obtain great technical success and a substantial degree of Soviet cooperation," the program

also carried a substantial "*risk* that a vigorous BMD research program could bring on an offensive and defensive arms race, and a further risk that BMD deployment, if it took place without Soviet cooperation, could create severe instabilities."[57]

Lieutenant General Daniel O. Graham, director of High Frontier, called the conclusions of the report "ridiculous" and based on "political" rather than "technological" judgments. He resigned in protest from the twenty-man OTA advisory panel after seeing an earlier draft of the report. Representative Les Aspin, however, greeted the recommendations with the following wry observation: "What this means is that after spending billions and billions of dollars, we could find that we have brought ourselves greater instability than the world has ever confronted in the atomic age."[58]

The Pentagon quickly challenged the Congressional study's assertion that defenses might increase the risk of nuclear war. "We would not deploy" such defenses, the Pentagon said, "unless it was proved that they would contribute to military stability by foiling the advantages of a sneak attack and making defense cheaper than offense." The Pentagon also disputed the report's conclusion that the administration seemed to have a more limited goal in mind such as defending U.S. ICBM forces from surprise attack. While "a future President" might choose a limited use for the strategic defense program "[t]he goal of our research, however, is not, and cannot be, simply to protect our retaliatory forces from attack."[59]

In 1985 the debate about how far the administration could go in testing new anti-missile defenses without violating the ABM Treaty grew. The Treaty states that the parties pledge "not to develop, test, or deploy ABM systems or components which are sea-based, air-based, space-based, or mobile-land-based." But administration officials came up with something they called the "broad interpretation," focusing on "Agreed Statement D" of the ABM Treaty.[60] Statement D says that "in the event ABM systems based on other physical principles and including other components capable of substituting for ABM interceptor missiles, ABM launchers, or ABM radars are created in the future, specific limitations on such systems and their components would be subject to discussion." Officials argued that in theory the United States could test and produce space-based systems just so long as they were not deployed. However, officials who negotiated the Treaty said that "Agreed Statement D" was not a loophole but an open-ended statement intended

to gather all possible future technical developments under the umbrella of the ABM Treaty.

To build support for SDI among the United States' allies, Secretary of Defense Caspar Weinberger held out the lure of defense in Europe from intermediate-range Soviet ballistic missiles. "The President's SDI program is directed against the whole spectrum of offensive nuclear ballistic missiles, not just short-range missiles aimed at the U.S. Indeed, if the research succeeds, it may free Europe from the specter of Soviet intermediate-range missiles. . . . Allied countries participating in SDI research would accrue benefits to their industrial-technical bases. . . . SDI capability against intermediate nuclear forces would enhance conventional deterrence by increasing survivability of NATO's defenses in Europe—thus reducing opportunities for the Warsaw Pact to see advantage in attacking."[61]

Lieutenant General Abrahamson and Under Secretary for Defense, Policy, Fred Ikle told the Senate Armed Services Committee Subcommittee on Strategic and Theater Nuclear Forces that the United States "must accelerate" research in methods of shooting down shorter range missiles as well as those of intercontinental range. The administration was keen to reassure European allies that the United States was not intending to erect a shield only on North America, leaving its allies exposed. These officials also took care to point out there was technological compatibility in the two plans because the technologies needed for anti-tactical missile defense were closely related to those needed in the final or terminal state of continental defense, consisting of several layers of anti-missile weapons.[62]

The Pentagon also came under attack because key assessments about SDI were being made by the same private contractors that would build the systems and stand to gain from contracts. "It's an enormous potential conflict of interest," said William Proxmire, who had failed to convince Congress to establish an independent science advisory group on strategic defense. The New York–based Council on Economic Priorities wrote that the program "is rife with potential for conflict of interest." Former arms control negotiator Paul C. Warnke said, "People who know that the forward movement of the project will bring them billions and billions of dollars in business can hardly be disinterested."

According to *New York Times* correspondent David Sanger, "The

Pentagon has often sought the advice of contractors in developing weapons, but in the case of missile defense, the contractors are playing a far greater role in decision-making than before. In the past, contractors have served chiefly as advisers on the design of individual weapons, whose prototypes could be thoroughly tested. Contractors involved in the missile-defense studies, however, are designing entire systems, requiring that judgments be made about how a host of components, which can be tested individually, might work together. Many believe those individual judgments will be impossible to verify because the entire system may never be tested— even after the Pentagon builds its National Test Bed Facility to attempt large-scale battle simulations."[63]

Ten companies were initially involved in major studies of a seven-layer space defense system. In the summer of 1985, five were chosen for the second stage of study, receiving $5 million each to take a year-long look at defensive system architecture. Three were major defense contractors: TRW Inc., Martin Marietta Corporation, and Rockwell International. The other two, Sparta Inc. and Science Applications International Corporation, were specialists in computer modeling and strategic systems analysis. The biggest contractor, Boeing Aerospace, had contracts worth $130 million. Seventy-seven percent of SDI research money went to the districts of congressmen who serve on the House or Senate Armed Services or Appropriations Committees.[64]

What did the public think about SDI? Public-opinion polls portrayed a confused picture. One Roper poll asked the following question: "President Reagan has proposed that the United States build a space-based defense system against incoming missiles. Many people think that this is a good idea because it would give us an advantage over the Russians in this area, which would help deter a Soviet attack. Many others feel that a space-based defense system is a bad idea because it would escalate the arms race and increase the risk of nuclear confrontation with Russia. How do you feel— do you think the United States should or should not build a space-based defense?" When the poll was taken in August 1984, 54 percent of the respondents said the United States should not go ahead, 34 percent said yes, and 12 percent were undecided. When the poll was taken again in March 1985, 52 percent said no, 36 percent yes, and 12 percent were undecided. But by July 1985, 43 percent were saying no, 35 percent yes, and 22 percent were un-

decided. A Gallup poll taken in January 1985 had 52 percent of Americans wanting "to see the U.S. go ahead with deployment" of a space-based system against nuclear attack. A *New York Times/Daniel Yankelovich* survey in May 1985 had 51 percent of Americans agreeing that "building star wars is a good idea," 35 percent believing it to be a "bad idea," and 14 percent "not sure."[65]

On November 20, 1985, the Pentagon announced it had recently destroyed a mock-up of a Soviet SS-18 booster with a hardened plastic pellet fired by an electromagnetic rail gun, an experimental kinetic-energy weapon that could be deployed in space to destroy enemy missiles. The Pentagon also released photographs of a Titan missile booster that had been destroyed by a chemical laser at White Sands Missile Range, New Mexico.[66]

But there were reports that tests of the much more technically sophisticated X-ray laser were the result of dishonest research and cover-ups. A March 23 test of the X-ray laser that was billed as successful apparently wasn't because monitoring instruments had been excited by X rays to emit light and therefore the brightness they measured was much greater than what the device actually produced, making the result completely unreliable. Ray Kidder, a physicist at Los Alamos and skeptic of "Star Wars," was quoted as saying: "The public is getting swindled by one side that has access to classified information and can say whatever it wants and not go to jail, whereas we [the skeptics] can't say whatever we want. We would go to jail, that's the difference."[67] Dr. David Lorge Parnas, a computer software specialist, resigned in June 1985 from the President's panel on space-based missile defense because the United States could not ever have confidence that computer software for such a system would ever work, that it always would be vulnerable to "catastrophic failure."[68]

President Reagan signed the act containing a House-Senate compromise authorization of $2.75 billion for the SDI for FY 1986 on November 8, 1985. Congress approved the $2.75 billion Defense Appropriations Bill for SDI in December 1985, a compromise figure between the Senate's $2.96 billion and the House's $2.5 billion.[69] In a year's-end speech to a German-U.S. seminar in Bonn, West Germany, U.S. Secretary of Defense Caspar Weinberger predicted that the United States might be able to deploy a space-based anti-missile shield using ground-based lasers by the mid-1990s. "In the past, we thought that a ground-based laser sys-

tem would not be available until the turn of the century. . . . [but] breakthroughs [in research] convince us that a ground-based laser missile-defense system with space-based elements may be feasible by the mid-1990s."[70]

On December 6, 1985, thirty members of Congress sent a letter to the Secretary of Defense urging him to postpone a $30 million test (code-named "Goldstone") of an X-ray laser because of reported flaws in the experiment's design. The letter, drafted by Representative William Green (R.-N.Y.), stated: "We are disturbed that, at this time of skyrocketing deficits and cutbacks in defense spending, money is being wasted in a test that does not provide accurate data. . . . Even those who support the Space Defense Initiative should realize that fudging tests and wasting money will undermine confidence in, and support for, the program."[71]

On December 31, 1985, Weinberger declared in his new Defense Guidance Statement (used by military services to devise their long-term programs) that SDI shares the "highest priority" among Pentagon programs and would be sheltered from the budget cuts required in the current fiscal year owing to the budget-balancing law. The new Defense Guidance (DG) would remain in force for two years in order to encourage Congress to move toward the establishment of a two-year military budget to avoid delays and uncertainties in military programs. In an apparent effort to reassure European critics of SDI, the DG also said that research on defense against short-range missiles should be conducted "as a hedge against Soviet improvements in tactical ballistic missile accuracy."[72]

On February 4, 1986, Weinberger sent his new budget to Congress proposing $4.8 billion for SDI research, a 75 percent increase over FY 1986.[73] The Energy Department also sought $603 million for nuclear power and nuclear weapons related to SDI, up from $288 million in FY 1986, which would come on top of the DoD request for $4.8 billion. About $250 million was to be used for underground test explosions in the Nevada desert to help develop directed-energy weapons.

Weinberger told the NATO defense ministers in March that space defense research would not be abandoned in order to reach an arms control agreement with the Soviet Union. "I advised my colleagues that strategic defense is one of the very highest priorities of our Government and one of the highest priorities of our Presi-

dent, that it is not a bargaining chip; it will not be set aside in response to any demand in connection with any arms reduction agreement."[74]

MORE OPPOSITION

On March 17, a staff report done for Senators William Proxmire, J. Bennett Johnston, and Lawton Chiles (D.-Fla.), based on extensive interviews and briefings conducted with top SDIO officials, argued that "Congress should maintain a certain degree of skepticism over claims of tremendous advances in SDI research ... compared to the task at hand ... SDI has moved ahead by inches." It argued that "a closer look should be taken at whether boost-phase intercept can ever be made to work and whether space-based assets can ever be made survivable. If the evidence shows that boost-phase intercept cannot work and space-based assets cannot be made survivable, with or without arms control, serious questions should be raised about the feasibility of implementing the President's vision of a comprehensive strategic defense." The authors of the report were "struck by myriad uncertainties and unknowns at every turn in the program—uncertainties and unknowns that bear directly on the effectiveness of a comprehensive ballistic missile defense. ... And much of that uncertainty will likely remain, for even with strategic defenses in place, the U.S. would never be able to adequately test the system under realistic conditions. ... It would seem inevitable that faced with these uncertainties, both the U.S. and the U.S.S.R. would deem it necessary to maintain a highly secure and effective antisatellite capability to ensure that at the onset of a nuclear conflict they did not suddenly discover their adversary's defense intact and their own defense debilitated. Thus, both sides would have strategic defenses in place with separate ASAT weapons poised to destroy the other's defense. This situation does not strike us as a stable environment for the future."[75]

In response to congressional opposition, the President warned in July that reductions in spending on strategic defenses would jeopardize chances of reaching an arms control agreement with the Soviet Union and of a successful summit meeting with Soviet leader Mikhail Gorbachev. The President hoped to stave off deeper budget reductions than those already approved by the House and Senate Armed Services Committees. The administration requested

a total of $5.4 billion in anti-missile research for FY 1987, of which about $600 million was sought for the Energy Department's work for SDIO. The Senate Armed Services Committee voted to reduce the request to $3.95 billion, and the House Armed Services Committee approved $3.77 billion. Critics of the anti-missile program in both Houses threatened to offer amendments in the floor debate to cut the total to $3.1 billion, a figure only 3 percent higher than spending in 1986.[76]

On April 19, 1987, former Secretaries of Defense Robert S. McNamara and Harold Brown, testifying before the Defense Subcommittee of the Senate Appropriations Committee on the Reagan administration's request, said they believed the cost of building and operating an anti-missile defense system could reach astronomical proportions without providing an effective deterrent. They stressed that to be workable a defense system would have to be able to shoot missiles and warheads, survive if attacked, and be effective against enemy countermeasures, as well as worth the cost per unit of defense. They believed that spending should be limited to $2.5 billion.[77]

Top administration officials promised that they would deliver cost goals for SDI in the next budget request to Congress. Figures given in briefings were running between $87 billion and $174 billion for the space system alone.[78] But data supplied by Senate investigators suggested estimates of $1 trillion or more, with an annual cost for maintenance and modernization of $200 billion in 1986 dollars.[79]

Momentum grew for holding down the line on the amount of money spent on strategic defense. Forty-six senators, nine Republicans and thirty-seven Democrats, sent a letter to the Senate Armed Services Committee in May calling for a 3 percent real growth in expenditures for SDI in FY 1987. The senators were concerned that the SDI program was being rushed to meet an unrealistic schedule. They did not want the Armed Services Committee to slash vital defense programs in order to increase SDI funding. This figure put funding at $2.95 billion, or only $200 million above the 1986 budget. The Gramm-Rudman-Hollings deficit-reduction law also seemed to account for the growing desire to put restraints on SDI research. The Senate and House had adopted budgets that would reduce the deficit to the Gramm-Rudman-Hollings target of $144 billion for 1987; both budgets called for cuts in Reagan's defense

requests. But beyond these financial concerns there were growing worries about the merits of the program itself, whether SDI would protect populations or hard targets such as missile silos, how it would impact on arms control, and what the Soviets might do to counter it.[80]

The White House quickly responded to the Senate challenge. Deputy White House Press Secretary Larry Speakes charged that the reduction made by Congress to the FY 1986 budget had already slowed progress in several key areas of the program and narrowed the range of technologies that researchers could explore. Further cuts, Speakes said, "would seriously compound these problems and would set back the prospects for an informed decision in the 1990s on whether to proceed with full-scale development of effective strategic defenses."[81]

On June 2, a General Accounting Office study requested by Representative Samuel Stratton (D.-N.Y.), Chairman of the House Subcommittee on Procurement and Military Nuclear Affairs, found that the X-ray laser program DoD was conducting in collaboration with the Department of Energy had "many unresolved issues." GAO's review concluded that although "there was no 'design flaw' in the diagnostic instrumentation as mentioned in a *Los Angeles Times* article," analysis of test data by Lawrence Livermore scientists "raised questions about the accuracy of some experimental data."[82]

On June 3, 1986, Reagan issued a special statement appealing to Congress to continue to finance SDI and the nuclear force buildup program. He warned Congress that it was on the verge of imperiling the nation's security and undercutting American negotiating efforts at Geneva. The White House's response to the letter from the forty-six senators urging only a 3 percent increase in the SDI budget was that the President worries that "every dollar taken from our strategic programs is a victory for potential aggressors. Every cut or delay weakens our cause in Geneva and adds materially to the ultimate cost of deterrence."[83]

Later in June more than 1,600 scientists in major government and industrial laboratories, many working on SDI research, petitioned lawmakers to slow the growth of funding for anti-missile research. The goal of developing a way to render nuclear weapons obsolete "is not feasible in the foreseeable future," the scientists and engineers said in an open letter to the Senate. "The more limited goal of developing partial defenses against ballistic missiles

does not fundamentally alter the current policy of deterrence, yet it represents a significant escalation of the arms race and runs the risk of jeopardizing existing arms control treaties and future negotiations." J. Carson Mark, former head of nuclear weapons design at Los Alamos, said the SDI is certain to prompt Soviet efforts to counter it. "It is almost certainly a much simpler technical task to counter an SDI system than to establish a fault-free system in the first place."[84]

Congress handed President Reagan a severe setback as committees in both Houses voted for reductions in SDI funding on June 24, 1986. The House Armed Services Committee voted on June 19 to cut $1.7 billion from the administration's request for $5.4 billion in SDI funds for FY 1987, and the Senate Armed Services Committee on June 20 voted a $1.4 billion SDI funding cut. The Senate Budget Reduction Amendment was sponsored by none other than Senator Sam Nunn and Senator William Cohen (R.-Maine), defense "hawks," who pointed out that administration proposals for SDI were "vague" and "confusing." The two senators said they wanted to see less emphasis placed on long-term projects and more effort spent on short-term defenses that counter immediate threats to U.S. forces. The Senate and House votes came shortly after Representative Les Aspin warned the administration that its funding request for SDI was in "serious trouble" in Congress. Aspin also said that many conservative members of the House were convinced that SDI was too expensive in light of the size of the federal deficit.[85] The possibility that SDI would violate the ABM Treaty also had some lawmakers worried even though Lieutenant General Abrahamson assured Congress that the current test program would be conducted within Treaty limitations—although the test effort might conflict with a narrow reading of the Treaty by around 1989.

Weinberger assailed Congress for its "unwisdom" in trying to "slash" SDI and pointed to a successful recent test of the anti-missile missile the Flexible Lightweight Agile Guided Experiment (FLAGE), which destroyed a simulated enemy warhead during a test in June at White Sands. The target missile was launched from a navy F-4 jet, making it the first time a moving target had been destroyed by a defensive missile relying entirely on an on-board guidance system.[86]

Five former senior policymakers suggested that Reagan seek an agreement with the Soviets that would put off testing of space-

based weapons for up to ten years. They also said that the United States should continue to abide by a restrictive interpretation of the ABM Treaty and to abide by numerical limits on long-range missiles in the unratified SALT II Treaty. The signatories of the 3,500-word letter were Harold Brown (Carter's Defense Secretary), Melvin Laird (Nixon's Defense Secretary), James R. Schlesinger (Defense Secretary under Nixon and Ford), Brent Scowcroft (Ford's National Security Adviser), and Cyrus Vance (Secretary of State under Carter). The group expressed its belief that limited defenses of missiles was possible by the end of the century but that "a significant degree of protection of the population, if feasible at all in the face of countermeasures, would be decades away."[87]

In September, a secret test took place in which one space vehicle tracked and successfully intercepted another vehicle. Both crafts had been lofted into space by a Delta rocket. The experiment was known as the Delta 180 space experiment, and others in the Delta series would follow. It eliminated much of the skepticism within the SDIO about the feasibility of attaining a near-term attack capability against missiles in the boost phase. In this experiment, off-the-shelf technology was used to acquire and track a U.S. missile during its boost phase. According to John E. Pike of the Federation of American Scientists, the experiment would be useful in developing systems for attacking warheads and missiles in space. But the test also raised the thorny issue of compliance with the ABM Treaty, which restricts the research and testing of anti-missile systems.[88]

At the Reykjavík, Iceland summit meeting between President Reagan and Soviet leader Mikhail Gorbachev, held October 11–12, SDI and the ABM Treaty proved to be the major stumbling blocks to a new arms control agreement on offensive missile reductions. Under the draft American text, "both sides would agree to confine itself to research, development, and testing which is permitted by the ABM Treaty for a period of five years, through 1991, during which time a 50 percent reduction of strategic nuclear arsenals would be achieved. . . . At the end of 10 years, with all offensive ballistic missiles eliminated, either side would be free to deploy defenses." Gorbachev proposed that "the U.S.S.R. and the United States undertake for a period of 10 years not to take advantage of the right of withdrawing from the ABM Treaty. . . . Testing of all space elements of anti-ballistic defense in space is

prohibited except for research and testing in laboratories." When Reagan and Gorbachev met, Gorbachev indicated that he would agree to the ten-year deal on ballistic missiles only if the United States would "strengthen" the ABM Treaty by confining all SDI research to the laboratory and agreeing not to develop space weapons. The Soviets thus made the entire arms control package conditional on an American agreement to limit testing and research of space-based technologies for ballistic missile defense to the laboratory.[89] President Reagan refused on the grounds that research, testing, and development of space-based systems are permissible under the ABM Treaty. The conference dissolved without agreement, even though on their return from Reykjavík U.S. officials tried to portray the meeting as a success.[90]

On October 16, 1986, Congress approved a compromise Defense Authorization Bill that provided only $3.5 billion in funds for SDI research, a substantial cut of $1.8 billion from Reagan's original request. As part of the House-Senate compromise, the bill extended a ban on anti-satellite weapons and urged Reagan to abide by the unratified SALT II Treaty. A majority of the Senate Armed Services Committee urged that the SDI program put emphasis on the goal of defending military targets instead of population defenses.[91]

THE BATTLE OVER THE ABM TREATY

On December 1, 1986, Senator Carl Levin (D.-Mich.) wrote to Secretary of State George Shultz after conducting his own review of the ABM Treaty negotiating record with key members of the U.S. SALT I delegation, Ambassador Gerard Smith, Raymond Garthoff, Sidney Graybeal, John Rhinelander, and General Royal Allison. "Based on my review," he wrote, "I have concluded that Judge Sofaer's [the State Department's legal adviser] interpretation of the Treaty is incorrect and that the process he used to develop and justify the interpretation is fatally flawed. ... I believe that: (1) Judge Sofaer has provided Congress with an incomplete and misleading analysis of the record in an effort to justify his interpretation of the ABM Treaty; (2) the process used by Judge Sofaer to review the negotiating record was fatally flawed; (3) our national interest requires that the administration authorize a new and independent review of the ABM Treaty."[92]

At a White House meeting shortly before Christmas President Reagan was given a detailed briefing on SDI by Secretary of Defense Caspar Weinberger, SDIO Director Lieutenant General James Abrahamson, and Assistant Secretary of Defense Richard Perle. The shield described at the meeting consisted primarily of space-based sensors and orbiting battle stations that would fire a volley of chemical homing rockets at Soviet ballistic missiles shortly after launch. Ground-based rockets would also attack Soviet warheads in space. The mid-course weaponry, called the Exoatmospheric Reentry Vehicle Interception System (ERIS), was an outgrowth of the 1984 homing overlay experiment. The presentation was widely interpreted as an effort to nudge Reagan to move the SDI program from research to development, a decision that would require modification if not abandonment of the ABM Treaty. According to Attorney General Edwin Meese, who also attended the meeting, SDI proponents were anxious to get sufficient momentum in the program so that it could not be "tampered with by future administrations." The system that was envisioned was much closer to Daniel Graham's "high frontier" concept of using existing, "off-the shelf" rather than advanced technologies.[93]

Senior Reagan administration officials actively began promoting the idea of early deployment of defenses against missiles with some units installed in space in the early 1990s. At a briefing at the National Press Club and then later in a speech to the U.S. Space Foundation in Colorado Springs in January 1987, Secretary of Defense Weinberger said the system would include several types of interceptors combined in such a way as to defend the entire continent, not just military facilities. Phase 1 "could include both ground- and space-based components operating to detect, track, and destroy ballistic missiles in the boost and late mid-course phases of flight."[94] He also declared that the proposal would promote progress in arms control. "I suspect that one of the reasons there are talks in Geneva now, and have been the last year or so, is because we are working on this." However, Weinberger's comments did not go over well with Secretary of State Shultz, who was leading the action within the administration to keep arms control negotiations alive and use SDI as a bargaining chip. Shultz reportedly believed that SDI would not be deployable until the twenty-first century and that the best compromise with the Soviets would be to confine SDI to research and development and forgo deployment

for a significant period of time in exchange for Soviet reductions in their offensive weapons. Prohibition on rapid deployment would be a key part of the deal.[95]

Weinberger's proposal for early deployment of a partial defense was attacked by Senator Albert Gore, a member of the Senate Armed Services Committee: "This is a formula for accelerating the arms race, and the end of any meaningful arms control efforts." Two key members of the Senate Appropriations Committee's Defense Subcommittee, J. Bennett Johnston and William Proxmire, said that they had financial and technical objections to the plans being drafted by the Pentagon and that it was too early to deploy defenses in space. Proxmire said early deployment would violate his amendment to the FY 1986 Defense Authorization Act requiring that before deployment a President certify that the SDI system "(A) . . . is survivable (that is, the system is able to maintain a sufficient degree of effectiveness to fulfill its mission even in the face of determined attacks against it); (b) . . . is cost effective at the margin to the extent that the system is able to maintain its effectiveness against the offense at less cost than it would take to develop offensive countermeasures and proliferate the ballistic missiles necessary to overcome it."[96] (These were the Nitze criteria and were written into a National Security Directive in 1985.) The senators threatened to block funds for the project. Similarly in the House, Representative Charles E. Bennett (D.-Fla.) recommended freezing SDIO's budget at the previous year's levels.[97]

Skepticism was growing among scientific experts that a rudimentary system could shoot down attacking enemy missiles. The initial system promoted by the administration would not have lasers, particle-beam weapons, or other kinds of exotic weaponry. Some believed that such a system would be especially vulnerable to attack. Said Harvard physicist Ashton Carter, "I see problems being swept under the rug in the interests of getting consensus on early deployment. It may be possible to put a system like this in place, but it is not clear that it would have any military value." Suspicion increased that SDIO officials were lowering the performance requirement of a defense system and had not yet developed a full "system architecture" because many basic engineering issues remained unresolved.[98]

Work leaked out that the push for early deployment of a rudimentary defense was causing a shift in budgetary and research

priorities, with delays in more exotic programs, including X-ray lasers, chemical lasers, particle beams, and free-electron lasers, and acceleration of kinetic-energy weapons research. In response to congressional reductions, the administration cut the FY 1986 budget for kinetic-energy weapons by 27 percent and for beam weapons by only 12 percent. These were reversed in FY 1987 when beam weaponry took a 48 percent cut and kinetic weapons only a 16 percent cut.[99]

At a meeting on February 3, 1987, with Secretary of State George Shultz, Defense Secretary Caspar Weinberger, ACDA Director Kenneth Adelman, Ambassador Edward Rowny, Arms Control negotiator Paul Nitze, National Security Adviser Frank Carlucci, Attorney General Edwin Meese, and JCS Chairman Admiral William Crowe, the President apparently decided to shift to the broad interpretation of the ABM Treaty in order to permit tests of some of the new potential technologies for space-based defense. Excerpts from the minutes of the meeting follow (direct quotes are indicated by quotation marks; brackets are in the original).

Mr. Weinberger. Question is, "Do we deploy incrementally? Go to LCI [the legally correct interpretation of the ABM Treaty]?" Later we could go with lasers, particle beams, and so forth. But we need a specific program. . . . "We need phased deployment because you can't do it all at once." [Reminds President of December briefing on phased deployment.] "It is an area defense, not a point defense, and it's stabilizing."

Mr. Shultz. "I didn't know we made decisions in December, but I have talked to Abe [Abe Sofaer, the State Department's Legal Adviser] twice, and all the chiefs individually, and am impressed by what I've heard." Notes that "the chiefs have been skeptical on going back on the ABM Treaty." Don't start on phase 1 unless "you have some idea on where you're going beyond. . . . I agree with Crowe that we're not in a position to confront the decision."

Mr. Reagan inquires about Soviet reaction.

Mr. Shultz. "It's hard to say what the Soviets would so." There have been no indications from Geneva, and we should feel them out. The problem with deployment even for 1993 is that some tests [Delta 181] require broad interpretation of the ABM Treaty, or LCI.

Mr. Weinberger. The Soviets have an agenda. . . . They want to prohibit something. "We shouldn't debate with the Soviets what can and can't be prohibited."

Mr. Shultz. "We should see what we can find out, if we can't find it, then negotiate with the Soviet Union."

Mr. Reagan. "Why don't we just go ahead on the assumption that this is what we're doing and it's right. . . . We're not going nearly as far as them." Notes a magazine article on Soviet "star wars" program. "Don't ask the Soviets. Tell them." The United States can move ahead. "I'll say I've reevaluated. I see the price tag and I'm willing to pay."[100]

However, appearing at a Senate Armed Services Committee hearing immediately afterward Shultz said: "The question of deployment has to be governed by the content of the program and the consistency with the criteria that have been set by the President." He said that Reagan was sticking with the Nitze criteria and that the President might want to shift to the broad interpretation of the ABM Treaty "sometime soon" but "until then I'll tell him what I think on the subject." Said one State Department official, "my hunch is that the White House is letting Weinberger and the right wing bring up early deployment as a straw man to make it appear going to a broad interpretation of the ABM Treaty is a moderate compromise. They would be able to accelerate the timetable for research, but avoid any firm decision on deployment."[101]

Senator Sam Nunn, Chairman of the Senate Armed Services Committee, warned of an impending constitutional crisis on the interpretation of the ABM Treaty if the administration went ahead with the broad interpretation. Later that month, administration officials announced that Reagan had signed National Security Decision Directive 161 on ABM interpretation and early deployment instructing American negotiators in Geneva not to negotiate or even discuss limits on ABM systems more restrictive than the broad interpretation and to consult with the allies and Congress about the need for the broad interpretation. The directive also ordered DoD to produce by the end of April a detailed list of experiments that could be conducted under the broad interpretation, a proposed timetable, and an assessment of the tests' importance, and it directed the State Department to complete its analysis of the legal issues in the broad interpretation by the end of April.[102]

American negotiators in Geneva reportedly discussed a deal with the senators observers group—Albert Gore, Claiborne Pell (D.-R.I.), Arlen Specter (R.-Penn.), Ted Stevens, Richard Lugar (R.-Ind.), and Don Nickles (R.-Okla.)—on SDI testing. Under the suggested com-

promise, the Senate would support a "respectable level" of funding for SDI yet to be determined and would defer legislation endorsing the narrow interpretation of the ABM Treaty, while the administration, in return, would postpone any tests that might violate the narrow interpretation of the ABM Treaty and would instruct the American delegation to explore with the Soviets "an appropriate way" of limiting future research.[103]

Senator Sam Nunn took the offensive. In a three-part brief issued on March 11, 1987, he challenged the administration's case for a broadened interpretation of the ABM Treaty to allow testing and development of space-based defensive weapons. After reviewing the classified negotiating record he found no evidence of a single statement confirming that testing and development of space-based "exotic" technologies are allowed; he also found a compendium of unequivocal statements to the effect that the treaty bans everything other than research on ABM systems that are firmly based on land. The case for reinterpretation rests on "ambiguities and omissions" and at least one instance of "complete and total misrepresentation." Said Nunn, "the Reagan Administration's unilateral interpretation of the ABM Treaty constitutes a fundamental constitutional challenge to the Senate as a whole with respect to its powers and prerogatives in this area. . . . In effect, the Reagan Administration is telling the Senate not only that the executive branch is free to ignore the meaning of the treaty as originally described to the Senate of the United States, but also other nations who are party to such treaties can disregard what the executive branch told the Senate at the time of ratification."[104]

The administration also told Congress it needed a lot more money to go ahead with testing of SDI systems and subsystems. The SDIO's budget request was for $5.22 billion in FY 1988 and $6.28 billion in FY 1989. Congress had cut $3 billion from SDIO's budget requests for FY 1985 to FY 1987. DoD's supplemental request of $2.8 billion for FY 1987 included $500 million for SDIO. Funding requests for SDIO in FY 1988 and FY 1989 were for five major programs in surveillance, acquisition, tracking, and kill assessment; directed-energy weapons development; kinetic-energy weapons development; systems analysis; and battle management. The first (surveillance, acquisition, tracking, and kill assessment) was targeted for the largest individual share of the SDI budget in FY 1988–1989 ($1.5 billion for 1988 and $1.8 billion for 1989) because of

its applicability to all phases of any layered ballistic missile defense system.[105] In addition, the Energy Department requested $481 million in FY 1988 to support SDIO in weapons research.

On April 8, 1987, the House Armed Services Committee voted to permit tests of anti-missile systems that might be deployed in the next decade by overturning an earlier decision by one of its subcommittees that would have blocked tests of any weapon that might serve as a basis for the first stages of a strategic defense. The Committee, however, cut Reagan's SDI request for $5.7 billion to $3.8 billion. This was subsequently amended by Committee Chairman Les Aspin, who offered an amended Authorization Bill that reflected the subcommittee's efforts to reconcile programs under their jurisdiction within the Joint Resolution. The Aspin substitute amendment recommended funding SDI at $3.6 billion. Of these funds, $200 million would be transferred to the air force for the Boost Surveillance Tracking Satellite and Advanced Launch System.[106]

The administration also issued its third annual SDI report in April. The report stated that "incremental deployment of defenses is the only likely means of deployment" and would help "lay the groundwork for the deployment of subsequent phases."[107] At a press conference following release of the report, Lieutenant General Abrahamson said SDI had three planned phases and that the first phase, with kinetic-energy weapons, could be deployed in the early to middle 1990s and cost $40 billion to $60 billion.[108] However, a panel of the American Physical Society, the nations's largest professional society for physicists, declared that so many breakthroughs would be required to develop laser and particle-beam weapons that it would take at least a decade of intensive research to determine whether strategic defense would be feasible. The report did not call the goal impossible but said it was "highly questionable" whether the SDI system would survive an attack on it. Co-chairmen of the fifteen-member panel were Nicolaas Bloembergen, a Harvard Nobel Prize–winning physicist, and C. K. N. Patel, an executive director in research at A.T. & T.'s Bell Laboratories. The SDIO admitted that the report appears to be "an objective independent appraisal of various technologies" but found its "conclusions to be subjective and unduly pessimistic about our capability to bring to fruition the specific technologies needed for a full-scale development decision in the 1990s."[109]

The Senate Armed Services Committee voted 12–8 in May to prohibit tests conflicting with the narrow interpretation of the ABM Treaty. In a report released later along with the Committee's FY 1988 Defense Authorization Bill, the Committee said that SDI "should be dedicated to developing survivable and cost-effective defense options for enhancing the survivability of U.S. retaliatory forces and command, control, and communications."[110]

The same month, the United States proposed confidence-building measures at the Geneva talks to promote cooperative transition from an offense-dominant world to a defense-dominant one. Under the proposal, both the United States and the Soviet Union would commit through 1994 not to withdraw from the ABM Treaty, as long as the Soviet Union agreed to offensive force reductions coupled with elimination of all strategic ballistic missiles after ten years. "After 1994, either side could deploy defensive systems of its own choosing, unless mutually agreed otherwise." The United States also proposed that the two countries "annually exchange data on their planned strategic defense activities." The United States was prepared to restrain its testing programs by the terms of the ABM Treaty until 1994, but it was not interested in amending the Treaty to put in more severe restrictions than existed before the broad interpretation.

On May 9, Weinberger sent Reagan a report of what testing would be permitted under the broad interpretation but barred under the narrow: (1) Tiered Hierarchy Overlayed Research (THOR), a series of experiments testing interception capability of warheads and dummies during mid-course flight; (2) SLBM intercept, space-based sensors and interceptor rockets to be employed against an SLBM with dummy warheads and decoys; (3) Laser Integrated Space Experiment (LISE), a test of a space-based chemical laser in 1990; (4) Sensor Integrated Discrimination Experiment (SIDE), where space-based and other sensors would attempt to discriminate between dummy warheads and decoys out of a rocket fired from Vandenberg Air Force Base in California, scheduled for 1990. Weinberger argued that if the United States did not accept the broad interpretation, it would be forced to terminate development testing. But other officials accused DoD of making the list of tests as long as it could in order to defend the need to adopt the broad interpretation.[111]

The House voted 219–199 for a reduction in SDI funds to $3.1

billion as an amendment to the DoD FY 1988 Defense Authorization Bill ($2.85 billion for DoD's SDI program and $297 million to the Department of Energy's). Les Aspin argued that the spending cut represented a figure at which the House could bargain with the Senate level of $4.5 billion, which had been voted upon. The House also rejected 302–121 an amendment offered by Jack Kemp (R.-N.Y.) requiring DoD to achieve an operational Star Wars capability by 1993. It voted without objection an amendment proposed by Dennis Hertel (D.-Mich.) the "[t]he Secretary of Defense may not deploy any antiballistic missile system unless such deployment is specifically authorized by law." It voted to adhere to the traditional interpretation of the ABM Treaty in a substitute amendment to the FY 1988 Defense Authorization Bill as offered by Les Aspin. It rejected by 216–203 an amendment proposed by Frank McCloskey (D.-Ind.) to prohibit testing of a space-based kinetic-kill vehicle, but voted for the same prohibition (229–188) against ASAT testing in space as passed in 1986.[112]

On May 13, the administration released the first two parts of the second Sofaer study supporting the broad interpretation of the ABM Treaty. In his fifty-page report, Sofaer argued that the negotiating record did not limit the United States to the narrow interpretation of the ABM Treaty, and claimed it would not be logical to expect the Soviet Union to be bound by the Senate ratification proceedings. Sofaer also declared that the Senate had failed to attach any understandings to the ratification which would have been legally binding on the Soviet Union.[113] On May 19, the Senate Foreign Relations Committee reported favorably on House Resolution 167, which endorsed the traditional interpretation of the ABM Treaty. The same day Senator Sam Nunn issued the final installment of his own report on the ABM Treaty and said that the Sofaer report contained "basic flaws." Earlier Nunn said the administration's position meant that all future ratification procedures would include making the negotiating record public. "I think there are some people in the State Department and in the White House who need to do some rethinking where the slippery slope of ABM interpretation is leading"[114]

THE TESTING CONTINUES

On May 21, 1987, a FLAGE missile successfully intercepted a LANCE missile at the White Sands testing range at a height of 12,000 feet.

It used data from the White Sands tracking radars until the last two seconds of its 72-second flight when it was on its own homing radar. According to Lieutenant General John Wells of the U.S. Army Strategic Defense Command, the experiment, the first time the system had been used on such a small target, was a "proof of principle" of the homing radar.

A week later, SDIO chiefs gave a secret briefing to key members of Congress on near-term deployment options. A two-tiered system could be deployed in 1994–1995 using ERIS and SBKKV (space-based kinetic-kill vehicle) but it would be only 20 to 30 percent effective. And a three-tiered system using HEDI (high endoatmospheric defense interceptor, a kinetic-energy weapon program that would destroy incoming warheads in the atmosphere and would help to counter the threat from submarine-launched missiles), which would add some mid-course discrimination capability, could be operational in the late 1990s. This system, SDIO officials predicted, would be 70 to 90 percent effective but discrimination capability would be a primary hurdle to be overcome.[115]

A month later, Ambassador Paul Nitze said that the United States should drop its opposition to ABM Treaty interpretation talks and admitted that he was at odds with National Security Adviser Frank Carlucci on this one. He hoped Reagan would change his mind about negotiating with the Soviets on this issue. Reagan believed that negotiations would lead to limitations on the SDI program and did not want to negotiate on that basis.

By mid-June the Senate still had not permitted a vote on the FY 1988 Defense Authorization Bill—the Republican minority was employing a filibuster to prevent the bill from coming to the floor. The Republicans opposed measures that would require approval of both Houses before the administration could conduct tests that conflicted with the narrow interpretation of the ABM Treaty.

But the fact that SDI was in trouble did not hamper the Pentagon. In June and July, the Pentagon's Defense Acquisition Board, chaired by Under Secretary for Defense, Acquisition, Richard Godwin, approved SDIO's five-year plan for demonstrating and validating the elements of a first-phase strategic defense system. The DAB approved the entire proposal, thus clearing the way for technical demonstration of elements comprising a first-phase system based largely on kinetic-energy weapon interceptors.

For boost-phase attack, the systems under consideration would rely on some 5,000–10,000 rockets stored in satellites in low-earth

orbit. Each satellite could launch a number of chemical-fuel rockets which would destroy ballistic missiles emerging from the atmosphere by colliding with them. These space-based kinetic-kill vehicles would pick up the missiles after warning from sensor satellites. ERIS would rely on U.S.-based rockets launched from the ground to attack warheads after they had been released from the "bus" atop the missile. The rocket would distinguish the warhead from decoys and collide with it. In 1987 DoD was spending some $500 million to build eight rockets for testing, scheduled for completion in 1990 or 1991, at which point flight testing data would be available to determine feasibility.[116]

The DAB qualified its Milestone I approval of the first six strategic defense system (SDS) elements with the directive that the second group of elements must receive Milestone I approval before the Board would approve Milestone II, or full-scale development, of the first six elements. The first phase would defend against attacking missiles in their boost, post-boost, and mid-course phases of flight. SDIO did not include a terminal layer of defense in the first phase because, according to SDIO head Lieutenant General Abrahamson, the greatest effectiveness would be achieved by overcoming enemy missiles in the boost and post-boost phases. Abrahamson said the purpose of the system was not silo defense; it was designed to create substantial uncertainty for Soviet attack planners so that they would be unsure how many of their missiles would get through and therefore be deterred from attacking in the first place. According to Alan Mense, DIO deputy chief scientist, "The operational definition of SDI is to develop technologies that devalue Soviet offensive ballistic missiles in the mind of the Soviet offensive mission planner. What we're trying to achieve is a zero launch rate . . . one of the real and foremost values of defense is to prevent wars from starting."[117]

DAB also received the report of the Defense Science Board, chaired by Charles Everett, former president of the MITRE Corporation. One of the Science Board's key conclusions was deleted from the report because DSB was not asked to comment on whether it should approve the system. That conclusion read: "As a consequence of the current gaps in system design and key technologies, there is presently no way of confidently assessing: (1) system performance against requirements; (2) system cost; (3) schedule. Therefore . . . a decision can be considered whenever sufficient

progress is made to formulate with confidence a system concept. . . ."[118]

At the end of July, the Soviets tabled a draft treaty on space weapons providing for mutual non-withdrawal from the ABM Treaty for a period of ten years, a mutual commitment to confine work on space-based ABM systems to research in laboratories and banning all ABM activity in space, an agreement on a list of devices that cannot be put into space, and a commitment to further talk on ASAT systems and "space-earth" armaments once the agreement went into effect. American negotiator Henry Cooper said the proposal contained some interesting "new details" but asserted that the Soviets were intent on restricting the SDI program, which the President was not about to let them do.

As if to underscore the President's intent, in August the United States started construction of the SDI national test bed at Colorado Springs where scientists would run one of the world's largest collections of supercomputers to simulate a wide variety of possible Star Wars and defensive battles.

The State Department publicly released the third part of Sofaer's report on the ABM Treaty in September.[119] Sofaer said, "During negotiation of clarifying interpretations and at other times between 1972 and 1978, the Soviets repeatedly expressed the view that the treaty was intended to regulate conventional ABM systems. U.S. negotiators disagreed with this view, but accepted the Soviet text for purposes of interpretation."[120]

Senate Republicans also agreed to lift their filibuster against the Defense Authorization Bill. Some had come to believe that they had a better chance of modifying or deleting language on SDI now that an arms control agreement on intermediate-range forces was closer. Republican leader Robert Dole (Kansas) introduced a resolution asking Congress not to write laws affecting arms control that was in negotiation.

At the September 15–18 Shultz-Shevardnadze meeting in Washington, the Soviets offered a detailed list of objects not to be launched into space, including limits on size of mirrors and speed of interceptors. Shultz once again reaffirmed U.S. commitment not to agree to restrictions "that make it harder to pursue the Strategic Defense Initiative."[121]

Congress was obviously intent on tying the administration's hands. On September 17, 1987, the Senate voted 58–38 for the Nunn-

Levin provision to ban SDI work that violated the traditional interpretation of the ABM Treaty. A provision failed 59–35 that stated "Congress must not act to further the interests of the Soviet Union by unilaterally adopting Soviet negotiating positions that have been rejected by the United States government." Instead the Senate passed a provision that said, "Neither the Congress nor the President should take actions which are unilateral concessions to the Soviet Union." Nunn warned that if Reagan vetoed the bill "my own vote would be to give them less money for SDI, I'm not playing games here." An amendment to cut $800 million from the SDI budget failed on a 51–50 vote on September 22 when Vice-President George Bush was called upon to break the tie. The funding was left at $4.5 billion. Thirteen Democrats, mostly conservative Southerners, joined thirty-seven Republicans and the Vice-President in voting against it. Nine Republicans joined forty-one Democrats in support of it.[122]

Weinberger approved the DAB recommendation for work on six systems in Phase 1 of SDI in September. He said that the experiments could be performed without violating the ABM Treaty and that the tests would not violate the Nunn-Levin amendment. However, in a position paper the Union of Concerned Scientists said that proposed tests would violate even the broad interpretation. National Security Council Adviser Frank Carlucci said Weinberger's announcement was overdue and "We intend to develop it [SDI] as rapidly as we can and deploy it when it's ready. Until we negotiate a strategic arms agreement, there's absolutely no reason why we shouldn't proceed with the tests and even after we negotiate one, it is still our intention to go forward with the SDI program."[123]

Nitze still wanted to discuss the scope of space testing with the Soviets and to offer counterproposals but senior Pentagon officials feared discussion would put the United States on the "slippery slope" toward unacceptable and unverifiable limits on SDI. Nitze was overruled.

On September 20, the Senate Foreign Relations Committee reported favorably on a resolution submitted by Senator Joseph Biden (R.-Del.) supporting the traditional interpretation of the ABM Treaty. The report accompanying the amendment stated, "The Administration's theory of treaty-making, having cast a dark cloud over the Senate's consideration of all future treaties, could severely complicate and greatly prolong the committee considera-

tion of an INF treaty—and thereby jeopardize early ratification of that treaty."[124]

A week later, U.S. officials in Geneva announced that they had been negotiating the meaning of the ABM Treaty with the Soviets and probing the Soviets about the meaning of their draft treaty tabled in July. The United States had told the Soviets it would restrain its SDI program within the broad interpretation for a seven-year no-withdrawal period and informed them that it did not want to renegotiate the Treaty or strengthen it.[125]

On October 5, a U.S. Navy high-energy chemical laser beam successfully struck a drone target and destroyed the vital components of the missile, which then went into a spin and was destroyed on impact. SDI testing was continuing on a steady course.

In a final bid to get the United States to concede to discussion limiting SDI testing, Gorbachev refused to set a summit date without agreement on SDI limitations in his October 22–23 meetings in Moscow with Secretary of State Shultz. It looked as if the much-touted Washington summit to sign an INF agreement was off. Senator Nunn took the opportunity to criticize the administration for its unwillingness to discuss with the U.S.S.R. limits on SDI testing. But then on October 30 Soviet Foreign Minister Schevardnadze visited Washington and the two sides announced that Gorbachev would indeed visit the United States on December 7 to sign the INF agreement.

On October 28,1987, the House Appropriations Committee cut SDI funding to $2.8 billion and banned deployment of SBKKVs. It looked like there might be an embarrassing showdown between the administration and Congress just before the summit. From October 28 through November 17, White House Chief of Staff Howard Baker and new DoD head Frank Carlucci met with four representatives of the House and Senate Armed Services Committees—Representatives Les Aspin and William Dickinson (R.-Ala.) and Senators Sam Nunn and John Warner—to work out a compromise that would avoid confrontation before the December summit. Said one administration official, "It looks like we have found ways to accommodate each other without compromising basic principles. It should be seen as part of a process of trying to rebuild trust between the Administration and the mainstream members of the Armed Services Committees." Under the compromise, Congress stipulated that funds approved for FY 1988 would be

used only for the current schedule of SDI tests. The bill would prohibit development and testing of ABM systems that were not fixed and ground based (unless the President submits a report to Congress and the development of the test is approved by Joint Resolution), require human involvement in SDI battle management systems, and prohibit deployment unless specifically authorized. The ASAT testing ban would also be extended but bills for a comprehensive test ban would be abandoned. SDI spending was set at $3.99 billion ($3.6 billion for RDT&E, $380 million for DoE programs, and $123 million for military construction), compromising between the House and the Senate. The compromise Defense Authorization Bill was passed by the House on November 19 and by the Senate on November 20.

Some, however, charged that the administration-Congress compromise on SDI had a big loophole. John Pike of the Federation of American Scientists warned that the ban on FY 1988 tests "has no substantial impact on the SDI program whatsoever." He noted that if SDIO justified a test not on the basis of the broad interpretation but on a basis used in the past, a test could go forward if it actually involved an "adjunct" but not a "component" of the system. "Basically, they'll go all the way up to deployment, claiming that the things they're testing aren't components. . . . I'm concerned that in driving a stake in the heart of the broad interpretation, Congress has signed on to a version of the traditional interpretation you could drive a Mack truck through."[126]

At the Washington summit between President Reagan and Soviet leader Gorbachev, the Soviets stated they were no longer demanding strict limits on all forms of SDI testing. Nevertheless, the Reagan administration continued to assert that the language of the ABM Treaty and the negotiating record supported a "broad interpretation" that would permit expanded testing of SDI components. Just five days before the summit, Reagan accused the Soviets of flouting the ABM Treaty by shifting two-radar installations to the vicinity of Moscow and Kiev and making improvements to the already challenged radar at Krasnoyarsk.[127]

Although negotiators at the Washington summit reached a compromise agreement on strategic offensive weapons to limit ballistic missile warheads to 4,900 apiece within an overall limit of 6,000 warheads (a figure covering both ICBMs and sea-based cruise mis-

siles) SDI continued to remain a major sticking point and a much-hoped-for breakthrough on strategic and space weapons did not emerge. Hopes would have to be deferred to the spring of 1988 and the planned Moscow summit.

Reagan did not seem to want to give up his dream for the future. As if to underscore its commitment to SDI, the administration let it be known that the Pentagon had begun top-secret ground tests of a new two-million-watt Alpha laser which, if deployed in space, would be powerful enough to damage or destroy orbiting targets. Built by TRW Inc., the laser is chemically powered by a combustion of fuels similar to those used in rocket engines, but is much lighter than ordinary chemical lasers. The laser is scheduled for testing in space in 1990.[128]

In an exchange of televised New Years' greetings on January 1, 1988, while praising the recently signed arms control treaty on INF, President Reagan said that he was "committed to pursuing" his Strategic Defense Initiative.[129] The President's tone did not augur well for continuing negotiations between the United States and the Soviet Union on strategic defense.

The domestic debate over SDI also entered a new phase in January when Senator Sam Nunn recommended in a speech before the Arms Control Association that the government explore the possibility of building a limited defense against accidental launches by other nations. While acknowledging that the decision would hinge on cost and technical feasibility, Nunn suggested that the system might be space based. He urged the administration to negotiate with the Soviets on what anti-missile devices might be tested in space under the ABM Treaty even if it would require a U.S.-Soviet amendment to the Treaty. "I can envision certain defensive deployments that could be in the interest of both our nation and the Soviet Union," Nunn said.[130]

As Nunn tried to pick his way through what was obviously becoming a political minefield as to what form SDI should take, the Pentagon announced on February 8, 1988, that a Delta 181 rocket had launched a three-ton military satellite in space that had succeeded in using a battery of sensors to track fifteen mock enemy targets for the anti-missile program. At $250 million this was the Pentagon's most costly and complex experiment yet undertaken for the SDI program. The experiment's success would prove cru-

cial to the development of orbiting battle stations, which would have to track accurately literally thousands of enemy targets in space.[131]

CONCLUSION

Predictions are dangerous. But there is little doubt that during the five years since President Reagan first enunciated his vision of a world without ballistic missiles, SDI has developed into a sizable research program sucking billions of taxpayer dollars while employing thousands of scientists, engineers, and researchers across the nation. Although it will be some time, if ever, before a defensive system is actually deployed, it is obvious that the Reagan administration was intent on paving the road for future deployment by undermining the foundations of the ABM Treaty and accelerating the research and development schedule for SDI while embarking on an ambitious testing program. In the final year of the Reagan presidency, SDI acquired a momentum that future administrations may find hard to stop. As *New York Times* correspondent William Broad, an astute observer of the program, remarks: "Whatever the outcome . . . military advocates of Star Wars will almost certainly keep looking for technical solutions or innovations. The scientists will continue their research. The 21st century will no doubt be every bit as different as the one that preceded it. New military technology will no doubt evolve from the billions of dollars of new research. The days of the hard-cased nuclear missile are probably numbered."[132]

But SDI has not been driven simply by technology. It has also been the result of political choices and compromises in which the President and Congress have been willing or unwitting players. The program's fate will ultimately depend on its political rather than technological momentum.

11

□

CONCLUSION

Predictable, inevitable, wasteful. These adjectives summarize the story behind America's arsenal. Most controversial weapons systems inevitably get built and predictably end up costing the American taxpayer far more than they should. This book has tried to explain why. In the early stages of research and development, a program enjoying strong bureaucratic and political support will obtain enough seed money—which can run into the hundreds of millions of dollars for a program like SDI—to move ahead. As it enters the prototype development and production stage, a program will become increasingly contentious as its bureaucratic and political opponents fight to limit the resources it gets. Ensuing budgetary instability causes program stretch-outs, cost overruns, and other difficulties. Nevertheless, major weapons programs enjoying strong political backing are rarely canceled and usually obtain sufficient funding to remain viable. Like giant octopuses, they survive even if they lose some tentacles.

The story is the same for every weapons system and program examined in this book: the Trident submarine and missile, the B-1 bomber, the air-launched cruise missile, the MX missile, and the M-1 tank. The jury is still out on the Midgetman missile and Ronald Reagan's Strategic Defense Initiative but, if history is any guide, undoubtedly these programs will survive the vagaries of the political and budgetary process and eventually be deployed, although the final product may bear little resemblance to what was originally envisioned.

Reasonable men and women can differ about priorities. One thing is certain: America's weapons are too often bought without

any sort of priorities whatsoever. Cooperation and "consensus building" in the bureaucracy and in Congress ensure that key trade-offs and fundamental resource-allocation questions are almost never addressed. To the extent that they are addressed, political and bureaucratic accommodation takes precedence over administrative and economic efficiency and other economic, social, or military objectives. The challenge for reform is to restructure the acquisitions and budgetary process so that these criteria are more explicitly addressed when making decisions about funding for new weapons.

This book shows that the root of the problem is deceptively obvious: bureaucratic and political interests approach weapons acquisition and defense budget issues as non–zero-sum games; that is, as games where there are rewards and payoffs to all parties from cooperation or collusion. As discussed earlier, governmental behavior is not marked by "pure cooperation"; rather, it involves a mixture of "competitive-cooperative" strategies where competition nevertheless has well-defined limits. This behavior characterizes political relationships within the bureaucracy, in Congress, and between Congress and the President. The problem, however, is that compromise waters down priorities and spreads scarce resources too thinly among competing programs. Over the long term, costs are inflated, development is delayed, programs are changed, and the final result is a weapon that nobody really wants. For a system like MX, for example, critics wanted to cancel the program. Supporters of MX, however, wanted to deploy the missile in a way that would remedy perceived vulnerabilities in the land-based leg of the strategic triad of forces. They invented a variety of basing schemes, none of which was popular. The compromise to emerge from the political battles that followed satisfied nobody. It was to put MX in refurbished Minuteman silos and perhaps some missiles on rail cars in a mobile basing scheme to enhance survivability. Most would agree this did not solve the ICBM vulnerability problem (some would even argue it made it worse by creating a high-value target for the Soviets). The air force was unhappy because it did not get the large fleet of missiles it sought to improve its own hard-target, prompt counterforce capability. Would it have been better not to have built and deployed the system at all? Most would say yes. A minority would argue "better some than none." But critics and supporters of MX alike would almost certainly agree

that resources were wasted, the original rationale for deployment was not achieved, and the cost of the system was excessive.

Similarly, in the B-1 bomber, special interests successfully evaded President Carter's decision to cancel production. This was more an instance of downright collusion between the air force and Congress. Research and development funds were successfully channeled to the program's prime contractor, Rockwell International, so that prototype development could continue and the project kept alive. When the program was revived by President Reagan, the system was rushed into production and a new set of operational requirements tacked on to the original design. The plane entered service without all of its working parts in order, leading many to question whether it should have been built in the first place.

The M-1 tank and the Trident submarine and missile programs likewise managed to generate enough bureaucratic and political enthusiasm to ensure production. But again, a series of political compromises watered down budgetary support for these programs, contributing to cost overruns and production and development difficulties. So far, advocates of SDI have managed to secure a "consensus" within Congress on research and development so that the program's future is assured just so long as it does not move too rapidly into testing and deployment. But history runs the danger of repeating itself if the program generates momentum and political support for deployment increases.

Incremental programming and budgetary processes combined with long lead times for weapons development, sometimes as long as fifteen to twenty years as in the B-1 bomber, enable major weapons programs to outlive the political lives of their sponsors and critics alike. In the process, political accountability is eroded and weapons develop an uncontrollable life of their own. The system is in obvious need of reform. What is to be done?

First, development lead times for new weapons systems must be shortened. Second, the programming and budgeting cycle correspondingly must be lengthened to accommodate the prolonged development cycle of modern weapons systems. Third, the programming and budgetary process must be restructured to make it more competitive, less cooperative, among the players so that tradeoffs are addressed squarely and resources are allocated more efficiently. Incremental approaches to budgeting must be eliminated

and stakes raised so that legislators confront the total life-cycle costs of a system. Efficiency mandates that there be real "winners" and "losers" in budgetary allocation decisions. It means that some programs are funded and others are not. Occasionally it means that none among competing programs gets funded. In short, the weapons acquisition and budgetary process must be restructured so that it becomes more of a zero-sum game.

REFORMS

Congress. Congress is a prime target for reform. Many note the growing involvement of Congress in foreign and defense policy issues in recent years: the Boland amendment prohibiting aid to the Contras, the Cooper-Church amendment limiting aid to Indochina, the War Powers Resolution of 1973, the Jackson-Vanik amendment. The growth of congressional staffs and an increasing proliferation of committees and subcommittees to deal with foreign policy and defense issues are further indications of this involvement. Some interpret these developments as evidence of greater activism and Congress's increasing tendency to micromanage defense and foreign policy.

For major weapons programs, the level of congressional interest and involvement is uneven. For every weapons program where Congress immersed itself in the details, there are cases where it did not. When opposition to a new system is strong, particularly among the public and scientific or expert community, Congress takes a more active interest in procurement and deployment questions. Growing public opposition to nuclear weapons in the early 1980s, coupled with the emergence of the nuclear freeze movement, had a significant impact on congressional attitudes toward MX procurement. Failure to find a suitable basing mode for the system also tempered congressional enthusiasm. The level of congressional interest and debate on MX is striking compared to its quiescence in the Trident II missile and the B-1B bomber decisions. Congress has not vetoed the actual development and/or deployment of a major strategic weapons system; it has usually only acted to affect the rate of development and/or numbers deployed of a system by shaving the budget. Once a program finds its way into appropriations it tends to stay there.[1]

Right now, effective congressional oversight of the defense bud-

get simply does not exist. Instead, Congress fusses about certain line-by-line items in the budget while ignoring others. The defense budget is parceled into many different budgets in the budgetary resolution, authorization, appropriations, and sequestering process. Coherence is lost. The number of hurdles the defense budget must go through as it runs the legislative gauntlet is bewildering. At times Congress seems to chase its own tail. Even congressmen themselves admit they often do not know what is going on. Confusion and budgetary incrementalism thus weaken political accountability. Simplifying the authorization and appropriations process while reducing the number of steps the budget must go through is patently necessary. An overhaul not just of the defense budget but of the budget system as a whole is required if real reform is to be achieved. This should be seriously considered, although it will be extraordinarily difficult to achieve. In the meantime, more modest initiatives should be pursued far more vigorously than they have been. These include passing authorization and appropriation bills on schedule so that different stages of the budgetary and legislative cycle are synchronized, reducing the number of budgetary resolutions so that the resolutions that are voted have some significance, and developing a longer term perspective on budgeting by moving to multiyear authorization and appropriations, if not for the defense budget as a whole, then for major programs. None of these ideas is new, but the political will to implement them is sorely lacking. Take the following:

1. In May 1984, after two years of extensive and detailed study, the Beilenson Task Force of the House Rules Committee recommended a number of important changes to the 1974 budget act. These included accelerating the annual budgeting timetable, limiting the number of binding budget resolutions to one, and developing a longer term perspective on budgeting by adopting one-year-ahead-of-time authorization, multiyear authorization, and a single budget resolution of more binding planning numbers for two years beyond the fiscal year under consideration. These measures would help Congress put the budgeting process in a multiyear perspective and improve the quality of congressional oversight. They would also help bring the costs of a program over the course of several years up front thereby making program funding more stable.[2]

These recommendations have yet to be adopted and implemented by Congress.

2. The Congressional Budget Office and the President's Blue Ribbon Commission on Defense Management (Packard Commission) both recommended that Congress establish "milestone authorizations" at each stage of the weapons systems "life cycle" instead of annual authorizations. This would be akin to the DSARC / DAB review process in the Pentagon. The reviews would be conducted by the armed services and appropriations committees accordingly. By forcing the Pentagon to provide proper documentation for program review, this procedure would help secure programs from shifting political winds.[3]

These recommendations have been implemented only for very selective authorizations in the 1987 Defense Authorization Act.

3. The Packard Commission recommended that the President issue at the outset of his Administration, and thereafter as required, provisional five-year budget levels to the Department of Defense (DoD). "These budget levels would reflect competing demands on the federal budget and projected gross national product and revenues would come from the recommendations of the NSC and the Office of Management and Budget." The President would then select a military program and associated budget level which would be binding on the Administration. DoD would then develop a five-year defense plan and two-year defense budget which would conform to the President's plan. A two-year defense budget would then be submitted to Congress which Congress would be asked to approve.[4]

Two-year budgets were initiated for FY 1988–1989. However, Congress did not complete full authorization because the FY 1989 targets fell outside the Gramm-Rudman-Hollings budgetary ceilings and appropriations under the new system are still annual. Although some initial steps have been made toward strengthening the planning, programming, and budgeting systems within DoD, they fall well short of the Packard Commission's recommendations for a full five-year budget plan.

4. The Packard Commission recommended that Congress and the Administration simplify and recode all federal statutes governing procurement legislation into one regulatory package.

Some of this was done through the Acquisition Streamlining Initiative but Congress has yet to take any action and efforts to update the Federal Acquisition Regulations and the Defense Acquisition Regulations have consistently lagged behind the introduction of new laws.

5. The Packard Commission and various senators have recommended that DoD and the armed services committees in Congress should expand use of multiyear procurement for major research, development, and pro-

curement programs and treat them differently from operations, maintenance, and personnel which are dealt with on an annual basis.[5]

Congress has authorized multiyear funding for some programs. But
major, controversial weapons programs are still subject to annual
congressional authorization.

These recommendations, if adopted and properly implemented,
would substantially improve congressional oversight and control
of the defense budget. They are a good place to start, but it will
take concerted public pressure and leadership from within Congress to see them through.

The Pentagon. DoD has received the greatest attention in recent
acquisition reforms. As a result of the Packard Commission's recommendations and the Goldwater-Nichols Act a new position of
Under Secretary of Defense, Acquisitions, was established; a Defense Acquisition Board was created to replace the old Defense
Systems Acquisitions Review Council; and a variety of measures
were taken to streamline and improve the acquisitions sytem within
DoD. However, these reforms have not gone far enough:

- The Under Secretary of Defense, Acquisitions, has limited power over
  the armed services in acquisitions and does not enjoy the levels of authority envisioned in the Packard Commission's report.
- Only some programs qualify for special streamlined acquisition management status.
- The Defense Acquisition Board represents only a modest change and
  improvement from the DSARC.
- The increased role of the Defense Advanced Research Projects Agency,
  especially in prototype development, has led to DARPA organization
  setup but no funding.

The close relationship between DoD and the Office of Management and Budget also is not changed by these reforms. A major
problem with the current budgetary and programming system is
that instead of acting as devil's advocate, OMB has become DoD's
accomplice. Ties between DoD and OMB are strengthened by OMB
representation on the Defense Resources Board, which sets key
programming and budgetary priorities. If fiscal priorities are to guide
the budgetary process and limits to defense spending are to be
effectively imposed, the relationship between DoD and OMB will

have to become more adversarial, perhaps by limiting contact between the two departments to well-defined points in the budgetary cycle when defense spending is brought in line with fiscal policy objectives.

Defense Industries. Since 1984, Congress has passed a series of acquisitions laws, including the Competition in Contracting Act and the Defense Procurement Reform Act, to regulate the defense industry. Criminal and civil codes have been vigorously enforced to prevent fraud, waste, and abuse by defense contractors. The number of audits, inspections, and reviews of defense corporations has increased, causing some to complain about the amount of time and money spent on oversight.[6] Nevertheless, this effort is necessary if real abuses are to be curbed and government / industry accountability improved. The list of recommendations by the Packard Commission and other governmental studies yet to be fully implemented includes:

- Strengthening of civil and criminal laws including the Civil False Claims Act.
- Expanded involvement by industry in an industrial self-governance code of ethics which only major firms participate in now.
- Removal of DoD barriers to contractor self-governance and improved industrial self-governance.
- Adoption of cost-reduction and efficiency improvement measures.
- Removal of duplication in government auditing of contractors which is only partially addressed by the Defense Authorization Act.[7]

These reforms will require leadership from the President and Congress. Organizational and budgetary reform is no substitute for sound management and strong political leadership. Bad political management contributed to the difficulties of weapons development in some of the cases discussed in this book. For example, President Carter failed to anticipate the depth and degree of political hostility to the multiple-protective-shelter basing scheme for MX. Even a strong President like Ronald Reagan had difficulty finding the right formula to satisfy Congress on MX basing. If compromises are not to be patched together at the eleventh hour, leadership, planning, and foresight in both branches of government are required.

ANALYTIC CONCLUSIONS

A number of important analytic conclusions also stem from the case studies of particular weapons systems in this book. These have to do with the role of new technology, the impact of the arms race, the role of military strategy and doctrine, and the impact of arms control on weapons development. These four factors feed into domestic debates about new weapons programs but in ways that differ depending on the system involved.

Technology. The older a weapon is in its life cycle, the more likely that a search for a replacement will be initiated. System obsolescence therefore determines whether a defense system becomes the subject of intense research and development. This is one of the more underrated yet important aspects of weapons development. For example, the early evolution of the B-1 and the MX missile represented attempts to deal with the problem of aging systems: the B-52 bomber in the former case and the Minuteman missile in the latter. Similarly, the Underwater Long-Range Missile System which eventually evolved into the Trident submarine program was designed to replace the aging Polaris / Poseidon submarine force. Likewise the M-1 Abrams tank was developed to replace the increasingly obsolescent M-60 tank series.

Though it is a powerful argument, the "rust-out" rationale for new weapons programs does not go unchallenged. Opponents of Trident believed that the longevity of the Polaris / Poseidon force could be extended through modernization. Similarly, critics of B-1 believed that the B-52 bomber force was sufficiently durable to last into the 1990s when new Stealth technologies would be available to develop a radically new penetration bomber. Modernization of "old" systems therefore usually proceeds in tandem with new weapons development in response to countervailing pressures from those who seek to prolong the life of current systems.

In the design process, defense planners will often look to new technologies in order to build the most advanced and sophisticated system possible. But those technologies must be compatible with the established missions and traditions of the armed services. Technologies—no matter how advanced—that are incompatible with fundamental missions get a lukewarm reception. For example, the air force did all it could to block the development of

the air-launched cruise missile because the system was considered a threat to the survival of the B-1 manned-bomber program. In the final *quid pro quo,* it reluctantly accepted the missile only if the B-1 program was allowed to continue. As technology for the ALCM improved, the air force's enthusiasm for the ALCM as a standoff weapon increased and it is now accepted as a potent complement to the air-breathing leg of the strategic triad.

The air force was lukewarm toward the Midgetman mobile missile program and fought to have the program cut from the defense budget. The specifications for the missile were drawn up by Congress, which imposed strict limits on the size and payload of the missile. The air force would prefer to have a larger missile that could carry several MIRVed warheads.

Technological innovation is therefore a necessary but not sufficient condition for new weapons development. New technologies must also be compatible with the traditional missions of the services and provide a means for enhancing existing capabilities. When they are not, they will be resisted or ignored. The services have traditionally had a rather conservative attitude toward technological innovation. The same cannot be said about the civilian leadership in the Department of Defense or of Congress, which have tended to be more forward looking in the application of new technologies and strategic concepts. It was civilian defense analysts in DoD who first grasped the new possibilities of microprocessor computers and advanced guidance systems for the cruise missile. Similarly, Congress viewed a mobile, single-warhead missile as a way to reestablish strategic stability and restore the viability of the U.S. land-based, intercontinental ballistic missile force. But politicians can also exaggerate and place unwarranted faith in technology. This is all too apparent in the Strategic Defense Initiative. Ronald Reagan's vision of an invulnerable defensive shield against ballistic missiles is not shared by even the most ardent supporters of SDI in the scientific and technical community.

The march of new technology is therefore neither inevitable nor ineluctable. The selection of new technologies will depend on the kinds of bargains and compromises that are struck among a complex set of bureaucratic, institutional, and political interests. The outcome of these bargains is often difficult to predict.

Arms Race Influences. Action-reaction models of arms races are accurate depictions of the early stages of weapons development,

particularly regarding basic research and development, because weapons designers will be most concerned about anticipating new threats from the international environment. But enormous uncertainty characterizes the measurement of these threats and the nature and direction of Soviet programs. Other factors therefore come into play as programs move beyond the very initial research and development stages. These include the possibilities and limitations of new technology, service needs and missions, and bargains struck among competing domestic interests.

However, the threat of new Soviet programs and capabilities continues to play an important role as projects move to higher stages of development. As the level of resources required by a program grows, its sponsors may project the external threat more vividly and characterize it in terms of greater rather than less certainty. For instance, both Trident and MX were justified to meet the growing threat posed by increasing accuracy and payloads of the Soviet ICBM force. SDI has been justified as a research program to provide "insurance" against accelerated Soviet efforts in ballistic missile defense. The level of tension in the international environment may also affect the level of resources devoted to specific programs.[8] The B-1 bomber was the unintended beneficiary of the Soviet invasion of Afghanistan and the Iranian hostage crisis, which reinforced congressional and domestic fears that President Carter was weak on defense.

But threats may also be downplayed and underrated if they jeopardize new programs and threaten traditional service missions. The air force consistently downplayed the threat of Soviet air defenses to the future of the manned bomber in its efforts to build support for B-1 deployment. The army likewise defended the M-1 against those who argued that advances in anti-tank weaponry and precision-guided munitions were fast rendering the tank obsolete as a fighting vehicle. Little doubt exists that intelligence and threat assessments are highly politicized assets in weapons programs. But the way the threat is portrayed largely depends on whether it adds to or detracts from the rationale for a new or ongoing program.

Doctrine and Force Posture. In an ideal world, a direct relationship would exist between doctrine and military composition and force posture but, as many have noted, in the real world there is a disjunction between the two. Although military doctrine helps

to explain general trends in the selection of new weapons systems, weapons and doctrine seem to develop in tandem more often than not. It is the old question of whether the tail wags the dog. For example, the shift toward counterforce weapons in the 1970s, including the development of the Trident II and MX missiles, paralleled the shift in American doctrine to counterforce and war-fighting strategies enshrined in National Security Decision Memorandum 242 and subsequently in Presidential Directive 59. More often than not, the architects of new strategic thinking and concepts were also the strongest supporters of new weapons systems. For instance, Secretary of Defense James Schlesinger, who served under Presidents Nixon and Ford, was a key supporter of MX and the principal architect of the new look in American strategic doctrine. However, factors such as bureaucratic and budgetary politics, Congress, and others discussed above are more important in explaining the pace, scope, and timing of weapons programs than is military or strategic doctrine per se.

Arms Control. Critics of arms control argue that the internal bargaining that goes on during the negotiation of arms control agreements accelerates rather than retards the arms race.[9] This study supports the internal "bargaining-chip" hypothesis about weapons development. For example, the Pentagon's acceptance of SALT I was conditional on the acceleration of a number of new programs including the Trident missile and submarine system and the cruise missile. The bargain struck to obtain support for SALT I helped save Trident from its critics within the administration and in Congress. Similarly, the MX missile was kept alive because the Carter administration found itself forced to give its support to MX in order to secure congressional support for the SALT II agreements.

An administration intent on building and deploying a system in the face of strong opposition in Congress may also use the argument that a system is necessary to get the Soviets to the table in arms control. Reagan tied MX developments to arms control in an effort to defuse growing sentiment for a nuclear weapons freeze in the early 1980s. Reagan also argued that SDI research and development was a key factor in bringing the Soviets back to the table in arms control talks on intermediate and strategic nuclear force reductions in 1985. Without SDI, Reagan administration of-

ficials argued, the Soviets would not have been willing to make the concessions they did.

A recent examination of U.S.-Soviet arms control asserts "that militarily significant constraints on any particular category of weapons elude negotiations if either side strongly prefers unfettered freedom of action with regard to the weapons in question. . . . If either party has tested the weapon or invested heavily in it, the difficulties confronting arms control are compounded."[10] Although antiballistic missile defense was effectively arrested by arms control in the 1970s, the Reagan administration's commitment to and investment in SDI research created major new problems for arms control. In particular, the Antiballistic Missile Treaty's limits on testing of new and exotic technologies for ballistic missile defense have become a contentious issue in the debate over the "broad" versus "narrow" interpretation of the Treaty, as discussed in Chapter 10.

Arms control obviously affects the magnitude and pace of weapons development, procurement, and deployment, but instances where development of a new weapons system has been stopped dead in its tracks are rare. Systems that have moved beyond the advanced research and development stage therefore will not likely be stopped by arms control although the numbers and form of deployment will be affected. For example, the SALT II protocols limited deployment numbers of long-range ALCMs and prohibited land-mobile launchers for heavy missiles, and the recent INF Treaty will see the removal, after deployment, of several hundred intermediate-range nuclear missiles from Europe.

This book has argued that the way America buys its weapons is a supremely political process and one plagued by inefficiency, waste, and political mismanagement. This judgment may seem harsh. But much-needed reform will occur only if the public recognizes the severity of the problem and pressure for reform grows. Leadership in the Congress and by the President is also required to ensure that reform is carried out and that defense is based on what the nation can afford. Too much horse trading afflicts the weapons acquisition process today. Our story is one of failed leadership and institutions out of control. It is a story of "unguided missiles" where politics too often substitutes for sound planning and prudent public policy.

Appendix A

□

COMPETITIVE-COOPERATIVE BEHAVIOR IN THE DEFENSEBUDGET

The purpose of this appendix is to elaborate upon some of the key theoretical assumptions that underlie the discussion of the politics of the defense budgetary process in Chapters 3 and 4. These assumptions are rooted in oligopoly theory and game theory. This book argues that the relationship among key bureaucratic and political actors in the Pentagon, within the executive branch, and in Congress on defense budget and weapons procurement matters is essentially "competitive-cooperative" and similar to the oligopolistic behavior of firms in the economic marketplace. The reasons for this are found in a number of factors including the incremental nature of the defense budgetary process, the limited number of key bureaucratic and institutional interests, and decision-making processes characterized by regular and frequent interaction among the players. This model of decision making, most notably as it applies to the relationship among bureaucratic interests within the executive branch, is intended to refine and elaborate upon current models of decision making that stress the more competitive aspects of political and bureaucratic behavior in government. Before explaining this model further, it must be stressed at the outset that the analogy to oligopoly theory and game theory is intended to be illustrative and suggestive rather than definitively proven or conclusive. The model is offered as a set of postulates about political and bureaucratic preferences and relationships in an effort to link them into a more coherent and rigorous analytic framework. It thus seeks to provide a "first-order" approximation of the problems of weapons procurement and the defense budget discussed in this book.

"BUREAUCRATIC POLITICS" MODEL OF GOVERNMENT

Students of government have long since recognized that it is a mistake to view "government" as a unitary, rational actor. In his pathfinding study

of the Cuban missile crisis, Graham Allison challenged the prevailing tendency of political scientists to view governmental outputs as the choices of a single decision maker (the rational actor model) or as an "organizational output" partially coordinated by a unified group of leaders (the organizational process model). Instead, Allison offered a third variant of governmental behavior that he labeled the "governmental" or "bureaucratic politics" paradigm. Allison argued, "The 'leaders' who sit on top of government organizations are not a monolithic group. Rather, each individual in this group is, in his own right, a player in a central, competitive game. The name of the game is politics: bargaining along regularized circuits among players positioned hierarchically within the government. Government behavior can thus be understood . . . as results of these bargaining games."[1] Each player's preferences and perceptions are colored by his or her position within the government bureaucracy: "The factors that encourage organizational parochialism also exert pressure upon the players who occupy positions on top of (or within) these organizations. . . . The games into which the player can enter and the advantages with which he plays enhance these pressures."[2] According to Allison, government decision making is best characterized as a process of conflict, bargaining, and compromise—what political scientist Charles Lindbloom calls "the science of muddling through."[3]

> The decisions and actions of government are intranational political resultants: resultants in the sense that what happens is not chosen as a solution to a problem but rather from compromise, conflict, and confusion of officials with diverse interests and unequal influence; political in the sense that the activity from which decisions and actions emerge is best characterized as bargaining along regularized channels among individual members of the government.[4]

Allison appears to give greater emphasis to the more competitive aspects of bureaucratic political behavior, however. He suggests that outcomes depend on "bargaining advantages, skill and will in us[ing] bargaining advantages, and the other players' perceptions of the first two ingredients. The sources of bargaining advantages include formal authority and responsibility . . . expertise and control over information . . . personal persuasiveness, etc."[5] Strategy and gamesmanship are therefore less important than "power," "control," and an individual's personal authority within the organizational setting.

Some scholars have taken this argument one step further asserting that government players do in fact approach bureaucratic "games" as zero sum (what one gains the other loses) where the objective is to "win" by

defeating or outmaneuvering competitors. Interservice rivalry is one such manifestation of the bureaucratic politics paradigm. For example, in his important study of the development of the Polaris submarine system, Harvey Sapolsky argues that the success of the program depended largely on the ability of its bureaucratic proponents "to eliminate competitors, outmaneuver reviewing agencies, and co-opt congressmen, admirals, journalists, and academicians." Sapolsky argues "that success requires skills in bureaucratic politics. Only through the exercise of such skills does a favorable environment yield sustained support for a program."[6] This perspective is to some extent shared by Robert Art in his study of the TFX airplane. Art saw the development of the TFX primarily in terms of internal politics at the Pentagon and the conflicts that arose between a strong Secretary of Defense, Robert McNamara, who wanted the air force and navy to collaborate on a joint aircraft, and the services, each of which wanted a system that would meet its own special combat needs. Art argues that "McNamara accomplished something that no Secretary of Defense before him had done." He overrode the interests of the services and forced them to accept a plane that neither wanted.[7]

This view of decision making is flawed insofar as it overlooks the cooperative elements of government behavior and action. To the extent that some, like Allison, do allow for cooperative behavior in their models of government, they fail to specify the causes of this behavior or to indicate when bureaucratic conflict and competition are likely to give way to cooperation. Moreover, from the point of view of weapons procurement and defense budgets, this approach cannot explain the high levels of bureaucratic and political cooperation that inform certain stages of this process. Oligopoly theory and game theory provide a more rigorous basis for explaining the "competitive-cooperative" political relationship among the players involved in the weapons procurement aspect of the defense budget.

OLIGOPOLY THEORY

According to the pure theory of oligopolistic pricing, each firm in the economic marketplace chooses to market the quantity of output that maximizes its own profits, assuming the quantities marketed by rivals to be fixed. Thus, for any industry there theoretically exists a determinate and stable price-quantity equilibrium. The equilibrium price depends on the number of sellers. With a single seller, the monopoly price results. As the number of sellers increases, the equilibrium price declines until eventually there are so many sellers the price approaches equality with

marginal cost. The competitive equilibrium price is therefore more closely reached as the number of sellers increases.[8]

This particular model of oligopolistic pricing, advanced by Augustin Cournot in the nineteenth century, was criticized by later economists for assuming that the quantity of output supplied by firms is the key decision variable, as opposed to price. Subsequent models tried to incorporate more complex reaction assumptions into their explanations of oligopolistic behavior. Edward Chamberlain asserted that recognition of "mutual interdependence" in a market when the number of sellers is small and products are standardized facilitates cooperation and the setting of prices at or near the monopoly level.

> If each seeks his maximum profit rationally and intelligently, he will realize that when there are only two or a few sellers his own move has a considerable effect upon his competitors, and that this makes it idle to suppose that they will accept without retaliation the losses he forces upon them. Since the result of a cut by any one is inevitably to decrease his own profits, no one will cut, and although the sellers are entirely independent, the equilibrium result is the same as though there were a monopolistic agreement among them.[9]

Chamberlain argued that when sellers are few in number, no formal collusion is necessary to maintain price and output decisions. However, "when cost functions and/or market shares vary from firm to firm within an oligopolistic industry, conflicts arise that, unless resolved through formal collusive agreements, interfere with the maximization of collective monopoly profits."[10] If unresolved, these conflicts will eventually undermine the industry's solution to its joint profit-maximizing solution.

Economists have since identified a number of important institutional mechanisms that may facilitate cooperation among firms in oligopolistic settings. These include overt and covert agreements, price leadership, rules of thumb, and the use of focal points.[11] A brief word about each follows.

Overt and Covert Agreements. Collusion among firms is an ancient economic pratice. As Adam Smith remarked, "people of the same trade seldom meet together, even for the merriment and diversion, but the conversation ends in a conspiracy against the public, or in some contrivance to raise prices." In the United States price-fixing agreements are prohibited by law but many violations go undetected. European and Japanese laws are more tolerant of such behavior and hundreds of cartel arrangements have been registered with the European Economic Community Commission.

Agreements to abide by particular prices on standard products may

also be reached informally through gentlemen's agreements without formal collusion. When product lines are complex and finished products vary significantly in quality, finish, packaging, etc., collusion may be over product detail or charges for extras. Another widely used approach is to insert restrictive provisions into patent licenses when several firms hold a strong patent position on the same product(s). The entrance of new producers can therefore be blocked by the refusal to grant licenses. Direct or indirect output restrictions can also be incorporated directly into the licensing agreement. Control over the members of a cartel may also be enforced by requiring them to market their products through a central sales bureau, as was the case of soft coal producers in Appalachia during the depression.

Price Leadership. To maintain an oligopolistic market structure, firms may also coordinate their behavior by allowing one of their members to serve as a price leader. "Price leadership implies a set of industry practices or customs under which list price changes are normally announced by a specific firm accepted as the leader by others, who follow the leader's initiatives." The leader may dominate an industry and set prices by taking into account the reactions of marginal producers. Or, the price leader may simply act as a barometer, setting prices that might otherwise emerge under competition.

Rules of Thumb. Another "informal" price-fixing mechanism is the "rule-of-thumb" pricing formula whereby firms set prices according to a "cost-plus" principle that takes into account a normal profit margin and a percentage return on invested capital which is added to the unit cost to calculate product price. This mechanism works better if firms face the same unit costs and use roughly the same formula.

Focal Points and Tacit Coordination. Coordinated action over prices may also take place through a process of tacit communication whereby the parties come to rest their decision on a common focal point. Thomas Schelling explains this process as follows:

> When a man loses his wife in a department store without any prior understanding on where to meet if they get separated, the chances are good that they will find each other. It is likely that each will think of some obvious place to meet, so obvious that each will be sure that the other is sure that it is "obvious" to both of them. One does not simply predict where the other will go, since the other will go where he predicts the first to go, which is wherever the first predicts the second to predict the first to go, and so ad infinitum. Not "What would I do if I were she?" but "What would I do if she were wondering what I would do if I were she . . . ?" What is

necessary is to coordinate predictions, to read the same message in the common situation, to identify the one course of action that their expectations of the other can converge on. They must "mutually recognize" some unique signal that coordinates the expectation of the other. We cannot be sure they will meet, nor would all couples read the same signal; but the chances are certainly a great deal better than if they pursued a random course of search.[12]

The focal points "may owe their prominence to analogy, symmetry, precedent, aesthetic considerations, or even the accident of arrangement." They may also be based on simple rules like "split the difference." As F. N. Scherer notes, "Focal points also play a role in explicit, across-the-table bargaining when a solution is difficult to reach despite free communication because a concession by one party generates an expectation in the other's mind that further concessions may be extracted. Focal points provide a barrier each recognizes as a natural place for further concessions to be resisted, and thus they facilitate convergence upon a unique solution ... the automobile salesperson who works out the arithmetic for a rock bottom price of $2,507.63 is almost pleading to be relieved of $7.63."[13] This insight has also been incorporated into oligopoly theory. Firms will tacitly set their prices at some focal point thereby encouraging their competitors to follow suit without undercutting.

In sum, when firms are in a potentially competitive relationship they will nevertheless cooperate when their numbers are few and they recognize their mutual interest in avoiding competitive pricing strategies and harmful competition that would reduce profits as prices approach competitive equilibrium. Formal and informal methods of communication will help to promote cooperation in an oligopolistic setting by enabling firms to anticipate the reactions and behavior of others so that prices stay at or close to monopoly equilibrium.

GAME THEORY

Game theory also provides an extremely useful set of insights into the roots of cooperation among potential competitors. Most important is the attention it gives to the structure of the decision-making environment. Game theory shows that situations where adversaries play a game once and have little chance of meeting again will tend to elicit competitive behavior. By contrast, adversaries will tend to cooperate if they are forced to interact repeatedly with each other in an ongoing game.[14] To understand why consider the following.

Prisoners' Dilemma. Suppose two cowboys are arrested by an unscrupulous sheriff on the trumped-up charge of murder. They are held in two

Figure A-1. **Prisoners' Dilemma**

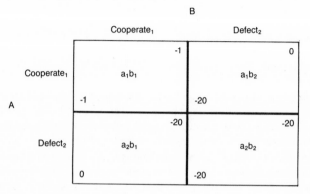

separate, adjoining jail cells and are prevented from speaking to each other. Each prisoner is told that he will be allowed to go free if he turns state's evidence against the other, as long as the other has not confessed to the crime. (The one who hasn't confessed will get life imprisonment.) However, if both "confess" they will each get twenty-year sentences. If both plead innocent, they will get shorter sentences (one year maximum in prison).

The payoff structure in this game is illustrated in Figure A-1. The question is what should each prisoner do?

If neither prisoner can communicate with the other, neither can be sure that he won't be double-crossed if he says nothing, or that his betrayal would be detected in time for counteraction. Faced with this dilemma, each prisoner is better off confessing, which means a twenty-year life sentence for each. Honest cooperation, however, would have meant a one-year sentence, with the possibility of parole for good behavior in a few months.

The difficulty here is an absence of communication. "The outcome of the prisoners' dilemma situation thus is directly related not to the wisdom or stupidity of the 'prisoners,' but to the presence or absence of devices that assure each side that it will know in time if the other is about to cheat, devices whose presence generally would make cooperation safe and advisable."[15] When communication is possible and relatively free and rapid between parties they will play the game differently. Thus, if there is a hole in the wall between the two adjoining cells and the two prisoners are able to remain in constant communication with each other so that one knows the other is not confessing, they could both get off with light sentences.

Few situations in real life conform to the prisoners' dilemma game.

But the example shows how the structure of a situation will affect decision-making choices and encourage "defection" if communication or trust between two individuals is not possible.

Communication, however, is not the only way to get two individuals to cooperate. Some rivalries or conflicts are continuous while others are discontinuous or "one-shot" affairs. Game theorists have found that the likelihood of cooperation among self-seeking egoists increases when a game like prisoners' dilemma is played by the same participants indefinitely.[16] Maximization of joint benefits is more likely when a rivalry is continuous and repeated experience under stable conditions affords an opportunity for learning to cooperate and for trust to develop. Moreover, in a repetitious or continuous game, one party can threaten its rivals with damaging retaliation tomorrow if cooperation is not forthcoming today. The threat of future sanctions or penalties will also serve as an inducement to cooperation.

Continuity of Players. If one player is unlikely to be around for whatever reason, the incentive to defect becomes stronger. As Caesar explained when Pompey's allies stopped cooperating with Pompey, "They regarded his [Pompey's] prospects as hopeless and acted according to the common rule by which a man's friends become his enemies in adversity."[17]

Long-Term Interaction. An "iterated" or repeated game enables strategies of reciprocity to be used, which increase the likelihood of cooperation. They establish a direct connection between the current behavior of the actor and his anticipation of future benefits. In the prisoners' dilemma game, for example, iteration enhances cooperation because a current defection will reduce the likelihood of cooperation in the future. It is unprofitable for a challenger to defect because he knows that the other player will defect in the next move.

Long-term interaction increases the stability of cooperation. "Any member of Congress who is perceived as likely to be defeated in the next election may have some difficulty doing legislative business with his colleagues on the usual basis of trust and credit." Similarly, "a visiting professor is likely to receive poor treatment by other faculty members compared to the way these same people treat their regular colleagues."[18]

We are all familiar with the difference between the way people treat one another in small towns and in big cities. The friendliness, decency, and common courtesy found in small towns are the result of proximity and the possibility for frequent social interaction among the inhabitants.

Strangers may be ruder and less helpful to each other in a big city in part because there is less chance they will run into each other again.

Low Discount Rates for Future Payoffs. For cooperation to continue working, players must continue to place a relatively high value on future payoffs from the game relative to the present. If they discount future payoffs too heavily, cooperation will break down. Take, for example, Rousseau's metaphor of the stag hunt. A group of hunters is chasing a stag. It requires the efforts of all four of them to trap it. If they are successful they will have food for a week. If they are not, they will go hungry. One hunter sees a hare run by during the chase. If he catches it, all four will lose the stag, but he will have enough food to satisfy his immediate hunger. His temptation to cooperate or defect will be affected, among other factors, by the value he places on the desirability of eating now versus later. If his discount rate is high, he will go for the hare; if it is low, he will stay with the hunt.

Kenneth Oye suggests that linkage tactics may also enhance the prospects for cooperation. For example, the temptation to defect in a deal promising $30 billion for a billion barrels of oil may be reduced if the deal is broken up into a series of payments and deliveries. Cooperation in arms reduction or in territorial disengagement may be difficult if the reduction or disengagement must be achieved in one jump. But "[i]f a reduction or disengagement can be sliced up into increments, the problem of cooperation may be rendered more tractable." Oye also suggests that "strategies of issue-linkage can be used to alter payoff structures and to interject elements of iterativeness to single-play situations." This means linking good behavior in one game to the outcome in another.

Short games tend to be conflictual and create strong incentives to "defect" by going for the maximum payoff to the individual. But games with longer "shadows of the future" tend to elicit cooperative behavior among adversaries and a view of outcomes as non-zero sum. These games are characterized by continuity, regular and frequent interactions among players, and low discount rates for future payoffs.

A number of caveats are in order, however. First, the number of players in a game will tend to affect the likelihood of cooperation and the opportunities for recognition of mutual interests. As the number of players increases and communication among parties and exchange of information become more difficult, cooperation tends to break down. Second, as the number of players increases the problem of identifying defectors and imposing penalties increases. Threatening violators with sanctions can lead to wholesale defections and a breakdown of the entire system. Third, numbers increase the likelihood of heterogeneous preferences and

different utility functions among actors. As Kenneth Oye further explains: "Cooperative behavior rests on the calculations of expected utility— merging discount rates, payoff structures, and anticipated behavior of other players. Discount rates and approaches to calculation are likely to vary across actors, and the prospects for mutual cooperation may decline as the number of players and the probable heterogeneity of actors increases."[19]

But a large number of players does not necessarily mean that cooperation will break down. Social scientists have identified a number of other factors that can help to lengthen "the shadow of the future" and increase the likelihood of cooperation in games where the numbers of players is large. The prospects for cooperation may be enhanced by informal or formal sets of rules and norms. "[C]onventions provide rules of thumb that can diminish transaction and information costs ... collective enforcement mechanisms both decrease the likelihood of autonomous defection and permit selective punishment of violators or norms."[20] Robert Keohane has demonstrated that international regimes like the International Monetary Fund (IMF), the General Agreement on Tariffs and Trade (GATT), and the International Energy Agency (IEA) fostered cooperation among their members long after the United States stopped being the world's policeman.[21]

But norms may also emerge "informally" via an evolutionary process of adaptation and adjustment that does not assume rational calculation by the actors involved. Robert Axelrod, for example, suggests that "metanorms" can help get norms started and protect them once established. "By linking vengefulness against nonpunishers with vengefulness against defectors, the metanorm provides a mechanism by which the norm against defection becomes self-policing." Another mechanism is dominance of one group by another, one such example being apartheid in South Africa, which is enforced by the economic, political, and military power of the white minority. Still another way for norms to be maintained is via internalization. "Norms frequently become internalized. This means that violating an established norm is psychologically painful even if the direct material benefits are positive." Reputation may also strengthen norms. "For example, if there is a norm dictating that people should dress for dinner, and you don't, then others might make some quite general inferences about you." The signal given also contains information about the future behavior of the defector in a variety of situations. Finally, norms may be supported by voluntary membership in a group or organization whereby membership means accepting a set of commitments or obligations that reduce the incentive to defect.[22]

In sum, even when incentives to defect are strong norms and rules may provide a powerful mechanism for regulating conflict in groups where

the number of players is large and no central authority exists to enforce compliance among them.

THE WEAPONS ACQUISITION AND DEFENSE BUDGETARY PROCESS

It is the argument of this book that the weapons acquisition and defense budgetary process is marked by "competitive-cooperative" behavior akin to that noted by economists in oligopolistic settings and by game theorists in iterated or repetitive games. Weapons acquisition and budgetary "games" are viewed by their bureaucratic and congressional participants as non-zero sum and, even when they are not, competitors will behave cooperatively. The reasons for this are as follows.

First, the number of players and institutional interests in the formulation of the defense budget is limited. In the bureaucracy, the key institutions are the Office of the Secretary of Defense, the armed services, the Joint Chiefs of Staff, and the Office of Management and Budget (OMB). In the Congress, the key players are the Armed Services Committees and the Appropriations Committees of both Houses. Although each set of government players represents a much broader constituency of interests, the number of players involved in making key decisions is actually quite small. Moreover, in the Congress, where the number of actors is potentially large, institutionalized norms favoring "consensus" and political accommodation of competing interests facilitate cooperative approaches to decision making.

Second, the defense budget process through which weapons programs are funded is characterized by regular and frequent action among the players. The defense budget must be drafted each year. It engages a common group of players who meet regularly to decide upon important resource allocation decisions. In the Pentagon this includes the members of the Defense Resources Board whose membership includes representatives from OMB. In the Congress this includes the members of the House and Senate Armed Services and Appropriations Committees. Moreover, the two branches of government are involved in continuous communication and contact with the other as Pentagon and congressional staffs meet to thrash out the details of the defense budget behind closed doors and officials from the Pentagon appear to testify before the Senate and House.

Third, a combination of long lead times for new weapons development and the fractionated and incremental nature of the budgetary process encourage cooperative approaches to decision making in the bureaucracy and in Congress. Although there has been some movement to multiyear authorization, funds are rarely committed to the entire life-

cycle costs of a program as a lump sum. The formulation of the defense budget is a continuous game involving the same groups of actors and interests from year to year, although the potential for conflict and breakdown of cooperation between the executive branch and Congress obviously increases as a President approaches the end of his term and Congress anticipates that it will be dealing with a new administration.

Fourth, institutional processes facilitate bargaining and coordination. Unlike the economic marketplace, governmental actors can negotiate directly with each other because there are no formal prohibitions against collusion. Analogs to the various methods of communication found in the oligopolistic environment can also be found. For instance, the Department of Defense and Secretary of Defense play a role that is remarkably similar to the price leader in oligopoly. DoD and the Secretary of Defense establish the initial requirements for the defense budget to which other bureaucratic and governmental interests like OMB must respond. The privileged position of DoD as purveyor of information and the principal source of expertise on defense matters gives it a powerful voice in establishing budgetary requirements and setting funding levels for different programs. "Rules of thumb" and "focal points" are also evident in bargaining behavior within the bureaucracy and between the Congress and the executive branch of government on defense acquisition and budget matters. DoD tries to anticipate what level of resources Congress is willing to appropriate for particular programs in the defense budget and adjusts its own estimates accordingly—what Richard Stubbing calls the "cut-insurance game." This is the political analog to the "cost-plus" formula in oligopolistic pricing. Similarly, bargaining between the two Houses of Congress over the defense budget in what eventually becomes the Joint Resolution on Defense bears a strong resemblance to Schelling's notion of "focal points" in tacit or overt bargaining processes. The House and Senate leadership respectively know what sort of cuts or increases to the defense budget the other will accept. This facilitates compromise by establishing defined parameters to negotiation. The same pattern of behavior also manifests itself between the President and Congress, although Gramm-Rudman-Hollings and budgetary deficits have obviously made agreement on budgetary matters, including defense, more difficult because of conflicting interests and priorities. Finally, the entire process is greased by a set of political norms which encourage cooperative approaches to decision making when priorities and preferences conflict. Les Aspin identifies this as the search for a consensus that makes sense to the "common sense middle." Others speak of it as "pluralism" which is rooted in a shared sense of common political values.

COMPETITION AND COOPERATION DURING THE LIFE CYCLE OF WEAPONS SYSTEMS

The level or degree of political competition (or conversely cooperation) of course varies with intensity over time. In the case of the defense budget, the degree of bureaucratic conflict and interservice rivalry seems to be affected, in the first instance, by the level of resources being entertained for any given program. There are a number of distinct stages through which a weapons system must pass which run from basic research and engineering to prototype development, to testing, to procurement, to deployment, and, eventually, to modernization. In the early stages of research and development, the level of resources commanded by a program is usually quite small. Most interesting or potentially significant programs, therefore, receive some level of funding although few R&D programs are sufficiently promising to move beyond this stage.

When a decision is required on production and deployment, which usually absorb the lion's share of costs in relation to total program development, interservice rivalry and service conflict with civilian managers in the Department of Defense intensify. Not all programs can be funded and a finite level of resources ensures that not all weapons desired by the services can be built. The more acutely a service believes a particular weapon is essential to its overall mission and objectives, the more intensively it will lobby for it and challenge programs advanced by other services that are in direct competition for scarce funds.[23] To the extent that a major weapons program involves a sizable share of the overall defense budget, the debate will engage other interested parties in the executive branch and in Congress (for instance, the Secretary of Defense, the President, the Office of Management and Budget, the armed services, and the House and Senate Appropriations Committees and Subcommittees).

Once a system achieves maturity, it generates its own political constituency, not only in the Pentagon, but also in the industrial contracting community.[24] As this constituency grows, the system acquires a momentum of its own, just as bureaucratic analysts predict. Once a system has moved into the production stage, it becomes extremely difficult to halt. This is because internal bargaining processes over budgetary and procurement choices, not only within the Pentagon but also in the Pentagon's relationship with the Office of Management and Budget, are usually not viewed as zero sum; that is, there are rewards or payoffs to all parties from cooperative behavior. A program will therefore not get all of the funds and resources its sponsors want, but, by the same token, it will rarely be killed. The relationship can be expressed in the form of the simplified diagram in Figure A-2.

Thus there are points in the weapons acquisition and procurement

Figure A-2. **Relationship between Program Expenditure and Level of Interservice Rivalry and Bureaucratic Competition.**

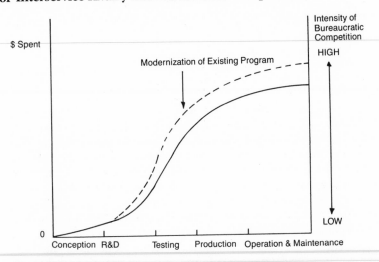

cycle that are characterized by greater levels of competition among bureaucratic and institutional interests. Empirically this was borne out in case studies of particular programs. Decisions about weapons production involving major resource allocation decisions such as those required to move a program into advanced prototype development and testing or production and deployment under conditions of relative scarcity witnessed increased interservice rivalry and greater conflict among government departments and Congress. This suggests that empirically the degree of cooperation among institutional actors is affected by their perception of the costs and stakes involved. Where fundamental institutional interests and "core" values are involved, competition and conflict are likely to be greater than in circumstances and conditions where stakes and perceptions of cost are lower (for example, a decision to fund a new R&D program). The relationship can be expressed formally as follows:

The expected utility of bureaucratic player j is:

$$U_j = \frac{\sum_{t=z}^{T} \sum_{w=1}^{W} P_{jtw}(\cdot F_{zj}) \times U_j(B_{tw} - \sum_{j \neq i}^{I} D_{itw})}{(1+r)^t}$$

where

B_{tw} = total defense budget available at time t in state w;
D_{itw} = expenditure on defense system i at time t in state w;

U_j = utility of bureaucratic player j;
P_{jtw} = bureaucratic player j's subjective probability of state w at time t;
t = $1 \ldots T$ periods of time;
w = $1 \ldots W$ states of nature;
i = $1 \ldots I$ bureaucratic players;
F_{zj} = information available to player j at time z; and B_{tw} and D_{itw} are functions of the strategies available adopted by all bureaucratic players.

Assuming bureaucratic players are expected utility maximizers, the equation shown above states that a player's expected utility is a function of his or her share of the total defense budget, that is, the money spent on the player's particular weapons system. This share has been defined residually as the total defense budget less the money spent on the weapons systems of other players. This point emphasizes the fact that all players are competing for a share of the defense budget.

The probability weights used in the expected value calculation are conditional probabilities. They are conditional on the information and strategies available to each player at each particular point in time. The above equation can be used to demonstrate how the ideas and concepts discussed previously affect a bureaucratic player's well-being. For example, if another weapons system is in the conception stage of its life cycle, then a player's *ex ante* probability of it being a threat to his or her own weapon system will be small, given that most weapons programs do not survive beyond the initial stages. This will be reflected in a low probability of large expenditures on this competing weapons system at later points in time. Thus a competing weapons system will be assigned a small penalty for potential claims to future defense procurement budgets. Also, because the current expenditures of a competing weapons system in its conceptual stage are small there is also an associated small penalty for its use of the current defense budget. However, the cost of not cooperating with another bureaucratic player seeking approval for budget allocations in the initial phases of its life cycle could be very high if non-cooperation results in cancellation of one's own weapons system either now or later on. Note that the effects of discounting also serve to reduce the current cost of future budget displacement of competing weapons systems.

Figure A-3 illustrates that as a program progresses through its life cycle and the dollar expenditures per unit of time increase, the probability of cancellation decreases or, conversely, the probability of program continuity increases. By the same token, the probability that some cuts will be made to planned program expenditures increases. This reinforces the notion that cooperation is greatest when weapons systems are in the initial phases of their life cycles than when they are in the later phases of

Figure A-3. **Relationship between Program Continuity and Likelihood of Some Cuts to Program Budget.**

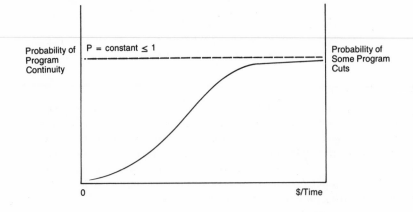

their life cycles. Clearly the costs of cooperation increase as a program progresses because it becomes a greater threat to the weapons systems and programs of other bureaucratic players. In these later stages of the life cycle, a program will be more exposed to hostile political and fiscal pressures in the bureaucracy and in Congress.

Just as the oligopolist has limited control over demand shifts or a shift in the price of inputs, bureaucratic and military sponsors of a new weapons program have limited control over their political and budgetary environment. Changes in this environment may undermine the old political and budgetary consensus as the members of Congress and other political actors find themselves facing new pressures when called upon to vote for a program in a new authorization or appropriations bill. It may take a while for a new political consensus or cooperative equilibrium to establish itself. Economists speak of "sequential equilibria" whereby at each point in time a system has to find a new equilibrium point where a new oligopolistic price can emerge. Similarly, with each stage or step in the budgetary process, the political coalition of forces may likewise shift. From the point of view of the weapons contractor, the budgetary and programming process may appear highly unstable. The actual level of funding a program will receive in any given year is therefore uncertain. However, from the viewpoint of the defense budget as a whole, each sequential equilibrium is not very different from the previous one as the budget moves from authorization to appropriations, leading one to the conclusion that the process is relatively stable when viewed as a whole

over time. As discussed earlier, competition will rarely degenerate to the point where a major program is canceled simply because some cooperation (that is, compromise) will always be forthcoming. Otherwise the budgetary process and norms or rules of cooperation that inform it would break down.

Thus even games that have a long "shadow of the future" witness intensified competition if stakes are high, substantial financial resources are involved, and core institutional values are at stake. The probability that a program will be displaced in the budget by other programs as it moves toward production and deployment is high. This does not mean that a major program will be canceled, but the probability increases that the levels of funding sought by its sponsors will not be achieved.

Cooperation and oligopoly theories have important applications to the budgetary process and political setting but the results must be treated cautiously. There are obviously other important factors at work on the behavior of actors and institutions in the real world that are not captured fully by these theories. As the case studies illustrate, variables such as technological innovation, military doctrine, arms control, military intelligence, and perceptions of the Soviet threat also have an important impact on weapons acquisition and procurement decisions and feed into domestic debates over weapons and budgets. The impact of these variables is more thoroughly discussed in the concluding chapter of this book.

SELECTION OF CASES

The cases for this book were chosen because they involved different weapons programs and different branches of the armed services, and different military roles and missions covering the spectrum from the strategic to the conventional. One would, *a priori,* expect to find some variations in political behavior rather than common patterns. Since the argument is a general proposition about political behavior, it was important to select cases where it could be tested and where there would be solid grounds for disproving it. It was also important to select cases where outcomes varied—hence the selection of the B-1 bomber, a major program that was canceled but then resurrected by a later President. If the proposition about "competitive-cooperative" behavior holds in different cases, we can be more confident about its generalizability.[25]

At the same time, however, it was important to find cases where one would be comparing roughly similar areas of public policy and there was a rough similarity in certain kinds of external and internal factors influencing policy—hence the emphasis on *major* weapons procurement

programs and systems. Otherwise, the variation (or absence of variation) in policy behavior and outcomes among the cases might be explained as the consequence of the independent influence of other factors (for example, the size of a program in the budget).[26] It was important to select a policy sector where one could "control" in a general way for a variety of independent external and internal influences on policy (such as those influences mentioned above).

Appendix B

□

Historical Trends in Defense Spending

Table B-1. Department of Defense—B/A by Appropriation* (dollars in millions)

	FY 1983	FY 1984	FY 1985	FY 1986†	FY 1987	FY 1988	FY 1989
Current Dollars							
Military Personnel	45,688	64,866	67,773	67,794	73,761	78,308	81,559
Retired Pay	16,155	—‡	—‡	—‡	—‡	—‡	—‡
Operation & Maintenance	66,540	70,950	77,803	74,888	78,536	86,563	91,460
Procurement	80,355	86,161	96,842	92,506	85,174	83,974	94,624
Research, Development, Test and Evaluation	22,798	26,867	31,327	33,609	35,994	43,749	44,287
Special Foreign Currency Program	4	3	9	2	4	—	—
Military Construction	4,512	4,510	5,517	5,281	5,131	6,599	6,903
Family Housing & Homeowners Assistance Program	2,712	2,669	2,890	2,803	3,121	3,485	3,682
Revolving & Management Funds	1,075	2,774	5,088	5,235	651	1,201	1,132
Trust Funds, Receipts & Deductions	-365	-650	-447	-729	-675	-726	-742
Proposed Legislation	—	—	—	—	—	142	384
Total—Direct Program (B/A)	239,474	258,150	286,802	281,390	281,695	303,295	323,290

Constant FY 1988 Dollars

Military Personnel	54,252	74,868	75,321	72,588	77,148	78,308	78,366
Retired Pay	19,154	—‡	—‡	—‡	—‡	—‡	—‡
Operation and Maintenance	75,541	79,433	84,420	81,296	83,425	86,563	88,266
Procurement	94,502	97,918	106,678	98,698	87,935	83,974	91,876
Research, Development, Test and Evaluation	26,912	30,595	34,549	36,046	37,354	43,749	42,855
Special Foreign Currency Program	4	3	10	2	4	—	—
Military Construction	5,333	5,157	6,103	5,668	5,320	6,599	6,699
Family Housing & Homeowners Assistance Program	3,137	2,997	3,153	2,987	3,236	3,485	3,562
Revolving & Management Funds	1,267	3,149	5,587	5,586	673	1,201	1,094
Trust Funds, Receipts & Deductions	−430	−768	−491	−777	−698	−726	−717
Proposed Legislation	—	—	—	—	—	142	371
Total—Direct Program (B/A)	**279,671**	**293,383**	**315,331**	**302,094**	**294,397**	**303,295**	**312,372**

*Numbers may not add to totals due to rounding. [B/A = budgetary authority.]

†Lower Budget Authority in the Military Personnel Accounts in FY 1986 reflects the congressional direction to finance $4.5 billion for the military pay raise and retirement accrual costs by transfers from prior year unobligated balances.

‡Retired Pay accrual included in Military Personnel Appropriation.

Source: Caspar W. Weinberger, Secretary of Defense, *Annual Report to the Congress, Fiscal Year 1988* (Washington, D.C.: U.S. Government Printing Office, January 1, 1987), p. 325.

Table B-2. Department of Defense—B/A by Component* (dollars in millions)

	FY 1983	FY 1984	FY 1985	FY 1986†	FY 1987	FY 1988	FY 1989
Current Dollars							
Department of the Army	57,529	68,664‡	74,270‡	73,128‡	74,525‡	80,102‡	84,747‡
Department of the Navy	81,854	87,365‡	99,015‡	96,113‡	95,345‡	102,343‡	108,693‡
Department of the Air Force	74,074	90,851‡	99,420‡	94,870‡	93,833‡	100,437‡	107,235‡
Defense Agencies/OSD/JCS	9,256	10,746	13,126	15,520	16,641	19,070	20,919
Defense-wide	16,761	524	970	1,759	1,352	1,342	1,696
Total—Direct Program (B/A)	**239,474**	**258,150**	**286,802**	**281,390**	**281,695**	**303,295**	**323,290**
Constant FY 1988 Dollars							
Department of the Army	68,293	79,046‡	82,446‡	78,911‡	78,037‡	80,102‡	81,851‡
Department of the Navy	95,341	99,137‡	108,774‡	103,105‡	99,598‡	102,343‡	105,070‡
Department of the Air Force	85,028	102,112‡	108,388‡	101,322‡	97,926‡	100,437‡	103,551‡
Defense Agencies/OSD/JCS	11,141	12,493	14,656	16,876	17,413	19,070	20,260
Defense-wide	19,868	596	1,068	1,880	1,399	1,342	1,640
Total—Direct Program (B/A)	**279,671**	**293,383**	**315,331**	**302,094**	**294,397**	**303,295**	**312,372**

*Numbers may not add to totals due to rounding. [B/A = budgetary authority.]

†Lower Budget Authority in the Military Personnel Accounts in FY 1986 reflects the congressional direction to finance $4.5 billion for the military pay raise and retirement accrual costs by transfers from prior year unobligated balances.

‡Includes Retired Pay accrual.

Source: Caspar W. Weinberger, Secretary of Defense, *Annual Report to the Congress, Fiscal Year 1988* (Washington, D.C.: U.S. Government Printing Office, January 1, 1987). p. 326.

Table B-3. Federal Budget Trends (dollars in millions)

Fiscal Year	Federal Outlays as a % of GNP	DoD Outlays as a % of Federal Outlays	DoD Outlays as a % of GNP	Non-DoD Outlays as a % of Federal Outlays	Non-DoD Outlays as a % of GNP	DoD Outlays as a % of Net Public Spending*
1950	16.0	27.5	4.4	72.5	11.6	18.5
1955	17.6	51.5	9.1	48.5	8.6	35.6
1960	18.2	45.0	8.2	55.0	10.0	30.3
1965	17.5	38.8	6.8	61.2	10.7	25.2
1970	19.8	39.4	7.8	60.6	12.0	25.5
1971	19.9	35.4	7.0	64.6	12.8	22.4
1972	20.0	32.6	6.5	67.4	13.5	20.6
1973	19.1	29.8	5.7	70.2	13.4	19.0
1974	19.0	28.8	5.5	71.2	13.5	18.3
1975	21.8	25.5	5.6	74.5	16.2	16.5
1976	21.9	23.6	5.2	76.4	16.7	15.4
1977	21.1	23.4	4.9	76.6	16.2	15.5
1978	21.1	22.5	4.7	77.5	16.4	15.2
1979	20.5	22.8	4.7	77.2	15.8	15.4
1980	22.2	22.5	5.0	77.5	17.2	15.3
1981	22.7	23.0	5.2	77.0	17.5	15.8
1982	23.7	24.5	5.8	75.5	17.9	16.7
1983	24.3	25.4	6.2	74.6	18.2	17.3
1984	23.1	25.9	6.0	74.1	17.1	17.5
1985	24.0	25.9	6.2	74.1	17.8	17.7
1986	23.8	26.8	6.4	73.2	17.4	18.1
1987	23.0	27.0	6.2	73.0	16.8	17.8
1988	21.7	28.2	6.1	71.8	15.5	18.1
1989	21.1	28.4	6.0	71.6	15.1	18.1

*Federal, State, and Local net spending excluding government enterprises (such as the postal service and public utilities) except for any support these activities receive from tax funds.

Source: Caspar W. Weinberger, Secretary of Defense, *Annual Report to the Congress, Fiscal Year 1988* (Washington, D.C.: U.S. Government Printing Office, January 1, 1987), p. 327.

Table B-4. Defense Shares of Economic Aggregates

| Fiscal Year | DoD as a Percentage of Public Employment | | DoD as a Percentage of National Labor Force | | National Income Accounts Percentage of Total Purchases | | |
	Federal	Federal State & Local	Direct Hire (DoD)	Including Industry	National Defense*	Total Federal	State & Local
1965	71.3	29.3	5.0	7.8	7.3	9.8	9.8
1966	73.0	30.6	5.6	9.0	7.5	10.0	10.0
1967	74.1	31.5	6.0	10.0	8.7	11.0	10.4
1968	74.0	31.3	6.1	10.0	9.0	11.4	10.8
1969	73.2	30.1	5.9	9.4	8.5	10.8	11.0
1970	72.3	27.7	5.3	8.1	7.9	10.1	11.4
1971	68.3	24.3	4.6	7.0	7.1	9.3	12.0
1972	66.0	21.5	4.0	6.2	6.6	9.0	12.0
1973	65.0	20.4	3.7	5.8	6.0	8.2	11.8
1974	63.8	19.4	3.5	5.5	5.6	7.7	12.0
1975	62.9	18.6	3.4	5.3	5.7	8.1	12.8
1976	62.5	18.1	3.3	5.0	5.4	7.8	12.7
1977	62.5	17.5	3.2	5.0	5.1	7.6	11.9
1978	61.9	17.0	3.1	4.8	4.9	7.3	11.8
1979	61.1	16.5	2.9	4.7	4.8	7.1	11.5
1980	61.3	16.5	2.8	4.7	5.1	7.5	11.8
1981	62.4	17.1	2.8	4.7	5.4	7.8	11.4
1982	63.2	17.4	2.8	4.9	6.0	8.4	11.5
1983	63.5	17.6	2.9	5.1	6.3	8.7	11.6
1984	63.5	17.6	2.8	5.3	6.2	8.1	11.2
1985	63.3	17.5	2.9	5.5	6.4	8.7	11.5
1986	62.9	17.2	2.8	5.5	6.6	8.9	11.7
1987	63.1	17.2	2.8	5.5	6.6	9.0	11.8

*Includes Department of Defense—military, atomic energy defense activities, and other defense-related activities, such as emergency management and maintenance of strategic stockpiles and the Selective Service System.

Source: Caspar W. Weinberger, Secretary of Defense, *Annual Report to the Congress, Fiscal Year 1988* (Washington, D.C.: U.S. Government Printing Office, January 1, 1987), p. 327.

Notes

1. INTRODUCTION

[1] Alexander Hamilton, "No. 23," *The Federalist Papers* (New York: The American Library, 1961), pp. 153–154.

2. THE WEAPONS ACQUISITION CYCLE

[1] Alexander Kossiakoff, "Conception of New Defense Systems and the Role of Government R&D Centers," in Franklin A. Long and Judith Reppy, eds., *The Genesis of New Weapons: Decision Making for Military R&D* (New York: Pergamon Press, 1980), p. 63.

[2] Gordon Adams, *The Iron Triangle: The Politics of Defense Contracting* (New York: Council on Economic Priorities, 1981), p. 96.

[3] Quoted in ibid.

[4] Quoted in ibid., p. 98.

[5] Ibid., p. 101.

[6] Sheila Tobias, Peter Goudinoff, Stefan Leader, and Shelah Leader, *What Kinds of Guns Are They Buying for Your Butter? A Beginner's Guide to Defense, Weaponry, and Military Spending* (New York: William Morrow, 1982), p. 247.

[7] Reported in James Fallows, *National Defense* (New York: Random House, 1981), p. 65.

[8] Quoted in ibid., p. 66.

[9] Kossiakoff, "Conception of New Defense Systems," p. 69.

[10] A simplified but useful description of the different stages of the weapons-acquisition process is to be found in Mark Rovner, *Defense Dollars and Sense: A Common Cause Guide to the Defense Budget Process* (Washington, D.C.: Common Cause, 1983), pp. 22–23.

[11] Harold Brown, *Thinking About National Security: Defense and Foreign Policy in a Dangerous World* (Boulder, Colo.: Westview Press, 1983), p. 242.

[12] Kossiakoff, "Conception of New Defense Systems," p. 80.

[13] U.S. Department of Defense, *The Defense Acquisition Board,* Directive No. 5000.49, September 1, 1987, pp. 2–4. The program procedures are explained in U.S. Department of Defense, *Defense Acquisition Program Procedures,* Directive No. 5000.2, September 1, 1987.

[14] Thomas McNaugher, "Weapons Procurement: The Futility of Reform," *International Security,* Vol. 12, No. 2 (Fall 1987), p. 89.

[15] Ibid., p. 91.

[16] Under new acquisition guidelines the services can sometimes move to the next stage without necessarily obtaining full DAB approval.

[17] Tobias et al., *What Kinds of Guns Are They Buying for Your Butter?,* p. 279.

[18] The Boston Study Group, *Winding Down: The Price of Defense* (San Francisco: W. H. Freeman, 1982), p. 234.

[19] Fallows, *National Defense,* p. 105.

[20] McNaugher, "Weapons Procurement," pp. 92–93.

[21] For a more detailed discussion, see General Dynamics Corporation, *Fiscal Life Cycles of Defense Systems* (Pomona, Cal.: General Dynamics Corporation, 1983).

[22] This problem is discussed in Gerard Smith, *Doubletalk: The Story of SALT I* (Lanham, Md.: University Press of America, 1985).

[23] Richard A. Stubbing, *The Defense Game* (New York: Harper and Row, 1986), p.6.

[24] For a provocative and timely discussion of this problem, see William E. Burrows, *Deep Black: Space Espionage and National Security* (New York: Random House, 1987).

[25] For further discussion see Stubbing, *The Defense Game*, pp. 3–28; and Jeffrey T. Richelson, *The U.S. Intelligence Community* (Cambridge, Mass.: Ballinger, 1985). A comprehensive history of the intelligence community is also to be found in Tyrus G. Fain, ed., *The Intelligence Community: History, Organization, and Issues* (New York: R. R. Bowker, 1977).

[26] In addition, the OJCS publishes a Joint Strategic Capabilities Plan every two years on forces, logistics, and intelligence for the commanders of the unified and specified commands. The Joint Long-Range Strategic Appraisal, which is published every five years, is used to provide a general framework for outlining broad force structuring implications and to assess military policies, plans, and programs having mid- to long-term implications.

[27] President's Blue Ribbon Commission on Defense Management, *An Interim Report to the President,* Washington, D.C., February 28, 1986, p. 5.

[28] A useful guide to the Packard proposals and list of those which have been implemented is found in the CSIS Defense Acquisition Study, *U.S. Defense Acquisition: A Process in Trouble* (Washington, D.C.: The Center for Strategic and International Studies, Georgetown University, March 1987), pp. 75–78.

[29] "Defense Acquisition Improvement Act of 1986," *Laws of the 99th Congress-Second Session, 1986,* Vol. 3 (St. Paul, Minn.: West Publishing Co., 1986), pp. 100 STAT.3910–3917); and *Congressional Quarterly Almanac* (1986) (Washington, D.C.: U.S. Government Printing Office, 1987), p. 475.

[30] The Defense Acquisition Board was initially named the Joint Requirements and Management Board.

[31] Arnold F. Kirk, "Under Secretary of Defense Acquisition," *National Defense,* Vol. 71, No. 424 (January 1987), p. 33.

3. THE PENTAGON AND THE DEFENSE BUDGET

[1] One popular study, for example, notes that "politics affects defense procurement in several ways. Bureaucratic politics, in the form of interservice rivalry, is one. The Army, Navy, and Air Force compete with one another for resources and tend to view any weapon that serves their own particular missions as 'successful.'" It goes on to point out that "[t]here has been a great deal of competition over 'roles and missions,' and one reason for this is that with the enlargement of a military responsibility (that is, a new mission) comes the opportunity to purchase new weapons to carry out that task." See Sheila Tobias, Peter Goudinoff, Stefan Leader, and Shelah Leader, *What Kinds of Guns Are They Buying for Your Butter? A Beginner's Guide to Defense, Weaponry, and Military Spending* (New York: William Morrow, 1982), p. 243. Another study notes that weapons are usually selected by individual services and that these forces are designed to meet the special organizational missions and priorities of each service. "Thus, the armed services design the structure of their forces as if they intended to fight *independent* land, sea, air, and amphibious wars." See Barry M. Blechman and William J. Lynn, eds., *Toward a More Effective Defense: Report of the Defense Reorganization Project* (Cambridge, Mass.: Ballinger, 1985), p. 91.

[2] One might well ask whose interests are reflected in the final outcome of collective decisions—the majority, the minority, or a single individual? The Nobel Prize–winning economist Kenneth Arrow has argued that social choices often represent the interests of

no one or of anyone. See Kenneth Arrow, *Social Choice and Individual Values* (New York: John Wiley, 1951).

[3] See Alain C. Enthoven and K. Wayne Smith, *How Much Is Enough? Shaping the Defense Program, 1961–1969* (New York: Harper and Row, 1972), pp. 71–72.

[4] Quoted in ibid., p. 35.

[5] Ibid., pp. 48–72.

[6] Laurence E. Lynn, Jr. and Richard I. Smith, "Can the Secretary of Defense Make a Difference?," *International Security,* Vol. 7, No. 1 (Summer 1982), pp. 52–53.

[7] The following discussion is drawn from Mark Rovner, *Defense Dollars and Sense: A Common Cause Guide to the Defense Budget Process* (Washington, D.C.: Common Cause, 1983), pp. 18–26.

[8] The DRB, the key organizational player in the defense budgetary process, was created in 1979 under the Carter administration with a membership of six top DoD officials. Under the Reagan administration the membership list was expanded to seventeen and includes the Chairman of the JCS; the Deputy Secretary of Defense; the various Under Secretaries of Defense; the Comptroller and other Assistant Secretaries of Defense; the Director of Program Analysis and Evaluation; the Director of the Defense Advanced Research Agency; the different service Secretaries; and the Associate Director for National Security Affairs of the Office of Management and Budget. See John M. Collins, *U.S. Defense Planning: A Critique* (Boulder, Colo.: Westview Press, 1982), pp. 42–47.

[9] Richard A. Stubbing, *The Defense Game* (New York: Harper and Row, 1986), p. 71.

[10] Arnold Kanter, *Defense Politics: A Budgetary Perspective* (Chicago: The University of Chicago Press, 1979), pp. 25–28.

[11] Quoted in Samuel P. Huntington, *The Common Defense: Strategic Programs in National Politics* (New York: Columbia University Press, 1961), p. 162.

[12] Rovner, *Defense Dollars and Sense,* p. 22.

[13] Committee on Armed Services, House of Representatives, *Defense Procurement Policies and Procedures: Cost Management and Control: Hearing Before the Special Panel on Defense Procurement Procedures,* H.A.S.C. No. 97-311, 97th Congress, 1st Session (Washington, D.C.: U.S. Government Printing Office, 1981), pp. 69–70.

[14] See Stephen Kirby and Andrew Cox, "Defense Budgeting and Accountability: Britain and the United States," *Review of International Studies,* Vol. 9, No. 3 (1983), p. 176.

[15] Programs are approved at three funding levels: basic, minimum, and enhanced. Cost data and zero based budgeting techniques are used to develop a priority list of programs at different budgetary levels; that is, programs are ranked in accordance with their contribution to defense objectives. Programs ranked below a particular level are eventually dropped before the budget is submitted by the President to Congress. See Lawrence J. Korb, "The Defense Budgetary Process: The Process and Problems of Linking Policy and Force Structure through the Defense Budget Process," *Policy Studies Journal,* Vol. 8, No. 1 (1979), pp. 92–98.

[16] Stubbing, *The Defense Game,* p. 77.

[17] Ibid., pp. 78–79.

[18] See Robert J. Art, *The TFX Decision: McNamara and the Military* (Boston: Little, Brown, 1968).

[19] This is the subject of Robert J. Coulam's *Illusions of Choice: The F-111 and the Problems of Weapons Acquisition Reform* (Princeton: Princeton University Press, 1977).

[20] Tobias et al., *What Kinds of Guns Are They Buying for Your Butter?,* p. 270.

[21] The President's role in the actual preparation of the budget tends to be quite modest and has usually been limited to the establishment of aggregate budget limits and priorities and occasionally supervision of pet agencies or programs. See Kim Quaile Hill and John Patrick Plumlee, "Presidential Success in Budgetary Policymaking: A Longitudinal Analysis," *Presidential Studies Quarterly,* Vol. 12, No. 2 (Spring 1982), pp. 174–185.

[22] Rovner, *Defense Dollars and Sense,* p. 25.

[23] David A. Stockman, *The Triumph of Politics: The Inside Story of the Reagan Revolution* (New York: Avon Books, 1987), p. 117.

[24] Ibid., pp. 302–303. Weinberger, however, resisted these cuts and the resulting compromise growth figure was above the SGA level.

[25] Robert Komer, "Strategymaking in the Pentagon," in Robert J. Art, Vincent Davis, and

Samuel P. Huntington, eds., *Reorganizing America's Defense: Leadership in War and Peace* (Washington, D.C.: Pergamon Brassey's, 1985), pp. 218–219.

[26] Needless to say, this is not the only aspect of the defense budget that has been subject to rising costs in recent years. Military and civilian salaries and a high ratio of support to combat manpower are probably more responsible for the sharp rise in the price of defense. See Barry M. Blechman and Edward R. Fried, "Controlling the Defense Budget," *Foreign Affairs*, Vol. 54, No. 2 (January 1976), pp. 233–249.

[27] General Accounting Office, *DoD's Defense Acquisition Program: A Status Report*, NSIAD-86-148 (July 1986), p. 13; and Congressional Budget Office, *Effects of Weapons Procurement Stretch-Outs on Costs and Schedules* (Washington, D.C.: Congressional Budget Office, November 1987), pp. 2–3.

[28] General Accounting Office, *The Defense Budget: A Look at Budgetary Resources, Accomplishments, and Problems*, GAO / PLRD-83-62 (Washington, D.C.: U.S. General Accounting Office, April 27, 1983), pp. ii–v.

[29] United States Senate Committee on Armed Services, *Hearing before the Subcommittee on Defense Acquisition Policy*, 99th Congress, 1st Session, S. Hrg. 99–112, Pt. 4, February 20, 1985 (Washington, D.C.: U.S. Government Printing Office, 1985), p. 10.

[30] General Accounting Office, *Defense Budget Increases: How Well Are They Planned and Spent?* PLRD-82-62 (Washington, D.C.: U.S. General Accounting Office, April 13, 1982), pp. 57–60.

[31] Jacques S. Gansler, "Report of the Working Group on Weapons Acquisition," in Barry M. Blechman and William J. Lynn, eds., *Toward a More Effective Defense: Report of the Defense Reorganization Project* (Cambridge, Mass.: Ballinger, 1985), p. 89. See also Jacques S. Gansler, *The Defense Industry* (Cambridge, Mass.: M.I.T. Press, 1980).

4. CONGRESS AND THE DEFENSE BUDGET

[1] Elizabeth Drew, "A Political Journal," *The New Yorker*, Vol. 159, No. 18 (June 26, 1983), p. 39.

[2] David Mayhew, for instance, argues that congressmen are "single-minded seekers of re-election." Their position on issues is determined by their constituents' interests and a desire to claim benefits for them. See David Mayhew, *Congress: The Electoral Connection* (New Haven: Yale University Press, 1974). This view is shared by Francis Orlando Wilcox, *Congress, the Executive, and Foreign Policy* (New York: Harper and Row, 1971).

[3] This has led many to stress the role of bargaining and to emphasize the role of political institutions as aggregators and adjusters of group interests. The outcome of this bargaining process is one of "partisan mutual adjustment" whereby the public interest is defined in terms of the aggregation or sum of particular interests [see Arthus Maas, *Congress and the Common Good* (New York: Basic Books, 1983), pp. 3–4]. Others argue that because Congress deals with literally hundreds of complex issues, many of which are beyond the scope or competence of the individual legislator, congressional committees like Ways and Means, Appropriations, Foreign Affairs, etc., play a decisive role in shaping and defining the legislative agenda [see Richard F. Fenno, Jr., *Congressmen in Committees* (Boston: Little Brown, 1973)]. Congressmen will often take their cues on important voting decisions from their more informed colleagues and the reports of the specialized committees. But the question of "influence" is difficult to measure: congressmen are likely to take their cues from a variety of different sources, such as their party, constituents, and particular interest groups. What determines how a congressman will vote on any particular issue is fraught with imprecision [see Robert A. Pastor, *Congress and the Politics of U.S. Foreign Economic Policy 1929–1976* (Berkeley: University of California Press, 1980), pp. 38–41; and Aage R. Clausen, *How Congressmen Decide: A Policy Focus* (New York: St. Martin's Press, 1973)].

[4] This is the view advanced by Maas in *Congress and the Common Good*.

[5] Les Aspin, "Congress, the Defense Budget, and Arms Control Talks," *Atlantic Community Quarterly*, Vol. 22, No. 4 (Winter 1984 / 85), p. 317.

[6] Robert Axelrod, *The Evolution of Cooperation* (New York: Basic Books, 1984), p. 18. Nelson Polsby has also produced data which show that in the House "the overall stability of membership, as measured by the mean terms of members (total number of terms served

divided by total number of Representatives), has been on the rise" since the eighteenth century. See Nelson W. Polsby, "The Institutionalization of the U.S. House of Representatives," *American Political Science Review,* Vol. 62 (1968), p. 146. Samuel Patterson argues that "incumbent candidates for both House and Senate seats have a marked tendency to be reelected," but that the "incumbency effect" is more pronounced in the House than it is in the Senate, where incumbents have not done quite so well in recent elections. See Samuel C. Patterson, "The Semi-Sovereign Congress," in Anthony King, ed., *The New American Political System* (Washington, D.C.: American Enterprise Institute, 1978), pp. 141–142.

[7] Richard A. Stubbing, *The Defense Game* (New York: Harper and Row, 1986), p. 39.

[8] Gregg Easterbrook, "What's Wrong With Congress?," *The Atlantic,* Vol. 254, No. 6 (December 1984), pp. 58–59.

[9] Quoted in ibid., p. 59.

[10] Quoted in ibid., p. 60.

[11] Mark Rovner, *Defense Dollars and Sense: A Common Cause Guide to the Defense Budget Process* (Washington, D.C.: Common Cause, 1983), p. 27.

[12] Ibid.

[13] Maas, *Congress and the Common Good,* p. 122.

[14] Stephen Kirby and Andrew Cox, "Defense Budgeting and Accountability: Britain and the United States," *Review of International Studies,* Vol. 9, No. 3 (1983), p. 183.

[15] Michael Ganley, "House and Senate Democrats Could End Up Far Apart on Defense Issues," *Armed Forces Journal International,* Vol. 124, No. 7 (February 1987), pp. 8–12.

[16] James M. Lindsay, "Congress and Defense Policy: 1961 to 1986," *Armed Forces and Society,* Vol. 13, No. 3 (Spring 1987), p. 373.

[17] Robert J. Art, "Congress and the Defense Budget: Enhancing Policy Oversight," *Political Science Quarterly,* Vol. 100, No. 2 (Summer 1985), pp. 227–248. Also published in Robert J. Art, Vincent Davis, and Samuel P. Huntington, *Reorganizing America's Defense: Leadership in War and Peace* (Washington, D.C.: Pergamon Brassey's, 1985), pp. 405–428.

[18] Art, "Congress and the Defense Budget," p. 232.

[19] Quoted in Captain Brent Baker, "National Defense and the Congressional Role," *Naval War College Review,* Vol. 35, No. 4 (July–August 1982), p. 9.

[20] See Michael J. Malbin, *Unelected Representatives: Congressional Staffs and the Future of Representative Government* (New York: Basic Books, 1980).

[21] The CSIS Acquisition Study, *U.S. Defense Acquisition: A Process in Trouble* (Washington, D.C.: The Center for Strategic and International Studies, Georgetown University, March 1987), p. 18.

[22] "National Defense and the Congressional Role," p. 7. For an in-depth treatment of how Congress deals with entitlement programs see Kent Weaver, *Automatic Government* (Washington, D.C.: The Brookings Institution, 1988).

[23] Easterbrook, "What's Wrong with Congress?," p. 61.

[24] Quoted in John F. Morton, "Congress Is Numb to the Numbers," *Armed Forces Journal International,* Vol. 125, No. 5 (December 1987), p. 12.

[25] Quoted in Michael Ganley, "DoD Suffers Sharpest Budget Cuts Ever as Congress Heads Home for Elections," *Armed Forces Journal International,* Vol. 124, No. 4 (November 1986), p. 18.

[26] Rovner, *Defense Dollars and Sense,* p. 30.

[27] Maas, *Congress and the Common Good,* p. 131.

[28] Ibid., p. 132.

[29] Robert L. Bledsoe and Roger Handberg, "Changing Times: Congress and Defense," *Armed Forces and Society,* Vol. 6, No.3 (Spring 1980), pp. 415–429.

[30] Maas, *Congress and the Common Good,* p. 131. Maas also points out that although House committees have been increasingly subject to floor challenges in recent years with the democratization of Congress, this is not the case with the House Appropriations Committee, which has successfully maintained its strong position.

[31] Stubbing, *The Defense Game,* pp. 96–97.

[32] Carl J. Friedrich, *Constitutional Government and Democracy* (Boston: Little, Brown, 1941), pp. 589–591, and quoted in Pastor, *Congress and the Politics of U.S. Foreign Economic Policy,* p. 52.

[33] Pastor, *Congress and the Politics of U.S. Foreign Economic Policy,* p. 61.

[34] Arnold Kanter, "Congress and the Defense Budget: 1960–1970," *American Political Science Review,* Vol. 66, No. 1 (1972), pp. 129–143.

[35] Bledsoe and Handberg, "Changing Times," pp. 423–425.

[36] The following discussion is drawn from Joshua M. Epstein's extremely useful and incisive study *The 1987 Defense Budget* (Washington, D.C.: The Brookings Institution, 1986), pp. 4–9.

[37] Ibid., p. 5. But as Epstein correctly points out, the slow-money accounts must also be reduced today if the deficit is to be reduced tomorrow. If they are not, and the Gramm-Rudman-Hollings trigger is avoided, the fast-money accounts will be cut even more in the future.

[38] Ibid., p. 7.

[39] Congressional Budget Office, *Reducing the Deficit: Spending and Revenue Options: A Report to the Senate and House Committees of the Budget,* Part II (Washington, D.C.: U.S. Government Printing Office, January 1987), pp. 13–62. Also see Michael Ganley, "Defense Buildup Will Slow, but Outlays Will Increase 38% over Next Five Years," *Armed Forces Journal International,* Vol. 124, No. 8 (March 1987), pp. 8, 10.

[40] Quoted in John F. Morton, "The DoD Budget: Numbers Uncertain, Further Cuts Expected," *Armed Forces Journal International,* Vol. 125, No. 3 (October 1987), p. 18.

[41] L. Edgar Prina, "Why Defense Costs So Much," *Policy Review,* No. 28 (Spring 1984), p. 83.

[42] Les Aspin, "The Defense Budget and Foreign Policy: The Role of Congress," *Daedulus,* Vol. 104, No. 3 (1975), p. 156.

[43] Gordon Adams, *The B-1 Bomber: An Analysis of Its Strategic Utility, Cost, Constituency, and Economic Impact* (New York: Council on Economic Priorities, 1976), p. 15.

[44] Aspin, "The Defense Budget and Foreign Policy," p. 157.

[45] Bledsoe and Handberg, "Changing Times," p. 417.

[46] Quoted in Committee on Armed Services, United States Senate, *Hearing Before the Subcommittee on Defense Acquisition Policy, Part 3* (S. Hrg. 99–112), 99th Congress, January 30, 1985, p. 12.

[47] CSIS, *U.S. Defense Acquisition,* p. 57.

[48] Pat Towell, "Senate Record of Its Homework on Defense Issues Has Become Visible," *Armed Forces Journal International,* Vol. 125, No. 3, (October 1987), p. 14.

[49] Quoted in Committee on Armed Services, United States Senate, *Defense Procurement Process: Hearing Before the Task Force on Selected Defense Procurement Matters, Part II* (S. Hrg. 98-1256), 98th Congress, September 20, 1984, p. 158.

[50] CSIS, *U.S. Defense Acquisition,* p. 57. The DoD Defense Reorganization Bill would eliminate about two-thirds of the more than 400 defense reports now required by Congress from the President and DoD. The Bill, however, lists 149 separate current reporting requirements that have not been eliminated, and Congress has not eliminated any reports it might require "to be submitted on time." In FY 1987 authorization and appropriation bills Congress requested an additional 90 reports under this new authority. See Michael Ganley, "Is Congress Adding to, Not Reducing, the Number of DoD Reports It Requires Annually?," *Armed Forces Journal International,* Vol. 124, No. 6 (January 1987), p. 14.

[51] By contrast, the Senate changed 450 of the 731 line items in the Pentagon's FY 1984 request. The Senate also changed 710 of the 1,129 items in the DoD appropriations request. See Michael Ganley, "Near Record Number of Amendments and Floor Time Spent on FY88 DoD Bill," *Armed Forces Journal International,* Vol. 124, No. 12 (July 1987), p. 8.

[52] Quoted in Committee on Armed Services, *Defense Procurement Process,* p. 158.

[53] Robert J. Art, "Congress and the Defense Budget: New Procedures and Old Realities," in Barry M. Blechman and William J. Lynn, eds., *Toward a More Effective Defense: Report of the Defense Organization Project* (Cambridge, Mass.: Ballinger, 1985), p. 158.

[54] Committee on Armed Services, United States Senate, "Statement of General Lawrence A. Skantze, Commander, Air Force Systems Command," *Defense Procurement Process: Hearing before the Task Force on Selected Defense Procurement Matters, Part I,* S. Hrg. 98-1256, 98th Congress, 2nd Session, September 13, 1984 (Washington, D.C.: U.S. Government Printing Office, 1985), pp. 6–9.

[55] These are discussed in Art, "Congress and the Defense Budget," and also by John J. Hamre, "Potential New Patterns of Congressional Review of Defense Budget Authority," in

Blechman and Lynn, eds., *Toward a More Effective Defense,* pp. 169–180.

[56] John H. Cushman, Jr., "Congress Presses for 2-Year Military Budgets," *New York Times,* April 12, 1987.

[57] Michael Ganley, "First Ever Two-Year Pentagon Budgets for Some Programs Likely This Year," *Armed Forces Journal International,* Vol. 124, No. 9 (April 1987), p. 12.

[58] Art, "Congress and the Defense Budget," pp. 161–162.

[59] Benjamin F. Schemmer, "Pentagon Spending Will Grow 21% Faster than Its New Two-Year Budget Suggests," *Armed Forces Journal International,* Vol. 124, No. 10 (February 1987), pp. 15–19.

[60] Paul Mann, "U.S. Defense Absorbs Third Annual Decline, But No Major Weapon Cancellations Result," *Aviation Week and Space Technology,* January 4, 1988, pp. 28–29; and John F. Morton, "Outlay Concerns in Congress: Making 'Wacky,'" *Armed Forces Journal International,* Vol. 125, No. 6 (January 1988), pp. 10, 12.

5. THE TRIDENT SUBMARINE AND MISSILE

[1] For a good overview of the Polaris / Poseidon program see R. A. Furman, "The Fleet Ballistic Missile System: Polaris to Trident," *Journal of Spacecraft,* Vol. 15, No. 5 (September / October 1978), pp. 265–286.

[2] D. Douglas Dalgleish and Larry Schweikart, *Trident* (Carbondale and Edwardsville, Ill.: Southern Illinois University Press, 1984), pp. 41–120.

[3] Norman Polmar and Thomas B. Allen, *Rickover* (New York: Simon and Schuster, 1982), p. 565.

[4] Ibid., p. 566.

[5] Quoted in ibid., p. 567.

[6] Quoted in Dalgleish and Schweikart, *Trident,* p. 43.

[7] However, there is still some controversy whether Rickover determined the size of the submarine or not. According to Admiral Isaac Kidd, Jr., former Chief of Navy Matériel, "the missile sized the submarine." Early designs of what later became the Trident II or D-5 missile put displacement at 60 tons, 42 feet long, 7 feet in diameter. However, Rickover also felt that a larger reactor would make the submarine quieter by reducing hull vibrations and strain on the engine. He told the Joint Committee that the plant necessary for Trident had "to be very quiet so as to make the ship difficult to detect." But "[a]lmost equally important to quietness, in my opinion, will be a high speed capability" in order to break "contact with the enemy if the ship is detected and . . . also insure that the ship has adequate power for control and recovery from casualties." These considerations were not part of the STRAT-X directives and major design issues came later. See Polmar and Allen, *Rickover,* p. 568.

[8] Barry E. Carter and John D. Steinbruner, "Trident," in *Commission on the Organization of Government for the Conduct of Foreign Policy* (Murphy Commission), Vol. 4, Appendix K (Washington, D.C.: U.S. Government Printing Office, June 1975), pp. 177–178.

[9] Ibid., p. 178.

[10] Dalgleish and Schweikart, *Trident,* p. 46.

[11] Ibid., p. 63.

[12] William Beecher, "Laird Says Soviet Threat Speeds Up," The *New York Times,* January 8, 1970, pp. A1, A15.

[13] Polmar and Allen, *Rickover,* p. 569.

[14] Dalgleish and Schweikart, *Trident,* p. 46.

[15] Ibid., p. 47.

[16] Carter and Steinbruner, "Trident," p. 178.

[17] The deadlock on the submarine issue persisted right until the end of the talks (see Hedrick Smith, "Deadlock on Submarines Said to Persist in Vienna," The *New York Times,* January 12, 1972, pp. A1, A13).

[18] Dalgleish and Schweikart, *Trident,* p. 50; see also William Beecher, "$83-Billion Request for Defense Accelerates New Upward Trend," The *New York Times,* January 25, 1972, p. A16.

[19] Dalgleish and Schweikart, *Trident,* p. 51.

[20] Ibid.

[21] Drew Middleton, "Plan for Undersea Missile System Opposed," The *New York Times,* March 4, 1972, p. A11.

[22] Carter and Steinbruner, "Trident," p. 176. See also George W. Rathjens and Jack P. Ruina, "Trident," in K. Tsipis, A. H. Cahn, and B. Feld, eds., *The Future of the Sea-Based Deterrent* (Cambridge, Mass.: M.I.T. Press, 1974).

[23] Carter and Steinbruner, "Trident," p. 176.

[24] Dalgleish and Schweikart, *Trident,* p. 50.

[25] Ibid., p. 50.

[26] Ibid. See also Middleton, "Plan for Undersea Missile System Opposed."

[27] Herbert Scoville, Jr., "Missile Submarine and National Security," *Scientific American,* Vol. 226, No. 6 (June 1972), p. 27. See also "Navy R&D: Will Congress Have the Nerve to Spear Trident?," *Science,* Vol. 180, No. 4083 (April 20, 1973), pp. 281–284.

[28] Dalgleish and Schweikart, *Trident,* p. 55.

[29] John Finney, "Support of Pacts Is Linked by Laird to New Arms Fund," The *New York Times,* June 7, 1972, pp. A1, A11. See also United States Senate, Committee on Armed Services, *Hearings on the Military Implications of the Treaty on the Limitation of ABM Systems and the Interim Agreement on Limitation of Offensive Arms,* 92nd Congress, 2nd Session (Washington, D.C.: U.S. Government Printing Office, June and July 1972), pp. 333, 335, 367–368, 468–469; and United States Senate, Committee on Foreign Relations, *Hearings on the Strategic Arms Limitation Agreements,* 92nd Congress, 2nd Session (Washington, D.C.: U.S. Government Printing Office, June and July 1972), pp. 256–271.

[30] Dalgleish and Schweikart, *Trident,* p. 54.

[31] Ibid., p. 56.

[32] Bernard Gwertzman, "Senators Indicate Support at Arms Control Accords Hearing," The *New York Times,* June 20, 1972, p. A3.

[33] Bernard Gwertzman, "Fulbright and Laird Clash at Hearing on Arms Limitation Accords," The *New York Times,* June 22, 1972, p. A10.

[34] Carter and Steinbruner, "Trident," p. 179.

[35] John Finney, "Senate Endorses Rise in Spending for Nuclear Sub," The *New York Times,* July 28, 1972, pp. A1, A13.

[36] "Defense Cost Growth," The *New York Times,* July 27, 1972, p. A30.

[37] Dalgleish and Schweikart, *Trident,* p. 58.

[38] Ibid., p. 59.

[39] Ibid., p. 60.

[40] John Finney, "Trident Fund Cut by Senate Panel," The *New York Times,* August 2, 1973, p. A8. This followed an earlier recommendation by the Committee's subcommittee on research and development to cut funds from the program. See John W. Finney, "Senate Unit Cuts Trident Program," The *New York Times,* July 11, 1973, pp. A1, A15; "Slowing the Trident," The *New York Times,* July 19, 1973, p. A34; and "Senate Unit Cuts Missile Projects Sought by Pentagon," The *New York Times,* July 20, 1973, p. A7.

[41] John W. Finney, "Goldwater Shift May Aid Trident," The *New York Times,* August 3, 1973, p. A59; "Senators Restore Funds for Trident," The *New York Times,* August 4, 1973, p. A55; and "Close, But Butter Still Runs Second to Guns," The *New York Times,* August 5, 1973, p. IV3.

[42] Dalgleish and Schweikart, *Trident,* pp. 63–64.

[43] Ibid., p. 65.

[44] Quoted in Polmar and Allen, *Rickover,* p. 570.

[45] Ibid., p. 570.

[46] Richard Witkin, "Navy Cost Expert Scores Trident Submarine Contract; Aspin Seeks Inquiry," The *New York Times,* August 15, 1974, p. A21.

[47] Dalgleish and Schweikart, *Trident,* p. 84.

[48] "Aspin Charges Navy Hides Trident Costs," The *New York Times,* April 22, 1974, p. 70.

[49] Dalgleish and Schweikart, *Trident,* p. 85.

[50] Polmar and Allen, *Rickover,* p. 572.

[51] Ibid., p. 573.

[52] Matthew L. Wald, "Navy, Electric Boat Enjoy a Renewed Partnership," The *New York Times,* November 15, 1981, p. VIII2.

[53] Polmar and Allen, *Rickover,* p. 573.

[54] John W. Finney, "Pentagon Chief Sees Pact Leading to Arms Build-Up," The *New York Times,* December 7, 1974, pp. A1, A13.

[55] John W. Finney, "Pentagon Seeking Funds for More Deadly Trident," The *New York Times,* February 7, 1975, p. A29.

[56] Dalgleish and Schweikart, *Trident,* p. 90.

[57] Ibid., p. 93. See also John W. Finney, "House Approves a $2 Billion Rise in Arms Spending," The *New York Times,* April 10, 1976, pp. A1, A13.

[58] "Trident Submarine Is Opposed by Udall," The *New York Times,* April 19, 1976, p. A30.

[59] Dalgleish and Schweikart, *Trident,* p. 92.

[60] Drew Middleton, "Navy Lays Keel for Trident Sub," The *New York Times,* April 11, 1976, p. A30.

[61] Dalgleish and Schweikart, *Trident,* p. 98.

[62] Polmar and Allen, *Rickover,* p. 578.

[63] Dalgleish and Schweikart, *Trident,* p. 100.

[64] Ibid., p. 102.

[65] "Senate Unit Seeks Submarine Cheaper than Trident," The *New York Times,* June 14, 1978, p. A7.

[66] Quoted in Dalgleish and Schweikart, *Trident,* p. 104.

[67] U.S. General Accounting Office, *Report to the Secretary of Defense: Trident II System: Status and Reporting,* GAO / NSIAD-84-86, May 15, 1984, pp. 22–24.

[68] Richard Burt, "Sea-and-Land Missile Sought by Pentagon," The *New York Times,* April 24, 1978, p. A11.

[69] Dalgleish and Schweikart, *Trident,* p. 105.

[70] These had to do with the missile's range and payload characteristics. See "Trident in Trouble: New Missile May Resemble Poseidon, After All," *Science,* Vol. 191, No. 4222 (January 9, 1976), pp. 50–51.

[71] Polmar and Allen, *Rickover,* p. 574.

[72] Dalgleish and Schweikart, *Trident,* p. 106.

[73] Polmar and Allen, *Rickover,* p. 577.

[74] Dalgleish and Schweikart, *Trident,* p. 108. There were also reports from the navy that the Trident missile programs were proceeding successfully. See "Trident Missile Capabilities Advance," *Aviation Week and Space Technology,* June 16, 1980, pp. 91–100.

[75] Many of these problems were resolved by the time the first Trident was launched. See Matthew L. Wald, "Calmer Waters for Electric Boat," The *New York Times,* April 14, 1979, pp. D1, D5.

[76] Richard Burt, "Pentagon Reports Serious Difficulties in Trident Program," The *New York Times,* November 25, 1980, pp. A1, A7.

[77] Dalgleish and Schweikart, *Trident,* p. 109.

[78] Ibid., p. 114.

[79] Ibid., p. 117.

[80] Richard Halloran, "Reagan Expanding Trident Program," The *New York Times,* February 6, 1983, p. A17.

[81] Report by the Comptroller General to the Congress of the United States, *Alternatives to Consider in Planning Integrated Logistics Support for the Trident Submarine,* LCD-79-415, September 28, 1979.

[82] Thomas Downey, "Against Trident II," The *New York Times,* February 11, 1982, p. A35.

[83] Michael F. Altfeld and Stephen J. Cimbala, "Trident II for Prompt Counterforce?: A Critical Assessment," *Defense Analysis,* Vol. 3, No. 4 (December 1987), pp. 349–359.

[84] Quoted in Philip M. Boffey, "Trident's Technology May Make It a Potent Rival to Land-Based Missiles," The *New York Times,* July 13, 1982, pp. C1, C3.

[85] Quoted in Wayne Biddle, "New Trident Missile Bears a Payload of Apprehension," The *New York Times,* September 9, 1984, p. IV3. See also "An Alternative to the MX,"

Science, Vol. 216, No. 21 (May 1982), pp. 828–832.

[86] Congressional Budget Office, *Trident II Missiles: Capability, Costs, and Alternatives* (Washington, D.C.: U.S. Government Printing Office, July 1986), p. 25. It should also be noted that the Reagan administration decided not to deploy a controversial twelve-warhead version of the Trident II missile, relying instead on an eight-warhead version in a new warhead-counting arrangement developed at the Washington 1987 summit meeting [see Matthew Bunn, "Deployment of 12-Warhead Trident Cancelled," *Arms Control Today,* Vol. 18, No. 1 (January / February 1988), p. 25].

[87] William M. Arkin, "Sleight of Hand with Trident II," *Bulletin of the Atomic Scientists,* Vol. 40, No. 10 (December 1984), p. 5.

6. MX AND MIDGETMAN

[1] "First 10 MX Missiles Placed on Alert," The *New York Times,* December 24, 1986, p. D16.

[2] Lauren H. Holland and Robert A. Hoover, *The MX Decision: A New Direction in U.S. Weapons Procurement Policy?* (Boulder, Colo.: Westview Press, 1985), p. 243. Useful chronologies of the MX story are also found in John Edwards, *Superweapon: The Making of MX* (New York: W.W. Norton, 1982); and Paul Stockton, "Arms Development and Arms Control: The Strange Case of the MX Missile," in Allan P. Sindler, ed., *American Politics and Public Policy* (Washington, D.C.: Congressional Quarterly Press, 1982), pp. 225–253.

[3] Holland and Hoover, *The MX Decision,* p. 124.

[4] Paul Stockton quoted in ibid., p. 125.

[5] Ibid., p. 125.

[6] Ibid., p. 126.

[7] "Shell Game," *Scientific American,* Vol. 236, No. 3 (March 1977), pp. 58–61.

[8] Ibid.

[9] Robert C. Aldridge, "The Missile Shell Game," *The Nation,* Vol. 226, No. 18 (May 13, 1978), pp. 560–563.

[10] Cecil Brownlow, "DoD Leans to Land-Based MX," *Aviation Week and Space Technology,"* February 17, 1975, pp. 14–15.

[11] Holland and Hoover, *The MX Decision,* p. 130.

[12] Ibid., p. 131.

[13] Ibid.

[14] Leon Sloss and Marc Dean Millot, "U.S. Nuclear Strategy in Evolution," *Strategic Review,* Vol. 12, No. 1 (Winter 1984), p. 23.

[15] Ibid.

[16] Holland and Hoover, *The MX Decision,* p. 132.

[17] Ibid., p. 134.

[18] Ibid., p. 135.

[19] Ibid., p. 137.

[20] Wayne Biddle, "The Silo Busters, Misguided Missiles: The MX Project," *Harpers,* Vol. 259, No. 1555 (December 1979), p. 49.

[21] Drew Middleton, "Three Arms Development Options Seen for Carter," The *New York Times,* April 1, 1977, p. A8.

[22] Biddle, "The Silo Busters," pp. 50–51.

[23] Aldridge, "The Missile Shell Game," p. 562.

[24] The trench method would have required digging a 5- to 25-mile-long trench for each missile. For 200–300 missiles this would have meant approximately 4,000 miles of trenches, or more than the entire distance across the continental United States. Inside each tunnel would be a track for the transporter / launcher vehicle of the missiles. The roof of the tunnel would be made of interlocking keystones that could withstand great pressure from above but could easily be pushed out of the way when the transporter rose to fire the missile.

[25] "Baseless Missiles," *Scientific American,* Vol. 239, No. 2 (August 1978), p. 68.

[26] According to Herbert Scoville, Jr., the Soviets successfully tested their first MIRV in the summer of 1973 and began deploying MIRVed warheads on their missiles in late 1975.

See Herbert Scoville, Jr., *MX: Prescription for Disaster* (Cambridge, Mass.: M.I.T. Press, 1981), p. 66.

[27] Richard Burt, "Search for an Invulnerable Missile," The *New York Times Magazine,* May 27, 1979, p. 34.

[28] Holland and Hoover, *The MX Decision,* p. 142. See also Edwards, *Superweapon,* pp. 165–168.

[29] M. Callahan, B. T. Feld, E. Hadjimichael, and K. M. Tsipis, "The MX Missile: An Arms Control Impact Statement," Program in Science and Technology, Department of Physics, Massachusetts Institute of Technology, Cambridge, Massachusetts, March 1978, pp. 1–3. See also Stephen M. Meyer, "MAPS for the MX Missile," *Bulletin of the Atomic Scientists,* Vol. 35, No. 6 (June 1979), pp. 26–29.

[30] Holland and Hoover, *The MX Decision,* pp. 144–145.

[31] Ibid., p. 144; see also Edwards, *Superweapon,* p. 169.

[32] Burt, "Search for an Invulnerable Missile," p. 40.

[33] Holland and Hoover, *The MX Decision,* p. 145.

[34] Ibid.

[35] Ibid., p. 155.

[36] Biddle, "The Silo Busters," p. 58.

[37] Domestic political opposition to these negotiations, however, was quite strong from the outset. See William J. Lanouette, "The Battle to Shape and Sell the New Arms Control Treaty," *National Journal,* December 31, 1977, pp. 1984–1993.

[38] Holland and Hoover, *The MX Decision,* p. 158.

[39] See U.S. Senate Committee on Armed Services, 96th Congress, 2nd Session, Report 96-1054, *Military Implications of the Proposed SALT II Treaty Relating to the National Defense* (Washington, D.C.: U.S. Government Printing Office, December 4, 1980), pp. 15–17; and *Hearings on the Military Implications of the Treaty on the Limitation of Strategic Offensive Arms and Protocol Thereto (SALT II Treaty),* Part 3 (Washington, D.C.: U.S. Government Printing Office, October 1979), pp. 876–899.

[40] U.S. Senate Committee on Foreign Relations, 96th Congress., 1st Session, Report 96-14, *The SALT II Treaty* (Washington, D.C.: U.S. Government Printing Office, November 19, 1979), p. 159.

[41] See Stephen J. Flanagan, "SALT II," in Albert Carnesale and Richard N. Haass, eds., *Superpower Arms Control: Setting the Record Straight* (Cambridge, Mass.: Ballinger, 1987), pp. 120–121; and Stephen J. Flanagan, "The Domestic Politics of SALT II: Implications for the Foreign Policy Process," in John Spanier and Joseph Nogee, eds., *Congress, the Presidency and American Foreign Policy* (New York: Pergamon Press, 1982), pp. 44–76.

[42] Holland and Hoover, *The MX Decision,* p. 158.

[43] Richard Burt, "Pentagon Includes Two New Missiles in its 1979 Budget," The *New York Times,* November 15, 1978, pp. A1, A11. See also Edwards, *Superweapon,* pp. 203–204.

[44] Eliot Marshall, "MX Missile to Roam 200 Racetracks," *Science,* Vol. 206, No. 4415 (October 12, 1979), pp. 198–200.

[45] Congressional Budget Office, *The MX Missile and Multiple Protective Structure Basing: Long-Term Budgetary Implications* (Washington, D.C.: U.S. Government Printing Office, June 1979), pp. xviii–xxiii.

[46] James Fallows, "The Politics of the MX," *Technology Review,* Vol. 83, No. 6 (May / June 1981), pp. 22–23.

[47] Quoted in Paul Stockton, "Arms Development and Arms Control," p. 246.

[48] Holland and Hoover, *The MX Decision,* p. 160.

[49] Ibid., p. 161. See also Stockton, "Arms Development and Arms Control," pp. 246–247.

[50] Jeffrey M. Lenorovitz, "MX Impact Hearings Stir Criticism," *Aviation Week and Space Technology,* Vol. 112, No. 6 (February 11, 1980), pp. 17–18. See also Scoville, *MX,* pp. 112–117.

[51] "Taking Aim at the MX Missile," *Time,* Vol. 115, No. 14 (April 7, 1980), p. 23.

[52] "Air Force Reverses Position, Backs Horizontal Basing," *Aviation Week and Space Technology,* Vol. 110, No. 10 (March 10, 1980), pp. 21–22.

[53] Committee on the Present Danger, *The 1980 Crisis and What We Should Do about It,* Washington, D.C., 1980, p. 15.

[54] Scoville, *MX,* p. 114.

[55] Holland and Hoover, *The MX Decision,* pp. 169–170.

[56] Desmond Ball, "The Development of the SIOP, 1960–1983," in Desmond Ball and Jeffrey Richelson, eds., *Strategic Nuclear Targeting* (Ithaca: Cornell University Press, 1986), p. 77.

[57] Ibid.

[58] Ibid., p. 176.

[59] Ibid., p. 177.

[60] Richard Halloran, "Weinberger Is Pressed to Decide on New Bomber and MX Basing," The *New York Times,* July 14, 1983, p. A15.

[61] "Background Statement from White House on MX Missile and B-1 Bomber," The *New York Times,* October 3, 1981, p. A12.

[62] Steven V. Roberts, "MX Decision Wins Praise but B-1 Plan Faces Test," and William E. Schmidt, "Political Leaders in Utah and Nevada Applaud Decision on the MX," The *New York Times,* October 3, 1981, p. A14.

[63] Christopher Paine, "Running in Circles with the MX," *Bulletin of the Atomic Scientists,* Vol. 37, No. 10 (December 1981), p. 8.

[64] R. Jeffrey Smith, "Air Force Takes Aim at a Big Bird," *Science,* Vol. 216, No. 4543 (April 16, 1982), pp. 270–273.

[65] Martin Tolchin, "Democrats Assail Military Program," The *New York Times,* October 4, 1981, p. A40; and Steven Weisman, "Aides Say Reagan Never Advocated Carter's MX Plan," The *New York Times,* October 4, 1981, pp. A1, A40.

[66] Office of Technology Assessment, *MX Missile Basing* (Washington, D.C.: U.S. Government Printing Office, September 1981), pp. 4–5.

[67] Richard Halloran, "Joint Chiefs' Head Says He Preferred Carter's MX Plan," The *New York Times,* October 6, 1981, pp. A1, A30.

[68] Richard Halloran, "House Panel Votes B-1 but Turns Down MX," The *New York Times,* October 29, 1981, p. A17.

[69] Holland and Hoover, *The MX Decision,* p. 182.

[70] "Senate Votes to Delay Funds for B-1 Bomber and MX," The *New York Times,* November 7, 1981, p. A18.

[71] Richard Halloran, "Two Weapons Facing Capitol Questions," The *New York Times,* November 1, 1981, pp. A1, A32.

[72] R. Jeffrey Smith, "A Last Go-Around for the MX Missile," *Science,* Vol. 218, No. 4575 (November 26, 1982), pp. 865–866.

[73] Holland and Hoover, *The MX Decision,* p. 224.

[74] Ibid., p. 226.

[75] Ibid., p. 227.

[76] Ibid., p. 228.

[77] See *Report of the President's Commission on Strategic Forces* (Washington, D.C.: The White House, 1983), pp. 8–17.

[78] Elizabeth Drew, "A Political Journal," *The New Yorker,* Vol. 59, No. 18 (June 26, 1983), p. 50.

[79] Quoted in ibid., p. 51.

[80] Holland and Hoover, *The MX Decision,* p. 237.

[81] Quoted in Drew, "A Political Journal," p. 60.

[82] Holland and Hoover, *The MX Decision,* p. 238.

[83] Quoted in Drew, "A Political Journal," p. 56.

[84] Ibid., p. 61.

[85] Holland and Hoover, *The MX Decision,* p. 240; and Drew, "A Political Journal," p. 64.

[86] Holland and Hoover, *The MX Decision,* p. 240.

[87] See Martin Tolchin, "House Bars Cut in Funds to MX and B-1 Plane," The *New York Times,* November 2, pp. A1, A2; and Martin Tolchin, "Senate Approves Funds for the MX," The *New York Times,* November 8, 1983, p. A20.

[88] Ball, "Development of the SIOP, 1960–1983," p. 80.

[89] Quoted in Sloss and Millot, "U.S. Nuclear Strategy in Evolution," p. 25.

[90] Steven V. Roberts, "House Gives Final Approval to $1.5 Billion MX Purchase," The *New York Times,* March 29, 1985, pp. A1, A14, and "Presidential Persuasion Wins Another

Round," The *New York Times*, March 31, 1985, p. E1.

[91] This was under a deal worked out with Congress in order to avoid defeat on the President's $232 billion Defense Authorization Bill (Steven V. Roberts, "Senate's Chiefs and President in MX Accord," The *New York Times*, May 24, 1985, pp. A1, A13).

[92] Steven V. Roberts, "Reagan Yields to Limit of 50 on MX Missiles," The *New York Times*, May 22, 1985, pp. A1, A23.

[93] Bill Keller, "Doubts Increase Over Future of U.S. Land-Based Missiles," The *New York Times*, June 17, 1985, pp. A1, A17.

[94] Jonathan E. Medalia, *MX, Midgetman, and Titan Missile Programs* (Washington, D.C.: Congressional Research Service, April 18, 1986), pp. 2–3.

[95] Fred Hiatt, "Midgetman Won't Be Shielded from Budget Cuts," *The Washington Post*, January 10, 1986, p. A8.

[96] John Morrocco, "Perle: Single-Warhead ICBM a Waste of Funds," *Defense News*, Vol. 1, No. 6, p. 1; and "Cap Criticizes Midgetman Costs," *Defense Week*, March 17, 1986, p. 7.

[97] Bill Keller, "Panel Said to Back Small Main Missile," The *New York Times*, February 2, 1986, pp. A1, A24.

[98] *Report of the Defense Science Board Task Force on Small Intercontinental Ballistic Missile Modernization* (Washington, D.C.: Office of the Under Secretary for Research and Engineering, March 1986), pp. 8–15. The GAO also completed a similar study for Congress; see General Accounting Office, *Report to Congress: ICBM Modernization: Status, Survivable Basing Issues, and Need to Reestablish a National Consensus*, GAO/NSIAD-86-200 (Washington, D.C.: U.S. Government Printing Office, September 1986).

[99] "Redesigned Midgetman Could Save $20 Billion," *Aviation Week and Space Technology*, February 24, 1986, p. 20.

[100] Michael R. Gordon, "Reagan Orders a Study to Decide If U.S. Should Build New Missile," The *New York Times*, April 25, 1986, pp. A1, A36; and Peter Grier, "Hazy Future for U.S. Missiles," *Christian Science Monitor*, May 16, 1986, p. 1.

[101] David Silverberg, "Officials Work to Launch Midgetman Compromise," *Defense News*, July 21, 1986, pp. 1, 17.

[102] Michael A. Gordon, "Pentagon Pressed on Small Missiles," The *New York Times*, June 25, 1986, pp. A1, A15.

[103] John D. Morrocco, "Defense Official Challenges Continuing SICBM Development," *Aviation Week and Space Technology*, March 16, 1987, pp. 18–19; and Peter Adams, "Opinions Differ on Role of Midgetman Missile," *Defense News*, March 9, 1987, p. 26.

[104] John D. Morrocco, "Reagan Will Pursue Rail-Based MX, Full-Scale Midgetman Development," *Aviation Week and Space Technology*, January 5, 1987, pp. 20, 21.

[105] Howard Siller, "Chain Says Mobile MX Needed," *Omaha World-Herald*, June 11, 1987, p. 21.

[106] Subcommittee on Research and Development and Subcommittee on Procurement and Military Nuclear Systems, Committee on Armed Services, U.S. House of Representatives, *The MX Missile Inertial Measurement Unit: A Program Review*, 100th Congress, 1st Session, 76-143 (Washington, D.C.: U.S. Government Printing Office, August 1987), p. 10.

[107] Ibid., p. 4. The air force was quick to seize on this argument to defend the MX. Brigadier General Charles A. May, responding to the report, attributed the system's problems to congressional reductions in funds for buying MX missiles, saying there was "no connection" between rescheduling and "any alleged problems." See Michael R. Gordon, "Air Force Backs Its MX Program Against Critics," The *New York Times*, August 24, 1987, p. A1.

7. B-1 BOMBER

[1] Ronald Huisken, *The Origin of the Strategic Cruise Missile* (New York: Praeger, 1981), p. 60.

[2] Michael Edward Brown, "Flying Blind: Decision Making in the U.S. Strategic Bomber Program," unpublished Ph.D. dissertation, Cornell University, 1983.

[3] Ibid., p. 262.

[4] Ibid., p. 171.

[5] Ibid., p. 267.

[6] Ibid., p. 276.

[7] Ibid., p. 277.

[8] Huisken, *Origin of the Strategic Cruise Missile,* p. 63.

[9] Brown, "Flying Blind," pp. 278–279.

[10] Ibid., p. 285.

[11] Ibid., pp. 288–290.

[12] Ibid., p. 291.

[13] Quoted in Huisken, *Origin of the Strategic Cruise Missile,* p. 63.

[14] Nick Kotz, *Wild Blue Yonder: Money, Politics, and the B-1 Bomber* (New York: Pantheon Books, 1988), p. 84.

[15] Quoted in Brown, "Flying Blind," p. 294.

[16] Ibid., pp. 294–295.

[17] Ibid., p. 296.

[18] Huisken, *Origin of the Strategic Cruise Missile,* p. 64.

[19] Brown, "Flying Blind," pp. 298–299.

[20] Quoted in ibid., p. 301.

[21] Ibid., pp. 303–304.

[22] Ibid., p. 310.

[23] Ibid., pp. 314–315.

[24] Cecil Brownlow, "Major Incentives Offered for B-1," *Aviation Week and Space Technology,* June 15, 1970, pp. 12–13. But Rockwell subsequently lost the incentive fee because of program stretch-outs ("Rockwell to lose B-1 Incentive Fees," *Aviation Week and Space Technology,* July 23, 1973, p. 23).

[25] In 1971 in its preliminary design review, the USAF requested 297 more alterations to the aircraft design ("Design Review of B-1 'Favorable,' " *Aviation Week and Space Technology,* November 8, 1971, p. 17).

[26] Charles A. Sorrels, *U.S. Cruise Missile Programs: Development, Deployment and Implications for Arms Control* (New York: McGraw-Hill, 1983), p. 17.

[27] Brown, "Flying Blind," p. 319.

[28] Quoted in ibid., p. 320.

[29] Donald C. Winston, "Defense Cut Bid Threatens B-1 Bomber," *Aviation Week and Space Technology,* May 10, 1971, pp. 16–17.

[30] Brown, "Flying Blind," p. 321.

[31] Ibid., p. 322.

[32] Ibid., p. 328.

[33] Ibid., pp. 322–323.

[34] "Bombers Away," *Scientific American,* Vol. 228, No. 5 (May 1973), pp. 42–43.

[35] Quoted in Sorrels, *U.S. Cruise Missile Programs,* p. 7.

[36] Quoted in John F. Finney, "Who Needs the B-1," The *New York Times Magazine,* July 25, 1976, p. 27.

[37] See "$100 Million Slashed from B-1, Senate Unit Cuts Other Weapons," *Aviation Week and Space Technology,* August 6, 1973, p. 23; Cecil Brownlow, "Proposed Cuts Could Cripple B-1 Project," *Aviation Week and Space Technology,* August 27, 1973, p. 18; and Katherine Johnsen, "House Turns Back Move to Kill B-1, Minuteman Improvements," *Aviation Week and Space Technology,* May 27, 1974, pp. 17–18; and "Senate Turns Back Amendment to Slash B-1 by $255 Million," *Aviation Week and Space Technology,* June 10, 1974, p. 18.

[38] Brown, "Flying Blind," p. 324. See also "Air Force Seeks to Avoid Break in B-1," *Aviation Week and Space Technology,* July 15, 1974, pp. 117–122; and "USAF Presses B-1 Cost Effort," *Aviation Week and Space Technology,* October 28, 1974, p. 22.

[39] "Broad Coalition Attacks B-1 Funding," *Aviation Week and Space Technology,* May 12, 1975, p. 18; and "USAF Counters Proxmire's B-1 Charges," *Aviation Week and Space Technology,* March 12, 1975, p. 14.

[40] Robert J. Art and Stephen E. Ockenden, "The Domestic Politics of Cruise Missile Development, 1970–1980," in Richard K. Betts, ed., *Cruise Missiles: Technology, Strategy, Politics* (Washington, D.C.: The Brookings Institution, 1981), p. 372.

[41] See Deborah Shapley, "The B-1 and the Cruise Missile: To Have and Have Not," *Sci-*

ence, Vol. 193, No. 4250 (July 23, 1976), pp. 303–305; Eugene Kozicharow, "Senate Move to Delay B-1 Faces Conference Action," *Aviation Week and Space Technology,* May 31, 1976, pp. 14–15; Katherine Johnsen, "Conferees Compromise on B-1 Funding," *Aviation Week and Space Technology,* September 6, 1976, p. 41; and Cecil Brownlow, "B-1 Production Plan Approved," *Aviation Week and Space Technology,* December 6, 1976, p. 12.

[42] Kotz, *Wild Blue Yonder,* p. 129.

[43] Ibid., p. 135.

[44] Nicholas Wade, "Death of the B-1: The Events Behind Carter's Decision," *Science,* Vol. 197, No. 4303 (August 5, 1977), pp. 536–539.

[45] Brown, "Flying Blind," p. 374.

[46] Ibid.

[47] Art and Ockenden, "The Domestic Politics of Cruise Missile Development," p. 377.

[48] Jimmy Carter, *Keeping Faith: Memoirs of a President* (Toronto: Bantam Books, 1982), p. 82.

[49] Quoted in "Carter Blocks Production of B-1," *Aviation Week and Space Technology,* July 4, 1977, pp. 14–16. Congress's reaction was mixed with support for the President's decision being stronger in the Senate than House. See Katherine Johnsen, "Support for B-1 Decision Seen Mixed in Congress," *Aviation Week and Space Technology,* July 1, 1977, pp. 21–22, and The *New York Times,* July 1, 1977, pp. A1, A10–11.

[50] Quoted in Huisken, *Origin of the Strategic Cruise Missile,* p. 81.

[51] Brown, "Flying Blind," p. 326.

[52] Carter, *Keeping Faith,* p. 83.

[53] Nicholas Wade, "B-1 Raises Head from Grave," *Science,* Vol. 198, No. 4313 (October 14, 1977), p. 177; Clarence A. Robinson, Jr., "House Unit Overturns B-1, MC Funding Cuts," *Aviation Week and Space Technology,* October 3, 1977, pp. 21–22; and Martin Tolchin, "Senate Rejects Use of B-1 Bomber Funds," The *New York Times,* February 2, 1978, p. A7.

[54] Kotz, *Wild Blue Yonder,* p. 184.

[55] Ibid., pp. 190–193.

[56] Brown, "Flying Blind," p. 332.

[57] Quoted in Sorrels, *U.S. Cruise Missile Programs,* p. 36. See also Kotz, *Wild Blue Yonder,* pp. 193–194.

[58] The Stealth bomber is being developed by the Northrop Corporation. It is a highly secret "black box," program about which there is little information available in the public record. For a useful article that has stitched together what little information there is, see Wayne Biddle, "The Real Secret of Stealth," *Discover,* Vol. 7, No. 7 (February 1986), pp. 20–31.

[59] Richard Halloran, "Air Force Seeks New Bomber and Development of a Radar-Evading Plane," The *New York Times,* February 14, 1981, p. A9; Richard Halloran, "Reagan Moving on Start of Fleet of New Bombers," The *New York Times,* February 22, 1981, pp. A1, A23; and Clarence A. Robinson, Jr., "USAF Recommends New Combat Aircraft," *Aviation Week and Space Technology,* May 11, 1981, pp. 18–20.

[60] Julia Malone, "New Design Touches $200 Million Price Tag, and All—B-1 May Yet Fly," *Christian Science Monitor,* June 4, 1973, p. 3; and Alton J. Marsh, "Bomber Faces Opposition in House Funding Group," *Aviation Week and Space Technology,* October 12, 1973, pp. 23–25.

[61] Quoted in Sorrels, *U.S. Cruise Missile Programs,* pp. 36–37.

[62] Brown, "Flying Blind," pp. 336–337.

[63] "Senate Hearing Criticizes B-1 Based on CIA, GAO Reports," *Aviation Week and Space Technology,* November 2, 1981, pp. 20–21; "GAO Report Questions USAF B-1B Cost Estimates," *Aviation Week and Space Technology,* November 16, 1981, pp. 18–19; and "USAF Reaffirms B-1B Costs in Face of GAO Disclosures," *Aviation Week and Space Technology,* June 28, 1982, pp. 29–30.

[64] "House Defeats Efforts to Kill MX, B-1B Funds," *Aviation Week and Space Technology,* November 7, 1983, p. 23.

[65] Paul Mann, "Law Prohibits Diversion of Funding to B-1 Bomber," *Aviation Week and Space Technology,* October 8, 1984, pp. 17–19; Eugene Kozicharow, "Some USAF Planners Promote Extended Production of B-1B," *Aviation Week and Space Technology,* February 25, 1985, pp. 50–51; Paul Mann, "Key Senator Seeks Arms Project Curb," *Aviation Week*

and Space Technology, March 4, 1985, pp. 16–17; and William H. Gregory, "Decision on B-1," *Aviation Week and Space Technology,* March 25, 1985, p. 13.

[66] Wayne Biddle, "U.S. Faces Bomber Choice," The *New York Times,* February 11, 1985, pp. D1, D5; and Nicholas D. Kristoff, "Rockwell Layoffs Viewed as a Trend," The *New York Times,* May 30, 1986, pp. D1, D9.

[67] John H. Cushman, "$500 Million in Extra Expense Is Forecast for B-1B Bomber," The *New York Times,* May 4, 1986, p. A1.

[68] "First B-1 Bomber in Operation," The *New York Times,* October 4, 1986, p. A21; and Richard L. Berke, "U.S. Withholds $250 Million Over Flaws in New Bomber," The *New York Times,* December 4, 1986, p. B27, and December 5, 1986, p. A31.

[69] General Larry D. Welch, Chief of Staff, U.S. Air Force, before Subcommittee on the Department of Defense, *Hearings Before a Subcommittee of the Committee on Appropriations, House of Representatives: Department of Defense Appropriations for 1988, Pt. 2,* 100th Congress, 1st Session, 71-918-0 (Washington, D.C.: U.S. Government Printing Office, 1987), p. 609; see also pp. 603–613, 621–623, and 699–704.

[70] "Debut of the Wrong Bomber," The *New York Times,* December 12, 1986, p. A34; John H. Cushman, Jr., "Air Force to Seek Funds for Bomber," The *New York Times,* January 8, 1987, p. B9; David E. Sanger, "Contractor Reorganizes B-1B Bomber Project," The *New York Times,* January 9, 1987, pp. D1, D3; and "Aspin Criticizes Bomber Cost," The *New York Times,* February 13, 1987, p. A19.

[71] Subcommittee on Research and Development and Subcommittee on Procurement and Military Nuclear Systems, Committee on Armed Services, House of Representatives, *The B-1: A Program Review,* 100th Congress, 1st Session (Washington, D.C.: U.S. Government Printing Office, March 30, 1987), pp. 1–2. See also Subcommittee on Research and Development and Subcommittee on Procurement and Military Nuclear Systems, Committee on Armed Services, House of Representatives, *Hearings on National Defense Authorization Act for FY 1988/89–H.R. 1748: Review of Air Force B-1B Program,* H.A.S.C. 100–8, 100th Congress, 1st Session (Washington, D.C.: U.S. Government Printing Office, 1987).

[72] Ibid., p. 17.

[73] "Panel Assails Air Force on B-1B Bomber Program," The *New York Times,* March 3, 1987, p. A25; and "Congress Questions Cost of B-1B Recovery Program," *Aviation Week and Space Technology,* March 2, 1987, pp. 28–29.

[74] General Lawrence A. Skantze, "B-1B: A Timely Lesson in Risk Management," *Aviation Week and Space Technology,* March 23, 1987, p. 11; "House Panel Warns of Future Risks in B-1B Program Costs and Schedule," *Aviation Week and Space Technology,* April 6, 1987, pp. 20–21; and Paul Mann, "B-1B Bomber Inquiry Triggers Aspin Probe of Stealth Weapons," *Aviation Week and Space Technology,* March 23, 1987, pp. 18–20.

8. THE AIR-LAUNCHED CRUISE MISSILE

[1] Kenneth P. Werrell, *The Evolution of the Cruise Missile* (Washington, D.C.: U.S. Government Printing Office, September 1985), pp. 41–78.

[2] Quoted in ibid., p. 103.

[3] Ibid., pp. 125–128.

[4] Robert J. Art and Stephen E. Ockenden, "The Domestic Politics of Cruise Missile Development, 1970–1980," in Richard K. Betts, ed., *Cruise Missiles: Technology, Strategy, Politics* (Washington, D.C.: The Brookings Institution, 1981), pp. 360–361.

[5] Ibid., p. 366.

[6] Huisken, *The Origin of the Strategic Cruise Missile* (New York: Praeger, 1981), p. 65. See also Art and Ockenden, "The Domestic Politics of Cruise Missile Development," pp. 366–367.

[7] Huisken, *Origin of the Strategic Cruise Missile,* p. 66.

[8] Art and Ockenden, "The Domestic Politics of Cruise Missile Development," pp. 367–368.

[9] Huisken, *Origin of the Strategic Cruise Missile,* p. 67.

[10] Ibid., p. 69.

[11] Quoted in ibid., p. 69.

12 Ibid., p. 70.

13 Ibid., p. 71.

14 Art and Ockenden, "The Domestic Politics of Cruise Missile Development," pp. 368–369.

15 Werrell, *The Evolution of the Cruise Missile,* p. 149.

16 Art and Ockenden, "The Domestic Politics of Cruise Missile Development," p. 371.

17 Huisken, *Origin of the Strategic Cruise Missile,* p. 75.

18 Charles A. Sorrels, *U.S. Cruise Missile Programs: Development, Deployment and Implications for Arms Control* (New York: McGraw-Hill, 1983), p. 19.

19 Quoted in Huisken, *Origin of the Strategic Cruise Missile,* p. 76.

20 Art and Ockenden, "The Domestic Politics of Cruise Missile Development," p. 395.

21 Huisken, *Origin of the Strategic Cruise Missile,* p. 77.

22 Ibid., pp. 78–79.

23 Committee on Armed Services, House of Representatives, *Hearings before the Special Panel on Defense Procurement Procedures: Defense Procurement Policies and Procedures: Cost Management and Control,* 1st Session, 97th Congress, H201–9 (Washington, D.C.: U.S. Government Printing Office, 1981), p. 597.

24 Werrell, *The Evolution of the Cruise Missile,* p. 177.

25 Ibid., p. 178.

26 Quoted in ibid.

27 Stephen J. Flanagan, "SALT II," in Albert Carnesale and Richard N. Haass, eds., *Superpower Arms Control: Setting the Record Straight* (Cambridge, Mass.: Ballinger, 1987), pp. 122–123.

28 Huisken, *Origin of the Strategic Cruise Missile,* p. 86; and Werrell, *The Evolution of the Cruise Missile,* p. 184.

29 "The Air-Launched Cruise Missile," *DMS Market Intelligence Report,* 1983, p. 1.

30 Committee on Armed Services, House of Representatives, *Hearings on H.R. 5167, Department of Defense Authorization of Appropriations for Fiscal Year 1985,* 98th Congress, 2nd Session, H.A.S.C. No 98-341 (Washington, D.C.: U.S. Government Printing Office, 1984), pp. 356–357; and Committee on Armed Services, United States Senate; *Hearings on S. 674, to Authorize Appropriations for Fiscal Year 1986 . . . Part 7: Strategic and Theater Nuclear Forces,* Pt. 7, 99th Congress, 1st Session, S. Hrg. 99-58 (Washington, D.C.: U.S. Government Printing Office, 1985), pp. 3684–3685.

31 Werrell, *The Evolution of the Cruise Missile,* pp. 185–187.

32 Committee on Armed Services, House of Representatives, "Written Statement of Col. Joseph G. Rutter," *Hearings before the Special Panel on Defense Procurement Procedures: Defense Procurement Policies and Procedures: Cost Management and Control,* pp. 523–524.

33 Ibid., p. 517.

34 Ibid., p. 553.

35 Ibid., p. 580.

36 Quoted in ibid., p. 605.

37 Werrell, *The Evolution of the Cruise Missile,* p. 210.

38 Reported in *Current News,* Department of Defense, January 7, 1987, p. 1.

39 Werrell, *The Evolution of the Cruise Missile,* p. 206.

9. THE M-1 ABRAMS TANK

1 Quoted in Nicholas Wade, "Tank Can Run, Shoot and Vanish in a Puff of Smoke," *Science,* Vol. 201. No. 4355 (August 11, 1978), p. 511.

2 Drew Middleton, "Soviet Introducing New Tank in Europe," The *New York Times,* March 16, 1980, p. A7.

3 Martin S. Miller, Jr., and Konrad Schreier, Jr., "The U.S. Main Battle Tank—Today and Tomorrow," *International Defense Review,* Vol. 6, No. 6 (November 1973), p. 57.

4 Nicholas Wade, "NATO Builds a Better Battle Tank But May Still Lose the Battle," *Science,* Vol. 201, No. 4351 (July 14, 1978), p. 136. See also John W. Finney, "Army Buying Its New Tank: A $4.5 Billion Decision," The *New York Times,* July 18, 1978, p. D3.

[5] Warren Weaver, Jr., "Tank Fund Halted for a Cost Study," The *New York Times*, August 9, 1969, pp. A1–A2.

[6] Quoted in Wade, "NATO Builds a Better Battle Tank," p. 136.

[7] Brooke Nihart, "Main Battle Tank Still in Trouble with Congress, OSD," *Armed Forces Journal International*, Vol. 108, No. 20 (June 1971), pp. 36–37. See also John W. Finney, "Senate Panel Limits Plans to Expand ABM System," The *New York Times*, August 5, 1971, p. 11.

[8] "MBT-70 Killed," *Armed Forces Journal International*, Vol. 109, No. 6 (February 1972), p. 19.

[9] Drew Middleton, "Pentagon Approves Plans for Superior Battle Tank for 1980's," The *New York Times*, April 24, 1973, p. A6.

[10] Quoted in Miller and Schreier, "The U.S. Main Battle Tank," p. 59.

[11] Ibid., p. 59.

[12] Fred Schreier, "The XM-1 Program: A Synopsis," in "A Tank Designed to Cost—The US Army's XM-1," *International Defense Review*, Vol. 10, No. 3 (April 1977), p. 460.

[13] "XM-1 Competition Underway," *Armed Forces Journal International*, Vol. 110, No. 8 (April 1973), p. 18.

[14] Schreier, "A Tank Designed to Cost," p. 459.

[15] R. D. M. Furlong, "The XM-1 Tank Program—A Status Report," *International Defense Review*, Vol. 9, No. 3 (June 1976), pp. 481–482.

[16] F. Clifton Berry, Jr., "Solving the 144-inch 'Mystery,'" *Armed Forces Journal International*, Vol. 114, No. 10 (June 1977), pp. 18, 20.

[17] Quoted in Wade, "NATO Builds a Better Battle Tank," p. 136.

[18] Robert Gillette, "Military R&D: Hard Lessons of an Electronic War," *Science*, Vol. 182, No. 4112 (November 9, 1973), p. 560.

[19] "M1 Abrams MBT," *Jane's Armour and Artillery, 1986–87* (London: Jane's Publishing Company, 1986), p. 117. See also "Chrysler, GM Win Tank Prototypes," *Armed Forces Journal International*, Vol. 110, No. 11 (July 1973), pp. 22–23; and "Contract Awards," The *New York Times*, June 29, 1973, p. B54.

[20] Quoted in David C. Isby, *Weapons and Tactics of the Soviet Army* (London: Jane's Publishing Company, 1981), p. 145.

[21] Quoted in Gillette, "Military R&D," p. 560.

[22] John W. Finney, "Pentagon Asks West Germans to Enter Competition for Order for New Tank," The *New York Times*, January 17, 1975, p. A43.

[23] John W. Finney, "G.A.O. Assails Army's Plans for New Battle Tank," The *New York Times*, June 30, 1976, p. A8.

[24] Schreier, "The XM-1 Program," p. 460.

[25] Drew Middleton, "U.S. Ground Forces Get Latest Weapons Systems," The *New York Times*, May 28, 1974, pp. 1, 31.

[26] Drew Middleton, "Will the Tank Survive?," The *New York Times*, November 24, 1985, p. F12.

[27] Wade, "NATO Builds a Better Battle Tank," p. 137.

[28] Quoted in Phil Patton, "Battle Over the New U.S. Tank," The *New York Times*, June 1, 1980, p. F83.

[29] "Tank Designers Stress Technology Instead of More Weight." The *New York Times*, December 19, 1980, p. A16. See also "Tank Test Bed Program" and "Future Close Combat Vehicle System," *Jane's Armour and Artillery 1986–87*, pp. 115–116.

[30] Quoted in Wade, "NATO Builds a Better Battle Tank," p. 138. See also John W. Finney, "U.S. Weighing Use of a German Tank," The *New York Times*, February 13, 1976, p. A13.

[31] Furlong, "The XM-1 Tank Program," p. 481.

[32] "New U.S. MBT Candidates Said to Test Out in 'Dead Heat,'" *Armed Forces Journal International*, Vol. 113, No. 8 (April 1976), p. 18.

[33] "Army Accepts XM-1 Tank Prototypes," *Armed Forces Journal International*, Vol. 113, No. 6 (February 1976), p. 13.

[34] Quoted in Wade, "NATO Builds a Better Battle Tank," p. 138. See also John W. Finney, "U.S. Army Blocks German Tank Project," The *New York Times*, July 15, 1976, p. A6.

[35] "XM-1, Leopard II Stakes Raised; AWACS Hostage?," *Armed Forces Journal International*, Vol. 113, No. 8 (April 1976), p. 14.

[36] John W. Finney, "U.S. and Bonn Reach Tank Compromise," The *New York Times,* August 5, 1976, pp. A1, 5.

[37] Quoted in "US-FRG Tank Decision for January 1977," *International Defense Review,* Vol. 9, No. 5 (October 1976), p. 709.

[38] "XM-1: NATO Standardization Breakthrough, or Rumsfeld's TFX?," *Armed Forces Journal International,* Vol. 114, No. 1 (September 1976), p. 26.

[39] Ibid., p. 26.

[40] Ibid., p. 22.

[41] R. D. M. Furlong and R. B. Penegelley, "Main Armament for the XM-1 Tank—Storm Over the Selection Process," *International Defense Review,* Vol. 9, No. 6 (December 1976), p. 989. See also "U.S. Army Comments on XM-1 and Leopard II Tank Programs," *International Defense Review,* Vol. 9, No. 6 (December 1976), pp. 905–906.

[42] Quoted in Furlong and Penegelley, "Main Armament for the XM-1 Tank," p. 990.

[43] Quoted in F. Clifton Berry, Jr., "House Panel Slams XM-1 Delay," *Armed Forces Journal International,* Vol. 114, No. 2 (October 1976), p. 34.

[44] "U.S. Army Comments," p. 905.

[45] Benjamin F. Schemmer, "XM-1 Cost Proposals Changed by Wide Margins," *Armed Forces Journal International,* Vol. 114, No. 5 (January 1977), p. 20.

[46] F. Clifton Berry, Jr., "Army Selects Chrysler to Develop XM-1 Tank," *Armed Forces Journal International,* Vol. 114, No. 4 (December 1976), p. 6.

[47] Schreier, "The XM-1 Program," p. 460.

[48] "How Germany's Leopard 2 Tank Failed the Test," *Armed Forces Journal International,* Vol. 114, No. 8 (April 1977), p. 12.

[49] "U.S. Tank Gun Trials Produce Surprises," *International Defense Review,* Vol. 10, No. 1 (January 1977), pp. 21–22.

[50] For the progression of talks with the Germans, see John W. Finney, "Rift with Germans Over Tank Widening," The *New York Times,* March 8, 1977, p. 7; David Binder, "Bonn Defense Chief Asserts U.S. Risks Clash Over Tanks," The *New York Times,* March 16, 1977, p. A9; and David Binder, "U.S. and Bonn Gaining on Tank Components," The *New York Times,* March 17, 1977, p. A12.

[51] Quoted in "House Group Fears Rift Over NATO Tank," The *New York Times,* October 21, 1977, p. A7.

[52] Ibid., p. A7.

[53] "Select XM-1 Gun on Merit, Not Politics, Congress Warns," *Armed Forces Journal International,* Vol. 115, No. 3 (November 1977), p. 10.

[54] "XM1 Tank Gun Trials—Round 2," *International Defense Review,* Vol. 10, No. 6 (December 1977), pp. 1028–1029.

[55] "U.S. Army Selects German Smoothbore Gun for XM-1 Tank," *International Defense Review,* Vol. 11, No. 2 (March 1978), p. 145. See also "U.S. 120mm Tank Gun Decision Under Fire," *International Defense Review,* Vol. 11, No. 5 (July 1978), pp. 665–667.

[56] Quoted in "Better Reasons Behind Army's 120mm XM-1 Gun Choice than Made Public?," *Armed Forces Journal International,* Vol. 115, No. 7 (March 1978), p. 14.

[57] Quoted in "U.S. 120mm Tank Gun Decision Under Fire," p. 666.

[58] "U.S. Army Explains XM-1 Gun Choice," *International Defense Review,* Vol. 11, No. 3 (April 1978), p. 441.

[59] R. L. Janisch, "7 of 11 XM-1 Pilot Vehicles Downed by Engine Failure," *Armed Forces Journal International,* Vol. 116, No. 2 (October 1978), p. 12. Subsequent modifications reduced the problem. R. L. Janisch, "XM-1 Engine Problems Drop 50% Since Modifications," *Armed Forces Journal International,* Vol. 116, No. 4 (December 1978), p. 16, and "XM-1 Tank Engine Fixes," *International Defense Review,* Vol. 12, No. 2 (March 1979), p. 157.

[60] Schreier, "The XM-1 Program," p. 460.

[61] Janisch, "XM-1 Engine Problems Drop," p. 16.

[62] Quoted in ibid., p. 16. See also "XM-1 Tank Engine Fixes," p. 157.

[63] "XM-1 Engine Failed on Average of Once Every 338 Miles in Tests," *Armed Forces Journal International,* Vol. 116, No. 9 (May 1979), p. 16.

[64] "New Concern Over XM-1 Engine Problems," *Armed Forces Journal International,* Vol. 116, No. 8 (April 1979), p. 26.

[65] Ibid., p. 16.

[66] Quoted in "XM-1 Production to Be Delayed?," *International Defense Review,* Vol. 12, No. 4 (May 1979), p. 479.

[67] Quoted in "XM-1 Gets Limited Production Go-Ahead Despite Failings," *International Defense Review,* Vol. 12, No. 5 (July 1979), p. 697. See also "Pentagon to Produce New Tank Despite Call for Additional Tests," The *New York Times,* May 9, 1979, p. A14; and Robin J. Stein, "Army to Buy 110 XM-1s in '80, Future Buys Uncertain," *Armed Forces Journal International,* Vol. 116, No. 10 (June 1979), p. 12.

[68] "XM-1 Engine Failed," p. 16. See also "XM-1 Production to be Delayed," pp. 479–480.

[69] "Senate Wants XM-1 Back-Up Engine," *Armed Forces Journal International,* Vol. 116, No. 11 (July 1979), p. 14.

[70] *Jane's Armour and Artillery 1986–87,* p. 117. See also "XM-1 Long-Lead Items Authorized," *International Defense Review,* Vol. 13, No. 1 (January 1980), p. 24.

[71] "Army, XM-1 May Be 3 to 7 Tons Overweight," *Armed Forces Journal International,* Vol. 117, No. 4 (December 1979), p. 14. See also Benjamin Schemmer, "XM-1 Mobility Fixes Prove Out; Weight Growth Poses New Dilemma," *Armed Forces Journal International,* Vol. 117, No. 5 (January 1980), pp. 16, 32a.

[72] Quoted in "First Production XM-1 Handed Over," *International Defense Review,* Vol. 13, No. 3 (March 1980), p. 318.

[73] Ibid., p. 318.

[74] Quoted in "Army Gets Its First Production XM-1," *Armed Forces Journal International,* Vol. 117, No. 87 (March 1980), p. 20.

[75] Quoted in Middleton, "Battle Over the New U.S. Tank," p. 81.

[76] Quoted in "First Production XM-1s," p. 317.

[77] Quoted in Richard Halloran, "Army's New Main Battle Tank Christened Amid Debate," The *New York Times,* February 29, 1980, p. A12.

[78] "Army Says Tank Proves Itself," The *New York Times,* March 6, 1982, p. A9.

[79] Charles Mohr, "Tests of M-1 Tank Give Mixed Results," The *New York Times,* September 20, 1982, p. B15.

[80] Drew Middleton, "British Expert Says M-1 Tank May Be Hailed as Innovation," The *New York Times,* February 25, 1982, p. B17. See also "Tests of M-1 Tank," p. B15; and Middleton, "Battle Over the New U.S. Tank," p. 82.

[81] Benjamin F. Schemmer, "Press Reports that Leopard II Beat M-1 in Swiss Shoot-Off Are Premature," *Armed Forces Journal International,* Vol. 120, No. 10 (May 1983), pp. 62, 66, 69.

[82] Major subcontractors for the M-1 are Avco-Lycoming, Stanford, Connecticut (engine); Cadillac Gage Company, Warren, Michigan (turret drive and stabilization system); Computing Devices Company, Ottawa, Canada (ballistic computer); Detroit Diesel Allison Division, Indianapolis, Indiana (transmission and final drives); Hughes Aircraft Company, El Segundo, California (laser-range finder and thermal imaging system); Kollmorgen Corporation, Northampton, Massachusetts (gunner's auxiliary sight); and Singer Kearfott Division, Clifton, New Jersey (line-of-sight data link).

[83] "Carter Orders 'Highest National Priority' for XM-1, M-X and Pershing II Programs," *Armed Forces Journal International,* Vol. 117, No. 9 (May 1980), p. 17.

[84] "Chrysler Schedule Held Lagging in Building XM-1 Tank for Army," The *New York Times,* December 18, 1980, p. A20. See also Reps. Dan Daniel and William L. Dickinson, "The Great Tank Engine War of 1983," *Armed Forces Journal International,* Vol. 121, No. 2 (September 1983), pp. 32–34; and "Tank Designers Stress Technology," p. A16.

[85] Quoted in "Tank Costs Up Fivefold, with Inflation Blamed," The *New York Times,* July 22, 1981, p. A15.

[86] For part of this debate see "The Troubled Tank," The *New York Times,* October 22, 1982, p. 26; Maj.-Gen. Duard D. Ball, "M-1; The World's 'Most Survivable' Tank," The *New York Times,* November 23, 1982, p. A28; and "Aren't Four Tanks Better than One?," The *New York Times,* December 1, 1982, p. A30.

[87] "US/FRG 120 mm Tank Gun Agreement Details," *International Defense Review,* Vol. 12, No. 5 (July 1979), pp. 697–698.

[88] *Jane's Armour and Artillery 1986–87,* pp. 119–120. See also D. H. Jenkins, "Abrams and Leopard 2—A User's View of the Heavyweights," *International Defense Review,* Vol.

14, No. 12 (December 1981) p. 1664; and Wolfgang Schneider, "Uprating the M1 Tank," *International Defense Review*, Vol. 19, No. 10 (October 1986), pp. 1495–1500.

[89] Drew Middleton, "Soviet Introducing New Tank," p. 7.

[90] "U.S. Tanks Can't Kill Russia's Latest Ones in Head-on Combat," *Armed Forces Journal International*, Vol. 120, No. 10 (May 1983), p. 70.

[91] Andrew Cockburn, "The Russians Coming? In a Nonexistent Tank?," The *New York Times*, November 22, 1982, p. A19. See also Deborah G. Meyer, "The Great T80 Debate: Is It or Isn't It a New Tank?," *Armed Forces Journal International*, Vol. 102, No. 10 (May 1983), p. 70.

[92] *Jane's Armour and Artillery 1986–87*, p. 118.

[93] Daniel and Dickinson, "The Great Tank Engine War," p. 31.

[94] Ibid., pp. 30–38. See also Chris Meyer, "DeLauer Calls Army's: M-1 Engine Study 'Lousy,' But Still Supports Dual Sourcing," *Armed Forces Journal International*, Vol. 121, No. 10 (May 1984), p. 14.

[95] "Warranties for Tanks," The *New York Times*, May 2, 1983, p. D2.

[96] Quoted in Daniel and Dickinson, "The Great Tank Engine War," p. 34.

[97] "New Systems Pose Huge 'Bow Wave' for Army Budget," *Armed Forces Journal International*, Vol. 115, No. 10 (June 1978), pp. 10–12.

[98] Daniel and Dickinson, "The Great Tank Engine War," p. 34.

10. THE STRATEGIC DEFENSE INITIATIVE

[1] "Appendix A: The Conclusion of President Reagan's March 23, 1983, Speech on Defense Spending and Defensive Technology," in Steven E. Miller and Steven Van Evera, eds., *The Star Wars Controversy: An International Security Reader* (Princeton: Princeton University Press, 1986), pp. 257–258.

[2] William J. Broad, " 'Star Wars' Traced to Eisenhower Era," The *New York Times*, October 28, 1986, pp. C1, C3. See also David N. Schwartz, "Past and Present: The Historical Legacy," in Ashton B. Carter and David N. Schwartz, eds., *Ballistic Missile Defense* (Washington, D.C.: The Brookings Institution, 1984, pp. 332–343. For a comprehensive discussion of the history of anti-satellite weapons programs and technologies, which are not treated here, see Paul B. Stares, *Space Weapons and U.S. Strategy: Origins and Development* (London: Croom Helm, 1985); Paul Stares, *Space and National Security* (Washington, D.C.: The Brookings Institution, 1987); and Bhupendra Jasani, *Space Weapons and International Security* (Oxford: Stockholm International Peace Research Institute and Oxford University Press, 1987).

[3] See Fen Osler Hampson, "SALT I Interim Agreement and ABM Treaty," in Albert Carnesale and Richard N. Haass, eds., *Superpower Arms Control: Setting the Record Straight* (Cambridge, Mass.: Ballinger, 1987), pp. 65–103.

[4] See William J. Broad, *Star Warriors: A Penetrating Look into the Lives of the Young Scientists Behind Our Space Age Weaponry* (New York: Simon and Schuster, 1985). See also Lord Solly Zuckerman, "The Wonders of Star Wars," The *New York Review of Books*, January 30, 1986, pp. 32–40; and Christopher Lee, *War in Space* (London: Hamish Hamilton, 1986).

[5] Tom Mangold, "The Birth of SDI," *World Press Review*, March 17, 1987, pp. 17–19.

[6] William J. Broad, "Reagan's 'Star Wars' Bid: Many Ideas Converging," The *New York Times*, March 4, 1985, p. 1. See also " 'Star Wars': Where Does It Stand?," The *New York Times*, September 28, 1985, p. A4.

[7] Quoted in ibid.

[8] Ibid.

[9] Quoted in William J. Broad, "Space Weapon Idea Now Being Weighed Was Assailed in '82," The *New York Times*, May 4, 1987, pp. A1, B10.

[10] John Bardeen, "The Strategic Defense Initiative: 'Star Wars,' " The *New York Times*, September 13, 1985, p. A8.

[11] Quoted in Senator Larry Pressler, *Star Wars: The Strategic Defense Initiative Debates in Congress* (New York: Praeger, 1986), pp. 66–69.

[12] Fred S. Hofman, *Ballistic Missile Defenses and U.S. National Security: Summary*

Report (Washington, D.C.: Future Security Strategy Study, October 1983), in Miller and Van Evera, *The Star Wars Controversy,* p. 281. See also Fred S. Hoffman, "The SDI in U.S. Nuclear Strategy," *International Security,* Vol. 10, No. 1 (Summer 1985), pp. 13–24.

[13] Department of Defense, *The Strategic Defense Initiative* (Washington, D.C.: April 1984), in Miller and Van Evera, *The Star Wars Controversy,* p. 301.

[14] Ibid., p. 302.

[15] Ashton B. Carter, *Directed Energy Missile Defense in Space* (Washington, D.C.: Office of Technology Assessment, April 1984), in Miller and Van Evera, *The Star Wars Controversy,* p. 175.

[16] Ibid., pp. 253–254.

[17] John A. Adam and Mark A Fischetti, "Star Wars: SDI: The Grand Experiment," *IEEE Spectrum,* September 1986, p. 34.

[18] Reuters, April 24, 1984, p. 7.

[19] Clarence A. Robinson, Jr., "Strategic Defense Group Speeds Efforts," *Aviation Week and Space Technology,* Vol. 120, No. 24 (June 11, 1984), pp. 16–17.

[20] Quoted in Lord Solly Zuckerman, "Nuclear War: Can Anything Stop the Rain," The *New York Times Book Review,* January 20, 1985, p. 6.

[21] United States Information Agency, "USIA Wireless File, Microtext Edition," April 25, 1984, pp. E1–E2, F1, G1, H1.

[22] David Holzman, "A Cheap Ballistic-Missile Defense?," *Technology Review,* August/September 1984, pp. 73–74; and Clarence A. Robinson, Jr., "BMD Homing Interceptor Destroys Reentry Vehicle," *Aviation Week and Space Technology,* June 18, 1984, pp. 19–20.

[23] Quoted in Wayne Biddle, "How High Will Star Wars Fly?" The *New York Times,* December 30, 1984, p. E1.

[24] Ibid.

[25] John Tirman, ed., *The Fallacy of Star Wars: Based on Studies Conducted by the Union of Concerned Scientists* (New York: Vintage Books, 1983). A more recent study by the Congressional Research Service concluded that "most or all of the [SDI] weapon concepts that do prove feasible could in principle be used either offensively or defensively" ("Study Finds that SDI Could Be Offensive Threat to Soviets," *Aviation Week and Space Technology,* November 30, 1987, p. 23). These issues are also the subject of Charles L. Glaser, "Do We Want the Missile Defenses We Can Build?," *International Security,* Vol. 10, No. 1 (Summer 1985), pp. 25–57.

[26] Union of Concerned Scientists, "Space-Based Missile Defense," Briefing Paper, Cambridge, Massachusetts, September 1984.

[27] William J. Broad, "Reduced Goal Set on Reagan's Plan for Space Defense," The *New York Times,* December 23, 1984, pp. A1, A14.

[28] Quoted in ibid., p. A14.

[29] Ibid.

[30] Quoted in Charles Mohr, "What Moscow Might Do in Replying to 'Star Wars,'" The *New York Times,* March 6, 1985, pp. A1, B8.

[31] Philip M. Boffey, "Dark Side of 'Star Wars': System Could Also Attack," The *New York Times,* March 7, 1985, pp. A1, A24.

[32] Charles L. Glaser, "Star Wars Bad Even If It Works," *Bulletin of the Atomic Scientists,* Vol. 41 (March 1985), p. 13.

[33] "Reagan Presses Call for Antimissile Plan Before Space Group," The *New York Times,* March 30, 1985, p. A1.

[34] Quoted in *The Arms Control Reporter* (Brookline, Mass.: Institute for Defense and Disarmament Studies, 1985), p. 575.B.13.

[35] Bill Keller, "Weinberger Backs Antimissile Plan," The *New York Times,* April 12, 1985, p. A1.

[36] United States Department of Defense, *Soviet Military Power* (Washington, D.C.: U.S. Government Printing Office, March 1986), p. 3.

[37] Quoted in Thomas K. Longstreth, John E. Pike, and John B. Rhinelander, *The Impact of U.S. and Soviet Ballistic Missile Defense Programs and the ABM Treaty,* 3rd ed. (Washington, D.C.: National Campaign to Save the ABM Treaty, March 1985), p. 31.

[38] Office of the Press Secretary, The White House, *The President's Unclassified Report on Soviet Noncompliance with Arms Control Agreements,* December 23, 1985, p. 3. It is

interesting to note that publication of the 1986 and 1987 reports on Soviet noncompliance were delayed because of internal struggles between the State Department and the Pentagon over the nature and degree of Soviet violations.

[39] Quoted in Longstreth et al., *The Impact of U.S. and Soviet Ballistic Missile Defense Programs and the ABM Treaty,* p. 58.

[40] Report of a Working Group, *Compliance and the Future of Arms Control* (Palo Alto, Cal.: Center for International Security and Arms Control, Stanford University, February 12, 1987), pp. i, ii.

[41] This was confirmed in an on-site inspection of the facilities at the Krasnoyarsk radar site by a congressional delegation in September 1987. There was also evidence that the Soviet Union was making significant changes in its policy toward verification of arms control agreements. See Congressional Research Service for the Subcommittee on Arms Control, International Security and Science, Committee on Foreign Affairs, *Verifying Arms Control Agreements: The Soviet View,* 100th Congress, 1st Session, 72–183 (Washington, D.C.: U.S. Government Printing Office, 1987).

[42] "What the Soviets Are Doing," *Time,* June 23, 1986, p. 19.

[43] Albert Gore, Jr., "Reassess the Focus of 'Star Wars,'" The *New York Times,* June 3, 1985, p. A9.

[44] The breakdown of expenditures is outlined in U.S. Department of Defense, *Report to Congress on the Strategic Defense Initiative* (Washington, D.C.: Department of Defense, 1985). For a sustained, in-depth examination of the macroeconomic consequences of SDI, see Barry M. Blechman and Victor A. Utgoff, "The Macroeconomics of Strategic Defense," *International Security,* Vol. 11, No. 3 (Winter 1986–87), pp. 33–70.

[45] Quoted in Philip M. Boffey, " 'Star Wars' and Mankind: Consequences for the Future," The *New York Times,* March 8, 1985, pp. A1, A14.

[46] These amendments and debates are reported in Pressler, *Star Wars,* pp. 69–70.

[47] Ibid., p. 71.

[48] Ibid., pp. 80–83.

[49] Steven V. Roberts, "Senate Rejects $1.1 Billion Cut in Antimissile Plan," The *New York Times,* June 5, 1985, p. A19.

[50] Steven V. Roberts, " $2.5 Billion Voted in House for Work on Missile Shield," The *New York Times,* June 21, 1985, p. A1.

[51] "House Amendments Would Set Commissions to Monitor SDI," *Aviation Week and Space Technology,* July 8, 1985, p. 23.

[52] United States Embassy (Ottawa), "SDI Laser Experiment Successful," News Release (85–43), June 25, 1985; and William J. Broad, "Laser Beam Hits 8-Inch Target in Space," The *New York Times,* June 22, 1985, p. A11.

[53] "Reagan Vows to Act on Antimissile Plan," The *New York Times,* July 14, 1985, p. A21.

[54] Phil Gailey, "President Presses Plans to Develop Weapons in Space," The *New York Times,* August 23, 1985, p. A1.

[55] Quoted in Ivor Peterson, "U.S. Activates Unit for Space Defense," The *New York Times,* September 24, 1985, p. A1.

[56] Colin Campbell, " 'Star Wars' Forces Press for Boycott," The *New York Times,* September 13, 1985, p. A1.

[57] Office of Technology Assessment, *Strategic Defenses: Ballistic Missile Defense Technologies, Anti-Satellite Weapons, Countermeasures, and Arms Control* (Princeton: Princeton University Press, 1986), pp. 33–34.

[58] Quoted in Charles A. Mohr, "Antimissile Shield Held to Raise Risk of a Nuclear War," The *New York Times,* September 25, 1985, p. A1.

[59] Bill Keller, "Pentagon Disputes Report on Missile Defense," The *New York Times,* September 26, 1985, p. A1.

[60] "Statement by Abraham D. Sofaer, Legal Adviser, Department of State, before the Subcommittee on Arms Control, International Security, and Science of the House Foreign Affairs Committee, Washington, D.C., October 22, 1985," *Current Policy,* No. 755 (Washington, D.C.: Bureau of Public Affairs, United States Department of State, October 1985).

[61] Caspar Weinberger, "SDI: Realities and Misconceptions," *The Christian Science Monitor,* October 17, 1985, p. 16. For a comprehensive and invaluable discussion of the Euro-

pean response to SDI, see Ivo H. Daalder, *The SDI Challenge to Europe* (Cambridge, Mass.: Ballinger, 1987).

[62] Charles Mohr, " 'Star Wars' Chief Presses Research," The *New York Times,* October 31, 1985, p.A1.

[63] David E. Sanger, "Pentagon and Critics Dispute Roles of Space Arms Designers," The *New York Times,* November 5, 1985, pp. C1, C3.

[64] Peter Grier, "Star Wars: Will It Work?," *The Christian Science Monitor,* November 12, 1985, pp. 30–31. See also William D. Hartung et al., *The Strategic Defense Initiative: Costs, Contractors and Consequences* (New York: Council on Economic Priorities, 1985), pp. 24–32.

[65] Ibid., p. 31.

[66] David E. Sanger, " 'Star Wars' Chief Expecting Speed-Up After the Meeting," The *New York Times,* November 21, 1985, p. A16.

[67] Flora Lewis, "A 'Star Wars' Cover-Up," The *New York Times,* December 3, 1985, p. A26, and "The Scientific Gag Rule," The *New York Times,* January 14, 1986, p. A25.

[68] Michael Gordon, "Scientist Assails 'Star Wars' Plan," The *New York Times,* December 4, 1985, p. A1. See also David L. Parnas, "Software Aspects of Strategic Defense Systems," *American Scientist,* Vol. 73 (1985), pp. 432–440; and Herbert Lin, "The Development of Software for Ballistic Missile Defense," *Scientific American* (December 1985), pp. 32–39.

[69] Pressler, *Star Wars,* p. 92.

[70] "Star Wars Timetable Moving Up, U.S. Says," *The Globe and Mail,* December 6, 1985, p. 1.

[71] Quoted in William J. Broad, "30 Lawmakers Urge Delay in Laser Weapon Test," The *New York Times,* December 7, 1985, p. A10.

[72] Bill Keller, "Missile Shield Program Gets Pentagon's Highest Priority," *The New York Times,* January 29, 1986, p. A11.

[73] Bill Keller, "No. 1 Weapon in 1987 Budget Is Missile Shield," The *New York Times,* February 5, 1986, p. A1.

[74] Quoted in James M. Markham, "No 'Star Wars' Deals, U.S. Says," The *New York Times,* March 22, 1986, p. A4.

[75] Douglas Waller, James Bruce, and Douglas Cook, *SDI: Progress and Challenges: Staff Report Submitted to Senator William Proxmire, Senator J. Bennett Johnston and Senator Lawton Chiles* (Washington, D.C., March 17, 1986), pp. 3–4.

[76] Charles Mohr, "Reagan Makes Plea for Antimissile Funds," The *New York Times,* August 1, 1986, p. A1.

[77] Charles Mohr, "McNamara and Brown Question Missile Defense," The *New York Times,* April 11, 1986, p. A6. See also George W. Ball, "Reagan's Ramboism—The Fantasy of Star Wars and the Danger of Real Wars," *The Christian Science Monitor,* April 28, 1986, p. 18.

[78] Charles Mohr, " 'Cost Goals' for Missile Defense Program Expected in Next Budget," The *New York Times,* April 25, 1986, p. A36.

[79] William Proxmire, "When You Talk about 'Star Wars' You're Talking Trillions," *The Christian Science Monitor,* May 19, 1986, p. 13.

[80] Charlotte Sailkowski, " 'Star Wars' Defense System Is Losing Steam with Senators," *The Christian Science Monitor,* May 23, 1986, p. 12.

[81] "Strategic Defense Initiative," *Defense R&D Update,* Headline #2, June 1986, pp. 24–28.

[82] "GAO Study Finds X-Ray Laser Program Has Unresolved Issues," *Star Wars Intelligence Report,* No. 14, June 10, 1986.

[83] Gerald M. Boyd, "President Urges Congress to Back His Arms Buildup," The *New York Times,* June 4, 1986, pp. A1, A13. The same month DoD released its second report on SDI to Congress. See Department of Defense, *Report to Congress on the Strategic Defense Initiative* (Washington, D.C.: U.S. Department of Defense, June 1986).

[84] Charlotte Sailkowski, " 'Star Wars' Under the Gun," *The Christian Science Monitor,* June 20, 1986, p.1.

[85] "Reagan Suffers Setback on SDI Money; Rep. Aspin Says Funding in Trouble," *Star Wars Intelligence Report,* June 24, 1986; and John L. Cushman, "Cuts Said to Set Back Plan on Missile Defense," The *New York Times,* June 27, 1986, p. A26.

[86] "Weinberger Assails Senate Effort to Limit SDI Funds" and "Soviets Want to Fight,

Survive Nuclear War, Abrahamson Says," *Star Wars Intelligence Report,* July 8, 1986.

[87] Charles Mohr, "Delay in 'Star Wars' Tests Urged by 5 Former U.S. Policy Makers," The *New York Times,* August 17, 1986, pp. A1, A10. Another high-level group also expressed skepticism about the desirability of rapid development and deployment of strategic defenses. See The Aspen Strategy Group, *The Strategic Defense Initiative and American Security* (Lanham, Md.: University Press of America, 1987).

[88] Michael R. Gordon, "First Space-Based Test in Missile Defense Readied," The *New York Times,* September 5, 1986, p. A13; and Michael R. Gordon, "How Secret Should a Space Test Be?," The *New York Times,* September 13, 1986, p. A7.

[89] Paul H. Nitze, "Permitted and Prohibited Activities Under the ABM Treaty," *Current Policy,* No. 886 (Washington, D.C.: Bureau of Public Affairs, United States Department of State, November 1986).

[90] See Fen Osler Hampson, "Arms Control and East-West Relations," in Brian W. Tomlin and Maureen Appel Molot, eds., *Canada Among Nations* (Toronto: James Lorimer, 1987), pp. 37–40.

[91] Philip Boffey, "Obstacles Force Narrower Focus on 'Star Wars,'" The *New York Times,* October 19, 1986, pp. A1, A14.

[92] Carl Levin, "Letter to Secretary of State George Shultz," United States Senate, Washington, D.C., December 1, 1986.

[93] R. Jeffrey Smith, "The Push Is On for SDI," *The Washington Post National Weekly Edition,* February 2, 1987, pp. 8–9.

[94] *The Arms Control Reporter: A Chronicle of Treaties, Negotiations, Proposals* (Brookline, Mass.: Institute for Defense and Disarmament Studies, 1987), p. 575.B.188.

[95] John H. Cushman, Jr., "Partial Antimissile Deployment Weighed," The *New York Times,* January 16, 1987, p. A3; and Strobe Talbott, "A Shield Against Arms Control," *Time,* February 2, 1987, p. 23.

[96] *Congressional Record,* July 29, 1986, H6500.

[97] John H. Cushman, Jr., "2 Key Senators Vow to Defeat Missile Shield Plan," The *New York Times,* January 21, 1987, p. A14; and "Pentagon Secretly Prepares Plan for Missile Defense in Mid-1990s," The *New York Times,* April 8, 1987, p. A18.

[98] David E. Sanger, "Many Experts Doubt 'Star Wars' Could Be Effective by the Mid-90s," The *New York Times,* February 11, 1987, pp. B1, B13; Trish Gilmartin, "Early Deployment Battle Looms Before Congress," *Defense News,* February 2, 1987, pp. 1, 16; Richard Ruquist, "SDI Early Deployment: How Survivable? How Cost-Effective?" and "The Physicists Size Up SDI," *Arms Control Today,* Vol. 17, No. 6 (July/August 1987), pp. 18–19, 28–32.

[99] William J. Broad, "'Star Wars' Push Dimming Prospect for Exotic Arms," The *New York Times,* March 9, 1987, pp. A1, B6.

[100] Quoted and reported in the *Arms Control Reporter* (1987), p. 575.D.15.

[101] *Arms Control Reporter* (1987), p. 575.B.194.

[102] Ibid., pp. 575.B.199–575.B.200.

[103] Ibid., pp. 575.B.208–575.B.209.

[104] Senator Sam Nunn, "Interpretation of the ABM Treaty, Part I," *Congressional Record,* 100th Congress, 1st Session, Vol. 133, No. 38, March 11, 1987; "Part II," *Congressional Record,* 100th Congress, 1st Session, Vol. 133, No. 39, March 12, 1987; "Part III," *Congressional Record,* 100th Congress, 1st Session, Vol. 133, No. 40, March 13, 1987; and "Part IV," *Congressional Record,* 100th Congress, 1st Session, Vol. 133, No. 82, May 20, 1987.

[105] Brendan M. Greeley, Jr., "SDIO Continues Research Across Broad Technology Base," *Aviation Week and Space Technology,* March 9, 1987, pp. 38–43.

[106] "Anti-Missile Tests Approved by House Committee," The *New York Times,* April 9, 1987; and Steven A. Hildreth, *The Strategic Defense Initiative: Program Facts,* Issue Brief No. IB85170 (Washington, D.C.: Congressional Research Service, January 6, 1988), p. 13.

[107] Strategic Defense Initiative Organization, *Report to the Congress on the Strategic Defense Initiative* (Washington, D.C.: U.S. Department of Defense, April 1987), p. II-11.

[108] *Arms Control Reporter* (1987), p. 575.B.224. A staff report released by the Federation of American Scientists said that the SBI (Space-Based Interceptor) or "hit-to-kill" kinetic-energy weapons could not be tested legally even under the administration's broad interpretation of the ABM Treaty. See Thomas K. Longstreth, *Space-Based Interceptors for Star Wars: Untestable Under Any Interpretation of the ABM Treaty* (Washington, D.C.:

Federation of American Scientists, October 22, 1987); and Alan B. Sherr, "Sound Legal Reasoning or Policy Expedient? The 'New Interpretation' of the ABM Treaty," *International Security,* Vol. 11, No. 3 (Winter 1986–87), pp. 71–93.

[109] Philip M. Boffey, "Physicists Express 'Star Wars' Doubt: Long Delays Seen," The *New York Times,* April 23, 1987, p. A1; and David E. Sanger, "Missile Defense: New Turn in Debate," The *New York Times,* April 24, 1987, p. A8.

[110] *Arms Control Reporter* (1987), p. 575.B.225. There was also strong criticism of the Pentagon's plan to set up a special SDI advisory research institute. See Michael Gordon, "Senate Democrats Question Plan for 'Star Wars' Advisory Institute," The *New York Times,* May 7, 1987, p. A12; and Harry R. Finlay, "Proposed Strategic Defense Institute," United States General Accounting Office, Washington, D.C., May 6, 1987.

[111] *Arms Control Reporter* (1987), pp. 575.B.227–575.B.228.

[112] Ibid., pp. 575.B.231–575.B.238.

[113] Office of the Legal Adviser, *The ABM Treaty: Part I: Treaty Language and Negotiating History* and *Part II: Ratification Process* (Washington, D.C.: U.S. Department of State, May 11, 1987). See also "Sofaer's Last Stand?," *Arms Control Today,* Vol. 17, No. 8 (October 1987), pp. 14–16; John B. Rhinelander and James P. Rubin, "Mission Accomplished: An Insider's Account of the ABM Treaty Negotiating Record," and Raymond L. Garthoff, "History Confirms the Traditional Meaning; U.S. and Subsequent Practice Under the ABM Treaty," *Arms Control Today,* Vol. 17, No. 7 (September 1987), pp. 3–14, 15–19; and Gerard C. Smith et al., "Early Dismantlement of the ABM Treaty," *Arms Control Today,* Vol. 17, No. 2 (March 1987), pp. 3–5.

[114] *Arms Control Reporter* (1987), pp. 603.B.132–603.B.133. The same month Senator Dan Quayle (R.-Ind.) released the declassified 41-page "Report to Congress on the Strategic Defense Initiative Deployment Schedule," which was required under a Quayle-authored provision of the 1987 Defense Authorization Bill detailing what SDI technologies "can be developed or deployed within 5 to 10 years to defend against significant military threats and help accomplish critical military missions." See Senator Dan Quayle, "Declassified Pentagon Section 215 Report on Near-Term Applications of SDI Technologies," Washington, D.C., May 13, 1987.

[115] *Arms Control Reporter* (1987), pp. 575.B.234–575.B.235.

[116] Ibid., pp. 575.E.1–575.E.2.

[117] "Strategic Defense Initiative: Blueprint for a Layered Defense," *Aviation Week and Space Technology,* November 23, 1987, pp. 48–49; and "Strategic Defense Initiative: Defense Acquisition Board Completes First Review of SDI Program," *Defense R&D Update,* July 1987.

[118] *Arms Control Reporter* (1987), p. 575.B.241.

[119] Office of the Legal Adviser, *The ABM Treaty: Part III: Subsequent Practice* (Washington, D.C.: U.S. Department of State, September 9, 1987).

[120] Quoted in *Arms Control Reporter* (1987), p. 603.B.140.

[121] Ibid., p. 575.B.250.

[122] Jonathan Fuerbringer, "Senate Defeats Proposal to Advance White House 'Star Wars' Initiative," The *New York Times,* September 18, 1987, p. A6, and "Bush Breaks Tie on 'Star Wars,' " The *New York Times,* September 23, 1987, p. A3.

[123] *Arms Control Reporter* (1987), pp. 575.B.251–575.B.252.

[124] Ibid., p. 603.B.141.

[125] Ibid., p. 575.B.254.

[126] Ibid., pp. 575.B.266–575.B.267.

[127] "Reagan Says Soviets Violated Treaty," *The Globe and Mail,* December 3, 1987, p. 1.

[128] William J. Broad, "Anti-Missile Laser Given First Tests for Use in Space," The *New York Times,* January 3, 1987, pp. A1, A18.

[129] Joel Brinkley, "Reagan's Greetings, in Soviet Exchange, Have a Barbed Edge," The *New York Times,* January 2, 1987, pp. A1, A6. The importance of strategic defenses was underscored in the report of the Commission on Integrated Long-Term Strategy, co-chaired by Fred Ikle, Under Secretary of Defense, Policy, and Albert Wohlstetter, President of Pan Heuristics. The report stated that U.S. "conventional and nuclear posture should be based on a mix of offensive and defensive systems" and that "[t]he evolutionary development of missile defenses should be continued" because "ballistic missile defense, complemented in

some measure by air defense and a cruise missile defense, can improve the protection of the U.S. National Command Authorities, increase confidence in the country's ability to keep control of its forces in a war, and thus make it easier to ensure that our nuclear deterrent is not hair-triggered." See Report of the Commission on Integrated Long-Term Strategy, *Discriminate Deterrence* (Washington, D.C.: U.S. Department of Defense, January 1988), p. 52.

[130] Paul Mann, "Nunn Redirects Antimissile Debate Proposing Accidental Launch Shield," *Aviation Week and Space Technology,* January 25, 1988, p. 18.

[131] William J. Broad, "Military Satellite Launched to Test Antimissile Plan," The *New York Times,* February 9, 1988, pp. A1, A29, and "Military Satellite Test Is Rated Success," The *New York Times,* February 10, 1988, p. A18.

[132] William J. Broad, "Star Wars Is Coming, But Where Is It Going?," The *New York Times Magazine,* December 6, 1987, p. 90.

11. CONCLUSION

[1] O. Davis, M. Dempster, and A. Wildavsky, "A Theory of the Budgetary Process," *The American Political Science Review,* Vol. 60, No. 3 (September 1966), pp. 529–547. These authors show that changes in particular budgetary appropriations are incremental and that major shifts in spending for particular programs occur only gradually.

[2] See Robert J. Art, "Congress and the Defense Budget: New Procedures and Old Realities," in Barry M. Blechman and William J. Lynn, eds., *Toward a More Effective Defense: Report of the Defense Reorganization Project* (Cambridge, Mass.: Ballinger, 1985), pp. 154–157.

[3] Ibid., p. 160. See also President's Blue Ribbon Commission on Defense Management, *An Interim Report to the President,* Washington, D.C., February 28, 1986, p. 6; and The CSIS Defense Acquisition Study, *U.S. Defense Acquisition: A Process in Trouble* (Washington, D.C.: The Center for Strategic and International Studies, Georgetown University, March 1987), p. 75.

[4] *An Interim Report to the President,* pp. 7–8.

[5] *An Interim Report to the President,* p. 16. See also Art, "Congress and the Defense Budget," p. 160; and CSIS Defense Acquisition Study, *U.S. Defense Acquisition,* p. 49.

[6] CSIS Defense Acquisition Study, *U.S. Defense Acquisition,* pp. 29–30.

[7] See ibid., pp. 49–50, 77–78.

[8] Bruce Russett, "International Interactions and Processes: The Internal vs. External Debate Revisited," in Ada W. Finifter, ed., *Political Science: The State of the Discipline* (Washington, D.C.: The American Political Science Association, 1983), p. 546.

[9] Robert J. Bresler and Robert C. Gray, "The Bargaining Chip and SALT," *World Politics,* Vol. 92, No. 1 (Spring 1977), pp. 65–88.

[10] Albert Carnesale and Richard N. Haass, eds., *Superpower Arms Control: Lessons Learned from Experience* (Cambridge, Mass.: Ballinger and Harper and Row, 1983), p. 333.

APPENDIX A

[1] Graham T. Allison, *Essence of Decision: Explaining the Cuban Missile Crisis* (Boston: Little, Brown, 1971), p. 144.

[2] Ibid., pp. 166–167.

[3] Charles E. Lindbloom, *The Intelligence of Democracy* (New York: Basic Books, 1965); and Charles E. Lindbloom and David Braybrooke, *A Strategy of Decision* (Glencoe, Ill.: Free Press, 1963).

[4] Allison, *Essence of Decision,* p. 163.

[5] Ibid., pp. 168–169.

[6] See Harvey M. Sapolsky, *The Polaris System Development: Bureaucratic and Programmatic Success in Government* (Cambridge, Mass.: Harvard University Press, 1972), pp. 244–246.

[7] Robert J. Art, *The TFX Decision: McNamara and the Military* (Boston: Little, Brown, 1968), p. 158.

[8] F. N. Scherer, *Industrial Market Structure and Economic Performance,* 2nd ed. (Chicago: Rand McNally, 1980), pp. 152–153.

[9] Quoted in ibid., p. 155.

[10] Ibid., p. 160.

[11] This discussion is drawn from Scherer, *Industrial Market Structure and Economic Performance,* pp. 169–196. Oligopolistic producers will also maintain inventories and order backlogs to provide buffers and adjust production imbalances to changes in demand.

[12] Thomas C. Schelling, *The Strategy of Conflict* (Cambridge, Mass.: Harvard University Press, 1960), p. 54.

[13] Scherer, *Industrial Market Structure and Economic Performance,* p. 190.

[14] Robert Axelrod, *The Evolution of Cooperation* (New York: Basic Books, 1984).

[15] George H. Quester, *The Future of Nuclear Deterrence* (Lexington, Mass.: Lexington Books, 1986), p. 33.

[16] Robert Axelrod organized a computer tournament in which an international team of professional game theorists played prisoners' dilemma on a repetitive or "iterated" basis. Each entrant was asked to write a program that used a decision rule to select a cooperative or noncooperative choice on each move. The winner of the game, Professor Anatol Rapoport of the University of Toronto, used a TIT FOR TAT strategy which started with a cooperative choice and continued to reward cooperation by the other player with cooperation until the end of the game. If the other player defected, he was penalized with a defection, but subsequently "forgiven" with cooperation. In successive rounds of the tournament the TIT FOR TAT strategy won the game. According to Axelrod, "What accounts for TIT FOR TAT's robust success is its combination of being nice, retaliatory, forgiving, and clear. Its niceness prevents it from getting into unnecessary trouble. Its retaliation discourages the other side from persisting whenever defection is tried. Its forgiveness helps to restore mutual cooperation. And its clarity makes it intelligible to the other player, thereby eliciting long-term cooperation." See Axelrod, *The Evolution of Cooperation,* p. 54.

[17] Ibid., p. 59.

[18] Ibid., p. 60.

[19] Kenneth A. Oye, "Explaining Cooperation Under Anarchy: Hypotheses and Strategies," in Kenneth A. Oye, ed., *Cooperation Under Anarchy* (Princeton: Princeton University Press, 1986), Chapter 1, p. 19.

[20] Ibid., p. 20. See also Duncan Snidal, "Coordination versus Prisoners' Dilemma: Implications for International Cooperation and Regimes," *The American Political Science Review,* Vol. 79, No. 4 (December 1985), pp. 923–942.

[21] See Robert O. Keohane, *After Hegemony: Cooperation and Discord in the World Economy* (Princeton: Princeton University Press, 1984).

[22] Robert Axelrod, "An Evolutionary Approach to Norms," *The American Political Science Review,* Vol. 80, No. 4 (December 1986), pp. 1102–1107.

[23] The level of interservice rivalry will be affected by presidential priorities and the context of the overall defense budget, that is, whether the total defense budget is expanding, staying more or less constant, or shrinking. If it is expanding, as it has under Reagan, one would expect the degree of interservice competition to be less intense than it would be in an administration with a more austere approach to defense spending (for example, under Dwight Eisenhower). And one would expect the degree of bureaucratic competition between the Department of Defense and other agencies to be most intense during periods when DoD has been singled out for special budgetary increases or, conversely, special budget cuts.

[24] The foremost study of the structure of the defense industry and its relation to the U.S. economy is Jacques Gansler's *The Defense Industry* (Cambridge, Mass.: MIT Press, 1980).

[25] This is the equivalent of Harry Eckstein's "crucial-case" test of a theory. See "Case Study and Theory in Political Science," in Fred I. Greenstein and Nelson W. Polsby, eds., *Strategies of Inquiry: Handbook of Political Science,* Vol. 7 (Reading, Mass.: Addison-Wesley, 1975), pp. 113–123.

[26] The need for compatibility in independent variables is discussed in Alexander L. George, "Case Studies and Theory Development: The Method of Structured Focused Comparison," in Paul G. Lauren, ed., *Diplomatic History: New Approaches* (New York: Free Press, 1979), pp. 54–57.

GLOSSARY

Air-Launched Cruise Missile (ALCM): Small unmanned airplane-like vehicles armed with nuclear weapons.

Antiballistic Missile (ABM) Treaty: This treaty limits the deployment of antiballistic missile systems of the U.S. and Soviet Union to specific deployment areas (currently one site) and technical characteristics. Of unlimited duration it is subject to review every five years.

Anti-Submarine Warfare (ASW): Methods of warfare utilizing specialized sensors, data-processing techniques, weapons platforms, and weapons to search, identify, and destroy submarines.

B-1B Bomber: A medium-weight, intercontinental, penetrating, four-seat strategic bomber designed to replace the aging B-52 bomber.

Ballistic Missile Defense (BMD): Systems for defense against missiles that follow trajectories resulting from gravity and aerodynamic drag. This term is used interchangeably with ABM systems.

Command, Control, and Communications (C³): Systems and procedures that ensure that the President, senior civilian and military officials, and U.S. strategic forces remain in communication with each other.

Defense Systems Acquisitions Review Council (DSARC): A committee within the Defense Department, established in the post-McNamara reform era, that reviews and evaluates weapons systems at various stages of their development. It has since been replaced by the Defense Acquisitions Board (DAB).

Endoatmospheric Defense: ABM systems that operate within the earth's atmosphere.

Exchange Ratio: The number of nuclear weapons that must be used by an attacker to destroy one nuclear weapon belonging to an adversary.

Exoatmospheric Defense: ABM systems that operate outside the atmosphere.

Fratricide: The destruction of one nuclear warhead by another.

Ground-Launched Cruise Missile (GLCM): A cruise missile fired from a ground-based launcher.

Hard Target: Anything built to withstand the blast effects of a nuclear weapon, like a "hardened" command post or ICBM silo. By contrast, a "soft" target, like a military base or city, would suffer catastrophic damage from a nearby nuclear explosion.

Intercontinental Ballistic Missile (ICBM): A ballistic missile with a range of 3,000 to 8,000 nautical miles.

Intermediate-Range Ballistic Missile (IRBM): A land-based missile with a range of 2,500 to 3,000 nautical miles.

Kinetic-Energy Weapon: A weapon that uses a nonexplosive projectile moving at high speed to destroy a target on impact.

Laser: A device for producing an intense beam of light. A laser weapon may destroy a target by heating, melting, or vaporizing its surface.

Layered Defense: An antiballistic missile system consisting of both an exoatmospheric and an endoatmospheric defense.

Maneuvering Reentry Vehicle (MaRV): A nuclear warhead that can be maneuvered to evade ABM defenses.

Minuteman: An ICBM deployed by the United States in two models: Minuteman II, armed with a single nuclear weapon; and Minuteman III, armed with three independently targetable nuclear weapons.

Multiple Independently Targetable Reentry Vehicle (MIRV): A package of two or more reentry vehicles that can be carried by a single ballistic missile and guided to separate targets.

Multiple Protective Shelter (MPS): A basing mode for land-based missiles in which the missiles are deployed among a large number of hardened structures intended to provide protection against nearby nuclear detonations.

MX Missile: Missile X or missile experimental, an ICBM carrying up to ten independently targetable nuclear weapons.

North American Aerospace Defense Command (NORAD): A joint U.S.-Canadian military command responsible for outer space, airspace surveillance, and air defense of the North American continent.

Particle Beam Weapon: A weapon that emits a beam of atoms or subatomic particles accelerated to nearly the speed of light to destroy a target.

Planning, Programming, and Budgeting System (PPBS): The system devised by Robert McNamara in the 1960s for planning defense budgets in the Department of Defense.

Polaris: The first generation of submarine-launched ballistic missiles; also refers to the submarines that carried them.

Poseidon: The second generation of submarine-launched ballistic missiles and submarines.

Rail Gun: A weapon using electromagnetic launching to fire hypervelocity projectiles.

Reentry Vehicle (RV): Reentry vehicles contain nuclear weapons.

Safeguard: An antiballistic missile system deployed in the United States in the

early 1970s containing ABM radars and exoatmospheric and endoatmospheric interceptors.

SALT: An acronym for bilateral negotiations between the United States and Soviet Union in the 1960s and 1970s on the subject of Strategic Arms Limitation Talks.

Sea-Launched Cruise Missile (SLCM): A cruise missile fired from a naval surface vessel or submarine.

Silo: A vertical structure housing an ICBM and its launch support equipment that has been constructed to withstand the effects of a nearby nuclear explosion.

Single Integrated Operational Plan (SIOP): The preplanned nuclear attack options prepared for the consideration of the President by the Department of Defense.

SSBN: Designator of the nuclear-powered fleet of ballistic, missile-carrying submarines deployed by the United States, the Soviet Union, France, and the United Kingdom.

START: An acronym for bilateral negotiations between the United States and Soviet Union in the 1980s on Strategic Arms Reduction Talks.

Stealth Bomber: A popular term for a new type of aircraft that would be nearly invisible to enemy radar because of the use of a combination of electronic countermeasures and an airframe designed to absorb radar waves.

Strategic Defense Initiative (SDI): A research and technology program to explore key technologies associated with concepts for defense against ballistic missiles, including technologies to work in outer space.

Strategic Triad: The three different types of platforms used by the United States to deliver strategic nuclear weapons: ICBMs, submarines carrying SLBMs, and bombers carrying gravity bombs, short-range attack missiles, and long-range cruise missiles.

Submarine-Launched Ballistic Missile (SLBM): A ballistic missile carried in or attached to and launched from a submarine.

Throw Weight: The "weight" that is placed on a trajectory toward the target by the central boost phase of the missile including the reentry vehicle(s), warheads(s), decoys, and the post-boost vehicle used for independently targetable warheads.

Transporter-Erector-Launcher (TEL): A vehicle designed for an earlier version of MPS that would have been used to transport the MX missile, erect it into a vertical position, and launch it.

Trident Missile: A modern submarine-launched ballistic missile deployed by the United States that comes in two versions: Trident I and Trident II, the latter being larger and more accurate.

Trident Submarine: A very large nuclear-powered, ballistic missile–carrying submarine being deployed by the United States that carries twenty-four missiles.

Warhead: That part of the missile, bomb, or munition that contains explosives intended to do damage.

X Ray: Electromagnetic radiation resulting from either the release of energy from electrons changing orbits about the nucleus or the collision of charged particles with the electromagnetic field of the nucleus.

Yield: The energy released by an explosion, generally measured in terms of kilotons or megatons of TNT required to produce the same energy release.

INDEX

Why does time exist? } p. 139
Why does space exist? }
Bean story (in cabin) p. 97

Rich relatives p. 134

Primeval Drive — p. 139

129-130 Ain'tributes

Tone' Words